RUDYARD
KIPLING

COLLECTED
STORIES

As a young writer living in Lahore during the time of the British Raj, Rudyard Kipling (1865–1936) was possessed by an enormous subject – India; and his genius for rendering its beauty and strangeness was even then so fully formed that we have to look to the likes of Shakespeare and Dickens to find writers equally precocious. What is even more astonishing, and what this selection of his stories from his entire career reveals, is the fact that he continuously grew and developed. The work he did toward the end of his long writing life is even better than that which marked its splendid beginnings.

EVERYMAN,
I WILL GO WITH THEE,
AND BE THY GUIDE,
IN THY MOST NEED
TO GO BY THY SIDE

RUDYARD KIPLING

Collected Stories

Selected and introduced
by Robert Gottlieb

EVERYMAN'S LIBRARY

Alfred A. Knopf New York Toronto

199

THIS IS A BORZOI BOOK

PUBLISHED BY ALFRED A. KNOPF, INC.

This selection first included in Everyman's Library, 1994
Copyright © 1994 by David Campbell Publishers Ltd.
Introduction Copyright © 1994 by Robert Gottlieb
Bibliography and Chronology Copyright © 1994 by David
Campbell Publishers Ltd.
Typography by Peter B. Willberg

ISBN 0-679-43592-1
LC 94-5854

Library of Congress Cataloging-in-Publication Data
Kipling, Rudyard, 1865–1936.
[Short stories. Selections]
Collected stories / Rudyard Kipling.
p. cm.—(Everyman's library)
Includes bibliographical references.
ISBN 0-679-43592-1: $23.00
I. Title.
PR4852 1994
823'.8—dc20
94-5854
CIP

Book Design by Barbara de Wilde and Carol Devine Carson

Printed and bound in Germany by
Mohndruck Graphische Betriebe GmbH, Gütersloh

RUDYARD KIPLING

CONTENTS

———

RUDYARD KIPLING

Everything about Kipling is extreme – the abundance of his talent, his precocity, his early fame and success, the variety of literary forms he mastered, the passionate admiration and loathing he evoked in critics and readers, the contradictions within him, the contradictions in the way he has been perceived, both during his life and after his death.

About his precocity, there can be no contradictions. Born on 30 December 1865, he had seen his early 'Schoolboy Lyrics' printed (privately, by his mother) by the time he was sixteen. By the time he was twenty-one, poems and stories were appearing in profusion in both India and England. By the time he was twenty-five, he had published the stories collected in *Plain Tales from the Hills*, *Soldiers Three*, *The Story of the Gadsbys*, *In Black and White*, *Under the Deodars*, *The Phantom Rickshaw*, and *Wee Willie Winkie*; had completed his famous, if flawed, novel *The Light that Failed*; and had suffered a breakdown. By thirty he had published his *Barrack-Room Ballads* and the two volumes of *The Jungle Books*, and was completing *Captains Courageous*. At thirty-five, he had *Stalky & Co.* and *Kim* behind him. At forty, he had written the *Just So Stories* and had twice refused a knighthood. (Later, he was to twice refuse the Order of Merit.) At forty-one he won the Nobel Prize. Not even Dickens, the writer he in so many ways resembles, got off to a faster start. Yet despite this extraordinary level of early performance and success, and although his output after forty was to be smaller in quantity and less to the public taste than what preceded it, his finest work was still to come.

Kipling's most ardent admirers would not suggest that he is a writer on the level of Shakespeare and Dickens, yet he shares with them – and with no other major English writer of fiction or drama – this brilliant, prolific beginning. His limitless facility, combined with his uncanny powers of observation and an unabashed passion for the very act of writing, propelled him through scores of stories and a vast amount of poetry in half a dozen years. Reading this early work – all of it polished and professional, even those stories that are slight or formulaic – one senses a young man's sheer joy in having so great a subject, India, to grapple with, and his absolute confidence that he can master it. At this point, he is (again, like Dickens) working as a journalist, devouring the world around him and rushing to report everything he sees. He had spent his early childhood in India and had returned there as a very young man, and he knew it inside out – the British sahibs and memsahibs, of course, but also the enlisted men, both English and 'native'; the Sikhs, the Pathans, the Afghans; the water boys and the elephant drivers; the half-castes and priests and merchants and lepers; even the dogs and the snakes and the polo ponies. He knew how the government administered and how the bureaucracy stifled. He recognized the thrills of colonial ambition and the perils of colonial isolation. He realized what England had done for and to India, and what India had done for and to the English. And his great luck was that this knowledge, in tandem with his formidable gifts, gave him an exotic and fascinating world with which to attract a large public; he was like a traveller returning from outer space with the first solid news about Mars. Almost overnight, Kipling captured the attention of English-speaking readers everywhere with his revelations of the India that was the heart of Victoria's empire.

India, then, is almost exclusively the subject of Kipling's early career. But there is one significant exception, and that is 'Baa Baa, Black Sheep', the famous account of his anguished years as a small boy in England, to which his parents had exiled him and his even younger sister (he was six, she was only three) to be educated and, as it were, Englished in the care of foster parents. This story (to the extent that it *is* a story and not a superficially altered burst of autobiography) of the child Rudyard's six years of torment in what he calls the House of Desolation is an isolated, and therefore especially unsettling, account of the great trauma of his life – what he clearly felt to be an abandonment into misery and degradation. We cannot know how literally accurate the details of his humiliation at the hands of the 'Holloways' are – he more or less corroborated them many years later in his formal autobiography, and his sister, in her old age, further confirmed them –

but we certainly sense that this is an accurate account of his feelings; feelings that until much later in his life are almost totally missing from his work. Dickens, suffering a comparable if less severe trauma in his months in the blacking factory, did not write about it directly until *David Copperfield*, when he was nearly forty, but his emotions about that time permeate *Oliver Twist*, *Nicholàs Nickleby*, *The Old Curiosity Shop*, and *Dombey and Son*, all of which involve tormented and endangered children. Kipling appears to have lived in a peculiar state of denial: not only does the crucial event of his young life go unrecorded except in this one story, but his profound sense of the blackness of life is suppressed for many years.

One can, however, infer the severity of the trauma from the insistence of two themes in his work, one reflecting his idea of who he was before he was damaged, the other reflecting his unquenchable rage at what had been done to him, yet neither acknowledging, even obliquely, the event itself. In a series of somewhat cloying stories, Kipling presents a little boy who not only lives in a paradise of adoring parents and servants (the idealized India of his earliest youth) but has total power over his environment. In 'Tod's Amendment', 'Wee Willie Winkie', 'Son of his Father', and others – all of them both fantasies of unrestricted power and elegies for a lost kingdom – the little boy easily and gaily dominates his world, and woe to them who try to frustrate him. And then, in literally dozens of stories dealing with childhood, adolescence, and adulthood, emerges the theme of revenge. It is as if Dumas had gone on writing *The Count of Monte Cristo* over and over again. Most blatantly, almost all the episodes in *Stalky & Co.*, Kipling's romanticized reinvention of his schooldays, involve the success of the three young heroes at getting their own back (and then some) at schoolmates or masters who have displeased them – in one story, 'The Moral Reformers', revenge takes the form of physical abuse amounting to sadism. It isn't mere late-Victorian squeamishness that prompted a reviewer, in 1899, to refer to *Stalky*'s 'piling on of youthful brutality beyond all need'.

Revenge is by far the most frequent hinge to Kipling's stories: husbands kill unfaithful wives; obnoxious officials are taught lessons; downtrodden employees punish employers; boors are humiliated (sadistically, again, in 'A Friend's Friend'); uppity young subalterns are put in their place. Hoaxes, elaborate practical jokes, physical punishment, public disgraces – all these provide the mechanisms by which Kipling's anger is compulsively rekindled and assuaged. But were it not for 'Baa Baa, Black Sheep', and corroborating biographical data, we would find it impossible to understand Kipling's violent swings between idyllic happiness and savage resentment. Reticent in life, silent in his fiction, he gives us only two clues to the intensity of his suppressed suffering: this one story, and the nervous breakdown of 1890 (of 'overwork'). There are many instances of tragedy punctuating the Indian stories, but these are observed, impersonal tragedies. George Moore put it succinctly: 'Mr. Kipling has seen much more than he has felt.' This freeze on emotion and self-examination left him most at ease in the world of boys and boy-men whose strongest bonds are with each other, in school or as comrades-in-arms. (Or with animals: David Malouf, in his libretto for Michael Berkeley's opera 'Baa Baa, Black Sheep', makes a powerful case for considering Mowgli among the creatures of *The Jungle Books* as a mirror image or projection of the boy Punch among the Holloways.)

One psychological peculiarity that strikes the reader is that the people whose actions led to the trauma – the mother and father who, for whatever good reasons, dispatched Kipling to the House of Desolation – are not punished or even reprimanded in his fiction. (Or in life: Kipling was always touchingly devoted to both his parents.) Perhaps if he could have brought himself to blame he would have found it easier to forgive. As it is, his fathers and mothers are usually idealized, off-stage, or dead: Kim is not the only orphan in his fiction.

Strangely, movingly, it is only when Kipling himself is punished as a parent – by the loss of his beloved daughter Josephine at the age of six (in 1899) and, more decisively, by the loss of his son, John, in the war in 1915 – that he begins to expose his feelings to himself and to deal with them in fiction. So that, emerging from this second House of Desolation by confronting it, he begins to evolve from his compulsive need

INTRODUCTION

for revenge to a new embrace of healing. His most complex
and profound stories come toward the end, one of them –
'Dayspring Mishandled', written in 1928 – a long, convoluted
work in which a lifelong and diabolical plan for revenge gives
way at last to pity and regret. Bruised by the torrent of
Kipling's revenge tragedies and comedies, we come away from
this story uncertain who is most relieved by its therapeutic
resolution – its central character, Kipling, or ourselves.

Acts of healing are to be found throughout these later stories
– from the healing of a house seemingly inhabited by ghosts
('The House Surgeon') to the healing of breakdown ('An
Habitation Enforced') to the healing of shell-shock in a
surprising number of post-war works. In fact, and significantly, whereas Kipling's interest in the wars of his youth lay
in the way soldiers lived and fought, and in the adventure of
battle, the First World War stories are almost entirely concerned with the effect of war on people, combatants and non-
combatants alike. These stories – even the notoriously violent
'Mary Postgate' – are about pain endured rather than pain
inflicted.

If we can now readily isolate the themes of Paradise Lost and
revenge in Kipling's early stories, at the time they were written
what would have registered most was their actual material –
the specifics. Kipling's passion for detail, his descriptive
powers, and his dogged insistence on understanding how
everything works remain consistent over forty years. In the
beginning, it is the workings of India – *everything* about India –
that grips him; that is why the hundred or so Indian tales are
even more impressive taken together than read singly – they
add up to an immense and convincing record of a way of life. It
is only when India recedes and other subjects catch his
attention that one comes to realize that the question of how
things work – *any* things – is as important to Kipling as India
itself. He wants to know, and to dramatize, not only how wars
are fought and countries governed but how ships are sailed and
hedges are trimmed; how inanimate objects operate and how
animals think. He digs into the technicalities of cars, radios,
airplanes, as they emerge into general use. (Sometimes these
stories are pure exercises in scientific popularization, yet in

RUDYARD KIPLING

'Wireless' the excitements of early radio are made the basis, or background, of serious fiction.) Since most readers' first impressions of Kipling are of nineteenth-century India and of the children's books, and because his early start as a writer, in the 1880s, places him for us as a late Victorian, it is startling to find references throughout the later work to such phenomena as Hollywood and 'Kodaking', and to come upon a line like this one from 'Dayspring Mishandled': 'This was before the days of Freud.' But these oddities do not strike one as modern touches worked up by Kipling to demonstrate that he is still on top of things; clearly, they are further reflections of his ceaseless curiosity about the world and its workings.

This curiosity extended to the future and how *it* would work – as in 'With the Night Mail', a powerful and original piece of science-fiction. And, more and more, he tried to explain the past – not only in the *Puck of Pook's Hill* stories, in which England's history is anatomized for young readers through the magic of Puck, but in the late historical/religious stories, in which he approaches the narratives of early Christianity and the rituals of Heaven and Hell with the same vigorous need to explicate them that he felt for the mechanics of the Indian bureaucracy and the mysteries of the steam engine.

His very virtuosity often led him into exaggeration and self-parody in this kind of story. Much of the collection *The Day's Work* is uncomfortable to read – especially the coyness of having locomotives and ship engines and folksy Vermont horses (one named Tedda Gabler!) think aloud. Yet even in this questionable genre the reader can be amused and convinced, as by 'The Maltese Cat', about a polo match seen from the point of view of the ponies, in which ingenuity and exciting action blunt the cuteness. It was this direction in Kipling's fiction that Henry James deplored in a famous letter of 1897: 'In his earliest time I thought he perhaps contained the seeds of an English Balzac; but I have quite given that up in proportion as he has come steadily from the less simple in subject to the more simple – from the Anglo-Indians to the natives, from the natives to the Tommies, from the Tommies to the quadrupeds, from the quadrupeds to the fish, and from the fish to the engines and screws...' But James balances this

xvi

justified disparagement in a letter written a year earlier ('I am laid low by the absolute uncanny talent – the prodigious special faculty of it ... He's a rum 'un – one of the very few first *talents* of the time'), and in another letter two years later, in which after expressing his disgust at Kipling's 'loud brazen verse' he goes on to say, 'His talent I think quite diabolically great.' (James Joyce, too, as Norman Page points out in his invaluable *A Kipling Companion*, cited Kipling – along with d'Annunzio and Tolstoy – as one of the nineteenth century's 'greatest natural talents'.) Alas, James didn't live to read those stories in which Kipling's talent was to be applied to material that James would certainly have found more congenial than talking locomotives – in fact, on occasion, to semi-Jamesian données, as in 'Dayspring Mishandled'.

James's ambivalence about Kipling is particularly worth noting because it presages the ambivalence of so much of the criticism and comment to come. No writer of the period – except perhaps James himself – has been so worried over, so condemned and reclaimed. Certainly no writer of the period has had so many remarkable explicators, among them T. S. Eliot, W. H. Auden, C. S. Lewis, George Orwell, Edmund Wilson, Lionel Trilling, Randall Jarrell, Angus Wilson, Kingsley Amis. And there is important work being done on Kipling today – by duelling biographers and by outstanding critics like J. M. S. Tompkins and Craig Raine. Eliot was primarily concerned with reconsidering the poetry, but he shares with his fellow critics the urge to rescue Kipling – or to place him; their efforts underlining the fact that, given his 'diabolically great' talent, he has to be acknowledged and dealt with. However difficult a specimen he is to pin down, and however much one may dislike aspects of his mind and manner, he cannot be ignored.

Much of the problem is political. Because India shifted so abruptly from being Britain's great colonial achievement to being Britain's great colonial shame, and because of the strident jingoism of many of Kipling's poems and pronouncements, by the First World War he had become identified as the foremost spokesman for British imperialism – as politically incorrect as a writer can be. Although the India tales are far more ambivalent about Britain's role in the subcontinent than might at first appear, and although Kipling in the 1920s wrote with anguish about the recent war, he was labelled then and thereafter as a reactionary, a glorifier of war and an imperialist. (Shakespeare has suffered similar accusations in regard to the shamelessly propagandistic and Tudor-flattering history plays.) Norman Page quotes that canny belletrist Bonamy Dobrée as saying, as early as 1929, 'It will only be possible to give him his rightful place when the political heats of his day have become coldly historical.' That moment may have come: surely we can now read and judge the stories as fiction, and the poems as poetry, without feeling apologetic about responding to their genius. But with the cooling of political heat comes the responsibility to identify the nature of that genius.

Some of the difficulty in doing so lies in the multiplicity of Kipling's interests, in his uncanny aptitude for impersonating other writers, and in the nature of his growth as an artist. In his early work he can remind us of near-contemporaries like Mark Twain (the two writers admired each other); Robert Louis Stevenson (in 1889, Henry James writes to Stevenson, 'We'll tell you all about Rudyard Kipling – your nascent rival; he has killed one immortal – Rider Haggard; the star of the hour, aged 24 . . .'); Conan Doyle; H. G. Wells; Jules Verne; even Wilde and Pinero. Here is a typical exchange of dialogue from 'A Second-Rate Woman', one of the Mrs. Hauksbee stories of Anglo-Indian social life:

> Mrs. Mallowe – 'I always prefer to believe the best of everybody. It saves so much trouble.'
> Mrs. Hauksbee – 'Very good. I prefer to believe the worst. It saves useless expenditure of sympathy.'

Kipling wasn't really interested in tossing off epigrams à la Wilde; he was echoing the kind of hard chatter he heard from his mother and other clever women of her kind. But he was also tapping into a literary vein of the moment, unable to resist his talent for mimicry.

And just as he couldn't help testing diverse literary styles and genres, he couldn't dampen his enthusiasm for dialect – as with Mulvaney's Irish speech throughout the *Soldiers Three* stories, or a Pathan's, as in 'Dray Wara Yow Dee', or a Sikh's, in 'A Sahibs' War', or a Frenchman's turn of phrase in 'The Bull that Thought'. His descriptive power – his eye – was as acute as that of any English writer, and his ear was equally acute. Dickens indulged his love of melodrama in his famous readings and theatricals; the more timid Kipling becomes instead a ventriloquist, performing on the page in a series of monologues whose content often matters less to him (and to us) than the verisimilitude of the narrator's voice.

Another kind of story is set within a formal frame, with an anonymous 'I' introducing the action and commenting on it (and sometimes subtly undermining it). In this, Kipling suggests Conrad, the other great documenter of imperialism. But the trajectories of the two careers are almost diametrically opposite. Conrad, born eight years before Kipling but not publishing his first book until 1895, moves from the ornamental and literary *Almayer's Folly* and *An Outcast of the Islands* to the profound intuition and despair of his middle period to the potboilers of the years before his death, in 1924. Kipling begins with all the easy brio of an indefatigable born journalist and moves through a somewhat confused and self-conscious middle period, when his first great subject has dried up for him, into a final period that reveals a new depth of feeling and of understanding.

In the best of these latter stories – undoubtedly evoked by the death of his children and the devastation of the war – Kipling is a changed man, although we still note his insatiable curiosity about how things work and his extraordinary facility; there are stories of this period that could easily have been written thirty years before. But there are also the superb war stories – in particular, the implacable 'Mary Postgate' and the mystical 'The Gardener'. And there are stories – the above-mentioned included – in which women are no longer either the clever and manipulating matrons of Simla or the foolish (or worse) young girls who trap or undo wholesome young men but are formidable protagonists. (One of these, 'The Wish House,' with its grim awareness of old age and approaching death, its evocation of passion and sacrifice, its supernatural ambiguities, and the sheer genius of its dialogue, dialect, and detail, can make a solid claim to be considered

RUDYARD KIPLING

Kipling's finest story.) And there are the religious stories. All of this later work may or may not appear to us more valuable than the best of the early work, but it unquestionably helps us chart a progression that would have surprised Henry James – from the brilliantly simple to the brilliantly complex, and from a focus on the external world to a probing of the interior – a progression that no one could have imagined in the early years and that reminds us of how hard a worker and how complicated a man Kipling was. Ironically, by the time he was producing his most intricate and charged work, the literary world had left him far behind. When he died, in 1936, he must have seemed as ancient and irrelevant as a dinosaur to readers of Lawrence, Joyce, Woolf, Forster, Hemingway, Faulkner, Waugh. Not only was he a political throwback but his defining qualities of observation, curiosity, and energy – his very facility – would have seemed hopelessly out of date. Though not to the young. The children's books, at least, have remained staples from the time of their writing until now.

In this compressed account, I am neglecting large areas of Kipling's work – the poems, which continue to stir and amuse, and the longer prose works, of which the acknowledged masterpiece is *Kim*. (Those poems written as preambles or postscripts to many of the later stories are, of course, included in the text.) I am also excluding from the collection the work Kipling did expressly for children – the *Just So Stories*, *The Jungle Books*, and all but one of the *Puck of Pook's Hill* reconstructions of English history. (The exception, 'Dymchurch Flit', is conspicuously different in tone and approach from the rest.) Since the *Stalky* stories have probably been read as much by grown men as by boys, I have included the first of them, 'In Ambush', to suggest both their charm and their retrogressive attitudes.

In general, there is comforting agreement among the various anthologizers and commentators as to which are the best of Kipling's stories, though there is occasional disagreement, too. For instance, Angus Wilson, in his perceptive book *The Strange Ride of Rudyard Kipling*, cannot embrace 'Mrs. Bathurst', a story that others, myself among them, find powerful and

INTRODUCTION

moving. (Craig Raine is particularly helpful on this impacted and ambiguous story.) But almost all critics would include on their list of Kipling's best 'Baa Baa, Black Sheep', 'The Man Who Would Be King', 'The Wish House', 'The Gardener', 'On Greenlow Hill', 'The Bridge-Builders', and 'Mary Postgate'. The space this volume has been granted by the generosity of the Everyman editors has made it possible to reprint here not only the stories I think are Kipling's very strongest but also works chosen to demonstrate the wide scope of his interest and techniques. (They appear in the order they hold in the official complete works.) 'Mrs. Hauksbee Sits Out' is representative of the amusing playlets he enjoyed composing – an entire sequence of them, 'The Story of the Gadsbys', is too long to include; 'The City of Dreadful Night' is a virtuoso display of descriptive writing; 'Jews in Shushan' a surprising expression of Kipling's sympathies; 'A Bank Fraud' shows the attractive side of his sentimentality; 'The Strange Ride of Morrowbie Jukes' has a powerful allegorical quality; 'A Wayside Comedy' is startlingly explicit about sexual relationships. 'The Mark of the Beast' is a horror story, 'With the Night Mail' is science-fiction, 'The House Surgeon' has ghosts. 'The Drums of the Fore and Aft' is an extraordinary depiction of battle. 'The Head of the District' displays Kipling's consummate grasp of how Victoria's India *worked*. 'Love-o'-Women' confronts passion, 'Without Benefit of Clergy' confronts love. 'The Man Who Would Be King' is, among other things, a superb adventure (and was made into a superb John Huston movie, Michael Caine and Sean Connery joining Ronald Colman, Victor McLaglen, Lionel Barrymore, Walter Huston, Stewart Granger, David Niven, Errol Flynn, Cary Grant, Douglas Fairbanks, Jr., Spencer Tracy, and Sabu in a long line of Kipling film heroes). And 'The Bridge-Builders' is both a lesson in engineering and a compelling religious phantasmagoria.

Of course, each of these stories is other things, too – Kipling would not be the finest writer of short stories in English if his work could be so easily reduced and pigeonholed. That he was far less successful as a novelist suggests his limitations but does not detract from his achievement: reading the entire body of his stories only confirms James's recognition of his prodigious talent. In fact, there has been no writer since Dickens whose talent was so immediately apparent to readers and critics alike; no talent so lavish and so fluent. If through most of his life Kipling used this fluency, or facility, to hide behind, the mask itself is never less than spellbinding.

Robert Gottlieb

SELECT BIBLIOGRAPHY

THE TEXT
There are complete hardcover editions of Kipling's work to be found in second-hand bookstores, and Penguin has in print all the individual volumes of Kipling's stories, each with a useful introduction and with helpful apparatus. There are various collections of prose and poetry, perhaps the most useful of which is *A Choice of Kipling's Prose*, selected and with an introduction by Craig Raine, 1987. There is inevitable overlap with this volume, but Raine includes some very interesting non-fiction, and his introduction is excellent.

BIOGRAPHIES
The 'standard' work is probably still C. E. Carrington's *Rudyard Kipling: His Life and Work*, 1955; 3rd edition 1978. Other important efforts are Lord Birkenhead's *Rudyard Kipling*, 1978; Philip Mason's *Kipling: The Glass, the Shadow and the Fire*, 1975; and Martin Seymour-Smith's provocative *Rudyard Kipling*, 1989.

CRITICISM
The most influential modern work is J. M. S. Tompkins' *The Art of Rudyard Kipling*, 1959. Angus Wilson's *The Strange Ride of Rudyard Kipling*, 1977, is perhaps more valuable for its critical appreciations than for its biographical insights, although they are interesting, too. There are several comprehensive anthologies of criticism and commentary: John Gross's *Rudyard Kipling: The Man, His Work and His World*, 1972; Andrew Rutherford's *Kipling's Mind and Art*, 1964; and Elliot L. Gilbert's *Kipling and His Critics*, 1966. Within these volumes can be found essays by Lionel Trilling, Edmund Wilson, George Orwell, Randall Jarrell, T. S. Eliot, etc. There is also Kingley Amis's *Rudyard Kipling and His World*, 1975, and J. I. M. Stewart's *Rudyard Kipling*, 1962. Finally, Norman Page's *The Kipling Companion*, 1984, is an essential compendium of data.

CHRONOLOGY

DATE	AUTHOR'S LIFE	LITERARY CONTEXT
1865	Birth of Rudyard Kipling (30 December) to John Lockwood Kipling and Alice Kipling (née Macdonald) in Bombay. Kipling's father is Professor of Architectural Sculpture at the government School of Art in Bombay.	Gaskell: *Wives and Daughters*. Carroll: *Alice's Adventures in Wonderland*. Dickens: *Our Mutual Friend*. Chatterji: *Durgeśanandini*. Dostoevsky: *Crime and Punishment* (1866).
1868	Kipling accompanies his mother to England. Birth of his sister, Alice Macdonald Kipling ('Trix') in London. Return to Bombay.	Browning: *The Ring and the Book*. Dostoevsky: *The Idiot*. Collins: *The Moonstone*. Tolstoy: *War and Peace* (1869).
1871	Kiplings leave Bombay for England. The children are taken to Southsea to be cared for by Mrs Pryse Agar Holloway. Parents return to Bombay.	Dostoevsky: *The Devils*. Carroll: *Through the Looking Glass*. Turgenev: 'Spring Torrents' (1872). Abdullah Bilgrami: *The Romance of Amir-Hamzah*.
1875	Kipling's parents move from Bombay to Lahore where his father is to be director of the School of Art and curator of Lahore Museum.	
1877	Kipling's mother returns to England, taking her children from the care of Mrs Holloway. They spend a summer in Epping and then take lodgings in London.	Tolstoy: *Anna Karenina*. James: *The American*. Flaubert: *Trois Contes*.
1878	Kipling enters the United Services College, Westward Ho!, North Devon. Kipling's father arrives in England (the first time Kipling has seen him since 1871): they go to Paris where John Lockwood Kipling is in charge of Indian exhibit at the Paris Exhibition.	Hardy: *Return of the Native*. Swinburne: *Poems and Ballads*.
1880	Kipling meets Florence Garrard.	Dostoevsky: *The Brothers Karamazov*. Henty: *The Young Buglers*.

HISTORICAL EVENTS

End of American Civil War. Assassination of Lincoln.

Foundation of Ku Klux Klan in US.
Suez Canal opens (1869).

Paris Commune. Abolition of purchase of army commissions. Trade Unions legalized in Britain. End of Franco-Prussian War.

Carnarvon revives Grey's proposal for South African Federation. Public Health Act in Britain. Prince of Wales visits India. Telephone invented by Alexander Graham Bell (1876).

Queen Victoria proclaimed Empress of India in Delhi. Annexation of Transvaal; 9th Kafir War.

Congress of Berlin. Afghan War. Paris World Exhibition.

Liberal Majority; Gladstone becomes Prime Minister. Transvaal Boers declare Republic.

DATE	AUTHOR'S LIFE	LITERARY CONTEXT
1881	Edits United Service College's *Chronicle*. *Schoolboy Lyrics* privately printed in Lahore.	James: *The Portrait of a Lady*.
1882	Sails from London to join parents in Lahore and begin work on the *Civil and Military Gazette (CMG)* as assistant to the editor.	Ibsen: *An Enemy of the People*.
1883	Kipling's mother returns to England to collect 'Trix'. Kipling's first visit to Simla. The family are re-united in Lahore for Christmas.	Nietzsche: *Thus Spake Zarathustra*. Stevenson: *Treasure Island*.
1884	Writes series of special reports on 'The Viceroy at Patiala' – his first major piece of work for the *CMG*. Engagement to Florence Garrard broken off. A volume of verse parodies by Kipling and his sister published as *Echoes*.	Twain: *Huckleberry Finn*. Huysmans: *A Rebours*. Maupassant: *Claire de Lune*; *Miss Harriet*. Henty: *With Clive in India*. Nazir Ahmad: *The Repentance of Nussooh* (in translation).
1885	Conceives idea of 'Mother Maturin', his never published novel of India. From March–April Kipling is special correspondent of *CMG* at meeting of Viceroy of India and Amir of Afghanistan in Rawalpinda. Walking tour in Himalayas. *Quartette* published – the work of all four Kiplings.	Zola: *Germinal*. Maupassant: *Bel-Ami*. Haggard: *King Solomon's Mines*. Stevenson: *A Child's Garden of Verses*. Pinero: *The Magistrate*.
1886	Joins Masonic Lodge 'Hope and Perseverance', no. 782, Lahore. *Departmental Ditties*. At Simla.	Stevenson: *Dr Jekyll and Mr Hyde*; *Kidnapped*. James: *The Bostonians*. Hardy: *The Mayor of Casterbridge*.
1887	Begins work at *The Pioneer*, Allahabad.	Haggard: *She*.
1888	*Plain Tales from the Hills*. Takes up editorship of *CMG* in editor's absence. Moves into Belvedere, Allahabad. *Soldiers Three*, first of the 'Indian Railway Library' series.	Wilde: *The Happy Prince and Other Tales*. Zola: *La Terre*. James: *The Aspern Papers*.
1889	Leaves India from Calcutta en route to Japan and the United States. Writes *From Sea to Sea*	Twain: *A Connecticut Yankee at King Arthur's Court*. Jerome: *Three Men in a Boat*.

CHRONOLOGY

HISTORICAL EVENTS

Tsar Alexander II assassinated. Opening of Natural History Museum in South Kensington.

Married Women's Property Act.

Ripon attempts to place British and Indian magistrates on equal terms.

Third Reform Bill. Gladstone restores autonomy of Transvaal.

Fall of Khartoum. Salisbury becomes Prime Minister. First Indian National Congress.

Gladstone becomes Prime Minister. First Home Rule for Ireland Bill. Greenwich bomb outrage.

Queen Victoria's Golden Jubilee. 'Bloody Sunday' (police attack demonstrators in Trafalgar Square: 200 injured and 3 killed.) Match girls' strike in London. Gladstone's First Home Rule Bill defeated. Wilhelm II becomes Kaiser.

Large central area of the Indian territory opened; huge land rush. London Dock Strike. Eiffel Tower built.

DATE	AUTHOR'S LIFE	LITERARY CONTEXT
1889 cont.	travelling across US. Arrives in Liverpool; engaged to Caroline Taylor. Stories and verses appear in *Macmillan's* and *St James's Gazette*. Kipling now sought after by London editors. Retains A. P. Watt as literary agent.	Stevenson: *The Master of Ballantrae*.
1890	'Indian Railway Library' stories republished in England, beginning with *Soldiers Three*. Severe illness; engagement to Caroline Taylor broken off. Subject of leading article in *The Times*. Kipling's parents arrive in England and stay from May until September. First meeting with Caroline Balestier.	Ibsen: *Hedda Gabler*. James: *The Tragic Muse*. Wilde: *The Picture of Dorian Gray*. Maupassant: *L'Inutile Beauté*.
1891	Complete edition of *The Light that Failed*. Travels to New York. *Life's Handicap*. Sails on world tour visiting Cape Town, New Zealand, Australia and finally Lahore, India. Returns to England in December.	Hardy: *Tess of the d'Urbervilles*. Gissing: *New Grub Street*. Doyle: *The Adventures of Sherlock Holmes*.
1892	Marries Caroline Balestier (January); honeymoon to US, Canada, Japan. *Barrack-Room Ballads*; *The Naulahka*. Takes up residence in Brattleboro, Vermont. Birth of first child, Josephine (December).	Zola: *Le Débâcle*. Wilde: *Lady Windermere's Fan*. Whitman: *Leaves of Grass*, 3rd edition.
1893	*Many Inventions*. Kiplings move into a house designed and built for them north of Brattleboro.	Doyle: *Memoirs of Sherlock Holmes*. Pinero: *The Second Mrs Tanqueray*. Twain: *Pudd'nhead Wilson*.
1894	Trip to England. *The Jungle Book*. Makes speech at Westward Ho! Returns to Vermont.	Shaw: *Arms and the Man*. Hope: *The Prisoner of Zenda*.
1895	In Washington, DC (February). In England (July–August). *The Second Jungle Book*.	Crane: *The Red Badge of Courage*. Hardy: *Jude the Obscure*. Wells: *The Time Machine*. Wilde: *The Importance of Being Earnest*.

HISTORICAL EVENTS

Fall of Bismarck. Parnell resigns as Irish Nationalist leader.

James Keir Hardie elected MP; first Independent Labour Party Member.

Indian Councils Act. Resignation of Salisbury; Gladstone Prime Minister for fourth and last time.

Gladstone's second Irish Home Rule Bill rejected by Lords.

Dreyfus affair. Nicholas II becomes Tsar. Gladstone resigns, having split Liberals over Home Rule.

Salisbury again Prime Minister after Liberal defeat.

RUDYARD KIPLING

DATE	AUTHOR'S LIFE	LITERARY CONTEXT
1896	Birth of second daughter, Elsie (February). Sails for England and takes up residence at Maidencombe, Devon. *The Seven Seas*.	Conrad: *An Outcast of the Islands*. Housman: *A Shropshire Lad*. Stevenson: *Weir of Hermiston*. Wells: *The Island of Doctor Moreau*.
1897	Moves to London and then to Rottingdean. Birth of son, John (August). *Captain's Courageous*.	Conrad: *The Nigger of the Narcissus*. Wells: *The Invisible Man*.
1989	Takes family to Cape Town. *The Day's Work*; *A Fleet in Being*.	Wells: *The War of the Worlds*. Hardy: *Wessex Poems*.
1899	Sails with family for New York; Children ill on arrival – death of Josephine (March). Family return to England: Kipling never returns to US. *From Sea to Sea*; *Stalky & Co.*, 'The White Man's Burden'.	Chekhov: *The Lady with the Little Dog*. Tolstoy: *Resurrection*.
1900	Visits South Africa and works on the staff of *The Friend*. From now until 1908 Kipling in South Africa from January to March.	Conrad: *Lord Jim*. Freud: *The Interpretation of Dreams*. Dreiser: *Sister Carrie*.
1901	Returns to England. With Channel Fleet on manoeuvres. *Kim*. Returns to South Africa.	Mann: *Buddenbrooks*. Yeats: *Poems*.
1902	*Just So Stories*.	James: *The Wings of the Dove*.
1903	*The Five Nations*.	James: *The Ambassadors*. London: *Call of the Wild*. Conrad: *Typhoon*. Shaw: *Man and Superman*. Ahmad: *The Bride's Mirror* (in translation). Butler: *The Way of All Flesh*.
1904	*Traffics and Discoveries*.	Chekhov: *The Cherry Orchard*. Conrad: *Nostromo*. James: *The Golden Bowl*.
1905	*Puck of Pook's Hill*.	Wells: *Kipps*. Wharton: *The House of Mirth*.
1906		Sinclair: *The Jungle*.
1907	Receives honorary degrees at Durham and Oxford. Canadian tour. Awarded Nobel Prize.	Conrad: *The Secret Agent*.
1908	Honorary degree from Cambridge. Motor tour through north of England. *Letters to the Family*.	Forster: *A Room with a View*.

xxx

HISTORICAL EVENTS

Jameson Raid in South Africa; British negotiations with Boers fail.

Royal Commission reports on agricultural depression.

War between Spain and USA. Curies discover radium.

Boer War (until 1902). First Hague Conference.

Russia occupies Manchuria.

Queen Victoria dies. Assassination of President McKinley in US; succeeded by Roosevelt.

Resignation of Salisbury; Balfour Prime Minister.
Emmeline Pankhurst founds the Women's Social and Political Union.

Russo-Japanese War (until 1905).

Royal Commission on Poor Law. Bengal Partition: unrest in India.

Anglo-Russian Entente.
Second Hague Conference.

Asquith becomes Prime Minister. Austria annexes Bosnia and Herzegovina.
Formation of Muslim League in India.

DATE	AUTHOR'S LIFE	LITERARY CONTEXT
1909	*Actions and Reactions*; *Abaft the Funnel*.	Wells: *Tono-Bungay* and *Ann Veronica*.
1910	*Rewards and Fairies*. Death of Alice Kipling.	Forster: *Howards End*.
1911	Death of Kipling's father. *A History of England*, with C. R. L. Fletcher. Tours of France and Ireland.	Brooke: *Poems*. Pound: *Canzoni*.
1912	Motor tour in west of England. *Songs from Books*.	Mann: *Death in Venice*. Alain-Fournier: *Le Grand Meaulnes*. Tagore: *Gitanjali: Song Offering*.
1913	Voyage to Egypt and up the Nile. Kipling's play, *The Harbour Watch*, produced.	Lawrence: *Sons and Lovers*. Wharton: *The Custom of the Country*. Cather: *O Pioneers!* Proust: *Swann's Way*. Gorky: *Childhood*.
1914	Speech on Ulster at Tunbridge Wells. Secures commission in Irish Guards for John Kipling from Lord Roberts.	Joyce: *Dubliners*. Burroughs: *Tarzan of the Apes*.
1915	John Kipling reported wounded and missing. His body is never found. Kipling has gastritis; onset of permanent illness. *France at War*, *The Fringes of the Fleet* and *The New Army in Training*.	Lawrence: *The Rainbow*. Conrad: *Victory*. Ford: *The Good Soldier*. Buchan: *The Thirty-Nine Steps*. Maugham: *Of Human Bondage*. Muhammad Iqbal: *The Secrets of the Self*.
1916	*Sea Warfare*.	Joyce: *A Portrait of the Artist as a Young Man*. Hardy: *Selected Poems*.
1917	Joins War Graves Commission. Visits Italian front. *A Diversity of Creatures*.	Eliot: 'The Love Song of J. Alfred Prufrock'. Shaw: *Pygmalion*.
1918	*The Eyes of Asia*.	Strachey: *Eminent Victorians*. Cather: *My Antonia*.
1919	*The Years Between*.	Woolf: *Night and Day*. Shaw: *Heartbreak House*. Maugham: *The Moon and Sixpence*. Tagore: *The Home and the World*.
1920	Honorary degree from the University of Edinburgh. Visit to French battlefields, including Chalkpit Wood, where John Kipling was lost. *Letters of Travel*.	Lawrence: *Women in Love*. Mansfield: *Bliss*. Fitzgerald: *This Side of Paradise*. Owen: *Poems*.

CHRONOLOGY

HISTORICAL EVENTS

Lloyd George introduces People's Budget. Blériot flies across Channel.

Death of Edward VII. Liberals back in power.

Coronation of George V. Agadir crisis. Suffragette riots. Chinese Revolution.

First Balkan War. Sinking of *Titanic*.

Second Balkan War.

Outbreak of World War I.

Asquith forms coalition government with Balfour. Rasputin effective ruler of Russia.

First battle of the Somme. Lloyd George becomes Prime Minister.

Russian Revolution. US joins war. Third battle of Ypres.

Armistice. Women over thirty gain vote.

Versailles peace conference. Hitler founds National Socialist German Workers' Party. Punjab riots.

Formation of League of Nations. Prohibition in the US.

DATE	AUTHOR'S LIFE	LITERARY CONTEXT
1921	Visits Algiers. Honorary degrees from the Sorbonne and the University of Strasbourg.	Huxley: *Crome Yellow*.
1922	Tour to Gibraltar and Spain. Visit to French cemeteries; hears King George's address at Boulogne. In London nursing home for examination – has abdominal operation.	Eliot: *The Waste Land*. Joyce: *Ulysses*. Hašek: *The Good Soldier Švejk*. Ahmed Ali: *Ocean of Night*. Mansfield: *The Garden Party*.
1923	Rectorial address at St Andrew's. *The Irish Guards in the Great War; Land and Sea Tales*.	Huxley: *Antic Hay*. Hitler: *Mein Kampf*.
1924	Elsie Kipling marries George Bambridge.	Forster: *A Passage to India*. Shaw: *St Joan*. Ford: *Parade's End*. Mann: *The Magic Mountain*. Tagore: *Gora*.
1925	Motor tours through France and west of England. Seriously ill with pneumonia.	Eliot: *Poems 1909–1925*. Dreiser: *An American Tragedy*. Fitzgerald: *The Great Gatsby*. Woolf: *Mrs Dalloway*. Kafka: *The Trial*.
1926	*Debits and Credits*.	Kafka: *The Castle*. Gide: *The Counterfeiters*.
1927	Voyage to Brazil from January to April. Kipling attends the opening of Indian War Memorial in France.	Woolf: *To the Lighthouse*. Hemingway: *Men Without Women*.
1928	Kipling a pallbearer at funeral of Thomas Hardy. *A Book of Words*.	Lawrence: *Lady Chatterley's Lover; The Woman Who Rode Away*. Bulgakov: *The Master and Margarita*. Waugh: *Decline and Fall*. Maugham: *Ashenden*.
1929	Visits war graves in Egypt and Palestine.	Remarque: *All Quiet on the Western Front*. Graves: *Goodbye to All That*. Hemingway: *A Farewell to Arms*. Faulkner: *The Sound and the Fury*.
1930	Voyage to Jamaica and then Bermuda where Kipling's wife, having been ill, is hospitalized. At dedication of monument, Dud Corner, Loos, to the missing (including John Kipling). *Thy Servant a Dog*.	Faulkner: *As I Lay Dying*. Hammett: *The Maltese Falcon*. Crane: *The Bridge*. Freud: *Civilization and its Discontents*. Musil: *The Man without Qualities*. Maugham: *Cakes and Ale*.

CHRONOLOGY

RUDYARD KIPLING

DATE	AUTHOR'S LIFE	LITERARY CONTEXT
1931	In nursing home for examination: doctors conclude against an operation.	Prem Chand: *Deliverance*.
1932	Tour of the Midlands in new Rolls Royce. Kipling made honorary fellow of Magdalene College, Cambridge.	Faulkner: *Light in August*. Huxley: *Brave New World*. Iqbal: *Javid-Nama*.
1933	Kipling is diagnosed as having duodenal ulcer. Elected to Institut de France. *Souvenirs of France*.	Hemingway: *Winner Take Nothing*.
1934	*Collected Dog Stories*.	Fitzgerald: *Tender is the Night*. Miller: *Tropic of Cancer*. Waugh: *A Handful of Dust*.
1935	Begins his autobiography.	Eliot: *Murder in the Cathedral*.
1936	Kipling is taken ill in London and dies in Middlesex hospital (18 January).	Faulkner: *Absalom, Absalom!* Prem Chand: *Godan*.
1937	*Something of Myself* posthumously published.	Steinbeck: *Of Mice and Men*. Hemingway: *To Have and Have Not*.

CHRONOLOGY

HISTORICAL EVENTS

Financial crisis in Britain. London Round Table Conference on India: Ghandi insists on all-India government; opposed by Muslims of Pakistan.

Hunger marches in Britain. F. D. Roosevelt's landslide victory.

Hitler becomes Chancellor of Germany. Nazi persecution of Jews begins. 'New Deal' announced by Roosevelt in US.

Riots in Paris.

Italy invade Abyssinia. Baldwin Prime Minister after resignation of Macdonald.
Spanish civil war begins. Abdication crisis in Britain.

Japanese invade China. Attempts are made to appease Hitler. Discovery of Fascist plot in Paris. Baldwin retires and Neville Chamberlain becomes Prime Minister. Punjab becomes autonomous province of India.

RUDYARD KIPLING
COLLECTED STORIES

—

IN THE HOUSE OF SUDDHOO

IN THE HOUSE OF SUDDHOO

* * *

A stone's throw out on either hand
From that well-ordered road we tread,
    And all the world is wild and strange:
Churel and ghoul and *Djinn* and sprite
Shall bear us company to-night,
For we have reached the Oldest Land
    Wherein the powers of Darkness range.

From the Dusk to the Dawn

THE house of Suddhoo, near the Taksali Gate, is two-storeyed, with four carved windows of old brown wood, and a flat roof. You may recognise it by five red hand-prints arranged like the Five of Diamonds on the whitewash between the upper windows. Bhagwan Dass the grocer and a man who says he gets his living by seal-cutting live in the lower storey with a troop of wives, servants, friends, and retainers. The two upper rooms used to be occupied by Janoo and Azizun and a little black-and-tan terrier that was stolen from an Englishman's house and given to Janoo by a soldier. To-day, only Janoo lives in the upper rooms. Suddhoo sleeps on the roof generally, except when he sleeps in the street. He used to go to Peshawar in the cold weather to visit his son who sells curiosities near the Edwardes' Gate, and then he slept under a real mud roof. Suddhoo is a great friend of mine, because his cousin had a son who secured, thanks to my recommendation, the post of head-messenger to a big firm in the Station. Suddhoo says that God will make me a Lieutenant-Governor one of these days. I daresay his prophecy will come true. He is very, very old, with white hair and no teeth worth showing, and he has outlived his wits

– outlived nearly everything except his fondness for his son at Peshawar. Janoo and Azizun are Kashmiris, Ladies of the City, and theirs was an ancient and more or less honourable profession; but Azizun has since married a medical student from the North-West and has settled down to a most respectable life somewhere near Bareilly. Bhagwan Dass is an extortionate and an adulterator. He is very rich. The man who is supposed to get his living by seal-cutting pretends to be very poor. This lets you know as much as is necessary of the four principal tenants in the house of Suddhoo. Then there is Me of course; but I am only the chorus that comes in at the end to explain things. So I do not count.

Suddhoo was not clever. The man who pretended to cut seals was the cleverest of them all – Bhagwan Dass only knew how to lie – except Janoo. She was also beautiful, but that was her own affair.

Suddhoo's son at Peshawar was attacked by pleurisy, and old Suddhoo was troubled. The seal-cutter man heard of Suddhoo's anxiety and made capital out of it. He was abreast of the times. He got a friend in Peshawar to telegraph daily accounts of the son's health. And here the story begins.

Suddhoo's cousin's son told me, one evening, that Suddhoo wanted to see me; that he was too old and feeble to come personally, and that I should be conferring an everlasting honour on the house of Suddhoo if I went to him. I went; but I think, seeing how well off Suddhoo was then, that he might have sent something better than an *ekka*, which jolted fearfully, to haul out a future Lieutenant-Governor to the City on a muggy April evening. The *ekka* did not run quickly. It was full dark when we pulled up opposite the door of Ranjit Singh's Tomb near the main gate of the Fort. Here was Suddhoo, and he said that, by reason of my condescension, it was absolutely certain that I should become a Lieutenant-Governor while my hair was yet black. Then we talked about the weather, and the state of my health, and the wheat crops, for fifteen minutes, in the Huzuri Bagh, under the stars.

Suddhoo came to the point at last. He said that Janoo had told him that there was an order of the *Sirkar* against magic, because it was feared that magic might one day kill the Empress of India. I didn't know anything about the state of the law; but I fancied that something interesting was going to happen. I said that so far from magic being discouraged by the Government, it was highly commended. The greatest officials of the State practised it themselves. (If the Financial Statement isn't magic, I don't know what is.) Then, to encourage him further, I said that, if there was any *jadoo* afoot, I had not the least objection to giving it my countenance and sanction, and to seeing that it was clean *jadoo* – white magic, as distinguished from the unclean *jadoo* which kills folk. It took a long time before Suddhoo admitted that this was just what he had asked me to come for. Then he told me, in jerks and quavers, that the man who said he cut seals was a sorcerer of the cleanest kind; that every day he gave Suddhoo news of the sick son in Peshawar more quickly than the lightning could fly, and that this news was always corroborated by the letters. Further, that he had told Suddhoo how a great danger was threatening his son, which could be removed by clean *jadoo*; and, of course, heavy payment. I began to see exactly how the land lay, and told Suddhoo that I also understood a little *jadoo* in the Western line, and would go to his house to see that everything was done decently and in order. We set off together; and on the way Suddhoo told me that he had paid the seal-cutter between one hundred and two hundred rupees already; and the *jadoo* of that night would cost two hundred more. Which was cheap, he said, considering the greatness of his son's danger; but I do not think he meant it.

The lights were all cloaked in the front of the house when we arrived. I could hear awful noises from behind the seal-cutter's shop-front, as if some one were groaning his soul out. Suddhoo shook all over, and while we groped our way upstairs told me that the *jadoo* had begun. Janoo and Azizun met us at the stair-head, and told us that the *jadoo*-work was coming off in their rooms, because there was more space there. Janoo is a lady of a freethinking turn of mind. She whispered that the *jadoo* was an invention to get money out of Suddhoo, and that the seal-cutter would go to a hot place when he died. Suddhoo was nearly crying with fear and old age. He kept walking up and down the room in the half-light, repeating his son's name over and over again, and asking Azizun if the seal-cutter ought not to make a reduction in the case of his own landlord. Janoo pulled me over to the shadow in the recess of the carved bow-windows. The boards were up, and the rooms were only lit by one tiny oil-lamp. There was no chance of my being seen if I stayed still.

Presently the groans below ceased, and we heard steps on the staircase. That was the seal-cutter. He stopped outside the door as the terrier barked and Azizun fumbled at the chain, and he told Suddhoo to blow out the lamp. This left the place in jet darkness, except for the red glow from the two *huqas* that belonged to Janoo and Azizun. The seal-cutter came in, and I heard Suddhoo throw himself down on the floor and groan. Azizun caught her breath, and Janoo backed on to one of the beds with a shudder. There was a clink of something metallic, and then shot up a pale blue-green flame near the ground. The light was just enough to show Azizun, pressed against one corner of the room with the terrier between her knees; Janoo, with her hands clasped, leaning forward as she sat on the bed; Suddhoo, face down, quivering, and the seal-cutter.

I hope I may never see another man like that seal-cutter. He was stripped to the waist, with a wreath of white jasmine as thick as my wrist round his forehead, a salmon-coloured loin-cloth round his middle, and a steel bangle on each ankle. This was not awe-inspiring. It was the face of the man that turned me cold. It was a blue-grey in the first place. In the second, the eyes were rolled back till you could only see the whites of them; and, in the third, the face was the face of a demon – a ghoul – anything you please except of the sleek, oily old ruffian who sat in the daytime over his turning-lathe

downstairs. He was lying on his stomach with his arms
turned and crossed behind him, as if he had been thrown
down pinioned. His head and neck were the only parts of
him off the floor. They were nearly at right angles to the
body, like the head of a cobra at spring. It was ghastly. In
the centre of the room, on the bare earth floor, stood a big,
deep, brass basin, with a pale blue-green light floating in the
centre like a night-light. Round that basin the man on the
floor wriggled himself three times. How he did it I do not
know. I could see the muscles ripple along his spine and fall
smooth again; but I could not see any other motion. The
head seemed the only thing alive about him, except that slow
curl and uncurl of the labouring back-muscles. Janoo from
the bed was breathing seventy to the minute; Azizun held her
hands before her eyes; and old Suddhoo, fingering at the dirt
that had got into his white beard, was crying to himself. The
horror of it was that the creeping, crawly thing made no
sound – only crawled! And, remember, this lasted for ten
minutes, while the terrier whined, and Azizun shuddered,
and Janoo gasped, and Suddhoo cried.

I felt the hair lift at the back of my head and my heart
thump like a thermantidote paddle. Luckily, the seal-cutter
betrayed himself by his most impressive trick and made me
calm again. After he had finished that unspeakable triple
crawl, he stretched his head away from the floor as high as
he could and sent out a jet of fire from his nostrils. Now I
knew how fire-spouting is done – I can do it myself – so I
felt at ease. The business was a fraud. If he had only kept to
that crawl without trying to raise the effect, goodness knows
what I might not have thought. Both the girls shrieked at the
jet of fire, and the head dropped, chin down, on the floor,
with a thud; the whole body lying then like a corpse with its
arms trussed. There was a pause of five full minutes after
this, and the blue-green flame died down. Janoo stooped to
settle one of her anklets, while Azizun turned her face to the
wall and took the terrier in her arms. Suddhoo put out an
arm mechanically to Janoo's *huqa*, and she slid it across the

floor with her foot. Directly above the body and on the wall were a couple of flaming portraits, in stamped-paper frames, of the Queen and the Prince of Wales. They looked down on the performance, and, to my thinking, seemed to heighten the grotesqueness of it all.

Just when the silence was getting unendurable, the body turned over and rolled away from the basin to the side of the room, where it lay stomach up. There was a faint "plop" from the basin – exactly like the noise a fish makes when it takes a fly – and the green light in the centre revived.

I looked at the basin, and saw, bobbing in the water, the dried, shrivelled, black head of a native baby – open eyes, open mouth, and shaved scalp. It was worse, being so very sudden, than the crawling exhibition. We had no time to say anything before it began to speak.

Read Poe's account of the voice that came from the mesmerised dying man, and you will realise less than one half of the horror of that head's voice.

There was an interval of a second or two between each word, and a sort of "ring, ring, ring" in the note of the voice, like the timbre of a bell. It pealed slowly, as if talking to itself, for several minutes before I got rid of my cold sweat. Then the blessed solution struck me. I looked at the body lying near the doorway, and saw, just where the hollow of the throat joins on the shoulders, a muscle that had nothing to do with any man's regular breathing twitching away steadily. The whole thing was a careful reproduction of the Egyptian teraphin that one reads about sometimes; and the voice was as clever and as appalling a piece of ventriloquism as one could wish to hear. All this time the head was "lip-lip-lapping" against the side of the basin, and speaking. It told Suddhoo, on his face again whining, of his son's illness and of the state of the illness up to the evening of that very night. I always shall respect the seal-cutter for keeping so faithfully to the time of the Peshawar telegrams. It went on to say that skilled doctors were night and day watching over the man's life; and that he would eventually recover if the fee to the potent sorcerer, whose servant was the head in the basin, were doubled.

Here the mistake from the artistic point of view came in. To ask for twice your stipulated fee in a voice that Lazarus might have used when he rose from the dead is absurd. Janoo, who is really a woman of masculine intellect, saw this as quickly as I did. I heard her say, "*Asli nahin! Fareib!*" scornfully under her breath; and just as she said so, the light in the basin died out, the head stopped talking, and we heard the room-door creak on its hinges. Then Janoo struck a match, lit the lamp, and we saw that head, basin, and seal-cutter were gone. Suddhoo was wringing his hands and explaining to any one who cared to listen, that, if his chances of eternal salvation depended on it, he could not raise another two hundred rupees. Azizun was nearly in hysterics in the corner; while Janoo sat down composedly on one of the beds to discuss the probabilities of the whole thing being a *bunao*, or "make-up."

I explained as much as I knew of the seal-cutter's way of *jadoo*; but her argument was much more simple – "The magic that is always demanding gifts is no true magic," said she. "My mother told me that the only potent love-spells are those which are told you for love. This seal-cutter man is a liar and a devil. I dare not tell, do anything, or get anything done, because I am in debt to Bhagwan Dass the *bunnia* for two gold rings and a heavy anklet. I must get my food from his shop. The seal-cutter is the friend of Bhagwan Dass, and he would poison my food. A fool's *jadoo* has been going on for ten days, and has cost Suddhoo many rupees each night. The seal-cutter used black hens and lemons and *mantras* before. He never showed us anything like this till to-night. Azizun is a fool, and will be a *purdahnashin* soon. Suddhoo has lost his strength and his wits. See now! I had hoped to get from Suddhoo many rupees while he lived, and many more after his death; and behold, he is spending everything on that offspring of a devil and a she-ass, the seal-cutter!"

Here I said, "But what induced Suddhoo to drag me into

the business? Of course I can speak to the seal-cutter, and he shall refund. The whole thing is child's talk — shame — and senseless."

"Suddhoo *is* an old child," said Janoo. "He has lived on the roofs these seventy years, and is as senseless as a milch- goat. He brought you here to assure himself that he was not break-ing any law of the *Sirkar*, whose salt he ate many years ago. He worships the dust off the feet of the seal-cutter, and that cow-devourer has forbidden him to go and see his son. What does Suddhoo know of your laws or the lightning-post? I have to watch his money going day by day to that lying beast below."

Janoo stamped her foot on the floor and nearly cried with vexation; while Suddhoo was whimpering under a blanket in the corner, and Azizun was trying to guide the pipe-stem to his foolish old mouth.

* * *

Now, the case stands thus. Unthinkingly, I have laid my-self open to the charge of aiding and abetting the seal-cutter in obtaining money under false pretences, which is forbidden by Section 420 of the Indian Penal Code. I am helpless in the matter for these reasons. I cannot inform the Police. What witnesses would support my statements? Janoo refuses flatly, and Azizun is a veiled woman somewhere near Bareilly — lost in this big India of ours. I dare not again take the law into my own hands, and speak to the seal-cutter; for certain am I that, not only would Suddhoo disbelieve me, but this step would end in the poisoning of Janoo, who is bound hand and foot by her debt to the *bunnia*. Suddhoo is an old dotard; and whenever we meet mumbles my idiotic joke that the *Sirkar* rather patronises the Black Art than otherwise. His son is well now; but Suddhoo is completely under the in-fluence of the seal-cutter, by whose advice he regulates the affairs of his life. Janoo watches daily the money that she hoped to wheedle out of Suddhoo taken by the seal-cutter, and becomes daily more furious and sullen.

She will never tell, because she dare not; but, unless something happens to prevent her, I am afraid that the seal-cutter will die of cholera – the white arsenic kind – about the middle of May. And thus I shall be privy to a murder in the House of Suddhoo.

BEYOND THE PALE

BEYOND THE PALE

* * *

Love heeds not caste nor sleep a broken bed. I went in search of love and lost myself.

Hindu Proverb

A MAN should, whatever happens, keep to his own caste, race and breed. Let the White go to the White and the Black to the Black. Then, whatever trouble falls is in the ordinary course of things – neither sudden, alien nor unexpected.

This is the story of a man who wilfully stepped beyond the safe limits of decent everyday society, and paid for it heavily.

He knew too much in the first instance; and he saw too much in the second. He took too deep an interest in native life; but he will never do so again.

Deep away in the heart of the City, behind Jitha Megji's *bustee*, lies Amir Nath's Gully, which ends in a dead-wall pierced by one grated window. At the head of the Gully is a big cowbyre, and the walls on either side of the Gully are without windows. Neither Suchet Singh nor Gaur Chand approve of their women-folk looking into the world. If Durga Charan had been of their opinion, he would have been a happier man to-day, and little Bisesa would have been able to knead her own bread. Her room looked out through the grated window into the narrow dark Gully where the sun never came and where the buffaloes wallowed in the blue slime. She was a widow, about fifteen years old, and she prayed the Gods, day and night, to send her a lover; for she did not approve of living alone.

One day, the man – Trejago his name was – came into Amir Nath's Gully on an aimless wandering; and, after he had passed the buffaloes, stumbled over a big heap of cattle-food.

17

Then he saw that the Gully ended in a trap, and heard a little laugh from behind the grated window. It was a pretty little laugh, and Trejago, knowing that, for all practical purposes, the old "Arabian Nights" are good guides, went forward to the window, and whispered that verse of "The Love Song of Har Dyal" which begins:–

Can a man stand upright in the face of the naked Sun; or a Lover in the Presence of his Beloved?
If my feet fail me, O Heart of my Heart, am I to blame, being blinded by the glimpse of your beauty?

There came the faint *tchink* of a woman's bracelets from behind the grating, and a little voice went on with the song at the fifth verse:–

Alas! alas! Can the Moon tell the Lotus of her love when the Gate of Heaven is shut and the clouds gather for the rains?
They have taken my Beloved, and driven her with the pack-horses to the North.
There are iron chains on the feet that were set on my heart.
Call to the bowmen to make ready—

The voice stopped suddenly, and Trejago walked out of Amir Nath's Gully, wondering who in the world could have capped "The Love Song of Har Dyal" so neatly.

Next morning, as he was driving to office, an old woman threw a packet into his dogcart. In the packet was the half of a broken glass-bangle, one flower of the blood-red *dhak*, a pinch of *bhusa* or cattle-food, and eleven cardamoms. That packet was a letter – not a clumsy compromising letter, but an innocent, unintelligible lover's epistle.

Trejago knew far too much about these things, as I have said. No Englishman should be able to translate object-letters. But Trejago spread all the trifles on the lid of his office-box and began to puzzle them out.

A broken glass-bangle stands for a Hindu widow all India over; because when her husband dies, a woman's bracelets are broken on her wrists. Trejago saw the meaning of the little bit of the glass. The flower of the *dhak* means diverse-

ly "desire," "come," "write," or "danger," according to the
other things with it. One cardamom means "jealousy"; but
when any article is duplicated in an object-letter, it loses its
symbolic meaning and stands merely for one of a number
indicating time, or, if incense, curds, or saffron be sent also,
place. The message ran then – "A widow – *dhak* flower and
bhusa – at eleven o'clock." The pinch of *bhusa* enlightened
Trejago. He saw – this kind of letter leaves much to instinct-
ive knowledge – that the *bhusa* referred to the big heap of
cattle-food over which he had fallen in Amir Nath's Gully,
and that the message must come from the person behind the
grating; she being a widow. So the message ran then – "A
widow, in the Gully in which is the heap of *bhusa*, desires
you to come at eleven o'clock."

Trejago threw all the rubbish into the fireplace and
laughed. He knew that men in the East do not make love
under windows at eleven in the forenoon, nor do women fix
appointments a week in advance. So he went, that very night
at eleven, into Amir Nath's Gully, clad in a *boorka*, which
cloaks a man as well as a woman. Directly the gongs of the
City made the hour, the little voice behind the grating took
up "The Love Song of Har Dyal" at the verse where the
Pathan girl calls upon Har Dyal to return. The song is really
pretty in the Vernacular. In English you miss the wail of it.
It runs something like this–

> Alone upon the housetops to the North
>   I turn and watch the lightning in the sky,–
> The glamour of thy footsteps in the North,
>   *Come back to me, Beloved, or I die!*
>
> Below my feet the still bazar is laid,
>   Far, far below the weary camels lie,–
> The camels and the captives of thy raid.
>   *Come back to me, Beloved, or I die!*
>
> My father's wife is old and harsh with years,
>   And drudge of all my father's house am I.
> My bread is sorrow and my drink is tears,
>   *Come back to me, Beloved, or I die!*

As the song stopped, Trejago stepped up under the grating and whispered – "I am here."

Bisesa was good to look upon.

That night was the beginning of many strange things, and of a double life so wild that Trejago to-day sometimes wonders if it were not all a dream. Bisesa, or her old handmaiden who had thrown the object-letter, had detached the heavy grating from the brick-work of the wall; so that the window slid inside, leaving only a square of raw masonry into which an active man might climb.

In the day-time, Trejago drove through his routine of office-work, or put on his calling-clothes and called on the ladies of the Station; wondering how long they would know him if they knew of poor little Bisesa. At night, when all the City was still, came the walk under the evil-smelling *boorka*, the patrol through Jitha Megji's *bustee*, the quick turn into Amir Nath's Gully between the sleeping cattle and the dead walls, and then, last of all, Bisesa, and the deep, even breathing of the old woman who slept outside the door of the bare little room that Durga Charan allotted to his sister's daughter. Who or what Durga Charan was, Trejago never inquired; and why in the world he was not discovered and knifed never occurred to him till his madness was over, and Bisesa . . . But this comes later.

Bisesa was an endless delight to Trejago. She was as ignorant as a bird; and her distorted versions of the rumours from the outside world that had reached her in her room, amused Trejago almost as much as her lisping attempts to pronounce his name – "Christopher." The first syllable was always more than she could manage, and she made funny little gestures with her roseleaf hands, as one throwing the name away, and then, kneeling before Trejago, asked him, exactly as an Englishwoman would do, if he were sure he loved her. Trejago swore that he loved her more than any one else in the world. Which was true.

After a month of this folly, the exigencies of his other life compelled Trejago to be especially attentive to a lady of his acquaintance. You may take it for a fact that anything of this kind is not only noticed and discussed by a man's own race, but by some hundred and fifty natives as well. Trejago had to walk with this lady and talk to her at the Band-stand, and once or twice to drive with her; never for an instant dreaming that this would affect his dearer, out-of-the-way life. But the news flew, in the usual mysterious fashion, from mouth to mouth, till Bisesa's duenna heard of it and told Bisesa. The child was so troubled that she did the household work evilly, and was beaten by Durga Charan's wife in consequence.

A week later, Bisesa taxed Trejago with the flirtation. She understood no gradations and spoke openly. Trejago laughed and Bisesa stamped her little feet – little feet, light as marigold flowers, that could lie in the palm of a man's one hand.

Much that is written about Oriental passion and impulsiveness is exaggerated and compiled at second-hand, but a little of it is true; and when an Englishman finds that little, it is quite as startling as any passion in his own proper life. Bisesa raged and stormed, and finally threatened to kill herself if Trejago did not at once drop the alien Memsahib who had come between them. Trejago tried to explain, and to show her that she did not understand these things from a Western standpoint. Bisesa drew herself up, and said simply–

"I do not. I know only this – it is not good that I should have made you dearer than my own heart to me, Sahib. You are an Englishman. I am only a black girl," – she was fairer than bar-gold in the Mint, – "and the widow of a black man."

Then she sobbed and said – "But on my soul and my Mother's soul, I love you. There shall no harm come to you, whatever happens to me."

Trejago argued with the child, and tried to soothe her, but she seemed quite unreasonably disturbed. Nothing would satisfy her save that all relations between them should end. He was to go away at once. And he went. As he dropped out of the window, she kissed his forehead twice, and he walked home wondering.

A week, and then three weeks, passed without a sign from Bisesa. Trejago, thinking that the rupture had lasted quite long enough, went down to Amir Nath's Gully for the fifth time in the three weeks, hoping that his rap at the sill of the shifting grating would be answered. He was not disappointed.

There was a young moon, and one stream of light fell down into Amir Nath's Gully, and struck the grating, which was drawn away as he knocked. From the black dark, Bisesa held out her arms into the moonlight. Both hands had been cut off at the wrists, and the stumps were nearly healed.

Then, as Bisesa bowed her head between her arms and sobbed, some one in the room grunted like a wild beast, and something sharp – knife, sword, or spear – thrust at Trejago in his *boorka*. The stroke missed his body, but cut into one of the muscles of the groin, and he limped slightly from the wound for the rest of his days.

The grating went into its place. There was no sign whatever from inside the house – nothing but the moonlight strip on the high wall, and the blackness of Amir Nath's Gully behind.

The next thing Trejago remembers, after raging and shouting like a madman between those pitiless walls, is that he found himself near the river as the dawn was breaking, threw away his *boorka* and went home bareheaded.

* * *

What was the tragedy – whether Bisesa had, in a fit of causeless despair, told everything, or the intrigue had been discovered and she tortured to tell; whether Durga Charan knew his name, and what became of Bisesa – Trejago does not know to this day. Something horrible had happened, and the thought of what it must have been comes upon Trejago in the night now and again, and keeps him company till the morning. One special feature of the case is that he does not know where lies the front of Durga Charan's house. It may open on to a courtyard common to two or more houses, or it may lie behind any one of the gates of Jitha Megji's *bustee*. Trejago cannot tell. He cannot get Bisesa – poor little Bisesa – back again. He has lost her in the City where each man's house is as guarded and as unknowable as the grave; and the grating that opens into Amir Nath's Gully has been walled up.

But Trejago pays his calls regularly, and is reckoned a very decent sort of man.

There is nothing peculiar about him, except a slight stiffness, caused by a riding-strain, in the right leg.

A BANK FRAUD

A BANK FRAUD

* * *

He drank strong waters and his speech was coarse;
   He purchased raiment and forbore to pay;
He stuck a trusting junior with a horse,
   And won Gymkhanas in a doubtful way.
Then, 'twixt a vice and folly, turned aside
To do good deeds and straight to cloak them, lied.

The Mess Room

IF Reggie Burke were in India now, he would resent this
tale being told; but as he is in Hong Kong and won't see
it, the telling is safe. He was the man who worked the big
fraud on the Sind and Sialkote Bank. He was manager of an
upcountry Branch, and a sound practical man with a large
experience of native loan and insurance work. He could com-
bine the frivolities of ordinary life with his work, and yet do
well. Reggie Burke rode anything that would let him get up,
danced as neatly as he rode, and was wanted for every sort
of amusement in the Station.

As he said himself, and as many men found out rather to
their surprise, there were two Burkes, both very much at
your service. "Reggie Burke," between four and ten, ready for
anything from a hot-weather gymkhana to a riding- picnic,
and, between ten and four, "Mr. Reginald Burke, Manager
of the Sind and Sialkote Branch Bank." You might play polo
with him one afternoon and hear him express his opinions
when a man crossed; and you might call on him next morning
to raise a two-thousand-rupee loan on a five-hundred-pound
insurance policy, eighty pounds paid in premiums. He would
recognise you, but you would have some trouble in recognising him.

The Directors of the Bank – it had its headquarters in Calcutta and its General Manager's word carried weight with the Government – picked their men well. They had tested Reggie up to a fairly severe breaking-strain. They trusted him just as much as Directors ever trust Managers. You must see for yourself whether their trust was misplaced.

Reggie's Branch was in a big Station, and worked with the usual staff – one Manager, one Accountant, both English, a Cashier, and a horde of native clerks; besides the Police patrol at nights outside. The bulk of its work, for it was in a thriving district, was *hoondi* and accommodation of all kinds. A fool has no grip of this sort of business; and a clever man who does not go about among his clients, and know more than a little of their affairs, is worse than a fool. Reggie was young-looking, clean-shaved, with a twinkle in his eye, and a head that nothing short of a gallon of the Gunners' Madeira could make any impression on.

One day, at a big dinner, he announced casually that the Directors had shifted on to him a Natural Curiosity, from England, in the Accountant line. He was perfectly correct. Mr. Silas Riley, Accountant, was a most curious animal – a long, gawky, rawboned Yorkshireman, full of the savage self-conceit that blossoms only in the best county in England. Arrogance was a mild word for the mental attitude of Mr. S. Riley. He had worked himself up, after seven years, to a Cashier's position in a Huddersfield Bank; and all his experience lay among the factories of the North. Perhaps he would have done better on the Bombay side, where they are happy with one-half per cent. profits, and money is cheap. He was useless for Upper India and a wheat Province, where a man wants a large head and a touch of imagination if he is to turn out a satisfactory balance-sheet.

He was wonderfully narrow-minded in business, and, being new to the country, had no notion that Indian banking is totally distinct from Home work. Like most clever self-made men, he had much simplicity in his nature; and, somehow or other, had construed the ordinarily polite terms of his

letter of engagement into a belief that the Directors had
chosen him on account of his special and brilliant talents, and
that they set great store by him. This notion grew and crys-
tallised; thus adding to his natural North-country conceit.
Further, he was delicate, suffered from some trouble in his
chest, and was short in his temper.

You will admit that Reggie had reason to call his new
Accountant a Natural Curiosity. The two men failed to hit it
off at all. Riley considered Reggie a wild, feather-headed
idiot, given to Heaven only knew what dissipation in low
places called "Messes," and totally unfit for the serious and
solemn vocation of banking. He could never get over Reggie's
look of youth and "you-be-damned" air; and he couldn't
understand Reggie's friends – clean-built, careless men in the
Army – who rode over to big Sunday breakfasts at the Bank,
and told sultry stories till Riley got up and left the room.
Riley was always showing Reggie how the business ought to
be conducted, and Reggie had more than once to remind him
that seven years' limited experience between Huddersfield
and Beverley did not qualify a man to steer a big up-country
business. Then Riley sulked, and referred to himself as a
pillar of the Bank and a cherished friend of the Directors,
and Reggie tore his hair. If a man's English subordinates fail
him in India, he comes to a hard time indeed, for native help
has strict limitations. In the winter Riley went sick for weeks
at a time with his lung complaint, and this threw more work
on Reggie. But he preferred it to the everlasting friction
when Riley was well.

One of the Travelling Inspectors of the Bank discovered
these collapses and reported them to the Directors. Now
Riley had been foisted on the Bank by an M. P., who wanted
the support of Riley's father, who, again, was anxious to get
his son out to a warmer climate because of those lungs. The
M. P. had interest in the Bank; but one of the Directors
wanted to advance a nominee of his own; and, after Riley's
father had died, he made the rest of the Board see that an
Accountant who was sick for half the year had better give

place to a healthy man. If Riley had known the real story of his appointment, he might have behaved better; but, knowing nothing, his stretches of sickness alternated with restless, persistent, meddling irritation of Reggie, and all the hundred ways in which conceit in a subordinate situation can find play. Reggie used to call him striking and hair-curling names behind his back as a relief to his own feelings; but he never abused him to his face, because he said, "Riley is such a frail beast that half of his loathsome conceit is due to pains in the chest."

Late one April, Riley went very sick indeed. The Doctor punched him and thumped him, and told him he would be better before long. Then the Doctor went to Reggie and said – "Do you know how sick your Accountant is?" – "No!" said Reggie – "The worse the better, confound him! He's a clacking nuisance when he's well. I'll let you take away the Bank Safe if you can drug him silent for this hot weather."

But the Doctor did not laugh – "Man, I'm not joking," he said. "I'll give him another three months in his bed and a week or so more to die in. On my honour and reputation that's all the grace he has in this world. Consumption has hold of him to the marrow."

Reggie's face changed at once into the face of "Mr. Reginald Burke," and he answered, "What can I do?" – "Nothing," said the Doctor. "For all practical purposes the man is dead already. Keep him quiet and cheerful, and tell him he's going to recover. That's all. I'll look after him to the end, of course."

The Doctor went away, and Reggie sat down to open the evening mail. His first letter was one from the Directors, intimating for his information that Mr. Riley was to resign, under a month's notice, by the terms of his agreement, telling Reggie that their letter to Riley would follow, and advising Reggie of the coming of a new Accountant, a man whom Reggie knew and liked.

Reggie lit a cheroot, and, before he had finished smoking, he had sketched the outline of a fraud. He put away – burked

– the Directors' letter, and went in to talk to Riley, who was as ungracious as usual, and fretting himself over the way the Bank would run during his illness. He never thought of the extra work on Reggie's shoulders, but solely of the damage to his own prospects of advancement. Then Reggie assured him that everything would be well, and that he, Reggie, would confer with Riley daily on the management of the Bank. Riley was a little soothed, but he hinted in as many words that he did not think much of Reggie's business capacity. Reggie was humble. And he had letters in his desk from the Directors that a Gilbarte or a Hardie might have been proud of!

The days passed in the big darkened house, and the Directors' letter of dismissal to Riley came and was put away by Reggie, who, every evening, brought the books to Riley's room, and showed him what had been going forward, while Riley snarled. Reggie did his best to make statements pleasing to Riley, but the Accountant was sure that the Bank was going to rack and ruin without him. In June, as the lying in bed told on his spirit, he asked whether his absence had been noted by the Directors, and Reggie said that they had written most sympathetic letters hoping that he would be able to resume his valuable services before long. He showed Riley the letters; and Riley said that the Directors ought to have written to him direct. A few days later, Reggie opened Riley's mail in the half-light of the room, and gave him the sheet – not the envelope – of a letter to Riley from the Directors. Riley said he would thank Reggie not to interfere with his private papers, specially as Reggie knew he was too weak to open his own letters. Reggie apologised.

Then Riley's mood changed, and he lectured Reggie on his evil ways: his horses and his bad friends. "Of course, lying here on my back, Mr. Burke, I can't keep you straight; but when I'm well I *do* hope you'll pay some heed to my words." Reggie, who had dropped polo, and dinners, and tennis and all, to attend to Riley, said that he was penitent, and settled Riley's head on the pillow and heard him fret and contradict in hard, dry, hacking whispers, without a sign of impatience. This, at the end of a heavy day's office work, doing double duty, in the latter half of June.

When the new Accountant came, Reggie told him the facts of the case, and announced to Riley that he had a guest staying with him. Riley said that he might have had more consideration than to entertain his "doubtful friends" at such a time. Reggie made Carron, the new Accountant, sleep at the Club in consequence. Carron's arrival took some of the heavy work off his shoulders, and he had time to attend to Riley's exactions – to explain, soothe, invent, and settle and re-settle the poor wretch in bed, and to forge complimentary letters from Calcutta. At the end of the first month Riley wished to send some money home to his mother. Reggie sent the draft. At the end of the second month Riley's salary came in just the same. Reggie paid it out of his own pocket, and, with it, wrote Riley a beautiful letter from the Directors.

Riley was very ill indeed, but the flame of his life burnt unsteadily. Now and then he would be cheerful and confident about the future, sketching plans for going Home and seeing his mother. Reggie listened patiently when the office-work was over, and encouraged him.

At other times Riley insisted on Reggie reading the Bible and grim "Methody" tracts to him. Out of these tracts he pointed morals directed at his Manager. But he always found time to worry Reggie about the working of the Bank, and to show him where the weak points lay.

This indoor, sickroom life and constant strains wore Reggie down a good deal, and shook his nerves, and lowered his billiard play by forty points. But the business of the Bank, and the business of the sickroom, had to go on, though the glass was 116° in the shade.

At the end of the third month Riley was sinking fast, and had begun to realise that he was very sick. But the conceit that made him worry Reggie kept him from believing the worst. "He wants some sort of mental stimulant if he is to drag on," said the Doctor. "Keep him interested in life if you care about his living." So Riley, contrary to all the laws of business and the finance, received a 25-per-cent. rise of salary from the Directors. The "mental stimulant" succeeded beautifully. Riley was happy and cheerful, and, as is often the case in consumption, healthiest in mind when the body was weakest. He lingered for a full month, snarling and fretting about the Bank, talking of the future, hearing the Bible read, lecturing Reggie on sin, and wondering when he would be able to move abroad.

But at the end of September, one mercilessly hot evening, he rose up in his bed with a little gasp, and said quickly to Reggie – "Mr. Burke, I am going to die. I know it in myself. My chest is all hollow inside, and there's nothing to breathe with. To the best of my knowledge I have done nowt" – he was returning to the talk of his boyhood – "to lie heavy on my conscience. God be thanked, I have been preserved from the grosser forms of sin; and I counsel *you*, Mr. Burke . . ."

Here his voice died down, and Reggie stooped over him.

"Send my salary for September to my Mother . . . done great things with the Bank if I had been spared . . . mistaken policy . . . no fault of mine . . ."

Then he turned his face to the wall and died.

Reggie drew the sheet over Its face, and went out into the verandah, with his last "mental stimulant" – a letter of condolence and sympathy from the Directors – unused in his pocket.

"If I'd been only ten minutes earlier," thought Reggie, "I might have heartened him up to pull through another day."

PIG

PIG

* * *

Go, stalk the red deer o'er the heather,
  Ride, follow the fox if you can!
But, for pleasure and profit together,
  Allow me the hunting of Man,—
The chase of the Human, the search for the Soul
  To its ruin, – the hunting of Man.

The Old Shikarri

I BELIEVE the difference began in the matter of a horse,
with a twist in his temper, whom Pinecoffin sold to
Nafferton and by whom Nafferton was nearly slain. There
may have been other causes of offence; the horse was the
official stalking-horse. Nafferton was very angry; but Pinecoffin laughed, and said that he had never guaranteed the
beast's manners. Nafferton laughed too, though he vowed
that he would write off his fall against Pinecoffin if he waited
five years. Now, a Dalesman from beyond Skipton will
forgive an injury when the Strid lets a man live; but a
South Devon man is as soft as a Dartmoor bog. You can see
from their names that Nafferton had the race-advantage of
Pinecoffin. He was a peculiar man, and his notions of
humour were cruel. He taught me a new and fascinating
form of *shikar*. He hounded Pinecoffin from Mithankot to
Jagadri, and from Gurgaon to Abbottabad – up and across
the Punjab, a large Province, and in places remarkably dry.
He said that he had no intention of allowing Assistant Commissioners to "sell him pups," in the shape of ramping,
screaming countrybreds, without making their lives a burden
to them.

Most Assistant Commissioners develop a bent for some

37

special work after their first hot weather in the country. The
boys with digestions hope to write their names large on the
Frontier, and struggle for dreary places like Bannu and
Kohat. The bilious ones climb into the Secretariat. Which is
very bad for the liver. Others are bitten with a mania for
District work, Ghuznivide coins or Persian poetry; while
some, who come of farmers' stock, find that the smell of the
Earth after the Rains gets into their blood, and calls them to
"develop the resources of the Province." These men are en-
thusiasts. Pinecoffin belonged to their class. He knew a great
many facts bearing on the cost of bullocks, and temporary
wells, and opium-scrapers, and what happens if you burn too
much rubbish on a field in the hope of enriching used-up
soil. All the Pinecoffins come of a landholding breed, and so
the land only took back her own again. Unfortunately – most
unfortunately for Pinecoffin – he was a Civilian as well as a
farmer. Nafferton watched him, and thought about the horse.
Nafferton said, "See me chase that boy till he drops!" I said,
"You can't get your knife into an Assistant Commissioner."
Nafferton told me that I did not understand the administration of the Province.

Our Government is rather peculiar. It gushes on the agricultural and general information side, and will supply a
moderately respectable man with all sorts of "economic statistics," if he speaks to it prettily. For instance, you are interested in gold-washing in the sands of the Sutlej. You pull the
string, and find that it wakes up half a dozen Departments,
and finally communicates, say, with a friend of yours in the
Telegraph, who once wrote some notes on the customs of the
gold-washers when he was on construction work in their part
of the Empire. He may or may not be pleased at being ordered to write out everything he knows for your benefit. This
depends on his temperament. The bigger man you are, the
more information and the greater trouble can you raise.

Nafferton was not a big man; but he had the reputation of
being very "earnest." An "earnest" man can do much with a
Government. There was an earnest man once who nearly

wrecked . . . but all India knows *that* story. I am not sure
what real "earnestness" is. A very fair imitation can be manufactured by neglecting to dress decently, by mooning about
in a dreamy, misty sort of way, by taking office-work home
after staying in office till seven, and by receiving crowds of
native gentlemen on Sundays. That is one sort of "earnestness."

Nafferton cast about for a peg whereon to hang his earnestness, and for a string that would communicate with Pinecoffin. He found both. They were Pig. Nafferton became an
earnest inquirer after Pig. He informed the Government that
he had a scheme whereby a very large percentage of the
British Army in India could be fed, at a very large saving, on
Pig. Then he hinted that Pinecoffin might supply him with
the "varied information necessary to the proper inception of
the scheme." So the Government wrote on the back of the
letter, "Instruct Mr. Pinecoffin to furnish Mr. Nafferton with
any information in his power." Government is very prone to
writing things on the backs of letters which, later, lead to
trouble and confusion.

Nafferton had not the faintest interest in Pig, but he knew
that Pinecoffin would flounce into the trap. Pinecoffin was
delighted at being consulted about Pig. The Indian Pig is not
exactly an important factor in agricultural life; but Nafferton
explained to Pinecoffin that there was room for improvement, and corresponded direct with that young man.

You may think that there is not much to be evolved from
Pig. It all depends how you set to work. Pinecoffin, being a
Civilian and wishing to do things thoroughly, began with an
essay on the Primitive Pig, the Mythology of the Pig, and the
Dravidian Pig. Nafferton filed that information – twenty-
seven foolscap sheets – and wanted to know about the dis-
tribution of the Pig in the Punjab, and how it stood the
Plains in the hot weather. From this point onwards remember that I am giving you only the barest outlines of the affair
– the guy-ropes, as it were, of the web that Nafferton spun
round Pinecoffin.

Pinecoffin made a coloured Pig-population map, and collected observations on the comparative longevity of Pig (*a*) in the sub-montane tracts of the Himalayas, and (*b*) in the Rechna Doab. Nafferton filed that, and asked what sort of people looked after Pig. This started an ethnological excursus on swineherds, and drew from Pinecoffin long tables showing the proportion per thousand of the caste in the Derajat. Nafferton filed that bundle, and explained that the figures which he wanted referred to the Cis-Sutlej states, where he understood that Pigs were very fine and large, and where he proposed to start a Piggery. By this time, Government had quite forgotten their instructions to Mr. Pinecoffin. They were like the gentlemen, in Keats' poem, who turned well-oiled wheels to skin other people. But Pinecoffin was just entering into the spirit of the Pig-hunt, as Nafferton well knew he would do. He had a fair amount of work of his own to clear away; but he sat up of nights reducing Pig to five places of decimals for the honour of his Service. He was not going to appear ignorant of so easy a subject as Pig.

Then Government sent him on special duty to Kohat, to "inquire into" the big, seven-foot ironshod spades of that District. People had been killing each other with those peaceful tools; and Government wished to know "whether a modified form of agricultural implement could not, tentatively and as a temporary measure, be introduced among the agricultural population without needlessly or unduly exacerbating the existing religious sentiments of the peasantry."

Between those spades and Nafferton's Pig, Pinecoffin was rather heavily burdened.

Nafferton now began to take up "(*a*) The food-supply of the indigenous Pig, with a view to the improvement of its capacities as a flesh-former. (*b*) The acclimatisation of the exotic Pig, maintaining its distinctive peculiarities." Pinecoffin replied exhaustively that the exotic Pig would become merged in the indigenous type; and quoted horse-breeding statistics to prove this. The side-issue was debated, at great length on Pinecoffin's side, till Nafferton owned that he had been in the wrong, and moved the previous question. When Pinecoffin had quite written himself out about flesh-formers, and fibrins, and glucose, and the nitrogenous constituents of maize and lucerne, Nafferton raised the question of expense. By this time Pinecoffin, who had been transferred from Kohat, had developed a Pig theory of his own, which he stated in thirty-three folio pages – all carefully filed by Nafferton. Who asked for more.

These things took ten months, and Pinecoffin's interest in the potential Piggery seemed to die down after he had stated his own views. But Nafferton bombarded him with letters on "the Imperial aspect of the scheme, as tending to officialise the sale of pork, and thereby calculated to give offence to the Mahommedan population of Upper India." He guessed that Pinecoffin would want some broad, free-hand work after his niggling, stippling, decimal details. Pinecoffin handled the latest development of the case in masterly style, and proved that no "popular ebullition of excitement was to be apprehended." Nafferton said that there was nothing like Civilian insight in matters of this kind, and lured him up a by-path – "the possible profits to accrue to the Government from the sale of hog-bristles." There is an extensive literature of hog-bristles, and the shoe, brush, and colour-man's trades recognise more varieties of bristles than you would think possible. After Pinecoffin had wondered a little at Nafferton's rage for information, he sent back a monograph, fifty-one pages, on "Products of the Pig." This led him, under Nafferton's tender handling, straight to the Cawnpore factories, the trade in hogskin for saddles – and thence to the tanners. Pinecoffin wrote that pomegranate-seed was the best cure for hog-skin, and suggested – for the past fourteen months had wearied him – that Nafferton should "raise his pigs before he tanned them."

Nafferton went back to the second section of his fifth question. How could the exotic Pig be brought to give as much pork as it did in the West and yet "assume the essentially hirsute characteristics of its Oriental congener"? Pinecoffin felt dazed, for he had forgotten what he had written sixteen months before, and fancied that he was about to reopen the entire question. He was too far involved in the hideous tangle to retreat, and, in a weak moment, he wrote, "Consult my first letter." Which related to the Dravidian Pig. As a matter of fact, Pinecoffin had still to reach the acclimatisation stage; having gone off on a side-issue on the merging of types.

Then Nafferton really unmasked his batteries! He complained to the Government, in stately language, of "the paucity of help accorded to me in my earnest attempts to start a potentially remunerative industry, and the flippancy with which my requests for information are treated by a gentleman whose pseudo-scholarly attainments should at least have taught him the primary differences between the Dravidian and the Berkshire variety of the genus *Sus*. If I am to understand that the letter to which he refers me contains his serious views on the acclimatisation of a valuable, though possibly uncleanly, animal, I am reluctantly compelled to believe," etc. etc.

There was a new man at the head of the Department of Castigation. The wretched Pinecoffin was told that the Service was made for the Country, and not the Country for the Service, and that he had better begin to supply information about Pigs.

Pinecoffin answered insanely that he had written everything that could be written about Pig, and that some furlough was due to him.

Nafferton got a copy of that letter, and sent it, with the essay on the Dravidian Pig, to a down-country paper which printed both in full. The essay was rather high-flown; but if the Editor had seen the stacks of paper, in Pinecoffin's handwriting, on Nafferton's table, he would not have been so sarcastic about the "nebulous discursiveness and blatant self-sufficiency of the modern Competition-*wallah*, and his utter inability to grasp the practical issues of a practical question." Many friends cut out these remarks and sent them to Pinecoffin.

I have already stated that Pinecoffin came of a soft stock.
This last stroke frightened and shook him. He could not
understand it; but he felt that he had been, somehow, shamelessly betrayed by Nafferton. He realised that he had
wrapped himself up in the Pig-skin without need, and that
he could not well set himself right with his Government. All
his acquaintances asked after his "nebulous discursiveness"
or his "blatant self-sufficiency," and this made him miserable.

He took a train and went to Nafferton, whom he had not
seen since the Pig business began. He also took the cutting
from the paper, and blustered feebly and called Nafferton
names, and then died down to a watery, weak protest of the
"I-say-it's-too-bad-you-know" order.

Nafferton was very sympathetic.

"I'm afraid I've given you a good deal of trouble, haven't
I?" said he.

"Trouble!" whimpered Pinecoffin; "I don't mind the
trouble so much, though that was bad enough; but what I
resent is this showing up in print. It will stick to me like a
burr all through my service. And I *did* do my best for your
interminable swine. It's too bad of you – on my soul it is!"

"I don't know," said Nafferton. "Have you ever been
stuck with a horse? It isn't the money I mind, though that is
bad enough; but what I resent is the chaff that follows, especially from the boy who stuck me. But I think we'll cry quits
now."

Pinecoffin found nothing to say save bad words; and
Nafferton smiled ever so sweetly, and asked him to dinner.

ON GREENHOW HILL

ON GREENHOW HILL

* * *

To Love's low voice she lent a careless ear;
Her hand within his rosy fingers lay,
A chilling weight. She would not turn or hear;
But with averted face went on her way.
But when pale Death, all featureless and grim,
Lifted his bony hand, and beckoning
Held out his cypress-wreath, she followed him,
And Love was left forlorn and wondering,
That she who for his bidding would not stay,
At Death's first whisper rose and went away.

Rivals

"Ohé, Ahmed Din! Shafiz Ullah ahoo! Bahadur Khan, where
are you? Come out of the tents, as I have done, and fight
against the English. Don't kill your own kin! Come out to
me!"

The deserter from a native corps was crawling round the
outskirts of the camp, firing at intervals, and shouting invi-
tations to his old comrades. Misled by the rain and the darkness, he came to the English wing of the camp, and with his
yelping and rifle-practice disturbed the men. They had been
making roads all day, and were tired.

Ortheris was sleeping at Learoyd's feet. "Wot's all that?"
he said thickly. Learoyd snored, and a Snider bullet ripped
its way through the tent wall. The men swore. "It's that
bloomin' deserter from the Aurangabadis," said Ortheris.
"Git up, some one, an' tell 'im 'e's come to the wrong shop."

"Go to sleep, little man," said Mulvaney, who was steaming nearest the door. "I can't arise an' expaytiate with him.
'Tis rainin' entrenchin' tools outside."

" 'Tain't because you bloomin' can't. It's 'cause you bloomin' won't, ye long, limp, lousy, lazy beggar, you. 'Ark to 'im 'owlin'!"

"Wot's the good of argifying? Put a bullet into the swine! 'E's keepin' us awake!" said another voice.

A subaltern shouted angrily, and a dripping sentry whined from the darkness –

" 'Tain't no good, sir. I can't see 'im. 'E's 'idin' somewhere down 'ill."

Ortheris tumbled out of his blanket. "Shall I try to get 'im, sir?" said he.

"No," was the answer. "Lie down. I won't have the whole camp shooting all round the clock. Tell him to go and pot his friends."

Ortheris considered for a moment. Then, putting his head under the tent wall, he called, as a 'bus conductor calls in a block, " 'Igher up, there! 'Igher up!"

The men laughed, and the laughter was carried down wind to the deserter, who, hearing that he had made a mistake, went off to worry his own regiment half a mile away. He was received with shots; the Aurangabadis were very angry with him for disgracing their colours.

"An' that's all right," said Ortheris, withdrawing his head as he heard the hiccough of the Sniders in the distance. "S'elp me Gawd, tho', that man's not fit to live – messin' with my beauty-sleep this way."

"Go out and shoot him in the morning, then," said the subaltern incautiously. "Silence in the tents now. Get your rest, men."

Ortheris lay down with a happy little sigh, and in two minutes there was no sound except the rain on the canvas and the all-embracing and elemental snoring of Learoyd.

The camp lay on a bare ridge of the Himalayas, and for a week had been waiting for a flying column to make connection. The nightly rounds of the deserter and his friends had become a nuisance.

In the morning the men dried themselves in hot sunshine

and cleaned their grimy accoutrements. The native regiment was to take its turn of road-making that day while the Old Regiment loafed.

"I'm goin' to lay for a shot at that man," said Ortheris, when he had finished washing out his rifle. "'E comes up the watercourse every evenin' about five o'clock. If we go and lie out on the north 'ill a bit this afternoon we'll get 'im."

"You're a bloodthirsty little mosquito," said Mulvaney, blowing blue clouds into the air. "But I suppose I will have to come wid you. Fwhere's Jock?"

"Gone out with the Mixed Pickles, 'cause 'e thinks 'isself a bloomin' marksman," said Ortheris with scorn.

The "Mixed Pickles" were a detachment of picked shots, generally employed in clearing spurs of hills when the enemy were too impertinent. This taught the young officers how to handle men, and did not do the enemy much harm. Mulvaney and Ortheris strolled out of camp, and passed the Aurangabadis going to their road-making.

"You've got to sweat to-day," said Ortheris genially. "We're going to get your man. You didn't knock 'im out last night by any chance, any of you?"

"No. The pig went away mocking us. I had one shot at him," said a private. "He's my cousin, and *I* ought to have cleared our dishonour. But good luck to you."

They went cautiously to the north hill, Ortheris leading, because, as he explained, "this is a long-range show, an' I've got to do it." His was an almost passionate devotion to his rifle, which, by barrack-room report, he was supposed to kiss every night before turning in. Charges and scuffles he held in contempt, and, when they were inevitable, slipped between Mulvaney and Learoyd, bidding them to fight for his skin as well as their own. They never failed him. He trotted along, questing like a hound on a broken trail, through the wood of the north hill. At last he was satisfied, and threw himself down on the soft pine-needle slope that commanded a clear view of the watercourse and a brown, bare hillside beyond it. The trees made a scented darkness in which an army corps could have hidden from the sun-glare without.

" 'Ere's the tail o' the wood," said Ortheris. " 'E's got to come up the watercourse, 'cause it gives 'im cover. We'll lay 'ere. 'Tain't not 'arf so bloomin' dusty neither."

He buried his nose in a clump of scentless white violets. No one had come to tell the flowers that the season of their strength was long past, and they had bloomed merrily in the twilight of the pines.

"This is something like," he said luxuriously. "Wot a 'evinly clear drop for a bullet acrost! How much d'you make it, Mulvaney?"

"Seven hunder. Maybe a trifle less, bekaze the air's so thin."

Wop! wop! wop! went a volley of musketry on the rear face of the north hill.

"Curse them Mixed Pickles firin' at nothin'! They'll scare arf the country."

"Thry a sightin' shot in the middle of the row," said Mulvaney, the man of many wiles. "There's a red rock yonder he'll be sure to pass. Quick!"

Ortheris ran his sight up to six hundred yards and fired. The bullet threw up a feather of dust by a clump of gentians at the base of the rock.

"Good enough!" said Ortheris, snapping the scale down. "You snick your sights to mine or a little lower. You're always firin' high. But remember, first shot to me. O Lordy! but it's a lovely afternoon."

The noise of the firing grew louder, and there was a tramping of men in the wood. The two lay very quiet, for they knew that the British soldier is desperately prone to fire at anything that moves or calls. Then Learoyd appeared, his tunic ripped across the breast by a bullet, looking ashamed of himself. He flung down on the pine-needles, breathing in snorts.

"One o' them damned gardeners o' th' Pickles," said he, fingering the rent. "Firin' to th' right flank, when he knowed I was there. If I knew who he was I'd 'a' rippen the hide offan him. Look at ma tunic!"

ON GREENHOW HILL

"That's the spishil trustability av a marksman. Thrain him to hit a fly wid a stiddy rest at seven hunder, an' he'll loose on anythin' he sees or hears up to th' mile. You're well out av that fancy-firin' gang, Jock. Stay here."

"Bin firin' at the bloomin' wind in the bloomin' tree-tops," said Ortheris with a chuckle. "I'll show you some firin' later on."

They wallowed in the pine-needles, and the sun warmed them where they lay. The Mixed Pickles ceased firing, and returned to camp, and left the wood to a few scared apes. The watercourse lifted up its voice in the silence, and talked foolishly to the rocks. Now and again the dull thump of a blasting-charge three miles away told that the Aurangabadis were in difficulties with their road-making. The men smiled as they listened and lay still, soaking in the warm leisure. Presently Learoyd, between the whiffs of his pipe –

"Seems queer – about 'im yonder – desertin' at all."

" 'E'll be a bloomin' side queerer when I've done with 'im," said Ortheris. They were talking in whispers, for the stillness of the wood and the desire of slaughter lay heavy upon them.

"I make no doubt he had his reasons for desertin'; but, my faith! I make less doubt ivry man has good reason for killin' him," said Mulvaney.

"Happen there was a lass tewed up wi' it. Men do more than more for th' sake of a lass."

"They make most av us 'list. They've no manner av right to make us desert."

"Ah; they make us 'list, or their fathers do," said Learoyd softly, his helmet over his eyes.

Ortheris's brows contracted savagely. He was watching the valley. "If it's a girl I'll shoot the beggar twice over, an' second time for bein' a fool. You're blasted sentimental all of a sudden. Thinkin' o' your last near shave?"

"Nay, lad; Ah was but thinkin' o' what had happened."

"An' fwhat has happened, ye lumberin' child av calamity, that you're lowing like a cow-calf at the back av the pasture,

an' suggestin' invidious excuses for the man Stanley's goin'
to kill. Ye'll have to wait another hour yet, little man. Spit it
out, Jock, an' bellow melojus to the moon. It takes an earth-
quake or a bullet graze to fetch aught out av you. Discoorse,
Don Juan! The a-moors av Lotharius Learoyd! Stanley, kape
a rowlin' rig'mintal eye on the valley."

"It's along o' yon hill there," said Learoyd, watching the
bare sub-Himalayan spur that reminded him of his Yorkshire
moors. He was speaking more to himself than his fellows.
"Ay," said he, "Rumbolds Moor stands up ower Skipton
town, an' Greenhow Hill stands up ower Pately Brig. I
reckon you've never heeard tell o' Greenhow Hill, but yon
bit o' bare stuff, if there was nobbut a white road windin', is
like it; strangely like. Moors an' moors an' moors, wi' never
a tree for shelter, an' grey houses wi' flagstone rooves, and
pewits cryin', an' a windhover goin' to and fro just like these
kites. And cold! A wind that cuts you like a knife. You could
tell Greenhow Hill folk by the red-apple colour o' their
cheeks an' nose-tips, and their blue eyes driven into pin-
points by the wind. Miners mostly, burrowin' for lead i' th'
hillsides, followin' the trail of th' ore-vein same as a field-rat.
It was the roughest minin' I ever seen. Yo'd come on a bit
o' creakin' wood windlass like a well-head, an' you was let
down i' th' bight of a rope, fendin' yoursen off the side wi'
one hand, carryin' a candle stuck in a lump o' clay with
t'other, an' clickin' hold of a rope with t'other hand."

"An' that's three of them," said Mulvaney. "Must be a
good climate in those parts."

Learoyd took no heed.

"An' then yo' came to a level, where you crept on
your hands and knees through a mile o' windin' drift, an' you
come out into a cave-place as big as Leeds Town-hall,
with a' engine pumpin' water from workin's 'at went deeper
still. It's a queer country, let alone minin', for the hill is
full of those natural caves, an' the rivers an' the becks drops
into what they call pot-holes, an' come out again miles
away."

"Wot was you doin' there?" said Ortheris.

"I was a young chap then, an' mostly went wi' 'osses, leadin' coal and lead ore; but at th' time I'm tellin' on I was drivin' the waggon-team i' th' big sumph. I didn't belong to that country-side by rights. I went there because of a little difference at home, an' at fust I took up wi' a rough lot. One night we'd been drinkin', an' I must ha' hed more than I could stand, or happen th' ale was none so good. Though i' them days, by for God, I never seed bad ale." He flung his arms over his head, and gripped a vast handful of white violets. "Nah," said he, "I never seed the ale I could not drink, the 'bacca I could not smoke, nor the lass I could not kiss. Well, we mun have a race home, the lot on us. I lost all th' others, an' when I was climbin' ower one of them walls built o' loose stones, I comes down into the ditch, stones and all, an' broke my arm. Not as I knawed much about it, for I fell on th' back av of my head, an' was knocked stupid like. An' when I come to mysen it were mornin', an' I were lyin' on the settle i' Jesse Roantree's house-place, an' 'Liza Roantree was settin' sewin'. I ached all over, and my mouth were like a lime-kiln. She gave me a drink out of a china mug wi' gold letters – 'A Present from Leeds' – as I looked at many and many a time at after. 'Yo're to lie still while Dr. Warbottom comes, because your arm's broken, and father has sent a lad to fetch him. He found yo' when he was goin' to work, an' carried you here on his back,' sez she. 'Oa!' sez I; an' I shet my eyes, for I felt ashamed o' mysen. 'Father's gone to his work these three hours, an' he said he'd tell 'em to get somebody to drive the tram.' The clock ticked, an' a bee comed in the house, an' they rung i' my head like mill-wheels. An' she give me another drink an' settled the pillow. 'Eh, but yo're young to be getten drunk an' such like, but yo' won't do it again, will yo'?' – 'Noa,' sez I, 'I wouldn't if she'd not but stop they mill-wheels clatterin'.' "

"Faith, it's a good thing to be nursed by a woman when you're sick!" said Mulvaney. "Dir' cheap at the price av twenty broken heads."

Ortheris turned to frown across the valley. He had not been nursed by many women in his life.

"An' then Dr. Warbottom comes ridin' up, an' Jesse Roantree along with 'im. He was a high-larned doctor, but he talked wi' poor folks same as theirsens. 'What's ta bin agaate on naa?' he sings out. 'Brekkin' tha thick head?' An' he felt me all ovver. 'That's none broken. Tha' nobbut knocked a bit sillier than ordinary, an' that's daaft eneaf.' An' soa he went on, callin' me all the names he could think on, but settin' my arm, wi' Jesse's help, as careful as could be. 'Yo' mun let the big oaf bide here a bit, Jesse,' he says, when he hed strapped me up an' given me a dose o' physic; 'an' you an' Liza will tend him, though he's scarcelins worth the trouble. An' tha'll lose tha work,' sez he, 'an' tha'll be upon th' Sick Club for a couple o' months an' more. Doesn't tha think tha's a fool?' "

"But whin was a young man, high or low, the other av a fool, I'd like to know?" said Mulvaney. "Sure, folly's the only safe way to wisdom, for I've thried it."

"Wisdom!" grinned Ortheris, scanning his comrades with uplifted chin. "You're bloomin' Solomons, you two, ain't you?"

Learoyd went calmly on, with a steady eye like an ox chewing the cud.

"And that was how I come to know 'Liza Roantree. There's some tunes as she used to sing – aw, she were always singin' – that fetches Greenhow Hill before my eyes as fair as yon brow across there. And she would learn me to sing bass, an' I was to go to th' chapel wi' 'em, where Jesse and she led the singin', th' old man playin' the fiddle. He was a strange chap, old Jesse, fair mad wi' music, an' he made me promise to learn the big fiddle when my arm was better. It belonged to him, and it stood up in a big case alongside o' th' eight-day clock; but Willie Satterthwaite, as played it in the chapel, had getten deaf as a door-post, and it vexed Jesse, as he had to rap him ower his head wi' th' fiddle-stick to make him give ower sawin' at th' right time.

"But there was a black drop in it all, an' it was a man in a black coat that brought it. When th' Primitive Methodist preacher came to Greenhow, he would always stop wi' Jesse Roantree, an' he laid hold of me from th' beginning. It seemed I wor a soul to be saved, and he meaned to do it. At th' same time I jealoused 'at he were keen o' savin' 'Liza Roantree's soul as well, and I could ha' killed him many a time. An' this went on till one day I broke out, an' borrowed th' brass for a drink from 'Liza. After fower days I come back, wi' my tail between my legs, just to see 'Liza again. But Jesse were at home an' th' preacher – th' Reverend Amos Barraclough. 'Liza said naught, but a bit o' red come into her face as were white of a regular thing. Says Jesse, tryin' his best to be civil, 'Nay, lad, it's like this. You've getten to choose which way it's goin' to be. I'll ha' nobody across ma doorstep as goes a-drinkin', an' borrows my lass's money to spend i' their drink. Ho'd tha tongue, 'Liza,' sez he, when she wanted to put in a word 'at I were welcome to th' brass, and she were none afraid that I wouldn't pay it back. Then the Reverend cuts in, seein' as Jesse were losin' his temper, an' they fair beat me among them. But it were 'Liza, as looked an' said naught, as did more than either o' their tongues, an' soa I concluded to get converted."

"Fwhat?" shouted Mulvaney. Then, checking himself, he said softly, "Let be! Let be! Sure the Blessed Virgin is the mother of all religion an' most women; an' there's a dale av piety in a girl if the men would only let ut stay there. I'd ha' been converted myself under the circumstances."

"Nay, but," pursued Learoyd with a blush, "I meaned it."

Ortheris laughed as loudly as he dared, having regard to his business at the time.

"Ay, Ortheris, you may laugh, but you didn't know yon preacher Barraclough – a little white-faced chap, wi' a voice as 'u'd wile a bird off an a bush, and a way o' layin' hold of folks as made them think they'd never had a live man for a friend before. You never saw him, an' – an' – you never seed 'Liza Roantree – never seed 'Liza Roantree. . . . Happen it was as much 'Liza as th' preacher and her father, but anyways they all meaned it, an' I was fair 'shamed o' mysen, an' so I become what they call a changed character. And when I think on, it's hard to believe as yon chap going to prayer-meetin's, chapel, and class-meetin's were me. But I never had naught to say for mysen, though there was a deal o' shoutin', and old Sammy Strother, as were almost clemmed to death and doubled up with the rheumatics, would sing out, 'Joyful! Joyful!' and 'at it were better to go up to heaven in a coal-basket than down to hell i' a coach an' six. And he would put his poor old claw on my shoulder, sayin', 'Doesn't tha feel it, tha great lump? Doesn't tha feel it?' An' sometimes I thought I did, and then again I thought I didn't, an' how was that?"

"The iverlastin' nature av mankind," said Mulvaney. "An', furthermore, I misdoubt you were built for the Primitive Methodians. They're a new corps anyways. I hold by the Ould Church, for she's the mother of them all – ay, an' the father, too. I like her bekaze she's most remarkable regimintal in her fittings. I may die in Honolulu, Nova Zambra, or Cape Cayenne, but wherever I die, me bein' fwhat I am, an' a priest handy, I go under the same orders an' the same words an' the same unction as tho' the Pope himself come down from the roof av St. Peter's to see me off. There's neither high nor low, nor broad nor deep, nor betwixt nor between wid her, an' that's what I like. But mark you, she's no manner av Church for a wake man, bekaze she takes the body and the soul av him, onless he has his proper work to do. I remember when my father died that was three months comin' to his grave; begad he'd ha' sold the shebeen above our heads for ten minutes' quittance of purgathory. An' he did all he could. That's why I say ut takes a strong man to dale with the Ould Church, an' for that reason you'll find so many women go there. An' that same's a conundrum."

"Wot's the use o' worritin' 'bout these things?" said Ortheris. "You're bound to find all out quicker nor you want to, any'ow." He jerked the cartridge out of the breech-block into the palm of his hand. " 'Ere's my chaplain," he said, and made the venomous black-headed bullet bow like a marionette. " 'E's goin' to teach a man all about which is which, an' wot's true, after all, before sundown. But wot 'appened after that, Jock?"

"There was one thing they boggled at, and almost shut th' gate i' my face for, and that were my dog Blast, th' only one saved out o' a litter o' pups as was blowed up when a keg o' minin'-powder loosed off in th' store-keeper's hut. They liked his name no better than his business, which were fightin' every dog he comed across; a rare good dog, wi' spots o' black and pink on his face, one ear gone, and lame o' one side wi' being driven in a basket through an iron roof a matter of half a mile.

"They said I mun give him up 'cause he were worldly and low; and would I let mysen be shut out of heaven for the sake on a dog? 'Nay,' says I, 'if th' door isn't wide enough for th' pair on us, we'll stop outside, for we'll none be parted.' And th' preacher spoke up for Blast, as had a likin' for him from th' first – I reckon that was why I come to like th' preacher – and wouldn't hear o' changin' his name to Bless, as some o' them wanted. So th' pair on us became reg'lar chapel-members. But it's hard for a young chap o' my build to cut traces from the world, th' flesh, an' the devil all uv a heap. Yet I stuck to it for a long time, while th' lads as used to stand about th' town-end an' lean ower th' bridge, spittin' into th' beck o' a Sunday, would call after me, 'Sitha, Learoyd, when's ta bean to preach, 'cause we're comin' to hear tha.' – 'Ho'd tha jaw. He hasn't getten th' white choaker on ta morn,' another lad would say, and I had to double my fists hard i' th' bottom of my Sunday coat, and say to mysen, 'If 'twere Monday and I warn't a member o' the Primitive Methodists, I'd leather all th' lot of yond'.' That was th' hardest of all – to know that I could fight and I mustn't fight."

Sympathetic grunts from Mulvaney.

"So what wi' singin', practisin', and class-meetin's, and

th' big fiddle, as he made me take between my knees, I spent a deal o' time i' Jesse Roantree's house-place. But often as I was there, th' preacher fared to me to go oftener, and both th' old man an' th' young woman were pleased to have him. He lived i' Pately Brig, as were a goodish step off, but he come. He come all the same. I liked him as well or better as any man I'd ever seen i' one way, and yet I hated him wi' all my heart i' t'other, and we watched each other like cat and mouse, but civil as you please, for I was on my best behaviour, and he was that fair and open that I was bound to be fair with him. Rare good company he was if I hadn't wanted to wring his cliver little neck half of the time. Often and often when he was goin' from Jesse's I'd set him a bit on the road."

"See 'im 'ome, you mean?" said Ortheris.

"Ay. It's a way we have i' Yorkshire o' seein' friends off. Yon was a friend as I didn't want to come back, and he didn't want me to come back neither, and so we'd walk together towards Pately, and then he'd set me back again, and there we'd be wal two o'clock i' the mornin' settin' each other to an' fro like a blasted pair o' pendulums 'twixt hill and valley, long after th' light had gone out i' 'Liza's window, as both on us had been looking at, pretending to watch the moon."

"Ah!" broke in Mulvaney, "ye'd no chanst against the maraudin' psalm-singer. They'll take the airs an' the graces instid av the man nine times out av ten, an' they only find the blunder later – the wimmen."

"That's just where yo're wrong," said Learoyd, reddening under the freckled tan of his cheeks. "I was th' first wi' Liza, an' yo'd think that were enough. But th' parson were a steady-gaited sort o' chap, and Jesse were strong o' his side, and all th' women i' the congregation dinned it to 'Liza 'at she were fair fond to take up wi' a wastrel ne'er-do-weel like me, as was scarcelins respectable an' a fighting dog at his heels. It was all very well for her to be doing me good and saving my soul, but she must mind as she didn't do herself harm. They talk o' rich folk bein' stuck up an' genteel, but for cast-iron pride o' respectability there's naught like poor chapel folk. It's as cold as th' wind o' Greenhow Hill – ay, and colder, for 'twill never change. And now I come to think on it, one o' th' strangest things I know is 'at they couldn't abide th' thought o' soldiering. There's a vast o' fightin' i' th' Bible, and there's a deal of Methodists i' th' army; but to hear chapel folk talk yo'd think that soldierin' were next door, an' t'other side, to hangin'. I' their meetin's all their talk is o' fightin'. When Sammy Strother were stuck for summat to say in his prayers, he'd sing out, 'Th' sword o' th' Lord and o' Gideon." They were allus at it about puttin' on th' whole armour o' righteousness, an' fightin' the good fight o' faith. And then, atop o' 't all, they held a prayer-meetin' ower a young chap as wanted to 'list and nearly deafened him, till he picked up his hat and fair ran away. And they'd tell tales in th' Sunday-school o' bad lads as had been thumped and brayed for bird-nesting o' Sundays and playin' truant o' week-days, and how they took to wrestlin', dog-fightin', rabbit-runnin', and drinkin', till at last, as if 'twere a hepitaph on a gravestone, they damned him across th' moors wi', 'an' then he went and 'listed for a soldier,' an' they'd all fetch a deep breath, and throw up their eyes like a hen drinkin.' "

"Fwhy is ut?" said Mulvaney, bringing down his hand on his thigh with a crack. "In the name av God, fwhy is ut? I've seen ut, tu. They cheat an' they swindle an' they lie an' they slander, an' fifty things fifty times worse; but the last an' the worst by their reckonin' is to serve the Widdy honest. It's like the talk av children – seein' things all round."

"Plucky lot of fightin' good fights of whatsername they'd do if we didn't see they had a quiet place to fight in. And such fightin' as theirs is! Cats on the tiles. T'other callin' to which to come on. I'd give a month's pay to get some o' them broad-backed beggars in London sweatin' through a day's road-makin' an' a night's rain. They'd carry on a deal after-wards – same as we're supposed to carry on. I've bin turned out of a measly 'arf-licence pub down Lambeth way, full o' greasy kebmen, 'fore now," said Ortheris with an oath.

"Maybe you were dhrunk," said Mulvaney soothingly.

"Worse nor that. The Forders were drunk. *I* was wearin' the Queen's uniform."

"I'd no particular thought to be a soldier i' them days," said Learoyd, still keeping his eye on the bare hill opposite, "but this sort o' talk put it i' my head. They was so good, th' chapel folk, that they tumbled ower t'other side. But I stuck to it for 'Liza's sake, specially as she was learning me to sing the bass part in a horotorio as Jesse were gettin' up. She sung like a throstle hersen, and we had practisin's night after night for a matter of three months."

"I know what a horotorio is," said Ortheris pertly. "It's a sort of chaplain's sing-song – words all out of the Bible, and hullabaloojah choruses."

"Most Greenhow Hill folks played some instrument or t'other, an' they all sung so you might have heard them miles away, and they were so pleased wi' the noise they made they didn't fair to want anybody to listen. The preacher sung high seconds when he wasn't playin' the flute, an' they set me, as hadn't got far with the big fiddle, again' Willie Satterthwaite, to jog his elbow when he had to get a' gate playin'. Old Jesse was happy if ever a man was, for he were th' conductor an' th' first fiddle an' th' leadin' singer, beatin' time wi' his fiddle-stick, till at times he'd rap with it on the table, and cry out, 'Now, you mun all stop; it's my turn.' And he'd face round to his front, fair sweating wi' pride, to sing th' tenor solos. But he were grandest i' th' choruses, waggin' his head, flinging his arms round like a windmill, and singin' hisself black in the face. A rare singer were Jesse.

"Yo' see, I was not o' much account wi' 'em all exceptin' to 'Liza Roantree, and I had a deal o' time settin' quiet at meetings and horotorio practices to hearken their talk, and if it were strange to me at beginnin', it got stranger still at after, when I was shut on it, and could study what it meaned.

"Just after th' horotorios come off, 'Liza, as had allus been weakly like, was took very bad. I walked Dr. Warbottom's horse up and down a deal of times while he were inside, where they wouldn't let me go, though I fair ached to see her.

" 'She'll be better i' noo, lad – better i' noo,' he used to say. 'Tha mun ha' patience.' Then they said if I was quiet I might go in, and th' Reverend Amos Barraclough used to read to her lyin' propped up among th' pillows. Then she began to mend a bit, and they let me carry her on to th' settle, and when it got warm again she went about same as afore. Th' preacher and me and Blast was a deal together i' them days, and i' one way we was rare good comrades. But I could ha' stretched him time and again with a good will. I mind one day he said he would like to go down into th' bowels o' th' earth, and see how th' Lord had builded th' framework o' th' everlastin' hills. He were one of them chaps as had a gift o' sayin' things. They rolled off the tip of his cliver tongue, same as Mulvaaney here, as would ha' made a rare good preacher if he had nobbut given his mind to it. I lent him a suit o' miner's kit as almost buried th' little man, and his white face down i' th' coat-collar and hat-flap looked like the face of a boggart, and he cowered down i' th' bottom o' the waggon. I was drivin' a tram as led up a bit of an incline up to th' cave where th' engine was pumpin', and where th' ore was brought up and put into th' waggons as went down o' themselves, me puttin' th' brake on and th' horses a-trottin' after. Long as it was daylight we were good friends, but when we got fair into th' dark, and could nobbut see th' day shinin' at the hole like a lamp at a street-end, I feeled downright wicked. Ma religion dropped all away from me when I looked back at him as were always comin' between me and 'Liza. The talk was 'at they were to be wed when she got better, an' I couldn't get her to say yes or nay to it. He began to sing a hymn in his thin voice, and I came out wi' a chorus that was all cussin' an' swearin' at my horses, an' I began to know how I hated him. He were such a little chap, too. I could drop him wi' one hand down Garstang's

Copper-hole – a place where th' beck slithered ower th' edge on a rock, and fell wi' a bit of a whisper into a pit as no rope i' Greenhow could plumb."

Again Learoyd rooted up the innocent violets. "Ay, he should see th' bowels o' th' earth an' never naught else. I could take him a mile or two along th' drift, and leave him wi' his candle doused to cry hallelujah, wi' none to hear him and say amen. I was to lead him down th' ladder-way to th' drift where Jesse Roantree was workin', and why shouldn't he slip on th' ladder, wi' my feet on his fingers till they loosed grip, and I put him down wi' my heel? If I went fust down th' ladder I could click hold on him and chuck him over my head, so as he should go squshin' down the shaft, breakin' his bones at ev'ry timberin' as Bill Appleton did when he was fresh, and hadn't a bone left when he wrought to th' bottom. Niver a blasted leg to walk from Pately. Niver an arm to put round 'Liza Roantree's waist. Niver no more – niver no more."

The thick lips curled back over the yellow teeth, and that flushed face was not pretty to look upon. Mulvaney nodded sympathy, and Ortheris, moved by his comrade's passion, brought up the rifle to his shoulder, and searched the hillside for his quarry, muttering ribaldry about a sparrow, a spout, and a thunder-storm. The voice of the watercourse supplied the necessary small talk till Learoyd picked up his story.

"But it's none so easy to kill a man like yon. When I'd given up my horses to th' lad as took my place and I was showin' th' preacher th' workin's, shoutin' into his ear across th' clang o' th' pumpin'-engines, I saw he were afraid o' naught; and when the lamplight showed his black eyes, I could feel as he was masterin' me again. I were no better nor Blast chained up short and growlin' i' the depths of him while a strange dog went safe past.

" 'Th'art a coward and a fool,' I said to mysen; an' I wrestled i' my mind again' him till, when we come to Garstang's Copper-hole, I laid hold o' the preacher and lifted him up over my head and held him into the darkest on it.

'Now, lad,' I says, 'it's to be one or t'other on us – thee or me – for 'Liza Roantree. Why, isn't thee afraid for thysen?' I says, for he was still i' my arms as a sack. 'Nay; I'm but afraid for thee, my poor lad, as knows naught,' says he. I set him down on th' edge, an' th' beck run stiller, an' there was no more buzzin' in my head like when th' bee come through th' window o' Jesse's house. 'What dost tha mean?' says I.

" 'I've often thought as thou ought to know,' says he, 'but 'twas hard to tell thee. 'Liza Roantree's for neither on us, nor for nobody o' this earth. Dr. Warbottom says – and he knows her, and her mother before her – that she is in a decline, and she cannot live six months longer. He's known it for many a day. Steady, John! Steady!' says he. And that weak little man pulled me further back and set me again' him, and talked it all over quiet and still, me turnin' a bunch o' candles in my hand, and counting them ower and ower again as I listened. A deal on it were th' regular preachin' talk, but there were a vast lot as made me begin to think as he were more of a man than I'd ever given him credit for, till I were cut as deep for him as I were for mysen.

"Six candles we had, and we crawled and climbed all that day while they lasted, and I said to mysen, ' 'Liza Roantree hasn't six months to live.' And when we came into th' day-light again we were like dead men to look at, an' Blast come behind us without so much as waggin' his tail. When I saw 'Liza again she looked at me a minute and says, 'Who's telled tha? For I see tha knows.' And she tried to smile as she kissed me, and I fair broke down.

"Yo' see, I was a young chap i' them days, and had seen naught o' life, let alone death, as is allus a-waitin'. She telled me as Dr. Warbottom said as Greenhow air was too keen, and they were goin' to Bradford, to Jesse's brother David, as worked i' a mill, and I mun hold up like a man and a Christian, and she'd pray for me. Well, and they went away, and the preacher that same back end o' th' year were appointed to another circuit, as they call it, and I were left alone on Greenhow Hill.

"I tried, and I tried hard, to stick to th' chapel, but 'tweren't th' same thing at after. I hadn't 'Liza's voice to follow i' th' singin', nor her eyes a-shinin' acrost their heads. And i' th' class meetings they said as I mun have some experiences to tell, and I hadn't a word to say for mysen.

"Blast and me moped a good deal, and happen we didn't behave ourselves ower well, for they dropped us and wondered however they'd come to take us up. I can't tell how we got through th' time, while i' th' winter I gave up my job and went to Bradford. Old Jesse were at th' door o' th' house, in a long street o' little houses. He'd been sendin' th' children 'way as were clatterin' their clogs in th' causeway, for she were asleep.

" 'Is it thee?' he says; 'but you're not to see her. I'll none have her wakened for a nowt like thee. She's goin' fast, and she mun go in peace. Thou'lt never be good for naught i' th' world, and as long as thou live thou'lt never play the big fiddle. Get away, lad, get away!' So he shut the door softly i' my face.

"Nobody never made Jesse my master, but it seemed to me he was about right, and I went away into the town and knocked up against a recruiting sergeant. The old tales o' th' chapel folk came buzzin' into my head. I was to get away, and this were th' regular road for the likes o' me. I 'listed there and then, took th' Widow's shillin', and had a bunch o' ribbons pinned i' my hat.

"But next day I found my way to David Roantree's door, and Jesse came to open it. Says he, 'Thou's come back again wi' th' devil's colours flyin' – thy true colours, as I always telled thee.'

"But I begged and prayed of him to let me see her nobbut to say good-bye, till a woman calls down th' stairway, 'She says John Learoyd's to come up.' Th' old man shifts aside in a flash, and lays his hand on my arm, quite gentle like. 'But thou'lt be quiet, John,' says he, 'for she's rare and weak. Thou was allus a good lad.'

"Her eyes were all alive wi' light, and her hair was thick

on the pillow round her, but her cheeks were thin – thin to frighten a man that's strong. 'Nay, father, yo' mayn't say th' devil's colours. Them ribbons is pretty.' An' she held out her hands for th' hat, an' she put all straight as a woman will wi' ribbons. 'Nay, but what they're pretty,' she says. 'Eh, but I'd ha' liked to see thee i' thy red coat, John, for thou was allus my own lad – my very own lad, and none else.'

"She lifted up her arms, and they come round my neck i' a gentle grip, and they slacked away, and she seemed fainting. 'Now yo' mun get away, lad,' says Jesse, and I picked up my hat and I came downstairs.

"Th' recruiting sergeant were waitin' for me at th' corner public-house. 'Yo've seen your sweetheart?' says he. 'Yes, I've seen her,' says I. 'Well, we'll have a quart now, and you'll do your best to forget her,' says he, bein' one o' them smart, bustlin' chaps. 'Ay, sergeant,' says I. 'Forget her.' And I've been forgettin' her ever since."

He threw away the wilted clump of white violets as he spoke. Ortheris suddenly rose to his knees, his rifle at his shoulder, and peered across the valley in the clear afternoon light. His chin cuddled the stock, and there was a twitching of the muscles of the right cheek as he sighted; Private Stanley Ortheris was engaged on his business. A speck of white crawled up the watercourse.

"See that beggar? . . . Got 'im."

Seven hundred yards away, and a full two hundred down the hillside, the deserter of the Aurangabadis pitched forward, rolled down a red rock, and lay very still, with his face in a clump of blue gentians, while a big raven flapped out of the pine wood to make investigation.

"That's a clean shot, little man," said Mulvaney.

Learoyd thoughtfully watched the smoke clear away. "Happen there was a lass tewed up wi' him, too," said he.

Ortheris did not reply. He was staring across the valley with the smile of the artist who looks on the completed work.

"LOVE-O'-WOMEN"

* * *

A lamentable tale of things
Done long ago, and ill done.

THE horror, the confusion, and the separation of the
murderer from his comrades were all over before I
came. There remained only on the barrack-square the blood
of man calling from the ground. The hot sun had dried it to
a dusky gold-beater-skin film, cracked lozenge-wise by the
heat, and as the wind rose each lozenge, rising a little, curled
up at the edges as if it were a dumb tongue. Then a heavier
gust blew all away down wind in grains of dark-coloured
dust. It was too hot to stand in the sunshine before breakfast.
The men were all in barracks talking the matter over. A knot
of soldiers' wives stood by one of the entrances to the married quarters, while inside a woman shrieked and raved with
wicked filthy words.

A quiet and well-conducted sergeant had shot down in
broad daylight just after early parade one of his own corpo-
rals, had then returned to barracks and sat on a cot till the
guard came for him. He would, therefore, in due time be
handed over to the High Court for trial. Further, but this he
could hardly have considered in his scheme of revenge,
he would horribly upset my work; for the reporting of the
trial would fall on me without a relief. What that trial would
be like I knew even to weariness. There would be the rifle
carefully uncleaned, with the fouling marks about breech and
muzzle, to be sworn to by half a dozen superfluous privates;
there would be heat, reeking heat, till the wet pencil slipped
sideways between the fingers; and the punkah would swish
and the pleaders would jabber in the verandahs, and his

69

Commanding Officer would put in certificates of the prisoner's moral character, while the jury would pant and the summer uniforms of the witnesses would smell of dye and soaps; and some abject barrack-sweeper would lose his head in cross-examination, and the young barrister who always defended soldiers' cases for the credit that they never brought him, would say and do wonderful things, and would then quarrel with me because I had not reported him correctly. At the last, for he surely would not be hanged, I might meet the prisoner again, ruling blank account-forms in the Central Jail, and cheer him with the hope of a wardership in the Andamans.

The Indian Penal Code and its interpreters do not treat murder, under any provocation whatever, in a spirit of jest. Sergeant Raines would be very lucky indeed if he got off with seven years, I thought. He had slept the night upon his wrongs, and had killed his man at twenty yards before any talk was possible. That much I knew. Unless, therefore, the case was doctored a little, seven years would be his least; and I fancied it was exceedingly well for Sergeant Raines that he had been liked by his Company.

That same evening – no day is so long as the day of a murder – I met Ortheris with the dogs, and he plunged defiantly into the middle of the matter. "I'll be one o' the witnesses," said he. "I was in the verandah when Mackie came along. 'E come from Mrs. Raines's quarters. Quigley, Parsons, an' Trot, they was in the inside verandah, so they couldn't 'ave 'eard nothing. Sergeant Raines was in the verandah talkin' to me, an' Mackie 'e come along acrost the square an' 'e sez, 'Well,' sez 'e, ' 'ave they pushed your 'elmet off yet, Sergeant?' 'e sez. An' at that Raines 'e catches 'is breath an' 'e sez, 'My Gawd, I can't stand this!' sez 'e, an' 'e picks up my rifle an' shoots Mackie. See?"

"But what were you doing with your rifle in the outer verandah an hour after parade?"

"Cleanin' 'er," said Ortheris, with the sullen brassy stare that always went with his choice lies.

He might as well have said that he was dancing naked, for at no time did his rifle need hand or rag on her twenty minutes after parade. Still the High Court would not know his routine.

"Are you going to stick to that – on the Book?" I asked.

"Yes. Like a bloomin' leech."

"All right, I don't want to know any more. Only remember that Quigley, Parsons, and Trot couldn't have been where you say without hearing something; and there's nearly certain to be a barrack-sweeper who was knocking about the square at the time. There always is."

" 'Twasn't the sweeper. It was the beastie. 'E's all right."

Then I knew that there was going to be some spirited doctoring, and I felt sorry for the Government Advocate who would conduct the prosecution.

When the trial came on I pitied him more, for he was always quick to lose his temper, and made a personal matter of each lost cause. Raines's young barrister had for once put aside his unslaked and Welling passion for alibis and insanity, had forsworn gymnastics and fireworks, and worked soberly for his client. Mercifully the hot weather was yet young, and there had been no flagrant cases of barrack-shootings up to the time; and the jury was a good one, even for an Indian jury, where nine men out of every twelve are accustomed to weighing evidence. Ortheris stood firm and was not shaken by any cross-examination. The one weak point in his tale – the presence of his rifle in the outer verandah – went unchallenged by civilian wisdom, though some of the witnesses could not help smiling. The Government Advocate called for the rope; contending throughout that the murder had been a deliberate one. Time had passed, he argued, for that reflection which comes so naturally to a man whose honour is lost. There was also the Law, ever ready and anxious to right the wrongs of the common soldier if, indeed, wrong had been done. But he doubted much whether there had been any sufficient wrong. Causeless suspicion over-long brooded upon had led, by his theory, to deliberate crime. But his attempts to minimise the motive failed. The most disconnected witness knew – had known for weeks – the causes of offence, and the prisoner, who naturally was the last of all to know, groaned in the dock while he listened. The one question that the trial circled round was whether Raines had fired under sudden and blinding provocation given that very morning, and in the summing up it was clear that Ortheris's evidence told. He had contrived, most artistically, to suggest that he personally hated the Sergeant, who had come into the verandah to give him a talking to for insubordination. In a weak moment the Government Advocate asked one question too many. "Beggin' *your* pardon, sir," Ortheris replied, " 'e was callin' me a dam' impudent little lawyer." The Court shook. The jury brought it in a killing, but with every provocation and extenuation known to God or man, and the Judge put his hand to his brow before giving sentence, and the Adam's apple in the prisoner's throat went up and down mercury-pumping before a cyclone.

In consideration of all considerations, from his Commanding Officer's certificate of good conduct to the sure loss of pension, service, and honour, the prisoner would get two years, to be served in India, and – there need be no demonstration in Court. The Government Advocate scowled and picked up his papers; the guard wheeled with a clash, and the prisoner was relaxed to the Secular Arm, and driven to the jail in a broken-down *ticca-gharri*.

His guard and some ten or twelve military witnesses, being less important, were ordered to wait till what was officially called the cool of the evening before marching back to cantonments. They gathered together in one of the deep red brick verandahs of a disused lock-up and congratulated Ortheris, who bore his honours modestly. I sent my work into the office and joined them. Ortheris watched the Government Advocate driving off to lunch.

"That's a nasty little bald-'eaded little butcher, that is," he said. " 'E don't please me. 'E's got a colley dog wot *do*, though. I'm goin' up to Murree in a week. That dawg'll bring fifteen rupees anywheres."

"You had better spend it in Masses," said Terence, unbuckling his belt, for he had been on the prisoner's guard, standing helmeted and bolt upright for three long hours.

"Not me," said Ortheris cheerfully. "Gawd'll put it down to B Comp'ny's barrick damages one o' these days. You look strapped, Terence."

"Faith, I'm not so young as I was. That guard–mountin' wears on the sole av the fut, and this" – he sniffed contemptuously at the brick verandah – "is as hard setting as standin'!"

"Wait a minute. I'll get the cushions out of my cart," I said.

" 'Strewth – sofies! We're going it gay," said Ortheris, as Terence dropped himself section by section on the leather cushions, saying prettily, "May you niver want a soft place wheriver you go, an' power to share ut wid a frind. Another for yourself? That's good. It lets me sit longways. Stanley, pass me a poipe. Augrrh! An' that's another man gone all to pieces bekaze av a woman. I must ha' been on forty or fifty prisoners' gyards, first an' last, an' I hate ut new ivry time."

"Let's see. You were on Losson's, Lancey's, Dugard's, and Stebbins's, that I can remember," I said.

"Ay, an' before that an' before that – scores av thim," he answered with a worn smile. " 'Tis betther to die than to live for thim, though. Whin Raines comes out – he'll be changin' his kit at the jail now – he'll think that too. He shud ha' shot himself an' the woman by rights, an' made a clean bill av all. Now he's left the woman – she tuk tay wid Dinah Sunday gone last – an' he's left himself. Mackie's the lucky man."

"He's probably getting it hot where he is," I ventured, for I knew something of the dead Corporal's record.

"Be sure av that," said Terence, spitting over the edge of the verandah. "But fwhat he'll get there is light marchin'–ordher to fwhat he'd ha' got here if he'd lived."

"Surely not. He'd have gone on and forgotten like the others."

"Did ye know Mackie well, Sorr?" said Terence.

"He was on the Pattiala guard of honour last winter, and I went out shooting with him in an *ekka* for the day, and I found him rather an amusing man."

"Well, he'll ha' got shut av amusemints, excipt turnin' from wan side to the other, these few years to come. I knew Mackie, an' I've seen too many to be mistuk in the muster av wan man. He might ha' gone on an' forgot, as you say, Sorr, but he was a man wid an educashin, an' he used ut for his schames, an' the same educashin, an' talkin', an' all that made him able to do fwhat he had a mind to wid a woman, that same wud turn back again in the long run an' tear him alive. I can't say fwhat that I mane to say bekaze I don't know how, but Mackie was the spit an' livin' image av a man that I saw march the same march *all but*; an' 'twas worse for him that he did not come by Mackie's ind. Wait while I remimber now. 'Twas fwhin I was in the Black Tyrone, an' he was drafted us from Portsmouth; an' fwhat was his misbegotten name? Larry – Larry Tighe ut was; an' wan of the draft said he was a gentleman ranker, an' Larry tuk an' three parts killed him for saying so. An' he was a big man, an' a strong man, an' a handsome man, an' that tells heavy in practice wid some women, but, takin' thim by an' large, not wid all. Yet 'twas wid all that Larry dealt – *all* – for he 'ud put the comether on any woman that trod the green earth av God, an' he knew ut. Like Mackie that's roastin' now, he knew ut; an' niver did he put the comether on any woman save an' excipt for the black shame. 'Tis not me that shud be talkin', dear knows, dear knows, but the most av my mis – misalli'nces was for pure devilry, an' mighty sorry I have been whin harm came; an' time an' again wid a girl, ay, an' a woman too, for the matter av that, whin I have seen by the eyes av her that I was makin' more throuble than I talked, I have hild off an' let be for the sake av the mother that bore me. But Larry, I'm thinkin', he was suckled by a she-devil, for he niver let wan go that came nigh to listen to him. 'Twas his business, as if it might ha' bin sinthry-go. He was a good soldier too. Now there was the Colonel's governess – an' he a privit too! – that was never known in barracks; an' wan av the Major's maids, and she was promised to a man; an' some more outside; an' fwhat ut was amongst us we'll never know till Judgment Day! 'Twas the nature av the baste to put the comether on the best av thim – not the prettiest by any manner av manes – but the like av such woman as you cud lay your hand on the Book an' swear there was niver thought av foolishness in. An' for that very reason, mark you, he was niver caught. He came close to ut wanst or twice, but caught he niver was, an' that cost him more at the ind than the beginnin'. He talked to me more than most, bekaze he tould me, barrin' the accident av my educashin, I'd ha' been the same kind av divil he was. 'An' is ut like,' he wud say, houldin' his head high – 'is ut like that I'd iver be thrapped? For fwhat am I when all's said an' done?' he sez. 'A damned privit,' sez he. 'An' is ut like, think you, that thim I know wud be connect wid a privit like me? Number tin thousand four hundred an' sivin,' he sez, grinnin'. I knew by the turn av his spache whin he was not takin' care to talk rough that he was a gentleman ranker.

" 'I do not undherstan' ut at all,' I sez; 'but I know,' sez I, 'that the divil looks out av your eyes, an' I'll have no share wid you. A little fun by way av amusemint where 't will do no harm, Larry, is right and fair, but I am mistook if 'tis any amusemint to you,' I sez.

" 'You are much mistook,' he sez. 'An' I counsel you not to judge your betters.'

" 'My betthers!' I sez. 'God help you, Larry. There's no betther in this. 'Tis all bad, as you will find for yoursilf.'

" 'You're not like me,' he says, tossin' his head.

" 'Praise the Saints, I am not,' I sez. 'Fwhat I have done I have done an' been crool sorry for. Fwhin your time comes,' sez I, 'ye'll remimber fwhat I say.'

" 'An' whin that time comes,' sez he, 'I'll come to you for ghostly consolation, Father Terence,' an' at that he wint off afther some more divil's business – for to get expayrience, he tould me. He was wicked – rank wicked – wicked as all Hell!

I'm not construct by nature to go in fear av any man, but, begad, I was afraid av Larry. He'd come in to barricks wid his cap on three hairs, an' lie on his cot and stare at the ceilin', and now an' again he'd fetch a little laugh, the like av a splash in the bottom av a well, an' by that I knew he was schamin' new wickedness, an' I'd be afraid. All this was long an' long ago, but ut hild me straight – for a while.

"I tould you, did I not, Sorr, that I was caressed an' pershuaded to lave the Tyrone on account av a throuble?"

"Something to do with a belt and a man's head, wasn't it?" Terence had never given me the exact facts.

"It was. Faith, ivry time I go on prisoner's gyard in coort I wondher fwhy I am not where the pris'ner is. But the man I struk tuk it in fair fight, an' he had the good sinse not to die. Considher now, fwhat wud ha' come to the Arrmy if he had! I was enthreated to exchange, an' my Commandin' Orf'cer pled wid me. I wint, not to be disobligin', an' Larry tould me he was powerful sorry to lose me, though fwhat I'd done to make him sorry I do not know. So to the Ould Rig'mint I came, lavin' Larry to go to the divil his own way, an' niver expectin' to see him again except as a shootin'-case in barricks. . . . Who's that lavin' the compound?" Terence's quick eye had caught sight of a white uniform skulking behind the hedge.

"The Sergeant's gone visiting," said a voice.

"Thin I command here, an' I will have no sneakin' away to the bazar, an' huntin' for you wid a pathrol at midnight. Nalson, for I know ut's you, come back to the verandah."

Nalson, detected, slunk back to his fellows. There was a grumble that died away in a minute or two, and Terence, turning on the other side, went on: –

"That was the last I saw av Larry for a while. Exchange is the same as death for not thinkin', an' by token I married Dinah, an' that kept me from remimberin' ould times. Thin we wint up to the Front, an' ut tore my heart in tu to lave Dinah at the Depôt in Pindi. Consequint whin I was at the

Front I fought circumspectuous till I warrmed up, an thin I fought double tides. You remimber fwhat I tould you in the gyard-gate av the fight at Silver's Theatre."

"Wot's that about Silver's Theayter!" said Ortheris quickly, over his shoulder.

"Nothin', little man. A tale that ye know. As I was sayin', afther that fight us av the Ould Rig'-mint an' the Tyrone was all mixed together takin' shtock av the dead, an' av coorse I wint about to find if there was any man that remimbered me. The second man I came acrost – an' how I'd missed him in the fight I do not know – was Larry, an' a fine man he looked, but oulder, by token that he had a call to be. 'Larry,' sez I, 'how is ut wid you?'

" 'Ye're callin' the wrong man,' he sez, wid his gentleman's smile; 'Larry has been dead these three years. They call him "Love-o'-Women" now,' he sez. By that I knew the ould divil was in him yet, but the ind av a fight is no time for the beginnin' av confession, so we sat down an' talked av times.

" 'They tell me you're a married man,' he sez, puffing slow at his poipe. 'Are ye happy?'

" 'I will be whin I get back to Depôt,' I sez. ' 'Tis a reconnaissance honeymoon now.'

" 'I'm married too,' he sez, puffin' slow an' more slow, an' stopperin' wid his forefinger.

" 'Sind you happiness,' I sez. 'That's the best hearin' for a long time.'

" 'Are ye av that opinion?' he sez; an' thin he began talkin' av the campaign. The sweat av Silver's Theatre was not dhry upon him, an' he was prayin' for more work. I was well contint to lie and listen to the cook-pot lids.

"Whin he got up off the ground he shtaggered a little, an' laned over all twisted.

" 'Ye've got more than ye bargained for,' I sez. 'Take an inventory, Larry. 'Tis like you're hurt.'

"He turned round stiff as a ramrod an' damned the eyes av me up an' down for an impartinent Irish-faced ape. If that had been in barricks, I'd ha' stretched him an' no more said;

but 'twas at the Front, an' afther such a fight as Silver's Theatre I knew there was no callin' a man to account for his timpers. He might as well ha' kissed me. Aftherwards I was well pleased I kept my fistes home. Then our Captain Crook – Cruik-na-bulleen – came up. He'd been talkin' to the little orf'cer bhoy av the Tyrone. 'We're all cut to windystraws,' he sez, 'but the Tyrone are damned short for noncoms. Go you over there, Mulvaney, an' be Deputy-Sergeant, Corp'ral, Lance, an' everything else ye can lay hands on till I bid you stop.'

"I wint over an' tuk hould. There was wan sergeant left standin', an' they'd pay no heed to him. The remnint was me, an' 'twas high time I came. Some I talked to, an' some I did not, but before night the bhoys av the Tyrone stud to attention, begad, if I sucked on my poipe above a whishper. Betune you an' me an' Bobs, I was commandin' the company, an' that was what Cruik had transferred me for, an' the little orf'cer bhoy knew ut, and I knew ut, but the comp'ny did not. And *there*, mark you, is the vartue that no money an' no dhrill can buy – the vartue av the ould soldier that knows his orf'cer's work an' does ut – at the salute!

"Thin the Tyrone, wid the Ould Rig'mint in touch, was sint maraudin' and prowlin' acrost the hills promishcuous an' unsatisfactory. 'Tis my privit opinion that a gin'ral does not know half his time fwhat to do wid three-quarthers his command. So he shquats on his hunkers an' bids thim run round an' round forninst him while he considhers on ut. Whin by the process av nature they get sejuced into a big fight that was none av their seekin', he sez: 'Obsarve my shuparior janius! I meant ut to come so.' We ran round an' about, an' all we got was shootin' into the camp at night, an' rushin' empty *sungars* wid the long bradawl, an' bein' hit from behind rocks till we was wore out – all except Love-o'-Women. That puppy-dog business was mate an' dhrink to him. Begad, he cud niver get enough av ut. Me well knowin' that it is just this desultorial campaignin' that kills the best men, an' suspicionin' that if I was cut the little orf'cer bhoy wud expind all his men in thryin' to get out, I wud lie most powerful doggo whin I heard a shot, an' curl my long legs behind a bowlder, an' run like blazes whin the ground was clear. Faith, if I led the Tyrone in rethreat wanst I led them forty times. Love-o'-Women wud stay pottin' an' pottin' from behind a rock, and wait till the fire was heaviest, an' thin stand up an' fire man-height clear. He wud lie out in camp too at night snipin' at the shadows, for he niver tuk a mouthful av slape. My commandin' orf'cer – save his little soul! – cud not see the beauty av my strategims, an' whin the Ould Rig'mint crossed us, an' that was wanst a week, he'd throt off to Cruik, wid his big blue eyes as round as saucers, an' lay an information against me. I heard thim wanst talkin' through the tent-wall, an' I nearly laughed.

" 'He runs – runs like a hare,' sez the little orf'cer bhoy. ' 'Tis demoralisin' my men.'

" 'Ye damned little fool,' sez Cruik, laughin'. 'He's larnin' you your business. Have ye been rushed at night yet?'

" 'No,' sez the child, wishful that he had been.

" 'Have you any wounded?' sez Cruik.

" 'No,' he sez. 'There was no chanst for that. They follow Mulvaney too quick,' he sez.

" 'Fwhat more do you want, thin?' sez Cruik. 'Terence is bloodin' you neat an' handy,' he sez. 'He knows fwhat you do not, an' that's that there's a time for ivrything. He'll not lead you wrong,' he sez, 'but I'd give a month's pay to larn fwhat he thinks av you.'

"That kept the babe quiet, but Love-o'-Women was pokin' at me for ivrything I did, an' specially my manoeuvres.

" 'Mr. Mulvaney,' he sez wan evenin', very contempshus, 'you're growin' very *jeldy* wid your feet. Among gentlemen,' he sez, 'among gentlemen that's called no pretty name.'

" 'Among privits 'tis different,' I sez. 'Get back to your tent. I'm sergeant here,' I sez.

"There was just enough in the voice av me to tell him he was playin' wid his life betune his teeth. He wint off, an' I noticed that this man that was contempshus set off from the halt wid a shunt as tho' he was bein' kicked behind. That same night there was a Pathan picnic in the hills about, an' firin' into our tents fit to wake the livin' dead. 'Lie down all,' I sez. 'Lie down an' kape still. They'll no more than waste ammunition.'

"I heard a man's feet on the ground, an' thin a 'Tini joinin' in the chorus. I'd been lyin' warm, thinkin' av Dinah an' all, but I crup out wid the bugle for to look round in case there was a rush, an' the 'Tini was flashin' at the fore-ind av the camp, an' the hill near by was fair flickerin' wid long-range fire. Undher the starlight I beheld Love-o'-Women settin' on a rock wid his belt and helmet off. He shouted wanst or twice, an' thin I heard him say: 'They should ha' got the range long ago. Maybe they'll fire at the flash.' Thin he fired again, an' that dhrew a fresh volley, and the long slugs that they chew in their teeth came floppin' among the rocks like tree-toads av a hot night. 'That's better,' sez Love-o'-Women. 'Oh Lord, how long, how long!' he sez, an' at that he lit a match an' held ut above his head.

" 'Mad,' thinks I, 'mad as a coot,' an' I tuk wan stip forward, an' the nixt I knew was the sole av my boot flappin' like a cavalry gydon an' the funny-bone av my toes tinglin'. 'Twas a clane-cut shot – a slug – that niver touched sock or hide, but set me bare-fut on the rocks. At that I tuk Love-o'-Women by the scruff an' threw him under a bowlder, an' whin I sat down I heard the bullets patterin' on that good stone.

" 'Ye may dhraw your own wicked fire,' I sez, shakin' him, 'but I'm not goin' to be kilt too.'

" 'Ye've come too soon,' he sez. 'Ye've come too soon. In another minute they cud not ha' missed me. Mother av God,' he sez, 'fwhy did ye not lave me be? Now 'tis all to do again,' an' he hides his face in his hands.

" 'So that's it,' I sez, shakin' him again. 'That's the manin' av your disobeyin' ordhers.'

" 'I dare not kill meself,' he sez, rockin' to and fro. 'My own hand wud not let me die, and there's not a bullet this month past wud touch me. I'm to die slow,' he sez. 'I'm to die slow. But I'm in hell now,' he sez, shriekin' like a woman. 'I'm in hell now!'

" 'God be good to us all,' I sez, for I saw his face. 'Will ye tell a man the throuble. If 'tis not murder, maybe we'll mend it yet.'

"At that he laughed. 'D'you remimber fwhat I said in the Tyrone barricks about comin' to you for ghostly consolation. I have not forgot,' he sez. 'That came back, an' the rest av my time is on me now, Terence. I've fought ut off for months an' months, but the liquor will not bite any more, Terence,' he sez. 'I can't get dhrunk.'

"Thin I knew he spoke the truth about bein' in hell, for whin liquor does not take hould, the sowl av a man is rotten in him. But me bein' such as I was, fwhat could I say to him?

" 'Di'monds an' pearls,' he begins again. 'Di'monds and pearls I have thrown away wid both hands – an' fwhat have I left? Oh, fwhat have I left?'

"He was shakin' an' thremblin' up against my shouldher, an' the slugs was singin' overhead, an' I was wonderin' whether my little bhoy wud have sinse enough to kape his men quiet through all this firin'.

" 'So long as I did not think,' sez Love-o'-Women, 'so long I did not see – I wud not see – but I can now, what I've lost. The time an' the place,' he sez, 'an' the very words I said whin ut pleased me to go off alone to hell. But thin, even thin,' he sez, wrigglin' tremenjus, 'I wud not ha' been happy. There was too much behind av me. How cud I ha' believed her sworn oath – me that have bruk mine again an' again for the sport av seein' thim cry. An' there are the others,' he sez. 'Oh, what will I do – what will I do?' He rocked back an' forward again, an' I think he was cryin' like wan av the women he dealt wid.

"The full half av fwhat he said was Brigade Ordhers to me, but from the rest an' the remnint I suspicioned some-thin' av his throuble. 'Twas the judgmint av God had grup the heel av him, as I tould him 'twould in the Tyrone barricks. The slugs was singin' over our rock more an' more, an' I sez for to divart him: 'Let bad alone,' I sez. 'They'll be thryin' to rush the camp in a minut'.'

"I had no more than said that whin a Pathan man crep' up on his belly wid his knife betune his teeth, not twinty yards from us. Love-o'-Women jumped up an' fetched a yell, an' the man saw him an' ran at him (he'd left his rifle under the rock) wid the knife. Love-o'-Women niver turned a hair, but by the Living Power, for I saw ut, a stone twisted under the Pathan man's feet an' he came down full sprawl, an' his knife wint tinklin' acrost the rocks! 'I tould you I was Cain,' sez Love-o'-Women. 'Fwhat's the use av killin' him? He's an honest man – by compare.'

"I was not dishputin' about the morils av Pathans that tide, so I dhropped Love-o'-Women's butt acrost the man's face, an' 'Hurry into camp,' I sez, 'for this may be the first av a rush.'

"There was no rush afther all, though we waited undher arms to give thim a chanst. The Pathan man must ha' come alone for the mischief, an' afther a while Love-o'-Women wint back to his tint wid that quare lurchin' sind-off in his walk that I cud niver undherstand. Begad, I pitied him, an' the more bekaze he made me think for the rest av the night av the day whin I was confirmed Corp'ril, not actin' Lef'tenant, an' my thoughts was not good.

"Ye can undherstand that afther that night we came to talkin' a dale together, an' bit by bit ut came out fwhat I'd suspicioned. The whole av his carr'in's on an' divilmints had come back on him hard as liquor comes back whin you've been on the dhrink for a wake. All he'd said an' all he'd done, an' only he cud tell how much that was, come back, an' there was niver a minut's peace in his sowl. 'Twas the Horrors widout any cause to see, an' yet, an' yet – fwhat am I talkin' av? He'd ha' taken the Horrors wid thankfulness. Beyon' the repentince av the man, an' that was beyon' the nature av man – awful, awful, to behould! – there was more that was worst than any repentince. Av the scores an' scores that he called over in his mind (an' they were dhrivin' him mad), there was, mark you, wan woman av all, an' she was not his wife, that cut him to the quick av his marrow. 'Twas there he said that he'd thrown away di'monds an' pearls past count, an' thin he'd begin again like a blind *byle* in an oil-mill, walkin' round an' round, to considher (him that was beyond all touch av being happy this side hell!) how happy he wud ha' been wid *her*. The more he considhered, the more he'd consate himself that he'd lost mighty happiness, an' thin he wud work ut all backwards, an' cry that he niver cud ha' been happy anyways.

"Time an' time an' again in camp, on p'rade, ay, an' in action, I've seen that man shut his eyes an' duck his head as you wud duck to the flicker av a bay'nit. For 'twas thin he tould me that the thought av all he'd missed came an' stud forninst him like red-hot irons. For what he'd done wid the others he was sorry, but he did not care; but this wan woman that I've tould of, by the Hilts av God she made him pay for all the others twice over! Niver did I know that a man cud enjure such tormint widout his heart crackin' in his ribs, an' I have been" – Terence turned the pipe-stem slowly between his teeth – "I have been in some black cells. All I iver suffered tho' was not to be talked of alongside av *him* . . . an' what could I do? Paternosters was no more than peas for his sorrow.

"Evenshually we finished our prom'nade acrost the hills, and thanks to me for the same, there was no casualties an' no glory. The campaign was comin' to an ind, an' all the rig'mints was bein' drawn together for to be sint back home. Love-o'-Women was mighty sorry bekaze he had no work to do, an' all his time to think in. I've heard that man talkin' to his belt-plate an' his side-arms while he was soldierin' thim, all to prevint himself from thinkin', an' ivry time he got up afther he had been settin' down or wint on from the halt, he'd start wid that kick an' traverse that I tould you of – his legs sprawlin' all ways to wanst. He wud niver go see the docthor, tho' I tould him to be wise. He'd curse me up an' down for my advice; but I knew he was no more a man to be reckoned wid than the little bhoy was a commandin' orf'cer, so I let his tongue run if it aised him.

"Wan day – 'twas on the way back – I was walkin' round camp wid him, an' he stopped an' struck ground wid his right fut three or four times doubtful. 'Fwhat is ut?' I sez. 'Is that ground?' sez he; an' while I was thinkin' his mind was goin', up comes the docthor, who'd been anatomisin' a dead bullock. Love-o'-Women starts to go on quick, an' lands me a kick on the knee while his legs was gettin' into marchin' ordher.

" 'Hould on there,' sez the docthor; an' Love-o'-Women's face, that was lined like a gridiron, turns red as brick.

" ' 'Tention,' says the docthor; an' Love-o'-Women stud so. 'Now shut your eyes,' sez the docthor. 'No, ye must not hould by your comrade.'

" ' 'Tis all up,' sez Love-o'-Women, trying to smile. 'I'd fall, docthor, an' you know ut.'

" 'Fall?' I sez. 'Fall at attention wid your eyes shut! Fwhat do ye mane?'

" 'The docthor knows,' he sez. 'I've hild up as long as I can, but begad I'm glad 'tis all done. But I will die slow,' he sez, 'I will die very slow.'

"I cud see by the docthor's face that he was mortial sorry for the man, an' he ordhered him to hospital. We wint back together, an' I was dumb-struck; Love-o'-Women was cripplin' and crumblin' at ivry step. He walked wid a hand on my shoulder all slued sideways, an' his right leg swingin' like a lame camel. Me not knowin' more than the dead fwhat ailed him, 'twas just as though the docthor's word had done ut all – as if Love-o'-Women had but been waitin' for the ordher to let go.

"In hospital he sez somethin' to the docthor that I could not catch.

" 'Holy shmoke!' sez the docthor, 'an' who are you to be givin' names to your diseases? 'Tis ag'in' all the regulations.'

" 'I'll not be a privit much longer,' sez Love-o'-Women in his gentleman's voice, an' the docthor jumped.

" 'Thrate me as a study, Docthor Lowndes,' he sez; an' that was the first time I'd iver heard a docthor called his name.

" 'Good-bye, Terence,' sez Love-o'-Women. ' 'Tis a dead man I am widout the pleasure av dyin'. You'll come an' set wid me sometimes for the peace av my soul.'

"Now I had been minded to ask Cruik to take me back to the Ould Rig'mint, for the fightin' was over, an' I was wore out wid the ways av the bhoys in the Tyrone; but I shifted my will, an' hild on, an' wint to set wid Love-o'-Women in the hospital. As I have said, Sorr, the man bruk all to little pieces undher my hand. How long he had hild up an' forced himself fit to march I cannot tell, but in hospital but two days later he was such as I hardly knew. I shuk hands wid him, an' his grip was fair strong, but his hands wint all ways to wanst, an' he cud not button his tunic.

" 'I'll take long an' long to die yet,' he sez, 'for the ways av sin they're like interest in the rig'mintal savin's-bank – sure, but a damned long time bein' paid.'

"The docthor sez to me quiet one day, 'Has Tighe there anythin' on his mind?' he sez. 'He's burnin' himself out.'

" 'How shud I know, Sorr?' I sez, as innocent as putty.

" 'They call him Love-o'-Women in the Tyrone, do they not?' he sez. 'I was a fool to ask. Be wid him all you can. He's houldin' on to your strength.'

" 'But fwhat ails him, docthor,' I sez.

" 'They call ut Locomotus attacks us,' he sez, 'bekaze,' sez he, 'ut attacks us like a locomotive, if ye know fwhat that manes. An' ut comes,' sez he, lookin' at me, 'ut comes from bein' called Love-o'-Women.'

" 'You're jokin', docthor,' I sez.

" 'Jokin'!' sez he. 'If iver you feel that you've got a felt sole in your boot instead av a Government bull's-wool, come to me,' he sez, 'an' I'll show you whether 'tis a joke.'

"You would not belave ut, Sorr, but that an' seein'

Love-o'-Women overtuk widout warnin' put the cowld fear
av attacks us on me so strong that for a week an' more I was
kickin' my toes against stones an' stumps for the pleasure av
feelin' them hurt.

"An' Love-o'-Women lay in the cot (he might have gone
down wid the wounded before an' before, but he asked to
stay wid me), and fwhat there was in his mind had full swing
at him night an' day an' ivry hour av the day an' the night,
an' he withered like beef rations in a hot sun, an' his eyes
was like owls' eyes, an' his hands was mut'nous.

"They was gettin' the rig'mints away wan by wan, the
campaign bein' inded, but as ushuil they was behavin' as if
niver a rig'mint had been moved before in the mem'ry av
man. Now, fwhy is that, Sorr? There's fightin' in an' out
nine months av the twelve somewhere in the Army. There
has been – for years an' years an' years, an' I wud ha' thought
they'd begin to get the hang av providin' for throops. But no!
Ivry time it's like a girls' school meetin' a big red bull whin
they're goin' to church; an' 'Mother av God,' sez the Commissariat an' the railways an' the Barrick-masters, 'fwhat will
we do now?' The ordhers came to us av the Tyrone an' the
Ould Rig'mint an' half a dozen more to go down, and there
the ordhers stopped dumb. We wint down, by the special
grace av God – down the Khaiber anyways. There was sick
wid us, an' I'm thinkin' that some av them was jolted to
death in the doolies, but they was anxious to be kilt so if they
cud get to Peshawur alive the sooner. I walked by Love-o'-
Women – there was no marchin', an' Love-o'-Women was
not in a stew to get on. 'If I'd only ha' died up there!' sez he
through the doolie-curtains, an' then he'd twist up his eyes
an' duck his head for the thoughts that came to him.

"Dinah was in Depôt at Pindi, but I wint circumspectuous, for well I knew 'tis just at the rump-ind av all things
that his luck turns on a man. By token I had seen a dhriver
of a batthery goin' by at a trot singin' 'Home, swate home'
at the top av his shout, and takin' no heed to his bridle-hand
– I had seen that man dhrop under the gun in the middle of

a word, and come out by the limber like – like a frog on a
pavestone. No. I wud *not* hurry, though, God knows, my
heart was all in Pindi. Love-o'-Women saw fwhat was in my
mind, an' 'Go on, Terence,' he sez, 'I know fwhat's waitin''
for you.' 'I will not,' I sez. ' 'Twill kape a little yet.'

"Ye know the turn of the pass forninst Jumrood and the
nine mile road on the flat to Peshawur? All Peshawur was
along that road day and night waitin' for frinds – men,
women, childer, and bands. Some av the throops was camped
round Jumrood, an' some went on to Peshawur to get away
down to their cantonmints. We came through in the early
mornin', havin' been awake the night through, and we dhruv
sheer into the middle av the mess. Mother av Glory, will I
ever forget that comin' back? The light was not fair lifted,
and the furst we heard was 'For 'tis my delight av a shiny
night,' frum a band that thought we was the second four
comp'nies av the Lincolnshire. At that we was forced to sind
them a yell to say who we was, an' thin up wint 'The wearin''
av the Green.' It made me crawl all up my backbone, not
havin' taken my brequist. Thin, right smash into our rear,
came fwhat was left av the Jock Elliotts – wid four pipers an'
not half a kilt among thim, playin' for the dear life, an'
swingin' their rumps like buck rabbits, an' a native rig'mint
shrieking blue murther. Ye niver heard the like. There was
men cryin' like women that did – an' faith I do not blame
thim. Fwhat bruk me down was the Lancers' Band – shinin'
an' spick like angels, wid the ould dhrum-horse at the head
an' the silver kettle-dhrums an' all an' all, waitin' for their
men that was behind us. They shtruck up the Cavalry
Canter, an', begad, those poor ghosts that had not a sound
fut in a throop they answered to ut, the men rockin' in their
saddles. We thried to cheer them as they wint by, but ut
came out like a big gruntin' cough, so there must have been
many that was feelin' like me. Oh, but I'm forgettin'! The
Fly-by-Nights was waitin' for their second battalion, an'
whin ut came out, there was the Colonel's horse led at the
head – saddle-empty. The men fair worshipped him, an' he'd

died at Ali Musjid on the road down. They waited till the remnint av the battalion was up, and thin – clane against ordhers, for who wanted *that* chune that day? – they wint back to Peshawur slow-time an' tearin' the bowils out av ivry man that heard, wid 'The Dead March.' Right across our line they wint, an' ye know their uniforms are as black as the Sweeps, crawlin' past like the dead, an' the other bands damnin' them to let be.

"Little they cared. The carpse was wid them, an' they'd ha' taken ut so through a Coronation. Our ordhers was to go into Peshawur, an' we wint hot-fut past the Fly-by-Nights, not singin', to lave that chune behind us. That was how we tuk the road of the other corps.

" 'Twas ringin' in my ears still whin I felt in the bones of me that Dinah was comin', an' I heard a shout, an' thin I saw a horse an' a tattoo latherin' down the road, hell to shplit, under women. I knew – I knew! Wan was the Tyrone Colonel's wife – ould Beeker's lady – her gray hair flyin' an' her fat round carkiss rowlin' in the saddle, an' the other was Dinah, that shud ha' been at Pindi. The Colonel's lady she charged at the head av our column like a stone wall, an' she all but knocked Beeker off his horse throwin' her arms round his neck an' blubberin', 'Me bhoy! me bhoy!' an' Dinah wheeled left an' came down our flank, an' I let a yell that had suffered inside av me for months, and – Dinah came. Will I iver forget that while I live! She'd come on pass from Pindi, an' the Colonel's lady had lint her the tattoo. They'd been huggin' an' cryin' in each other's arms all the long night.

"So she walked along wid her hand in mine, askin' forty questions to wanst, an' beggin' me on the Virgin to make oath that there was not a bullet consaled in me, unbeknownst somewhere, an' thin I remimbered Love-o'-Women. He was watchin' us, an' his face was like the face av a divil that has been cooked too long. I did not wish Dinah to see ut, for whin a woman's runnin' over wid happiness she's like to be touched, for harm afterwards, by the laste little thing in life.

So I dhrew the curtain, an' Love-o'-Women lay back and groaned.

"Whin we marched into Peshawur, Dinah wint to barracks to wait for me, an' me feelin' so rich that tide, I wint on to take Love-o'-Women to hospital. It was the laste I cud do, an' to save him the dust an' the smother I turned the doolie-men down a road well clear av the rest av the throops, an we wint along, me talkin' through the curtains. Av a sudden I heard him say: —

" 'Let me look. For the Mercy av Hiven, let me look!' I had been so tuk up wid gettin' him out av the dust and thinkin' of Dinah that I had not kept my eyes about me. There was a woman ridin' a little behind av us, an', talkin' ut over wid Dinah afterwards, that same woman must ha' rid not far on the Jumrood road. Dinah said that she had been hoverin' like a kite on the left flank av the column.

"I halted the doolie to set the curtains, an' she rode by walkin'-pace, an' Love-o'-Women's eyes wint afther her as if he would fair haul her down from the saddle.

" 'Follow there,' was all he sez, but I niver heard a man spake in that voice before or since, an' I knew by those two wan words an' the look in his face that she was Di'monds-an'-Pearls that he'd talked av in his disthresses.

"We followed till she turned into the gate av a little house that stud near the Edwardes's Gate. There was two girls in the verandah, an' they ran in whin they saw us. Faith, at long eye-range ut did not take me a wink to see fwhat kind av house ut was. The throops bein' there an' all, there was three or four such, but afterwards the polis bade them go. At the verandah Love-o'-Women sez, catchin' his breath, 'Stop here,' an' thin, an' thin, wid a grunt that must ha' tore the heart up from his stomach, he swung himself out av the doolie, an' my troth he stud up on his feet wid the sweat pourin' down his face. If Mackie was to walk in here now I'd be less tuk back than I was thin. Where he'd dhrawn his power from, God knows — or the divil — but 't was a dead man walkin' in the sun wid the face av a dead man and the breath av a dead man held up by the Power, an' the legs an' the arms of the carpse obeyin' ordhers!

"The woman stud in the verandah. She'd been a beauty too, though her eyes was sunk in her head, an' she looked Love-o'-Women up an' down terrible. 'An',' she sez, kickin' back the tail av her habit, – 'An',' she sez, 'fwhat are you doin' *here*, married man?'

"Love-o'-Women said nothin', but a little froth came to his lips, an' he wiped ut off wid his hand an' looked at her an' the paint on her, an' looked, an' looked, an' looked.

" 'An' yet,' she sez, wid a laugh. (Did you hear Mrs. Raines laugh whin Mackie died? Ye did not? Well for you.) 'An' yet,' she sez, 'who but you have betther right,' sez she. 'You taught me the road. You showed me the way,' she sez. 'Ay, look,' she sez, 'for 'tis your work; you that tould me – d'you remimber it? – that a woman who was false to wan man cud be false to two. I have been that,' she sez, 'that an' more, for you always said I was a quick learner, Ellis. Look well,' she sez, 'for it is me that you called your wife in the sight av God long since!' An' she laughed.

"Love-o'-Women stud still in the sun widout answerin'. Thin he groaned an' coughed to wanst, an' I thought 'twas the death-rattle, but he niver tuk his eyes off her face not for a wink. Ye cud ha' put her eyelashes through the flies av an E.P. tent, they were so long.

" 'Fwhat do you do here?' she sez, word by word, 'that have taken away my joy in my man this five years gone – that have broken my rest an' killed my body an' damned my soul for the sake av seein' how 'twas done? Did your expayrience aftherwards bring you acrost any woman that gave you more than I did? Wud I not ha' died for you an' wid you, Ellis? Ye know that, man! If ever your lyin' sowl saw truth in uts life ye know that.'

"An' Love-o'-Women lifted up his head and said, 'I knew,' an' that was all. While she was spakin' the Power hild him up parade-set in the sun, an the sweat dhropped undher his helmet. 'Twas more an' more throuble for him to talk, an' his mouth was runnin' twistways.

" 'Fwhat do you do here?' she sez, an' her voice wint up. 'Twas like bells tollin' before. 'Time was whin you were quick enough wid your words, – you that talked me down to hell. Are ye dumb now?' An' Love-o'-Women got his tongue, an' sez simple, like a little child, 'May I come in?' he sez.

" 'The house is open day an' night,' she sez, wid a laugh; an' Love-o'-Women ducked his head an' hild up his hand as tho' he was gyardin'. The Power was on him still – it hild him up still, for, by my sowl, as I'll never save ut, he walked up the verandah steps that had been a livin' corpse in hospital for a month!

" 'An' now?' she sez, lookin' at him; an' the red paint stud lone on the white av her face like a bull's-eye on a target.

"He lifted up his eyes, slow an' very slow, an' he looked at her long an' very long, an' he tuk his spache betune his teeth wid a wrench that shuk him.

" 'I'm dyin', Aigypt – dyin',' he sez; ay, those were his words, for I remimber the name he called her. He was turnin' the death-colour, but his eyes niver rowled. They were set – set on her. Widout word or warnin' she opened her arms full stretch, an' 'Here!' she sez. (Oh, fwhat a golden mericle av a voice ut was!) 'Die here,' she sez; an' Love-o'-Women dhropped forward, an' she hild him up, for she was a fine big woman.

"I had no time to turn, bekaze that minut I heard the sowl quit him – tore out in the death-rattle – an' she laid him back in a long chair, an' she sez to me, 'Misther soldier,' she sez, 'will ye not go in an' talk to wan av the girls. This sun's too much for him.'

"Well I knew there was no sun he'd iver see, but I cud not spake, so I wint away wid the empty doolie to find the docthor. He'd been breakfastin' an' lunchin' ever since we'd come in, an' he was as full as a tick.

" 'Faith ye've got dhrunk mighty soon,' he sez, whin I'd tould him, 'to see that man walk. Barrin' a puff or two av life, he was a corpse before we left Jumrood. I've a great mind,' he sez, 'to confine you.'

" 'There's a dale av liquor runnin' about, docthor,' I sez, solemn as a hard-boiled egg. 'Maybe 'tis so, but will ye not come an' see the corpse at the house?'

" ' 'Tis dishgraceful,' he sez, 'that I would be expected to go to a place like that. Was she a pretty woman?' he sez, an' at that he set off double quick.

"I cud see that the two was in the verandah where I'd left them, an' I knew by the hang av her head an' the noise av the crows fwhat had happened. 'Twas the first and the last time that I'd ever known woman to use the pistol. They dread the shot as a rule, but Di'monds-an'-Pearls she did not – she did not.

"The docthor touched the long black hair av her head ('twas all loose upon Love-o'-Women's chest), an' that cleared the liquor out av him. He stud considherin' a long time, his hands in his pockets, an' at last he sez to me, 'Here's a double death from naturil causes; an' in the presint state av affairs the rig'mint will be thankful for wan grave the less to dig. *Issiwasti*,' he sez, '*Issiwasti*, Privit Mulvaney, these two will be buried together in the Civil Cemet'ry at my expinse, an' may the good God,' he sez, 'make it so much for me whin my time comes. Go to your wife,' he sez; 'go an' be happy. I'll see to this all.'

"I left him still considherin'. They was buried in the Civil Cemet'ry together, wid a Church of England service. There was too many buryin's thin to ask questions, an' the docthor – he ran away wid Major – Major Van Dyce's lady that year – he saw to ut all. Fwhat the right an' the wrong av Love-o'- Women an' Di'monds-an'-Pearls was I niver knew, an' I will niver know; but I've tould ut as I came acrost ut – here an' there in little pieces. *So*, being fwhat I am, an' knowin' fwhat I know, that's fwhy I say in this shootin'-case here, Mackie that's dead an' in hell is the lucky man. There are times, Sorr, whin 'tis betther for the man to die than to live, an' by con- sequince forty million times betther for the woman."

* * *

"H'up there!" said Ortheris. "It's time to go."

The witnesses and guard formed up in the thick white dust of the parched twilight and swung off, marching easy and whistling. Down the road to the green by the church I could hear Ortheris, the black Book-lie still uncleansed on his lips, setting, with a fine sense of the fitness of things, the shrill quick-step that runs –

> "Oh, do not despise the advice of the wise,
>   Learn wisdom from those that are older,
> And don't try for things that are out of your reach –
>   An' that's what the Girl told the Soldier!
>   Soldier! soldier!
>   Oh, that's what the Girl told the Soldier!"

THE DRUMS OF THE FORE
AND AFT

THE DRUMS OF THE FORE
AND AFT

IN the Army List they still stand as "The Fore and Fit
Princess Hohenzollern-Sigmaringen-Anspach's Merther-
Tydfilshire Own Royal Loyal Light Infantry, Regimental
District 329A," but the Army through all its barracks and
canteens knows them now as the "Fore and Aft." They may
in time do something that shall make their new title honourable, but at present they are bitterly ashamed, and the man
who calls them "Fore and Aft" does so at the risk of the head
which is on his shoulders.

Two words breathed into the stables of a certain Cavalry
Regiment will bring the men out into the streets with belts
and mops and bad language; but a whisper of "Fore and Aft"
will bring out this regiment with rifles.

Their one excuse is that they came again and did their
best to finish the job in style. But for a time all their world
knows that they were openly beaten, whipped, dumb-cowed,
shaking and afraid. The men know it; their officers know it;
the Horse Guards know it, and when the next war comes the
enemy will know it also. There are two or three regiments of
the Line that have a black mark against their names which
they will then wipe out; and it will be excessively inconvenient for the troops upon whom they do their wiping.

The courage of the British soldier is officially supposed to
be above proof, and, as a general rule, it is so. The exceptions
are decently shovelled out of sight, only to be referred to in
the freshest of unguarded talk that occasionally swamps a
Mess-table at midnight. Then one hears strange and horrible
stories of men not following their officers, of orders being
given by those who had no right to give them, and of disgrace
that, but for the standing luck of the British Army, might
have ended in brilliant disaster. These are unpleasant stories

to listen to, and the Messes tell them under their breath, sitting by the big wood fires, and the young officer bows his head and thinks to himself, please God, his men shall never behave unhandily.

The British soldier is not altogether to be blamed for occasional lapses; but this verdict he should not know. A moderately intelligent General will waste six months in mastering the craft of the particular war that he may be waging; a Colonel may utterly misunderstand the capacity of his regiment for three months after it has taken the field, and even a Company Commander may err and be deceived as to the temper and temperament of his own handful: wherefore the soldier, and the soldier of to-day more particularly, should not be blamed for falling back. He should be shot or hanged afterwards – to encourage the others; but he should not be vilified in newspapers, for that is want of tact and waste of space.

He has, let us say, been in the service of the Empress for, perhaps, four years. He will leave in another two years. He has no inherited morals, and four years are not sufficient to drive toughness into his fibre, or to teach him how holy a thing is his Regiment. He wants to drink, he wants to enjoy himself – in India he wants to save money – and he does not in the least like getting hurt. He has received just sufficient education to make him understand half the purport of the orders he receives, and to speculate on the nature of clean, incised, and shattering wounds. Thus, if he is told to deploy under fire preparatory to an attack, he knows that he runs a very great risk of being killed while he is deploying, and suspects that he is being thrown away to gain ten minutes' time. He may either deploy with desperate swiftness, or he may shuffle, or bunch, or break, according to the discipline under which he has lain for four years.

Armed with imperfect knowledge, cursed with the rudiments of an imagination, hampered by the intense selfishness of the lower classes, and unsupported by any regimental associations, this young man is suddenly introduced to an enemy who in eastern lands is always ugly, generally tall and hairy, and frequently noisy. If he looks to the right and the left and sees old soldiers – men of twelve years' service, who, he knows, know what they are about – taking a charge, rush, or demonstration without embarrassment, he is consoled and applies his shoulder to the butt of his rifle with a stout heart. His peace is the greater if he hears a senior, who has taught him his soldiering and broken his head on occasion, whispering: "They'll shout and carry on like this for five minutes. Then they'll rush in, and then we've got 'em by the short hairs!"

But, on the other hand, if he sees only men of his own term of service, turning white and playing with their triggers and saying: "What the Hell's up now?" while the Company Commanders are sweating into their sword-hilts and shouting: "Front rank, fix bayonets. Steady there – steady! Sight for three hundred – no, for five! Lie down, all! Steady! Front rank kneel!" and so forth, he becomes unhappy, and grows acutely miserable when he hears a comrade turn over with the rattle of fire-irons falling into the fender, and the grunt of a pole-axed ox. If he can be moved about a little and allowed to watch the effect of his own fire on the enemy he feels merrier, and may be then worked up to the blind passion of fighting, which is, contrary to general belief, controlled by a chilly Devil and shakes men like ague. If he is not moved about, and begins to feel cold at the pit of the stomach, and in that crisis is badly mauled and hears orders that were never given, he will break, and he will break badly, and of all things under the light of the Sun there is nothing more terrible than a broken British regiment. When the worst comes to the worst and the panic is really epidemic, the men must be e'en let go, and the Company Commanders had better escape to the enemy and stay there for safety's sake. If they can be made to come again they are not pleasant men to meet; because they will not break twice.

About thirty years from this date, when we have succeeded in half-educating everything that wears trousers, our

Army will be a beautifully unreliable machine. It will know too much and it will do too little. Later still, when all men are at the mental level of the officer of to-day, it will sweep the earth. Speaking roughly, you must employ either black-guards or gentlemen, or, best of all, blackguards commanded by gentlemen, to do butcher's work with efficiency and des-patch. The ideal soldier should, of course, think for himself – the "Pocket-book" says so. Unfortunately, to attain this virtue, he has to pass through the phase of thinking of him-self, and that is misdirected genius. A blackguard may be slow to think for himself, but he is genuinely anxious to kill, and a little punishment teaches him how to guard his own skin and perforate another's. A powerfully prayerful High-land Regiment, officered by rank Presbyterians, is, perhaps, one degree more terrible in action than a hard-bitten thou-sand of irresponsible Irish ruffians led by most improper young unbelievers. But these things prove the rule – which is that the midway men are not to be trusted alone. They have ideas about the value of life and an upbringing that has not taught them to go on and take the chances. They are carefully unprovided with a backing of comrades who have been shot over, and until that backing is re-introduced, as a great many Regimental Commanders intend it shall be, they are more liable to disgrace themselves than the size of the Empire or the dignity of the Army allows. Their officers are as good as good can be, because their training begins early, and God has arranged that a clean-run youth of the British middle classes shall, in the matter of backbone, brains, and bowels, surpass all other youths. For this reason a child of eighteen will stand up, doing nothing, with a tin sword in his hand and joy in his heart until he is dropped. If he dies, he dies like a gentleman. If he lives, he writes Home that he has been "potted," "sniped," "chipped," or "cut over," and sits down to besiege Government for a wound-gratuity until the next little war breaks out, when he perjures himself before a Medical Board, blarneys his Colonel, burns incense round his Adjutant, and is allowed to go to the Front once more.

Which homily brings me directly to a brace of the most finished little fiends that ever banged drum or tootled fife in the Band of a British Regiment. They ended their sinful career by open and flagrant mutiny and were shot for it. Their names were Jakin and Lew – Piggy Lew – and they were bold, bad drummer-boys, both of them frequently birched by the Drum-Major of the Fore and Aft.

Jakin was a stunted child of fourteen, and Lew was about the same age. When not looked after, they smoked and drank. They swore habitually after the manner of the Barrack-room, which is cold swearing and comes from between clenched teeth, and they fought religiously once a week. Jakin had sprung from some London gutter, and may or may not have passed through Dr. Barnardo's hands ere he arrived at the dignity of drummer-boy. Lew could remember nothing except the Regiment and the delight of listening to the Band from his earliest years. He hid somewhere in his grimy little soul a genuine love for music, and was most mistakenly furnished with the head of a cherub: insomuch that beautiful ladies who watched the Regiment in church were wont to speak of him as a "darling." They never heard his vitriolic comments on their manners and morals, as he walked back to barracks with the Band and matured fresh causes of offence against Jakin.

The other drummer-boys hated both lads on account of their illogical conduct. Jakin might be pounding Lew, or Lew might be rubbing Jakin's head in the dirt, but any attempt at aggression on the part of an outsider was met by the combined forces of Lew and Jakin; and the consequences were painful. The boys were the Ishmaels of the corps, but wealthy Ishmaels, for they sold battles in alternate weeks for the sport of the barracks when they were not pitted against other boys; and thus amassed money.

On this particular day there was dissension in the camp. They had just been convicted afresh of smoking, which is bad for little boys who use plug-tobacco, and Lew's contention was that Jakin had "stunk so 'orrid bad from keepin' the pipe in pocket," that he and he alone was responsible for the birching they were both tingling under.

"I tell you I 'id the pipe back o' barracks," said Jakin pacifically.

"You're a bloomin' liar," said Lew without heat.

"You're a bloomin' little barstard," said Jakin, strong in the knowledge that his own ancestry was unknown.

Now there is one word in the extended vocabulary of barrack-room abuse that cannot pass without comment. You may call a man a thief and risk nothing. You may even call him a coward without finding more than a boot whiz past your ear, but you must not call a man a bastard unless you are prepared to prove it on his front teeth.

"You might ha' kep' that till I wasn't so sore," said Lew sorrowfully, dodging round Jakin's guard.

"I'll make you sorer," said Jakin genially, and got home on Lew's alabaster forehead. All would have gone well and this story, as the books say, would never have been written, had not his evil fate prompted the Bazar-Sergeant's son, a long, employless man of five-and-twenty, to put in an appearance after the first round. He was eternally in need of money, and knew that the boys had silver.

"Fighting again," said he. "I'll report you to my father, and he'll report you to the Colour-Sergeant."

"What's that to you?" said Jakin with an unpleasant dilation of the nostrils.

"Oh! nothing to *me*. You'll get into trouble, and you've been up too often to afford that."

"What the Hell do you know about what we've done?" asked Lew the Seraph. "*You* aren't in the Army, you lousy, cadging civilian."

He closed in on the man's left flank.

"Jes' 'cause you find two gentlemen settlin' their diff' rences with their fists you stick in your ugly nose where you aren't wanted. Run 'ome to your 'arf-caste slut of a Ma – or we'll give you what-for," said Jakin.

The man attempted reprisals by knocking the boys' heads

together. The scheme would have succeeded had not Jakin punched him vehemently in the stomach, or had Lew refrained from kicking his shins. They fought together, bleeding and breathless, for half an hour, and, after heavy punishment, triumphantly pulled down their opponent as terriers pull down a jackal.

"Now," gasped Jakin, "I'll give you what-for." He proceeded to pound the man's features while Lew stamped on the outlying portions of his anatomy. Chivalry is not a strong point in the composition of the average drummer-boy. He fights, as do his betters, to make his mark.

Ghastly was the ruin that escaped, and awful was the wrath of the Bazar-Sergeant. Awful too was the scene in the Orderly-room when the two reprobates appeared to answer the charge of half-murdering a "civilian." The Bazar-Sergeant thirsted for a criminal action, and his son lied. The boys stood to attention while the black clouds of evidence accumulated.

"You little devils are more trouble than the rest of the Regiment put together," said the Colonel angrily. "One might as well admonish thistledown, and I can't well put you in cells or under stoppages. You must be birched again."

"Beg y' pardon, Sir. Can't we say nothin' in our own defence, Sir?" shrilled Jakin.

"Hey! What? Are you going to argue with *me*?" said the Colonel.

"No, Sir," said Lew. "But if a man come to you, Sir, and said he was going to report you, Sir, for 'aving a bit of a turn-up with a friend, Sir, an' wanted to get money out o' *you*, Sir —"

The Orderly-room exploded in a roar of laughter. "Well?" said the Colonel.

"That was what that measly *jarnwar* there did, Sir, and 'e'd 'a' *done* it, Sir, if we 'adn't prevented 'im. We didn't 'it 'im much, Sir. 'E 'adn't no manner o' right to interfere with us, Sir. I don't mind bein' birched by the Drum-Major, Sir, nor yet reported by *any* Corp'ral, but I'm – but I don't think it's fair, Sir, for a civilian to come an' talk over a man in the Army."

A second shout of laughter shook the Orderly-room, but the Colonel was grave.

"What sort of characters have these boys?" he asked of the Regimental Sergeant-Major.

"Accordin' to the Bandmaster, Sir," returned that revered official – the only soul in the Regiment whom the boys feared – "they do everything *but* lie, Sir."

"Is it like we'd go for that man for fun, Sir?" said Lew, pointing to the plaintiff.

"Oh, admonished – admonished!" said the Colonel testily, and when the boys had gone he read the Bazar-Sergeant's son a lecture on the sin of unprofitable meddling, and gave orders that the Bandmaster should keep the Drums in better discipline.

"If either of you come to practice again with so much as a scratch on your two ugly little faces," thundered the Band-master, "I'll tell the Drum-Major to take the skin off your backs. Understand that, you young devils."

Then he repented of his speech for just the length of time that Lew, looking like a seraph in red worsted embellish-ments, took the place of one of the trumpets – in hospital – and rendered the echo of a battle-piece. Lew certainly was a musician, and had often in his more exalted moments ex-pressed a yearning to master every instrument of the Band.

"There's nothing to prevent your becoming a Band-master, Lew," said the Bandmaster, who had composed waltzes of his own, and worked day and night in the interests of the Band.

"What did he say?" demanded Jakin after practice.

"Said I might be a bloomin' Bandmaster, an' be asked in to 'ave a glass o' sherry wine on Mess-nights."

"Ho! 'Said you might be a bloomin' non-combatant, did 'e! That's just about wot 'e would say. When I've put in my boy's service – it's a bloomin' shame that doesn't count for pension – I'll take on as a privit. Then I'll be a Lance in a year – knowin' what I know about the ins an' outs o' things. In three years I'll be a bloomin' Sergeant. I won't marry then, not I! I'll 'old on and learn the orf'cers' ways an' apply for exchange into a reg'ment that doesn't know all about me. Then I'll be a bloomin' orf'cer. Then I'll ask you to 'ave a glass o' sherry wine, *Mister* Lew, an' you'll bloomin' well 'ave to stay in the hanty-room while the Mess-Sergeant brings it to your dirty 'ands."

" 'S'pose I'm going to be a Bandmaster? Not I, quite. I'll be a orf'cer too. There's nothin' like takin' to a thing an' stickin' to it, the Schoolmaster says. The Reg'ment don't go 'ome for another seven years. I'll be a Lance then or near to."

Thus the boys discussed their futures, and conducted themselves piously for a week. That is to say, Lew started a flirtation with the Colour-Sergeant's daughter, aged thirteen – "not," as he explained to Jakin, "with any intention o' matrimony, but by way o' keepin' my 'and in." And the black-haired Cris Delighan enjoyed that flirtation more than previous ones, and the other drummer-boys raged furiously together, and Jakin preached sermons on the dangers of "bein' tangled along o' petticoats."

But neither love nor virtue would have held Lew long in the paths of propriety had not the rumour gone abroad that the Regiment was to be sent on active service, to take part in a war which, for the sake of brevity, we will call "The War of the Lost Tribes."

The barracks had the rumour almost before the Mess-room, and of all the nine hundred men in barracks, not ten had seen a shot fired in anger. The Colonel had, twenty years ago, assisted at a Frontier expedition; one of the Majors had seen service at the Cape; a confirmed deserter in E Company had helped to clear streets in Ireland; but that was all. The Regiment had been put by for many years. The overwhelming mass of its rank and file had from three to four years' service; the non-commissioned officers were under thirty years old; and men and sergeants alike had forgotten to speak of the stories written in brief upon the Colours – the New

Colours that had been formally blessed by an Archbishop in England ere the Regiment came away.

They wanted to go to the Front – they were enthusiastically anxious to go – but they had no knowledge of what war meant, and there was none to tell them. They were an educated regiment, the percentage of school-certificates in their ranks was high, and most of the men could do more than read and write. They had been recruited in loyal observance of the territorial idea; but they themselves had no notion of that idea. They were made up of drafts from an overpopulated manufacturing district. The system had put flesh and muscle upon their small bones, but it could not put heart into the sons of those who for generations had done overmuch work for overscanty pay, had sweated in drying-rooms, stooped over looms, coughed among white-lead, and shivered on lime-barges. The men had found food and rest in the Army, and now they were going to fight "niggers" – people who ran away if you shook a stick at them. Wherefore they cheered lustily when the rumour ran, and the shrewd, clerkly non-commissioned officers speculated on the chances of batta and of saving their pay. At Headquarters men said: "The Fore and Fit have never been under fire within the last generation. Let us, therefore, break them in easily by setting them to guard lines of communication." And this would have been done but for the fact that British Regiments were wanted – badly wanted – at the front, and there were doubtful Native Regiments that could fill the minor duties. "Brigade 'em with two strong Regiments," said Headquarters. "They may be knocked about a bit, but they'll learn their business before they come through. Nothing like a night-alarm and a little cutting-up of stragglers to make a Regiment smart in the field. Wait till they've had half a dozen sentries' throats cut."

The Colonel wrote with delight that the temper of his men was excellent, that the Regiment was all that could be wished, and as sound as a bell. The Majors smiled with a sober joy, and the subalterns waltzed in pairs down the

Mess-room after dinner, and nearly shot themselves at revolver-practice. But there was consternation in the hearts of Jakin and Lew. What was to be done with the Drums? Would the Band go to the Front? How many of the Drums would accompany the Regiment?

They took counsel together, sitting in a tree and smoking.

"It's more than a bloomin' toss-up they'll leave us be'ind at the Depôt with the women. You'll like that," said Jakin sarcastically.

" 'Cause o' Cris, y' mean? Wot's a woman, or a 'ole bloomin' Depôt o' women, 'longside o' the chanst of field-service? You know I'm as keen on goin' as you," said Lew.

" 'Wish I was a bloomin' bugler," said Jakin sadly. "They'll take Tom Kidd along, that I can plaster a wall with, an' like as not they won't take us."

"Then let's go an' make Tom Kidd so bloomin' sick 'e can't bugle no more. You 'old 'is 'ands an' I'll kick him," said Lew, wriggling on the branch.

"That ain't no good neither. We ain't the sort o' characters to presoom on our rep'tations – they're bad. If they have the Band at the Depôt we don't go, and no error *there*. If they take the Band we may get cast for medical unfitness. Are you medical fit, Piggy?" said Jakin, digging Lew in the ribs with force.

"Yus," said Lew with an oath. "The Doctor says your 'eart's weak through smokin' on an empty stummick. Throw a chest an' I'll try yer."

Jakin threw out his chest, which Lew smote with all his might. Jakin turned very pale, gasped, crowed, screwed up his eyes, and said – "That's all right."

"You'll do," said Lew. "I've 'eard o' men dying when you 'it 'em fair on the breastbone."

"Don't bring us no nearer goin', though," said Jakin. "Do you know where we're ordered?"

"Gawd knows, an' 'E won't split on a pal. Somewheres up to the Front to kill Pathans – hairy big beggars that turn you inside out if they get 'old o' you. They say their women are good-looking, too."

"Any loot?" asked the abandoned Jakin.

"Not a bloomin' anna, they say, unless you dig up the ground an' see what the niggers 'ave 'id. They're a poor lot." Jakin stood upright on the branch and gazed across the plain.

"Lew," said he, "there's the Colonel coming. 'Colonel's a good old beggar. Let's go an' talk to 'im."

Lew nearly fell out of the tree at the audacity of the suggestion. Like Jakin he feared not God, neither regarded he Man, but there are limits even to the audacity of a drummer-boy, and to speak to a Colonel was —

But Jakin had slid down the trunk and doubled in the direction of the Colonel. That officer was walking wrapped in thought and visions of a C. B. – yes, even a K. C. B., for had he not at command one of the best Regiments of the Line – the Fore and Fit? And he was aware of two small boys charging down upon him. Once before it had been solemnly reported to him that "the Drums were in a state of mutiny," Jakin and Lew being the ringleaders. This looked like an organised conspiracy.

The boys halted at twenty yards, walked to the regulation four paces, and saluted together, each as well set-up as a ramrod and little taller.

The Colonel was in a genial mood; the boys appeared very forlorn and unprotected on the desolate plain, and one of them was handsome.

"Well!" said the Colonel, recognising them. "Are you going to pull me down in the open? I'm sure I never interfere with you, even though" – he sniffed suspiciously – "you have been smoking."

It was time to strike while the iron was hot. Their hearts beat tumultuously.

"Beg y' pardon, Sir," began Jakin. "The Reg'ment's ordered on active service, Sir?"

"So I believe," said the Colonel courteously.

"Is the Band goin', Sir?" said both together. Then, without pause, "We're goin', Sir, ain't we?"

"You!" said the Colonel, stepping back the more fully to take in the two small figures. "You! You'd die in the first march."

"No, we wouldn't, Sir. We can march with the Reg'ment anywheres – p'rade an' anywhere else," said Jakin.

"If Tom Kidd goes 'e'll shut up like a clasp-knife," said Lew. "Tom 'as very-close veins in both 'is legs, Sir."

"Very how much?"

"Very-close veins, Sir. That's why they swells after long p'rade, Sir. If 'e can go, we can go, Sir."

Again the Colonel looked at them long and intently.

"Yes, the Band is going," he said as gravely as though he had been addressing a brother officer. "Have you any parents, either of you two?"

"No, Sir," rejoicingly from Lew and Jakin. "We're both orphans, Sir. There's no one to be considered of on our account, Sir."

"You poor little sprats, and you want to go up to the Front with the Regiment, do you? Why?"

"I've wore the Queen's Uniform for two years," said Jakin. "It's very 'ard, Sir, that a man don't get no recompense for doin' of 'is dooty, Sir."

"An' – an' if I don't go, Sir," interrupted Lew, "the Bandmaster 'e says 'e'll catch an' make a bloo – a blessed musician o' me, Sir. Before I've seen any service, Sir."

The Colonel made no answer for a long time. Then he said quietly: "If you're passed by the Doctor I dare say you can go. I shouldn't smoke if I were you."

The boys saluted and disappeared. The Colonel walked home and told the story to his wife, who nearly cried over it. The Colonel was well pleased. If that was the temper of the children, what would not the men do?

Jakin and Lew entered the boys' barrack-room with great stateliness, and refused to hold any conversation with their comrades for at least ten minutes. Then, bursting with pride,

Jakin drawled: "I've bin intervooin' the Colonel. Good old beggar is the Colonel. Says I to 'im, 'Colonel,' says I, 'let me go to the Front, along o' the Reg'ment.' – 'To the Front you shall go,' says 'e, 'an' I only wish there was more like you among the dirty little devils that bang the bloomin' drums.' Kidd, if you throw your 'courtrements at me for tellin' you the truth to your own advantage, your legs'll swell.'

None the less there was a Battle-Royal in the barrack-room, for the boys were consumed with envy and hate, and neither Jakin nor Lew behaved in conciliatory wise.

"I'm goin' out to say adoo to my girl," said Lew, to cap the climax. "Don't none o' you touch my kit because it's wanted for active service; me bein' specially invited to go by the Colonel."

He strolled forth and whistled in the clump of trees at the back of the Married Quarters till Cris came to him, and, the preliminary kisses being given and taken, Lew began to explain the situation.

"I'm goin' to the Front with the Reg'ment," he said valiantly.

"Piggy, you're a little liar," said Cris, but her heart misgave her, for Lew was not in the habit of lying.

"Liar yourself, Cris," said Lew, slipping an arm round her. "I'm goin'. When the Reg'ment marches out you'll see me with 'em, all galliant and gay. Give us another kiss, Cris, on the strength of it."

"If you'd on'y a-stayed at the Depôt – where you *ought* to ha' bin – you could get as many of 'em as – as you dam please," whimpered Cris, putting up her mouth.

"It's 'ard, Cris. I grant you it's 'ard. But what's a man to do? If I'd a-stayed at the Depôt, you wouldn't think anything of me."

"Like as not, but I'd 'ave you with me, Piggy. An' all the thinkin' in the world isn't like kissin'."

"An' all the kissin' in the world isn't like 'avin' a medal to wear on the front o' your coat."

"*You* won't get no medal."

"Oh, yus, I shall though. Me an' Jakin are the only acting-drummers that'll be took along. All the rest is full men, an' we'll get our medals with them."

"They might ha' taken anybody but you, Piggy. You'll get killed – you're so venturesome. Stay with me, Piggy darlin', down at the Depôt, an' I'll love you true, for ever."

"Ain't you goin' to do that *now*, Cris? You said you was."

"O' course I am, but th' other's more comfortable. Wait till you've growed a bit, Piggy. You aren't no taller than me now."

"I've bin in the Army for two years, an' I'm not goin' to get out of a chanst o' seein' service, an' don't you try to make me do so. I'll come back, Cris, an' when I take on as a man I'll marry you – marry you when I'm a Lance."

"Promise, Piggy."

Lew reflected on the future as arranged by Jakin a short time previously, but Cris's mouth was very near to his own.

"I promise, s'elp me Gawd!" said he.

Cris slid an arm round his neck.

"I won't 'old you back no more, Piggy. Go away an' get your medal, an' I'll make you a new button-bag as nice as I know how," she whispered.

"Put some o' your 'air into it, Cris, an' I'll keep it in my pocket so long's I'm alive."

Then Cris wept anew, and the interview ended. Public feeling among the drummer-boys rose to fever pitch, and the lives of Jakin and Lew became unenviable. Not only had they been permitted to enlist two years before the regulation boy's age – fourteen – but, by virtue, it seemed, of their extreme youth, they were allowed to go to the Front – which thing had not happened to acting-drummers within the knowledge of boy. The Band which was to accompany the Regiment had been cut down to the regulation twenty men, the surplus returning to the ranks. Jakin and Lew were attached to the Band as supernumeraries, though they would much have preferred being company buglers.

" 'Don't matter much," said Jakin after the medical

inspection. "Be thankful that we're 'lowed to go at all. The Doctor 'e said that if we could stand what we took from the Bazar-Sergeant's son we'd stand pretty nigh anything."

"Which we will," said Lew, looking tenderly at the ragged and ill-made housewife that Cris had given him, with a lock of her hair worked into a sprawling "L" upon the cover.

"It was the best I could," she sobbed. "I wouldn't let mother nor the Sergeant's tailor 'elp me. Keep it always, Piggy, an' remember I love you true."

They marched to the railway station, nine hundred and sixty strong, and every soul in cantonments turned out to see them go. The drummers gnashed their teeth at Jakin and Lew marching with the Band, the married women wept upon the platform, and the Regiment cheered its noble self black in the face.

"A nice level lot," said the Colonel to the Second-in-Command as they watched the first four companies entraining.

"Fit to do anything," said the Second-in-Command enthusiastically. "But it seems to me they're a thought too young and tender for the work in hand. It's bitter cold up at the Front now."

"They're sound enough," said the Colonel. "We must take our chance of sick casualties."

So they went northward, ever northward, past droves and droves of camels, armies of camp-followers, and legions of laden mules, the throng thickening day by day, till with a shriek the train pulled up at a hopelessly congested junction where six lines of temporary track accommodated six forty-waggon trains; where whistles blew, Babus sweated, and Commissariat officers swore from dawn till far into the night, amid the wind-driven chaff of the fodder-bales and the lowing of a thousand steers.

"Hurry up – you're badly wanted at the Front," was the message that greeted the Fore and Aft, and the occupants of the Red Cross carriages told the same tale.

" 'Tisn't so much the bloomin' fightin'," gasped a head-

bound trooper of Hussars to a knot of admiring Fore and
Afts. " 'Tisn't so much the bloomin' fightin', though there's
enough o' that. It's the bloomin' food an' the bloomin' climate. Frost all night 'cept when it hails, and b'iling sun all
day, and the water stinks fit to knock you down. I got my
'ead chipped like a egg; I've got pneumonia too, an' my guts
is all out o' order. 'Tain't no bloomin' picnic in those parts,
I can tell you."

"Wot are the niggers like?" demanded a private.

"There's some prisoners in that train yonder. Go an' look
at 'em. They're the aristocracy of the country. The common
folk are a dashed sight uglier. If you want to know what they
fight with, reach under my seat an' pull out the long knife
that's there."

They dragged out and beheld for the first time the grim,
bone-handled, triangular Afghan knife. It was almost as long
as Lew.

"That's the thing to j'int ye," said the trooper feebly. "It
can take off a man's arm at the shoulder as easy as slicing
butter. I halved the beggar that used that un, but there's
more of his likes up above. They don't understand thrustin',
but they're devils to slice."

The men strolled across the tracks to inspect the Afghan
prisoners. They were unlike any "niggers" that the Fore and
Aft had ever met – these huge, black-haired, scowling sons
of the Beni-Israel. As the men stared the Afghans spat freely
and muttered one to another with lowered eyes.

"My eyes! Wot awful swine!" said Jakin, who was in the
rear of the procession. "Say, ole man, how you got *puckrowed*,
eh? *Kiswasti* you wasn't hanged for your ugly face, hey?"

The tallest of the company turned, his leg-irons clanking
at the movement, and stared at the boy. "See!" he cried to
his fellows in Pushto. "They send children against us. What
a people, and what fools!"

"*Hya!*" said Jakin, nodding his head cheerily. "You go
down-country. *Khana* get, *peenikapana* get – live like a
bloomin' Raja *ke marfik*. That's a better *bandobust* than baynit

get it in your innards. Good-bye, ole man. Take care o' your
beautiful figure-'ead, an' try to look *kushy*."

The men laughed and fell in for their first march, when
they began to realise that a soldier's life is not all beer and
skittles. They were much impressed with the size and bestial
ferocity of the niggers whom they had now learned to call
"Pathans," and more with the exceeding discomfort of their
own surroundings. Twenty old soldiers in the corps would
have taught them how to make themselves moderately snug
at night, but they had no old soldiers, and, as the troops on
the line of march said, "they lived like pigs." They learned
the heart-breaking cussedness of camp-kitchens and camels
and the depravity of an E. P. tent and a wither-wrung mule.
They studied animalculœ, in water, and developed a few
cases of dysentery in their study.

At the end of their third march they were disagreeably
surprised by the arrival in their camp of a hammered iron
slug which, fired from a steady rest at seven hundred yards,
flicked out the brains of a private seated by the fire. This
robbed them of their peace for a night, and was the beginning of a long-range fire carefully calculated to that end. In
the daytime they saw nothing except an unpleasant puff of
smoke from a crag above the line of march. At night there
were distant spurts of flame and occasional casualties, which
set the whole camp blazing into the gloom and, occasionally,
into opposite tents. Then they swore vehemently and vowed
that this was magnificent but not war.

Indeed it was not. The Regiment could not halt for reprisals against the sharpshooters of the country-side. Its duty
was to go forward and make connection with the Scotch and
Goorkha troops with which it was brigaded. The Afghans
knew this, and knew too, after their first tentative shots, that
they were dealing with a raw regiment. Thereafter they
devoted themselves to the task of keeping the Fore and Aft
on the strain. Not for anything would they have taken equal
liberties with a seasoned corps – with the wicked little
Goorkhas, whose delight it was to lie out in the open on a

dark night and stalk their stalkers – with the terrible big men
dressed in women's clothes, who could be heard praying to
their God in the night-watches, and whose peace of mind no
amount of "sniping" could shake – or with those vile Sikhs,
who marched so ostentatiously unprepared and who dealt out
such grim reward to those who tried to profit by that unpre-
paredness. This white regiment was different – quite different. It slept like a hog, and, like a hog, charged in every
direction when it was roused. Its sentries walked with a footfall that could be heard for a quarter of a mile; would fire at
anything that moved – even a driven donkey – and when they
had once fired, could be scientifically "rushed" and laid out
a horror and an offence against the morning sun. Then
there were camp-followers who straggled and could be cut
up without fear. Their shrieks would disturb the white
boys, and the loss of their services would inconvenience
them sorely.

Thus, at every march, the hidden enemy became bolder
and the Regiment writhed and twisted under attacks it could
not avenge. The crowning triumph was a sudden night-rush
ending in the cutting of many tent-ropes, the collapse of the
sodden canvas, and a glorious knifing of the men who
struggled and kicked below. It was a great deed, neatly carried out, and it shook the already shaken nerves of the Fore
and Aft. All the courage that they had been required to exercise up to this point was the "two o'clock in the morning
courage"; and, so far, they had only succeeded in shooting
their comrades and losing their sleep.

Sullen, discontented, cold, savage, sick, with their uniforms dulled and unclean, the Fore and Aft joined their
Brigade.

"I hear you had a tough time of it coming up," said the
Brigadier. But when he saw the hospital-sheets his face fell.

"This is bad," said he to himself. "They're as rotten as
sheep." And aloud to the Colonel – "I'm afraid we can't
spare you just yet. We want all we have, else I should have
given you ten days to recover in."

The Colonel winced. "On my honour, Sir," he returned, "there is not the least necessity to think of sparing us. My men have been rather mauled and upset without a fair return. They only want to go in somewhere where they can see what's before them."

"Can't say I think much of the Fore and Fit," said the Brigadier in confidence to his Brigade-Major. "They've lost all their soldiering, and, by the trim of them, might have marched through the country from the other side. A more fagged-out set of men I never put eyes on."

"Oh, they'll improve as the work goes on. The parade gloss has been rubbed off a little, but they'll put on field polish before long," said the Brigade-Major. "They've been mauled, and they don't quite understand it."

They did not. All the hitting was on one side, and it was cruelly hard hitting with accessories that made them sick. There was also the real sickness that laid hold of a strong man and dragged him howling to the grave. Worst of all, their officers knew just as little of the country as the men themselves, and looked as if they did. The Fore and Aft were in a thoroughly unsatisfactory condition, but they believed that all would be well if they could once get a fair go-in at the enemy. Pot-shots up and down the valleys were unsatisfactory, and the bayonet never seemed to get a chance. Perhaps it was as well, for a long-limbed Afghan with a knife had a reach of eight feet, and could carry away lead that would disable three Englishmen.

The Fore and Aft would like some rifle-practice at the enemy – all seven hundred rifles blazing together. That wish showed the mood of the men.

The Goorkhas walked into their camp, and in broken, barrack-room English strove to fraternise with them: offered them pipes of tobacco and stood them treat at the canteen. But the Fore and Aft, not knowing much of the nature of the Goorkhas, treated them as they would treat any other "niggers," and the little men in green trotted back to their firm friends the Highlanders, and with many grins confided to them: "That dam white regiment no dam use. Sulky – ugh! Dirty – ugh! *Hya*, any tot for Johnny?" Whereat the Highlanders smote the Goorkhas as to the head, and told them not to vilify a British Regiment, and the Goorkhas grinned cavernously, for the Highlanders were their elder brothers and entitled to the privileges of kinship. The common soldier who touches a Goorkha is more than likely to have his head sliced open.

Three days later the Brigadier arranged a battle according to the rules of war and the peculiarity of the Afghan temperament. The enemy were massing in inconvenient strength among the hills, and the moving of many green standards warned him that the tribes were "up" in aid of the Afghan regular troops. A squadron and a half of Bengal Lancers represented the available Cavalry, and two screw-guns, borrowed from a column thirty miles away, the Artillery at the General's disposal.

"If they stand, as I've a very strong notion that they will, I fancy we shall see an infantry fight that will be worth watching," said the Brigadier. "We'll do it in style. Each regiment shall be played into action by its Band, and we'll hold the Cavalry in reserve."

"For *all* the reserve?" somebody asked.

"For all the reserve; because we're going to crumple them up," said the Brigadier, who was an extraordinary Brigadier, and did not believe in the value of a reserve when dealing with Asiatics. Indeed, when you come to think of it, had the British Army consistently waited for reserves in all its little affairs, the boundaries of Our Empire would have stopped at Brighton beach.

The battle was to be a glorious battle.

The three regiments debouching from three separate gorges, after duly crowning the heights above, were to converge from the centre, left, and right upon what we will call the Afghan army, then stationed towards the lower extremity of a flat-bottomed valley. Thus it will be seen that three sides of the valley practically belonged to the English, while the fourth was strictly Afghan property. In the event of defeat the Afghans had the rocky hills to fly to, where the fire from the guerrilla tribes in aid would cover their retreat. In the event of victory these same tribes would rush down and lend their weight to the rout of the British.

The screw-guns were to shell the head of each Afghan rush that was made in close formation, and the Cavalry, held in reserve in the right valley, were to gently stimulate the break-up which would follow on the combined attack. The Brigadier, sitting upon a rock overlooking the valley, would watch the battle unrolled at his feet. The Fore and Aft would debouch from the central gorge, the Goorkhas from the left, and the Highlanders from the right, for the reason that the left flank of the enemy seemed as though it required the most hammering. It was not every day that an Afghan force would take ground in the open, and the Brigadier was resolved to make the most of it.

"If we only had a few more men," he said plaintively, "we could surround the creatures and crumple 'em up thoroughly. As it is, I'm afraid we can only cut them up as they run. It's a great pity."

The Fore and Aft had enjoyed unbroken peace for five days, and were beginning, in spite of dysentery, to recover their nerve. But they were not happy, for they did not know the work in hand, and had they known, would not have known how to do it. Throughout those five days in which old soldiers might have taught them the craft of the game, they discussed together their misadventures in the past – how such an one was alive at dawn and dead ere the dusk, and with what shrieks and struggles such another had given up his soul under the Afghan knife. Death was a new and horrible thing to the sons of mechanics who were used to die decently of zymotic disease; and their careful conservation in barracks had done nothing to make them look upon it with less dread.

Very early in the dawn the bugles began to blow, and the Fore and Aft, filled with a misguided enthusiasm, turned out without waiting for a cup of coffee and a biscuit; and were rewarded by being kept under arms in the cold while the other regiments leisurely prepared for the fray. All the world knows that it is ill taking the breeks off a Highlander. It is much iller to try to make him stir unless he is convinced of the necessity for haste.

The Fore and Aft waited, leaning upon their rifles and listening to the protests of their empty stomachs. The Colonel did his best to remedy the default of lining as soon as it was borne in upon him that the affair would not begin at once, and so well did he succeed that the coffee was just ready when – the men moved off, their Band leading. Even then there had been a mistake in time, and the Fore and Aft came out into the valley ten minutes before the proper hour. Their Band wheeled to the right after reaching the open, and retired behind a little rocky knoll still playing while the Regiment went past.

It was not a pleasant sight that opened on the uninstructed view, for the lower end of the valley appeared to be filled by an army in position – real and actual regiments attired in red coats, and – of this there was no doubt – firing Martini-Henry bullets which cut up the ground a hundred yards in front of the leading company. Over that pockmarked ground the Regiment had to pass, and it opened the ball with a general and profound courtesy to the piping pickets; ducking in perfect time, as though it had been brazed on a rod. Being half capable of thinking for itself, it fired a volley by the simple process of pitching its rifle into its shoulder and pulling the trigger. The bullets may have accounted for some of the watchers on the hill side, but they certainly did not affect the mass of enemy in front, while the noise of the rifles drowned any orders that might have been given.

"Good God!" said the Brigadier, sitting on the rock high above all. "That Regiment has spoilt the whole show. Hurry up the others, and let the screw-guns get off."

But the screw-guns, in working round the heights, had

stumbled upon a wasp's nest of a small mud fort which they incontinently shelled at eight hundred yards, to the huge discomfort of the occupants, who were unaccustomed to weapons of such devilish precision.

The Fore and Aft continued to go forward, but with shortened stride. Where were the other regiments, and why did these niggers use Martinis? They took open order instinctively, lying down and firing at random, rushing a few paces forward and lying down again, according to the regulations. Once in this formation, each man felt himself desperately alone, and edged in towards his fellow for comfort's sake.

Then the crack of his neighbour's rifle at his ear led him to fire as rapidly as he could – again for the sake of the comfort of the noise. The reward was not long delayed. Five volleys plunged the files in banked smoke impenetrable to the eye, and the bullets began to take ground twenty or thirty yards in front of the firers, as the weight of the bayonet dragged down and to the right arms wearied with holding the kick of the leaping Martini. The Company Commanders peered helplessly through the smoke, the more nervous mechanically trying to fan it away with their helmets.

"High and to the left!" bawled a Captain till he was hoarse. "No good! Cease firing, and let it drift away a bit."

Three and four times the bugles shrieked the order, and when it was obeyed the Fore and Aft looked that their foe should be lying before them in mown swaths of men. A light wind drove the smoke to leeward, and showed the enemy still in position and apparently unaffected. A quarter of a ton of lead had been buried a furlong in front of them, as the ragged earth attested.

That was not demoralising to the Afghans, who have not European nerves. They were waiting for the mad riot to die down, and were firing quietly into the heart of the smoke. A private of the Fore and Aft spun up his company shrieking with agony, another was kicking the earth and gasping, and a third, ripped through the lower intestines by a jagged bullet, was calling aloud on his comrades to put him out of his pain. These were the casualties, and they were not soothing to hear or see. The smoke cleared to a dull haze.

Then the foe began to shout with a great shouting, and a mass – a black mass – detached itself from the main body, and rolled over the ground at horrid speed. It was composed of, perhaps, three hundred men, who would shout and fire and slash if the rush of their fifty comrades who were determined to die carried home. The fifty were Ghazis, half maddened with drugs and wholly mad with religious fanaticism. When they rushed the British fire ceased, and in the lull the order was given to close ranks and meet them with the bayonet.

Any one who knew the business could have told the Fore and Aft that the only way of dealing with a Ghazi rush is by volleys at long ranges; because a man who means to die, who desires to die, who will gain heaven by dying, must, in nine cases out of ten, kill a man who has a lingering prejudice in favour of life. Where they should have closed and gone forward, the Fore and Aft opened out and skirmished, and where they should have opened out and fired, they closed and waited.

A man dragged from his blankets half awake and unfed is never in a pleasant frame of mind. Nor does his happiness increase when he watches the whites of the eyes of three hundred six-foot fiends upon whose beards the foam is lying, upon whose tongues is a roar of wrath, and in whose hands are yard-long knives.

The Fore and Aft heard the Goorkha bugles bringing that regiment forward at the double, while the neighing of the Highland pipes came from the left. They strove to stay where they were, though the bayonets wavered down the line like the oars of a ragged boat. Then they felt body to body the amazing physical strength of their foes; a shriek of pain ended the rush, and the knives fell amid scenes not to be told. The men clubbed together and smote blindly – as often as not at their own fellows. Their front crumpled like paper,

and the fifty Ghazis passed on; their backers, now drunk with
success, fighting as madly as they.

Then the rear ranks were bidden to close up, and the
subalterns dashed into the stew – alone. For the rear-ranks
had heard the clamour in front, the yells and the howls of
pain, and had seen the dark stale blood that makes afraid.
They were not going to stay. It was the rushing of the camps
over again. Let their officers go to Hell, if they chose; they
would get away from the knives.

"Come on!" shrieked the subalterns, and their men, curs-
ing them, drew back, each closing into his neighbour and
wheeling round.

Charteris and Devlin, subalterns of the last company,
faced their death alone in the belief that their men would
follow.

"You've killed me, you cowards," sobbed Devlin, and
dropped, cut from the shoulder-strap to the centre of the
chest; and a fresh detachment of his men retreating, always
retreating, trampled him under foot as they made for the pass
whence they had emerged.

> I kissed her in the kitchen and I kissed her in the hall.
> Child'un, child'un, follow me!
> Oh Golly, said the cook, is he gwine to kiss us all?
> Halla – Halla – Halla – Hallelujah!

The Goorkhas were pouring through the left gorge and
over the heights at the double to the invitation of their
Regimental Quick-step. The black rocks were crowned with
dark green spiders as the bugles gave tongue jubilantly: –

> In the morning! In the morning by the bright light!
> When Gabriel blows his trumpet in the morning!

The Goorkha rear companies tripped and blundered over
loose stones. The front files halted for a moment to take stock
of the valley and to settle stray boot-laces. Then a happy
little sigh of contentment soughed down the ranks, and it was
as though the land smiled, for behold there below was the

enemy, and it was to meet them that the Goorkhas had doubled so hastily. There was much enemy. There would be amusement. The little men hitched their *kukris* well to hand, and gaped expectantly at their officers as terriers grin ere the stone is cast for them to fetch. The Goorkhas' ground sloped downward to the valley, and they enjoyed a fair view of the proceedings. They sat upon the boulders to watch, for their officers were not going to waste their wind in assisting to repulse a Ghazi rush more than half a mile away. Let the white men look to their own front.

"Hi! yi!" said the Subadar-Major, who was sweating profusely. "Dam fools yonder, stand close order! This is no time for close order, it is the time for volleys. Ugh!"

Horrified, amused, and indignant, the Goorkhas beheld the retirement of the Fore and Aft with a running chorus of oaths and commentaries.

"They run! The white men run! Colonel Sahib, may *we* also do a little running?" murmured Runbir Thappa, the Senior Jemadar.

But the Colonel would have none of it. "Let the beggars be cut up a little," said he wrathfully. "Serves 'em right. They'll be prodded into facing round in a minute." He looked through his field-glasses, and caught the glint of an officer's sword.

"Beating 'em with the flat – damned conscripts! How the Ghazis are walking into them!" said he.

The Fore and Aft, heading back, bore with them their officers. The narrowness of the pass forced the mob into solid formation, and the rear ranks delivered some sort of a wavering volley. The Ghazis drew off, for they did not know what reserve the gorge might hide. Moreover, it was never wise to chase white men too far. They returned as wolves return to cover, satisfied with the slaughter that they had done, and only stopping to slash at the wounded on the ground. A quarter of a mile had the Fore and Aft retreated, and now, jammed in the pass, was quivering with pain, shaken and demoralised with fear, while the officers, maddened beyond control, smote the men with the hilts and the flats of their swords.

"Get back! Get back, you cowards – you women! Right about face – column of companies, form – you hounds!" shouted the Colonel, and the subalterns swore aloud. But the Regiment wanted to go – to go anywhere out of the range of those merciless knives. It swayed to and fro irresolutely with shouts and outcries, while from the right the Goorkhas dropped volley after volley of cripple-stopper Snider bullets at long range into the mob of the Ghazis returning to their own troops.

The Fore and Aft Band, though protected from direct fire by the rocky knoll under which it had sat down, fled at the first rush. Jakin and Lew would have fled also, but their short legs left them fifty yards in the rear, and by the time the Band had mixed with the Regiment, they were painfully aware that they would have to close in alone and unsupported.

"Get back to that rock," gasped Jakin. "They won't see us there."

And they returned to the scattered instruments of the Band, their hearts nearly bursting their ribs.

"Here's a nice show for *us*," said Jakin, throwing himself full length on the ground. "A bloomin' fine show for British Infantry! Oh, the devils! They've gone and left us alone here! Wot'll we do?"

Lew took possession of a cast-off water-bottle, which naturally was full of canteen rum, and drank till he coughed again.

"Drink," said he shortly. "They'll come back in a minute or two – you see."

Jakin drank, but there was no sign of the Regiment's return. They could hear a dull clamour from the head of the valley of retreat, and saw the Ghazis slink back, quickening their pace as the Goorkhas fired at them.

"We're all that's left of the Band, an' we'll be cut up as sure as death," said Jakin.

"I'll die game, then," said Lew thickly, fumbling with his tiny drummer's sword. The drink was working on his brain as it was on Jakin's.

" 'Old on! I know something better than fightin'," said Jakin, stung by the splendour of a sudden thought due chiefly to rum. "Tip our bloomin' cowards yonder the word to come back. The Pathan beggars are well away. Come on, Lew! We won't get hurt. Take the fife an' give me the drum. The Old Step for all your bloomin' guts are worth! There's a few of our men coming back now. Stand up, ye drunken little defaulter. By your right – quick march!"

He slipped the drum-sling over his shoulder, thrust the fife into Lew's hand, and the two boys marched out of the cover of the rock into the open, making a hideous hash of the first bars of the "British Grenadiers."

As Lew had said, a few of the Fore and Aft were coming back sullenly and shamefacedly under the stimulus of blows and abuse; their red coats shone at the head of the valley, and behind them were wavering bayonets. But between this shattered line and the enemy, who with Afghan suspicion feared that the hasty retreat meant an ambush, and had not moved therefore, lay half a mile of level ground dotted only by the wounded.

The tune settled into full swing and the boys kept shoulder to shoulder, Jakin banging the drum as one possessed. The one fife made a thin and pitiful squeaking, but the tune carried far, even to the Goorkhas.

"Come on, you dogs!" muttered Jakin to himself. "Are we to play forhever?" Lew was staring straight in front of him and marching more stiffly than ever he had done on parade.

And in bitter mockery of the distant mob, the old tune of the Old Line shrilled and rattled: –

> Some talk of Alexander,
>   And some of Hercules;
> Of Hector and Lysander,
>   And such great names as these!

There was a far-off clapping of hands from the Goorkhas, and a roar from the Highlanders in the distance, but never a shot was fired by British or Afghan. The two little red dots moved forward in the open parallel to the enemy's front.

> But of all the world's great heroes
> There's none that can compare,
> With a tow-row-row-row-row-row,
> To the British Grenadier!

The men of the Fore and Aft were gathering thick at the entrance into the plain. The Brigadier on the heights far above was speechless with rage. Still no movement from the enemy. The day stayed to watch the children.

Jakin halted and beat the long roll of the Assembly, while the fife squealed despairingly.

"Right about face! Hold up, Lew, you're drunk," said Jakin. They wheeled and marched back: —

> Those heroes of antiquity
> Ne'er saw a cannon-ball,
> Nor knew the force o' powder,

"Here they come!" said Jakin. "Go on, Lew": —

> To scare their foes withal!

The Fore and Aft were pouring out of the valley. What officers had said to men in that time of shame and humiliation will never be known; for neither officers nor men speak of it now.

"They are coming anew!" shouted a priest among the Afghans. "Do not kill the boys! Take them alive, and they shall be of our faith."

But the first volley had been fired, and Lew dropped on his face. Jakin stood for a minute, spun round and collapsed, as the Fore and Aft came forward, the curses of their officers in their ears, and in their hearts the shame of open shame.

Half the men had seen the drummers die, and they made

no sign. They did not even shout. They doubled out straight across the plain in open order, and they did not fire.

"This," said the Colonel of Goorkhas, softly, "is the real attack, as it should have been delivered. Come on, my children."

"Ulu-lu-lu-lu!" squealed the Goorkhas, and came down with a joyful clicking of *kukris* – those vicious Goorkha knives.

On the right there was no rush. The Highlanders, cannily commending their souls to God (for it matters as much to a dead man whether he has been shot in a Border scuffle or at Waterloo), opened out and fired according to their custom, that is to say without heat and without intervals, while the screw-guns, having disposed of the impertinent mud fort aforementioned, dropped shell after shell into the clusters round the flickering green standards on the heights.

"Charrging is an unfortunate necessity," murmured the Colour-Sergeant of the right company of the Highlanders. "It makes the men sweer so, but I am thinkin' that it will come to a charrge if these black devils stand much longer. Stewarrt, man, you're firing into the eye of the sun, and he'll not take any harm for Government ammuneetion. A foot lower and a great deal slower! What are the English doing? They're very quiet, there in the centre. Running again?"

The English were not running. They were hacking and hewing and stabbing, for though one white man is seldom physically a match for an Afghan in a sheepskin or wadded coat, yet, through the pressure of many white men behind, and a certain thirst for revenge in his heart, he becomes capable of doing much with both ends of his rifle. The Fore and Aft held their fire till one bullet could drive through five or six men, and the front of the Afghan force gave on the volley. They then selected their men, and slew them with deep gasps and short hacking coughs, and groanings of leather belts against strained bodies, and realised for the first time that an Afghan attacked is far less formidable than an

Afghan attacking; which fact old soldiers might have told them.

But they had no old soldiers in their ranks.

The Goorkhas' stall at the bazar was the noisiest, for the men were engaged – to a nasty noise as of beef being cut on the block – with the *kukri*, which they preferred to the bayonet; well knowing how the Afghan hates the half-moon blade.

As the Afghans wavered, the green standards on the mountain moved down to assist them in a last rally. This was unwise. The Lancers, chafing in the right gorge, had thrice despatched their only subaltern as galloper to report on the progress of affairs. On the third occasion he returned, with a bullet-graze on his knee, swearing strange oaths in Hindustani, and saying that all things were ready. So that squadron swung round the right of the Highlanders with a wicked whistling of wind in the pennons of its lances, and fell upon the remnant just when, according to all the rules of war, it should have waited for the foe to show more signs of wavering.

But it was a dainty charge, deftly delivered, and it ended by the Cavalry finding itself at the head of the pass by which the Afghans intended to retreat; and down the track that the lances had made streamed two companies of the Highlanders, which was never intended by the Brigadier. The new development was successful. It detached the enemy from his base as a sponge is torn from a rock, and left him ringed about with fire in that pitiless plain. And as a sponge is chased round the bath-tub by the hand of the bather, so were the Afghans chased till they broke into little detachments much more difficult to dispose of than large masses.

"See!" quoth the Brigadier. "Everything has come as I arranged. We've cut their base, and now we'll bucket 'em to pieces."

A direct hammering was all that the Brigadier had dared to hope for, considering the size of the force at his disposal; but men who stand or fall by the errors of their opponents may be forgiven for turning Chance into Design. The bucketing went forward merrily. The Afghan forces were upon the run – the run of wearied wolves who snarl and bite over their shoulders. The red lances dipped by twos and threes, and, with a shriek, uprose the lance-butt, like a spar on a stormy sea, as the trooper cantering forward cleared his point. The Lancers kept between their prey and the steep hills, for all who could were trying to escape from the valley of death. The Highlanders gave the fugitives two hundred yards' law, and then brought them down, gasping and choking ere they could reach the protection of the boulders above. The Goorkhas followed suit; but the Fore and Aft were killing on their own account, for they had penned a mass of men between their bayonets and a wall of rock, and the flash of the rifles was lighting the wadded coats.

"We cannot hold them, Captain Sahib!" panted a Ressaidar of Lancers. "Let us try the carbine. The lance is good, but it wastes time."

They tried the carbine, and still the enemy melted away – fled up the hills by hundreds when there were only twenty bullets to stop them. On the heights the screw-guns ceased firing – they had run out of ammunition – and the Brigadier groaned, for the musketry fire could not sufficiently smash the retreat. Long before the last volleys were fired, the doolies were out in force looking for the wounded. The battle was over, and, but for want of fresh troops, the Afghans would have been wiped off the earth. As it was, they counted their dead by hundreds, and nowhere were the dead thicker than in the track of the Fore and Aft.

But the Regiment did not cheer with the Highlanders, nor did they dance uncouth dances with the Goorkhas among the dead. They looked under their brows at the Colonel as they leaned upon their rifles and panted.

"Get back to camp, you. Haven't you disgraced yourself enough for one day! Go and look to the wounded. It's all you're fit for," said the Colonel. Yet for the past hour the Fore and Aft had been doing all that mortal commander could expect. They had lost heavily because they did not know how to set about their business with proper skill, but they had borne themselves gallantly, and this was their reward.

A young and sprightly Colour-Sergeant, who had begun to imagine himself a hero, offered his water-bottle to a Highlander whose tongue was black with thirst. "I drink with no cowards," answered the youngster huskily, and, turning to a Goorkha, said, "*Hya*, Johnny! Drink water got it?" The Goorkha grinned and passed his bottle. The Fore and Aft said no word.

They went back to camp when the field of strife had been a little mopped up and made presentable, and the Brigadier, who saw himself a Knight in three months, was the only soul who was complimentary to them. The Colonel was heart-broken, and the officers were savage and sullen.

"Well," said the Brigadier, "they are young troops, of course, and it was not unnatural that they should retire in disorder for a bit."

"Oh, my only Aunt Maria!" murmured a junior Staff Officer. "Retire in disorder! It was a bally run!"

"But they came again, as we all know," cooed the Brigadier, the Colonel's ashy-white face before him, "and they behaved as well as could possibly be expected. Behaved beautifully, indeed. I was watching them. It's not a matter to take to heart, Colonel. As some German General said of his men, they wanted to be shooted over a little, that was all." To himself he said – "Now they're blooded I can give 'em responsible work. It's as well that they got what they did. 'Teach 'em more than half a dozen rifle flirtations, that will – later – run alone and bite. Poor old Colonel, though."

All that afternoon the heliograph winked and flickered on the hills, striving to tell the good news to a mountain forty miles away. And in the evening there arrived, dusty, sweating, and sore, a misguided Correspondent who had gone out to assist at a trumpery village-burning, and who had read off the message from afar, cursing his luck the while.

"Let's have the details somehow – as full as ever you can, please. It's the first time I've ever been left this campaign," said the Correspondent to the Brigadier; and the Brigadier, nothing loth, told him how an Army of Communication had been crumpled up, destroyed, and all but annihilated by the craft, strategy, wisdom, and foresight of the Brigadier.

But some say, and among these be the Goorkhas who watched on the hillside, that that battle was won by Jakin and Lew, whose little bodies were borne up just in time to fit two gaps at the head of the big ditch-grave for the dead under the heights of Jagai.

DRAY WARA YOW DEE

DRAY WARA YOW DEE

* * *

For jealousy is the rage of a man: therefore he will not spare in
the day of vengeance.

Prov. vi. 34

ALMONDS and raisins, Sahib? Grapes from Kabul? Or a
pony of the rarest if the Sahib will only come with me.
He is thirteen three, Sahib, plays polo, goes in a cart, carries
a lady and – Holy Kurshed and the Blessed Imams, it is the
Sahib himself! My heart is made fat and my eye glad. May
you never be tired! As is cold water in the Tirah, so is the
sight of a friend in a far place. And what do *you* in this
accursed land? South of Delhi, Sahib, you know the saying
– "Rats are the men and trulls the women." It was an order?
Ahoo! An order is an order till one is strong enough to dis-
obey. O my brother, O my friend, we have met in an auspicious hour! Is all well in the heart and the body and the
house? In a lucky day have we two come together again.

I am to go with you? Your favour is great. Will there be
picket-room in the compound? I have three horses and the
bundles and the horse-boy. Moreover, remember that the
police here hold me a horse-thief. What do these Lowland
bastards know of horse-thieves? Do you remember that time
in Peshawur when Kamal hammered on the gates of Jumrud
– mountebank that he was – and lifted the Colonel's horses
all in one night? Kamal is dead now, but his nephew has
taken up the matter, and there will be more horses amissing
if the Khaiber Levies do not look to it.

The Peace of God and the favour of His Prophet be upon
this house and all that is in it! Shafizullah, rope the mottled
mare under the tree and draw water. The horses can stand

135

in the sun, but double the felts over the loins. Nay, my friend, do not trouble to look them over. They are to sell to the Officer fools who know so many things of the horse. The mare is heavy in foal; the grey is a devil unlicked; and the dun – but you know the trick of the peg. When they are sold I go back to Pubbi, or, it may be, the Valley of Peshawur.

O friend of my heart, it is good to see you again. I have been bowing and lying all day to the Officer Sahibs in respect to those horses; and my mouth is dry for straight talk. *Auggrh!* Before a meal tobacco is good. Do not join me, for we are not in our own country. Sit in the verandah and I will spread my cloth here. But first I will drink. *In the name of God returning thanks, thrice!* This is sweet water, indeed – sweet as the water of Sheoran when it comes from the snows.

They are all well and pleased in the North – Khoda Baksh and the others. Yar Khan has come down with the horses from Kurdistan – six and thirty head only, and a full half pack-ponies – and has said openly in the Kashmir Serai that you English should send guns and blow the Amir into Hell. There are *fifteen* tolls now on the Kabul road; and at Dakka, when he thought he was clear, Yar Khan was stripped of all his Balkh stallions by the Governor! This is a great injustice, and Yar Khan is hot with rage. And of the others: Mahbub Ali is still at Pubbi, writing God knows what. Tugluq Khan is in jail for the business of the Kohat Police Post. Faiz Beg came down from Ismail-ki-Dhera with a Bokhariot belt for thee, my brother, at the closing of the year, but none knew whither thou hadst gone: there was no news left behind. The Cousins have taken a new run near Pakpattan to breed mules for the Government carts, and there is a story in Bazar of a priest. Oho! Such a salt tale! Listen —

Sahib, why do you ask that? My clothes are fouled because of the dust on the road. My eyes are sad because of the glare of the sun. My feet are swollen because I have washed them in bitter water, and my cheeks are hollow because the food here is bad. Fire burn your money! What do I want with it? I am rich and I thought you were my friend; but you are like the others – a Sahib. Is a man sad? Give him money, say the Sahibs. Is he dishonoured? Give him money, say the Sahibs. Hath he a wrong upon his head? Give him money, say the Sahibs. Such are the Sahibs, and such art thou – even thou.

Nay, do not look at the feet of the dun. Pity it is that I ever taught you to know the legs of a horse. Footsore? Be it so. What of that? The roads are hard. And the mare footsore? She bears a double burden, Sahib.

And now I pray you, give me permission to depart. Great favour and honour has the Sahib done me, and graciously has he shown his belief that the horses are stolen. Will it please him to send me to the Thana? To call a sweeper and have me led away by one of these lizard-men? I am the Sahib's friend. I have drunk water in the shadow of his house, and he has blackened my face. Remains there anything more to do? Will the Sahib give me eight annas to make smooth the injury and – complete the insult —?

Forgive me, my brother. I knew not – I know not now – what I say. Yes, I lied to you! I will put dust on my head – and I am an Afridi! The horses have been marched footsore from the Valley to this place, and my eyes are dim, and my body aches for the want of sleep, and my heart is dried up with sorrow and shame. But as it was my shame, so by God the Dispenser of Justice – by Allah-al-Mumit – it shall be my own revenge!

We have spoken together with naked hearts before this, and our hands have dipped into the same dish and thou hast been to me as a brother. Therefore I pay thee back with lies and ingratitude – as a Pathan. Listen now! When the grief of the soul is too heavy for endurance it may be a little eased by speech, and, moreover, the mind of a true man is as a well, and the pebble of confession dropped therein sinks and is no more seen. From the Valley have I come on foot, league by league, with a fire in my chest like the fire of the Pit. And why? Hast thou, then, so quickly forgotten our customs, among this folk who sell their wives and their daughters for silver? Come back with me to the North and be among men once more. Come back, when this matter is accomplished and I call for thee! The bloom of the peach-orchards is upon all the Valley, and *here* is only dust and a great stink. There is a pleasant wind among the mulberry trees, and the streams are bright with snow-water, and the caravans go up and the caravans go down, and a hundred fires sparkle in the gut of the Pass, and tent-peg answers hammer-nose, and pack-horse squeals to pack-horse across the drift smoke of the evening. It is good in the North now. Come back with me. Let us return to our own people! Come!

* * *

Whence is my sorrow? Does a man tear out his heart and make fritters thereof over a slow fire for aught other than a woman? Do not laugh, friend of mine, for your time will also be. A woman of the Abazai was she, and I took her to wife to staunch the feud between our village and the men of Ghor. I am no longer young? The lime has touched my beard? True. I had no need of the wedding? Nay, but I loved her. What saith Rahman: "Into whose heart Love enters, there is Folly *and naught else*. By a glance of the eye she hath blinded thee; and by the eyelids and the fringe of the eyelids taken thee into the captivity without ransom, *and naught else*." Dost thou remember that song at the sheep-roasting in the Pindi camp among the Uzbegs of the Amir?

The Abazai are dogs and their women the servants of sin. There was a lover of her own people, but of that her father told me naught. My friend, curse for me in your prayers, as I curse at each praying from the Fakr to the Isha, the name of Daoud Shah, Abazai, whose head is still upon his neck, whose hands are still upon his wrists, who has done me dishonour, who has made my name a laughing-stock among the women of Little Malikand.

I went into Hindustan at the end of two months – to Cherat. I was gone twelve days only; but I had said that I would be fifteen days absent. This I did to try her, for it is written: "Trust not the incapable." Coming up the gorge alone in the falling of the light, I heard the voice of a man singing at the door of my house; and it was the voice of Daoud Shah, and the song that he sang was "*Dray wara yow dee*" – "All three are one." It was as though a heel-rope had been slipped round my heart and all the Devils were drawing it tight past endurance. I crept silently up the hill-road, but the fuse of my matchlock was wetted with the rain, and I could not slay Daoud Shah from afar. Moreover, it was in my mind to kill the woman also. Thus he sang, sitting outside my house, and, anon, the woman opened the door, and I came nearer, crawling on my belly among the rocks. I had only my knife to my hand. But a stone slipped under my foot, and the two looked down the hill-side, and he, leaving his matchlock, fled from my anger, because he was afraid for the life that was in him. But the woman moved not till I stood in front of her, crying: "O woman, what is this that thou hast done?" And she, void of fear, though she knew my thought, laughed, saying: "It is a little thing. I loved him, and *thou* art a dog and cattle-thief coming by night. Strike!" And I, being still blinded by her beauty, for, O my friend, the women of the Abazai are very fair, said: "Hast thou no fear?" And she answered: "None – but only the fear that I do not die." Then said I: "Have no fear." And she bowed her head, and I smote it off at the neck-bone so that it leaped between my feet. Thereafter the rage of our people came upon me, and I hacked off the breasts, that the men of Little Malikand might know the crime, and cast the body into the water-course that flows to the Kabul river. *Dray wara yow dee! Dray wara yow dee!* The body without the head, the soul without light, and my own darkling heart – all three are one – all three are one!

That night, making no halt, I went to Ghor and de-manded news of Daoud Shah. Men said: "He is gone to Pubbi for horses. What wouldst thou of him? There is peace between the villages." I made answer: "Aye! The peace of treachery and the love that the Devil Atala bore to Gurel." So I fired thrice into the gate and laughed and went my way.

In those hours, brother and friend of my heart's heart, the moon and the stars were as blood above me, and in my mouth was the taste of dry earth. Also, I broke no bread, and my drink was the rain of the Valley of Ghor upon my face.

At Pubbi I found Mahbub Ali, the writer, sitting upon his charpoy, and gave up my arms according to your Law. But I was not grieved, for it was in my heart that I should kill Daoud Shah with my bare hands thus – as a man strips a bunch of raisins. Mahbub Ali said: "Daoud Shah has even now gone hot-foot to Peshawur, and he will pick up his horses upon the road to Delhi, for it is said that the Bombay Tramway Company are buying horses there by the truck-load; eight horses to the truck." And that was a true saying.

Then I saw that the hunting would be no little thing, for the man was gone into your borders to save himself against my wrath. And shall he save himself so? Am I not alive? Though he run northward to the Dora and the snow, or southerly to the Black Water, I will follow him, as a lover follows the footsteps of his mistress, and coming upon him I will take him tenderly – Aho! so tenderly! – in my arms, saying: "Well hast thou done and well shalt thou be repaid." And out of that embrace Daoud Shah shall not go forth with the breath in his nostrils. *Auggrh!* Where is the pitcher? I am as thirsty as a mother-mare in the first month.

Your Law! What is your Law to me? When the horses fight on the runs do they regard the boundary pillars; or do the kites of Ali Musjid forbear because the carrion lies under the shadow of the Ghor Kuttri? The matter began across the Border. It shall finish where God pleases. Here, in my own country, or in Hell. All three are one.

Listen now, sharer of the sorrow of my heart, and I will tell of the hunting. I followed to Peshawur from Pubbi, and

I went to and fro about the streets of Peshawur like a house-less dog, seeking for my enemy. Once I thought that I saw him washing his mouth in the conduit in the big square, but when I came up he was gone. It may be that it was he, and, seeing my face, he had fled.

A girl of the bazar said that he would go to Nowshera. I said: "O heart's heart, does Daoud Shah visit thee?" And she said: "Even so." I said: "I would fain see him, for we be friends parted for two years. Hide me, I pray, here in the shadow of the window shutter, and I will wait for his coming." And the girl said: "O Pathan, look into my eyes!" And I turned, leaning upon her breast, and looked into her eyes, swearing that I spoke the very Truth of God. But she answered: "Never friend waited friend with such eyes. Lie to God and the Prophet, but to a woman ye cannot lie. Get hence! There shall no harm befall Daoud Shah by cause of me."

I would have strangled that girl but for the fear of your Police; and thus the hunting would have come to naught. Therefore I only laughed and departed, and she leaned over the window-bar in the night and mocked me down the street. Her name is Jamun. When I have made my account with the man I will return to Peshawur and – her lovers shall desire her no more for her beauty's sake. She shall not be *Jamun*, but *Ak*, the cripple among trees. Ho! Ho! *Ak* shall she be!

At Peshawur I bought the horses and grapes, and the almonds and dried fruits, that the reason of my wanderings might be open to the Government, and that there might be no hindrance upon the road. But when I came to Nowshera he was gone, and I knew not where to go. I stayed one day at Nowshera, and in the night a Voice spoke in my ears as I slept among the horses. All night it flew round my head and would not cease from whispering. I was upon my belly, sleeping as the Devils sleep, and it may have been that the Voice was the voice of a Devil. It said: "Go south, and thou shalt come upon Daoud Shah." Listen, my brother and chiefest among friends – listen! Is the tale a long one? Think

how it was long to me. I have trodden every league of the
road from Pubbi to this place; and from Nowshera my guide
was only the Voice and the lust of vengeance.

To the Uttock I went, but that was no hindrance to me.
Ho! Ho! A man may turn the word twice, even in his trouble.
The Uttock was no *uttock* [obstacle] to me; and I heard the
Voice above the noise of the waters beating on the big rock,
saying: "Go to the right." So I went to Pindigheb, and in
those days my sleep was taken from me utterly, and the head
of the woman of the Abazai was before me night and day,
even as it had fallen between my feet. *Dray wara yow dee!
Dray wara yow dee!* Fire, ashes, and my couch, all three are
one – all three are one!

Now I was far from the winter path of the dealers who
had gone to Sialkot and so south by the rail and the Big Road
to the line of cantonments; but there was a Sahib in camp at
Pindigheb who bought from me a white mare at a good price,
and told me that one Daoud Shah had passed to Shahpur
with horses. Then I saw that the warning of the Voice was
true, and made swift to come to the Salt Hills. The Jhelum
was in flood, but I could not wait, and, in the crossing, a bay
stallion was washed down and drowned. Herein was God
hard to me – not in respect of the beast, of that I had no care
– but in this snatching. While I was upon the right bank
urging the horses into the water, Daoud Shah was upon the
left; for – *Alghias! Alghias!* – the hoofs of my mare scattered the
hot ashes of his fires when we came up the hither bank in the
light of morning. But he had fled. His feet were made swift by
the terror of Death. And I went south from Shahpur as the
kite flies. I dared not turn aside, lest I should miss my vengeance – which is my right. From Shahpur I skirted by the
Jhelum, for I thought that he would avoid the Desert of the
Rechna. But, presently, at Sahiwal, I turned away upon the
road to Jhang, Samundri, and Gugera, till, upon a night, the
mottled mare breasted the fence of the rail that runs to
Montgomery. And that place was Okara, and the head of the
woman of the Abazai lay upon the sand between my feet.

Thence I went to Fazilka, and they said that I was mad to bring starved horses there. The Voice was with me, and I was *not* mad, but only wearied, because I could not find Daoud Shah. It was written that I should not find him at Rania nor Bahadurgarh, and I came into Delhi from the west, and there also I found him not. My friend, I have seen many strange things in my wanderings. I have seen Devils rioting across the Rechna as the stallions riot in spring. I have heard the *Djinns* calling to each other from holes in the sand, and I have seen them pass before my face. There are no Devils, say the Sahibs? They are very wise, but they do not know all things about devils or – horses. Ho! Ho! I say to you who are laughing at my misery, that I have seen the Devils at high noon whooping and leaping on the shoals of the Chenab. And was I afraid? My brother, when the desire of a man is set upon one thing alone, he fears neither God nor Man nor Devil. If my vengeance failed, I would splinter the Gates of Paradise with the butt of my gun, or I would cut my way into Hell with my knife, and I would call upon Those who Govern there for the body of Daoud Shah. What love so deep as hate?

Do not speak. I know the thought in your heart. Is the white of this eye clouded? How does the blood beat at the wrist? There is no madness in my flesh, but only the vehemence of the desire that has eaten me up. Listen!

South of Delhi I knew not the country at all. Therefore I cannot say where I went, but I passed through many cities. I knew only that it was laid upon me to go south. When the horses could march no more, I threw myself upon the earth, and waited till the day. There was no sleep with me in that journeying; and that was a heavy burden. Dost thou know, brother of mine, the evil of wakefulness that cannot break – when the bones are sore for lack of sleep, and the skin of the temples twitches with weariness, and yet – there is no sleep – there is no sleep? *Dray wara yow dee! Dray wara yow dee!* The eye of the Sun, the eye of the Moon, and my own unrestful eyes – all three are one – all three are one!

There was a city the name whereof I have forgotten, and there the Voice called all night. That was ten days ago. It has cheated me afresh.

I have come hither from a place called Hamirpur, and, behold, it is my Fate that I should meet with thee to my comfort and the increase of friendship. This is a good omen. By the joy of looking upon thy face the weariness has gone from my feet, and the sorrow of my so long travel is forgotten. Also my heart is peaceful; for I know that the end is near.

It may be that I shall find Daoud Shah in this city going northward, since a Hillman will ever head back to his Hills when the spring warns. And shall he see those hills of our country? Surely I shall overtake him! Surely my vengeance is safe! Surely God hath him in the hollow of His hand against my claiming. There shall no harm befall Daoud Shah till I come; for I would fain kill him quick and whole with the life sticking firm in his body. A pomegranate is sweetest when the cloves break away unwilling from the rind. Let it be in the daytime, that I may see his face, and my delight may be crowned.

And when I have accomplished the matter and my Honour is made clean, I shall return thanks unto God, the Holder of the Scale of the Law, and I shall sleep. From the night, through the day, and into the night again I shall sleep; and no dream shall trouble me.

And now, O my brother, the tale is all told. *Ahi! Ahi! Alghias! Ahi!*

"THE CITY OF DREADFUL NIGHT"

"THE CITY OF DREADFUL NIGHT"

T HE dense wet heat that hung over the face of land, like a blanket, prevented all hope of sleep in the first instance. The cicalas helped the heat; and the yelling jackals the cicalas. It was impossible to sit still in the dark, empty, echoing house and watch the punkah beat the dead air. So, at ten o'clock of the night, I set my walking-stick on end in the middle of the garden, and waited to see how it would fall. It pointed directly down the moonlit road that leads to the City of Dreadful Night. The sound of its fall disturbed a hare. She limped from her form and ran across to a disused Mahomedan burial-ground, where the jawless skulls and rough-butted shank-bones, heartlessly exposed by the July rains, glimmered like mother o' pearl on the rain-channelled soil. The heated air and the heavy earth had driven the very dead upward for coolness' sake. The hare limped on; snuffed curiously at a fragment of a smoke-stained lamp-shard, and died out in the shadow of a clump of tamarisk trees.

The mat-weaver's hut under the lee of the Hindu temple was full of sleeping men who lay like sheeted corpses. Overhead blazed the unwinking eye of the Moon. Darkness gives at least a false impression of coolness. It was hard not to believe that the flood of light from above was warm. Not so hot as the Sun, but still sickly warm, and heating the heavy air beyond what was our due. Straight as a bar of polished steel ran the road to the City of Dreadful Night; and on either side of the road lay corpses disposed on beds in fantastic attitudes – one hundred and seventy bodies of men. Some shrouded all in white with bound-up mouths; some naked and black as ebony in the strong light; and one – that lay face upwards with dropped jaw, far away from the others – silvery white and ashen grey.

"A leper asleep; and the remainder wearied coolies, servants, small shopkeepers, and drivers from the hack-stand hard by. The scene – a main approach to Lahore city, and the night a warm one in August." This was all that there was to be seen; but by no means all that one could see. The witchery of the moonlight was everywhere; and the world was horribly changed. The long line of the naked dead, flanked by the rigid silver statue, was not pleasant to look upon. It was made up of men alone. Were the womenkind, then, forced to sleep in the shelter of the stifling mud-huts as best they might? The fretful wail of a child from a low mud-roof answered the question. Where the children are the mothers must be also to look after them. They need care on these sweltering nights. A black little bullet-head peeped over the coping, and a thin – a painfully thin – brown leg was slid over on to the gutter pipe. There was a sharp clink of glass bracelets; a woman's arm showed for an instant above the parapet, twined itself round the lean little neck, and the child was dragged back, protesting, to the shelter of the bed-stead. His thin, high-pitched shriek died out in the thick air almost as soon as it was raised; for even the children of the soil found it too hot to weep.

More corpses; more stretches of moonlit, white road; a string of sleeping camels at rest by the wayside; a vision of scudding jackals; *ekka*-ponies asleep – the harness still on their backs, and the brass-studded country carts, winking in the moonlight – and again more corpses. Wherever a grain cart atilt, a tree trunk, a sawn log, a couple of bamboos and a few handfuls of thatch cast a shadow, the ground is covered with them. They lie – some face downwards, arms folded, in the dust; some with clasped hands flung up above their heads; some curled up dog-wise; some thrown like limp gunny-bags over the side of the grain-carts; and some bowed with their brows on their knees in the full glare of the Moon. It would be a comfort if they were only given to snoring; but they are not, and the likeness to corpses is unbroken in all respects save one. The lean dogs snuff at them and turn away. Here and there a tiny child lies on his father's bedstead, and a protecting arm is thrown round it in every instance. But, for the most part, the children sleep with their mothers on the housetops. Yellow-skinned, white-toothed pariahs are not to be trusted within reach of brown bodies.

A stifling hot blast from the mouth of the Delhi Gate nearly ends my resolution of entering the City of Dreadful Night at this hour. It is a compound of all evil savours, animal and vegetable, that a walled city can brew in a day and a night. The temperature within the motionless groves of plantain and orange-trees outside the city walls seems chilly by comparison. Heaven help all sick persons and young children within the city tonight! The high house-walls are still radiating heat savagely, and from obscure side gullies fetid breezes eddy that ought to poison a buffalo. But the buffaloes do not heed. A drove of them are parading the vacant main street; stopping now and then to lay their ponderous muzzles against the closed shutters of a grain-dealer's shop, and to blow thereon like grampuses.

Then silence follows – the silence that is full of the night noises of a great city. A stringed instrument of some kind is just, and only just, audible. High overhead some one throws open a window, and the rattle of the wood-work echoes down the empty street. On one of the roofs a hookah is in full blast; and the men are talking softly as the pipe gutters. A little farther on, the noise of conversation is more distinct. A slit of light shows itself between the sliding shutters of a shop. Inside, a stubble-bearded, weary-eyed trader is balancing his account-books among the bales of cotton prints that surround him. Three sheeted figures bear him company, and throw in a remark from time to time. First he makes an entry, then a remark; then passes the back of his hand across his streaming forehead. The heat in the built-in street is fearful. Inside the shops it must be almost unendurable. But the work goes on steadily; entry, guttural growl, and uplifted hand-stroke succeeding each other with the precision of clockwork.

A policeman – turbanless and fast asleep – lies across the

road on the way to the Mosque of Wazir Khan. A bar of moonlight falls across the forehead and eyes of the sleeper, but he never stirs. It is close upon midnight, and the heat seems to be increasing. The open square in front of the Mosque is crowded with corpses; and a man must pick his way carefully for fear of treading on them. The moonlight stripes the Mosque's high front of coloured enamel work in broad diagonal bands; and each separate dreaming pigeon in the niches and corners of the masonry throws a squab little shadow. Sheeted ghosts rise up wearily from their pallets, and flit into the dark depths of the building. Is it possible to climb to the top of the great Minars, and thence to look down on the city? At all events, the attempt is worth making, and the chances are that the door of the staircase will be un-locked. Unlocked it is; but a deeply-sleeping janitor lies across the threshold, face turned to the Moon. A rat dashes out of his turban at the sound of approaching footsteps. The man grunts, open his eyes for a minute, turns round and goes to sleep again. All the heat of a decade of fierce Indian sum-mers is stored in the pitch-black, polished walls of the cork-screw staircase. Half-way up, there is something alive, warm, and feathery; and it snores. Driven from step to step as it catches the sound of my advance, it flutters to the top and reveals itself as a yellow-eyed, angry kite. Dozens of kites are asleep on this and the other Minars, and on the domes below. There is the shadow of a cool, or at least a less sultry breeze at this height; and, refreshed thereby, turn to look on the City of Dreadful Night.

Doré might have drawn it! Zola could describe it – this spectacle of sleeping thousands in the moonlight and in the shadow of the Moon. The roof-tops are crammed with men, women, and children; and the air is full of undistinguishable noises. They are restless in the City of Dreadful Night; and small wonder. The marvel is that they can even breathe. If you gaze intently at the multitude, you can see that they are almost as uneasy as a daylight crowd; but the tumult is sub-dued. Everywhere, in the strong light, you can watch the sleepers turning to and fro; shifting their beds and again resettling them. In the pit-like courtyards of the houses there is the same movement.

The pitiless Moon shows it all. Shows, too, the plains outside the city, and here and there a hand's-breadth of the Ravee without the walls. Shows lastly a splash of glittering silver on a house-top almost directly below the mosque Minar. Some poor soul has risen to throw a jar of water over his fevered body; the tinkle of the falling water strikes faintly on the ear. Two or three other men, in far-off corners of the City of Dreadful Night, follow his example, and the water flashes like heliographic signals. A small cloud passes over the face of the Moon, and the city and its inhabitants – clear drawn in black and white before – fade into masses of black and deeper black. Still the unrestful noise continues, the sigh of a great city overwhelmed with the heat, and of a people seeking in vain for rest. It is only the lower-class women who sleep on the house-tops. What must the torment be in the latticed zenanas, where a few lamps are still twinkling? There are footfalls in the court below. It is the *Muezzin* – faithful minister; but he ought to have been here an hour ago to tell the Faithful that prayer is better than sleep – the sleep that will not come to the city.

The *Muezzin* fumbles for a moment with the door of one of the Minars, disappears awhile, and a bull-like roar – a magnificent bass thunder – tells that he has reached the top of the Minar. They must hear the cry to the banks of the shrunken Ravee itself! Even across the courtyard it is almost overpowering. The cloud drifts by and shows him outlined in black against the sky, hands laid upon his ears, and broad chest heaving with the play of his lungs – "Allah ho Akbar"; then a pause while another *Muezzin* somewhere in the dir- ection of the Golden Temple takes up the call – "Allah ho Akbar." Again and again; four times in all; and from the bedsteads a dozen men have risen up already. – "I bear wit- ness that there is no God but God." What a splendid cry it is, the proclamation of the creed that brings men out of their beds by scores at midnight! Once again he thunders through the same phrase, shaking with the vehemence of his own voice; and then, far and near, the night air rings with "Mahomed is the Prophet of God." It is as though he were flinging his defiance to the far-off horizon, where the summer lightning plays and leaps like a bared sword. Every *Muezzin* in the city is in full cry, and some men on the roof-tops are beginning to kneel. A long pause precedes the last cry, "La ilaha Illallah," and the silence closes up on it, as the ram on the head of a cotton-bale.

The *Muezzin* stumbles down the dark stairway grumbling in his beard. He passes the arch of the entrance and disappears. Then the stifling silence settles down over the City of Dreadful Night. The kites on the Minar sleep again, snoring more loudly, the hot breeze comes up in puffs and lazy eddies, and the Moon slides down towards the horizon. Seated with both elbows on the parapet of the tower, one can watch and wonder over that heat-tortured hive till the dawn. "How do they live down there? What do they think of? When will they awake?" More tinkling of sluiced water-pots; faint jarring of wooden bedsteads moved into or out of the shadows; uncouth music of stringed instruments softened by distance into a plaintive wail, and one low grumble of far-off thunder. In the courtyard of the mosque the janitor, who lay across the threshold of the Minar when I came up, starts wildly in his sleep, throws his hands above his head, mutters something, and falls back again. Lulled by the snoring of the kites – they snore like over-gorged humans – I drop off into an uneasy doze, conscious that three o'clock has struck, and that there is a slight – a very slight – coolness in the atmosphere. The city is absolutely quiet now, but for some vagrant dog's love-song. Nothing save dead heavy sleep.

Several weeks of darkness pass after this. For the Moon has gone out. The very dogs are still, and I watch for the first light of the dawn before making my way homeward. Again the noise of shuffling feet. The morning call is about to begin, and my night watch is over. "Allah ho Akbar! Allah ho Akbar!" The east grows grey, and presently saffron; the dawn wind comes up as though the *Muezzin* had summoned it; and, as one man, the City of Dreadful Night rises from its bed and turns its face towards the dawning day. With return of life comes return of sound. First a low whisper, then a deep bass hum; for it must be remembered that the entire city is on the house-tops. My eyelids weighed down with the arrears of long deferred sleep, I escape from the Minar through the courtyard and out into the square beyond, where the sleepers have risen, stowed away the bedsteads, and are discussing the morning hookah. The minute's freshness of the air has gone, and it is as hot as at first.

"Will the Sahib, out of his kindness, make room?" What is it? Something borne on men's shoulders comes by in the half-light, and I stand back. A woman's corpse going down to the burning-ghat, and a bystander says, "She died at midnight from the heat." So the city was of Death as well as Night, after all.

WITHOUT BENEFIT OF CLERGY

WITHOUT BENEFIT OF CLERGY

* * *

> Before my Spring I garnered Autumn's gain,
> Out of her time my field was white with grain,
>   The year gave up her secrets to my woe.
> Forced and deflowered each sick season lay,
> In mystery of increase and decay;
>   I saw the sunset ere men saw the day,
>   Who am too wise in that I should not know.
>
> *Bitter Waters*

I

"BUT if it be a girl?"

"Lord of my life, it cannot be. I have prayed for so many nights, and sent gifts to Sheikh Badl's shrine so often, that I know God will give us a son – a man-child that shall grow into a man. Think of this and be glad. My mother shall be his mother till I can take him again, and the mullah of the Pattan mosque shall cast his nativity – God send he be born in an auspicious hour! – and then, and then thou wilt never weary of me, thy slave."

"Since when hast thou been a slave, my queen?"

"Since the beginning – till this mercy came to me. How could I be sure of thy love when I knew that I had been bought with silver?"

"Nay, that was the dowry. I paid it to thy mother."

"And she has buried it, and sits upon it all day long like a hen. What talk is yours of dower! I was bought as though I had been a Lucknow dancing-girl instead of a child."

"Art thou sorry for the sale?"

"I have sorrowed; but to-day I am glad. Thou wilt never cease to love me now? – answer, my king."

"Never – never. No."

"Not even though the *mem-log* – the white women of thy own blood – love thee? And remember, I have watched them driving in the evening; they are very fair."

"I have seen fire-balloons by the hundred. I have seen the moon, and – then I saw no more fire-balloons."

Ameera clapped her hands and laughed. "Very good talk," she said. Then with an assumption of great stateliness, "It is enough. Thou hast my permission to depart, – if thou wilt."

The man did not move. He was sitting on a low red-lacquered couch in a room furnished only with a blue and white floor-cloth, some rugs, and a very complete collection of native cushions. At his feet sat a woman of sixteen, and she was all but all the world in his eyes. By every rule and law she should have been otherwise, for he was an Englishman, and she a Mussulman's daughter bought two years before from her mother, who, being left without money, would have sold Ameera shrieking to the Prince of Darkness if the price had been sufficient.

It was a contract entered into with a light heart; but even before the girl had reached her bloom she came to fill the greater portion of John Holden's life. For her, and the withered hag her mother, he had taken a little house overlooking the great red-walled city, and found, – when the marigolds had sprung up by the well in the courtyard and Ameera had established herself according to her own ideas of comfort, and her mother had ceased grumbling at the inadequacy of the cooking-places, the distance from the daily market, and at matters of housekeeping in general, – that the house was to him his home. Any one could enter his bachelor's bunga-low by day or night, and the life that he led there was an unlovely one. In the house in the city his feet only could pass beyond the outer courtyard to the women's rooms; and when the big wooden gate was bolted behind him he was king in his own territory, with Ameera for queen. And there was going to be added to this kingdom a third person whose arrival Holden felt inclined to resent. It interfered with his perfect happiness. It disarranged the orderly peace of the house that was his own. But Ameera was wild with delight at the thought of it, and her mother not less so. The love of a man, and particularly a white man, was at the best an inconstant affair, but it might, both women argued, be held fast by a baby's hands. "And then," Ameera would always say, "then he will never care for the white *mem-log*. I hate them all – I hate them all."

"He will go back to his own people in time," said the mother; "but by the blessing of God that time is yet afar off."

Holden sat silent on the couch thinking of the future, and his thoughts were not pleasant. The drawbacks of a double life are manifold. The Government, with singular care, had ordered him out of the station for a fortnight on special duty in the place of a man who was watching by the bedside of a sick wife. The verbal notification of the transfer had been edged by a cheerful remark that Holden ought to think himself lucky in being a bachelor and a free man. He came to break the news to Ameera.

"It is not good," she said slowly, "but it is not all bad. There is my mother here, and no harm will come to me – unless indeed I die of pure joy. Go thou to thy work and think no troublesome thoughts. When the days are done I believe . . . nay, I am sure. And – and then I shall lay *him* in thy arms, and thou wilt love me for ever. The train goes to-night, at midnight is it not? Go now, and do not let thy heart be heavy by cause of me. But thou wilt not delay in returning? Thou wilt not stay on the road to talk to the bold white *mem-log*. Come back to me swiftly, my life."

As he left the courtyard to reach his horse that was tethered to the gate-post, Holden spoke to the white-haired old watchman who guarded the house, and bade him under certain contingencies despatch the filled-up telegraph-form that Holden gave him. It was all that could be done, and with the sensations of a man who has attended his own funeral

Holden went away by the night mail to his exile. Every hour of the day he dreaded the arrival of the telegram, and every hour of the night he pictured to himself the death of Ameera. In consequence his work for the State was not of first-rate quality, nor was his temper towards his colleagues of the most amiable. The fortnight ended without a sign from his home, and, torn to pieces by his anxieties, Holden returned to be swallowed up for two precious hours by a dinner at the club, wherein he heard, as a man hears in a swoon, voices telling him how execrably he had performed the other man's duties, and how he had endeared himself to all his associates. Then he fled on horseback through the night with his heart in his mouth. There was no answer at first to his blows on the gate, and he had just wheeled his horse round to kick it in when Pir Khan appeared with a lantern and held his stirrup.

"Has aught occurred?" said Holden.

"The news does not come from my mouth, Protector of the Poor, but —" He held out his shaking hand as befitted the bearer of good news who is entitled to a reward.

Holden hurried through the courtyard. A light burned in the upper room. His horse neighed in the gateway, and he heard a shrill little wail that sent all the blood into the apple of his throat. It was a new voice, but it did not prove that Ameera was alive.

"Who is there?" he called up the narrow brick staircase.

There was a cry of delight from Ameera, and then the voice of the mother, tremulous with old age and pride – "We be two women and – the – man – thy – son."

On the threshold of the room Holden stepped on a naked dagger, that was laid there to avert ill-luck, and it broke at the hilt under his impatient heel.

"God is great!" cooed Ameera in the half-light. "Thou hast taken his misfortunes on thy head."

"Ay, but how is it with thee, life of my life? Old woman, how is it with her?"

"She has forgotten her sufferings for joy that the child is born. There is no harm; but speak softly," said the mother.

"It only needed thy presence to make me all well," said Ameera. "My king, thou hast been very long away. What gifts hast thou for me? Ah, ah! It is I that bring gifts this time. Look, my life, look. Was there ever such a babe? Nay, I am too weak even to clear my arm from him."

"Rest then, and do not talk. I am here, *bachari* [little woman]."

"Well said, for there is a bond and a heel-rope [*peecharee*] between us now that nothing can break. Look – canst thou see in this light? He is without spot or blemish. Never was such a man-child. *Ya illah!* he shall be a pundit – no, a trooper of the Queen. And, my life, dost thou love me as well as ever, though I am faint and sick and worn? Answer truly."

"Yea. I love as I have loved, with all my soul. Lie still, pearl, and rest."

"Then do not go. Sit by my side here – so. Mother, the lord of this house needs a cushion. Bring it." There was an almost imperceptible movement on the part of the new life that lay in the hollow of Ameera's arm. "Aho!" she said, her voice breaking with love. "The babe is a champion from his birth. He is kicking me in the side with mighty kicks. Was there ever such a babe? And he is ours to us – thine and mine. Put thy hand on his head, but carefully, for he is very young, and men are unskilled in such matters."

Very cautiously Holden touched with the tips of his fingers the downy head.

"He is of the faith," said Ameera; "for lying here in the night-watches I whispered the call to prayer and the profession of faith into his ears. And it is most marvellous that he was born upon a Friday, as I was born. Be careful of him, my life; but he can almost grip with his hands."

Holden found one helpless little hand that closed feebly on his finger. And the clutch ran through his body till it settled about his heart. Till then his sole thought had been for Ameera. He began to realise that there was some one else in the world, but he could not feel that it was a veritable son with a soul. He sat down to think, and Ameera dozed lightly.

"Get hence, Sahib," said her mother under her breath. "It is not good that she should find you here on waking. She must be still."

"I go," said Holden submissively. "Here be rupees. See that my *baba* gets fat and finds all that he needs."

The chink of the silver roused Ameera. "I am his mother, and no hireling," she said weakly. "Shall I look to him more or less for the sake of money? Mother, give it back. I have born my lord a son."

The deep sleep of weakness came upon her almost before the sentence was completed. Holden went down to the court-yard very softly with his heart at ease. Pir Khan, the old watchman, was chuckling with delight. "This house is now complete," he said, and without further comment thrust into Holden's hands the hilt of a sabre worn many years ago when he, Pir Khan, served the Queen in the police. The bleat of a tethered goat came from the well-kerb.

"There be two," said Pir Khan, "two goats of the best. I bought them, and they cost much money; and since there is no birth-party assembled their flesh will be all mine. Strike craftily, Sahib! 'Tis an ill-balanced sabre at the best. Wait till they raise their heads from cropping the marigolds."

"And why?" said Holden, bewildered.

"For the birth-sacrifice. What else? Otherwise the child being unguarded from fate may die. The Protector of the Poor knows the fitting words to be said."

Holden had learned them once with little thought that he would ever speak them in earnest. The touch of the cold sabre-hilt in his palm turned suddenly to the clinging grip of the child up-stairs – the child that was his own son – and a dread of loss filled him.

"Strike!" said Pir Khan. "Never life came into the world but life was paid for it. See, the goats have raised their heads. Now! With a drawing cut!"

Hardly knowing what he did Holden cut twice as he mut-tered the Mahomedan prayer that runs: "Almighty! In place of this my son I offer life for life, blood for blood, head for head, bone for bone, hair for hair, skin for skin." The waiting horse snorted and bounded in his pickets at the smell of the raw blood that spurted over Holden's riding-boots.

"Well smitten!" said Pir Khan, wiping the sabre. "A swordsman was lost in thee. Go with a light heart, Heaven-born. I am thy servant, and the servant of thy son. May the Presence live a thousand years and . . . the flesh of the goats is all mine?" Pir Khan drew back richer by a month's pay. Holden swung himself into the saddle and rode off through the low-hanging wood-smoke of the evening. He was full of riotous exultation, alternating with a vast vague tenderness directed towards no particular object, that made him choke as he bent over the neck of his uneasy horse. "I never felt like this in my life," he thought. "I'll go to the club and pull myself together."

A game of pool was beginning, and the room was full of men. Holden entered, eager to get to the light and the company of his fellows, singing at the top of his voice –

> "In Baltimore a-walking, a lady I did meet!"

"Did you?" said the club-secretary from his corner. "Did she happen to tell you that your boots were wringing wet? Great goodness, man, it's blood!"

"Bosh!" said Holden, picking his cue from the rack. "May I cut in? It's dew. I've been riding through high crops. My faith! my boots are in a mess though!

> "And if it be a girl she shall wear a wedding-ring,
>   And if it be a boy he shall fight for his king,
>   With his dirk, and his cap, and his little jacket blue,
>   He shall walk the quarter-deck –"

"Yellow on blue – green next player," said the marker monotonously.

" 'He shall walk the quarter-deck,' – Am I green, marker? 'He shall walk the quarter-deck,' – eh! that's a bad shot, – 'As his daddy used to do!' "

"I don't see that you have anything to crow about," said a

zealous junior civilian acidly. "The Government is not exactly pleased with your work when you relieved Sanders."

"Does that mean a wigging from headquarters?" said Holden with an abstracted smile. "I think I can stand it."

The talk beat up round the ever-fresh subject of each man's work, and steadied Holden till it was time to go to his dark empty bungalow, where his butler received him as one who knew all his affairs. Holden remained awake for the greater part of the night, and his dreams were pleasant ones.

II

"How old is he now?"

"*Ya illah!* What a man's question! He is all but six weeks old; and on this night I go up to the housetop with thee, my life, to count the stars. For that is auspicious. And he was born on a Friday under the sign of the Sun, and it has been told to me that he will outlive us both and get wealth. Can we wish for aught better, beloved?"

"There is nothing better. Let us go up to the roof, and thou shalt count the stars – but a few only, for the sky is heavy with cloud."

"The winter rains are late, and maybe they come out of season. Come, before all the stars are hid. I have put on my richest jewels."

"Thou hast forgotten the best of all."

"*Ai!* Ours. He comes also. He has never yet seen the skies."

Ameera climbed the narrow staircase that led to the flat roof. The child, placid and unwinking, lay in the hollow of her right arm, gorgeous in silver-fringed muslin with a small skull-cap on his head. Ameera wore all that she valued most. The diamond nose-stud that takes the place of the Western patch in drawing attention to the curve of the nostril, the gold ornament in the centre of the forehead studded with tallow-drop emeralds and flawed rubies, the heavy circlet of beaten gold that was fastened round her neck by the softness of the pure metal, and the chinking curb-patterned silver anklets hanging low over the rosy ankle-bone. She was dressed in jade-green muslin as befitted a daughter of the Faith, and from shoulder to elbow and elbow to wrist ran bracelets of silver tied with floss silk, frail glass bangles slipped over the wrist in proof of the slenderness of the hand, and certain heavy gold bracelets that had no part in her country's ornaments but, since they were Holden's gift and fastened with a cunning European snap, delighted her immensely.

They sat down by the low white parapet of the roof, overlooking the city and its lights.

"They are happy down there," said Ameera. "But I do not think that they are as happy as we. Nor do I think the white *mem-log* are as happy. And thou?"

"I know they are not."

"How dost thou know?"

"They give their children over to the nurses."

"I have never seen that," said Ameera with a sigh, "nor do I wish to see. *Ahi!*" – she dropped her head on Holden's shoulder – "I have counted forty stars, and I am tired. Look at the child, love of my life, he is counting too."

The baby was staring with round eyes at the dark of the heavens. Ameera placed him in Holden's arms, and he lay there without a cry.

"What shall we call him among ourselves?" she said. "Look! Art thou ever tired of looking? He carries thy very eyes. But the mouth —"

"Is thine, most dear. Who should know better than I?"

" 'Tis such a feeble mouth. Oh, so small! And yet it holds my heart between its lips. Give him to me now. He has been too long away."

"Nay, let him lie; he has not yet begun to cry."

"When he cries thou wilt give him back – eh? What a man of mankind thou art! If he cried he were only the dearer to me. But, my life, what little name shall we give him?"

The small body lay close to Holden's heart. It was utterly
helpless and very soft. He scarcely dared to breathe for fear
of crushing it. The caged green parrot that is regarded as a
sort of guardian-spirit in most native households moved on
its perch and fluttered a drowsy wing.

"There is the answer," said Holden. "Mian Mittu has
spoken. He shall be the parrot. When he is ready he will talk
mightily and run about. Mian Mittu is the parrot in thy – in
the Mussulman tongue, is it not?"

"Why put me so far off?" said Ameera fretfully. "Let it
be like unto some English name – but not wholly. For he is
mine."

"Then call him Tota, for that is likest English."

"Ay, Tota, and that is still the parrot. Forgive me, my
lord, for a minute ago, but in truth he is too little to wear all
the weight of Mian Mittu for name. He shall be Tota – our
Tota to us. Hearest thou, O small one? Littlest, thou
art Tota." She touched the child's cheek, and he waking
wailed, and it was necessary to return him to his mother, who
soothed him with the wonderful rhyme of *Aré koko, Jaré
koko!* which says:

Oh crow! Go crow! Baby's sleeping sound,
And the wild plums grow in the jungle, only a penny a pound.
Only a penny a pound, *baba*, only a penny a pound.

Reassured many times as to the price of those plums, Tota
cuddled himself down to sleep. The two sleek, white well-
bullocks in the courtyard were steadily chewing the cud of
their evening meal; old Pir Khan squatted at the head of
Holden's horse, his police sabre across his knees, pulling
drowsily at a big water-pipe that croaked like a bull-frog in
a pond. Ameera's mother sat spinning in the lower verandah,
and the wooden gate was shut and barred. The music of a
marriage-procession came to the roof above the gentle hum
of the city, and a string of flying-foxes crossed the face of the
low moon.

"I have prayed," said Ameera after a long pause, "I have

prayed for two things. First, that I may die in thy stead if thy death is demanded, and in the second that I may die in the place of the child. I have prayed to the Prophet and to Beebee Miriam [the Virgin Mary]. Thinkest thou either will hear?"

"From thy lips who would not hear the lightest word?"

"I asked for straight talk, and thou hast given me sweet talk. Will my prayers be heard?"

"How can I say? God is very good."

"Of that I am not sure. Listen now. When I die, or the child dies, what is thy fate? Living, thou wilt return to the bold white *mem-log*, for kind calls to kind."

"Not always."

"With a woman, no; with a man it is otherwise. Thou wilt in this life, later on, go back to thine own folk. That I could almost endure, for I should be dead. But in thy very death thou wilt be taken away to a strange place and a paradise that I do not know."

"Will it be paradise?"

"Surely, for who would harm thee? But we two – I and the child – shall be elsewhere, and we cannot come to thee, nor canst thou come to us. In the old days, before the child was born, I did not think of these things; but now I think of them always. It is very hard talk."

"It will fall as it will fall. To-morrow we do not know, but to-day and love we know well. Surely we are happy now."

"So happy that it were well to make our happiness assured. And thy Beebee Miriam should listen to me; for she is also a woman. But then she would envy me! It is not seemly for men to worship a woman."

Holden laughed aloud at Ameera's little spasm of jealousy.

"Is it not seemly? Why didst thou not turn me from worship of thee, then?"

"Thou a worshipper! And of me? My king, for all thy sweet words, well I know that I am thy servant and thy slave, and the dust under thy feet. And I would not have it otherwise. See!"

Before Holden could prevent her she stooped forward and touched his feet; recovering herself with a little laugh she hugged Tota closer to her bosom. Then, almost savagely —

"Is it true that the bold white *mem-log* live for three times the length of my life? Is it true that they make their marriages not before they are old women?"

"They marry as do others – when they are women."

"That I know, but they wed when they are twenty-five. Is that true?"

"That is true."

"*Ya illah!* At twenty-five! Who would of his own will take a wife even of eighteen? She is a woman – ageing every hour. Twenty-five! I shall be an old woman at that age, and — Those *mem-log* remain young for ever. How I hate them!"

"What have they to do with us?"

"I cannot tell. I know only that there may now be alive on this earth a woman ten years older than I who may come to thee and take thy love ten years after I am an old woman, grey-headed, and the nurse of Tota's son. That is unjust and evil. They should die too."

"Now, for all thy years thou art a child, and shalt be picked up and carried down the staircase."

"Tota! Have a care for Tota, my lord! Thou at least art as foolish as any babe!" Ameera tucked Tota out of harm's way in the hollow of her neck, and was carried downstairs laughing in Holden's arms, while Tota opened his eyes and smiled after the manner of the lesser angels.

He was a silent infant, and, almost before Holden could realise that he was in the world, developed into a small gold-coloured little god and unquestioned despot of the house overlooking the city. Those were months of absolute happiness to Holden and Ameera – happiness withdrawn from the world, shut in behind the wooden gate that Pir Khan guarded. By day Holden did his work with an immense pity for such as were not so fortunate as himself, and a sympathy for small children that amazed and amused many mothers at the little station-gatherings. At nightfall he returned to

Ameera, – Ameera, full of the wondrous doings of Tota; how he had been seen to clap his hands together and move his fingers with intention and purpose – which was manifestly a miracle – how later, he had of his own initiative crawled out of his low bedstead on to the floor and swayed on both feet for the space of three breaths.

"And they were long breaths, for my heart stood still with delight," said Ameera.

Then Tota took the beasts into his councils – the well-bullocks, the little grey squirrels, the mongoose that lived in a hole near the well, and especially Mian Mittu, the parrot, whose tail he grievously pulled, and Mian Mittu screamed till Ameera and Holden arrived.

"O villain! Child of strength! This to thy brother on the house-top! *Tobah, tobah!* Fie! Fie! But I know a charm to make him wise as Suleiman and Aflatoun [Solomon and Plato]. Now look," said Ameera. She drew from an embroidered bag a handful of almonds. "See! we count seven. In the name of God!"

She placed Mian Mittu, very angry and rumpled, on the top of his cage, and seating herself between the babe and the bird she cracked and peeled an almond less white than her teeth. "This is a true charm, my life, and do not laugh. See! I give the parrot one half and Tota the other." Mian Mittu with careful beak took his share from between Ameera's lips, and she kissed the other half into the mouth of the child, who ate it slowly with wondering eyes. "This I will do each day of seven, and without doubt he who is ours will be a bold speaker and wise. Eh, Tota, what wilt thou be when thou art a man and I am grey-headed?" Tota tucked his fat legs into adorable creases. He could crawl, but he was not going to waste the spring of his youth in idle speech. He wanted Mian Mittu's tail to tweak.

When he was advanced to the dignity of a silver belt – which, with a magic square engraved on silver and hung round his neck, made up the greater part of his clothing – he staggered on a perilous journey down the garden to Pir Khan

and proffered him all his jewels in exchange for one little
ride on Holden's horse, having seen his mother's mother
chaffering with pedlars in the verandah. Pir Khan wept and
set the untried feet on his own grey head in sign of fealty,
and brought the bold adventurer to his mother's arms, vowing that Tota would be a leader of men ere his beard was
grown.

One hot evening, while he sat on the roof between his
father and mother watching the never-ending warfare of the
kites that the city boys flew, he demanded a kite of his own
with Pir Khan to fly it, because he had a fear of dealing with
anything larger than himself, and when Holden called him a
"spark," he rose to his feet and answered slowly in defence
of his new-found individuality, "*Hum 'park nahin hai. Hum
admi hai* [I am no spark, but a man]."

The protest made Holden choke and devote himself very
seriously to a consideration of Tota's future. He need hardly
have taken the trouble. The delight of that life was too perfect to endure. Therefore it was taken away as many things
are taken away in India – suddenly and without warning. The
little lord of the house, as Pir Khan called him, grew sorrowful and complained of pains who had never known the
meaning of pain. Ameera, wild with terror, watched him
through the night, and in the dawning of the second day the
life was shaken out of him by fever – the seasonal autumn
fever. It seemed altogether impossible that he could die,
and neither Ameera nor Holden at first believed the evidence
of the little body on the bedstead. Then Ameera beat her
head against the wall and would have flung herself down the
well in the garden had Holden not restrained her by main
force.

One mercy only was granted to Holden. He rode to his
office in broad daylight and found waiting him an unusually
heavy mail that demanded concentrated attention and hard
work. He was not, however, alive to this kindness of the
gods.

III

The first shock of a bullet is no more than a brisk pinch. The wrecked body does not send in its protest to the soul till ten or fifteen seconds later. Holden realised his pain slowly, exactly as he had realised his happiness, and with the same imperious necessity for hiding all trace of it. In the beginning he only felt that there had been a loss, and that Ameera needed comforting, where she sat with her head on her knees shivering as Mian Mittu from the house-top called *Tota! Tota! Tota!* Later all his world and the daily life of it rose up to hurt him. It was an outrage that any one of the children at the band-stand in the evening should be alive and clamorous, when his own child lay dead. It was more than mere pain when one of them touched him, and stories told by over-fond fathers of their children's latest performances cut him to the quick. He could not declare his pain. He had neither help, comfort, nor sympathy; and Ameera at the end of each weary day would lead him through the hell of self-questioning reproach which is reserved for those who have lost a child, and believe that with a little – just a little – more care it might have been saved.

"Perhaps," Ameera would say, "I did not take sufficient heed. Did I, or did I not? The sun on the roof that day when he played so long alone and I was – *ahi!* braiding my hair – it may be that the sun then bred the fever. If I had warned him from the sun he might have lived. But, oh my life, say that I am guiltless! Thou knowest that I loved him as I love thee. Say that there is no blame on me, or I shall die – I shall die!"

"There is no blame, – before God, none. It was written and how could we do aught to save? What has been, has been. Let it go, beloved."

"He was all my heart to me. How can I let the thought go when my arm tells me every night that he is not here? *Ahi! Ahi!* O Tota, come back to me – come back again, and let us be all together as it was before!"

"Peace, peace! For thine own sake, and for mine also, if thou lovest me – rest."

"By this I know thou dost not care; and how shouldst thou? The white men have hearts of stone and souls of iron. Oh, that I had married a man of mine own people – though he beat me – and had never eaten the bread of an alien!"

"Am I an alien – mother of my son?"

"What else – Sahib? . . . Oh, forgive me – forgive! The death has driven me mad. Thou art the life of my heart, and the light of my eyes, and the breath of my life, and – and I have put thee from me, though it was but for a moment. If thou goest away to whom shall I look for help? Do not be angry. Indeed, it was the pain that spoke and not thy slave."

"I know, I know. We be two who were three. The greater need therefore that we should be one."

They were sitting on the roof as of custom. The night was a warm one in early spring, and sheet-lightning was dancing on the horizon to a broken tune played by far-off thunder. Ameera settled herself in Holden's arms.

"The dry earth is lowing like a cow for the rain, and I – I am afraid. It was not like this when we counted the stars. But thou lovest me as much as before, though a bond is taken away? Answer!"

"I love more because a new bond has come out of the sorrow that we have eaten together, and that thou knowest."

"Yea, I knew," said Ameera in a very small whisper. "But it is good to hear thee say so, my life, who art so strong to help. I will be a child no more, but a woman and an aid to thee. Listen! Give me my *sitar* and I will sing bravely."

She took the light silver-studded *sitar* and began a song of the great hero Rajah Rasalu. The hand failed on the strings, the tune halted, checked, and at a low note turned off to the poor little nursery-rhyme about the wicked crow –

And the wild plums grow in the jungle, only a penny a pound.
Only a penny a pound, *baba* – only . . .

Then came the tears, and the piteous rebellion against fate

till she slept, moaning a little in her sleep, with the right arm thrown clear of the body as though it protected something that was not there. It was after this night that life became a little easier for Holden. The ever-present pain of loss drove him into his work, and the work repaid him by filling up his mind for nine or ten hours a day. Ameera sat alone in the house and brooded, but grew happier when she understood that Holden was more at ease, according to the custom of women. They touched happiness again, but this time with caution.

"It was because we loved Tota that he died. The jealousy of God was upon us," said Ameera. "I have hung up a large black jar before our window to turn the evil eye from us, and we must make no protestations of delight, but go softly underneath the stars, lest God find us out. Is that not good talk, worthless one?"

She had shifted the accent on the word that means "beloved," in proof of the sincerity of her purpose. But the kiss that followed the new christening was a thing that any deity might have envied. They went about henceforward saying, "It is naught, it is naught," and hoping that all the Powers heard.

The Powers were busy on other things. They had allowed thirty million people four years of plenty wherein men fed well and the crops were certain, and the birth-rate rose year by year; the districts reported a purely agricultural population varying from nine hundred to two thousand to the square mile of the overburdened earth; and the Member for Lower Tooting, wandering about India in pot-hat and frock-coat, talked largely of the benefits of British rule and suggested as the one thing needful the establishment of a duly qualified electoral system and a general bestowal of the franchise. His long-suffering hosts smiled and made him welcome, and when he paused to admire, with pretty picked words, the blossom of the blood-red *dhak*-tree that had flowered untimely for a sign of what was coming, they smiled more than ever.

It was the Deputy Commissioner of Kot-Kumharsen, staying at the club for a day, who lightly told a tale that made Holden's blood run cold as he overheard the end.

"He won't bother any one any more. Never saw a man so astonished in my life. By Jove, I thought he meant to ask a question in the House about it. Fellow-passenger in his ship – dined next him – bowled over by cholera and died in eighteen hours. You needn't laugh, you fellows. The Member for Lower Tooting is awfully angry about it; but he's more scared. I think he's going to take his enlightened self out of India."

"I'd give a good deal if he were knocked over. It might keep a few vestrymen of his kidney to their own parish. But what's this about cholera? It's full early for anything of that kind," said the warden of an unprofitable salt-lick.

"Don't know," said the Deputy Commissioner reflectively. "We've got locusts with us. There's sporadic cholera all along the north – at least we're calling it sporadic for decency's sake. The spring crops are short in five districts, and nobody seems to know where the rains are. It's nearly March now. I don't want to scare anybody, but it seems to me that Nature's going to audit her accounts with a big red pencil this summer."

"Just when I wanted to take leave, too!" said a voice across the room.

"There won't be much leave this year but there ought to be a great deal of promotion. I've come in to persuade the Government to put my pet canal on the list of famine-relief works. It's an ill wind that blows no good. I shall get that canal finished at last."

"Is it the old programme then," said Holden; "famine, fever, and cholera?"

"Oh, no. Only local scarcity and an unusual prevalence of seasonal sickness. You'll find it all in the reports if you live till next year. You're a lucky chap. *You* haven't got a wife to send out of harm's way. The hill-stations ought to be full of women this year."

"I think you're inclined to exaggerate the talk in the *bazars*," said a young civilian in the Secretariat. "Now I have observed —"

"I daresay you have," said the Deputy Commissioner, "but you've a great deal more to observe, my son. In the meantime, I wish to observe to you —" and he drew him aside to discuss the construction of the canal that was so dear to his heart. Holden went to his bungalow and began to understand that he was not alone in the world, and also that he was afraid for the sake of another – which is the most soul-satisfying fear known to man.

Two months later, as the Deputy had foretold, Nature began to audit her accounts with a red pencil. On the heels of the spring-reapings came a cry for bread, and the Government, which had decreed that no man should die of want, sent wheat. Then came the cholera from all four quarters of the compass. It struck a pilgrim-gathering of half a million at a sacred shrine. Many died at the feet of their god; the others broke and ran over the face of the land, carrying the pestilence with them. It smote a walled city and killed two hundred a day. The people crowded the trains, hanging on to the footboards and squatting on the roofs of the carriages, and the cholera followed them, for at each station they dragged out the dead and the dying. They died by the roadside, and the horses of the Englishmen shied at the corpses in the grass. The rains did not come, and the earth turned to iron lest man should escape death by hiding in her. The English sent their wives away to the hills and went about their work, coming forward as they were bidden to fill the gaps in the fighting-line. Holden, sick with fear of losing his chiefest treasure on earth, had done his best to persuade Ameera to go away with her mother to the Himalayas.

"Why should I go?" said she one evening on the roof.

"There is sickness, and people are dying, and all the white *mem-log* have gone."

"All of them?"

"All – unless perhaps there remain some old scald-head who vexes her husband's heart by running risk of death."

"Nay; who stays is my sister, and thou must not abuse her, for I will be a scald-head too. I am glad all the bold *mem-log* are gone."

"Do I speak to a woman or a babe? Go to the hills and I will see to it that thou goest like a queen's daughter. Think, child. In a red-lacquered bullock-cart, veiled and curtained, with brass peacocks upon the pole and red cloth hangings. I will send two orderlies for guard, and —"

"Peace! Thou art the babe in speaking thus. What use are those toys to me? *He* would have patted the bullocks and played with the housings. For his sake, perhaps, – thou hast made me very English – I might have gone. Now, I will not. Let the *mem-log* run."

"Their husbands are sending them, beloved."

"Very good talk. Since when hast thou been my husband to tell me what to do? I have but borne thee a son. Thou art only all the desire of my soul to me. How shall I depart when I know that if evil befall thee by the breadth of so much as my littlest finger-nail – is that not small? – I should be aware of it though I were in paradise. And here, this summer thou mayest die – *ai, janee*, die! – and in dying they might call to tend thee a white woman, and she would rob me in the last of thy love!"

"But love is not born in a moment or on a death-bed!"

"What dost thou know of love, stoneheart? She would take thy thanks at least, and, by God and the Prophet and Beebee Miriam the mother of thy Prophet, that I will never endure. My lord and my love, let there be no more foolish talk of going away. Where thou art, I am. It is enough." She put an arm round his neck and a hand on his mouth.

There are not many happinesses so complete as those that are snatched under the shadow of the sword. They sat together and laughed, calling each other openly by every pet name that could move the wrath of the gods. The city below them was locked up in its own torments. Sulphur fires blazed in the streets; the conches in the Hindu temples screamed and bellowed, for the gods were inattentive in those days. There was a service in the great Mahomedan shrine, and the call to prayer from the minarets was almost unceasing. They heard the wailing in the houses of the dead, and once the shriek of a mother who had lost a child and was calling for its return. In the grey dawn they saw the dead borne out through the city gates, each litter with its own little knot of mourners. Wherefore they kissed each other and shivered.

It was a red and heavy audit, for the land was very sick and needed a little breathing-space ere the torrent of cheap life should flood it anew. The children of immature fathers and undeveloped mothers made no resistance. They were cowed and sat still, waiting till the sword should be sheathed in November if it were so willed. There were gaps among the English, but the gaps were filled. The work of superintending famine-relief, cholera-sheds, medicine-distribution, and what little sanitation was possible, went forward because it was so ordered.

Holden had been told to keep himself in readiness to move to replace the next man who should fall. There were twelve hours in each day when he could not see Ameera, and she might die in three. He was considering what his pain would be if he could not see her for three months, or if she died out of his sight. He was absolutely certain that her death would be demanded – so certain that when he looked up from the telegram and saw Pir Khan breathless in the doorway, he laughed aloud. "And?" said he, —

"When there is a cry in the night and the spirit flutters into the throat, who has a charm that will restore? Come swiftly, Heaven-born! It is the black cholera."

Holden galloped to his home. The sky was heavy with clouds, for the long-deferred rains were near and the heat was stifling. Ameera's mother met him in the courtyard, whimpering, "She is dying. She is nursing herself into death. She is all but dead. What shall I do, Sahib?"

Ameera was lying in the room in which Tota had been

born. She made no sign when Holden entered, because the human soul is a very lonely thing, and, when it is getting ready to go away, hides itself in a misty borderland where the living may not follow. The black cholera does its work quietly and without explanation. Ameera was being thrust out of life as though the Angel of Death had himself put his hand upon her. The quick breathing seemed to show that she was either afraid or in pain, but neither eyes nor mouth gave any answer to Holden's kisses. There was nothing to be said or done. Holden could only wait and suffer. The first drops of the rain began to fall on the roof, and he could hear shouts of joy in the parched city.

The soul came back a little and the lips moved. Holden bent down to listen. "Keep nothing of mine," said Ameera. "Take no hair from my head. *She* would make thee burn it later on. That flame I should feel. Lower! Stoop lower! Remember only that I was thine and bore thee a son. Though thou wed a white woman to-morrow, the pleasure of receiving in thy arms thy first son is taken from thee for ever. Remember me when thy son is born – the one that shall carry thy name before all men. His misfortunes be on my head. I bear witness – I bear witness" – the lips were forming the words on his ear – "that there is no God but – thee, beloved!"

Then she died. Holden sat still, and all thought was taken from him, – till he heard Ameera's mother lift the curtain.

"Is she dead, Sahib?"

"She is dead."

"Then I will mourn, and afterwards take an inventory of the furniture in this house. For that will be mine. The Sahib does not mean to resume it? It is so little, so very little, Sahib, and I am an old woman. I would like to lie softly."

"For the mercy of God be silent a while. Go out and mourn where I cannot hear."

"Sahib, she will be buried in four hours."

"I know the custom. I shall go ere she is taken away. That matter is in thy hands. Look to it, that the bed on which – on which she lies —"

"Aha! That beautiful red-lacquered bed. I have long desired —"

"That the bed is left here untouched for my disposal. All else in the house is thine. Hire a cart, take everything, go hence, and before sunrise let there be nothing in this house but that which I have ordered thee to respect."

"I am an old woman. I would stay at least for the days of mourning, and the rains have just broken. Whither shall I go?"

"What is that to me? My order is that there is a going. The house gear is worth a thousand rupees, and my orderly shall bring thee a hundred rupees to-night."

"That is very little. Think of the cart-hire."

"It shall be nothing unless thou goest, and with speed. O woman, get hence and leave me with my dead!"

The mother shuffled down the staircase, and in her anxiety to take stock of the house-fittings forgot to mourn. Holden stayed by Ameera's side and the rain roared on the roof. He could not think connectedly by reason of the noise, though he made many attempts to do so. Then four sheeted ghosts glided dripping into the room and stared at him through their veils. They were the washers of the dead. Holden left the room and went out to his horse. He had come in a dead, stifling calm through ankle-deep dust. He found the courtyard a rain-lashed pond alive with frogs; a torrent of yellow water ran under the gate, and a roaring wind drove the bolts of the rain like buckshot against the mud walls. Pir Khan was shivering in his little hut by the gate, and the horse was stamping uneasily in the water.

"I have been told the Sahib's order," said Pir Khan. "It is well. This house is now desolate. I go also, for my monkey-face would be a reminder of that which has been. Concerning the bed, I will bring that to thy house yonder in the morning; but remember, Sahib, it will be to thee a knife turning in a green wound. I go upon a pilgrimage, and I will take no money. I have grown fat in the protection of the Presence whose sorrow is my sorrow. For the last time I hold his stirrup."

He touched Holden's foot with both hands and the horse sprang out into the road, where the creaking bamboos were whipping the sky, and all the frogs were chuckling. Holden could not see for the rain in his face. He put his hands before his eyes and muttered –

"Oh, you brute! You utter brute!"

The news of his trouble was already in his bungalow. He read the knowledge in his butler's eyes when Ahmed Khan brought in food, and for the first and last time in his life laid a hand upon his master's shoulder, saying, "Eat, Sahib, eat. Meat is good against sorrow. I also have known. Moreover, the shadows come and go, Sahib; the shadows come and go. These be curried eggs."

Holden could neither eat nor sleep. The heavens sent down eight inches of rain in that night and washed the earth clean. The waters tore down walls, broke roads, and scoured open the shallow graves on the Mahomedan burying-ground. All next day it rained, and Holden sat still in his house considering his sorrow. On the morning of the third day he received a telegram which said only, "Ricketts, Myndonie. Dying. Holden relieve. Immediate." Then he thought that before he departed he would look at the house wherein he had been master and lord. There was a break in the weather, and the rank earth steamed with vapour.

He found that the rains had torn down the mud pillars of the gateway, and the heavy wooden gate that had guarded his life hung lazily from one hinge. There was grass three inches high in the courtyard; Pir Khan's lodge was empty, and the sodden thatch sagged between the beams. A grey squirrel was in possession of the verandah, as if the house had been un-tenanted for thirty years instead of three days. Ameera's mother had removed everything except some mildewed matting. The *tick-tick* of the little scorpions as they hurried across the floor was the only sound in the house. Ameera's room and the other one where Tota had lived were heavy with mildew; and the narrow staircase leading to the roof was streaked and stained with rain-borne mud. Holden saw all these things, and came out again to meet in the road Durga Dass, his landlord, – portly, affable, clothed in white muslin, and driving a Cee-spring buggy. He was overlooking his property to see how the roofs stood the stress of the first rains.

"I have heard," said he, "you will not take this place any more, Sahib?"

"What are you going to do with it?"

"Perhaps I shall let it again."

"Then I will keep it on while I am away."

Durga Dass was silent for some time. "You shall not take it on, Sahib," he said. "When I was a young man I also —, but to-day I am a member of the Municipality. Ho! Ho! No. When the birds have gone what need to keep the nest? I will have it pulled down – the timber will sell for something always. It shall be pulled down, and the Municipality shall make a road across, as they desire, from the burning-ghaut to the city wall, so that no man may say where this house stood."

THE HEAD OF THE DISTRICT

THE HEAD OF THE DISTRICT

* * *

> There's a convict more in the Central Jail,
>   Behind the old mud wall;
> There's a lifter less on the Border trail,
>   And the Queen's Peace over all,
>   Dear boys,
>   The Queen's Peace over all.
>
> For we must bear our leader's blame,
>   On us the shame will fall,
> If we lift our hand from a fettered land,
>   And the Queen's Peace over all,
>   Dear boys,
>   The Queen's Peace over all!
>
> *The Running of Shindand*

I

THE Indus had risen in flood without warning. Last night it was a fordable shallow; to-night five miles of raving muddy water parted bank and caving bank, and the river was still rising under the moon. A litter borne by six bearded men, all unused to the work, stopped in the white sand that bordered the whiter plain.

"It's God's will," they said. "We dare not cross to-night, even in a boat. Let us light a fire and cook food. We be tired men."

They looked at the litter inquiringly. Within, the Deputy Commissioner of the Kot-Kumharsen district lay dying of fever. They had brought him across country, six fighting-men of a frontier clan that he had won over to the paths of a moderate righteousness, when he had broken down at the

185

foot of their inhospitable hills. And Tallantire, his assistant, rode with them, heavy-hearted as heavy-eyed with sorrow and lack of sleep. He had served under the sick man for three years, and had learned to love him as men associated in toil of the hardest learn to love – or hate. Dropping from his horse, he parted the curtains of the litter and peered inside.

"Orde – Orde, old man, can you hear? We have to wait till the river goes down, worse luck."

"I hear," returned a dry whisper. "Wait till the river goes down. I thought we should reach camp before the dawn. Polly knows. She'll meet me."

One of the litter-men stared across the river and caught a faint twinkle of light on the far side. He whispered to Tallantire, "There are his camp-fires, and his wife. They will cross in the morning, for they have better boats. Can he live so long?"

Tallantire shook his head. Yardley-Orde was very near to death. What need to vex his soul with hopes of a meeting that could not be? The river gulped at the banks, brought down a cliff of sand, and snarled the more hungrily. The litter-men sought for fuel in the waste – dried camel-thorn and refuse of the camps that had waited at the ford. Their sword-belts clinked as they moved softly in the haze of the moonlight, and Tallantire's horse coughed to explain that he would like a blanket.

"I'm cold too," said the voice from the litter. "I fancy this is the end. Poor Polly!"

Tallantire rearranged the blankets; Khoda Dad Khan, seeing this, stripped off his own heavy-wadded sheepskin coat and added it to the pile. "I shall be warm by the fire presently," said he. Tallantire took the wasted body of his chief into his arms and held it against his breast. Perhaps if they kept him very warm Orde might live to see his wife once more. If only blind Providence would send a three-foot fall in the river!

"That's better," said Orde faintly. "Sorry to be a nuisance, but is – is there anything to drink?"

They gave him milk and whisky, and Tallantire felt a little warmth against his own breast. Orde began to mutter.

"It isn't that I mind dying," he said. "It's leaving Polly and the district. Thank God! we have no children. Dick, you know, I'm dipped — awfully dipped — debts in my first five years' service. It isn't much of a pension, but enough for her. She has her mother at home. Getting there is the difficulty. And — and — you see, not being a soldier's wife —"

"We'll arrange the passage home, of course," said Tallantire quietly.

"It's not nice to think of sending round the hat; but, good Lord! how many men I lie here and remember that had to do it! Morten's dead — he was of my year. Shaughnessy is dead, and he had children; I remember he used to read us their school-letters; what a bore we thought him! Evans is dead — Kot-Kumharsen killed him! Ricketts of Myndonie is dead — and I'm going too. 'Man that is born of a woman is small potatoes and few in the hill.' That reminds me, Dick; the four Khusru Kheyl villages in our border want a one-third remittance this spring. That's fair; their crops are bad. See that they get it, and speak to Ferris about the canal. I should like to have lived till that was finished; it means so much for the North-Indus villages — but Ferris is an idle beggar — wake him up. You'll have charge of the district till my successor comes. I wish they would appoint you permanently; you know the folk. I suppose it will be Bullows, though. 'Good man, but too weak for frontier work; and he doesn't understand the priests. The blind priest at Jagai will bear watching. You'll find it in my papers, — in the uniform-case, I think. Call the Khusru Kheyl men up; I'll hold my last public audience. Khoda Dad Khan!"

The leader of the men sprang to the side of the litter, his companions following.

"Men, I'm dying," said Orde quickly, in the vernacular; "and soon there will be no more Orde Sahib to twist your tails and prevent you from raiding cattle."

"God forbid this thing!" broke out the deep bass chorus: "The Sahib is not going to die."

"Yes, he is; and then he will know whether Mahomed speaks truth, or Moses. But you must be good men when I am not here. Such of you as live in our borders must pay your taxes quietly as before. I have spoken of the villages to be gently treated this year. Such of you as live in the hills must refrain from cattle-lifting, and burn no more thatch, and turn a deaf ear to the voice of the priests, who, not knowing the strength of the Government, would lead you into foolish wars, wherein you will surely die and your crops be eaten by strangers. And you must not sack any caravans, and must leave your arms at the police-post when you come in; as has been your custom, and my order. And Tallantire Sahib will be with you, but I do not know who takes my place. I speak now true talk, for I am as it were already dead, my children, – for though ye be strong men, ye are children."

"And thou art our father and our mother," broke in Khoda Dad Khan with an oath. "What shall we do, now there is no one to speak for us, or to teach us to go wisely!"

"There remains Tallantire Sahib. Go to him; he knows your talk and your heart. Keep the young men quiet, listen to the old men, and obey. Khoda Dad Khan, take my ring. The watch and chain go to thy brother. Keep those things for my sake, and I will speak to whatever God I may encounter and tell him that the Khusru Kheyl are good men. Ye have my leave to go."

Khoda Dad Khan, the ring upon his finger, choked audibly as he caught the well-known formula that closed an interview. His brother turned to look across the river. The dawn was breaking, and a speck of white showed on the dull silver of the stream. "She comes," said the man under his breath. "Can he live for another two hours?" And he pulled the newly-acquired watch out of his belt and looked uncomprehendingly at the dial, as he had seen Englishmen do.

For two hours the bellying sail tacked and blundered up and down the river, Tallantire still clasping Orde in his arms, and Khoda Dad Khan chafing his feet. He spoke now and again of the district and his wife, but, as the end neared, more frequently of the latter. They hoped he did not know that she was even then risking her life in a crazy native boat to regain him. But the awful foreknowledge of the dying deceived them. Wrenching himself forward, Orde looked through the curtains and saw how near was the sail. "That's Polly," he said simply, though his mouth was wried with agony. "Polly and – the grimmest practical joke ever played on a man. Dick – you'll – have – to – explain."

And an hour later Tallantire met on the bank a woman in a gingham riding-habit and a sun-hat who cried out to him for her husband – her boy and her darling – while Khoda Dad Khan threw himself face-down on the sand and covered his eyes.

II

The very simplicity of the notion was its charm. What more easy to win a reputation for far-seeing statesmanship, originality, and, above all, deference to the desires of the people, than by appointing a child of the country to the rule of that country? Two hundred millions of the most loving and grateful folk under Her Majesty's dominion would laud the fact, and their praise would endure for ever. Yet he was indifferent to praise or blame, as befitted the Very Greatest of All the Viceroys. His administration was based upon principle, and the principle must be enforced in season and out of season. His pen and tongue had created the New India, teeming with possibilities – loud-voiced, insistent, a nation among nations – all his very own. Wherefore the Very Greatest of All the Viceroys took another step in advance, and with it counsel of those who should have advised him on the appointment of a successor to Yardley-Orde. There was a gentleman and a member of the Bengal Civil Service who had won his place and a university degree to boot in fair and open competition with the sons of the English. He was cultured, of the world, and, if report spoke truly, had wisely and, above all, sympathetically ruled a crowded district in South-Eastern Bengal. He had been to England and charmed many drawing-rooms there. His name, if the Viceroy recollected aright, was Mr. Grish Chunder Dé, M. A. In short, did anybody see any objection to the appointment, always on principle, of a man of the people to rule the people? The district in South-Eastern Bengal might with advantage, he apprehended, pass over to a younger civilian of Mr. G. C. Dé's nationality (who had written a remarkably clever pamphlet on the political value of sympathy in administration); and Mr. G. C. Dé could be transferred northward to Kot-Kumharsen. The Viceroy was averse, on principle, to interfering with appointments under control of the Provincial Governments. He wished it to be understood that he merely recommended and advised in this instance. As regarded the mere question of race, Mr. Grish Chunder Dé was more English than the English, and yet possessed of that peculiar sympathy and insight which the best among the best Service in the world could only win to at the end of their service.

The stern, black-bearded kings who sit about the Council-board of India divided on the step, with the inevitable result of driving the Very Greatest of All the Viceroys into the borders of hysteria, and a bewildered obstinacy pathetic as that of a child.

"The principle is sound enough," said the weary-eyed Head of the Red Provinces in which Kot-Kumharsen lay, for he too held theories. "The only difficulty is —"

"Put the screw on the District officials; brigade Dé with a very strong Deputy Commissioner on each side of him; give him the best assistant in the Province; rub the fear of God into the people beforehand; and if anything goes wrong, say that his colleagues didn't back him up. All these lovely little experiments recoil on the District-Officer in the end," said the Knight of the Drawn Sword with a truthful brutality that made the Head of the Red Provinces shudder. And on a tacit understanding of this kind the transfer was accomplished, as quietly as might be for many reasons.

It is sad to think that what goes for public opinion in India did not generally see the wisdom of the Viceroy's appointment. There were not lacking indeed hireling organs, notoriously in the pay of a tyrannous bureaucracy, who more than hinted that His Excellency was a fool, a dreamer of dreams, a doctrinaire, and, worst of all, a trifler with the lives of men. "The Viceroy's Excellence Gazette," published in Calcutta, was at pains to thank "Our beloved Viceroy for once more and again thus gloriously vindicating the potentialities of the Bengali nations for extended executive and administrative duties in foreign parts beyond our ken. We do not at all doubt that our excellent fellow-townsman, Mr. Grish Chunder Dé, Esq., M. A., will uphold the prestige of the Bengali, notwithstanding what underhand intrigue and *pesh-bundi* may be set on foot to insidiously nip his fame and blast his prospects among the proud civilians, some of which will now have to serve under a despised native and take orders too. How will you like that, Misters? We entreat our beloved Viceroy still to substantiate himself superiorly to race-prejudice and colour-blindness, and to allow the flower of this now *our* Civil Service all the full pays and allowances granted to his more fortunate brethren."

III

"When does this man take over charge? I'm alone just now, and I gather that I'm to stand fast under him."

"Would you have cared for a transfer?" said Bullows keenly. Then, laying his hand on Tallantire's shoulder: "We're all in the same boat; don't desert us. And yet, why the devil should you stay, if you can get another charge?"

"It was Orde's," said Tallantire simply.

"Well, it's Dé's now. He's a Bengali of the Bengalis, crammed with code and case law; a beautiful man so far as routine and deskwork go, and pleasant to talk to. They naturally have always kept him in his own home district, where all his sisters and his cousins and his aunts lived, somewhere south of Dacca. He did no more than turn the place into a pleasant little family preserve, allowed his subordinates to do what they liked, and let everybody have a chance at the shekels. Consequently he's immensely popular down there."

"I've nothing to do with that. How on earth am I to explain to the district that they are going to be governed by a Bengali? Do you – does the Government, I mean – suppose that the Khusru Kheyl will sit quiet when they once know? What will the Mahomedan heads of villages say? How will the police – Muzbi-Sikhs and Pathans – how will *they* work under him? We couldn't say anything if the Government appointed a sweeper; but my people will say a good deal, you know that. It's a piece of cruel folly!"

"My dear boy, I know all that, and more. I've represented it, and have been told that I am exhibiting 'culpable and puerile prejudice.' By Jove, if the Khusru Kheyl don't exhibit something worse than that I don't know the Border! The chances are that you will have the district alight on your hands, and I shall have to leave my work and help you pull through. I needn't ask you to stand by the Bengali man in every possible way. You'll do that for your own sake."

"For Orde's. I can't say that I care twopence personally."

"Don't be an ass. It's grievous enough, God knows, and the Government will know later on; but that's no reason for your sulking. *You* must try to run the district; *you* must stand between him and as much insult as possible; *you* must show him the ropes; *you* must pacify the Khusru Kheyl, and just warn Curbar of the Police to look out for trouble by the way. I'm always at the end of a telegraph-wire, and willing to peril my reputation to hold the district together. You'll lose yours, of course. If you keep things straight, and he isn't actually beaten with a stick when he's on tour, he'll get all the credit. If anything goes wrong, you'll be told that you didn't support him loyally."

"I know what I've got to do," said Tallantire wearily, "and I'm going to do it. But it's hard."

"The work is with us, the event is with Allah, – as Orde used to say when he was more than usually in hot water." And Bullows rode away.

That two gentlemen in Her Majesty's Bengal Civil Service should thus discuss a third, also in that service, and a cultured and affable man withal, seems strange and saddening. Yet listen to the artless babble of the Blind Mullah of Jagai, the priest of the Khusru Kheyl, sitting upon a rock overlooking the Border. Five years before, a chance-hurled shell from a screw-gun battery had dashed earth in the face of the Mullah, then urging a rush of Ghazis against half a dozen British bayonets. So he became blind, and hated the English none the less for the little accident. Yardley-Orde knew his failing, and had many times laughed at him therefor.

"Dogs you are," said the Blind Mullah to the listening tribesmen round the fire. "Whipped dogs! Because you listened to Orde Sahib and called him father and behaved as his children, the British Government have proven how they regard you. Orde Sahib ye know is dead."

"Ai! ai! ai!" said half a dozen voices.

"He was a man. Comes now in his stead, whom think ye? A Bengali of Bengal – an eater of fish from the South."

"A lie!" said Khoda Dad Khan. "And but for the small matter of thy priesthood, I'd drive my gun, butt first, down thy throat."

"Oho, art thou there, lickspittle of the English? Go in to-morrow across the Border to pay service to Orde Sahib's successor, and thou shalt slip thy shoes at the tent-door of a Bengali, as thou shalt hand thy offering to a Bengali's black fist. This I know; and in my youth, when a young man spoke evil to a Mullah holding the doors of Heaven and Hell, the gun-butt was not rammed down the Mullah's gullet. No!"

The Blind Mullah hated Khoda Dad Khan with Afghan hatred, both being rivals for the headship of the tribe; but the latter was feared for bodily as the other for spiritual gifts. Khoda Dad Khan looked at Orde's ring and grunted, "I go in to-morrow because I am not an old fool, preaching war against the English. If the Government, smitten with madness, have done this, then . . ."

"Then," croaked the Mullah, "thou wilt take out the young men and strike at the four villages within the Border?"

"Or wring thy neck, black raven of Jehannum, for a bearer of ill-tidings."

Khoda Dad Khan oiled his long locks with great care, put on his best Bokhara belt, a new turban-cap and fine green shoes, and accompanied by a few friends came down from the hills to pay a visit to the new Deputy Commissioner of Kot-Kumharsen. Also he bore tribute – four or five priceless gold mohurs of Akbar's time in a white handkerchief. These the Deputy Commissioner would touch and remit. The little ceremony used to be a sign that, so far as Khoda Dad Khan's personal influence went, the Khusru Kheyl would be good boys, – till the next time; especially if Khoda Dad Khan happened to like the new Deputy Commissioner. In Yardley-Orde's consulship his visit concluded with a sumptuous dinner and perhaps forbidden liquors; certainly with some wonderful tales and great good-fellowship. Then Khoda Dad Khan would swagger back to his hold, vowing that Orde Sahib was one prince and Tallantire Sahib another, and that whosoever went a-raiding into British territory would be flayed alive. On this occasion he found the Deputy Commissioner's tents looking much as usual. Regarding himself as privileged, he strode through the open door to confront a suave, portly Bengali in English costume, writing at a table. Unversed in the elevating influence of education, and not in the least caring for university degrees, Khoda Dad Khan promptly set the man down for a Babu – the native clerk of the Deputy Commissioner – a hated and despised animal.

"Ugh!" said he cheerfully. "Where's your master, Babu-jee?"

"I am the Deputy Commissioner," said the gentleman in English.

Now he overvalued the effects of university degrees, and stared Khoda Dad Khan in the face. But if from your earliest infancy you have been accustomed to look on battle, murder, and sudden death, if spilt blood affects your nerves as much as red paint, and, above all, if you have faithfully believed that the Bengali was the servant of all Hindustan, and that all Hindustan was vastly inferior to your own large, lustful self, you can endure, even though uneducated, a very large amount of looking over. You can even stare down a graduate of an Oxford college if the latter has been born in a hothouse, of stock bred in a hothouse, and fearing physical pain as some men fear sin; especially if your opponent's mother has frightened him to sleep in his youth with horrible stories of devils inhabiting Afghanistan, and dismal legends of the black North. The eyes behind the gold spectacles sought the floor. Khoda Dad Khan chuckled, and swung out to find Tallantire hard by. "Here," said he roughly, thrusting the coins before him, "touch and remit. That answers for *my* good behaviour. But, O Sahib, has the Government gone mad to send a black Bengali dog to us? And am I to pay service to such an one? And are you to work under him? What does it mean?"

"It is an order," said Tallantire. He had expected something of this kind. "He is a very clever S-sahib."

"He a Sahib! He's a *kala admi* – a black man – unfit to run at the tail of a potter's donkey. All the peoples of the earth have harried Bengal. It is written. Thou knowest when we of the North wanted women or plunder whither went we? To Bengal – where else? What child's talk is this of Sahib-dom – after Orde Sahib too! Of a truth the Blind Mullah was right."

"What of him?" asked Tallantire uneasily. He mistrusted that old man with his dead eyes and his deadly tongue.

"Nay, now, because of the oath that I sware to Orde Sahib when we watched him die by the river yonder, I will tell. In the first place, is it true that the English have set the heel of

the Bengali on their own neck, and that there is no more
English rule in the land?"

"I am here," said Tallantire, "and I serve the Maharanee
of England."

"The Mullah said otherwise, and further that because we
loved Orde Sahib the Government sent us a pig to show that
we were dogs who till now have been held by the strong
hand. Also that they were taking away the white soldiers, that
more Hindustanis might come, and that all was changing."

This is the worst of ill-considered handling of a very large
country. What looks so feasible in Calcutta, so right in Bombay, so unassailable in Madras, is misunderstood by the
North and entirely changes its complexion on the banks of
the Indus. Khoda Dad Khan explained as clearly as he could
that, though he himself intended to be good, he really could not
answer for the more reckless members of his tribe under the
leadership of the Blind Mullah. They might or they might
not give trouble, but they certainly had no intention whatever
of obeying the new Deputy Commissioner. Was Tallantire
perfectly sure that in the event of any systematic border-raid-
ing the force in the district could put it down promptly?

"Tell the Mullah if he talks any more fool's talk," said
Tallantire curtly, "that he takes his men on to certain death,
and his tribe to blockade, trespass-fine, and blood-money.
But why do I talk to one who no longer carries weight in the
counsels of the tribe?"

Khoda Dad Khan pocketed that insult. He had learned
something that he much wanted to know, and returned to his
hills to be sarcastically complimented by the Mullah, whose
tongue raging round the camp-fires was deadlier flame than
ever dung-cake fed.

IV

Be pleased to consider here for a moment the unknown
district of Kot-Kumharsen. It lay cut lengthways by the
Indus under the line of the Khusru hills – ramparts of useless
earth and tumbled stone. It was seventy miles long by fifty

broad, maintained a population of something less than two hundred thousand, and paid taxes to the extent of forty thousand pounds a year on an area that was by rather more than half sheer, hopeless waste. The cultivators were not gentle people, the miners for salt were less gentle still, and the cattle-breeders least gentle of all. A police-post in the top right-hand corner and a tiny mud fort in the top left-hand corner prevented as much salt-smuggling and cattle-lifting as the influence of the civilians could not put down; and in the bottom right-hand corner lay Jumala, the district headquarters – a pitiful knot of lime-washed barns facetiously rented as houses, reeking with frontier fever, leaking in the rain, and ovens in the summer.

It was to this place that Grish Chunder Dé was travelling, there formally to take over charge of the district. But the news of his coming had gone before. Bengalis were as scarce as poodles among the simple Borderers, who cut each other's heads open with their long spades and worshipped impartially at Hindu and Mahomedan shrines. They crowded to see him, pointing at him, and diversely comparing him to a gravid milch-buffalo, or a broken-down horse, as their limited range of metaphor prompted. They laughed at his police-guard, and wished to know how long the burly Sikhs were going to lead Bengali apes. They inquired whether he had brought his women with him, and advised him explicitly not to tamper with theirs. It remained for a wrinkled hag by the roadside to slap her lean breasts as he passed, crying, "I have suckled six that could have eaten six thousand of *him*. The Government shot them, and made this That a king!" Whereat a blue-turbaned huge-boned plough-mender shouted, "Have hope, mother o' mine! He may yet go the way of thy wastrels." And the children, the little brown puffballs, regarded curiously. It was generally a good thing for infancy to stray into Orde Sahib's tent, where copper coins were to be won for the mere wishing, and tales of the most authentic, such as even their mothers knew but the first half of. No! This fat black man could never tell them how

Pir Prith hauled the eye-teeth out of ten devils; how the big stones came to lie all in a row on top of the Khusru hills, and what happened if you shouted through the village-gate to the grey wolf at even, "Badl Khas is dead." Meantime Grish Chunder Dé talked hastily and much to Tallantire, after the manner of those who are "more English than the English," – of Oxford and "home," with much curious book-knowledge of bump-suppers, cricket-matches, hunting-runs, and other unholy sports of the alien. "We must get these fellows in hand," he said once or twice uneasily; "get them well in hand, and drive them on a tight rein. No use, you know, being slack with your district."

And a moment later Tallantire heard Debendra Nath Dé, who brotherliwise had followed his kinsman's fortune and hoped for the shadow of his protection as a pleader, whisper in Bengali, "Better are dried fish at Dacca than drawn swords at Delhi. Brother of mine, these men are devils, as our mother said. And you will always have to ride upon a horse!"

That night there was a public audience in a broken-down little town thirty miles from Jumala, when the new Deputy Commissioner, in reply to the greetings of the subordinate native officials, delivered a speech. It was a carefully thought out speech, which would have been very valuable had not his third sentence begun with three innocent words, "*Hamara hookum hai* – It is my order." Then there was a laugh, clear and bell-like, from the back of the big tent, where a few border land-holders sat, and the laugh grew and scorn mingled with it, and the lean, keen face of Debendra Nath Dé paled, and Grish Chunder, turning to Tallantire, spake: "*You* – you put up this arrangement." Upon that instant the noise of hoofs rang without, and there entered Curbar, the District Superintendent of Police, sweating and dusty. The State had tossed him into a corner of the province for seventeen weary years, there to check smuggling of salt, and to hope for promotion that never came. He had forgotten how to keep his white uniform clean, had screwed rusty spurs into patent-leather shoes, and clothed his head indifferently with a helmet or a turban. Soured, old, worn with heat and cold, he waited till he should be entitled to sufficient pension to keep him from starving.

"Tallantire," said he, disregarding Grish Chunder Dé, "come outside. I want to speak to you." They withdrew. "It's this," continued Curbar. "The Khusru Kheyl have rushed and cut up half a dozen of the coolies on Ferris's new canal-embankment; killed a couple of men and carried off a woman. I wouldn't trouble you about that – Ferris is after them and Hugonin, my assistant, with ten mounted police. But that's only the beginning, I fancy. Their fires are out on the Hassan Ardeb heights, and unless we're pretty quick there'll be a flare-up all along our Border. They are sure to raid the four Khusru villages on our side of the line; there's been bad blood between them for years; and you know the Blind Mullah has been preaching a holy war since Orde went out. What's your notion?"

"Damn!" said Tallantire thoughtfully. "They've begun quick. Well, it seems to me I'd better ride off to Fort Ziar and get what men I can there to picket among the lowland villages, if it's not too late. Tommy Dodd commands at Fort Ziar, I think. Ferris and Hugonin ought to teach the canal-thieves a lesson, and — No, we can't have the Head of the Police ostentatiously guarding the Treasury. You go back to the canal. I'll wire Bullows to come into Jumala with a strong police-guard, and sit on the Treasury. They won't touch the place, but it looks well."

"I – I – I insist upon knowing what this means," said the voice of the Deputy Commissioner, who had followed the speakers.

"Oh!" said Curbar, who, being in the Police, could not understand that fifteen years of education must, on principle, change the Bengali into a Briton. "There has been a fight on the Border, and heaps of men are killed. There's going to be another fight, and heaps more will be killed."

"What for?"

"Because the teeming millions of this district don't exactly

approve of you, and think that under your benign rule they
are going to have a good time. It strikes me that you had
better make arrangements. I act, as you know, by your
orders. What do you advise?"

"I – I take you all to witness that I have not yet assumed
charge of the district," stammered the Deputy Commissioner, not in the tones of the "more English."

"Ah, I thought so. Well, as I was saying, Tallantire, your
plan is sound. Carry it out. Do you want an escort?"

"No; only a decent horse. But how about wiring to headquarters?"

"I fancy, from the colour of his cheeks, that your superior
officer will send some wonderful telegrams before the night's
over. Let him do that, and we shall have half the troops of
the province coming up to see what's the trouble. Well, run
along, and take care of yourself – the Khusru Kheyl jab
upwards from below, remember. Ho! Mir Khan, give Tallantire Sahib the best of the horses, and tell five men to ride to
Jumala with the Deputy Commissioner Sahib Bahadur.
There is a hurry toward."

There was; and it was not in the least bettered by Debendra Nath Dé clinging to a policeman's bridle and demanding
the shortest, the very shortest way to Jumala. Now originality
is fatal to the Bengali. Debendra Nath should have stayed
with his brother, who rode steadfastly for Jumala on the
railway-line, thanking gods entirely unknown to the most
catholic of universities that he had not taken charge of the
district, and could still – happy resource of a fertile race! –
fall sick.

And I grieve to say that when he reached his goal two
policemen, not devoid of rude wit, who had been conferring
together as they bumped in their saddles, arranged an entertainment for his behoof. It consisted of first one and then the
other entering his room with prodigious details of war, the
massing of bloodthirsty and devilish tribes, and the burning
of towns. It was almost as good, said these scamps, as riding with Curbar after evasive Afghans. Each invention kept

the hearer at work for half an hour on telegrams which the sack of Delhi would hardly have justified. To every power that could move a bayonet or transfer a terrified man, Grish Chunder Dé appealed telegraphically. He was alone, his assistants had fled, and in truth he had not taken over charge of the district. Had the telegrams been despatched many things would have occurred; but since the only signaller in Jumala had gone to bed, and the station-master, after one look at the tremendous pile of paper, discovered that railway regulations forbade the forwarding of imperial messages, policemen Ram Singh and Nihal Singh were fain to turn the stuff into a pillow and slept on it very comfortably.

Tallantire drove his spurs into a rampant skewbald stallion with china-blue eyes, and settled himself for the forty-mile ride to Fort Ziar. Knowing his district blindfold, he wasted no time hunting for short cuts, but headed across the richer grazing-ground to the ford where Orde had died and been buried. The dusty ground deadened the noise of his horse's hoofs, the moon threw his shadow, a restless goblin, before him, and the heavy dew drenched him to the skin. Hillock, scrub that brushed against the horse's belly, unmetalled road where the whip-like foliage of the tamarisks lashed his forehead, illimitable levels of lowland furred with bent and speckled with drowsing cattle, waste, and hillock anew, dragged themselves past, and the skewbald was labouring in the deep sand of the Indus-ford. Tallantire was conscious of no distinct thought till the nose of the dawdling ferry-boat grounded on the farther side, and his horse shied snorting at the white headstone of Orde's grave. Then he uncovered, and shouted that the dead might hear, "They're out, old man! Wish me luck." In the chill of the dawn he was hammering with a stirrup-iron at the gate of Fort Ziar, where fifty sabres of that tattered regiment, the Belooch Beshaklis, were supposed to guard Her Majesty's interests along a few hundred miles of Border. This particular fort was commanded by a subaltern, who,

born of the ancient family of the Derouletts, naturally
answered to the name of Tommy Dodd. Him Tallantire
found robed in a sheepskin coat, shaking with fever like
an aspen, and trying to read the native apothecary's list of
invalids.

"So you've come, too," said he. "Well, we're all sick here,
and I don't think I can horse thirty men; but we're bub-bub-
bub-blessed willing. Stop, does this impress you as a trap or
a lie?" He tossed a scrap of paper to Tallantire, on which was
written painfully in crabbed Gurmukhi, "We cannot hold
young horses. They will feed after the moon goes down in
the four border villages issuing from the Jagai pass on the
next night." Then in English round hand – "Your sincere
friend."

"Good man!" said Tallantire. "That's Khoda Dad Khan's
work, I know. It's the only piece of English he could ever
keep in his head, and he is immensely proud of it. He is
playing against the Blind Mullah for his own hand – the
treacherous young ruffian!"

"Don't know the politics of the Khusru Kheyl, but if
you're satisfied, I am. That was pitched in over the gate-head
last night, and I thought we might pull ourselves together
and see what was on. Oh, but we're sick with fever here, and
no mistake! Is this going to be a big business, think you?"
said Tommy Dodd.

Tallantire gave him briefly the outlines of the case, and
Tommy Dodd whistled and shook with fever alternately.
That day he devoted to strategy, the art of war, and the
enlivenment of the invalids, till at dusk there stood ready
forty-two troopers, lean, worn, and dishevelled, whom
Tommy Dodd surveyed with pride, and addressed thus: "O
men! If you die you will go to Hell. Therefore endeavour to
keep alive. But if you go to Hell that place cannot be hotter
than this place, and we are not told that we shall there suffer
from fever. Consequently be not afraid of dying. File out
there!" They grinned, and went.

V

It will be long ere the Khusru Kheyl forget their night attack on the lowland villages. The Mullah had promised an easy victory and unlimited plunder; but behold, armed troopers of the Queen had risen out of the very earth, cutting, slashing, and riding down under the stars, so that no man knew where to turn, and all feared that they had brought an army about their ears, and ran back to the hills. In the panic of that flight more men were seen to drop from wounds inflicted by an Afghan knife jabbed upwards, and yet more from long-range carbine-fire. Then there rose a cry of treachery, and when they reached their own guarded heights, they had left, with some forty dead and sixty wounded, all their confidence in the Blind Mullah on the plains below. They clamoured, swore, and argued round the fires; the women wailing for the lost, and the Mullah shrieking curses on the returned.

Then Khoda Dad Khan, eloquent and unbreathed, for he had taken no part in the fight, rose to improve the occasion. He pointed out that the tribe owed every item of its present misfortune to the Blind Mullah, who had lied in every possible particular and talked them into a trap. It was undoubtedly an insult that a Bengali, the son of a Bengali, should presume to administer the Border, but that fact did not, as the Mullah pretended, herald a general time of licence and lifting; and the inexplicable madness of the English had not in the least impaired their power of guarding their marches. On the contrary, the baffled and out-generalled tribe would now, just when their food-stock was lowest, be blockaded from any trade with Hindustan until they had sent hostages for good behaviour, paid compensation for disturbance, and blood-money at the rate of thirty-six English pounds per head for every villager that they might have slain. "And ye know that those lowland dogs will make oath that we have slain scores. Will the Mullah pay the fines or must we sell our guns?" A low growl ran round the fires. "Now, seeing that all this is the Mullah's work, and that we have gained nothing but promises of Paradise thereby, it is in my heart that we of the Khusru Kheyl lack a shrine whereat to pray. We are weakened, and henceforth how shall we dare to cross into the Madar Kheyl border, as has been our custom, to kneel to Pir Sajji's tomb? The Madar men will fall upon us, and rightly. But our Mullah is a holy man. He has helped two score of us into Paradise this night. Let him therefore accompany his flock, and we will build over his body a dome of the blue tiles of Mooltan, and burn lamps at his feet every Friday night. He shall be a saint; we shall have a shrine; and there our women shall pray for fresh seed to fill the gaps in our fighting-tale. How think you?"

A grim chuckle followed the suggestion, and the soft *wheep, wheep* of unscabbarded knives followed the chuckle. It was an excellent notion, and met a long-felt want of the tribe. The Mullah sprang to his feet, glaring with withered eyeballs at the drawn death he could not see, and calling down the curses of God and Mahomed on the tribe. Then began a game of blind man's buff round and between the fires, whereof Khuruk Shah, the tribal poet, has sung in verse that will not die.

They tickled him gently under the armpit with the knife-point. He leaped aside screaming, only to feel a cold blade drawn lightly over the back of his neck, or a rifle-muzzle rubbing his beard. He called on his adherents to aid him, but most of these lay dead on the plains, for Khoda Dad Khan had been at some pains to arrange their decease. Men described to him the glories of the shrine they would build, and the little children, clapping their hands, cried, "Run, Mullah, run! There's a man behind you!" In the end, when the sport wearied, Khoda Dad Khan's brother sent a knife home between his ribs. "Wherefore," said Khoda Dad Khan with charming simplicity, "I am now Chief of the Khusru Kheyl!" No man gainsaid him; and they all went to sleep very stiff and sore.

On the plain below Tommy Dodd was lecturing on the beauties of a cavalry charge by night, and Tallantire, bowed on his saddle, was gasping hysterically because there was a sword dangling from his wrist flecked with the blood of the Khusru Kheyl, the tribe that Orde had kept in leash so well. When a Rajpoot trooper pointed out that the skewbald's right ear had been taken off at the root by some blind slash of its unskilled rider, Tallantire broke down altogether, and laughed and sobbed till Tommy Dodd made him lie down and rest.

"We must wait about till the morning," said he. "I wired to the Colonel, just before we left, to send a wing of the Beshaklis after us. He'll be furious with me for monopolising the fun, though. Those beggars in the hills won't give us any more trouble."

"Then tell the Beshaklis to go on and see what has happened to Curbar on the canal. We must patrol the whole line of the Border. You're quite sure, Tommy, that – that stuff was – was only the skewbald's ear?"

"Oh, quite," said Tommy. "You just missed cutting off his head. *I* saw you when we went into the mess. Sleep, old man."

Noon brought two squadrons of Beshaklis and a knot of furious brother officers demanding the court-martial of Tommy Dodd for "spoiling the picnic," and a gallop across country to the canal-works where Ferris, Curbar, and Hugonin were haranguing the terror-stricken coolies on the enormity of abandoning good work and high pay, merely because half a dozen of their fellows had been cut down. The sight of a troop of the Beshaklis restored wavering confidence, and the police-hunted section of the Khusru Kheyl had the joy of watching the canal-bank humming with life as usual, while such of their men as had taken refuge in the water-courses and ravines were being driven out by the troopers. By sundown began the remorseless patrol of the Border by police and trooper, most like the cow-boys' eternal ride round restless cattle.

"Now," said Khoda Dad Khan to his fellows, pointing out a line of twinkling fires below, "ye may see how far the old order changes. After their horse will come the little devil-guns that they can drag up to the tops of the hills, and, for aught I know, to the clouds when we crown the hills. If the tribe-council thinks good, I will go to Tallantire Sahib – who loves me – and see if I can stave off at least the blockade. Do I speak for the tribe?"

"Ay, speak for the tribe in God's name. How those accursed fires wink! Do the English send their troops on the wire – or is this the work of the Bengali?"

As Khoda Dad Khan went down the hill he was delayed by an interview with a hard-pressed tribesman, which caused him to return hastily for something he had forgotten. Then, handing himself over to the two troopers who had been chasing his friend, he claimed escort to Tallantire Sahib, then with Bullows at Jumala. The Border was safe, and the time for reasons in writing had begun.

"Thank Heaven," said Bullows, "that the trouble came at once. Of course we can never put down the reason in black and white, but all India will understand. And it is better to have a sharp, short outbreak than five years of impotent administration inside the Border. It costs less. Grish Chunder Dé has reported himself sick, and has been transferred to his own province without any sort of reprimand. He was strong on not having taken over the district."

"Of course," said Tallantire bitterly. "Well, what am I supposed to have done that was wrong?"

"Oh, you will be told that you exceeded all your powers, and should have reported, and written, and advised for three weeks until the Khusru Kheyl could really come down in force. But I don't think the authorities will dare to make a fuss about it. They've had their lesson. Have you seen Curbar's version of the affair? He can't write a report, but he can speak the truth."

"What's the use of the truth? He'd much better tear up the report. I'm sick and heart-broken over it all. It was so utterly unnecessary — except in that it rid us of the Babu."

Entered unabashed Khoda Dad Khan, a stuffed forage-net in his hand, and the troopers behind him.

"May you never be tired!" said he cheerily. "Well, Sahibs, that was a good fight, and Naim Shah's mother is in debt to you, Tallantire Sahib. A clean cut, they tell me, through jaw, wadded coat, and deep into the collar-bone. Well done! But I speak for the tribe. There has been a fault — a great fault. Thou knowest that I and mine, Tallantire Sahib, kept the oath we sware to Orde Sahib on the banks of the Indus."

"As an Afghan keeps his knife — sharp on one side, blunt on the other," said Tallantire.

"The better swing in the blow, then. But I speak God's truth. Only the Blind Mullah carried the young men on the tip of his tongue, and said that there was no more Border-law because a Bengali had been sent, and we need not fear the English at all. So they came down to avenge that insult and get plunder. Ye know what befell, and how far I helped. Now five score of us are dead or wounded, and we are all shamed and sorry, and desire no further war. Moreover, that ye may better listen to us, we have taken off the head of the Blind Mullah, whose evil counsels have led us to folly. I bring it for proof," — and he heaved on the floor the head. "He will give no more trouble, for *I* am chief now, and so I sit in a higher place at all audiences. Yet there is an offset to this head. That was another fault. One of the men found that black Bengali beast, through whom this trouble arose, wandering on horseback and weeping. Reflecting that he had caused loss of much good life, Alla Dad Khan, whom, if you choose, I will to-morrow shoot, whipped off this head, and I bring it to you to cover your shame, that ye may bury it. See, no man kept the spectacles, though they were of gold."

Slowly rolled to Tallantire's feet the crop-haired head of a spectacled Bengali gentleman, open-eyed, open-mouthed — the head of Terror incarnate. Bullows bent down. "Yet an-other blood-fine and a heavy one, Khoda Dad Khan, for this is the head of Debendra Nath, the man's brother. The Babu is safe long since. All but the fools of the Khusru Kheyl know that."

"Well, I care not for carrion. Quick meat for me. The thing was under our hills asking the road to Jumala, and Alla Dad Khan showed him the road to Jehannum, being, as thou sayest, but a fool. Remains now what the Government will do to us. As to the blockade —"

"Who art thou, seller of dog's flesh," thundered Tallantire, "to speak of terms and treaties? Get hence to the hills – go and wait there, starving, till it shall please the Government to call thy people out for punishment – children and fools that ye be! Count your dead, and be still. Rest assured that the Government will send you a *man*!"

"Ay," returned Khoda Dad Khan, "for we also be men."

As he looked Tallantire between the eyes, he added, "And by God, Sahib, may thou be that man!"

JEWS IN SHUSHAN

JEWS IN SHUSHAN

My newly purchased house furniture was, at the least, insecure; the legs parted from the chairs, and the tops from the tables, on the slightest provocation. But such as it was, it was to be paid for, and Ephraim, agent and collector for the local auctioneer, waited in the verandah with the receipt. He was announced by the Mahomedan servant as "Ephraim, Yahudi" – Ephraim the Jew. He who believes in the Brotherhood of Man should hear my Elahi Bukhsh grinding the second word through his white teeth with all the scorn he dare show before his master. Ephraim was, personally, meek in manner – so meek indeed that one could not understand how he had fallen into the profession of bill-collecting. He resembled an over-fed sheep, and his voice suited his figure. There was a fixed, unvarying mask of childish wonder upon his face. If you paid him, he was as one marvelling at your wealth; if you sent him away, he seemed puzzled at your hard-heartedness. Never was Jew more unlike his dread breed.

Ephraim wore list slippers and coats of duster-cloth, so preposterously patterned that the most brazen of British subalterns would have shied from them in fear. Very slow and deliberate was his speech, and carefully guarded to give offence to no one. After many weeks, Ephraim was induced to speak to me of his friends

"There be eight of us in Shushan, and we are waiting till there are ten. Then we shall apply for a synagogue, and get leave from Calcutta. To-day we have no synagogue; and I, only I, am Priest and Butcher to our people. I am of the tribe of Judah – I think, but I am not sure. My father was of the tribe of Judah, and we wish much to get our synagogue. I shall be a priest of that synagogue."

Shushan is a big city in the North of India, counting its dwellers by the ten thousand; and these eight of the Chosen People were shut up in its midst, waiting till time or chance sent them their full congregation.

Miriam, the wife of Ephraim, two little children, an orphan boy of their people, Ephraim's uncle Jackrael Israel, a white-haired old man, his wife Hester, a Jew from Cutch, one Hyem Benjamin, and Ephraim, Priest and Butcher, made up the list of the Jews in Shushan. They lived in one house, on the outskirts of the great city, amid heaps of salt-petre, rotten bricks, herds of kine, and a fixed pillar of dust caused by the incessant passing of the beasts to the river to drink. In the evening, the children of the City came to the waste place to fly their kites, and Ephraim's sons held aloof, watching the sport from the roof, but never descending to take part in it. At the back of the house stood a small brick enclosure, in which Ephraim prepared the daily meat for his people after the custom of the Jews. Once the rude door of the square was suddenly smashed open by a struggle from inside, and showed the meek bill-collector at his work, nostrils dilated, lips drawn back over his teeth, and his hands upon a half-maddened sheep. He was attired in strange raiment, having no relation whatever to duster coats or list slippers, and a knife was in his mouth. As he struggled with the animal between the walls, the breath came from him in thick sobs, and the nature of the man seemed changed. When the ordained slaughter was ended, he saw that the door was open and shut it hastily, his hand leaving a red mark on the timber, while his children from the neighbouring house-top looked down awe-stricken and open-eyed. A glimpse of Ephraim busied in one of his religious capacities was no thing to be desired twice.

Summer came upon Shushan, turning the trodden waste-ground to iron, and bringing sickness to the city.

"It will not touch us," said Ephraim confidently. "Before the winter we shall have our synagogue. My brother and his wife and children are coming up from Calcutta, and *then* I shall be the priest of the synagogue."

Jackrael Israel, the old man, would crawl out in the stifling evenings to sit on the rubbish-heap and watch the corpses being borne down to the river.

"It will not come near us," said Jackrael Israel feebly, "for we are the people of God, and my nephew will be priest of our synagogue. Let them die." He crept back to his house again and barred the door to shut himself off from the world of the Gentile.

But Miriam, the wife of Ephraim, looked out of the window at the dead as the biers passed, and said that she was afraid. Ephraim comforted her with hopes of the synagogue to be, and collected bills as was his custom.

In one night the two children died and were buried early in the morning by Ephraim. The deaths never appeared in the City returns. "The sorrow is my sorrow," said Ephraim; and this to him seemed a sufficient reason for setting at naught the sanitary regulations of a large, flourishing, and remarkably well-governed Empire.

The orphan boy, dependent on the charity of Ephraim and his wife, could have felt no gratitude, and must have been a ruffian. He begged for whatever money his protectors would give him, and with that fled down country for his life. A week after the death of her children Miriam left her bed at night and wandered over the country to find them. She heard them crying behind every bush, or drowning in every pool of water in the fields, and she begged the cartmen on the Grand Trunk Road not to steal her little ones from her. In the morning the sun rose and beat upon her bare head, and she turned into the cool, wet crops to lie down, and never came back, though Hyem Benjamin and Ephraim sought her for two nights.

The look of patient wonder on Ephraim's face deepened, but he presently found an explanation. "There are so few of us here, and these people are so many," said he, "that, it may be, our God has forgotten us."

In the house on the outskirts of the city old Jackrael Israel and Hester grumbled that there was no one to wait on them, and that Miriam had been untrue to her race. Ephraim went out and collected bills, and in the evenings smoked with Hyem Benjamin till, one dawning, Hyem Benjamin died, having first paid all his debts to Ephraim. Jackrael Israel and Hester sat alone in the empty house all day, and, when Ephraim returned, wept the easy tears of age till they cried themselves asleep.

A week later Ephraim, staggering under a huge bundle of clothes and cooking-pots, led the old man and woman to the railway station, where the bustle and confusion made them whimper.

"We are going back to Calcutta," said Ephraim, to whose sleeve Hester was clinging. "There are more of us there, and here my house is empty."

He helped Hester into the carriage and, turning back, said to me, "I should have been priest of the synagogue if there had been ten of us. Surely we must have been forgotten by our God."

The remnant of the broken colony passed out of the station on their journey south; while a subaltern, turning over the books on the bookstall, was whistling to himself "The Ten Little Nigger Boys."

But the tune sounded as solemn as the Dead March.

It was the dirge of the Jews in Shushan.

THE MAN WHO WOULD BE KING

THE MAN WHO WOULD BE KING

* * *

Brother to a Prince and fellow to a beggar if he be found
worthy.

THE Law, as quoted, lays down a fair conduct of life, and
one not easy to follow. I have been fellow to a beggar
again and again under circumstances which prevented either
of us finding out whether the other was worthy. I have still
to be brother to a Prince, though I once came near to kinship
with what might have been a veritable King and was
promised the reversion of a Kingdom – army, law-courts,
revenue and policy all complete. But, to-day, I greatly fear
that my King is dead, and if I want a crown I must go hunt
it for myself.

The beginning of everything was in a railway train upon
the road to Mhow from Ajmir. There had been a Deficit in
the Budget, which necessitated travelling, not Second-
class, which is only half as dear as First-class, but by Intermediate, which is very awful indeed. There are no cushions
in the Intermediate class, and the population are either
Intermediate, which is Eurasian, or native, which for a long
night journey is nasty, or Loafer, which is amusing though
intoxicated. Intermediates do not buy from refreshment-
rooms. They carry their food in bundles and pots, and buy
sweets from the native sweetmeat-sellers, and drink the roadside water. That is why in hot weather Intermediates are
taken out of the carriages dead, and in all weathers are most
properly looked down upon.

My particular Intermediate happened to be empty till I
reached Nasirabad, when a big black-browed gentleman in
shirt-sleeves entered, and, following the custom of Inter-

mediates, passed the time of day. He was a wanderer and a vagabond like myself, but with an educated taste for whisky. He told tales of things he had seen and done, of out-of-the-way corners of the Empire into which he had penetrated, and of adventures in which he risked his life for a few days' food.

"If India was filled with men like you and me, not knowing more than the crows where they'd get their next day's rations, it isn't seventy millions of revenue the land would be paying – it's seven hundred millions," said he; and as I looked at his mouth and chin I was disposed to agree with him.

We talked politics – the politics of Loaferdom, that sees things from the underside where the lath and plaster are not smoothed off – and we talked postal arrangements because my friend wanted to send a telegram back from the next station to Ajmir, the turning-off place from the Bombay to the Mhow line as you travel westward. My friend had no money beyond eight annas which he wanted for dinner, and I had no money at all, owing to the hitch in the Budget before mentioned. Further, I was going into a wilderness where, though I should resume touch with the Treasury, there were no telegraph offices. I was, therefore, unable to help him in any way.

"We might threaten a Station-master, and make him send a wire on tick," said my friend, "but that'd mean enquiries for you and for me, and I've got my hands full these days. Did you say you were travelling back along this line within any days?"

"Within ten," I said.

"Can't you make it eight?" said he. "Mine is rather urgent business."

"I can send your telegram within ten days if that will serve you," I said.

"I couldn't trust the wire to fetch him now I think of it. It's this way. He leaves Delhi on the 23d for Bombay. That means he'll be running through Ajmir about the night of the 23d."

"But I'm going into the Indian Desert," I explained.

"Well *and* good," said he. "You'll be changing at Marwar Junction to get into Jodhpore territory – you must do that – and he'll be coming through Marwar Junction in the early morning of the 24th by the Bombay Mail. Can you be at Marwar Junction on that time? 'Twon't be inconveniencing you because I know that there's precious few pickings to be got out of these Central India States – even though you pretend to be correspondent of the 'Backwoodsman.' "

"Have you ever tried that trick?" I asked.

"Again and again, but the Residents find you out, and then you get escorted to the Border before you've time to get your knife into them. But about my friend here. I *must* give him a word o' mouth to tell him what's come to me, or else he won't know where to go. I would take it more than kind of you if you was to come out of Central India in time to catch him at Marwar Junction, and say to him: 'He has gone South for the week.' He'll know what that means. He's a big man with a red beard, and a great swell he is. You'll find him sleeping like a gentleman with all his luggage round him in a Second-class apartment. But don't you be afraid. Slip down the window and say: 'He has gone South for the week,' and he'll tumble. It's only cutting your time of stay in those parts by two days. I ask you as a stranger – going to the West," he said with emphasis.

"Where have *you* come from?" said I.

"From the East," said he, "and I am hoping that you will give him the message on the Square – for the sake of my Mother as well as your own."

Englishmen are not usually softened by appeals to the memory of their mothers; but for certain reasons, which will be fully apparent, I saw fit to agree.

"It's more than a little matter," said he, "and that's why I asked you to do it – and now I know that I can depend on you doing it. A Second-class carriage at Marwar Junction, and a red-haired man asleep in it. You'll be sure to remember. I get out at the next station, and I must hold on there till he comes or sends me what I want."

"I'll give the message if I catch him," I said, "and for the sake of your Mother as well as mine I'll give you a word of advice. Don't try to run the Central India States just now as the correspondent of the 'Backwoodsman.' There's a real one knocking about here, and it might lead to trouble."

"Thank you," said he simply, "and when will the swine be gone? I can't starve because he's ruining my work. I wanted to get hold of the Degumber Rajah down here about his father's widow, and give him a jump."

"What did he do to his father's widow, then?"

"Filled her up with red pepper and slippered her to death as she hung from a beam. I found that out myself, and I'm the only man that would dare going into the State to get hush-money for it. They'll try to poison me, same as they did in Chortumna when I went on the loot there. But you'll give the man at Marwar Junction my message?"

He got out at a little roadside station, and I reflected. I had heard, more than once, of men personating correspondents of newspapers and bleeding small Native States with threats of exposure, but I had never met any of the caste before. They lead a hard life, and generally die with great suddenness. The Native States have a wholesome horror of English newspapers, which may throw light on their peculiar methods of government, and do their best to choke correspondents with champagne, or drive them out of their mind with four-in-hand barouches. They do not understand that nobody cares a straw for the internal administration of Native States so long as oppression and crime are kept within decent limits, and the ruler is not drugged, drunk, or diseased from one end of the year to the other. They are the dark places of the earth, full of unimaginable cruelty, touching the Railway and the Telegraph on one side, and, on the other, the days of Harun-al-Raschid. When I left the train I did business with divers Kings, and in eight days passed through many changes of life. Sometimes I wore dress–clothes and consorted with Princes and Politicals, drinking from crystal and eating from silver. Sometimes I lay out upon the ground and devoured what I could get, from a plate made of leaves, and drank the running water, and slept under the same rug as my servant. It was all in the day's work.

Then I headed for the Great Indian Desert upon the proper date, as I had promised, and the night Mail set me down at Marwar Junction, where a funny little, happy-go-lucky, native-managed railway runs to Jodhpore. The Bombay Mail from Delhi makes a short halt at Marwar. She arrived as I got in, and I had just time to hurry to her platform and go down the carriages. There was only one Second-class on the train. I slipped the window and looked down upon a flaming red beard, half covered by a railway rug. That was my man, fast asleep, and I dug him gently in the ribs. He woke with a grunt, and I saw his face in the light of the lamps. It was a great and shining face.

"Tickets again?" said he.

"No," said I. "I am to tell you that he is gone South for the week. He has gone South for the week!"

The train had begun to move out. The red man rubbed his eyes. "He has gone South for the week," he repeated. "Now that's just like his impidence. Did he say that I was to give you anything? 'Cause I won't."

"He didn't," I said, and dropped away, and watched the red lights die out in the dark. It was horribly cold because the wind was blowing off the sands. I climbed into my own train – not an Intermediate carriage this time – and went to sleep.

If the man with the beard had given me a rupee I should have kept it as a memento of a rather curious affair. But the consciousness of having done my duty was my only reward.

Later on I reflected that two gentlemen like my friends could not do any good if they foregathered and personated correspondents of newspapers, and might, if they black-mailed one of the little rat-trap states of Central India or Southern Rajputana, get themselves into serious difficulties. I therefore took some trouble to describe them as accurately as I could remember to people who would be interested in deporting them: and succeeded, so I was later informed, in having them headed back from the Degumber borders.

Then I became respectable, and returned to an Office where there were no Kings and no incidents outside the daily manufacture of a newspaper. A newspaper office seems to attract every conceivable sort of person, to the prejudice of discipline. Zenana-mission ladies arrive, and beg that the Editor will instantly abandon all his duties to describe a Christian prize-giving in a back slum of a perfectly inaccessible village; Colonels who have been overpassed for command sit down and sketch the outline of a series of ten, twelve, or twenty-four leading articles on Seniority *versus* Selection; missionaries wish to know why they have not been permitted to escape from their regular vehicles of abuse and swear at a brother-missionary under special patronage of the editorial We; stranded theatrical companies troop up to explain that they cannot pay for their advertisements, but on their return from New Zealand or Tahiti will do so with interest; inventors of patent punkah-pulling machines, carriage couplings and unbreakable swords and axle-trees call with specifications in their pockets and hours at their disposal; tea-companies enter and elaborate their prospectuses with the office pens; secretaries of ball-committees clamour to have the glories of their last dance more fully described; strange ladies rustle in and say: "I want a hundred lady's cards printed *at once*, please," which is manifestly part of an Editor's duty; and every dissolute ruffian that ever tramped the Grand Trunk Road makes it his business to ask for employment as a proof-reader. And, all the time, the telephone-bell is ringing madly, and Kings are being killed on the Continent, and Empires are saying – "You're another," and Mr. Gladstone is calling down brimstone upon the British Dominions, and the little black copy-boys are whining, "*kaa-pi chay-ha-yeh*" (copy wanted) like tired bees, and most of the paper is as blank as Modred's shield.

But that is the amusing part of the year. There are six other months when none ever come to call, and the thermometer walks inch by inch up to the top of the glass, and the office is darkened to just above reading-light, and the press-machines are red-hot of touch, and nobody writes anything but accounts of amusements in the Hill-stations or obituary notices. Then the telephone becomes a tinkling terror, because it tells you of the sudden deaths of men and women that you knew intimately, and the prickly-heat covers you with a garment, and you sit down and write: "A slight increase of sickness is reported from the Khuda Janta Khan District. The outbreak is purely sporadic in its nature, and, thanks to the energetic efforts of the District authorities, is now almost at an end. It is, however, with deep regret we record the death," etc.

Then the sickness really breaks out, and the less recording and reporting the better for the peace of the subscribers. But the Empires and the Kings continue to divert themselves as selfishly as before, and the Foreman thinks that a daily paper really ought to come out once in twenty-four hours, and all the people at the Hill-stations in the middle of their amusements say: "Good gracious! Why can't the paper be sparkling? I'm sure there's plenty going on up here."

That is the dark half of the moon, and, as the advertisements say, "must be experienced to be appreciated."

It was in that season, and a remarkably evil season, that the paper began running the last issue of the week on Saturday night, which is to say Sunday morning, after the custom of a London paper. This was a great convenience, for immediately after the paper was put to bed, the dawn would lower the thermometer from 96° to almost 84° for half an hour, and in that chill – you have no idea how cold is 84° on the grass until you begin to pray for it – a very tired man could get off to sleep ere the heat roused him.

One Saturday night it was my pleasant duty to put the paper to bed alone. A King or courtier or a courtesan or a

Community was going to die or get a new Constitution, or do something that was important on the other side of the world, and the paper was to be held open till the latest possible minute in order to catch the telegram.

It was a pitchy-black night, as stifling as a June night can be, and the *loo*, the red-hot wind from the westward, was booming among the tinder-dry trees and pretending that the rain was on its heels. Now and again a spot of almost boiling water would fall on the dust with the flop of a frog, but all our weary world knew that was only pretence. It was a shade cooler in the press-room than the office, so I sat there, while the type ticked and clicked, and the night-jars hooted at the windows, and the all but naked compositors wiped the sweat from their foreheads, and called for water. The thing that was keeping us back, whatever it was, would not come off, though the *loo* dropped and the last type was set, and the whole round earth stood still in the choking heat, with its finger on its lip, to wait the event. I drowsed, and wondered whether the telegraph was a blessing, and whether this dying man, or struggling people, might be aware of the inconvenience the delay was causing. There was no special reason beyond the heat and worry to make tension, but, as the clock-hands crept up to three o'clock and the machines spun their fly-wheels two and three times to see that all was in order, before I said the word that would set them off, I could have shrieked aloud.

Then the roar and rattle of the wheels shivered the quiet into little bits. I rose to go away, but two men in white clothes stood in front of me. The first one said: "It's him!" The second said: "So it is!" And they both laughed almost as loudly as the machinery roared, and mopped their foreheads. "We seed there was a light burning across the road, and we were sleeping in that ditch there for coolness, and I said to my friend here, 'The office is open. Let's come along and speak to him as turned us back from the Degumber State,' " said the smaller of the two. He was the man I had met in the Mhow train, and his fellow was the red-bearded man of Marwar Junction. There was no mistaking the eyebrows of the one or the beard of the other.

I was not pleased, because I wished to go to sleep, not to squabble with loafers. "What do you want?" I asked.

"Half an hour's talk with you, cool and comfortable, in the office," said the red-bearded man. "We'd *like* some drink – the Contrack doesn't begin yet, Peachey, so you needn't look – but what we really want is advice. We don't want money. We ask you as a favour, because we found out you did us a bad turn about Degumber State."

I led from the press-room to the stifling office with the maps on the walls, and the red-haired man rubbed his hands. "That's something like," said he. "This was the proper shop to come to. Now, Sir, let me introduce to you Brother Peachey Carnehan, that's him, and Brother Daniel Dravot, that is *me*, and the less said about our professions the better, for we have been most things in our time. Soldier, sailor, compositor, photographer, proof-reader, street-preacher, and correspondents of the 'Backwoodsman' when we thought the paper wanted one. Carnehan is sober, and so am I. Look at us first, and see that's sure. It will save you cutting into my talk. We'll take one of your cigars apiece, and you shall see us light up."

I watched the test. The men were absolutely sober, so I gave them each a tepid whisky and soda.

"Well *and* good," said Carnehan of the eyebrows, wiping the froth from his moustache. "Let me talk now, Dan. We have been all over India, mostly on foot. We have been boiler-fitters, engine-drivers, petty contractors, and all that, and we have decided that India isn't big enough for such as us."

They certainly were too big for the office. Dravot's beard seemed to fill half the room and Carnehan's shoulders the other half, as they sat on the big table. Carnehan continued: "The country isn't half worked out because they that governs it won't let you touch it. They spend all their blessed time in governing it, and you can't lift a spade, nor chip a rock, nor look for oil, nor anything like that without all the Government saying – 'Leave it alone, and let us govern.' Therefore, such *as* it is, we will let it alone, and go away to some other place where a man isn't crowded and can come to his own. We are not little men, and there is nothing that we are afraid of except Drink, and we have signed a Contrack on that. *Therefore*, we are going away to be Kings."

"Kings in our own right," muttered Dravot.

"Yes, of course," I said. "You've been tramping in the sun, and it's a very warm night, and hadn't you better sleep over the notion? Come to-morrow."

"Neither drunk nor sunstruck," said Dravot. "We have slept over the notion half a year, and require to see Books and Atlases, and we have decided that there is only one place now in the world that two strong men can Sar-a-*whack*. They call it Kafiristan. By my reckoning it's the top right-hand corner of Afghanistan, not more than three hundred miles from Peshawar. They have two-and-thirty heathen idols there, and we'll be the thirty-third and -fourth. It's a mountaineous country, and the women of those parts are very beautiful."

"But that is provided against in the Contrack," said Carnehan. "Neither Woman nor Liqu-or, Daniel."

"And that's all we know, except that no one has gone there, and they fight, and in any place where they fight a man who knows how to drill men can always be a King. We shall go to those parts and say to any King we find – 'D'you want to vanquish your foes?' and we will show him how to drill men; for that we know better than anything else. Then we will subvert that King and seize his Throne and establish a Dy-nasty."

"You'll be cut to pieces before you're fifty miles across the Border," I said. "You have to travel through Afghanistan to get to that country. It's one mass of mountains and peaks and glaciers, and no Englishman has been through it. The people are utter brutes, and even if you reached them you couldn't do anything."

"That's more like," said Carnehan. "If you could think us a little more mad we would be more pleased. We have come to you to know about this country, to read a book about it, and to be shown maps. We want you to tell us that we are fools and to show us your books." He turned to the bookcases.

"Are you at all in earnest?" I said.

"A little," said Dravot sweetly. "As big a map as you have got, even if it's all blank where Kafiristan is, and any books you've got. We can read, though we aren't very educated."

I uncased the big thirty-two-miles-to-the-inch map of India, and two smaller Frontier maps, hauled down volume INF–KAN of the "Encyclopædia Britannica," and the men consulted them.

"See here!" said Dravot, his thumb on the map. "Up to Jagdallak, Peachey and me know the road. We was there with Roberts' Army. We'll have to turn off to the right at Jagdallak through Laghmann territory. Then we get among the hills – fourteen thousand feet – fifteen thousand – it will be cold work there, but it don't look very far on the map."

I handed him Wood on the "Sources of the Oxus." Carnehan was deep in the "Encyclopædia."

"They're a mixed lot," said Dravot reflectively; "and it won't help us to know the names of their tribes. The more tribes the more they'll fight, and the better for us. From Jagdallak to Ashang. H'mm!"

"But all the information about the country is as sketchy and inaccurate as can be," I protested. "No one knows anything about it really. Here's the file of the 'United Services' Institute.' Read what Bellew says."

"Blow Bellew!" said Carnehan. "Dan, they're a stinkin' lot of heathens, but this book here says they think they're related to us English."

I smoked while the men pored over "Raverty," "Wood," the maps, and the "Encyclopædia."

"There is no use your waiting," said Dravot politely. "It's about four o'clock now. We'll go before six o'clock if you want to sleep, and we won't steal any of the papers. Don't you sit up. We're two harmless lunatics, and if you come to-morrow evening down to the Serai we'll say good-bye to you."

"You *are* two fools," I answered. "You'll be turned back at the Frontier or cut up the minute you set foot in Afghanistan. Do you want any money or a recommendation down-country? I can help you to the chance of work next week."

"Next week we shall be hard at work ourselves, thank you," said Dravot. "It isn't so easy being a King as it looks. When we've got our Kingdom in going order we'll let you know, and you can come up and help us to govern it."

"Would two lunatics make a Contrack like that?" said Carnehan, with subdued pride, showing me a greasy half-sheet of notepaper on which was written the following. I copied it, then and there, as a curiosity —

This Contract between me and you persuing witnesseth in the name of God — Amen and so forth.

(*One*) *That me and you will settle this matter together; i.e., to be Kings of Kafiristan.*

(*Two*) *That you and me will not, while this matter is being settled, look at any Liquor, nor any Woman black, white, or brown, so as to get mixed up with one or the other harmful.*

(*Three*) *That we conduct ourselves with Dignity and Discretion, and if one of us gets into trouble the other will stay by him.*

Signed by you and me this day.
Peachey Taliaferro Carnehan.
Daniel Dravot.
Both Gentlemen at Large.

"There was no need for the last article," said Carnehan, blushing modestly; "but it looks regular. Now you know the sort of men that loafers are — we *are* loafers, Dan, until we get out of India — and *do* you think that we would sign a

Contrack like that unless we was in earnest? We have kept away from the two things that make life worth having."

"You won't enjoy your lives much longer if you are going to try this idiotic adventure. Don't set the office on fire," I said, "and go away before nine o'clock."

I left them still poring over the maps and making notes on the back of the "Contrack." "Be sure to come down to the Serai to-morrow," were their parting words.

The Kumharsen Serai is the great four-square sink of humanity where the strings of camels and horses from the North load and unload. All the nationalities of Central Asia may be found there, and most of the folk of India proper. Balkh and Bokhara there meet Bengal and Bombay, and try to draw eye-teeth. You can buy ponies, turquoises, Persian pussy-cats, saddle-bags, fat-tailed sheep and musk in the Kumharsen Serai, and get many strange things for nothing. In the afternoon I went down to see whether my friends intended to keep their word or were lying there drunk.

A priest attired in fragments of ribbons and rags stalked up to me, gravely twisting a child's paper whirligig. Behind him was his servant bending under the load of a crate of mud toys. The two were loading up two camels, and the inhabitants of the Serai watched them with shrieks of laughter.

"The priest is mad," said a horse-dealer to me. "He is going up to Kabul to sell toys to the Amir. He will either be raised to honour or have his head cut off. He came in here this morning and has been behaving madly ever since."

"The witless are under the protection of God," stammered a flat-cheeked Usbeg in broken Hindi. "They foretell future events."

"Would they could have foretold that my caravan would have been cut up by the Shinwaris almost within shadow of the Pass!" grunted the Eusufzai agent of a Rajputana trading-house whose goods had been diverted into the hands of other robbers just across the Border, and whose misfortunes were the laughing-stock of the bazar. "Ohé, priest, whence come you and whither do you go?"

"From Roum have I come," shouted the priest, waving his whirligig; "from Roum, blown by the breath of a hundred devils across the sea! O thieves, robbers, liars, the blessing of Pir Khan on pigs, dogs, and perjurers! Who will take the Protected of God to the North to sell charms that are never still to the Amir? The camels shall not gall, the sons shall not fall sick, and the wives shall remain faithful while they are away, of the men who give me place in their caravan. Who will assist me to slipper the King of the Roos with a golden slipper with a silver heel? The protection of Pir Khan be upon his labours!" He spread out the skirts of his gaberdine and pirouetted between the lines of tethered horses.

"There starts a caravan from Peshawar to Kabul in twenty days, *Huzrut*," said the Eusufzai trader. "My camels go therewith. Do thou also go and bring us good luck."

"I will go even now!" shouted the priest. "I will depart upon my winged camels, and be at Peshawar in a day! Ho! Hazar Mir Khan," he yelled to his servant, "drive out the camels, but let me first mount my own."

He leaped on the back of his beast as it knelt, and, turning round to me, cried: "Come thou also, Sahib, a little along the road, and I will sell thee a charm – an amulet that shall make thee King of Kafiristan."

Then the light broke upon me, and I followed the two camels out of the Serai till we reached open road and the priest halted.

"What d'you think o' that?" said he in English. "Carnehan can't talk their patter, so I've made him my servant. He makes a handsome servant. 'Tisn't for nothing that I've been knocking about the country for fourteen years. Didn't I do that talk neat? We'll hitch on to a caravan at Peshawar till we get to Jagdallak, and then we'll see if we can get donkeys for our camels, and strike into Kafiristan. Whirligigs for the Amir, O Lor! Put your hand under the camel-bags and tell me what you feel."

I felt the butt of a Martini, and another and another.

"Twenty of 'em," said Dravot placidly. "Twenty of 'em and ammunition to correspond, under the whirligigs and the mud dolls."

"Heaven help you if you are caught with those things!" I said. "A Martini is worth her weight in silver among the Pathans."

"Fifteen hundred rupees of capital – every rupee we could beg, borrow, or steal – are invested on these two camels," said Dravot. "We won't get caught. We're going through the Khaiber with a regular caravan. Who'd touch a poor mad priest?"

"Have you got everything you want?" I asked, overcome with astonishment.

"Not yet, but we shall soon. Give us a memento of your kindness, *Brother*. You did me a service yesterday, and that time in Marwar. Half my Kingdom shall you have, as the saying is." I slipped a small charm compass from my watch-chain and handed it up to the priest.

"Good-bye," said Dravot, giving me his hand cautiously. "It's the last time we'll shake hands with an Englishman these many days. Shake hands with him, Carnehan," he cried, as the second camel passed me.

Carnehan leaned down and shook hands. Then the camels passed away along the dusty road, and I was left alone to wonder. My eye could detect no failure in the disguises. The scene in the Serai proved that they were complete to the native mind. There was just the chance, therefore, that Carnehan and Dravot would be able to wander through Afghanistan without detection. But, beyond, they would find death – certain and awful death.

Ten days later a native correspondent, giving me the news of the day from Peshawar, wound up his letter with: "There has been much laughter here on account of a certain mad priest who is going in his estimation to sell petty gauds and insignificant trinkets which he ascribes as great charms to H. H. the Amir of Bokhara. He passed through Peshawar and associated himself to the Second Summer caravan that goes to

Kabul. The merchants are pleased because through superstition they imagine that such mad fellows bring good fortune."

The two, then, were beyond the Border. I would have prayed for them, but, that night, a real King died in Europe, and demanded an obituary notice.

* * *

The wheel of the world swings through the same phases again and again. Summer passed and winter thereafter, and came and passed again. The daily paper continued, and I with it, and upon the third summer there fell a hot night, a night-issue, and a strained waiting for something to be telegraphed from the other side of the world, exactly as had happened before. A few great men had died in the past two years, the machines worked with more clatter, and some of the trees in the Office garden were a few feet taller. But that was all the difference.

I passed over to the press-room, and went through just such a scene as I have already described. The nervous tension was stronger than it had been two years before, and I felt the heat more acutely. At three o'clock I cried, "Print off," and turned to go, when there crept to my chair what was left of a man. He was bent into a circle, his head was sunk between his shoulders, and he moved his feet one over the other like a bear. I could hardly see whether he walked or crawled – this rag-wrapped, whining cripple who addressed me by name, crying that he was come back. "Can you give me a drink?" he whimpered. "For the Lord's sake, give me a drink!"

I went back to the office, the man following with groans of pain, and I turned up the lamp.

"Don't you know me?" he gasped, dropping into a chair, and he turned his drawn face, surmounted by a shock of grey hair, to the light.

I looked at him intently. Once before had I seen eyebrows that met over the nose in an inch-broad black band, but for the life of me I could not tell where.

"I don't know you," I said, handing him the whisky. "What can I do for you?"

He took a gulp of the spirit raw, and shivered in spite of the suffocating heat.

"I've come back," he repeated; "and I was the King of Kafiristan – me and Dravot – crowned Kings we was! In this office we settled it – you setting there and giving us the books. I am Peachey – Peachey Taliaferro Carnehan, and you've been setting here ever since – O Lord!"

I was more than a little astonished, and expressed my feelings accordingly.

"It's true," said Carnehan, with a dry cackle, nursing his feet, which were wrapped in rags. "True as gospel. Kings we were, with crowns upon our heads – me and Dravot – poor Dan – oh, poor, poor Dan, that would never take advice, not though I begged of him!"

"Take the whisky," I said, "and take your own time. Tell me all you can recollect of everything from beginning to end. You got across the border on your camels. Dravot dressed as a mad priest and you his servant. Do you remember that?"

"I ain't mad – yet, but I shall be that way soon. Of course I remember. Keep looking at me, or maybe my words will go all to pieces. Keep looking at me in my eyes, and don't say anything."

I leaned forward and looked into his face as steadily as I could. He dropped one hand upon the table and I grasped it by the wrist. It was twisted like a bird's claw, and upon the back was a ragged, red, diamond-shaped scar.

"No, don't look there. Look at me," said Carnehan. "That comes afterwards, but for the Lord's sake don't distrack me! We left with that caravan, me and Dravot playing all sorts of antics to amuse the people we were with. Dravot used to make us laugh in the evenings when all the people was cooking their dinners – cooking their dinners, and . . . what did they do then? They lit little fires with sparks that went into Dravot's beard, and we all laughed – fit to die. Little red fires they was, going into Dravot's big red beard – so funny." His eyes left mine, and he smiled foolishly.

"You went as far as Jagdallak with that caravan," I said at a venture, "after you had lit those fires. To Jagdallak, where you turned off to try to get into Kafiristan."

"No, we didn't neither. What are you talking about? We turned off before Jagdallak, because we heard the roads was good. But they wasn't good enough for our two camels – mine and Dravot's. When we left the caravan, Dravot took off all his clothes and mine too, and said we would be heathen, because the Kafirs didn't allow Mohammedans to talk to them. So we dressed betwixt and between, and such a sight as Daniel Dravot I never saw yet nor expect to see again. He burned half his beard, and slung a sheepskin over his shoulder, and shaved his head into patterns. He shaved mine, too, and made me wear outrageous things to look like a heathen. That was in a most mountaineous country, and our camels couldn't go along any more because of the mountains. They were tall and black, and coming home I saw them fight like wild goats – there are lots of goats in Kafiristan. And these mountains, they never keep still, no more than the goats. Always fighting they are, and don't let you sleep at night."

"Take some more whisky," I said very slowly. "What did you and Daniel Dravot do when the camels could go no further because of the rough roads that led into Kafiristan?"

"What did which do? There was a party called Peachey Taliaferro Carnehan that was with Dravot. Shall I tell you about him? He died out there in the cold. Slap from the bridge fell old Peachey, turning and twisting in the air like a penny whirligig that you can sell to the Amir. No; they was two for three ha'pence, those whirligigs, or I am much mistaken and woeful sore . . . And then these camels were no use, and Peachey said to Dravot – 'For the Lord's sake let's get out of this before our heads are chopped off,' and with that they killed the camels all among the mountains, not having anything in particular to eat, but first they took off the boxes with the guns and the ammunition, till two men came along driving four mules. Dravot up and dances in front of them, singing – 'Sell me four mules.' Says the first man – 'If you are rich enough to buy, you are rich enough to rob;' but before ever he could put his hand to his knife, Dravot breaks his neck over his knee, and the other party runs away. So Carnehan loaded the mules with the rifles that was taken off the camels, and together we starts forward into those bitter cold mountaineous parts, and never a road broader than the back of your hand."

He paused for a moment, while I asked him if he could remember the nature of the country through which he had journeyed.

"I am telling you as straight as I can, but my head isn't as good as it might be. They drove nails through it to make me hear better how Dravot died. The country was mountaineous and the mules were most contrary, and the inhabitants was dispersed and solitary. They went up and up, and down and down, and that other party, Carnehan, was imploring of Dravot not to sing and whistle so loud, for fear of bringing down the tremenjus avalanches. But Dravot says that if a King couldn't sing it wasn't worth being King, and whacked the mules over the rump, and never took no heed for ten cold days. We came to a big level valley all among the mountains, and the mules were near dead, so we killed them, not having anything in special for them or us to eat. We sat upon the boxes, and played odd and even with the cartridges that was jolted out.

"Then ten men with bows and arrows ran down that valley, chasing twenty men with bows and arrows, and the row was tremenjus. They was fair men – fairer than you or me – with yellow hair and remarkable well built. Says Dravot, unpacking the guns – 'This is the beginning of the business. We'll fight for the ten men,' and with that he fires two rifles at the twenty men, and drops one of them at two hundred yards from the rock where he was sitting. The other men began to run, but Carnehan and Dravot sits on the boxes picking them off at all ranges, up and down the valley. Then we goes up to the ten men that had run across the snow too, and they fires a footy little arrow at us. Dravot he shoots above their heads, and they all falls down flat. Then he walks over them and kicks them, and then he lifts them up and shakes hands all round to make them friendly like. He calls them and gives them the boxes to carry, and waves his hand for all the world as though he was King already. They takes the boxes and him across the valley and up the hill into a pine wood on the top, where there was half a dozen big stone idols. Dravot he goes to the biggest – a fellow they call Imbra – and lays a rifle and a cartridge at his feet, rubbing his nose respectful with his own nose, patting him on the head, and saluting in front of it. He turns round to the men and nods his head, and says – 'That's all right. I'm in the know too, and all these old jim-jams are my friends.' Then he opens his mouth and points down it, and when the first man brings him food, he says – 'No;' and when the second man brings him food he says – 'No;' but when one of the old priests and the boss of the village brings him food, he says – 'Yes;' very haughty, and eats it slow. That was how we came to our first village, without any trouble, just as though we had tumbled from the skies. But we tumbled from one of those damned rope-bridges, you see, and – you couldn't expect a man to laugh much after that?"

"Take some more whisky and go on," I said. "That was the first village you came into. How did you get to be King?"

"I wasn't King," said Carnehan. "Dravot he was the King, and a handsome man he looked with the gold crown on his head, and all. Him and the other party stayed in that village, and every morning Dravot sat by the side of old Imbra, and the people came and worshipped. That was Dravot's order. Then a lot of men came into the valley, and Carnehan and Dravot picks them off with the rifles before they knew where they was, and runs down into the valley and up again the other side and finds another village, same as the first one, and the people all falls down flat on their faces, and Dravot says –

'Now what is the trouble between you two villages?' and the people points to a woman, as fair as you or me, that was carried off, and Dravot takes her back to the first village and counts up the dead – eight there was. For each dead man Dravot pours a little milk on the ground and waves his arms like a whirligig, and 'That's all right,' says he. Then he and Carnehan takes the big boss of each village by the arm and walks them down into the valley, and shows them how to scratch a line with a spear right down the valley, and gives each a sod of turf from both sides of the line. Then all the people comes down and shouts like the devil and all, and Dravot says – 'Go and dig the land, and be fruitful and multiply,' which they did, though they didn't understand. Then we asks the names of things in their lingo – bread and water and fire and idols and such, and Dravot leads the priest of each village up to the idol, and says he must sit there and judge the people, and if anything goes wrong he is to be shot.

"Next week they was all turning up the land in the valley as quiet as bees and much prettier, and the priests heard all the complaints and told Dravot in dumb show what it was about. 'That's just the beginning,' says Dravot. 'They think we're Gods.' He and Carnehan picks out twenty good men and shows them how to click off a rifle, and form fours, and advance in line, and they was very pleased to do so, and clever to see the hang of it. Then he takes out his pipe and his baccy-pouch and leaves one at one village, and one at the other, and off we two goes to see what was to be done in the next valley. That was all rock, and there was a little village there, and Carnehan says – 'Send 'em to the old valley to plant,' and takes 'em there and gives 'em some land that wasn't took before. They were a poor lot, and we blooded 'em with a kid before letting 'em into the new Kingdom. That was to impress the people, and then they settled down quiet, and Carnehan went back to Dravot, who had got into another valley, all snow and ice and most mountaineous. There was no people there, and the Army got afraid, so Dravot shoots one of them, and goes on till he finds some people in a village, and the Army explains that unless the people wants to be killed they had better not shoot their little matchlocks; for they had matchlocks. We makes friends with the priest, and I stays there alone with two of the Army, teaching the men how to drill; and a thundering big Chief comes across the snow with kettle-drums and horns twanging, because he heard there was a new God kicking about. Carnehan sights for the brown of the men half a mile across the snow and wings one of them. Then he sends a message to the Chief that, unless he wished to be killed, he must come and shake hands with me and leave his arms behind. The Chief comes alone first, and Carnehan shakes hands with him and whirls his arms about, same as Dravot used, and very much surprised that Chief was, and strokes my eyebrows. Then Carnehan goes alone to the Chief, and asks him in dumb show if he had an enemy he hated. 'I have,' says the Chief. So Carnehan weeds out the pick of his men, and sets the two of the Army to show them drill, and at the end of two weeks the men can manœuvre about as well as Volunteers. So he marches with the Chief to a great big plain on the top of a mountain, and the Chief's men rushes into a village and takes it; we three Martinis firing into the brown of the enemy. So we took that village too, and I gives the Chief a rag from my coat and says, 'Occupy till I come;' which was scriptural. By way of a reminder, when me and the Army was eighteen hundred yards away, I drops a bullet near him standing on the snow, and all the people falls flat on their faces. Then I sends a letter to Dravot wherever he be by land or by sea."

At the risk of throwing the creature out of train, I interrupted – "How could you write a letter up yonder?"

"The letter? – Oh! – The letter! Keep looking at me between the eyes, please. It was a string-talk letter, that we'd learned the way of it from a blind beggar in the Punjab."

I remember that there had once come to the office a blind man with a knotted twig and a piece of string which he wound round the twig according to some cipher of his own.

He could, after the lapse of days or hours, repeat the sentence which he had reeled up. He had reduced the alphabet to eleven primitive sounds; and he tried to teach me his method, but I could not understand.

"I sent that letter to Dravot," said Carnehan; "and told him to come back because this Kingdom was growing too big for me to handle, and then I struck for the first valley, to see how the priests were working. They called the village we took along with the Chief, Bashkai, and the first village we took, Er-Heb. The priests at Er-Heb was doing all right, but they had a lot of pending cases about land to show me, and some men from another village had been firing arrows at night. I went out and looked for that village, and fired four rounds at it from a thousand yards. That used all the cartridges I cared to spend, and I waited for Dravot, who had been away two or three months, and I kept my people quiet.

"One morning I heard the devil's own noise of drums and horns, and Dan Dravot marches down the hill with his Army and a tail of hundreds of men, and, which was the most amazing, a great gold crown on his head. 'My Gord, Carnehan,' says Daniel, 'this is a tremenjus business, and we've got the whole country as far as it's worth having. I am the son of Alexander by Queen Semiramis, and you're my younger brother and a God too! It's the biggest thing we've ever seen. I've been marching and fighting for six weeks with the Army, and every footy little village for fifty miles has come in rejoiceful; and more than that, I've got the key of the whole show, as you'll see, and I've got a crown for you! I told 'em to make two of 'em at a place called Shu, where the gold lies in the rock like suet in mutton. Gold I've seen, and turquoise I've kicked out of the cliffs, and there's garnets in the sands of the river, and here's a chunk of amber that a man brought me. Call up all the priests and, here, take your crown.'

"One of the men opens a black hair bag, and I slips the crown on. It was too small and too heavy, but I wore it for the glory. Hammered gold it was – five pound weight, like a hoop of a barrel.

" 'Peachey,' says Dravot, 'we don't want to fight no more. The Craft's the trick, so help me!' and he brings forward that same Chief that I left at Bashkai – Billy Fish we called him afterwards, because he was so like Billy Fish that drove the big tank-engine at Mach on the Bolan in the old days. 'Shake hands with him,' says Dravot, and I shook hands and nearly dropped, for Billy Fish gave me the Grip. I said nothing, but tried him with the Fellow Craft Grip. He answers all right, and I tried the Master's Grip, but that was a slip. 'A Fellow Craft he is!' I says to Dan. 'Does he know the word?' – 'He does,' says Dan, 'and all the priests know. It's a miracle! The Chiefs and the priests can work a Fellow Craft Lodge in a way that's very like ours, and they've cut the marks on the rocks, but they don't know the Third Degree, and they've come to find out. It's Gord's Truth. I've known these long years that the Afghans knew up to the Fellow Craft Degree, but this is a miracle. A God and a Grand-Master of the Craft am I, and a Lodge in the Third Degree I will open, and we'll raise the head priests and the Chiefs of the villages.'

" 'It's against all the law,' I says, 'holding a Lodge without warrant from any one; and you know we never held office in any Lodge.'

" 'It's a master-stroke o' policy,' says Dravot. 'It means running the country as easy as a four-wheeled bogie on a down grade. We can't stop to enquire now, or they'll turn against us. I've forty Chiefs at my heel, and passed and raised according to their merit they shall be. Billet these men on the villages, and see that we run up a Lodge of some kind. The temple of Imbra will do for the Lodge-room. The women must make aprons as you show them. I'll hold a levee of Chiefs to-night and Lodge to-morrow.'

"I was fair run off my legs, but I wasn't such a fool as not to see what a pull this Craft business gave us. I showed the priests' families how to make aprons of the degrees, but for Dravot's apron the blue border and marks was made of turquoise lumps on white hide, not cloth. We took a great square stone in the temple for the Master's chair, and little stones for the officers' chairs, and painted the black pavement with white squares, and did what we could to make things regular.

"At the levee which was held that night on the hill-side with big bonfires, Dravot gives out that him and me were Gods and sons of Alexander, and Past Grand-Masters in the Craft, and was come to make Kafiristan a country where every man should eat in peace and drink in quiet, and specially obey us. Then the Chiefs come round to shake hands, and they were so hairy and white and fair it was just shaking hands with old friends. We gave them names according as they was like men we had known in India – Billy Fish, Holly Dilworth, Pikky Kergan, that was Bazar-master when I was at Mhow, and so on, and so on.

"*The* most amazing miracles was at Lodge next night. One of the old priests was watching us continuous, and I felt uneasy, for I knew we'd have to fudge the Ritual, and I didn't know what the men knew. The old priest was a stranger come in from beyond the village of Bashkai. The minute Dravot puts on the Master's apron that the girls had made for him, the priest fetches a whoop and a howl, and tries to overturn the stone that Dravot was sitting on. 'It's all up now,' I says. 'That comes of meddling with the Craft without warrant!' Dravot never winked an eye, not when ten priests took and tilted over the Grand-Master's chair – which was to say the stone of Imbra. The priest begins rubbing the bottom end of it to clear away the black dirt, and presently he shows all the other priests the Master's Mark, same as was on Dravot's apron, cut into the stone. Not even the priests of the temple of Imbra knew it was there. The old chap falls flat on his face at Dravot's feet and kisses 'em. 'Luck again,' says Dravot, across the Lodge to me; 'they say it's the missing Mark that no one could understand the why of. We're more than safe now.' Then he bangs the butt of his gun for a gavel and says: 'By virtue of the authority vested in me by my own right hand and the help of Peachey, I declare myself

Grand-Master of all Freemasonry in Kafiristan in this the Mother Lodge o' the country, and King of Kafiristan equally with Peachey!' At that he puts on his crown and I puts on mine – I was doing Senior Warden – and we opens the Lodge in most ample form. It was a amazing miracle! The priests moved in Lodge through the first two degrees almost without telling, as if the memory was coming back to them. After that, Peachey and Dravot raised such as was worthy – high priests and Chiefs of far-off villages. Billy Fish was the first, and I can tell you we scared the soul out of him. It was not in any way according to Ritual, but it served our turn. We didn't raise more than ten of the biggest men, because we didn't want to make the Degree common. And they was clamouring to be raised.

" 'In another six months,' says Dravot, 'we'll hold another Communication, and see how you are working.' Then he asks them about their villages, and learns that they was fighting one against the other, and were sick and tired of it. And when they wasn't doing that they was fighting with the Mohammedans. 'You can fight those when they come into our country,' says Dravot. 'Tell off every tenth man of your tribes for a Frontier guard, and send two hundred at a time to this valley to be drilled. Nobody is going to be shot or speared any more so long as he does well, and I know that you won't cheat me, because you're white people – sons of Alexander – and not like common, black Mohammedans. You are *my* people, and by God,' says he, running off into English at the end – 'I'll make a damned fine Nation of you, or I'll die in the making!'

"I can't tell all we did for the next six months, because Dravot did a lot I couldn't see the hang of, and he learned their lingo in a way I never could. My work was to help the people plough, and now and again go out with some of the Army and see what the other villages were doing, and make 'em throw rope-bridges across the ravines which cut up the country horrid. Dravot was very kind to me, but when he walked up and down in the pine wood pulling that bloody red beard of his with both fists I knew he was thinking plans I could not advise about, and I just waited for orders.

"But Dravot never showed me disrespect before the people. They were afraid of me and the Army, but they loved Dan. He was the best of friends with the priests and the Chiefs; but any one could come across the hills with a complaint, and Dravot would hear him out fair, and call four priests together and say what was to be done. He used to call in Billy Fish from Bashkai, and Pikky Kergan from Shu, and an old Chief we called Kafuzelum – it was like enough to his real name – and hold councils with 'em when there was any fighting to be done in small villages. That was his Council of War, and the four priests of Bashkai, Shu, Khawak, and Madora was his Privy Council. Between the lot of 'em they sent me, with forty men and twenty rifles, and sixty men carrying turquoises, into the Ghorband country to buy those hand-made Martini rifles, that come out of the Amir's workshops at Kabul, from one of the Amir's Herati regiments that would have sold the very teeth out of their mouths for turquoises.

"I stayed in Ghorband a month, and gave the Governor there the pick of my baskets for hush-money, and bribed the Colonel of the regiment some more, and, between the two and the tribes-people, we got more than a hundred hand-made Martinis, a hundred good Kohat Jezails that'll throw to six hundred yards, and forty man-loads of very bad ammunition for the rifles. I came back with what I had, and distributed 'em among the men that the Chiefs sent in to me to drill. Dravot was too busy to attend to those things, but the old Army that we first made helped me, and we turned out five hundred men that could drill, and two hundred that knew how to hold arms pretty straight. Even those corkscrewed, hand-made guns was a miracle to them. Dravot talked big about powder-shops and factories, walking up and down in the pine wood when the winter was coming on.

" 'I won't make a Nation,' says he; 'I'll make an Empire! These men aren't niggers; they're English! Look at their eyes – look at their mouths. Look at the way they stand up. They sit on chairs in their own houses. They're the Lost Tribes, or something like it, and they've grown to be English. I'll take a census in the spring if the priests don't get frightened. There must be a fair two million of 'em in these hills. The villages are full o' little children. Two million people – two hundred and fifty thousand fighting men – and all English! They only want the rifles and a little drilling. Two hundred and fifty thousand men ready to cut in on Russia's right flank when she tries for India! Peachey, man,' he says, chewing his beard in great hunks, 'we shall be Emperors – Emperors of the Earth! Rajah Brooke will be a suckling to us. I'll treat with the Viceroy on equal terms. I'll ask him to send me twelve picked English – twelve that I know of – to help us govern a bit. There's Mackray, Sergeant-pensioner at Segowli – many's the good dinner he's given me, and his wife a pair of trousers. There's Donkin, the Warder of Tounghoo Jail; there's hundreds that I could lay my hand on if I was in India. The Viceroy shall do it for me; I'll send a man through in the spring for those men, and I'll write for a dispensation from the Grand Lodge for what I've done as Grand-Master. That – and all the Sniders that'll be thrown out when the native troops in India take up the Martini. They'll be worn smooth, but they'll do for fighting in these hills. Twelve English, a hundred thousand Sniders run through the Amir's country in driblets – I'd be content with twenty thousand in one year – and we'd be an Empire. When everything was shipshape, I'd hand over the crown – this crown I'm wearing now – to Queen Victoria on my knees, and she'd say: "Rise up, Sir Daniel Dravot." Oh, it's big! It's big, I tell you! But there's so much to be done in every place – Bashkai, Khawak, Shu, and everywhere else.'

" 'What is it?' I says. 'There are no more men coming in to be drilled this autumn. Look at those fat, black clouds. They're bringing the snow.'

" 'It isn't that,' says Daniel, putting his hand very hard on my shoulder; 'and I don't wish to say anything that's against you, for no other living man would have followed me and made me what I am as you have done. You're a first-class Commander-in-Chief, and the people know you; but – it's a big country, and somehow you can't help me, Peachey, in the way I want to be helped.'

" 'Go to your blasted priests, then!' I said, and I was sorry when I made that remark, but it did hurt me sore to find Daniel talking so superior when I'd drilled all the men, and done all he told me.

" 'Don't let's quarrel, Peachey,' says Daniel, without curs-ing. 'You're a King too, and the half of this Kingdom is yours; but can't you see, Peachey, we want cleverer men than us now – three or four of 'em, that we can scatter about for our Deputies. It's a hugeous great State, and I can't always tell the right thing to do, and I haven't time for all I want to do, and here's the winter coming on, and all.' He put half his beard into his mouth, all red like the gold of his crown.

" 'I'm sorry, Daniel,' says I. 'I've done all I could. I've drilled the men and shown the people how to stack their oats better; and I've brought in those tinware rifles from Ghor-band – but I know what you're driving at. I take it Kings always feel oppressed that way.'

" 'There's another thing too,' says Dravot, walking up and down. 'The winter's coming, and these people won't be giv-ing much trouble, and if they do we can't move about. I want a wife.'

" 'For Gord's sake leave the women alone!' I says. 'We've both got all the work we can, though I *am* a fool. Remember the Contrack, and keep clear o' women.'

" 'The Contrack only lasted till such time as we was Kings; and Kings we have been these months past,' says Dravot, weighing his crown in his hand. 'You go get a wife too, Peachey – a nice, strappin', plump girl that'll keep you warm in the winter. They're prettier than English girls, and we can take the pick of 'em. Boil 'em once or twice in hot water, and they'll come out like chicken and ham.'

" 'Don't tempt me!' I says. 'I will not have any dealings with a woman not till we are a dam' side more settled than we are now. I've been doing the work o' two men, and you've been doing the work o' three. Let's lie off a bit, and see if we can get some better tobacco from Afghan country and run in some good liquor; but no women.'

" 'Who's talking o' *women*?' says Dravot. 'I said *wife* – a Queen to breed a King's son for the King. A Queen out of the strongest tribe, that'll make them your blood-brothers, and that'll lie by your side and tell you all the people thinks about you and their own affairs. That's what I want.'

" 'Do you remember that Bengali woman I kept at Mogul Serai when I was a plate-layer?' says I. 'A fat lot o' good she was to me. She taught me the lingo and one or two other things; but what happened? She ran away with the Station-Master's servant and half my month's pay. Then she turned up at Dadur Junction in tow of a half-caste, and had the impidence to say I was her husband – all among the drivers in the running-shed too!'

" 'We've done with that,' says Dravot; 'these women are whiter than you or me, and a Queen I will have for the winter months.'

" 'For the last time o' asking, Dan, do *not*,' I says. 'It'll only bring us harm. The Bible says that Kings ain't to waste their strength on women, 'specially when they've got a new raw Kingdom to work over.'

" 'For the last time of answering, I will,' said Dravot, and he went away through the pine-trees looking like a big red devil, the sun being on his crown and beard and all.

"But getting a wife was not as easy as Dan thought. He put it before the Council, and there was no answer till Billy Fish said that he'd better ask the girls. Dravot damned them all round. 'What's wrong with me?' he shouts, standing by the idol Imbra. 'Am I a dog or am I not enough of a man for your wenches? Haven't I put the shadow of my hand over this country? Who stopped the last Afghan raid?' It was me really, but Dravot was too angry to remember. 'Who bought your guns? Who repaired the bridges? Who's the Grand-Master of the sign cut in the stone?' says he, and he thumped his hand on the block that he used to sit on in Lodge, and at Council, which opened like Lodge always. Billy Fish said nothing, and no more did the others. 'Keep your hair on, Dan,' said I; 'and ask the girls. That's how it's done at Home, and these people are quite English.'

" 'The marriage of the King is a matter of State,' says Dan, in a white-hot rage, for he could feel, I hope, that he was going against his better mind. He walked out of the Council-room, and the others sat still, looking at the ground.

" 'Billy Fish,' says I to the Chief of Bashkai, 'what's the difficulty here? A straight answer to a true friend.'

" 'You know,' says Billy Fish. 'How should a man tell you who knows everything? How can daughters of men marry Gods or Devils? It's not proper.'

"I remembered something like that in the Bible; but if, after seeing us as long as they had, they still believed we were Gods, it wasn't for me to undeceive them.

" 'A God can do anything,' says I. 'If the King is fond of a girl he'll not let her die.'

" 'She'll have to,' said Billy Fish. 'There are all sorts of Gods and Devils in these mountains, and now and again a girl marries one of them and isn't seen any more. Besides, you two know the Mark cut in the stone. Only the Gods know that. We thought you were men till you showed the sign of the Master.'

"I wished then that we had explained about the loss of the genuine secrets of a Master-Mason at the first go-off; but I said nothing. All that night there was a blowing of horns in a little dark temple half-way down the hill, and I heard a girl crying fit to die. One of the priests told us that she was being prepared to marry the King.

" 'I'll have no nonsense of that kind,' says Dan. 'I don't want to interfere with your customs, but I'll take my own wife.'

" 'The girl's a little bit afraid,' says the priest. 'She thinks she's going to die, and they are a-heartening of her up down in the temple.'

" 'Hearten her very tender, then,' says Dravot, 'or I'll hearten you with the butt of a gun so you'll never want to be heartened again.' He licked his lips, did Dan, and stayed up walking about more than half the night, thinking of the wife that he was to get in the morning. I wasn't any means comfortable, for I knew that dealings with a woman in foreign parts, though you was a crowned King twenty times over, could not but be risky. I got up very early in the morning while Dravot was asleep, and I saw the priests talking together in whispers, and the Chiefs talking together too, and they looked at me out of the corners of their eyes.

" 'What is up, Fish?' I says to the Bashkai man, who was wrapped up in his furs and looking splendid to behold.

" 'I can't rightly say,' says he; 'but if you can make the King drop all this nonsense about marriage, you'll be doing him and me and yourself a great service.'

" 'That I do believe,' says I. 'But sure, you know, Billy, as well as me, having fought against and for us, that the King and me are nothing more than two of the finest men that God Almighty ever made. Nothing more, I do assure you.'

" 'That may be,' says Billy Fish, 'and yet I should be sorry if it was.' He sinks his head upon his great fur cloak for a minute and thinks. 'King,' says he, 'be you man or God or Devil, I'll stick by you to-day. I have twenty of my men with me, and they will follow me. We'll go to Bashkai until the storm blows over.'

"A little snow had fallen in the night, and everything was white except the greasy fat clouds that blew down and down from the north. Dravot came out with his crown on his head, swinging his arms and stamping his feet, and looking more pleased than Punch.

" 'For the last time, drop it, Dan,' says I in a whisper; 'Billy Fish here says that there will be a row.'

" 'A row among my people!' says Dravot. 'Not much. Peachey, you're a fool not to get a wife too. Where's the girl?' says he with a voice as loud as the braying of a jackass. 'Call up all the Chiefs and priests, and let the Emperor see if his wife suits him.'

"There was no need to call any one. They were all there leaning on their guns and spears round the clearing in the centre of the pine wood. A lot of priests went down to the little temple to bring up the girl, and the horns blew fit to wake the dead. Billy Fish saunters round and gets as close to Daniel as he could, and behind him stood his twenty men with matchlocks. Not a man of them under six feet. I was next to Dravot, and behind me was twenty men of the regular Army. Up comes the girl, and a strapping wench she was, covered with silver and turquoises, but white as death, and looking back every minute at the priests.

" 'She'll do,' said Dan, looking her over. 'What's to be afraid of, lass? Come and kiss me.' He puts his arm round her. She shuts her eyes, gives a bit of a squeak, and down goes her face in the side of Dan's flaming red beard.

" 'The slut's bitten me!' says he, clapping his hand to his neck, and, sure enough, his hand was red with blood. Billy Fish and two of his matchlock-men catches hold of Dan by the shoulders and drags him into the Bashkai lot, while the priests howls in their lingo, – 'Neither God nor Devil, but a man!' I was all taken aback, for a priest cut at me in front, and the Army behind began firing into the Bashkai men.

" 'God A'mighty!' says Dan. 'What is the meaning o' this?'

" 'Come back! Come away!' says Billy Fish. 'Ruin and Mutiny is the matter. We'll break for Bashkai if we can.'

"I tried to give some sort of orders to my men – the men o' the regular Army – but it was no use, so I fired into the brown of 'em with an English Martini and drilled three beggars in a line. The valley was full of shouting, howling creatures, and every soul was shrieking, 'Not a God nor a Devil, but only a man!' The Bashkai troops stuck to Billy

Fish all they were worth, but their matchlocks wasn't half as good as the Kabul breech-loaders, and four of them dropped. Dan was bellowing like a bull, for he was very wrathy; and Billy Fish had a hard job to prevent him running out at the crowd.

" 'We can't stand,' says Billy Fish. 'Make a run for it down the valley! The whole place is against us.' The matchlock-men ran, and we went down the valley in spite of Dravot. He was swearing horrible and crying out he was a King. The priests rolled great stones on us, and the regular Army fired hard, and there wasn't more than six men, not counting Dan, Billy Fish, and Me, that came down to the bottom of the valley alive.

"Then they stopped firing, and the horns in the temple blew again. 'Come away – for Gord's sake come away!' says Billy Fish. 'They'll send runners out to all the villages before ever we get to Bashkai. I can protect you there, but I can't do anything now.'

"My own notion is that Dan began to go mad in his head from that hour. He stared up and down like a stuck pig. Then he was all for walking back alone and killing the priests with his bare hands; which he could have done. 'An Emperor am I,' says Daniel, 'and next year I shall be a Knight of the Queen.'

" 'All right, Dan,' says I; 'but come along now while there's time.'

" 'It's your fault,' says he, 'for not looking after your Army better. There was mutiny in the midst, and you didn't know – you damned engine-driving, plate-laying, missionary's-pass-hunting hound!' He sat upon a rock and called me every foul name he could lay tongue to. I was too heart-sick to care, though it was all his foolishness that brought the smash.

" 'I'm sorry, Dan,' says I, 'but there's no accounting for natives. This business is our Fifty-Seven. Maybe we'll make something out of it yet, when we've got to Bashkai.'

" 'Let's get to Bashkai, then,' says Dan, 'and, by God, when I come back here again I'll sweep the valley so there isn't a bug in a blanket left!'

"We walked all that day, and all that night Dan was stumping up and down on the snow, chewing his beard and muttering to himself.

" 'There's no hope o' getting clear,' said Billy Fish. 'The priests will have sent runners to the villages to say that you are only men. Why didn't you stick on as Gods till things was more settled? I'm a dead man,' says Billy Fish, and he throws himself down on the snow and begins to pray to his Gods.

"Next morning we was in a cruel bad country – all up and down, no level ground at all, and no food either. The six Bashkai men looked at Billy Fish hungry-way as if they wanted to ask something, but they said never a word. At noon we came to the top of a flat mountain all covered with snow, and when we climbed up into it, behold, there was an Army in position waiting in the middle!

" 'The runners have been very quick,' says Billy Fish, with a little bit of a laugh. 'They are waiting for us.'

"Three or four men began to fire from the enemy's side, and a chance shot took Daniel in the calf of the leg. That brought him to his senses. He looks across the snow at the Army, and sees the rifles that we had brought into the country.

" 'We're done for,' says he. 'They are Englishmen, these people, – and it's my blasted nonsense that has brought you to this. Get back, Billy Fish, and take your men away; you've done what you could, and now cut for it. Carnehan,' says he, 'shake hands with me and go along with Billy. Maybe they won't kill you. I'll go and meet 'em alone. It's me that did it. Me, the King!'

" 'Go!' says I. 'Go to Hell, Dan. I'm with you here. Billy Fish, you clear out, and we two will meet those folk.'

" 'I'm a Chief,' says Billy Fish, quite quiet. 'I stay with you. My men can go.'

"The Bashkai fellows didn't wait for a second word, but ran off; and Dan and Me and Billy Fish walked across to where the drums were drumming and the horns were horning. It was cold – awful cold. I've got that cold in the back of my head now. There's a lump of it there."

The punkah-coolies had gone to sleep. Two kerosene lamps were blazing in the office, and the perspiration poured down my face and splashed on the blotter as I leaned forward. Carnehan was shivering, and I feared that his mind might go. I wiped my face, took a fresh grip of the piteously mangled hands, and said: "What happened after that?"

The momentary shift of my eyes had broken the clear current.

"What was you pleased to say?" whined Carnehan. "They took them without any sound. Not a little whisper all along the snow, not though the King knocked down the first man that set hand on him – not though old Peachey fired his last cartridge into the brown of 'em. Not a single solitary sound did those swines make. They just closed up tight, and I tell you their furs stunk. There was a man called Billy Fish, a good friend of us all, and they cut his throat, Sir, then and there, like a pig; and the King kicks up the bloody snow and says: 'We've had a dashed fine run for our money. What's coming next?' But Peachey, Peachey Taliaferro, I tell you, Sir, in confidence as betwixt two friends, he lost his head, Sir. No, he didn't neither. The King lost his head, so he did, all along o' one of those cunning rope-bridges. Kindly let me have the paper-cutter, Sir. It tilted this way. They marched him a mile across that snow to a rope-bridge over a ravine with a river at the bottom. You may have seen such. They prodded him behind like an ox. 'Damn your eyes!' says the King. 'D'you suppose I can't die like a gentleman?' He turns to Peachey – Peachey that was crying like a child. 'I've brought you to this, Peachey,' says he. 'Brought you out of your happy life to be killed in Kafiristan, where you was late Commander-in-Chief of the Emperor's forces. Say you forgive me, Peachey.' – 'I do,' says Peachey. 'Fully and freely do I forgive you, Dan.' – 'Shake hands, Peachey,' says he. 'I'm going now.' Out he goes, looking neither right nor left, and when he was plumb in the middle of those dizzy dancing ropes, 'Cut, you beggars,' he shouts; and they cut, and old Dan fell, turning round and round and round, twenty thousand miles, for he took half an hour to fall till he struck the water, and I could see his body caught on a rock with the gold crown close beside.

"But do you know what they did to Peachey between two pine-trees? They crucified him, Sir, as Peachey's hands will show. They used wooden pegs for his hands and his feet; and he didn't die. He hung there and screamed, and they took him down next day, and said it was a miracle that he wasn't dead. They took him down – poor old Peachey that hadn't done them any harm – that hadn't done them any —"

He rocked to and fro and wept bitterly, wiping his eyes with the back of his scarred hands and moaning like a child for some ten minutes.

"They was cruel enough to feed him up in the temple, because they said he was more of a God than old Daniel that was a man. Then they turned him out on the snow, and told him to go home, and Peachey came home in about a year, begging along the roads quite safe; for Daniel Dravot he walked before and said: 'Come along, Peachey. It's a big thing we're doing.' The mountains they danced at night, and the mountains they tried to fall on Peachey's head, but Dan he held up his hand, and Peachey came along bent double. He never let go of Dan's hand, and he never let go of Dan's head. They gave it to him as a present in the temple, to remind him not to come again, and though the crown was pure gold, and Peachey was starving, never would Peachey sell the same. You knew Dravot, Sir! You knew Right Worshipful Brother Dravot! Look at him now!"

He fumbled in the mass of rags round his bent waist; brought out a black horsehair bag embroidered with silver thread; and shook therefrom on to my table – the dried, withered head of Daniel Dravot! The morning sun that had long been paling the lamps struck the red beard and blind, sunken eyes; struck, too, a heavy circlet of gold studded with raw turquoises, that Carnehan placed tenderly on the battered temples.

"You be'old now," said Carnehan, "the Emperor in his 'abit as he lived – the King of Kafiristan with his crown upon his head. Poor old Daniel that was a monarch once!"

I shuddered, for, in spite of defacements manifold, I recognised the head of the man of Marwar Junction. Carnehan rose to go. I attempted to stop him. He was not fit to walk abroad. "Let me take away the whisky, and give me a little money," he gasped. "I was a King once. I'll go to the Deputy Commissioner and ask to set in the Poorhouse till I get my health. No, thank you, I can't wait till you get a carriage for me. I've urgent private affairs – in the south – at Marwar."

He shambled out of the office and departed in the direction of the Deputy Commissioner's house. That day at noon I had occasion to go down the blinding hot Mall, and I saw a crooked man crawling along the white dust of the roadside, his hat in his hand, quavering dolorously after the fashion of street-singers at Home. There was not a soul in sight, and he was out of all possible earshot of the houses. And he sang through his nose, turning his head from right to left: –

> "The Son of Man goes forth to war,
>   A golden crown to gain;
> His blood-red banner streams afar –
>   Who follows in his train?"

I waited to hear no more, but put the poor wretch into my carriage and drove him off to the nearest missionary for eventual transfer to the Asylum. He repeated the hymn twice while he was with me, whom he did not in the least recognise, and I left him singing it to the missionary.

Two days later I enquired after his welfare of the Superintendent of the Asylum.

"He was admitted suffering from sun-stroke. He died early yesterday morning," said the Superintendent. "Is it true that he was half an hour bareheaded in the sun at midday?"

"Yes," said I, "but do you happen to know if he had anything upon him by any chance when he died?"

"Not to my knowledge," said the Superintendent.

And there the matter rests.

"THE FINEST STORY
IN THE WORLD"

"THE FINEST STORY IN THE WORLD"

*   *   *

> "Or ever the knightly years were gone
>   With the old world to the grave,
> I was a king in Babylon
>   And you were a Christian slave."
>
> *W. E. Henley*

HIS name was Charlie Mears; he was the only son of his mother, who was a widow, and he lived in the north of London, coming into the City every day to work in a bank. He was twenty years old and suffered from aspirations. I met him in a public billiard-saloon where the marker called him by his first name, and he called the marker "Bullseyes." Charlie explained, a little nervously, that he had only come to the place to look on, and since looking on at games of skill is not a cheap amusement for the young, I suggested that Charlie should go back to his mother.

That was our first step towards better acquaintance. He would call on me sometimes in the evenings instead of running about London with his fellow-clerks; and before long, speaking of himself as a young man must, he told me of his aspirations, which were all literary. He desired to make himself an undying name chiefly through verse, though he was not above sending stories of love and death to the penny-in-the-slot journals. It was my fate to sit still while Charlie read me poems of many hundred lines, and bulky fragments of plays that would surely shake the world. My reward was his unreserved confidence, and the self-revelations and troubles of a young man are almost as holy as those of a maiden. Charlie had never fallen in love, but was anxious to do so at the first opportunity; he believed in all things good and all things honourable, but at the same time was curiously careful to let me see that he knew his way about the world as befitted a bank-clerk on twenty-five shillings a week. He rhymed "dove" with "love" and "moon" with "June," and devoutly believed that they had never so been rhymed before. The long lame gaps in his plays he filled up with hasty words of apology and description, and swept on, seeing all that he intended to do so clearly that he esteemed it already done, and turned to me for applause.

I fancy that his mother did not encourage his aspirations, and I know that his writing-table at home was the edge of his washstand. This he told me almost at the outset of our acquaintance, when he was ravaging my bookshelves, and a little before I was implored to speak the truth as to his chances of "writing something really great, you know." Maybe I encouraged him too much, for, one night, he called on me, his eyes flaming with excitement, and said breathlessly: –

"Do you mind – can you let me stay here and write all this evening? I won't interrupt you, I won't really. There's no place for me to write in at my mother's."

"What's the trouble?" I said, knowing well what that trouble was.

"I've a notion in my head that would make the most splendid story that was ever written. Do let me write it out here. It's *such* a notion!"

There was no resisting the appeal. I set him a table; he hardly thanked me, but plunged into the work at once. For half an hour the pen scratched without stopping. Then Charlie sighed and tugged his hair. The scratching grew slower; there were more erasures; and at last ceased. The finest story in the world would not come forth.

"It looks such awful rot now," he said mournfully. "And yet it seemed so good when I was thinking about it. What's wrong?"

I could not dishearten him by saying the truth. So I answered: "Perhaps you don't feel in the mood for writing."

"Yes, I do – except when I look at this stuff. Ugh!"

"Read me what you've done," I said.

He read, and it was wondrous bad, and he paused at all the specially turgid sentences, expecting a little approval; for he was proud of those sentences, as I knew he would be.

"It needs compression," I suggested cautiously.

"I hate cutting my things down. I don't think you could alter a word here without spoiling the sense. It reads better aloud than when I was writing it."

"Charlie, you're suffering from an alarming disease afflicting a numerous class. Put the thing by, and tackle it again in a week."

"I want to do it at once. What do you think of it?"

"How can I judge from a half-written tale? Tell me the story as it lies in your head."

Charlie told, and in the telling there was everything that his ignorance had so carefully prevented from escaping into the written word. I looked at him, wondering whether it were possible that he did not know the originality, the power of the notion that had come in his way? It was distinctly a Notion among notions. Men had been puffed up with pride by ideas not a tithe as excellent and practicable. But Charlie babbled on serenely, interrupting the current of pure fancy with samples of horrible sentences that he proposed to use. I heard him out to the end. It would be folly to allow his thought to remain in his own inept hands, when I could do so much with it. Not all that could be done indeed; but, oh so much!

"What do you think?" he said at last. "I fancy I shall call it 'The Story of a Ship.'"

"I think the idea is pretty good; but you won't be able to handle it for ever so long. Now I —"

"Would it be of any use to you? Would you care to take it? I should be proud," said Charlie promptly.

There are few things sweeter in this world than the guileless, hot-headed, intemperate, open admiration of a junior. Even a woman in her blindest devotion does not fall into the gait of the man she adores, tilt her bonnet to the angle at which he wears his hat, or interlard her speech with his pet oaths. And Charlie did all these things. Still it was necessary to salve my conscience before I possessed myself of Charlie's thought.

"Let's make a bargain. I'll give you a fiver for the notion," I said.

Charlie became a bank-clerk at once.

"Oh, that's impossible. Between two pals, you know, if I may call you so, and speaking as a man of the world, I couldn't. Take the notion, if it's any use to you. I've heaps more."

He had – none knew this better than I – but they were the notions of other men.

"Look at it as a matter of business – between men of the world," I returned. "Five pounds will buy you any number of poetry-books. Business is business, and you may be sure I shouldn't give that price unless —"

"Oh, if you put it *that* way," said Charlie, visibly moved by the thought of the books. The bargain was clinched with an agreement that he should at unstated intervals come to me with all the notions that he possessed, should have a table of his own to write at, and unquestioned right to inflict upon me all his poems and fragments of poems. Then I said, "Now tell me how you came by this idea."

"It came by itself." Charlie's eyes opened a little.

"Yes, but you told me a great deal about the hero that you must have read before somewhere."

"I haven't any time for reading, except when you let me sit here, and on Sundays I'm on my bicycle or down the river all day. There's nothing wrong about the hero, is there?"

"Tell me again and I shall understand clearly. You say that your hero went pirating. How did he live?"

"He was on the lower deck of this ship-thing that I was telling you about."

"What sort of ship?"

"It was the kind rowed with oars, and the sea spurts through the oar-holes and the men row sitting up to their knees in water. Then there's a bench running down between the two lines of oars, and an overseer with a whip walks up and down the bench to make the men work."

"How do you know that?"

"It's in the tale. There's a rope running overhead, looped to the upper deck, for the overseer to catch hold of when the ship rolls. When the overseer misses the rope once and falls among the rowers, remember the hero laughs at him and gets licked for it. He's chained to his oar of course – the hero."

"How is he chained?"

"With an iron band round his waist fixed to the bench he sits on, and a sort of handcuff on his left wrist chaining him to the oar. He's on the lower deck where the worst men are sent, and the only light comes from the hatchways and through the oar-holes. Can't you imagine the sunlight just squeezing through between the handle and the hole and wobbling about as the ship rolls?"

"I can, but I can't imagine your imagining it."

"How could it be any other way? Now you listen to me. The long oars on the upper deck are managed by four men to each bench, the lower ones by three, and the lowest of all by two. Remember it's quite dark on the lowest deck, and all the men there go mad. When a man dies at his oar on that deck he isn't thrown overboard, but cut up in his chains and stuffed through the oar-hole in little pieces."

"Why?" I demanded, amazed, not so much at the information as the tone of command in which it was flung out.

"To save trouble and to frighten the others. It needs two overseers to drag a man's body up to the top deck; and if the men at the lower-deck oars were left alone, of course they'd stop rowing and try to pull up the benches by all standing up together in their chains."

"You've a most provident imagination. Where have you been reading about galleys and galley-slaves?"

"Nowhere that I remember. I row a little when I get the chance. But, perhaps, if you say so, I may have read something."

He went away shortly afterwards to deal with booksellers, and I wondered how a bank-clerk aged twenty could put into my hands, with a profligate abundance of detail, all given with absolute assurance, the story of extravagant and blood-thirsty adventure, riot, piracy, and death in unnamed seas. He had led his hero a desperate dance through revolt against the overseers, to command of a ship of his own, and the ultimate establishment of a kingdom on an island "some-where in the sea, you know;" and, delighted with my paltry five pounds, had gone out to buy the notions of other men, that these might teach him how to write. I had the consola-tion of knowing that this notion was mine by right of pur-chase; and I thought that I could make something of it.

When next he came to me he was drunk – royally drunk – on many poets for the first time revealed to him. His pupils were dilated, his words tumbled over each other, and he wrapped himself in quotations – as a beggar would enfold himself in the purple of Emperors. Most of all was he drunk with Longfellow.

"Isn't it splendid? Isn't it superb?" he cried, after hasty greetings. Listen to this –

> " 'Wouldst thou,' – so the helmsman answered,
>   'Know the secret of the sea?
> Only those who brave its dangers
>   Comprehend its mystery.'

"By gum!

> " 'Only those who brave its dangers
>   Comprehend its mystery,' "

he repeated twenty times, walking up and down the room and forgetting me. "But *I* can understand it too," he said to himself. "I don't know how to thank you for that fiver. And this; listen –

> " 'I remember the black wharves and the slips
>   And the sea-tides tossing free;
> And the Spanish sailors with bearded lips,

> And the beauty and mystery of the ships,
> And the magic of the sea.'

"I haven't braved any dangers, but I feel as if I knew all about it."

"You certainly seem to have a grip of the sea. Have you ever seen it?"

"When I was a little chap I went to Brighton once; we used to live in Coventry, though, before we came to London. I never saw it,

> " 'When descends on the Atlantic
> The gigantic
> Storm-wind of the Equinox.' "

He shook me by the shoulder to make me understand the passion that was shaking himself.

"When that storm comes," he continued, "I think that all the oars in the ship that I was talking about get broken, and the rowers have their chests smashed in by the oar-heads bucking. By the way, have you done anything with that notion of mine yet?"

"No. I was waiting to hear more of it from you. Tell me how in the world you're so certain about the fittings of the ship. You know nothing of ships."

"I don't know. It's as real as anything to me until I try to write it down. I was thinking about it only last night in bed, after you had lent me 'Treasure Island'; and I made up a whole lot of new things to go into the story."

"What sort of things?"

"About the food the men ate; rotten figs and black beans and wine in a skin bag, passed from bench to bench."

"Was the ship built so long ago as *that*?"

"As what? I don't know whether it was long ago or not. It's only a notion, but sometimes it seems just as real as if it was true. Do I bother you with talking about it?"

"Not in the least. Did you make up anything else?"

"Yes, but it's nonsense." Charlie flushed a little.

"Never mind; let's hear about it."

"Well, I was thinking over the story, and after awhile I got out of bed and wrote down on a piece of paper the sort of stuff the men might be supposed to scratch on their oars with the edges of their handcuffs. It seemed to make the thing more life-like. It *is* so real to me, y'know."

"Have you the paper on you?"

"Ye–es, but what's the use of showing it? It's only a lot of scratches. All the same, we might have 'em reproduced in the book on the front page."

"I'll attend to those details. Show me what your men wrote."

He pulled out of his pocket a sheet of notepaper, with a single line of scratches upon it, and I put this carefully away.

"What is it supposed to mean in English?" I said.

"Oh, I don't know. I mean it to mean 'I'm beastly tired.' It's great nonsense," he repeated, "but all those men in the ship seem as real as real people to me. Do do something to the notion soon; I should like to see it written and printed."

"But all you've told me would make a long book."

"Make it, then. You've only to sit down and write it out."

"Give me a little time. Have you any more notions?"

"Not just now. I'm reading all the books I've bought. They're splendid."

When he had left I looked at the sheet of notepaper with the inscription upon it. Then I took my head tenderly between both hands, to make certain that it was not coming off or turning round. Then . . . but there seemed to be no interval between leaving my rooms and finding myself arguing with a policeman outside a door marked *Private* in a corridor of the British Museum. All I demanded, as politely as possible, was "the Greek antiquity man." The policeman knew nothing except the rules of the Museum, and it became necessary to forage through all the houses and offices inside the gates. An elderly gentleman called away from his lunch put an end to my search by holding the notepaper between finger and thumb and sniffing at it scornfully.

"What does this mean? H'mm," said he. "So far as I can ascertain it is an attempt to write extremely corrupt Greek on the part" – here he glared at me with intention – "of an extremely illiterate – ah – person." He read slowly from the paper, *"Pollock, Erckmann, Tauchnitz, Henniker"* – four names familiar to me.

"Can you tell me what the corruption is supposed to mean – the gist of the thing?" I asked.

"I have been – many times – overcome with weariness in this particular employment. That is the meaning." He returned me the paper, and I fled without a word of thanks, explanation, or apology.

I might have been excused for forgetting much. To me of all men had been given the chance to write the most marvellous tale in the world, nothing less than the story of a Greek galley-slave, as told by himself. Small wonder that his dreaming had seemed real to Charlie. The Fates that are so careful to shut the doors of each successive life behind us had, in this case, been neglectful, and Charlie was looking, though that he did not know, where never man had been permitted to look with full knowledge since Time began. Above all, he was absolutely ignorant of the knowledge sold to me for five pounds; and he would retain that ignorance; for bank-clerks do not understand metempsychosis, and a sound commercial education does not include Greek. He would supply me – here I capered among the dumb gods of Egypt and laughed in their battered faces – with material to make my tale sure – so sure that the world would hail it as an impudent and vamped fiction. And I – I alone would know that it was absolutely and literally true. I – I alone held this jewel to my hand for the cutting and polishing. Therefore I danced again among the gods of the Egyptian court, till a policeman saw me and took steps in my direction.

It remained now only to encourage Charlie to talk, and here there was no difficulty. But I had forgotten those accursed books of poetry. He came to me time after time, as useless as a surcharged phonograph – drunk on Byron,

Shelley, or Keats. Knowing now what the boy had been in his past lives, and desperately anxious not to lose one word of his babble, I could not hide from him my respect and interest. He misconstrued both into respect for the present soul of Charlie Mears, to whom life was as new as it was to Adam, and interest in his readings: he stretched my patience to breaking point by reciting poetry – not his own now, but that of others. I wished every English poet blotted out of the memory of mankind. I blasphemed the mightiest names of song because they had drawn Charlie from the path of direct narrative, and would, later, spur him to imitate them; but I choked down my impatience until the first flood of enthusiasm should have spent itself and the boy returned to his dreams.

"What's the use of my telling you what *I* think, when these chaps wrote things for the angels to read?" he growled, one evening. "Why don't you write something like theirs?"

"I don't think you're treating me quite fairly," I said, speaking under strong restraint.

"I've given you the story," he said shortly, replunging into "Lara."

"But I want the details."

"The things I make up about that damned ship that you call a galley? They're quite easy. You can just make 'em up for yourself. Turn up the gas a little, I want to go on reading."

I could have broken the gas-globe over his head for his amazing stupidity. I could indeed make up things for myself did I only know what Charlie did not know that he knew. But since the doors were shut behind me, I could only wait his youthful pleasure and strive to keep him in good temper. One minute's want of guard might spoil a priceless revelation: now and again he would toss his books aside – he kept them in my rooms, for his mother would have been shocked at the waste of good money had she seen them – and launched into his sea dreams. Again I cursed all the poets of

England. The plastic mind of the bank-clerk had been over-laid, coloured, and distorted by that which he had read, and the result as delivered was a confused tangle of other voices most like the mutter and hum through a City telephone in the busiest part of the day.

He talked of the galley – his own galley, had he but known it – with illustrations borrowed from the "Bride of Abydos." He pointed the experiences of his hero with quotations from "The Corsair," and threw in deep and desperate moral reflections from "Cain" and "Manfred," expecting me to use them all. Only when the talk turned on Longfellow were the jarring cross-currents dumb, and I knew that Charlie was speaking the truth as he remembered it.

"What do you think of this?" I said one evening, as soon as I understood the medium in which his memory worked best, and, before he could expostulate, read him nearly the whole of "The Saga of King Olaf."

He listened open-mouthed, flushed, his hands drumming on the back of the sofa where he lay, till I came to the Song of Einar Tamberskelver and the verse: –

> "Einar then, the arrow taking
> From the loosened string,
> Answered, 'That was Norway breaking
> 'Neath thy hand, O King.' "

He gasped with pure delight of sound.

"That's better than Byron, a little?" I ventured.

"Better! Why, it's *true*! How could he have known?"

I went back and repeated: –

> " 'What was that?' said Olaf, standing
> On the quarter-deck,
> 'Something heard I like the stranding
> Of a shattered wreck.' "

"How could he have known how the ships crash and the oars rip out and go *z-zzp* all along the line? Why, only the other night . . . But go back, please, and read 'The Skerry of Shrieks' again."

"No, I'm tired. Let's talk. What happened the other night?"

"I had an awful dream about that galley of ours. I dreamed I was drowned in a fight. You see, we ran alongside another ship in harbour. The water was dead still except where our oars whipped it up. You know where I always sit in the galley?" He spoke haltingly at first, under the fine English fear of being laughed at.

"No. That's news to me," I answered meekly, my heart beginning to beat.

"On the fourth oar from the bow on the right side on the upper deck. There were four of us at that oar, all chained. I remember watching the water and trying to get my handcuffs off before the row began. Then we closed up on the other ship, and all their fighting men jumped over our bulwarks, and my bench broke and I was pinned down with the three other fellows on top of me, and the big oar jammed across our backs."

"Well?" Charlie's eyes were alive and alight. He was looking at the wall behind my chair.

"I don't know how we fought. The men were trampling all over my back, and I lay low. Then our rowers on the left side – tied to their oars, you know – began to yell and back water. I could hear the water sizzle, and we spun round like a cockchafer, and I knew, lying where I was, that there was a galley coming up, bow on, to ram us on the left side. I could just lift up my head and see her sail over the bulwarks. We wanted to meet her bow to bow, but it was too late. We could only turn a little bit because the galley on our right had hooked herself on to us and stopped our moving. Then, by gum! there was a crash! Our left oars began to break as the other galley – the moving one, y'know – stuck her nose into them. Then the lower-deck oars shot up through the deck-planking, butt first, and one of them jumped clear up into the air and came down again close at my head."

"How was that managed?"

"The moving galley's bow was plunking them back through their own oar-holes, and I could hear no end of a shindy in the decks below. Then her nose caught us nearly in the middle, and we tilted sideways, and the fellows in the right-hand galley unhitched their hooks and ropes, and threw things on to our upper deck – arrows, and hot pitch or something that stung, and we went up and up on the left side, and the right side dipped, and I twisted my head round and saw the water stand still as it topped the right bulwarks; and then it curled over and crashed down on the whole lot of us on the right side, and I felt it hit my back, and I woke."

"One minute, Charlie. When the sea topped the bulwarks, what did it look like?" I had my reasons for asking. A man of my acquaintance had once gone down with a leaking ship in a still sea, and had seen the water-level pause for an instant ere it fell on the deck.

"It looked just like a banjo-string drawn tight, and it seemed to stay there for years," said Charlie.

Exactly! The other man had said: "It looked like a silver wire laid down along the bulwarks, and I thought it was never going to break." He had paid everything except the bare life for this little valueless piece of knowledge, and I had travelled ten thousand weary miles to meet him and take his knowledge at second hand. But Charlie, the bank-clerk on twenty-five shillings a week, who had never been out of sight of a made road, knew it all. It was no consolation to me that once in his lives he had been forced to die for his gains. I also must have died scores of times, but behind me, because I could have used my knowledge, the doors were shut!

"And then?" I said, trying to put away the devil of envy.

"The funny thing was, though, in all the row I didn't feel a bit astonished or frightened. It seemed as if I'd been in a good many fights, because I told my next man so when the row began. But that cad of an overseer on my deck wouldn't unloose our chains and give us a chance. He always said that we'd all be set free after a battle, but we never were; we never were." Charlie shook his head mournfully.

"What a scoundrel!"

"I should say he was. He never gave us enough to eat, and sometimes we were so thirsty that we used to drink salt-water. I can taste that salt-water still."

"Now tell me something about the harbour where the fight was fought."

"I didn't dream about that. I know it was a harbour, though, because we were tied up to a ring on a white wall, and all the face of the stone under water was covered with wood to prevent our ram getting chipped when the tide made us rock."

"That's curious. Our hero commanded the galley, didn't he?"

"Didn't he just! He stood by the bows and shouted like a good un. He was the man who killed the overseer."

"But you were all drowned together, Charlie, weren't you?"

"I can't make that fit quite," he said, with a puzzled look. "The galley must have gone down with all hands, and yet I fancy that the hero went on living afterwards. Perhaps he climbed into the attacking ship. I wouldn't see that, of course. I was dead, you know."

He shivered slightly and protested that he could remember no more.

I did not press him further, but to satisfy myself that he lay in ignorance of the workings of his own mind, deliberately introduced him to Mortimer Collins's "Transmigration," and gave him a sketch of the plot before he opened the pages.

"What rot it all is!" he said frankly, at the end of an hour. "I don't understand his nonsense about the Red Planet Mars and the King, and the rest of it. Chuck me the Longfellow again."

I handed him the book and wrote out as much as I could remember of his description of the sea-fight, appealing to him from time to time for confirmation of fact or detail. He would answer without raising his eyes from the book, as assuredly as though all his knowledge lay before him on the printed page. I spoke under the normal key of my voice that the current might not be broken, and I know that he was not aware of what he was saying, for his thoughts were out on the sea with Longfellow.

"Charlie," I asked, "when the rowers on the galleys mutinied how did they kill their overseers?"

"Tore up the benches and brained 'em. That happened when a heavy sea was running. An overseer on the lower deck slipped from the centre plank and fell among the rowers. They choked him to death against the side of the ship with their chained hands quite quietly, and it was too dark for the other overseer to see what had happened. When he asked he was pulled down too and choked, and the lower deck fought their way up deck by deck, with the pieces of the broken benches banging behind 'em. How they howled!"

"And what happened after that?"

"I don't know. The hero went away – red hair and red beard and all. That was after he had captured our galley, I think."

The sound of my voice irritated him, and he motioned slightly with his left hand as a man does when interruption jars.

"You never told me he was red-headed before or that he captured your galley," I said, after a discreet interval.

Charlie did not raise his eyes.

"He was as red as a red bear," said he abstractedly. "He came from the north; they said so in the galley when he looked for rowers – not for slaves, but free men. Afterwards – years and years afterwards – news came from another ship, or else he came back —"

His lips moved in silence. He was rapturously retasting some poem before him.

"Where had he been, then?" I was almost whispering that the sentence might come gently to whichever section of Charlie's brain that was working on my behalf.

"To the Beaches – the Long and Wonderful Beaches!" was the reply after a minute of silence.

"To Furdurstrandi?" I asked, tingling from head to foot.

"Yes, to Furdurstrandi" – he pronounced the word in a new fashion. "And I too saw —" The voice failed.

"Do you know what you have said?" I shouted incautiously.

He lifted his eyes, fully roused now. "No!" he snapped. "I wish you'd let a chap go on reading. Hark to this: –

    " 'But Othere, the old sea-captain,
      He neither paused nor stirred
        Till the king listened, and then
        Once more took up his pen
      And wrote down every word.

    " 'And to the King of the Saxons
      In witness of the truth,
        Raising his noble head,
        He stretched his brown hand and said,
    "Behold this walrus tooth." '

By Jove, what chaps those must have been, to go sailing all over the shop, never knowing where they'd fetch the land! Hah!"

"Charlie," I pleaded, "if you'll only be sensible for a minute or two I'll make our hero in our tale every inch as good as Othere."

"Umph! Longfellow wrote that poem. I don't care about writing things any more. I want to read." He was thoroughly out of tune now, and raging over my own ill-luck, I left him.

Conceive yourself at the door of the world's treasure-house guarded by a child – an idle, irresponsible child playing knuckle-bones – on whose favour depends the gift of the key, and you will imagine one-half my torment. Till that evening Charlie had spoken nothing that might not lie within the experiences of a Greek galley-slave. But now, or there was no virtue in books, he had talked of some desperate adventure of the Vikings, of Thorfin Karlsefne's sailing to Wineland, which is America, in the ninth or tenth century. The battle in the harbour he had seen; and his own death he had described. But this was a much more startling plunge

into the past. Was it possible that he had skipped half a
dozen lives and was then dimly remembering some episode
of a thousand years later? It was a maddening jumble, and
the worst of it was that Charlie Mears in his normal condition was the last person in the world to clear it up. I could
only wait and watch, but I went to bed that night full of the
wildest imaginings. There was nothing that was not possible
if Charlie's detestable memory only held good.

I might rewrite the Saga of Thorfin Karlsefne as it had
never been written before, might tell the story of the first
discovery of America, myself the discoverer. But I was entirely at Charlie's mercy, and so long as there was a three-
and-sixpenny Bohn volume within his reach Charlie would
not tell. I dared not curse him openly; I hardly dared jog his
memory, for I was dealing with the experiences of a thousand
years ago, told through the mouth of a boy of to-day; and a
boy of to-day is affected by every change of tone and gust of
opinion, so that he must lie even when he most desires to
speak the truth.

I saw no more of Charlie for nearly a week. When next I
met him it was in Gracechurch Street with a bill-book
chained to his waist. Business took him over London Bridge,
and I accompanied him. He was very full of the importance
of that book and magnified it. As we passed over the Thames
we paused to look at a steamer unloading great slabs of white
and brown marble. A barge drifted under the steamer's stern
and a lonely ship's cow in that barge bellowed. Charlie's face
changed from the face of the bank-clerk to that of an unknown and – though he would not have believed this – a
much shrewder man. He flung out his arm across the parapet
of the bridge and laughing very loudly, said: –

"When they heard *our* bulls bellow the Skrœlings ran
away!"

I waited only for an instant, but the barge and the cow
had disappeared under the bows of the steamer before I
answered.

"Charlie, what do you suppose are Skrœlings?"

"Never heard of 'em before. They sound like a new kind of sea-gull. What a chap you are for asking questions!" he replied. "I have to go to the cashier of the Omnibus Company yonder. Will you wait for me and we can lunch somewhere together? I've a notion for a poem."

"No, thanks. I'm off. You're sure you know nothing about Skrœlings?"

"Not unless he's been entered for the Liverpool Handicap." He nodded and disappeared in the crowd.

Now it is written in the Saga of Eric the Red, or that of Thorfin Karlsefne, that nine hundred years ago, when Karlsefne's galleys came to Leif's booths, which Leif had erected in the unknown land called Markland, which may or may not have been Rhode Island, the Skrœlings – and the Lord He knows who these may or may not have been – came to trade with the Vikings, and ran away because they were frightened at the bellowing of the cattle which Thorfin had brought with him in the ships. But what in the world could a Greek slave know of that affair? I wandered up and down among the streets trying to unravel the mystery, and the more I considered it, the more baffling it grew. One thing only seemed certain, and that certainty took away my breath for the moment. If I came to full knowledge of anything at all, it would not be one life of the soul in Charlie Mears's body, but half a dozen – half a dozen several and separate existences spent on blue water in the morning of the world!

Then I walked round the situation.

Obviously if I used my knowledge I should stand alone and unapproachable until all men were as wise as myself. That would be something, but manlike I was ungrateful. It seemed bitterly unfair that Charlie's memory should fail me when I needed it most. Great Powers above – I looked up at them through the fog smoke – did the Lords of Life and Death know what this meant to me? Nothing less than eternal fame of the best kind, that comes from One, and is shared by one alone. I would be content – remembering Clive, I stood astounded at my own moderation, – with the mere right to tell one story, to work out one little contribution to the light literature of the day. If Charlie were permitted full recollection for one hour – for sixty short minutes – of existences that had extended over a thousand years – I would forego all profit and honour from all that I should make of his speech. I would take no share in the commotion that would follow throughout the particular corner of the earth that calls itself "the world." The thing should be put forth anonymously. Nay, I would make other men believe that they had written it. They would hire bull-hided self-advertising Englishmen to bellow it abroad. Preachers would found a fresh conduct of life upon it, swearing that it was new and that they had lifted the fear of death from all mankind. Every Orientalist in Europe would patronise it discursively with Sanskrit and Pali texts. Terrible women would invent unclean variants of the men's belief for the elevation of their sisters. Churches and religions would war over it. Between the hailing and restarting of an omnibus I foresaw the scuffles that would arise among half a dozen denominations all professing "the doctrine of the True Metempsychosis as applied to the world and the New Era"; and saw, too, the respectable English newspapers shying, like frightened kine, over the beautiful simplicity of the tale. The mind leaped forward a hundred – two hundred – a thousand years. I saw with sorrow that men would mutilate and garble the story; that rival creeds would turn it upside down till, at last, the western world, which clings to the dread of death more closely than the hope of life, would set it aside as an interesting superstition and stampede after some faith so long forgotten that it seemed altogether new. Upon this I changed the terms of the bargain that I would make with the Lords of Life and Death. Only let me know, let me write, the story with sure knowledge that I wrote the truth, and I would burn the manuscript as a solemn sacrifice. Five minutes after the last line was written I would destroy it all. But I must be allowed to write it with absolute certainty.

There was no answer. The flaming colours of an Aquarium poster caught my eye, and I wondered whether it would be wise or prudent to lure Charlie into the hands of the professional mesmerist there, and whether, if he were under his power, he would speak of his past lives. If he did, and if people believed him . . . but Charlie would be frightened and fluttered, or made conceited by the interviews. In either case he would begin to lie, through fear or vanity. He was safest in my own hands.

"They are very funny fools, your English," said a voice at my elbow, and turning round I recognised a casual acquaintance, a young Bengali law student, called Grish Chunder, whose father had sent him to England to become civilised. The old man was a retired native official, and on an income of five pounds a month contrived to allow his son two hundred pounds a year, and the run of his teeth in a city where he could pretend to be the cadet of a royal house, and tell stories of the brutal Indian bureaucrats who ground the faces of the poor.

Grish Chunder was a young, fat, full-bodied Bengali, dressed with scrupulous care in frock-coat, tall hat, light trousers, and tan gloves. But I had known him in the days when the brutal Indian Government paid for his university education, and he contributed cheap sedition to *Sachi Durpan*, and intrigued with the wives of his fourteen-year-old schoolmates.

"That is very funny and very foolish," he said, nodding at the poster. "I am going down to the Northbrook Club. Will you come too?"

I walked with him for some time. "You are not well," he said. "What is there on your mind? You do not talk."

"Grish Chunder, you've been too well educated to believe in a God, haven't you?"

"Oah, yes, *here*! But when I go home I must conciliate popular superstition, and make ceremonies of purification, and my women will anoint idols."

"And hang up *tulsi* and feast the *purohit*, and take you

back into caste again and make a good *khuttri* of you again, you advanced social Freethinker. And you'll eat *desi* food, and like it all, from the smell in the courtyard to the mustard oil over you."

"I shall very much like it," said Grish Chunder unguardedly. "Once a Hindu – always a Hindu. But I like to know what the English think they know."

"I'll tell you something that one Englishman knows. It's an old tale to you."

I began to tell the story of Charlie in English, but Grish Chunder put a question in the vernacular, and the history went forward naturally in the tongue best suited for its telling. After all, it could never have been told in English. Grish Chunder heard me, nodding from time to time, and then came up to my rooms, where I finished the tale.

"*Beshak*," he said philosophically. "*Lekin darwaza band hai*. [Without doubt, but the door is shut.] I have heard of this remembering of previous existences among my people. It is of course an old tale with us, but to happen to an Englishman – a cow-fed *Mlechh* – an outcast. By Jove, that is most peculiar!"

"Outcast yourself, Grish Chunder! You eat cow-beef every day. Let's think the thing over. The boy remembers his incarnations."

"Does he know that?" said Grish Chunder quietly, swinging his legs as he sat on my table. He was speaking in his English now.

"He does not know anything. Would I speak to you if he did? Go on!"

"There is no going on at all. If you tell that to your friends they will say you are mad and put it in the papers. Suppose, now, you prosecute for libel."

"Let's leave that out of the question entirely. Is there any chance of his being made to speak?"

"There is a chance. Oah, yess! But *if* he spoke it would mean that all this world would end now – *instanto* – fall down

on your head. These things are not allowed, you know. As I
said, the door is shut."

"Not a ghost of a chance?"

"How can there be? You are a Christi-án, and it is forbidden to eat, in your books, of the Tree of Life, or else you
would never die. How shall you all fear death if you all know
what your friend does not know that he knows? I am afraid
to be kicked, but I am not afraid to die, because I know what
I know. You are not afraid to be kicked, but you are afraid
to die. If you were not, by God! you English would be all
over the shop in an hour, upsetting the balances of power,
and making commotions. It would not be good. But no fear.
He will remember a little and a little less, and he will call it
dreams. Then he will forget altogether. When I passed my
First Arts Examination in Calcutta that was all in the cram-
book on Wordsworth. 'Trailing clouds of glory,' you know."

"This seems to be an exception to the rule."

"There are no exceptions to rules. Some are not so hard-
looking as others, but they are all the same when you touch.
If this friend of yours said so-and-so and so-and-so, indicating that he remembered all his lost lives, or one piece of a
lost life, he would not be in the bank another hour. He would
be what you called sack because he was mad, and they would
send him to an asylum for lunatics. You can see that, my
friend."

"Of course I can, but I wasn't thinking of him. His name
need never appear in the story."

"Ah! I see. That story will never be written. You can try."

"I am going to."

"For your own credit and for the sake of money, *of*
course?"

"No. For the sake of writing the story. On my honour,
that will be all."

"Even then there is no chance. You cannot play with the
Gods. It is a very pretty story now. As they say, Let it go on
that – I mean at that. Be quick; he will not last long."

"How do you mean?"

"What I say. He has never, so far, thought about a woman."

"Hasn't he, though!" I remembered some of Charlie's confidences.

"I mean no woman has thought about him. When that comes, *bus – hogya* – all up! I know. There are millions of women here. Housemaids, for instance. They kiss you behind doors."

I winced at the thought of my story being ruined by a housemaid. And yet nothing was more probable.

Grish Chunder grinned.

"Yes – also pretty girls – cousins of his house, and perhaps *not* of his house. One kiss that he gives back again and remembers will cure all this nonsense, or else —"

"Or else what? Remember he does not know that he knows."

"I know that. Or else, if nothing happens, he will become immersed in the trade and the financial speculations like the rest. It must be so. You can see that it must be so. But the woman will come first, *I* think."

There was a rap at the door, and Charlie charged in impetuously. He had been released from office; and by the look in his eyes I could see that he had come over for a long talk; most probably with poems in his pockets. Charlie's poems were very wearying, but sometimes they led him to talk about the galley.

Grish Chunder looked at him keenly for a minute.

"I beg your pardon," Charlie said uneasily; "I didn't know you had any one with you."

"I am going," said Grish Chunder.

He drew me into the lobby as he departed.

"That is your man," he said quickly. "I tell you he will never speak all you wish. That is rot – bosh! But he would be most good to make to see things. Suppose now we pretend that it was only play" – I had never seen Grish Chunder so excited – "and pour the ink-pool into his hand. Eh, what do you think? I tell you that he could see *anything* that a man could see. Let me get the ink and the camphor. He is a seer and he will tell us very many things."

"He may be all you say, but I'm not going to trust him to your gods and devils."

"They will not hurt him. He will only feel a little stupid and dull when he wakes up. You have seen boys look into the ink-pool before."

"That is the reason why I am not going to see it any more. You'd better go, Grish Chunder."

He went, insisting far down the staircase that it was throwing away my only chance of looking into the future.

This left me unmoved, for I was concerned for the past, and no peering of hypnotised boys into mirrors and ink-pools would help me to that. But I recognised Grish Chunder's point of view and sympathised with it.

"What a big black brute that was!" said Charlie, when I returned to him. "Well, look here, I've just done a poem; did it instead of playing dominoes after lunch. May I read it?"

"Let me read it to myself."

"Then you miss the proper expression. Besides, you always make my things sound as if the rhymes were all wrong."

"Read it aloud, then. You're like the rest of 'em."

Charlie mouthed me his poem, and it was not much worse than the average of his verses. He had been reading his books faithfully, but he was not pleased when I told him that I preferred my Longfellow undiluted with Charlie.

Then we began to go through the MS. line by line; Charlie parrying every objection and correction with:

"Yes, that may be better, but you don't catch what I'm driving at."

Charlie was, in one way at least, very like one kind of poet.

There was a pencil scrawl at the back of the paper, and "What's that?" I said.

"Oh, that's not poetry at all. It's some rot I wrote last night before I went to bed, and it was too much bother to hunt for rhymes; so I made it a sort of blank verse instead."

Here is Charlie's "blank verse": –

"We pulled for you when the wind was against us and the sails were low.
Will you never let us go?
We ate bread and onions when you took towns or ran aboard quickly when you were beaten back by the foe,
The captains walked up and down the deck in fair weather singing songs, but we were below,
We fainted with our chins on the oars and you did not see that we were idle for we still swung to and fro.
Will you never let us go?
The salt made the oar-handles like shark-skin; our knees were cut to the bone with salt cracks; our hair was stuck to our foreheads; and our lips were cut to our gums and you whipped us because we could not row.
Will you never let us go?
But in a little time we shall run out of the portholes as the water runs along the oar-blade, and though you tell the others to row after us you will never catch us till you catch the oar-thresh and tie up the winds in the belly of the sail. Aho!
Will you never let us go?"

"H'm. What's oar-thresh, Charlie?"

"The water washed up by the oars. That's the sort of song they might sing in the galley, y'know. Aren't you ever going to finish that story and give me some of the profits?"

"It depends on yourself. If you had only told me more about your hero in the first instance it might have been finished by now. You're so hazy in your notions."

"I only want to give you the general notion of it – the knocking about from place to place and the fighting and all that. Can't you fill in the rest yourself? Make the hero save a girl on a pirate-galley and marry her or do something."

"You're a really helpful collaborator. I suppose the hero went through some few adventures before he married."

"Well, then, make him a very artful card – a low sort of man – a sort of political man who went about making treaties and breaking them – a black-haired chap who hid behind the mast when the fighting began."

"But you said the other day that he was red-haired."

"I couldn't have. Make him black-haired of course. You've no imagination."

Seeing that I had just discovered the entire principles upon which our half-memory falsely called imagination is based, I felt entitled to laugh, but forbore, for the sake of the tale.

"You're right. *You're* the man with imagination. A black-haired chap in a decked ship," I said.

"No, an open ship – like a big boat."

This was maddening.

"Your ship has been built and designed, closed and decked in; you said so yourself," I protested.

"No, no, not that ship. That was open or half-decked because – By Jove you're right! You made me think of the hero as a red-haired chap. Of course if he were red, the ship would be an open one with painted sails."

Surely, I thought, he would remember now that he had served in two galleys at least – in a three-decked Greek one under the black-haired "political man," and again in a Viking's open sea-serpent under the man "red as a red bear" who went to Markland. My devil prompted me to speak.

"Why, of course, Charlie?" said I.

"I don't know. Are you making fun of me?"

The current was broken for the time being. I took up a note-book and pretended to make many entries in it.

"It's a pleasure to work with an imaginative chap like yourself," I said, after a pause. "The way that you've brought out the character of the hero is simply wonderful."

"Do you think so?" he answered with a pleased flush. "I often tell myself that there's more in me than my mo – than people think."

"There's an enormous amount in you."

"Then won't you let me send an essay on The Ways of Bank-Clerks to 'Tit-Bits,' and get the guinea prize?"

"That wasn't exactly what I meant, old fellow: perhaps it would be better to wait a little and go ahead with the galley-story."

"Ah, but I sha'n't get the credit of that. 'Tit-Bits' would publish my name and address if I win. What are you grinning at? They *would*."

"I know it. Suppose you go for a walk. I want to look through my notes about our story."

Now this reprehensible youth who left me, a little hurt and put back, might for aught he or I knew have been one of the crew of the *Argo* – had been certainly slave or comrade to Thorfin Karlsefne. Therefore he was deeply interested in guinea competitions. Remembering what Grish Chunder had said, I laughed aloud. The Lords of Life and Death would never allow Charlie Mears to speak with full knowledge of his pasts; and I must even piece out what he had told me with my own poor inventions while Charlie wrote of the ways of bank-clerks.

I got together and placed on one file all my notes; and the net result was not cheering. I read them a second time. There was nothing that might not have been compiled at second-hand from other people's books – except, perhaps, the story of the fight in the harbour. The adventures of a Viking had been written many times before; the history of a Greek galley-slave was no new thing, and though I wrote both, who could challenge or confirm the accuracy of my details? I might as well tell a tale of two thousand years hence. The Lords of Life and Death were as cunning as Grish Chunder had hinted. They would allow nothing to escape that might trouble or make easy the minds of men. Though I was convinced of this, yet I could not leave the tale alone. Exaltation followed reaction, not once, but twenty times in the next few weeks. My moods varied with the March sunlight and flying clouds. By night or in the beauty of a spring morning I perceived that I could write that tale and shift continents thereby. In the wet windy afternoons, I saw that the tale might indeed be written, but would be nothing more than a faked, false-varnished, sham-rusted piece of Wardour Street work at the end. Then I blessed Charlie in many ways – though it was no fault of his. He seemed to be busy with prize competitions, and I saw less and less of him as the weeks went by and the earth cracked and grew ripe to spring, and the buds swelled in their sheaths. He did not care to read or talk of what he had read, and there was a new ring of self-assertion in his voice. I hardly cared to remind him of the galley when we met; but Charlie alluded to it on every occasion, always as a story from which money was to be made.

"I think I deserve twenty-five per cent., don't I, at least," he said, with beautiful frankness. "I supplied all the ideas, didn't I?"

This greediness for silver was a new side in his nature. I assumed that it had been developed in the City, where Charlie was picking up the curious nasal drawl of the underbred City man.

"When the thing's done we'll talk about it. I can't make anything of it at present. Red-haired or black-haired hero – they are equally difficult."

He was sitting by the fire staring at the red coals. "I can't understand what you find so difficult. It's all as clear as mud to me," he replied. A jet of gas puffed out between the bars, took light, and whistled softly. "Suppose we take the red-haired hero's adventures first, from the time that he came south to my galley and captured it and sailed to the Beaches."

I knew better now than to interrupt Charlie. I was out of reach of pen and paper, and dared not move to get them lest I should break the current. The gas-jet puffed and whinnied, Charlie's voice dropped almost to a whisper, and he told a tale of the sailing of an open galley to Furdurstrandi, of sunsets on the open sea, seen under the curve of the one sail evening after evening when the galley's beak was notched into the centre of the sinking disc, and "we sailed by that, for we had no other guide," quoth Charlie. He spoke of a landing on an island and explorations in its woods, where the crew killed three men whom they found asleep under the pines. Their ghosts, Charlie said, followed the galley, swimming and choking in the water, and the crew cast lots and threw one of their number overboard as a sacrifice to the strange gods whom they had offended. Then they ate sea-weed when their provisions failed, and their legs swelled, and their leader, the red-haired man, killed two rowers who mutinied, and after a year spent among the woods they set sail for their own country, and a wind that never failed carried them back so safely that they all slept at night. This and much more Charlie told. Sometimes the voice fell so low that I could not catch the words, though every nerve was on the strain. He spoke of their leader, the red-haired man, as a pagan speaks of his God; for it was he who cheered them and slew them impartially as he thought best for their needs; and it was he who steered them for three days among floating ice, each floe crowded with strange beasts that "tried to sail with us," said Charlie, "and we beat them back with the handles of the oars."

The gas-jet went out, a burnt coal gave way, and the fire settled with a tiny crash to the bottom of the grate. Charlie ceased speaking, and I said no word.

"By Jove!" he said at last, shaking his head. "I've been staring at the fire till I'm dizzy. What was I going to say?"

"Something about the galley-book."

"I remember now. It's a quarter of the profits, isn't it?"

"It's anything you like when I've done the tale."

"I wanted to be sure of that. I must go now. I've – I've an appointment." And he left me.

Had not my eyes been held, I might have known that that broken muttering over the fire was the swan-song of Charlie Mears. But I thought it the prelude to further revelation. At last and at last I should cheat the Lords of Life and Death!

When next Charlie came to me I received him with rap-ture. He was nervous and embarrassed, but his eyes were very full of light, and his lips a little parted.

"I've done a poem," he said, and then, quickly: "It's the

best I've ever done. Read it." He thrust it into my hand and
retreated to the window.

I groaned inwardly. It would be the work of half an hour
to criticise – that is to say, praise – the poem sufficiently to
please Charlie. Then I had good reason to groan, for Charlie,
discarding his favourite centipede metres, had launched into
shorter and choppier verse, and verse with a motive at the
back of it. This is what I read: –

> "The day is most fair, the cheery wind
>   Halloos behind the hill
> Where he bends the wood as seemeth good,
>   And the sapling to his will!
> Riot, O wind; there is that in my blood
>   That would not have thee still!
>
> "She gave me herself, O Earth, O Sky;
>   Grey sea, she is mine alone!
> Let the sullen boulders hear my cry,
>   And rejoice tho' they be but stone!
>
> "Mine! I have won her, O good brown earth,
>   Make merry! 'Tis hard on Spring;
> Make merry; my love is doubly worth
>   All worship your fields can bring!
> Let the hind that tills you feel my mirth
>   At the early harrowing."

"Yes, it's the early harrowing, past a doubt," I said, with
a dread at my heart. Charlie smiled, but did not answer.

> "Red cloud of the sunset, tell it abroad;
>   I am victor. Greet me, O Sun,
> Dominant master and absolute lord
>   Over the soul of one!"

"Well?" said Charlie, looking over my shoulder.

I thought it far from well, and very evil indeed, when he
silently laid a photograph on the paper – the photograph of
a girl with a curly head and a foolish slack mouth.

"Isn't it – isn't it wonderful?" he whispered, pink to
the tips of his ears, wrapped in the rosy mystery of first

love. "I didn't know; I didn't think – it came like a thunder-clap."

"Yes. It comes like a thunderclap. Are you very happy, Charlie?"

"My God – she – she loves me!" He sat down repeating the last words to himself. I looked at the hairless face, the narrow shoulders already bowed by desk-work, and wondered when, where, and how he had loved in his past lives.

"What will your mother say?" I asked cheerfully.

"I don't care a damn what she says."

At twenty the things for which one does not care a damn should, properly, be many, but one must not include mothers in the list. I told him this gently; and he described Her, even as Adam must have described to the newly-named beasts the glory and tenderness and beauty of Eve. Incidentally I learned that She was a tobacconist's assistant with a weakness for pretty dress, and had told him four or five times already that She had never been kissed by a man before.

Charlie spoke on and on, and on; while I, separated from him by thousands of years, was considering the beginnings of things. Now I understood why the Lords of Life and Death shut the doors so carefully behind us. It is that we may not remember our first and most beautiful wooings. Were it not so, our world would be without inhabitants in a hundred years.

"Now, about that galley-story," I said still more cheerfully, in a pause in the rush of the speech.

Charlie looked up as though he had been hit. "The galley – what galley? Good heavens, don't joke, man! This is serious! You don't know how serious it is!"

Grish Chunder was right. Charlie had tasted the love of woman that kills remembrance, and the finest story in the world would never be written.

THE MARK OF THE BEAST

THE MARK OF THE BEAST

***

Your Gods and my Gods – do you or I know which are the stronger?

Native Proverb

E AST of Suez, some hold, the direct control of Providence ceases; Man being there handed over to the power of the Gods and Devils of Asia, and the Church of England Providence only exercising an occasional and modified supervision in the case of Englishmen.

This theory accounts for some of the more unnecessary horrors of life in India: it may be stretched to explain my story.

My friend Strickland of the Police, who knows as much of natives of India as is good for any man, can bear witness to the facts of the case. Dumoise, our doctor, also saw what Strickland and I saw. The inference which he drew from the evidence was entirely incorrect. He is dead now; he died in a rather curious manner, which has been elsewhere described.

When Fleete came to India he owned a little money and some land in the Himalayas, near a place called Dharmsala. Both properties had been left him by an uncle, and he came out to finance them. He was a big, heavy, genial, and inoffensive man. His knowledge of natives was, of course, limited, and he complained of the difficulties of the language.

He rode in from his place in the hills to spend New Year in the station, and he stayed with Strickland. On New Year's Eve there was a big dinner at the club, and the night was excusably wet. When men foregather from the uttermost ends of the Empire, they have a right to be riotous. The

Frontier had sent down a contingent o' Catch-'em-Alive-O's who had not seen twenty white faces for a year, and were used to ride fifteen miles to dinner at the next Fort at the risk of a Khyberee bullet where their drinks should lie. They profited by their new security, for they tried to play pool with a curled-up hedgehog found in the garden, and one of them carried the marker round the room in his teeth. Half a dozen planters had come in from the south and were talking "horse" to the Biggest Liar in Asia, who was trying to cap all their stories at once. Everybody was there, and there was a general closing up of ranks and taking stock of our losses in dead or disabled that had fallen during the past year. It was a very wet night, and I remember that we sang "Auld Lang Syne" with our feet in the Polo Championship Cup, and our heads among the stars, and swore that we were all dear friends. Then some of us went away and annexed Burma, and some tried to open up the Soudan and were opened up by Fuzzies in that cruel scrub outside Suakim, and some found stars and medals, and some were married, which was bad, and some did other things which were worse, and the others of us stayed in our chains and strove to make money on insufficient experiences.

Fleete began the night with sherry and bitters, drank champagne steadily up to dessert, then raw, rasping Capri with all the strength of whisky, took Benedictine with his coffee, four or five whiskies and sodas to improve his pool strokes, beer and bones at half-past two, winding up with old brandy. Consequently, when he came out, at half-past three in the morning, into fourteen degrees of frost, he was very angry with his horse for coughing, and tried to leapfrog into the saddle. The horse broke away and went to his stables; so Strickland and I formed a Guard of Dishonour to take Fleete home.

Our road lay through the bazar, close to a little temple of Hanuman, the Monkey-god, who is a leading divinity worthy of respect. All gods have good points, just as have all priests. Personally, I attach much importance to Hanuman, and am kind to his people – the great grey apes of the hills. One never knows when one may want a friend.

There was a light in the temple, and as we passed we could hear voices of men chanting hymns. In a native temple the priests rise at all hours of the night to do honour to their god. Before we could stop him, Fleete dashed up the steps, patted two priests on the back, and was gravely grinding the ashes of his cigar-butt into the forehead of the red stone image of Hanuman. Strickland tried to drag him out, but he sat down and said solemnly:

"Shee that? 'Mark of the B-beasht! *I* made it. Ishn't it fine?"

In half a minute the temple was alive and noisy, and Strickland, who knew what came of polluting gods, said that things might occur. He, by virtue of his official position, long residence in the country, and weakness for going among the natives, was known to the priests, and he felt unhappy. Fleete sat on the ground and refused to move. He said that "good old Hanuman" made a very soft pillow.

Then, without any warning, a Silver Man came out of a recess behind the image of the god. He was perfectly naked in that bitter, bitter cold, and his body shone like frosted silver, for he was what the Bible calls "a leper as white as snow." Also he had no face, because he was a leper of some years' standing, and his disease was heavy upon him. We two stooped to haul Fleete up, and the temple was filling and filling with folk who seemed to spring from the earth, when the Silver Man ran in under our arms, making a noise exactly like the mewing of an otter, caught Fleete round the body and dropped his head on Fleete's breast before we could wrench him away. Then he retired to a corner and sat mewing while the crowd blocked all the doors.

The priests were very angry until the Silver Man touched Fleete. That nuzzling seemed to sober them.

At the end of a few minutes' silence one of the priests came to Strickland and said, in perfect English, "Take your friend away. He has done with Hanuman, but Hanuman has not done with him." The crowd gave room and we carried Fleete into the road.

Strickland was very angry. He said that we might all three have been knifed, and that Fleete should thank his stars that he had escaped without injury.

Fleete thanked no one. He said that he wanted to go to bed. He was gorgeously drunk.

We moved on, Strickland silent and wrathful, until Fleete was taken with violent shivering fits and sweating. He said that the smells of the bazar were overpowering, and he wondered why slaughterhouses were permitted so near English residences. "Can't you smell the blood?" said Fleete.

We put him to bed at last, just as the dawn was breaking, and Strickland invited me to have another whisky and soda. While we were drinking he talked of the trouble in the temple, and admitted that it baffled him completely. Strickland hates being mystified by natives, because his business in life is to overmatch them with their own weapons. He has not yet succeeded in doing this, but in fifteen or twenty years he will have made some small progress.

"They should have mauled us," he said, "instead of mewing at us. I wonder what they meant. I don't like it one little bit."

I said that the Managing Committee of the temple would in all probability bring a criminal action against us for insulting their religion. There was a section of the Indian Penal Code which exactly met Fleete's offence. Strickland said he only hoped and prayed that they would do this. Before I left I looked into Fleete's room, and saw him lying on his right side, scratching his left breast. Then I went to bed, cold, depressed, and unhappy at seven o'clock in the morning.

At one o'clock I rode over to Strickland's house to inquire after Fleete's head. I imagined that it would be a sore one. Fleete was breakfasting and seemed unwell. His temper was gone, for he was abusing the cook for not supplying him with an underdone chop. A man who can eat raw meat after a wet night is a curiosity. I told Fleete this, and he laughed.

"You breed queer mosquitoes in these parts," he said. "I've been bitten to pieces, but only in one place."

"Let's have a look at the bite," said Strickland. "It may have gone down since this morning."

While the chops were being cooked, Fleete opened his shirt and showed us, just over his left breast, a mark, the perfect double of the black rosettes – the five or six irregular blotches arranged in a circle – on a leopard's hide. Strickland looked and said, "It was only pink this morning. It's grown black now."

Fleete ran to a glass.

"By Jove!" he said, "this is nasty. What is it?"

We could not answer. Here the chops came in, all red and juicy, and Fleete bolted three in a most offensive manner. He ate on his right grinders only, and threw his head over his right shoulder as he snapped the meat. When he had finished, it struck him that he had been behaving strangely, for he said apologetically, "I don't think I ever felt so hungry in my life. I've bolted like an ostrich."

After breakfast Strickland said to me, "Don't go. Stay here, and stay for the night."

Seeing that my house was not three miles from Strickland's, this request was absurd. But Strickland insisted, and was going to say something when Fleete interrupted by declaring in a shamefaced way that he felt hungry again. Strickland sent a man to my house to fetch over my bedding and a horse, and we three went down to Strickland's stables to pass the hours until it was time to go out for a ride. The man who has a weakness for horses never wearies of inspecting them; and when two men are killing time in this way they gather knowledge and lies the one from the other.

There were five horses in the stables, and I shall never forget the scene as we tried to look them over. They seemed to have gone mad. They reared and screamed and nearly tore up their pickets; they sweated and shivered and lathered and were distraught with fear. Strickland's horses used to know him as well as his dogs; which made the matter more curious. We left the stable for fear of the brutes throwing themselves in their panic. Then Strickland turned back and called me. The horses were still frightened, but they let us "gentle" and make much of them, and put their heads in our bosoms.

"They aren't afraid of *us*," said Strickland. "D'you know, I'd give three months' pay if Outrage here could talk."

But Outrage was dumb, and could only cuddle up to his master and blow out his nostrils, as is the custom of horses when they wish to explain things but can't. Fleete came up when we were in the stalls, and as soon as the horses saw him their fright broke out afresh. It was all that we could do to escape from the place unkicked. Strickland said, "They don't seem to love you, Fleete."

"Nonsense," said Fleete; "my mare will follow me like a dog." He went to her; she was in a loose-box; but as he slipped the bars she plunged, knocked him down, and broke away into the garden. I laughed, but Strickland was not amused. He took his moustache in both fists and pulled at it till it nearly came out. Fleete, instead of going off to chase his property, yawned, saying that he felt sleepy. He went to the house to lie down, which was a foolish way of spending New Year's Day.

Strickland sat with me in the stables and asked if I had noticed anything peculiar in Fleete's manner. I said that he ate his food like a beast; but that this might have been the result of living alone in the hills out of the reach of society as refined and elevating as ours, for instance. Strickland was not amused. I do not think that he listened to me, for his next sentence referred to the mark on Fleete's breast, and I said that it might have been caused by blister-flies, or that it was possibly a birth-mark newly born and now visible for the first time. We both agreed that it was unpleasant to look at, and Strickland found occasion to say that I was a fool.

"I can't tell you what I think now," said he, "because you

would call me a madman; but you must stay with me for the next few days, if you can. I want you to watch Fleete, but don't tell me what you think till I have made up my mind."

"But I am dining out to-night," I said.

"So am I," said Strickland, "and so is Fleete. At least if he doesn't change his mind."

We walked about the garden smoking, but saying nothing – because we were friends, and talking spoils good tobacco – till our pipes were out. Then we went to wake up Fleete. He was wide awake and fidgeting about his room.

"I say, I want some more chops," he said. "Can I get them?"

We laughed and said, "Go and change. The ponies will be round in a minute."

"All right," said Fleete. "I'll go when I get the chops – underdone ones, mind."

He seemed to be quite in earnest. It was four o'clock, and we had had breakfast at one; still, for a long time, he demanded those underdone chops. Then he changed into riding clothes and went out into the verandah. His pony – the mare had not been caught – would not let him come near. All three horses were unmanageable – mad with fear – and finally Fleete said that he would stay at home and get something to eat. Strickland and I rode out wondering. As we passed the temple of Hanuman, the Silver Man came out and mewed at us.

"He is not one of the regular priests of the temple," said Strickland. "I think I should peculiarly like to lay my hands on him."

There was no spring in our gallop on the race course that evening. The horses were stale, and moved as though they had been ridden out.

"The fright after breakfast has been too much for them," said Strickland.

That was the only remark he made through the remainder of the ride. Once or twice I think he swore to himself; but that did not count.

We came back in the dark at seven o'clock, and saw that there were no lights in the bungalow. "Careless ruffians my servants are!" said Strickland.

My horse reared at something on the carriage-drive, and Fleete stood up under its nose.

"What are you doing, grovelling about the garden?" said Strickland.

But both horses bolted and nearly threw us. We dismounted by the stables and returned to Fleete, who was on his hands and knees under the orange-bushes.

"What the devil's wrong with you?" said Strickland.

"Nothing, nothing in the world," said Fleete, speaking very quickly and thickly. "I've been gardening – botanising, you know. The smell of the earth is delightful. I think I'm going for a walk – a long walk – all night."

Then I saw that there was something excessively out of order somewhere, and I said to Strickland, "I am not dining out."

"Bless you!" said Strickland. "Here, Fleete, get up. You'll catch fever there. Come in to dinner and let's have the lamps lit. We'll all dine at home."

Fleete stood up unwillingly, and said, "No lamps – no lamps. It's much nicer here. Let's dine outside and have some more chops – lots of 'em and underdone – bloody ones with gristle."

Now a December evening in Northern India is bitterly cold, and Fleete's suggestion was that of a maniac.

"Come in," said Strickland sternly. "Come in at once."

Fleete came, and when the lamps were brought, we saw that he was literally plastered with dirt from head to foot. He must have been rolling in the garden. He shrank from the light and went to his room. His eyes were horrible to look at. There was a green light behind them, not in them, if you understand, and the man's lower lip hung down.

Strickland said, "There is going to be trouble – big trouble – to-night. Don't you change your riding-things."

We waited and waited for Fleete's reappearance, and ordered dinner in the meantime. We could hear him moving about his own room, but there was no light there. Presently from the room came the long-drawn howl of a wolf.

People write and talk lightly of blood running cold and hair standing up and things of that kind. Both sensations are too horrible to be trifled with. My heart stopped as though a knife had been driven through it, and Strickland turned as white as the tablecloth.

The howl was repeated, and was answered by another howl far across the fields.

That set the gilded roof on the horror. Strickland dashed into Fleete's room. I followed, and we saw Fleete getting out of the window. He made beast-noises in the back of his throat. He could not answer us when we shouted at him. He spat.

I don't quite remember what followed, but I think that Strickland must have stunned him with the long boot-jack or else I should never have been able to sit on his chest. Fleete could not speak, he could only snarl, and his snarls were those of a wolf, not of a man. The human spirit must have been giving way all day and have died out with the twilight. We were dealing with a beast that had once been Fleete.

The affair was beyond any human and rational experience. I tried to say "Hydrophobia," but the word wouldn't come, because I knew that I was lying.

We bound this beast with leather thongs of the punkah-rope, and tied its thumbs and big toes together, and gagged it with a shoe-horn, which makes a very efficient gag if you know how to arrange it. Then we carried it into the dining-room, and sent a man to Dumoise, the doctor, telling him to come over at once. After we had despatched the messenger and were drawing breath, Strickland said, "It's no good. This isn't any doctor's work." I, also, knew that he spoke the truth.

The beast's head was free, and it threw it about from side to side. Any one entering the room would have believed that we were curing a wolf's pelt. That was the most loathsome accessory of all.

Strickland sat with his chin in the heel of his fist, watching the beast as it wriggled on the ground, but saying nothing. The shirt had been torn open in the scuffle and showed the black rosette mark on the left breast. It stood out like a blister.

In the silence of the watching we heard something without mewing like a she-otter. We both rose to our feet, and, I answer for myself, not Strickland, felt sick — actually and physically sick. We told each other, as did the men in "Pinafore," that it was the cat.

Dumoise arrived, and I never saw a little man so unprofessionally shocked. He said that it was a heart-rending case of hydrophobia, and that nothing could be done. At least any palliative measures would only prolong the agony. The beast was foaming at the mouth. Fleete, as we told Dumoise, had been bitten by dogs once or twice. Any man who keeps half a dozen terriers must expect a nip now and again. Dumoise could offer no help. He could only certify that Fleete was dying of hydrophobia. The beast was then howling, for it had managed to spit out the shoe-horn. Dumoise said that he would be ready to certify to the cause of death, and that the end was certain. He was a good little man, and he offered to remain with us; but Strickland refused the kindness. He did not wish to poison Dumoise's New Year. He would only ask him not to give the real cause of Fleete's death to the public.

So Dumoise left, deeply agitated; and as soon as the noise of the cart-wheels had died away, Strickland told me, in a whisper, his suspicions. They were so wildly improbable that he dared not say them out aloud; and I, who entertained all Strickland's beliefs, was so ashamed of owning to them that I pretended to disbelieve.

"Even if the Silver Man had bewitched Fleete for polluting the image of Hanuman, the punishment could not have fallen so quickly."

As I was whispering this the cry outside the house rose again, and the beast fell into a fresh paroxysm of struggling till we were afraid that the thongs that held it would give way.

"Watch!" said Strickland. "If this happens six times I shall take the law into my own hands. I order you to help me."

He went into his room and came out in a few minutes with the barrels of an old shot-gun, a piece of fishing-line, some thick cord, and his heavy wooden bedstead. I reported that the convulsions had followed the cry by two seconds in each case, and the beast seemed perceptibly weaker.

Strickland muttered, "But he can't take away the life! He can't take away the life!"

I said, though I knew that I was arguing against myself, "It may be a cat. It must be a cat. If the Silver Man is responsible, why does he dare to come here?"

Strickland arranged the wood on the hearth, put the gun-barrels into the glow of the fire, spread the twine on the table, and broke a walking-stick in two. There was one yard of fishing-line, gut, lapped with wire, such as is used for *mahseer*-fishing, and he tied the two ends together in a loop.

Then he said, "How can we catch him? He must be taken alive and unhurt."

I said that we must trust in Providence, and go out softly with polo-sticks into the shrubbery at the front of the house. The man or animal that made the cry was evidently moving round the house as regularly as a night-watchman. We could wait in the bushes till he came by, and knock him over.

Strickland accepted this suggestion, and we slipped out from a bath-room window into the front verandah and then across the carriage-drive into the bushes.

In the moonlight we could see the leper coming round the corner of the house. He was perfectly naked, and from time to time he mewed and stopped to dance with his shadow. It was an unattractive sight, and thinking of poor Fleete, brought to such degradation by so foul a creature, I put away all my doubts and resolved to help Strickland from the heated gun-barrels to the loop of twine – from the loins to the head and back again – with all tortures that might be needful.

The leper halted in the front porch for a moment and we jumped out on him with the sticks. He was wonderfully strong, and we were afraid that he might escape or be fatally injured before we caught him. We had an idea that lepers were frail creatures, but this proved to be incorrect. Strickland knocked his legs from under him, and I put my foot on his neck. He mewed hideously, and even through my riding-boots I could feel that his flesh was not the flesh of a clean man.

He struck at us with his hand and feet-stumps. We looped the lash of a dog-whip round him, under the arm-pits, and dragged him backwards into the hall and so into the dining-room where the beast lay. There we tied him with trunk-straps. He made no attempt to escape, but mewed.

When we confronted him with the beast the scene was beyond description. The beast doubled backwards into a bow, as though he had been poisoned with strychnine, and moaned in the most pitiable fashion. Several other things happened also, but they cannot be put down here.

"I think I was right," said Strickland. "Now we will ask him to cure this case."

But the leper only mewed. Strickland wrapped a towel round his hand and took the gun-barrels out of the fire. I put the half of the broken walking-stick through the loop of fishing-line and buckled the leper comfortably to Strickland's bedstead. I understood then how men and women and little children can endure to see a witch burnt alive; for the beast was moaning on the floor, and though the Silver Man had no face, you could see horrible feelings passing through the slab that took its place, exactly as waves of heat play across red-hot iron – gun-barrels for instance.

Strickland shaded his eyes with his hands for a moment, and we got to work. This part is not to be printed.

* * *

The dawn was beginning to break when the leper spoke. His mewings had not been satisfactory up to that point. The beast had fainted from exhaustion, and the house was very still. We unstrapped the leper and told him to take away the evil spirit. He crawled to the beast and laid his hand upon the left breast. That was all. Then he fell face down and whined, drawing in his breath as he did so.

We watched the face of the beast, and saw the soul of Fleete coming back into the eyes. Then a sweat broke out on the forehead, and the eyes – they were human eyes – closed. We waited for an hour, but Fleete still slept. We carried him to his room and bade the leper go, giving him the bedstead, and the sheet on the bedstead to cover his nakedness, the gloves and the towels with which we had touched him, and the whip that had been hooked round his body. He put the sheet about him and went out into the early morning without speaking or mewing.

Strickland wiped his face and sat down. A night-gong, far away in the city, made seven o'clock.

"Exactly four-and-twenty hours!" said Strickland. "And I've done enough to ensure my dismissal from the service, besides permanent quarters in a lunatic asylum. Do you believe that we are awake?"

The red-hot gun-barrel had fallen on the floor and was singeing the carpet. The smell was entirely real.

That morning at eleven we two together went to wake up Fleete. We looked and saw that the black leopard-rosette on his chest had disappeared. He was very drowsy and tired, but as soon as he saw us, he said, "Oh! Confound you fellows. Happy New Year to you. Never mix your liquors. I'm nearly dead."

"Thanks for your kindness, but you're over time," said Strickland. "To-day is the morning of the second. You've slept the clock round with a vengeance."

The door opened, and little Dumoise put his head in. He had come on foot, and fancied that we were laying out Fleete.

"I've brought a nurse," said Dumoise. "I suppose that she can come in for . . . what is necessary."

"By all means," said Fleete cheerily, sitting up in bed. "Bring on your nurses."

Dumoise was dumb. Strickland led him out and explained that there must have been a mistake in the diagnosis. Dumoise remained dumb and left the house hastily. He considered that his professional reputation had been injured, and was inclined to make a personal matter of the recovery. Strickland went out too. When he came back, he said that he had been to call on the temple of Hanuman to offer redress for the pollution of the god, and had been solemnly assured that no white man had ever touched the idol, and that he was an incarnation of all the virtues labouring under a delusion. "What do you think?" said Strickland.

I said, "There are more things . . ."

But Strickland hates that quotation. He says that I have worn it threadbare.

One other curious thing happened which frightened me as much as anything in all the night's work. When Fleete was dressed he came into the dining-room and sniffed. He had a quaint trick of moving his nose when he sniffed. "Horrid doggy smell, here," said he. "You should really keep those terriers of yours in better order. Try sulphur, Strick."

But Strickland did not answer. He caught hold of the back of a chair, and, without warning, went into an amazing fit of hysterics. It is terrible to see a strong man overtaken with hysteria. Then it struck me that we had fought for Fleete's soul with the Silver Man in that room, and had disgraced ourselves as Englishmen forever, and I laughed and gasped and gurgled just as shamefully as Strickland, while Fleete thought that we had both gone mad. We never told him what we had done.

Some years later, when Strickland had married and was a church-going member of society for his wife's sake, we reviewed the incident dispassionately, and Strickland suggested that I should put it before the public.

I cannot myself see that this step is likely to clear up the mystery; because, in the first place, no one will believe a rather unpleasant story, and, in the second, it is well known to every right-minded man that the gods of the heathen are stone and brass, and any attempt to deal with them otherwise is justly condemned.

THE STRANGE RIDE OF
MORROWBIE JUKES

THE STRANGE RIDE OF
MORROWBIE JUKES

✳ ✳ ✳

Alive or dead – there is no other way.
Native Proverb

THERE is no invention about this tale. Jukes by accident stumbled upon a village that is well known to exist, though he is the only Englishman who has been there. A somewhat similar institution used to flourish on the outskirts of Calcutta, and there is a story that if you go into the heart of Bikanir, which is in the heart of the Great Indian Desert, you shall come across not a village but a town where the Dead who did not die but may not live have established their headquarters. And, since it is perfectly true that in the same Desert is a wonderful city where all the rich money-lenders retreat after they have made their fortunes (fortunes so vast that the owners cannot trust even the strong hand of the Government to protect them, but take refuge in the waterless sands), and drive sumptuous C-spring barouches, and buy beautiful girls and decorate their palaces with gold and ivory and Minton tiles and mother-o'-pearl, I do not see why Jukes's tale should not be true. He is a Civil Engineer, with a head for plans and distances and things of that kind, and he certainly would not take the trouble to invent imaginary traps. He could earn more by doing his legitimate work. He never varies the tale in the telling, and grows very hot and indignant when he thinks of the disrespectful treatment he received. He wrote this quite straightforwardly at first, but he has touched it up in places and introduced Moral Reflections: thus: –

In the beginning it all arose from a slight attack of fever.

My work necessitated my being in camp for some months between Pakpattan and Mubarakpur – a desolate sandy stretch of country, as every one who has had the misfortune to go there may know. My coolies were neither more nor less exasperating than other gangs, and my work demanded sufficient attention to keep me from moping, had I been inclined to so unmanly a weakness.

On the 23rd December, 1884, I felt a little feverish. There was a full moon at the time, and, in consequence, every dog near my tent was baying it. The brutes assembled in twos and threes and drove me frantic. A few days previously I had shot one loud-mouthed singer and suspended his carcass *in terrorem* about fifty yards from my tent-door, but his friends fell upon, fought for, and ultimately devoured the body: and, as it seemed to me, sang their hymns of thanksgiving afterwards with renewed energy.

The light-headedness which accompanies fever acts differently on different men. My irritation gave way, after a short time, to a fixed determination to slaughter one huge black-and-white beast who had been foremost in song and first in flight throughout the evening. Thanks to a shaking hand and a giddy head, I had already missed him twice with both barrels of my shot-gun, when it struck me that my best plan would be to ride him down in the open and finish him off with a hog-spear. This, of course, was merely the semi-delirious notion of a fever-patient; but I remember that it struck me at the time as being eminently practical and feasible.

I therefore ordered my groom to saddle Pornic and bring him round quietly to the rear of my tent. When the pony was ready, I stood at his head prepared to mount and dash out as soon as the dog should again lift up his voice. Pornic, by the way, had not been out of his pickets for a couple of days; the night air was crisp and chilly; and I was armed with a specially long and sharp pair of persuaders with which I had been rousing a sluggish cob that afternoon. You will easily believe, then, that when he was let go he went quickly. In one moment, for the brute bolted as straight as a die, the tent was left far behind, and we were flying over the smooth sandy soil at racing speed. In another we had passed the wretched dog, and I had almost forgotten why it was that I had taken horse and hog-spear.

The delirium of fever and the excitement of rapid motion through the air must have taken away the remnant of my senses. I have a faint recollection of standing upright in my stirrups, and of brandishing my hog-spear at the great white Moon that looked down so calmly on my mad gallop; and of shouting challenges to the camel-thorn bushes as they whizzed past. Once or twice, I believe, I swayed forward on Pornic's neck, and literally hung on by my spurs – as the marks next morning showed.

The wretched beast went forward like a thing possessed, over what seemed to be a limitless expanse of moonlit sand. Next, I remember, the ground rose suddenly in front of us, and as we topped the ascent I saw the waters of the Sutlej shining like a silver bar below. Then Pornic blundered heavily on his nose, and we rolled together down some unseen slope.

I must have lost consciousness, for when I recovered I was lying on my stomach in a heap of soft white sand, and the dawn was beginning to break dimly over the edge of the slope down which I had fallen. As the light grew stronger I saw I was at the bottom of a horseshoe-shaped crater of sand, opening on one side directly on to the shoals of the Sutlej. My fever had altogether left me, and, with the exception of a slight dizziness in the head, I felt no bad effects from the fall over night.

Pornic, who was standing a few yards away, was naturally a good deal exhausted, but had not hurt himself in the least. His saddle, a favourite polo one, was much knocked about, and had been twisted under his belly. It took me some time to put him to rights, and in the meantime I had ample opportunities of observing the spot into which I had so foolishly dropped.

At the risk of being considered tedious, I must describe it at length, inasmuch as an accurate mental picture of its peculiarities will be of material assistance in enabling the reader to understand what follows.

Imagine then, as I have said before, a horseshoe-shaped crater of sand with steeply-graded sand walls about thirty-five feet high. (The slope, I fancy, must have been about 65°.) This crater enclosed a level piece of ground about fifty yards long by thirty at its broadest part, with a rude well in the centre. Round the bottom of the crater, about three feet from the level of the ground proper, ran a series of eighty-three semicircular, ovoid, square, and multilateral holes, all about three feet at the mouth. Each hole on inspection showed that it was carefully shored internally with drift-wood and bamboos, and over the mouth a wooden drip-board projected, like the peak of a jockey's cap, for two feet. No sign of life was visible in these tunnels, but a most sickening stench pervaded the entire amphitheatre – a stench fouler than any which my wanderings in Indian villages have introduced me to.

Having remounted Pornic, who was as anxious as I to get back to camp, I rode round the base of the horseshoe to find some place whence an exit would be practicable. The inhabitants, whoever they might be, had not thought fit to put in an appearance, so I was left to my own devices. My first attempt to "rush" Pornic up the steep sand-banks showed me that I had fallen into a trap exactly on the same model as that which the ant-lion sets for its prey. At each step the shifting sand poured down from above in tons, and rattled on the drip-boards of the holes like small shot. A couple of ineffectual charges sent us both rolling down to the bottom, half choked with the torrents of sand; and I was constrained to turn my attention to the river-bank.

Here everything seemed easy enough. The sand-hills ran down to the river edge, it is true, but there were plenty of shoals and shallows across which I could gallop Pornic, and find my way back to *terra firma* by turning sharply to the

right or the left. As I led Pornic over the sands I was startled
by the faint pop of a rifle across the river; and at the same
moment a bullet dropped with a sharp "*whit*" close to Pornic's head.

There was no mistaking the nature of the missile – a
regulation Martini-Henry "picket." About five hundred
yards away a country-boat was anchored in midstream; and
a jet of smoke drifting away from its bows in the still morning air showed me whence the delicate attention had come.
Was ever a respectable gentleman in such an *impasse*? The
treacherous sand slope allowed no escape from a spot which
I had visited most involuntarily, and a promenade on the
river frontage was the signal for a bombardment from some
insane native in a boat. I'm afraid that I lost my temper very
much indeed.

Another bullet reminded me that I had better save my
breath to cool my porridge; and I retreated hastily up the
sands and back to the horseshoe, where I saw that the noise
of the rifle had drawn sixty-five human beings from the
badger-holes which I had up till that point supposed to be
untenanted. I found myself in the midst of a crowd of spectators – about forty men, twenty women, and one child who
could not have been more than five years old. They were all
scantily clothed in that salmon-coloured cloth which one
associates with Hindu mendicants, and, at first sight, gave me
the impression of a band of loathsome *fakirs*. The filth and
repulsiveness of the assembly were beyond all description,
and I shuddered to think what their life in the badger-holes
must be.

Even in these days, when local self-government has destroyed the greater part of a native's respect for a Sahib, I
have been accustomed to a certain amount of civility from
my inferiors, and on approaching the crowd naturally expected that there would be some recognition of my presence.
As a matter of fact, there was; but it was by no means what
I had looked for.

The ragged crew actually laughed at me – such laughter I

hope I may never hear again. They cackled, yelled, whistled, and howled as I walked into their midst; some of them literally throwing themselves down on the ground in convulsions of unholy mirth. In a moment I had let go Pornic's head, and, irritated beyond expression at the morning's adventure, commenced cuffing those nearest to me with all the force I could. The wretches dropped under my blows like nine-pins, and the laughter gave place to wails for mercy; while those yet untouched clasped me round the knees, imploring me in all sorts of uncouth tongues to spare them.

In the tumult, and just when I was feeling very much ashamed of myself for having thus easily given way to my temper, a thin, high voice murmured in English from behind my shoulder: "Sahib! Sahib! Do you not know me? Sahib, it is Gunga Dass, the telegraph-master."

I spun round quickly and faced the speaker.

Gunga Dass (I have, of course, no hesitation in mentioning the man's real name) I had known four years before as a Deccanee Brahmin lent by the Punjab Government to one of the Khalsia States. He was in charge of a branch telegraph-office there, and when I had last met him was a jovial, full-stomached portly Government servant with a marvellous capacity for making bad puns in English – a peculiarity which made me remember him long after I had forgotten his services to me in his official capacity. It is seldom that a Hindu makes English puns.

Now, however, the man was changed beyond all recognition. Caste-mark, stomach, slate-coloured continuations, and unctuous speech were all gone. I looked at a withered skeleton, turbanless and almost naked, with long matted hair and deep-set codfish-eyes. But for a crescent-shaped scar on the left cheek – the result of an accident for which I was responsible – I should never have known him. But it was indubitably Gunga Dass, and – for this I was thankful – an English-speaking native who might at least tell me the meaning of all that I had gone through that day.

The crowd retreated to some distance as I turned towards

the miserable figure and ordered him to show me some method of escaping from the crater. He held a freshly-plucked crow in his hand, and in reply to my question climbed slowly on a platform of sand which ran in front of the holes, and commenced lighting a fire there in silence. Dried bents, sand-poppies, and driftwood burn quickly; and I derived much consolation from the fact that he lit them with an ordinary sulphur match. When they were in a bright glow, and the crow was neatly spitted in front thereof, Gunga Dass began without a word of preamble: –

"There are only two kinds of men, Sar. The alive and the dead. When you are dead you are dead, but when you are alive you live." (Here the crow demanded his attention for an instant as it twirled before the fire in danger of being burnt to a cinder.) "If you die at home and do not die when you come to the ghât to be burnt, you come here."

The nature of the reeking village was made plain now, and all that I had known or read of the grotesque and the horrible paled before the fact just communicated by the ex-Brahmin. Sixteen years ago, when I first landed in Bombay, I had been told by a wandering Armenian of the existence, somewhere in India, of a place to which such Hindus as had the misfortune to recover from trance or catalepsy were conveyed and kept, and I recollect laughing heartily at what I was then pleased to consider a traveller's tale. Sitting at the bottom of the sand-trap, the memory of Watson's Hotel, with its swinging punkahs, white-robed servants, and the sallow-faced Armenian, rose up in my mind as vividly as a photograph, and I burst into a loud fit of laughter. The contrast was too absurd!

Gunga Dass, as he bent over the unclean bird, watched me curiously. Hindus seldom laugh, and his surroundings were not such as to move him that way. He removed the crow solemnly from the wooden spit and as solemnly devoured it. Then he continued his story, which I give in his own words: –

"In epidemics of the cholera you are carried to be burnt

almost before you are dead. When you come to the riverside
the cold air, perhaps, makes you alive, and then, if you are
only little alive, mud is put on your nose and mouth and you
die conclusively. If you are rather more alive, more mud is
put; but if you are too lively they let you go and take you
away. I was too lively, and made protestation with anger
against the indignities that they endeavoured to press upon
me. In those days I was Brahmin and proud man. Now I am
dead man and eat" – here he eyed the well-gnawed breastbone with the first sign of emotion that I had seen in him
since we met – "crows, and – other things. They took me
from my sheets when they saw that I was too lively and gave
me medicines for one week, and I survived successfully.
Then they sent me by rail from my place to Okara Station,
with a man to take care of me; and at Okara Station we met
two other men, and they conducted we three on camels, in the
night, from Okara Station to this place, and they propelled
me from the top to the bottom, and the other two succeeded,
and I have been here ever since two and a half years. Once I
was Brahmin and proud man, and now I eat crows."

"There is no way of getting out?"

"None of what kind at all. When I first came I made
experiments frequently, and all the others also, but we have
always succumbed to the sand which is precipitated upon our
heads."

"But surely," I broke in at this point, "the river-front is
open, and it is worth while dodging the bullets; while at
night —"

I had already matured a rough plan of escape which a
natural instinct of selfishness forbade me sharing with Gunga
Dass. He, however, divined my unspoken thought almost as
soon as it was formed; and, to my intense astonishment, gave
vent to a long, low chuckle of derision – the laughter, be it
understood, of a superior or at least of an equal.

"You will not" – he had dropped the Sir after his first
sentence – "make any escape that way. But you can try. I
have tried. Once only."

The sensation of nameless terror which I had in vain attempted to strive against overmastered me completely. My long fast – it was now close upon ten o'clock, and I had eaten nothing since tiffin on the previous day – combined with the violent agitation of the ride had exhausted me, and I verily believe that, for a few minutes, I acted as one mad. I hurled myself against the sand-slope. I ran round the base of the crater, blaspheming and praying by turns. I crawled out among the sedges of the river-front, only to be driven back each time in an agony of nervous dread by the rifle-bullets which cut up the sand round me – for I dared not face the death of a mad dog among that hideous crowd – and so fell, spent and raving, at the curb of the well. No one had taken the slightest notice of an exhibition which makes me blush hotly even when I think of it now.

Two or three men trod on my panting body as they drew water, but they were evidently used to this sort of thing, and had no time to waste upon me. Gunga Dass, indeed, when he had banked the embers of his fire with sand, was at some pains to throw half a cupful of fetid water over my head, an attention for which I could have fallen on my knees and thanked him, but he was laughing all the while in the same mirthless, wheezy key that greeted me on my first attempt to force the shoals. And so, in a half-fainting state, I lay till noon. Then, being only a man after all, I felt hungry, and said as much to Gunga Dass, whom I had begun to regard as my natural protector. Following the impulse of the outer world when dealing with natives, I put my hand into my pocket and drew out four annas. The absurdity of the gift struck me at once, and I was about to replace the money.

Gunga Dass, however, cried: "Give me the money, all you have, or I will get help, and we will kill you!"

A Briton's first impulse, I believe, is to guard the contents of his pockets; but a moment's thought showed me the folly of differing with the one man who had it in his power to make me comfortable, and with whose help it was possible that I might eventually escape from the crater. I gave him all the money in my possession, Rs. 9–8–5 – nine rupees, eight annas, and five pie – for I always keep small change as *bakshish* when I am in camp. Gunga Dass clutched the coins, and hid them at once in his ragged loin-cloth, looking round to assure himself that no one had observed us.

"*Now* I will give you something to eat," said he.

What pleasure my money could have given him I am unable to say; but inasmuch as it did please him, I was not sorry that I had parted with it so readily, for I had no doubt that he would have had me killed if I had refused. One does not protest against the doings of a den of wild beasts; and my companions were lower than any beasts. While I ate what Gunga Dass had provided, a coarse *chapatti* and a cupful of the foul well-water, the people showed not the faintest sign of curiosity – that curiosity which is so rampant, as a rule, in an Indian village.

I could even fancy that they despised me. At all events, they treated me with the most chilling indifference, and Gunga Dass was nearly as bad. I plied him with questions about the terrible village, and received extremely unsatisfactory answers. So far as I could gather, it had been in existence from time immemorial – whence I concluded that it was at least a century old – and during that time no one had ever been known to escape from it. (I had to control myself here with both hands, lest the blind terror should lay hold of me a second time and drive me raving round the crater.) Gunga Dass took a malicious pleasure in emphasising this point and in watching me wince. Nothing that I could do would induce him to tell me who the mysterious "They" were.

"It is so ordered," he would reply, "and I do not yet know any one who has disobeyed the orders."

"Only wait till my servant finds that I am missing," I retorted, "and I promise you that this place shall be cleared off the face of the earth, and I'll give you a lesson in civility, too, my friend."

"Your servants would be torn in pieces before they came near this place; and, besides, you are dead, my dear friend.

It is not your fault, of course, but none the less you are dead *and* buried."

At irregular intervals supplies of food, I was told, were dropped down from the land side into the amphitheatre, and the inhabitants fought for them like wild beasts. When a man felt his death coming on he retreated to his lair and died there. The body was sometimes dragged out of the hole and thrown on to the sand, or allowed to rot where it lay.

The phrase "thrown on to the sand" caught my attention, and I asked Gunga Dass whether this sort of thing was not likely to breed a pestilence.

"That," said he, with another of his wheezy chuckles, "you may see for yourself subsequently. You will have much time to make observations."

Whereat, to his great delight, I winced once more and hastily continued the conversation: "And how do you live here from day to day? What do you do?" The question elicited exactly the same answer as before – coupled with the information that "this place is like your European heaven; there is neither marrying nor giving in marriage."

Gunga Dass had been educated at a Mission School, and, as he himself admitted, had he only changed his religion "like a wise man," might have avoided the living grave which was now his portion. But as long as I was with him I fancy he was happy.

Here was a Sahib, a representative of the dominant race, helpless as a child and completely at the mercy of his native neighbours. In a deliberate, lazy way he set himself to torture me as a schoolboy would devote a rapturous half-hour to watching the agonies of an impaled beetle, or as a ferret in a blind burrow might glue himself comfortably to the neck of a rabbit. The burden of his conversation was that there was no escape "of no kind whatever," and that I should stay here till I died and was "thrown on to the sand." If it were possible to forejudge the conversation of the Damned on the advent of a new soul in their abode, I should say that they would speak as Gunga Dass did to me throughout that long afternoon. I was powerless to protest or answer; all my energies being devoted to a struggle against the inexplicable terror that threatened to overwhelm me again and again. I can compare the feeling to nothing except the struggles of a man against the overpowering nausea of the Channel passage – only my agony was of the spirit and infinitely more terrible.

As the day wore on, the inhabitants began to appear in full strength to catch the rays of the afternoon sun, which were now sloping in at the mouth of the crater. They assembled by little knots, and talked among themselves without even throwing a glance in my direction. About four o'clock, so far as I could judge, Gunga Dass rose and dived into his lair for a moment, emerging with a live crow in his hands. The wretched bird was in a most draggled and deplorable condition, but seemed to be in no way afraid of its master. Advancing cautiously to the river-front, Gunga Dass stepped from tussock to tussock until he had reached a smooth patch of sand directly in the line of the boat's fire. The occupants of the boat took no notice. Here he stopped, and, with a couple of dexterous turns of the wrist, pegged the bird on its back with outstretched wings. As was only natural, the crow began to shriek at once and beat the air with its claws. In a few seconds the clamour had attracted the attention of a bevy of wild crows on a shoal a few hundred yards away, where they were discussing something that looked like a corpse. Half a dozen crows flew over at once to see what was going on, and also, as it proved, to attack the pinioned bird. Gunga Dass, who had lain down on a tussock, motioned to me to be quiet, though I fancy this was a needless precaution. In a moment, and before I could see how it happened, a wild crow, who had grappled with the shrieking and helpless bird, was entangled in the latter's claws, swiftly disengaged by Gunga Dass, and pegged down beside its companion in adversity. Curiosity, it seemed, overpowered the rest of the flock, and almost before Gunga Dass and I had time to withdraw to the tussock, two more captives were struggling in the upturned claws of the decoys. So the chase – if I can give it

so dignified a name – continued until Gunga Dass had captured seven crows. Five of them he throttled at once, reserv-
ing two for further operations another day. I was a good deal
impressed by this, to me, novel method of securing food, and
complimented Gunga Dass on his skill.

"It is nothing to do," said he. "To-morrow you must do
it for me. You are stronger than I am."

This calm assumption of superiority upset me not a little,
and I answered peremptorily: "Indeed, you old ruffian? What
do you think I have given you money for?"

"Very well," was the unmoved reply. "Perhaps not to-
morrow, nor the day after, nor subsequently; but in the end,
and for many years, you will catch crows and eat crows, and
you will thank your European God that you have crows to
catch and eat."

I could have cheerfully strangled him for this; but judged
it best under the circumstances to smother my resentment.
An hour later I was eating one of the crows; and, as Gunga
Dass had said, thanking my God that I had a crow to eat.
Never as long as I live shall I forget that evening meal. The
whole population were squatting on the hard sand platform
opposite their dens, huddled over tiny fires of refuse and
dried rushes. Death, having once laid his hand upon these
men and forborne to strike, seemed to stand aloof from them
now; for most of our company were old men, bent and worn
and twisted with years, and women aged to all appearance as
the Fates themselves. They sat together in knots and talked
– God only knows what they found to discuss – in low
equable tones, curiously in contrast to the strident babble
with which natives are accustomed to make day hideous.
Now and then an access of that sudden fury which had possessed me in the morning would lay hold on a man or
woman; and with yells and imprecations the sufferer would
attack the steep slope until, baffled and bleeding, he fell back
on the platform incapable of moving a limb. The others
would never even raise their eyes when this happened, as
men too well aware of the futility of their fellows' attempts

and wearied with their useless repetition. I saw four such
outbursts in the course of that evening.

Gunga Dass took an eminently business-like view of my
situation, and while we were dining – I can afford to laugh
at the recollection now, but it was painful enough at the time
– propounded the terms on which he would consent to "do"
for me. My nine rupees, eight annas, he argued, at the rate
of three annas a day, would provide me with food for fifty-
one days, or about seven weeks; that is to say, he would be
willing to cater for me for that length of time. At the end of
it I was to look after myself. For a further consideration –
videlicet my boots – he would be willing to allow me to occupy the den next to his own, and would supply me with as
much dried grass for bedding as he could spare.

"Very well, Gunga Dass," I replied; "to the first terms I
cheerfully agree, but, as there is nothing on earth to prevent
my killing you as you sit here and taking everything that you
have" (I thought of the two invaluable crows at the time), "I
flatly refuse to give you my boots and shall take whichever
den I please."

The stroke was a bold one, and I was glad when I saw that
it had succeeded. Gunga Dass changed his tone immediately,
and disavowed all intention of asking for my boots. At the
time it did not strike me as at all strange that I, a Civil
Engineer, a man of thirteen years' standing in the Service,
and, I trust, an average Englishman, should thus calmly
threaten murder and violence against the man who had, for
a consideration it is true, taken me under his wing. I had left
the world, it seemed, for centuries. I was as certain then, as
I am now of my own existence, that in the accursed settle-
ment there was no law save that of the strongest; that the
living dead men had thrown behind them every canon of the
world which had cast them out; and that I had to depend for
my own life on my strength and vigilance alone. The crew
of the ill-fated *Mignonette* are the only men who would understand my frame of mind. "At present," I argued to myself, "I am strong and a match for six of these wretches. It is

imperatively necessary that I should, for my own sake, keep both health and strength until the hour of my release comes – if it ever does."

Fortified with these resolutions, I ate and drank as much as I could, and made Gunga Dass understand that I intended to be his master, and that the least sign of insubordination on his part would be visited with the only punishment I had it in my power to inflict – sudden and violent death. Shortly after this I went to bed. That is to say, Gunga Dass gave me a double armful of dried bents which I thrust down the mouth of the lair to the right of his, and followed myself, feet foremost; the hole running about nine feet into the sand with a slight downward inclination, and being neatly shored with timbers. From my den, which faced the river-front, I was able to watch the waters of the Sutlej flowing past under the light of a young moon and compose myself to sleep as best I might.

The horrors of that night I shall never forget. My den was nearly as narrow as a coffin, and the sides had been worn smooth and greasy by the contact of innumerable naked bodies, added to which it smelt abominably. Sleep was altogether out of the question to one in my excited frame of mind. As the night wore on, it seemed that the entire amphitheatre was filled with legions of unclean devils that, trooping up from the shoals below, mocked the unfortunates in their lairs.

Personally I am not of an imaginative temperament – very few Engineers are – but on that occasion I was as completely prostrated with nervous terror as any woman. After half an hour or so, however, I was able once more to calmly review my chances of escape. Any exit by the steep sand walls was, of course, impracticable. I had been thoroughly convinced of this some time before. It was possible, just possible, that I might, in the uncertain moonlight, safely run the gauntlet of the rifle-shots. The place was so full of terror for me that I was prepared to undergo any risk in leaving it. Imagine my delight, then, when after creeping stealthily to the river-front

I found that the infernal boat was not there. My freedom lay before me in the next few steps!

By walking out to the first shallow pool that lay at the foot of the projecting left horn of the horseshoe, I could wade across, turn the flank of the crater, and make my way inland. Without a moment's hesitation I marched briskly past the tussocks where Gunga Dass had snared the crows, and out in the direction of the smooth white sand beyond. My first step from the tufts of dried grass showed me how utterly futile was any hope of escape; for, as I put my foot down, I felt an indescribable drawing, sucking motion of the sand below. Another moment, and my leg was swallowed up nearly to the knee. In the moonlight the whole surface of the sand seemed to be shaken with devilish delight at my disappointment. I struggled clear, sweating with terror and exertion, back to the tussocks behind me, and fell on my face.

My only means of escape from the semicircle was protected with a quicksand!

How long I lay I have not the faintest idea; but I was roused at the last by the malevolent chuckle of Gunga Dass at my ear. "I would advise you, Protector of the Poor" (the ruffian was speaking English), "to return to your house. It is unhealthy to lie down here. Moreover, when the boat returns, you will most certainly be rifled at." He stood over me in the dim light of the dawn, chuckling and laughing to himself. Suppressing my first impulse to catch the man by the neck and throw him on to the quicksand, I rose sullenly and followed him to the platform below the burrows.

Suddenly, and futilely as I thought while I spoke, I asked: "Gunga Dass, what is the good of the boat if I can't get out *anyhow*?" I recollect that even in my deepest trouble I had been speculating vaguely on the waste of ammunition in guarding an already well protected foreshore.

Gunga Dass laughed again and made answer: "They have the boat only in daytime. It is for the reason that *there is a way*. I hope we shall have the pleasure of your company for much longer time. It is a pleasant spot when you have been here some years and eaten roast crow long enough."

I staggered, numbed and helpless, towards the fetid burrow allotted to me, and fell asleep. An hour or so later I was awakened by a piercing scream – the shrill, high-pitched scream of a horse in pain. Those who have once heard that will never forget the sound. I found some little difficulty in scrambling out of the burrow. When I was in the open, I saw Pornic, my poor old Pornic, lying dead on the sandy soil. How they had killed him I cannot guess. Gunga Dass explained that horse was better than crow, and "greatest good of greatest number is political maxim. We are now Republic, Mister Jukes, and you are entitled to a fair share of the beast. If you like, we will pass a vote of thanks. Shall I propose?"

Yes, we were a Republic indeed! A Republic of wild beasts penned at the bottom of a pit, to eat and fight and sleep till we died. I attempted no protest of any kind, but sat down and stared at the hideous sight in front of me. In less time almost than it takes me to write this, Pornic's body was divided, in some unclean way or other; the men and women had dragged the fragments on to the platform and were preparing their morning meal. Gunga Dass cooked mine. The almost irresistible impulse to fly at the sand walls until I was wearied laid hold of me afresh, and I had to struggle against it with all my might. Gunga Dass was offensively jocular till I told him that if he addressed another remark of any kind whatever to me I should strangle him where he sat. This silenced him till silence became insupportable, and I bade him say something.

"You will live here till you die like the other Feringhi," he said coolly, watching me over the fragment of gristle that he was gnawing.

"What other Sahib, you swine? Speak at once, and don't stop to tell me a lie."

"He is over there," answered Gunga Dass, pointing to a burrow-mouth about four doors to the left of my own. "You can see for yourself. He died in the burrow as you will die, and I will die, and as all these men and women and the one child will also die."

"For pity's sake tell me all you know about him. Who was he? When did he come, and when did he die?"

This appeal was a weak step on my part. Gunga Dass only leered and replied: "I will not – unless you give me something first."

Then I recollected where I was, and struck the man between the eyes, partially stunning him. He stepped down from the platform at once, and, cringing and fawning and weeping and attempting to embrace my feet, led me round to the burrow which he had indicated.

"I know nothing whatever about the gentleman. Your God be my witness that I do not. He was as anxious to escape as you were, and he was shot from the boat, though we all did all things to prevent him from attempting. He was shot here." Gunga Dass laid his hand on his lean stomach and bowed to the earth.

"Well, and what then? Go on!"

"And then – and then, Your Honour, we carried him into his house and gave him water, and put wet cloths on the wound, and he laid down in his house and gave up the ghost."

"In how long? In how long?"

"About half an hour after he received his wound. I call Vishnu to witness," yelled the wretched man, "that I did everything for him. Everything which was possible, that I did!"

He threw himself down on the ground and clasped my ankles. But I had my doubts about Gunga Dass's benevolence, and kicked him off as he lay protesting.

"I believe you robbed him of everything he had. But I can find out in a minute or two. How long was the Sahib here?"

"Nearly a year and a half. I think he must have gone mad. But hear me swear, Protector of the Poor! Won't Your Honour hear me swear that I never touched an article that belonged to him? What is Your Worship going to do?"

I had taken Gunga Dass by the waist and had hauled him on to the platform opposite the deserted burrow. As I did so I thought of my wretched fellow-prisoner's unspeakable misery among all these horrors for eighteen months, and the final agony of dying like a rat in a hole, with a bullet-wound in the stomach. Gunga Dass fancied I was going to kill him, and howled pitifully. The rest of the population, in the plethora that follows a full flesh meal, watched us without stirring.

"Go inside, Gunga Dass," said I, "and fetch it out."

I was feeling sick and faint with horror now. Gunga Dass nearly rolled off the platform, and howled aloud.

"But I am Brahmin, Sahib – a high-caste Brahmin. By your soul, by your father's soul, do not make me do this thing!"

"Brahmin or no Brahmin, by my soul and my father's soul, in you go!" I said, and, seizing him by the shoulders, I crammed his head into the mouth of the burrow, kicked the rest of him in, and, sitting down, covered my face with my hands.

At the end of a few minutes I heard a rustle and a creak; then Gunga Dass in a sobbing, choking whisper speaking to himself; then a soft thud – and I uncovered my eyes.

The dry sand had turned the corpse entrusted to its keeping into a yellow-brown mummy. I told Gunga Dass to stand off while I examined it. The body – clad in an olive-green hunting-suit much stained and worn, with leather pads on the shoulders – was that of a man between thirty and forty, above middle height, with light, sandy hair, long moustache, and a rough, unkempt beard. The left canine of the upper jaw was missing, and a portion of the lobe of the right ear was gone. On the second finger of the left hand was a ring – a shield-shaped blood-stone set in gold, with a monogram that might have been either "B. K." or "B. L." On the third finger of the right hand was a silver ring in the shape of a coiled cobra, much worn and tarnished. Gunga Dass deposited a handful of trifles he had picked out of the burrow

at my feet, and, covering the face of the body with my handkerchief, I turned to examine these. I give the full list in the
hope that it may lead to the identification of the unfortunate
man: –

1. Bowl of a brierwood pipe, serrated at the edge; much
worn and blackened; bound with string at the screw.

2. Two patent-lever keys; wards of both broken.

3. Tortoise-shell-handled penknife, silver or nickel, name-
plate marked with monogram "B. K."

4. Envelope, postmark undecipherable, bearing a Victorian stamp, addressed to "Miss Mon —" (rest illegible) –
"ham' – 'nt."

5. Imitation crocodile-skin note-book with pencil. First
forty-five pages blank; four and a half illegible; fifteen others
filled with private memoranda relating chiefly to three persons – a Mrs. L. Singleton, abbreviated several times to "Lot
Single," "Mrs. S. May," and "Garmison," referred to in
places as "Jerry" or "Jack."

6. Handle of small-sized hunting-knife. Blade snapped
short. Buck's horn, diamond-cut, with swivel and ring on the
butt; fragment of cotton cord attached.

It must not be supposed that I inventoried all these things
on the spot as fully as I have here written them down. The
note-book first attracted my attention, and I put it in my
pocket with a view to studying it later on. The rest of the
articles I conveyed to my burrow for safety's sake, and there,
being a methodical man, I inventoried them. I then returned
to the corpse and ordered Gunga Dass to help me to carry it
out to the river-front. While we were engaged in this, the
exploded shell of an old brown cartridge dropped out of one
of the pockets and rolled at my feet. Gunga Dass had not
seen it; and I fell to thinking that a man does not carry
exploded cartridge-cases, especially "browns," which will not
bear loading twice, about with him when shooting. In
other words, that cartridge-case had been fired inside the
crater. Consequently there must be a gun somewhere. I was
on the verge of asking Gunga Dass, but checked myself,

knowing that he would lie. We laid the body down on the edge of the quicksand by the tussocks. It was my intention to push it out and let it be swallowed up – the only possible mode of burial that I could think of. I ordered Gunga Dass to go away.

Then I gingerly put the corpse out on the quicksand. In doing so – it was lying face downward – I tore the frail and rotten khaki shooting-coat open, disclosing a hideous cavity in the back. I have already told you that the dry sand had, as it were, mummified the body. A moment's glance showed that the gaping hole had been caused by a gunshot wound; the gun must have been fired with the muzzle almost touching the back. The shooting-coat, being intact, had been drawn over the body after death, which must have been instantaneous. The secret of the poor wretch's death was plain to me in a flash. Some one of the crater, presumably Gunga Dass, must have shot him with his own gun – the gun that fitted the brown cartridges. He had never attempted to escape in the face of the rifle-fire from the boat.

I pushed the corpse out hastily, and saw it sink from sight literally in a few seconds. I shuddered as I watched. In a dazed, half-conscious way I turned to peruse the note-book. A stained and discoloured slip of paper had been inserted between the binding and the back, and dropped out as I opened the pages. This is what it contained: "*Four out from crow-clump; three left; nine out; two right; three back; two left; fourteen out; two left; seven out; one left; nine back; two right; six back; four right; seven back.*" The paper had been burnt and charred at the edges. What it meant I could not understand. I sat down on the dried bents, turning it over and over between my fingers, until I was aware of Gunga Dass standing immediately behind me with glowing eyes and outstretched hands.

"Have you got it?" he panted. "Will you not let me look at it also? I swear that I will return it."

"Got what? Return what?" I asked.

"That which you have in your hands. It will help us both." He stretched out his long, bird-like talons, trembling with eagerness.

"I could never find it," he continued. "He had secreted it about his person. Therefore I shot him, but nevertheless I was unable to obtain it."

Gunga Dass had quite forgotten his little fiction about the rifle-bullet. I heard him calmly. Morality is blunted by consorting with the Dead who are alive.

"What on earth are you raving about? What is it you want me to give you?"

"The piece of paper in the note-book. It will help us both. Oh, you fool! You fool! Can you not see what it will do for us? We shall escape!"

His voice rose almost to a scream, and he danced with excitement before me. I own I was moved at the chance of getting away.

"Do you mean to say that this slip of paper will help us? What does it mean?"

"Read it aloud! Read it aloud! I beg and I pray to you to read it aloud."

I did so. Gunga Dass listened delightedly, and drew an irregular line in the sand with his fingers.

"See now! It was the length of his gun-barrels without the stock. I have those barrels. Four gun-barrels out from the place where I caught crows. Straight out; do you mind me? Then three left. Ah! Now well I remember how that man worked it out night after night. Then nine out, and so on. Out is always straight before you across the quicksand to the North. He told me so before I killed him."

"But if you knew all this why didn't you get out before?"

"I did *not* know it. He told me that he was working it out a year and a half ago, and how he was working it out night after night when the boat had gone away, and he could get out near the quicksand safely. Then he said that we would get away together. But I was afraid that he would leave me behind one night when he had worked it all out, and so I shot him. Besides, it is not advisable that the men who once get in here should escape. Only I, and *I* am a Brahmin."

The hope of escape had brought Gunga Dass's caste back to him. He stood up, walked about, and gesticulated violently. Eventually I managed to make him talk soberly, and he told me how this Englishman had spent six months night after night in exploring, inch by inch, the passage across the quicksand; how he had declared it to be simplicity itself up to within about twenty yards of the river-bank after turning the flank of the left horn of the horseshoe. This much he had evidently not completed when Gunga Dass shot him with his own gun.

In my frenzy of delight at the possibilities of escape I recollect shaking hands wildly with Gunga Dass, after we had decided that we were to make an attempt to get away that very night. It was weary work waiting throughout the afternoon.

About ten o'clock, as far as I could judge, when the Moon had just risen above the lip of the crater, Gunga Dass made a move for his burrow to bring out the gun-barrels whereby to measure our path. All the other wretched inhabitants had retired to their lairs long ago. The guardian boat had drifted down-stream some hours before, and we were utterly alone by the crow-clump. Gunga Dass, while carrying the gun-barrels, let slip the piece of paper which was to be our guide. I stooped down hastily to recover it, and, as I did so, I was aware that the creature was aiming a violent blow at the back of my head with the gun-barrels. It was too late to turn round. I must have received the blow somewhere on the nape of my neck, for I fell senseless at the edge of the quicksand.

When I recovered consciousness, the Moon was going down, and I was sensible of intolerable pain in the back of my head. Gunga Dass had disappeared, and my mouth was full of blood. I lay down again and prayed that I might die without more ado. Then the unreasoning fury which I have before mentioned laid hold upon me, and I staggered inland towards the walls of the crater. It seemed that some one was

calling to me in a whisper – "Sahib! Sahib! Sahib!" exactly
as my bearer used to call me in the mornings. I fancied that
I was delirious until a handful of sand fell at my feet. Then
I looked up and saw a head peering down into the amphitheatre – the head of Dunnoo, my dog-boy, who attended to
my collies. As soon as he had attracted my attention, he held
up his hand and showed a rope. I motioned, staggering to
and fro the while, that he should throw it down. It was a
couple of leather punkah-ropes knotted together, with a loop
at one end. I slipped the loop over my head and under my
arms; heard Dunnoo urge something forward; was conscious
that I was being dragged, face downward, up the steep sand-
slope, and the next instant found myself choked and half-
fainting on the sand-hills overlooking the crater. Dunnoo,
with his face ashy grey in the moonlight, implored me not to
stay, but to get back to my tent at once.

It seems that he had tracked Pornic's footprints fourteen
miles across the sands to the crater; had returned and told
my servants, who flatly refused to meddle with any one,
white or black, once fallen into the hideous Village of the
Dead; whereupon Dunnoo had taken one of my ponies and
a couple of punkah-ropes, returned to the crater, and hauled
me out as I have described.

THE DISTURBER OF TRAFFIC

THE DISTURBER OF TRAFFIC

* * *

From the wheel and the drift of Things
  Deliver us, good Lord,
And we will meet the wrath of kings,
  The faggot, and the sword.

Lay not Thy toil before our eyes,
  Nor vex us with Thy wars,
Lest we should feel the straining skies
  O'ertrod by trampling stars.

A veil 'twixt us and Thee, dread Lord,
  A veil 'twixt us and Thee:
Lest we should hear too clear, too clear,
  And unto madness see!

Miriam Cohen

THE Brothers of the Trinity order that none unconnected with their service shall be found in or on one of their Lights during the hours of darkness; but their servants can be led to think otherwise. If you are fair-spoken and take an interest in their duties, they will allow you to sit with them through the long night and help to scare the ships into mid-channel.

Of the English south-coast Lights, that of St. Cecilia-under-the-Cliff is the most powerful, for it guards a very foggy coast. When the sea-mist veils all, St. Cecilia turns a hooded head to the sea and sings a song of two words once every minute. From the land that song resembles the bellowing of a brazen bull; but off-shore they understand, and the steamers grunt gratefully in answer.

Fenwick, who was on duty one night, lent me a pair of black glass spectacles, without which no man can look at the

337

Light unblinded, and busied himself in last touches to the lenses before twilight fell. The width of the English Channel beneath us lay as smooth and as many-coloured as the inside of an oyster-shell. A little Sunderland cargo-boat had made her signal to Lloyd's Agency, half a mile up the coast, and was lumbering down to the sunset, her wake lying white behind her. One star came out over the cliffs, the waters turned lead-colour, and St. Cecilia's Light shot out across the sea in eight long pencils that wheeled slowly from right to left, melted into one beam of solid light laid down directly in front of the tower, dissolved again into eight, and passed away. The light-frame of the thousand lenses circled on its rollers, and the compressed-air engine that drove it hummed like a blue-bottle under a glass. The hand of the indicator on the wall pulsed from mark to mark. Eight pulse-beats timed one half-revolution of the Light; neither more nor less.

Fenwick checked the first few revolutions carefully; he opened the engine's feed-pipe a trifle, looked at the racing governor, and again at the indicator, and said: "She'll do for the next few hours. We've just sent our regular engine to London, and this spare one's not by any manner so accurate."

"And what would happen if the compressed air gave out?" I asked, from curiosity.

"We'd have to turn the flash by hand, keeping an eye on the indicator. There's a regular crank for that. But it hasn't happened yet. We'll need all our compressed air to-night."

"Why?" said I. I had been watching him for not more than a minute.

"Look," he answered, and I saw that the dead sea-mist had risen out of the lifeless sea and wrapped us while my back had been turned. The pencils of the Light marched staggeringly across tilted floors of white cloud. From the balcony round the light-room the white walls of the light-house ran down into swirling, smoking space. The noise of the tide coming in very lazily over the rocks was choked down to a thick drawl.

"That's the way our sea-fogs come," said Fenwick, with an air of ownership. "Hark, now, to that little fool calling out 'fore he's hurt."

Something in the mist was bleating like an indignant calf; it might have been half a mile or half a hundred miles away.

"Does he suppose we've gone to bed?" continued Fenwick. "You'll hear us talk to him in a minute. He knows puffickly where he is, and he's carrying on to be told like if he was insured."

"Who is 'he'?"

"That Sunderland boat, o' course. Ah!"

I could hear a steam-engine hiss down below in the mist where the dynamos that fed the Light were clacking together. Then there came a roar that split the fog and shook the lighthouse.

"GIT-*toot*!" blared the fog-horn of St. Cecilia. The bleating ceased.

"Little fool!" Fenwick repeated. Then, listening: "Blest if that aren't another of them! Well, well, they always say that a fog do draw the ships of the sea together. They'll be calling all night, and so'll the siren. We're expecting some tea ships up-Channel. . . . If you put my coat on that chair, you'll feel more so fash, sir."

It is no pleasant thing to thrust your company upon a man for the night. I looked at Fenwick, and Fenwick looked at me; each gauging the other's capacities for boring and being bored. Fenwick was an old, clean-shaven, grey-haired man who had followed the sea for thirty years, and knew nothing of the land except the lighthouse in which he served. He fenced cautiously to find out the little that I knew, and talked down to my level till it came out that I had met a captain in the merchant service who had once commanded a ship in which Fenwick's son had served; and further, that I had seen some places that Fenwick had touched at. He began with a dissertation on pilotage in the Hugli. I had been privileged to know a Hugli pilot intimately. Fenwick had only seen the imposing and masterful breed from a ship's chains, and his intercourse had been cut down to "Quarter less five," and remarks of a strictly business-like nature. Hereupon he ceased to talk down to me, and became so amazingly technical that I was forced to beg him to explain every other sentence. This set him fully at his ease; and then we spoke as men together, each too interested to think of anything except the subject in hand. And that subject was wrecks, and voyages, and old-time trading, and ships cast away in desolate seas, steamers we both had known, their merits and demerits, lading, Lloyd's, and, above all, Lights. The talk always came back to Lights: Lights of the Channel; Lights on forgotten islands, and men forgotten on them; Lightships – two months' duty and one month's leave – tossing on kinked cables in ever-troubled tideways; and Lights that men had seen where never lighthouse was marked on the charts.

Omitting all those stories, and omitting also the wonderful ways by which he arrived at them, I tell here, from Fenwick's mouth, one that was not the least amazing. It was delivered in pieces between the roller-skate rattle of the revolving lenses, the bellowing of the fog-horn below, the answering calls from the sea, and the sharp tap of reckless night-birds that flung themselves at the glasses. It concerned a man called Dowse, once an intimate friend of Fenwick, now a waterman at Portsmouth, believing that the guilt of blood is on his head, and finding no rest either at Portsmouth or Gosport Hard.

* * *

. . . "And if anybody was to come to you and say, 'I know the Javva currents,' don't you listen to him; for those currents is never yet known to mortal man. Sometimes they're here, sometimes they're there, but they never runs less than five knots an hour through and among those islands of the Eastern Archipelagus. There's reverse currents in the Gulf of Boni – and that's up north in Celebes – that no man can explain; and through all those Javva passages from the Bali

Narrows, Dutch Gut, and Ombay, which I take it is the safest, they chop and they change, and they banks the tides fust on one shore and then on another, till your ship's tore in two. I've come through the Bali Narrows, stern first, in the heart o' the south-east monsoon, with a sou'-sou'-west wind blowing atop of the northerly flood, and our skipper said he wouldn't do it again, not for all Jamrach's. You've heard o' Jamrach's, sir?"

"Yes; and was Dowse stationed in the Bali Narrows?" I said.

"No, he was not at Bali, but much more east o' them passages, and that's Flores Strait, at the east end o' Flores. It's all on the way south to Australia when you're running through that Eastern Archipelagus. Sometimes you go through Bali Narrows if you're full-powered, and sometimes through Flores Strait, so as to stand south at once, and fetch round Timor, keeping well clear o' the Sahul Bank. Elseways, if you aren't full-powered, why it stands to reason you go round by the Ombay Passage, keeping careful to the north side. You understand that, sir?"

I was not full-powered, and judged it safer to keep to the north side – of Silence.

"And on Flores Strait, in the fairway between Adonare Island and the mainland, they put Dowse in charge of a screw-pile Light called the Wurlee Light. It's less than a mile across the head of Flores Strait. Then it opens out to ten or twelve mile for Solor Strait, and then it narrows again to a three-mile gut, with a topplin' flamin' volcano by it. That's old Loby Toby by Loby Toby Strait, and if you keep his Light and the Wurlee Light in a line you won't take much harm, not on the darkest night. That's what Dowse told me, and I can well believe him, knowing these seas myself; but you must ever be mindful of the currents. And there they put Dowse, since he was the only man that that Dutch government which owns Flores could find that would go to Wurlee and tend a fixed Light. Mostly they uses Dutch and Italians, Englishmen being said to drink when alone. I never could rightly find out what made Dowse accept of that position, but accept he did, and used to sit for to watch the tigers come out of the forests to hunt for crabs and such like round about the lighthouse at low tide. The water was always warm in those parts, as I know well, and uncommon sticky, and it ran with the tides as thick and smooth as hogwash in a trough. There was another man along with Dowse in the Light, but he wasn't rightly a man. He was a Kling. No, nor yet a Kling he wasn't, but his skin was in little flakes and cracks all over, from living so much in the salt water as was his usual custom. His hands was all webby-foot, too. He was called, I remember Dowse saying now, an Orange-Lord, on account of his habits. You've heard of an Orange-Lord, sir?"

"Orang-Laut?" I suggested.

"That's the name," said Fenwick, smacking his knee. "An Orang-Laut, of course, and his name was Challong; what they call a sea-gypsy. Dowse told me that that man, long hair and all, would go swimming up and down the straits just for something to do; running down on one tide and back again with the other, swimming side-stroke, and the tides going tremenjus strong. Elseways he'd be skipping about the beach along with the tigers at low tide, for he was most part a beast; or he'd sit in a little boat praying to old Loby Toby of an evening when the volcano was spitting red at the south end of the strait. Dowse told me that he wasn't a companionable man, like you and me might have been to Dowse.

"Now I can never rightly come at what it was that began to ail Dowse after he had been there a year or something less. He was saving of all his pay and tending to his Light, and now and again he'd have a fight with Challong and tip him off the Light into the sea. Then, he told me, his head began to feel streaky from looking at the tide so long. He said there was long streaks of white running inside it; like wall-paper that hadn't been properly pasted up, he said. The streaks, they would run with the tides, north and south, twice a day, accordin' to them currents, and he'd lie down on the planking – it was a screw-pile Light – with his eye to a crack and

watch the water streaking through the piles just so quiet as
hogwash. He said the only comfort he got was at slack water.
Then the streaks in his head went round and round like a
sampan in a tide-rip; but that was heaven, he said, to the
other kind of streaks – the straight ones that looked like
arrows on a wind-chart, but much more regular, and that was
the trouble of it. No more he couldn't ever keep his eyes off
the tides that ran up and down so strong, but as soon as ever
he looked at the high hills standing all along Flores Strait for
rest and comfort his eyes would be pulled down like to the
nesty streaky water; and when they once got there he
couldn't pull them away again till the tide changed. He told
me all this himself, speaking just as though he was talking of
somebody else."

"Where did you meet him?" I asked.

"In Portsmouth harbour, a-cleaning the brasses of a Ryde
boat, but I'd known him off and on through following the sea
for many years. Yes, he spoke about himself very curious,
and all as if he was in the next room laying there dead. Those
streaks, they preyed upon his intellecks, he said; and he made
up his mind, every time that the Dutch gunboat that attends
to the Lights in those parts come along, that he'd ask to be
took off. But as soon as she did come something went click
in his throat, and he was so took up with watching her masts,
because they ran longways, in the contrary direction to his
streaks, that he could never say a word until she was gone
away and her masts was under sea again. Then, he said, he'd
cry by the hour; and Challong swum round and round the
Light, laughin' at him and splashin' water with his webby-
foot hands. At last he took it into his pore sick head that the
ships, and particularly the steamers that came by, – there
wasn't many of them, – made the streaks, instead of the tides
as was natural. He used to sit, he told me, cursing every boat
that come along, – sometimes a junk, sometimes a Dutch
brig, and now and again a steamer rounding Flores Head and
poking about in the mouth of the strait. Or there'd come a
boat from Australia running north past old Loby Toby hunting

for a fair current, but never throwing out any papers that Challong might pick up for Dowse to read. Generally speaking, the steamers kept more westerly, but now and again they came looking for Timor and the west coast of Australia. Dowse used to shout to them to go round by the Ombay Passage, and not to come streaking past him, making the water all streaky, but it wasn't likely they'd hear. He says to himself after a month, 'I'll give them one more chance,' he says. 'If the next boat don't attend to my just representations,' – he says he remembers using those very words to Challong, – 'I'll stop the fairway.'

"The next boat was a Two-streak cargo-boat very anxious to make her northing. She waddled through under old Loby Toby at the south end of the strait, and she passed within a quarter of a mile of the Wurlee Light at the north end, in seventeen fathom o' water, the tide against her. Dowse took the trouble to come out with Challong in a little prow that they had, – all bamboos and leakage, – and he lay in the fairway waving a palm branch, and, so he told me, wondering why and what for he was making this fool of himself. Up come the Two-streak boat, and Dowse shouts: 'Don't you come this way again, making my head all streaky! Go round by Ombay, and leave me alone.' Some one looks over the port bulwarks and shies a banana at Dowse, and that's all. Dowse sits down in the bottom of the boat and cries fit to break his heart. Then he says, 'Challong, what am I a-crying for?' and they fetch up by the Wurlee Light on the half flood.

" 'Challong,' he says, 'there's too much traffic here, and that's why the water's so streaky as it is. It's the junks and the brigs and the steamers that do it,' he says; and all the time he was speaking he was thinking, 'Lord, Lord, what a crazy fool I am!' Challong said nothing, because he couldn't speak a word of English except say 'dam,' and he said that where you or me would say 'yes.' Dowse lay down on the planking of the Light with his eye to the crack, and he saw the muddy water streaking below, and he never said a word

till slack water, because the streaks kept him tongue-tied at
such times. At slack water he says, 'Challong, we must buoy
this fairway for wrecks,' and he holds up his hands several
times, showing that dozens of wrecks had come about in the
fairway; and Challong says, 'Dam.'

"That very afternoon he and Challong goes to Wurlee, the
village in the woods that the Light was named after, and buys
canes, – stacks and stacks of canes, and coir-rope thick and
fine, all sorts, – and they sets to work making square floats
by lashing of the canes together. Dowse said he took longer
over those floats than might have been needed, because he
rejoiced in the corners, they being square, and the streaks in
his head all running longways. He lashed the canes together,
criss-cross and thwartways – any way but longways, – and
they made up twelve-foot-square floats, like rafts. Then he
stepped a twelve-foot bamboo or a bundle of canes in the
centre, and to the head of that he lashed a big six-foot W
letter, all made of canes, and painted the float dark-green and
the W white, as a wreck-buoy should be painted. Between
them two they makes a round dozen of these new kind of
wreck-buoys, and it was a two months' job. There was no big
traffic, owing to it being on the turn of the monsoon, but
what there was Dowse cursed at, and the streaks in his head,
they ran with the tides, as usual.

"Day after day, so soon as a buoy was ready, Challong
would take it out, with a big rock that half sunk the prow
and a bamboo grapnel, and drop it dead in the fairway. He
did this day or night, and Dowse could see him of a clear
night, when the sea brimmed, climbing about the buoys with
the sea-fire dripping off him. They was all put into place,
twelve of them, in seventeen-fathom water; not in a straight
line, on account of a well-known shoal there, but slantways,
and two, one behind the other, mostly in the centre of the
fairway. You must keep the centre of those Javva currents,
for currents at the side is different, and in narrow water,
before you can turn a spoke, you get your nose took round
and rubbed upon the rocks and the woods. Dowse knew that

just as well as any skipper. Likeways he knew that no skipper daren't run through uncharted wrecks in a six-knot current. He told me he used to lie outside the Light watching his buoys ducking and dipping so friendly with the tide; and the motion was comforting to him on account of its being different from the run of the streaks in his head.

"Three weeks after he'd done his business up comes a steamer through Loby Toby Straits, thinking she'd run into Flores Sea before night. He saw her slow down; then she backed. Then one man and another came up on the bridge, and he could see there was a regular powwow, and the flood was driving her right on to Dowse's wreck-buoys. After that she spun round and went back south, and Dowse nearly killed himself with laughing. But a few weeks after that a couple of junks came shouldering through from the north, arm in arm, like junks go. It takes a good deal to make a Chinaman understand danger. They junks set well in the current, and went down the fairway, right among the buoys, ten knots an hour, blowing horns and banging tin pots all the time. That made Dowse very angry, he having taken so much trouble to stop the fairway. No boats run Flores Straits by night, but it seemed to Dowse that if junks'd do that in the day, the Lord knew but what a steamer might trip over his buoys at night; and he sent Challong to run a coir rope between three of the buoys in the middle of the fairway, and he fixed naked lights of coir steeped in oil to that rope. The tides was the only things that moved in those seas, for the airs was dead still till they began to blow, and *then* they would blow your hair off. Challong tended those lights every night after the junks had been so impident, – four lights in about a quarter of a mile hung up in iron skillets on the rope; and when they was alight, – and coir burns well, most like a lamp wick, – the fairway seemed more madder than anything else in the world. Fust there was the Wurlee Light, then these four queer lights, that couldn't be riding-lights, almost flush with the water, and behind them, twenty mile off, but the biggest light of all, there was the red top of old Loby

Toby volcano. Dowse told me that he used to go out in the prow and look at his handiwork, and it made him scared, being like no lights that ever was fixed.

"By and by some more steamers came along, snorting and snifting at the buoys, but never going through, and Dowse says to himself: 'Thank goodness, I've taught them not to come streaking through my water. Ombay Passage is good enough for them and the like of them.' But he didn't remember how quick that sort of news spreads among the shipping. Every steamer that fetched up by those buoys told another steamer and all the port officers concerned in those seas that there was something wrong with Flores Straits that hadn't been charted yet. It was block-buoyed for wrecks in the fairway, they said, and no sort of passage to use. Well, the Dutch, of course they didn't know anything about it. They thought our Admiralty Survey had been there, and they thought it very queer but neighbourly. You understand us English are always looking up marks and lighting sea-ways all the world over, never asking with your leave or by your leave, seeing that the sea concerns us more than any one else. So the news went to and back from Flores to Bali, and Bali to Probolingo, where the railway is that runs to Batavia. All through the Javva seas everybody got the word to keep clear o' Flores Straits, and Dowse, he was left alone except for such steamers and small craft as didn't know. They'd come up and look at the straits like a bull over a gate, but those nodding wreck-buoys scared them away. By and by the Admiralty Survey ship – the *Britomarte* I think she was – lay in Macassar Roads off Fort Rotterdam, alongside of the *Amboina*, a dirty little Dutch gunboat that used to clean there; and the Dutch captain says to our captain, 'What's wrong with Flores Straits?' he says.

" 'Blowed if I know,' says our captain, who'd just come up from the Angelica Shoal.

" 'Then why did you go and buoy it?' says the Dutchman.

" 'Blowed if I have,' says our captain. 'That's your lookout.'

" 'Buoyed it is,' said the Dutch captain, 'according to what they tell me; and a whole fleet of wreck-buoys, too.'

" 'Gummy!' says our captain. 'It's a dorg's life at sea, any way. I must have a look at this. You come along after me as soon as you can;' and down he skimmed that very night, round the heel of Celebes, three days' steam to Flores Head, and he met a Two-streak liner, very angry, backing out of the head of the strait; and the merchant captain gave our Survey ship something of his mind for leaving wrecks uncharted in those narrow waters and wasting his company's coal.

" 'It's no fault o' mine,' says our captain.

" 'I don't care whose fault it is,' says the merchant captain, who had come aboard to speak to him just at dusk. 'The fairway's choked with wreck enough to knock a hole through a dockgate. I saw their big ugly masts sticking up just under my forefoot. Lord ha' mercy on us!' he says, spinning round. 'The place is like Regent Street of a hot summer night.'

"And so it was. They two looked at Flores Straits, and they saw lights one after the other stringing across the fairway. Dowse, he had seen the steamers hanging there before dark, and he said to Challong: 'We'll give 'em something to remember. Get all the skillets and iron pots you can and hang them up alongside o' the regular four lights. We must teach 'em to go round by the Ombay Passage, or they'll be streaking up our water again!' Challong took a header off the light-house, got aboard the little leaking prow, with his coir soaked in oil and all the skillets he could muster, and he began to show his lights, four regulation ones and half a dozen new lights hung on that rope which was a little above the water. Then he went to all the spare buoys with all his spare coir, and hung a skillet-flare on every pole that he could get at – about seven poles. So you see, taking one with another, there was the Wurlee Light, four lights on the rope between the three centre fairway wreck-buoys that was hung out as a usual custom, six or eight extry ones that Challong had hung up on the same rope, and seven dancing flares that belonged to seven wreck-buoys – eighteen or twenty lights in all crowded into a mile of seventeen-fathom water, where no tide'd ever let a wreck rest for three weeks, let alone ten or twelve wrecks, as the flares showed.

"The Admiralty captain, he saw the lights come out one after another, same as the merchant skipper did who was standing at his side, and he said: –

" 'There's been an international catastrophe here or elseways,' and then he whistled. 'I'm going to stand on and off all night till the Dutchman comes,' he says.

" 'I'm off,' says the merchant skipper. 'My owners don't wish for me to watch illuminations. That strait's choked with wreck, and I shouldn't wonder if a typhoon hadn't driven half the junks o' China there.' With that he went away; but the Survey ship, she stayed all night at the head o' Flores Strait, and the men admired the lights till the lights was burning out, and then they admired more than ever.

"A little bit before morning the Dutch gunboat come flustering up, and the two ships stood together watching the lights burn out and out, till there was nothing left 'cept Flores Straits, all green and wet, and a dozen wreck-buoys, and Wurlee Light.

"Dowse had slept very quiet that night, and got rid of his streaks by means of thinking of the angry steamers outside. Challong was busy, and didn't come back to his bunk till late. In the very early morning Dowse looked out to sea, being, as he said, in torment, and saw all the navies of the world riding outside Flores Straits fairway in a half-moon, seven miles from wing to wing, most wonderful to behold. Those were the words he used to me time and again in telling the tale.

"Then, he says, he heard a gun fired with a most tremenjus explosion, and all them great navies crumbled to little pieces of clouds, and there was only two ships remaining, and a man-o'-war's boat rowing to the Light, with the oars going sideways instead o' longways as the morning tides, ebb or flow, would continually run.

" 'What the devil's wrong with this strait?' says a man in the boat as soon as they was in hailing distance. 'Has the whole English Navy sunk here, or what?'

" 'There's nothing wrong,' says Dowse, sitting on the platform outside the Light, and keeping one eye very watchful on the streakiness of the tide, which he always hated 'specially in the morning. 'You leave me alone and I'll leave you alone. Go round by the Ombay Passage, and don't cut up my water. You're making it streaky.' All the time he was saying that he kept on thinking to himself, 'Now that's foolishness, – now that's nothing but foolishness;' and all the time he was holding tight to the edge of the platform in case the streakiness of the tide should carry him away.

"Somebody answers from the boat, very soft and quiet, 'We're going round by Ombay in a minute, if you'll just come and speak to our captain and give him his bearings.'

"Dowse, he felt very highly flattered, and he slipped into the boat, not paying any attention to Challong. But Challong swum along to the ship after the boat. When Dowse was in the boat, he found, so he says, he couldn't speak to the sailors 'cept to call them 'white mice with chains about their neck,' and Lord knows he hadn't seen or thought o' white mice since he was a little bit of a boy and kept 'em in his handkerchief. So he kept himself quiet, and so they come to the Survey ship; and the man in the boat hails the quarterdeck with something that Dowse could not rightly understand, but there was one word he spelt out again and again, – m-a-d, mad, – and he heard some one behind him saying it backwards. So he had two words, – m-a-d, mad, d-a-m, dam; and he put those two words together as he come on the quarterdeck, and he says to the captain very slowly, 'I be damned if I am mad,' but all the time his eye was held like by the coils of rope on the belaying-pins, and he followed those ropes up and up with his eye till he was quite lost and comfortable among the rigging, which ran criss-cross, and slopeways, and up and down, and any way but straight along under his feet north and south. The deck-seams, they ran *that* way, and Dowse daresn't look at them. They was the same as the streaks of the water under the planking of the lighthouse.

"Then he heard the captain talking to him very kindly, and for the life of him he couldn't tell why; and what he wanted to tell the captain was that Flores Strait was too streaky, like bacon, and the steamers only made it worse; but all he could do was to keep his eye very careful on the rigging and sing: –

> 'I saw a ship a-sailing,
>   A-sailing on the sea;
> And oh, it was all lading
>   With pretty things for me!'

Then he remembered that was foolishness, and he started off to say about the Ombay Passage, but all he said was: 'The captain was a duck, – meaning no offence to you, sir, – but there was something on his back that I've forgotten.

> 'And when the ship began to move
>   The captain says, "Quack-quack." '

"He noticed the captain turn very red and angry, and he says to himself, 'My foolish tongue's run away with me again. I'll go forward;' and he went forward, and catched the reflection of himself in the binnacle brasses; and he saw that he was standing there and talking mother-naked in front of all them sailors, and he ran into the fo'c's'le howling most grievous. He must ha' gone naked for weeks on the Light, and Challong o' course never noticed it. Challong was swimmin' round and round the ship, sayin' 'dam' for to please the men and to be took aboard, because he didn't know any better.

"Dowse didn't tell what happened after this, but seemingly our Survey ship lowered two boats and went over to Dowse's buoys. They took one sounding, and then finding it was all correct they cut the buoys that Dowse and Challong had made, and let the tide carry 'em out through the Loby Toby end of the strait; and the Dutch gunboat, she sent two men ashore to take care o' the Wurlee Light, and the *Brito-marte*, she went away with Dowse, leaving Challong to try to follow them, a-calling 'dam – dam' all among the wake of the screw, and half heaving himself out of water and joining his webby-foot hands together. He dropped astern in five minutes, and I suppose he went back to the Wurlee Light. You can't drown an Orange-Lord, not even in Flores Strait on flood-tide.

"Dowse come across me when he came to England with the Survey ship, after being more than six months in her, and cured of his streaks by working hard and not looking over the side more than he could help. He told me what I've told you, sir, and he was very much ashamed of himself: but the trouble on his mind was to know whether he hadn't sent something or other to the bottom with his buoyings and his lightings and such like. He put it to me many times, and each time more and more sure he was that something had happened in the straits because of him. I think that distructed him, because I found him up at Fratton one day, in a red jersey, a-praying before the Salvation Army, which had produced him in their papers as a Reformed Pirate. They knew from his mouth that he had committed evil on the deep waters, – that was what he told them, – and piracy, which no one does now except Chineses, was all they knew of. I says to him: 'Dowse, don't be a fool. Take off that jersey and come along with me.' He says: 'Fenwick, I'm a-saving of my soul; for I do believe that I have killed more men in Flores Strait than Trafalgar.' I says: 'A man that thought he'd seen all the navies of the earth standing round in a ring to watch his foolish false wreck-buoys' (those was my very words I used) 'ain't fit to have a soul, and if he did he couldn't kill a flea with it. John Dowse, you was mad then, but you are a damn sight madder now. Take off that there jersey.'

"He took it off and come along with me, but he never got rid o' that suspicion that he'd sunk some ships a-cause of his foolishnesses at Flores Straits; and now he's a wherryman from Portsmouth to Gosport, where the tides run crossways and you can't row straight for ten strokes together. . . . So late as all this! Look!"

* * *

Fenwick left his chair, passed to the Light, touched something that clicked, and the glare ceased with a suddenness that was pain. Day had come, and the Channel needed St. Cecilia no longer. The sea-fog rolled back from the cliffs in trailed wreaths and dragged patches, as the sun rose and made the dead sea alive and splendid. The stillness of the morning held us both silent as we stepped on the balcony. A lark went up from the cliffs behind St. Cecilia, and we smelt a smell of cows in the lighthouse pastures below.

So you see we were both at liberty to thank the Lord for another day of clean and wholesome life.

MRS. HAUKSBEE SITS OUT

MRS. HAUKSBEE SITS OUT

AN UNHISTORICAL EXTRAVAGANZA

* * *

PERSONS CHIEFLY INTERESTED

HIS EXCELLENCY THE VICEROY AND GOVERNOR-GENERAL OF INDIA.

CHARLES HILTON HAWLEY (lieutenant at large).

LIEUTENANT-COLONEL J. SCRIFFSHAW (not so much at large).

MAJOR DECKER (a persuasive Irishman).

PEROO (an Aryan butler).

MRS. HAUKSBEE (a lady with a will of her own).

MRS. SCRIFFSHAW (a lady who believes she has a will of her own).

MAY HOLT (niece of the above).

ASSUNTA (an Aryan lady's-maid).

Aides-de-Camp, Dancers, Horses, and Devils as Required.

* * *

SCENE – *The imperial city of Simla, on a pine-clad mountain seven thousand feet above the level of the sea. Grey roofs of houses peering through green; white clouds going to bed in the valley below; purple clouds of sunset sitting on the peaks above. Smell of wood-smoke and pine-cones. A curtained verandah-room in* MRS. HAUKSBEE'S *house, overlooking Simla, shows* MRS. HAUKSBEE, *in black cachemire tea-gown opening over cream front, seated in a red-cushioned chair, her foot on a Khokand rug, Russian china tea-things on red lacquered table beneath red-shaded lamps. On a cushion at her feet,* MISS HOLT – *grey riding-habit, soft grey felt terai hat, blue and gold puggree, buff gauntlets in lap, and glimpse of spurred riding-boot. They have been talking as the twilight gathers.* MRS. HAUKSBEE *crosses over to piano in a natural pause of the conversation and begins to play.*

MAY: (*Without changing her position.*) Yes. That's nice. Play something.

MRS. H: What?

MAY: Oh! anything. Only I don't want to hear about sighing over tombs, and saying Nevermore.

MRS. H: Have you ever known me do that? May, you're in one of your little tempers this afternoon.

MAY: So would a Saint be. I've told you why. Horrid old *thing!* – isn't she?

MRS. H: (*Without prelude*) –

> Fair Eve knelt close to the guarded gate in the hush
> of an Eastern spring,
> She saw the flash of the Angel's sword, the gleam
> of the Angel's wing —

MAY: (*Impetuously.*) And now *you*'re laughing at me!

MRS. H: (*Shaking her head, continues the song for a verse; then crescendo*) –

> And because she was so beautiful, and because she
> could not see
> How fair were the pure white cyclamens crushed
> dying at her knee.

(That's the society of your aunt, my dear.)

> He plucked a Rose from the Eden Tree where the
> four great rivers met.

MAY: Yes. I know you're laughing at me. Now somebody's going to die, of course. They always do.

MRS. H: No. Wait and see what is going to happen. (*The puckers pass out of* MAY's *face as she listens*) –

> And though for many a Cycle past that Rose in the
> dust hath lain

With her who bore it upon her breast when she
    passed from grief and pain,

(*Retard*) –

There was never a daughter of Eve but once, ere the
    tale of her years be done,
Shall know the scent of the Eden Rose, but once
    beneath the sun!
Though the years may bring her joy or pain, fame,
    sorrow, or sacrifice,
The hour that brought her the scent of the Rose she
    lived it in Paradise!

(*Concludes with arpeggio chords.*)

MAY: (*Shuddering.*) Ah! don't. How good that is! What is it?

MRS. H: Something called "The Eden Rose." An old song to
a new setting.

MAY: Play it again!

MRS. H: (I thought it would tell.) No, dear. (*Returning to her
place by the tea-things.*) And so that amiable aunt of yours
won't let you go to the dance?

MAY: She says dancing's wicked and sinful; and it's only a
Volunteer ball, after all.

MRS. H: Then why are you so anxious to go?

MAY: Because she says I mustn't! Isn't that sufficient reason?
And because —

MRS. H: Ah, it's that "because" I want to hear about, dear.

MAY: Because I choose. Mrs. Hauksbee – *dear* Mrs.
Hauksbee – you will help me, won't you?

MRS. H: (*Slowly.*) Ye-es. Because *I* choose. Well?

MAY: In the first place, you'll take me under your wing,
won't you? And, in the second, you'll keep me there,
won't you?

MRS. H: That will depend a great deal on the Hawley Boy's
pleasure, won't it?

MAY: (*Flushing.*) Char – Mr. Hawley has nothing whatever
to do with it.

MRS. H: Of course not. But what will your aunt say?

MAY: She will be angry with *me*, but not with you. She is pious – oh! so pious! – and she would give anything to be put on that lady's committee for – what is it? – giving pretty dresses to half-caste girls. Lady Bieldar is the secretary, and she won't speak to Aunt on the Mall. You're Lady Bieldar's friend. Aunt daren't quarrel with you, and, besides, if I come here after dinner to-night, how are you to know that everything isn't correct?

MRS. H: On your own pretty head be the talking to! I'm willing to chaperon to an unlimited extent.

MAY: Bless you! and I'll love you *always* for it!

MRS. H: There, again, the Hawley Boy might have something to say. You've been a well-conducted little maiden so far, May. Whence this sudden passion for Volunteer balls? (*Turning down lamp and lowering voice as she takes the girl's hand.*) Won't you tell me? I'm not very young, but I'm not a grim griffin, and I think I'd understand, dear.

MAY: (*After a pause, and swiftly.*) His leave is nearly ended. He goes down to the plains to his regiment the day after to-morrow, and —

MRS. H: Has he said anything?

MAY: I don't know. I don't think so. Don't laugh at me, please! But I believe it would nearly break my heart if he didn't.

MRS. H: (*Smiling to herself.*) Poor child! And how long has this been going on?

MAY: Ever so long! Since the beginning of the world – or the beginning of the season. I couldn't help it. I didn't want to help it. And last time we met I was just as rude as I could be – and – and he thought I meant it.

MRS. H: How strange! Seeing that he is a man, too – (*half aloud*) – and probably with experiences of his own!

MAY: (*Dropping* MRS. H.'s *hand.*) I don't believe that, and – I won't. He couldn't!

MRS. H: No, dear. Of course he hasn't had experiences. Why should he? I was only teasing! But when do I pick you up to-night, and how?

MAY: Aunt's dining out somewhere – with goody-goody people. I dine alone with Uncle John – and he sleeps after dinner. I shall dress then. I simply daren't order my 'rickshaw. The trampling of four coolies in the verandah would wake the dead. I shall have Dandy brought round quietly, and slip away.

MRS. H: But won't riding crumple your frock horribly?

MAY: (*Rising*.) Not in the least, if you know how. I've ridden ten miles to a dance, and come in as fresh as though I had just left my brougham. A plain head hunting-saddle – swing up carefully – throw a waterproof over the skirt and an old shawl over the body, and there you are! Nobody notices in the dark, and Dandy knows when he feels a high heel that he must behave.

MRS. H: And what are you wearing?

MAY: My very, very bestest – slate body, smoke-coloured tulle skirt, and the loveliest steel-worked little shoes that ever were. Mother sent them. She doesn't know Aunt's views. That, and awfully pretty yellow roses – teeny-weeny ones. And you'll wait for me here, won't you – you angel! – at half-past nine? (*Shortens habit and whirls* MRS. H. *down the verandah. Winds up with a kiss.*) There!

MRS. H: (*Holding her at arm's length and looking into her eyes.*) And the next one will be given to —

MAY: (*Blushing furiously.*) Uncle John – when I get home.

MRS. H: Hypocrite! Go along, and be happy! (*As* MAY *mounts her horse in the garden.*) At half-past nine, then? And can you curl your own wig? But I shall be here to put the last touches to you.

MRS. H: (*In the verandah alone, as the stars come out.*) Poor child! Dear child! And Charley Hawley too! God gie us a guid conceit of oorselves! But I think they are made for each other! I wonder whether that Eurasian dress-reform committee is susceptible of improvements? I wonder whether – O youth, youth!

Enter PEROO, *the butler, with a note on a tray.*

MRS. H: (*Reading.*) "Help! help! help! The decorations are vile
– the Volunteers are fighting over them. The roses are just
beginning to come in. Mrs. Mallowe has a headache. I am
on a step-ladder and the verge of tears! Come and restore
order, if you have any regard for me! Bring things and
dress; and dine with us. – CONSTANCE." How vexatious!
But I must go, I suppose. I *hate* dressing in other people's
rooms – and Lady Bieldar takes all the chairs. But I'll tell
Assunta to wait for May. (*Passes into house, gives orders, and
departs. The clock-hands in the dining-room mark half-past
seven.*)

Enter ASSUNTA, *the lady's-maid, to* PEROO, *squatting on the
hearth-rug.*

ASSUNTA: Peroo, there is an order that I am to remain on
hand till the arrival of a young lady. (*Squats at his side.*)
PEROO: Hah!
ASSUNTA: I do not desire to wait so long. I wish to go to my
house.
PEROO: Hah!
ASSUNTA: My house is in the bazar. There is an urgency that
I should go there.
PEROO: To meet a lover?
ASSUNTA: No – black beast! To tend my children, who be
honest born. Canst thou say that of thine?
PEROO: (*Without emotion.*) That is a lie, and thou art a woman
of notoriously immoral carriage.
ASSUNTA: For this, my husband, who is a man, shall break
thy lizard's back with a bamboo.
PEROO: For that, I, who am much honoured and trusted in
this house, can, by a single word, secure his dismissal,
and, owing to my influence among the servants of this
town, can raise the bad name against ye both. Then ye will
starve for lack of employ.
ASSUNTA: (*Fawning.*) That is true. Thy honour is as great as

thy influence, and thou art an esteemed man. Moreover, thou art beautiful; especially as to thy moustachios.

PEROO: So other women, and of higher caste than thou, sweeper's wife, have told me.

ASSUNTA: The moustachios of a fighting-man – of a very swashbuckler! Ahi! Peroo, how many hearts hast thou broken with thy fine face and those so huge moustachios?

PEROO: (*Twirling moustache.*) One or two – two or three. It is a matter of common talk in the bazars. I speak not of the matter myself. (*Hands her betel-nut and lime wrapped in the leaf. They chew in silence.*)

ASSUNTA: Peroo!

PEROO: Hah!

ASSUNTA: I greatly desire to go away, and not to wait.

PEROO: Go, then!

ASSUNTA: But what wilt thou say to the mistress?

PEROO: That thou hast gone.

ASSUNTA: Nay, but thou must say that one came crying with news that my littlest babe was smitten with fever, and that I fled weeping. Else it were not wise to go.

PEROO: Be it so! But I shall need a little tobacco to solace me while I wait for the return of the mistress alone.

ASSUNTA: It shall come; and it shall be of the best. (A snake is a snake, and a bearer is a thieving ape till he dies!) I go. It was the fever of the child – the littlest babe of all – remember. (And now, if my lover finds I am late, he will beat me, judging that I have been unfaithful.) (*Exit.*)

At half-past nine enter tumultuously MAY, *a heavy shawl over her shoulders, skirt of smoke-coloured tulle showing beneath.*

MAY: Mrs. Hauksbee! Oh! she isn't here. And I dared not get Aunt's *ayah* to help. She would have told Uncle John – and I can't lace it myself. (PEROO *hands note.* MAY *reads.*) "So sorry. Dragged off to put the last touches to the draperies. Assunta will look after you." Sorry! You may well be sorry, wicked woman! Draperies, indeed! You never thought of mine, and – all up the back, too. (*To* PEROO.) Where's Assunta?

PEROO: (*Bowing to the earth.*) By your honoured favour, there came a man but a short time ago crying that the *ayah's* baby was smitten with fever, and she fled, weeping, to tend it. Her house is a mile hence. Is there any order?

MAY: How desperately annoying! (*Looking into fire, her eyes softening.*) Her baby! (*With a little shiver, passing right hand before eyes.*) Poor woman! (*A pause.*) But what am I to do? I can't even creep into the cloak-room as I am, and trust to some one to put me to rights; and the shawl's a horrid old plaid! Who invented dresses to lace up the back? It must have been a man! I'd like to put him into one! What *am* I to do? Perhaps the Colley-Haughton girls haven't left yet. They're sure to be dining at home. I might run up to their rooms and wait till they came. Eva wouldn't tell, I know. (*Remounts* DANDY, *and rides up the hill to house immediately above, enters glazed hall cautiously, and calls up staircase in an agonized whisper, huddling her shawl about her.*) Jenny! Eva! *Eva!* Jenny! They're out too, and, of course, their *ayah's* gone!

SIR HENRY COLLEY-HAUGHTON: (*Opening door of dining-room, where he has been finishing an after-dinner cigar, and stepping into hall.*) I thought I heard a – Miss Holt! I didn't know you were going with my girls. They've just left.

MAY: (*Confusedly.*) I wasn't. I didn't – that is, it was partly my fault. (*With desperate earnestness.*) Is Lady Haughton in?

SIR HENRY: She's with the girls. Is there anything that I can do? I'm going to the dance in a minute. Perhaps I might ride with you!

MAY: Not for worlds! Not for anything! It was a mistake. I hope the girls are quite well.

SIR HENRY: (*With bland wonder.*) Perfectly, thanks. (*Moves through hall towards horse.*)

MAY: (*Mounting in haste.*) No! Please don't hold my stirrup! I can manage perfectly, thanks! (*Canters out of the garden to side road shadowed by pines. Sees beneath her the lights of Simla town in orderly constellations, and on a bare ridge the*

illuminated bulk of the Simla Town-hall, shining like a cut-
paper transparency. The main road is firefly-lighted with the
moving 'rickshaw lamps all climbing towards the Town-hall.
The wind brings up a few bars of a waltz. A monkey in the
darkness of the wood wakes and croons dolefully.) And now,
where in the world am I to go? May, you bad girl! This
all comes of disobeying aunts and wearing dresses that
lace up the back, and – trusting Mrs. Hauksbee. Everybody is going. I must wait a little till that crowd has
thinned. Perhaps – perhaps Mrs. Lefevre might help me.
It's a horrid road to her poky little house, but she's very
kind, even if she is pious. (*Thrusts* DANDY *along an almost*
inaccessible path; halts in the shadow of a clump of rhododen-
dron, and watches the lighted windows of MRS. LEFEVRE'S
small cottage.) Oh! horror! so that's where Aunt is dining!
Back, Dandy, back! Dandy, dearest, step softly! (*Regains*
road, panting.) I'll never forgive Mrs. Hauksbee! – never!
And there's the band beginning "God Save the Queen,"
and that means the Viceroy has come; and Charley will
think I've disappointed him on purpose, because I was so
rude last time. And I'm all but ready. Oh! it's cruel, cruel!
I'll go home, and I'll go straight to bed, and Charley may
dance with any other horrid girl he likes! (*The last of the*
'rickshaw lights pass her as she reaches the main road. Clatter
of stones overhead and squeak of a saddle as a big horse picks
his way down a steep path above, and a robust baritone
chants –

> Our King went forth to Normandie
> With power of might and chivalry;
> The Lord for him wrought wondrously,
> Therefore now may England cry,
>   Deo Gratias!

Swings into main road, and the young moon shows a glimpse of
the cream and silver of the Deccan Irregular Horse uniform
under rider's opened cloak).
MAY: (*Leaning forward and taking reins short.*) That's Charley!

What a splendid voice! Just like a big, strong angel's! I wonder what he is so happy about? How he sits his horse! And he hasn't anything round his neck, and he'll catch his death of cold! If he sees me riding in this direction, he may stop and ask me why, and I can't explain. Fate's against me to-night. I'll canter past quickly. Bless you, Charley! (*Canters up the main road, under the shadow of the pines, as* HAWLEY *canters down.* DANDY's *hoofs keep the tune* "*There was never a daughter of Eve,*" *etc.* ALL EARTH *wakes, and tells the* STARS. *The* OCCUPANTS *of the Little Simla Cemetery stir in their sleep.*)

PINES OF THE CEMETERY (*to the* OCCUPANTS).

Lie still, lie still! O earth to earth returning!
    Brothers beneath, what wakes you to your pain?

The OCCUPANTS (*underground*).

Earth's call to earth – the old unstifled yearning,
        To clutch our lives again.

By summer shrivelled and by winter frozen,
    Ye cannot thrust us wholly from the light.
Do we not know, who were of old his chosen,
        Love rides abroad to-night?

By all that was our own of joy or sorrow,
    By Pain fordone, Desire snatched away!
By hopeless weight of that unsought To-morrow,
        Which is our lot to-day,

By vigil in our chambers ringing hollow,
    With Love's foot overhead to mock our dearth,
We who have come would speak for those who follow –
        Be pitiful, O Earth!

The DEVIL OF CHANCE, *in the similitude of a grey ape, runs out on the branch of an overhanging tree, singing –*

On a road that is pied as a panther's hide
    The shadows flicker and dance.
And the leaves that make them, my hand shall shake them –
    The hand of the Devil of Chance.

Echo from the SNOWS *on the Thibet road* –

The little blind Devil of Chance.

The DEVIL (*swinging branch furiously*) –

Yea, chance and confusion and error
The chain of their destiny wove;
And the horse shall be smitten with terror,
And the maiden made sure of her love!

DANDY *shies at the waving shadows, and cannons into* HAW-LEY'S *horse, off shoulder to off shoulder.* HAWLEY *catches the reins.*

The DEVIL *above* (*letting the branch swing back*) –

On a road that is pied as a panther's hide
The souls of the twain shall dance!
And the passions that shake them, my hand shall wake them –
The hand of the Devil of Chance.

Echo –

The little blind Devil of Chance.

HAWLEY: (*Recovering himself.*) Confou – er – hm! Oh, Miss Holt! And to what am I indebted for this honour?

MAY: Dandy shied. I hope you aren't hurt.

ALL EARTH, THE FLOWERS, THE TREES, and THE MOONLIGHT (*together to* HAWLEY). Speak now, or forever hold your peace!

HAWLEY: (*Drawing reins tighter, keeping his horse's off shoulder to* DANDY'S *side.*) My fault entirely. (It comes easily now.) Not much hurt, are you (*leaning off side, and putting his arm round her*), my May? It's awfully mean, I know, but I meant to speak weeks ago, only you never gave a fellow the chance – 'specially last time. (*Moistens his lips.*) I'm not fit – I'm utterly – (*in a gruff whisper*) – I'm utterly unworthy, and – and you aren't angry, May, are you? I thought you might have cared a little bit. *Do* you care, darl —?

MAY: (*Her head falling on his right shoulder. The arm tightens.*) Oh! don't – don't!

HAWLEY: (*Nearly tumbling off his horse.*) Only one, darling. We can talk at the dance.

MAY: But I can't go to the dance!

HAWLEY: (*Taking another promptly as head is raised.*) Nonsense! You *must*, dear, now. Remember I go down to my Regiment the day after to-morrow, and I sha'n't see you again. (*Catches glimpse of steel-grey slipper in stirrup.*) Why, you're dressed for it!

MAY: Yes, but I can't go! I've – torn my dress.

HAWLEY: Run along and put on a new one; only be quick. Shall I wait here?

MAY: No! Go away! Go at once!

HAWLEY: You'll find me opposite the cloak-room.

MAY: Yes, yes! Anything! Good-night!

HAWLEY *canters up the road, and the song breaks out again fortissimo.*

MAY: (*Absently, picking up reins.*) Yes, indeed. My king went forth to Normandie; and – I shall never get there. Let me think, though! Let me think! It's all over now – all over! I wonder what I ought to have said! I wonder what I did say! Hold up, Dandy; you need some one to order you about. It's nice to have some one nice to order you about. (*Flicks horse, who capers.*) Oh, don't jiggit, Dandy! I feel so trembly and faint. But I sha'n't see him for ever so long. . . . But we understand now. (DANDY *turns down path to* MRS. SCRIFFSHAW'S *house.*) And I wanted to go to the dance so much before, and now I want to go worse than ever! (*Dismounts, runs into house, and weeps with her head on the drawing-room table.*)

Enter SCRIFFSHAW, *grizzled Lieutenant-Colonel.*

SCRIFFSHAW: May! Bless my soul, what's all this? What's all this? (*Shawl slips.*) And, bless my soul, what's all *this*?

MAY: N-nothing. Only I'm miserable and wretched.

SCRIFFSHAW: But where have you been? I thought you were in your own room.

MAY: (*With icy desperation.*) I was, till you had fallen asleep. Then I dressed myself for a dance – this dance that Aunt has forbidden me to go to. Then I took Dandy out, and then – (*collapsing and wriggling her shoulders*) – doesn't it show enough?

SCRIFFSHAW: (*Critically.*) It does, dear. I thought those things – er – laced up the front.

MAY: This one doesn't. That's all. (*Weeps afresh.*)

SCRIFFSHAW: Then what are you going to do? Bless my soul, May, don't cry!

MAY: I *will* cry, and I'll sit here till Aunt comes home, and then she'll see what I've been trying to do, and I'll tell her that I hate her, and ask her to send me back to Calcutta!

SCRIFFSHAW: But – but if she finds you in this dress she'll be furiously angry with *me*!

MAY: For allowing me to put it on? So much the better. Then you'll know what it is to be scolded by Aunt.

SCRIFFSHAW: I knew that before you were born. (*Standing by* MAY's *bowed head.*) (She's my sister's child, and I don't think Alice has the very gentlest way with girls. I'm sure her mother wouldn't object if we took her to twenty dances. She can't find us amusing company – and Alice will be simply beside herself under any circumstances. I know her tempers after those "refreshing evenings" at the Lefevres'.) May, dear, don't cry like that!

MAY: I will! I will! I *will*! You – you don't know why!

SCRIFFSHAW: (*Revolving many matters.*) We may just as well be hanged for a sheep as a lamb.

MAY: (*Raising head swiftly.*) Uncle *John*!

SCRIFFSHAW: You see, my dear, your aunt can't be a scrap more angry than she will be if you don't take off that frock. She looks at the intention of things.

MAY: Yes; disobedience, of course. (And I'll only obey one person in the wide living world.) Well?

SCRIFFSHAW: Your aunt may be back at any moment. *I* can't face her.

MAY: Well?

SCRIFFSHAW: Let's go to the dance. I'll jump into my uniform, and then see if I can't put those things straight. We
may *just* as well be hanged for a sheep as a lamb. (And
there's the chance of a rubber.) Give me five minutes, and
we'll fly. (*Dives into his room, leaving* MAY *astounded.*)

SCRIFFSHAW: (*From the room.*) Tell them to bring round
Dolly Bobs. We can get away quicker on horseback.

MAY: But really, Uncle, hadn't you better go in a 'rickshaw?
Aunt says —

SCRIFFSHAW: We're in open mutiny now. We'll ride. (*Emerges in full uniform.*) There!

MAY: Oh, Uncle John! you look perfectly delightful – and so
martial, too!

SCRIFFSHAW: I was martial once. Suppose your aunt came
in? Let me see if I can lace those things of yours. That's
too tight – eh?

MAY: No! Much, much tighter. You must bring the edges
together. Indeed you must. And lace it *quick*! Oh! what if
Aunt should come? Tie it in a knot! Any sort of knot.

SCRIFFSHAW: (*Lacing bodice after a fashion of his own devising.*) Yes – yes! I see! Confound! That's all right! (*They
pass into the garden and mount their horses.*) Let go her
head! By Jove, May, how well you ride!

MAY: (*As they race through the shadows neck and neck.*) (Small
blame to me. I'm riding to my love.) Go along, Dandy
boy! Wasn't that Aunt's 'rickshaw that passed just now?
She'll come to the dance and fetch us back.

SCRIFFSHAW: (*After the gallop.*) Who cares?

SCENE. – *Main ball-room of the Simla Town-hall; dancing-floor
grooved and tongued teak, vaulted roof, and gallery round the walls.
Four hundred people dispersed in couples. Banners, bayonet-stars on
walls; red and gold, blue and gold, chocolate, buff, rifle-green, black,
and other uniforms under glare of a few hundred lamps. Cloak- and
supper-rooms at the sides, with alleys leading to Chinese-lanterned verandahs.* HAWLEY, *at entrance, receives* MAY *as she drops from her
horse and passes towards cloak-room.*

HAWLEY: (*As he pretends to rearrange shawl.*) Oh, my love, my love, my love!

MAY: (*Her eyes on the ground.*) Let me go and get these things off. I'm trying to control my eyes, but it is written on my face. (*Dashes into cloak-room.*)

NEWLY MARRIED WIFE OF CAPTAIN OF ENGINEERS TO HUSBAND: No need to ask what has happened *there*, Dick.

HUSBAND: No, bless 'em both, whoever they are!

HAWLEY: (*Under his breath.*) Damn his impertinence!

MAY *comes from cloak-room, having completely forgotten to do more than look at her face and hair in the glass.*

HAWLEY: Here's the programme, dear!

MAY: (*Returning it with pretty gesture of surrender.*) Here's the programme – dear!

HAWLEY *draws line from top to bottom, initials, and returns card.*

MAY: You can't! It's perfectly awful! But – I should have been angry if you hadn't. (*Taking his arm.*) Is it wrong to say that?

HAWLEY: It sounds delicious. We can sit out all the squares and dance all the round dances. There are heaps of square dances at Volunteer balls. Come along!

MAY: One minute! I want to tell my chaperon something.

HAWLEY: Come along! You belong to me now.

MAY: (*Her eyes seeking* MRS. HAUKSBEE, *who is seated on an easy-chair by an alcove.*) But it was so awfully sudden!

HAWLEY: My dear infant! When a girl throws herself literally into a man's arms —

MAY: I didn't! Dandy shied.

HAWLEY: Don't shy to conclusions. That man is never going to let her go. Come!

MAY *catches* MRS. H.'s *eye. Telegraphs a volume, and receives by return two. Turns to go with* HAWLEY.

MRS. H: (*As she catches sight of back of* MAY's *dress.*) Oh, horror! Assunta shall die to-morrow! (*Sees* SCRIFFSHAW *fluctuating uneasily among the chaperons, and following his niece's departure with the eye of an artist.*)

MRS. H: (*Furiously.*) Colonel Scriffshaw, you – *you* did that?

SCRIFFSHAW: (*Imbecilely.*) The lacing? Yes. I think it will hold.

MRS. H: You monster! Go and tell her. No, don't! (*Falling back in chair.*) I have lived to see every proverb I believed in a lie. The maid has forgotten her attire! (What a handsome couple they make! Anyhow, he doesn't care, and she doesn't know.) How did *you* come here, Colonel Scriffshaw?

SCRIFFSHAW: Strictly against orders. (*Uneasily.*) I'm afraid I shall have my wife looking for me.

MRS. H: I fancy you will. (*Sees reflection of herself in the mirrors – black-lace dinner dress, blood-red poinsettia at shoulder and girdle to secure single brace of black lace. Silver shoes, silver-handled black fan.*) (You're looking pretty to-night, dear. I wish your husband were here.) (*Aloud, to drift of expectant men.*) No, no, no! For the hundredth time, Mrs. Hauksbee is not dancing this evening. (Her hands are full, or she is in error. Now, the chances are that I sha'n't see May again till it is time to go, and I may see Mrs. Scriffshaw at any moment.) Colonel, *will* you take me to the supper-room? The hall's chilly without perpetual soups. (*Goes out on* COLONEL's *arm. Passing the cloak-room, sees portion of* MRS. SCRIFFSHAW's *figure.*) (Before me the Deluge!) If I were you, Colonel Scriffshaw, I'd go to the whist-room, and – stay there. (S. *follows the line of her eye, and blanches as he flies.*) She *has* come – to – take them home, and she is quite capable of it. What shall I do? (*Looks across the supper-tables. Sees* MAJOR DECKER, *a big black-haired Irishman, and attacks him among the meringues.*) Major Decker! Dear Major Decker! If ever I was a friend of yours, help me now!

MAJOR D: I will indeed. What is it?

MRS. H: (*Walking him back deftly in the direction of the cloak-*

room door.) I want you to be very kind to a very dear friend of mine – a Mrs. Scriffshaw. She doesn't come to dances much, and, being very sensitive, she feels neglected if no one asks her to dance. She really waltzes divinely, though you might not think it. There she is, walking out of the cloak-room now, in the high dress. *Please* come and be introduced. (*Under her eyelashes.*) You're an Irishman, Major, and you've got a way with you. (*Planting herself in front of* MRS. S.) Mrs. Scriffshaw, may I wah-wah-wah Decker? – wah-wah-wah Decker? – Mrs. Scuffles. (*Flies hastily.*) Saved for a moment! And now, if I can enlist the Viceroy on my side, I may do something.

MAJOR D: (*To* MRS. S.) The pleasure of a dance with you, Mrs. Scruffun?

MRS. SCRIFFSHAW: (*Backing, and filling in the doorway.*) Sir!

MAJOR D: (*Smiling persuasively.*) You've forgotten me, I see! I had the pleasure o' meeting you – (there's missionary in every line o' that head) – at – at – the last Presbyterian Conference.

MRS. S: (*Strict Wesleyan Methodist.*) I was never there.

MAJOR D: (*Retiring* en échelon *towards two easy-chairs.*) Were ye not, now? That's queer. Let's sit down here and talk over it, and perhaps we will strike a chord of mutual reminiscence. (*Sits down exhaustedly.*) And if it was not at the Conference, where was it?

MRS. S: (*Icily, looking for her husband.*) I apprehend that our paths in the world are widely different.

MAJOR D: (My faith! they are!) Not the least in the world. (MRS. S. *shudders.*) Are you sitting in a draught? Shall we try a turn at the waltz now?

MRS. S: (*Rising to the expression of her abhorrence.*) My husband is Colonel Scriffshaw. I should be much obliged if you would find him for me.

MAJOR D: (*Throwing up his chin.*) Scriffshaw, begad! I saw him just now at the other end of the room. (I'll get a dance out of the old woman, or I'll die for it.) We'll just waltz up there an' inquire. (*Hurls* MRS. S. *into the waltz. Revolves ponderously.*) (Mrs. Hauksbee has perjured herself – but not on my behalf. She's ruining my instep.) No, he's not at this end. (*Circling slowly.*) We'll just go back to our chairs again. If he won't dance with so magnificent a dancer as his wife, he doesn't deserve to be here, or anywhere else. (That's my own sound knee-cap she's kicking now.) (*Halts at point of departure.*) And now we'll watch for him here.

MRS. S: (*Panting.*) Abominable! Infamous!

MAJOR D: Oh, no! He's not so bad as that! Prob'bly playin' whist in the kyard-rooms. Will I look for him? (*Departs, leaving* MRS. S. *purple in the face among the chaperons, and passes* MRS. H. *in close conversation with a partner.*)

MAJOR D: (*To* MRS. H., *not noticing her partner.*) She's kicked me to pieces. She can dance no more than a Windsor chair, an' now she's sent me to look for her husband. You owe me something for this. . . . (The Viceroy, by Jove!)

MRS. H: (*Turning to her partner and concluding story.*) A base betrayal of confidence, of course; but the woman's absolutely without tact, and capable of making a scene at a minute's notice, besides doing her best to wreck the happiness of two lives, after her treatment at Major Decker's hands. But on the Dress Reform Committee, and under proper supervision, she would be most valuable.

HIS EXCELLENCY THE VICEROY AND GOVERNOR-GENERAL OF INDIA: (*Diplomatic uniform, stars, etc.*) But surely the work of keeping order among the waltzers is entrusted to abler hands. I cannot, cannot fight! I – I only direct armies.

MRS. H: No. But Your Excellency has not quite grasped the situation. (*Explains it with desperate speed, one eye on* MRS. S. *panting on her chair.*) So you see! Husband fled to the whist-room for refuge; girl with her lover, who goes down the day after to-morrow; and *she* is loose. She will be neither to hold nor to bind after the Major's onslaught, save by you. And on a committee – she really would —

HIS EXCELLENCY: I see. I am penetrated with an interest in Eurasian dress reform. I never felt so alive to the importance of committees before. (*Screwing up his eyes to see across the room.*) But pardon me – my sight is not so good as it has been – which of that line of Mothers in Israel do I attack! The wearied one who is protesting with a fan against this scene of riot and dissipation?

MRS. H: Can you doubt for a moment? I'm afraid your task is a heavy one, but the happiness of two —

HIS EXCELLENCY: (*Wearily.*) Hundred and fifty million souls? Ah, yes! And yet they say a Viceroy is overpaid. Let us advance. It will not talk to me about its husband's unrecognised merits, will it? You have no idea how inevitably the conversation drifts in that direction when I am left alone with a lady. They tell me of Poor Tom, or Dear Dick, or Persecuted Paul, before I have time to explain that these things are really regulated by my Secretaries. On my honour, I sometimes think that the ladies of India are polyandrous!

MRS. H: Would it be so difficult to credit that they love their husbands?

HIS EXCELLENCY: That also is possible. One of your many claims to my regard is that you have never mentioned your husband.

MRS. H: (*Sweetly.*) No; and as long as he is where he is, I have not the least intention of doing so.

HIS EXCELLENCY: (*As they approach the row of eminently self-conscious chaperons.*) And, by the way, where is he?

MRS. H: *lays her fan lightly over her heart, bows her head, and moves on.*

HIS EXCELLENCY: (*As the chaperons become more self-conscious, drifting to vacant chair at* MRS. S.'*s side.*) That also is possible. I do not recall having seen him elsewhere, at any rate. (*Watching* MRS. S.) How very like twenty thousand people that I could remember if I had time! (*Glides into vacant chair.* MRS. S. *colours to the temples; chaperons exchange glances. In a voice of strained honey.*) May I be pardoned for attacking you so brusquely on matters of public importance, Mrs. Scriffshaw? But my times are not my own, and I have heard so much about the good work you carry on so successfully. (*When she has quite recovered I may learn what that work was.*)

MRS. S., *in tones meant for the benefit of all the chaperons, discourses volubly, with little gasps, of her charitable mission work.*

HIS EXCELLENCY: How interesting! Of course, quite natural! What we want most on our dress reform committee is a firm hand and enormous local knowledge. Men are *so* tactless. You have been too proud, Mrs. Scriffshaw, to offer us your help in that direction. So, you see, I come to ask it as a favour. (*Gives* MRS. S. *to understand that the Eurasian dress reform committee cannot live another hour without her help and comfort.*)

FIRST AIDE: (*By doorway within eye-reach of* HIS EXCELLENCY.) What in the world is His Excellency tackling now?

SECOND AIDE: (*In attitude of fascination.*) Looks as if it had been a woman once. Anyhow, it isn't amusing him. I know that smile when he is in acute torment.

MRS. H: (*Coming up behind him.*) "Now the Serpent was more subtle than any beast of the field!"

SECOND AIDE: (*Turning.*) Ah! Your programme full, of course, Mrs. Hauksbee?

MRS. H: I'm not dancing, and you should have asked me before. You Aides have no manners.

FIRST AIDE: You must excuse him. Hugh's a blighted being. He's watching somebody dance with somebody else, and somebody's wanting to dance with him.

MRS. H: (*Keenly, under her eyebrows.*) You're too young for that rubbish.

SECOND AIDE: It's his imagination. *He*'s all right, but Government House duty is killing me. My heart's in the plains with a dear little, fat little, lively little nine-foot tiger. I want to sit out over that kill instead of watching over His Excellency.

MRS. H: Don't they let the Aides out to play, then?

SECOND AIDE: Not me. I've got to do most of Duggy's work while he runs after —

MRS. H: Never mind! A discontented Aide is a perpetual beast. One of you boys will take me to a chair, and then leave me. No, I don't want the delights of your conversation.

SECOND AIDE: (*As first goes off.*) When Mrs. Hauksbee is attired in holy simplicity it generally means – larks!

HIS EXCELLENCY: (*To* MRS. SCRIFFSHAW.) ... And so we all wanted to see more of you. I felt I was taking no liberty when I dashed into affairs of State at so short a notice. It was with the greatest difficulty I could find you. Indeed, I hardly believed my eyes when I saw you waltzing so divinely just now. (*She will first protest, and next perjure herself.*)

MRS. S: (*Weakly.*) But I assure you —

HIS EXCELLENCY: My eyes are not so old that they cannot recognise a good dancer when they see one.

MRS. S: (*With a simper.*) But only once in a way, Your Excellency.

HIS EXCELLENCY: (Of course.) That is too seldom – much too seldom. You should set our younger folk an example. These slow swirling waltzes are tiring. I prefer – as I see you do – swifter measures.

MAJOR D: (*Entering main door in strict charge of* SCRIFFSHAW, *who fears the judgment.*) Yes! she sent me to look for you, after giving me *the* dance of the evening. I'll never forget it!

SCRIFFSHAW: (*His jaw dropping.*) My – wife – danced – with – *you*! I mean – anybody!

MAJOR D: Anybody! Aren't I somebody enough? (*Looking across room.*) Faith! you're right, though! There she is in a corner, flirting with the Viceroy! I was not good enough for her. Well, it's no use to interrupt 'em.

SCRIFFSHAW: Certainly not! We'll – we'll get a drink and go back to the whist-rooms. (Alice must be mad! At any rate, I'm safe, I suppose.)

HIS EXCELLENCY *rises and fades away from* MRS.
SCRIFFSHAW's *side after a long and particular pressure of the
hand.* MRS. S. *throws herself back in her chair with the air of
one surfeited with similar attentions, and the chaperons begin to
talk.*

HIS EXCELLENCY: *Leaning over* MRS. H.'s *chair with an absolutely expressionless countenance.*) She is a truly estimable
lady – one that I shall count it an honour to number
among my friends. No! she will not move from her place,
because I have expressed a hope that, a little later on in
the dance, we may renew our very interesting conversation. And now, if I could only get my boys together, I
think I would go home. Have you seen any Aide who
looked as though a Viceroy belonged to him?

MRS. H: The feet of the young men are at the door without.
You leave early.

HIS EXCELLENCY: Have I not done enough?

MRS. H: (*Half rising from her chair.*) Too much, alas! Too
much! Look!

HIS EXCELLENCY: (*Regarding* MRS. SCRIFFSHAW, *who has
risen and is moving towards a side door.*) How interesting!
By every law known to me she should have waited in that
chair – such a comfortable chair – for my too tardy return.
But now she is loose! How has this happened?

MRS. H: (*Half to herself, shutting and opening fan.*) She is looking for May! I know it! Oh! why wasn't she isolated? One
of those women has taken revenge on Mrs. Scriffshaw's
new glory – *you* – by telling her that May has been sitting
out too much with Mr. Hawley.

HIS EXCELLENCY: Blame me! Always blame a Viceroy!
(MRS. H. *moves away.*) What are you meditating?

MRS. H: Following – watching – administering – anything! I
fly! I know where they are!

HIS EXCELLENCY: The plot thickens! May I come to administer?

MRS. H: (*Over her shoulder.*) If you can!

MRS. H. *flies down a darkened corridor speckled with occasional Chinese lanterns, and establishes herself behind a pillar as* MRS. S. *sweeps by to the darkest end, where* MAY *and* HAWLEY *are sitting very close together.* HIS EXCELLENCY *follows* MRS. H.

MRS. S: (*To both the invisibles.*) Well!

HIS EXCELLENCY: (*To* MRS. H. *in a whisper.*) Now, I should be afraid. I should run away.

MRS. S: (*In a high-pitched voice of the matron.*) May, go to the cloak-room at once, and wait till I come. I wonder you expect any one to speak to you after this! (MAY *hurries down corridor very considerably agitated.*)

HIS EXCELLENCY: (*As* MAY *passes, slightly raising his voice, and with all the deference due to half a dozen Duchesses.*) May an old man be permitted to offer you his arm, my dear? (*To* MRS. H.) I entreat – I *command* you to delay the catastrophe till I return!

MRS. H: (*Plunging into the darkness, and halting before a dead wall.*) Oh! I thought there was a way round! (*Pretends to discover the two.*) Mrs. Scriffshaw and Mr. Hawley! (*With exaggerated emphasis.*) Mrs. Scriffshaw – Oh! *Mrs.* Scriffshaw! – how truly shocking! What will that dear, good husband of yours say? (*Smothered chuckle from* HAWLEY, *who otherwise preserves silence. Snorts of indignation from* MRS. S.)

MRS. H: (*Hidden by pillar of observation.*) Now, in any other woman that would have been possibly weak – certainly vulgar. But I think it has answered the purpose.

HIS EXCELLENCY: (*Returning, and taking up his post at her side.*) Poor little girl! She was shaking all over. What an enormous amount of facile emotion exists in the young! What is about to —

MRS. S: (*In a rattling whisper to* HAWLEY.) Take me to some quieter place.

HAWLEY: On my word, you seem to be accustomed to *very* quiet places. I'm sorry I don't know any more secluded nook; but if you have anything to say —

MRS. S: Say, indeed! I wish you to understand that I consider your conduct abominable, sir!

HAWLEY: (*In level, expressionless voice.*) Yes? Explain yourself.

MRS. S: In the first place, you meet my niece at an entertainment of which I utterly disapprove —

HAWLEY: To the extent of dancing with Major Decker, the most notorious loose fish in the whole room? Yes.

MRS. S: (*Hotly.*) That was not my fault. It was entirely against my inclination.

HAWLEY: It takes two to make a waltz. Presumably, you are capable of expressing your wishes – are you not?

MRS. S: I did. It was – only – and I couldn't —

HAWLEY: (*Relentlessly.*) Well, it's a most serious business. I've been talking it over with May.

MRS. S: May!

HAWLEY: Yes, May; and she has assured me that you do not do – er – this sort of thing often. She *assured* me of that.

MRS. S: But by what right —

HAWLEY: You see, May has promised to marry me, and one can't be too careful about one's connections.

HIS EXCELLENCY: (*To* MRS. H.) That young man will go far! This is invention indeed.

MRS. H: He seems to have marched some paces already. (Blessed be the chance that led me to the Major! I can always say that I meant it.)

MRS. S: May has promised . . . this is worse than ever! And *I* was not consulted!

HAWLEY: If I had known the precise hour, you know, I might possibly have chosen to take you into my confidence.

MRS. S: May should have told *me*.

HAWLEY: You mustn't worry May about it. Is that perfectly clear to you?

HIS EXCELLENCY: (*To* MRS. H.) What a singularly flat, hopeless tone he has chosen to talk in – as if he were speaking to a coolie from a distance.

MRS. H: Yes. It's the one note that will rasp through her overstrained nerves.

HIS EXCELLENCY: You know him well?

MRS. H: I trained him.

HIS EXCELLENCY: Then *she* collapses.

MRS. H: If she does not, all my little faith in man is gone for ever.

MRS. S: (*To* HAWLEY.) This is perfectly monstrous! It's conduct utterly unworthy of a *man*, much less a gentleman. What do *I* know of you, or your connections, or your means?

HAWLEY: Nothing. How could you?

MRS. S: How could I? . . . Because – because I insist on knowing!

HAWLEY: Then am I to understand that you are anxious to marry me? Suppose we talk to the Colonel about that?

HIS EXCELLENCY: (*To* MRS. H.) Very far, indeed, will that young man go.

MRS. S: (*Almost weeping with anger.*) Will you let me pass? I – I want to go away. I've no language at my command that could convey to you —

HAWLEY: Then surely it would be better to wait here till the inspiration comes?

MRS. S: But this is insolence!

HAWLEY: You must remember that you drove May, who, by the way, is a woman, out of this place like a hen. That was insolence, Mrs. Scriffshaw – to her.

MRS. S: To her? She's my husband's sister's child.

HAWLEY: And she is going to do me the honour of carrying my name. I am accountable to your husband's sister in Calcutta. Sit down, please!

HIS EXCELLENCY: She will positively assault him in a minute. I can hear her preparing for a spring.

MRS. H: He will be able to deal with that too, if it happens. (I trained him. Bear witness, heaven and earth, I trained him, that his tongue should guard his head with my sex.)

MRS. S: (*Feebly.*) What shall I do? What *can* I do? (*Through her teeth.*) I hate you!

HIS EXCELLENCY: (*Critically.*) Weak. The end approaches.

MRS. S: *You*'re not the sort of man I should have chosen for anybody's husband.

HAWLEY: I can't say your choice seems particularly select – Major Decker, for instance. And believe me, you are not required to choose husbands for anybody.

(MRS. SCRIFFSHAW *looses all the double-thonged lightnings of her tongue, condemns* HAWLEY *as no gentleman, an impostor, possibly a bigamist, a defaulter, and every other unpleasant character she has ever read of; announces her unalterable intention of refusing to recognise the engagement, and of harrying* MAY *tooth and talon; and renews her request to be allowed to pass. No answer.*)

HIS EXCELLENCY: What a merciful escape! She might have attacked me on the chairs in this fashion. What will he do now?

MRS. H: I have faith – illimitable faith.

MRS. S: (*At the end of her resources.*) Well, what have you to say?

HAWLEY: (*In a placid and most insinuating drawl.*) Aunt Alice – give – me – a – kiss.

HIS EXCELLENCY: Beautiful! Oh! thrice beautiful! And my Secretaries never told me there were men like this in the Empire.

MRS. S: (*Bewilderedly, beginning to sob.*) Why – why *should* I?

HAWLEY: Because you will make – you really will – a delightful aunt-in-law, and it will save such a lot of trouble when May and I are married, and you have to accept me as a relation.

MRS. S: (*Weeping gently.*) But – but you're taking the management of affairs into your own hands.

HAWLEY: Quite so. They are my own affairs. And do you think that my aunt is competent to manage other people's affairs when she doesn't know whether she means to dance or sit out, and when she chooses the very worst —

MRS. S: (*Appealingly.*) Oh, don't – don't! Please, don't! (*Bursts into tears.*)

HIS EXCELLENCY: (*To* MRS. H.) Unnecessarily brutal, surely? She's crying.

MRS. H: No! It's nothing. We all cry – even the worst of us.

HAWLEY: Well?

MRS. S: (*Snuffling, with a rustle.*) There!

HAWLEY: No, no, no! I said give it to me! (*It is given.*)

HIS EXCELLENCY: (*Carried away.*) And I? What am I doing here, pretending to govern India, while that man languishes in a lieutenant's uniform?

MRS. H: (*Speaking very swiftly and distinctly.*) It rests with Your Excellency to raise him to honour. He should go down the day after to-morrow. A month at Simla, now, would mean Paradise to him, and one of your Aides is dying for a little tiger-shooting.

HIS EXCELLENCY: But would such an Archangel of Insolence condescend to run errands for me?

MRS. H: You can but try.

HIS EXCELLENCY: I shall be afraid of him; but we'll see if we can get the Commander-in-Chief to lend him to me.

HAWLEY: (*To* MRS. S.) There, there, there! It's nothing to make a fuss about, is it? Come along, Aunt Alice, and I'll tuck you into your 'rickshaw, and you shall go home quite comfy, and the Colonel and I will bring May home later. I go down to my regiment the day after to-morrow, worse luck! So you won't have me long to trouble you. But we quite understand each other, don't we? (*Emerges from the darkness, very tenderly escorting the very much shaken* MRS. SCRIFFSHAW.)

HIS EXCELLENCY: (*To* MRS. H. *as the captive passes.*) I feel as if I ought to salute that young man; but I must go to the ball-room. Send him to me as soon as you can. (*Drifts in direction of music.* HAWLEY *returns to* MRS. H.)

HAWLEY: (*Mopping his forehead.*) Phew! I have had easier duties.

MRS. H: How could you? How dared you? I builded better than I knew. It was cruel, but it was superb.

HAWLEY: Who taught me? Where's May?

MRS. H: In the cloak-room – being put to rights – I fervently trust.

HAWLEY: (*Guiltily.*) They wear their fringes so low on their foreheads that one can't —

MRS. H: (*Laughing.*) Oh, you goose! That wasn't it. His Excellency wants to speak to you! (HAWLEY *turns to ball-room as* MRS. H. *flings herself down in a chair.*)

MRS. H: (*Alone.*) For two seasons, at intervals, I formed the infant mind. Heavens, how raw he was in the beginning! And never once throughout his schooling did he disappoint you, dear. Never once, by word or look or sign, did he have the unspeakable audacity to fall in love with you. No, he chose his maiden, then he stopped his confidences, and conducted his own wooing, and in open fight slew his aunt-in-law. But he never, being a wholesome, dear, delightful boy, fell in love with you, Mrs. Hauksbee; and I wonder whether you liked it or whether you didn't. Which? . . . You certainly never gave him a chance . . . but that was the very reason why . . . (*Half aloud.*) Mrs. Hauksbee, you are an idiot!

Enters main ball-room just in time to see HIS EXCELLENCY *conferring with* HAWLEY, AIDES *in background.*

HIS EXCELLENCY: Have you any very pressing employment in the plains, Mr. Hawley?

HAWLEY: Regimental duty. Native Cavalry, sir.

HIS EXCELLENCY: And, of course, you are anxious to return at once?

HAWLEY: Not in the least, sir.

HIS EXCELLENCY: Do you think you could relieve one of my boys here for a month?

HAWLEY: Most certainly, sir.

SECOND AIDE: (*Behind* VICEROY's *shoulders, shouting in dumb show.*) My tiger! My tiger! My tigerling!

HIS EXCELLENCY: (*Lowering his voice and regarding* HAWLEY *between his eyes.*) But could we trust you – ahem! – not to

insist on ordering kisses at inopportune moments from –
people?

HAWLEY: (*Dropping eyes.*) Not when I'm on duty, sir.

HIS EXCELLENCY: (*Turning.*) Then I'll speak to the Commander-in-Chief about it.

MRS. H: (*As she sees gratified expression of the* VICEROY's *and*
HAWLEY's *lowered eyes.*) I am sometimes sorry that I am
a woman, but I'm very glad that I'm not a man, and – I
shouldn't care to be an angel. (MRS. SCRIFFSHAW *and*
MAY *pass – the latter properly laced, the former regarding the*
lacing.) So that's settled at last. (*To* MRS. S.) Your husband, Mrs. Scriffshaw? Yes, I know. But don't be too hard
on him. Perhaps he never did it, after all.

MRS. S: (*With a grunt of infinite contempt.*) Mrs. Hauksbee,
that man has tried to lace *me!*

MRS. H: (Then he's bolder than I thought. She will avenge all
her outrages on the Colonel.) May, come and talk to me
a moment, dear.

FIRST AIDE: (*To* HAWLEY, *as the* VICEROY *drifts away.*)
Knighted on the field of battle, by Jove! What the deuce
have you been doing to His Excellency?

SECOND AIDE: I'll bet on it that Mrs. Hauksbee is at the
bottom of this, somehow. I told her what I wanted, and –

HAWLEY: Never look a gift tiger in the mouth. It's apt to
bite. (*Departs in search of* MAY.)

HIS EXCELLENCY: (*To* MRS. H. *as he passes her sitting out with*
MAY.) No, I am not so afraid of your young friend. Have
I done well?

MRS. H: Exceedingly. (*In a whisper, including* MAY.) She is a
pretty girl, isn't she?

HIS EXCELLENCY: (*Regarding mournfully, his chin on his*
breast.) O youth, youth, youth! *Si la jeunesse savait – si la*
vieillesse pouvait.

MRS. H: (*Incautiously.*) Yes, but in this case we have seen
that youth did know quite as much as was good for it,
and — (*Stops.*)

HIS EXCELLENCY: And age had power, and used it. Sufficient reward, perhaps; but I hardly expected the reminder from *you*.

MRS. H: No. I won't try to excuse it. Perhaps the slip is as well, for it reminds me that I am but mortal, and in watching *you* controlling the destinies of the universe I thought I was as the gods!

HIS EXCELLENCY: Thank you! I go to be taken away. But it has been an interesting evening.

SCRIFFSHAW: (*Very much disturbed after the* VICEROY *has passed on, to* MRS. H.) Now, what in the world was wrong with my lacing? My wife didn't appear angry about my bringing May here. I'm informed she danced several dances herself. But she – she gave it me awfully in the supper-room for my – ahem! – lady's-maid's work. Fearfully she gave it me! What was wrong? It held, didn't it?

MAY: (*From her chair.*) It was beautiful, Uncle John. It was the best thing in the world you could have done. Never mind. I forgive you. (*To* HAWLEY, *behind her.*) No, Charley. No more dances for just a little while. Ask Mrs. Hauksbee now.

Alarums and Excursions. The ball-room is rent in twain as the VICEROY, AIDES, *etc., file out between Lines of Volunteers and Uniforms.*

BAND IN THE GALLERY –

> God save our gracious Queen,
> Heaven bless our noble Queen,
> God save the Queen!
> Send her victorious,
> Happy and glorious,
> Long to reign over us,
> God save the Queen!

HAWLEY: (*Behind* MRS. H.'s *chair.*) Amen, your Imperial
Majesty!

MRS. H: (*Looking up, head thrown back on left shoulder.*) Thank
you! Yes, you can have the next if you want it. Mrs.
Hauksbee isn't sitting out any more.

A WAYSIDE COMEDY

A WAYSIDE COMEDY

* * *

Because to every purpose there is time and judgment, therefore the misery of man is great upon him.

Eccles. viii. 6

FATE and the Government of India have turned the Station of Kashima into a prison; and, because there is no help for the poor souls who are now lying there in torment, I write this story, praying that the Government of India may be moved to scatter the European population to the four winds.

Kashima is bounded on all sides by the rock-tipped circle of the Dosehri hills. In Spring, it is ablaze with roses; in Summer, the roses die and the hot winds blow from the hills; in Autumn, the white mists from the *jhils* cover the place as with water, and in Winter the frosts nip everything young and tender to earth-level. There is but one view in Kashima – a stretch of perfectly flat pasture and plough-land, running up to the grey-blue scrub of the Dosehri hills.

There are no amusements, except snipe and tiger shooting; but the tigers have been long since hunted from their lairs in the rock-caves, and the snipe only come once a year. Narkarra – one hundred and forty-three miles by road – is the nearest station to Kashima. But Kashima never goes to Narkarra, where there are at least twelve English people. It stays within the circle of the Dosehri hills.

All Kashima acquits Mrs. Vansuythen of any intention to do harm; but all Kashima knows that she, and she alone, brought about their pain.

Boulte, the Engineer, Mrs. Boulte, and Captain Kurrell know this. They are the English population of Kashima, if

391

we except Major Vansuythen, who is of no importance whatever, and Mrs. Vansuythen, who is the most important of all.

You must remember, though you will not understand,
that all laws weaken in a small and hidden community where
there is no public opinion. When a man is absolutely alone
in a Station he runs a certain risk of falling into evil ways.
This risk is multiplied by every addition to the population
up to twelve – the Jury-number. After that, fear and con-
sequent restraint begin, and human action becomes less gro-
tesquely jerky.

There was deep peace in Kashima till Mrs. Vansuythen
arrived. She was a charming woman, every one said so everywhere; and she charmed every one. In spite of this, or, perhaps, because of this, since Fate is so perverse, she cared
only for one man, and he was Major Vansuythen. Had she
been plain or stupid, this matter would have been intelligible
to Kashima. But she was a fair woman, with very still grey
eyes, the colour of a lake just before the light of the sun
touches it. No man who had seen those eyes could, later on,
explain what fashion of woman she was to look upon. The
eyes dazzled him. Her own sex said that she was "not bad
looking, but spoilt by pretending to be so grave." And yet
her gravity was natural. It was not her habit to smile. She
merely went through life, looking at those who passed;
and the women objected while the men fell down and worshipped.

She knows and is deeply sorry for the evil she has done
to Kashima; but Major Vansuythen cannot understand why
Mrs. Boulte does not drop in to afternoon tea at least three
times a week. "When there are only two women in one Station, they ought to see a great deal of each other," says Major
Vansuythen.

Long and long before ever Mrs. Vansuythen came out of
those far-away places where there is society and amusement,
Kurrell had discovered that Mrs. Boulte was the one woman
in the world for him and – you dare not blame them. Kashima was as out of the world as Heaven or the Other Place,

and the Dosehri hills kept their secret well. Boulte had no concern in the matter. He was in camp for a fortnight at a time. He was a hard, heavy man, and neither Mrs. Boulte nor Kurrell pitied him. They had all Kashima and each other for their very, very own; and Kashima was the Garden of Eden in those days. When Boulte returned from his wanderings he would slap Kurrell between the shoulders and call him "old fellow," and the three would dine together. Kashima was happy then when the judgment of God seemed almost as distant as Narkarra or the railway that ran down to the sea. But the Government sent Major Vansuythen to Kashima, and with him came his wife.

The etiquette of Kashima is much the same as that of a desert island. When a stranger is cast away there, all hands go down to the shore to make him welcome. Kashima assembled at the masonry platform close to the Narkarra Road, and spread tea for the Vansuythens. That ceremony was reckoned a formal call, and made them free of the Station, its rights and privileges. When the Vansuythens were settled down, they gave a tiny house-warming to all Kashima; and that made Kashima free of their house, according to the immemorial usage of the Station.

Then the Rains came, when no one could go into camp, and the Narkarra Road was washed away by the Kasun River, and in the cup-like pastures of Kashima the cattle waded knee-deep. The clouds dropped down from the Dosehri hills and covered everything.

At the end of the Rains, Boulte's manner towards his wife changed and became demonstratively affectionate. They had been married twelve years, and the change startled Mrs. Boulte, who hated her husband with the hate of a woman who has met with nothing but kindness from her mate, and, in the teeth of this kindness, has done him a great wrong. Moreover, she had her own trouble to fight with – her watch to keep over her own property, Kurrell. For two months the Rains had hidden the Dosehri hills and many other things besides; but, when they lifted, they showed Mrs. Boulte that

her man among men, her Ted – for she called him Ted in
the old days when Boulte was out of earshot – was slipping
the links of the allegiance.

"The Vansuythen Woman has taken him," Mrs. Boulte
said to herself; and when Boulte was away, wept over her
belief, in the face of the over-vehement blandishments of
Ted. Sorrow in Kashima is as fortunate as Love, because
there is nothing to weaken it save the flight of Time. Mrs.
Boulte had never breathed her suspicion to Kurrell because
she was not certain; and her nature led her to be very certain
before she took steps in any direction. That is why she behaved as she did.

Boulte came into the house one evening, and leaned
against the door-posts of the drawing-room, chewing his
moustache. Mrs. Boulte was putting some flowers into a vase.
There is a pretence of civilisation even in Kashima.

"Little woman," said Boulte quietly, "do you care
for me?"

"Immensely," said she, with a laugh. "Can you ask it?"

"But I'm serious," said Boulte. "*Do* you care for me?"

Mrs. Boulte dropped the flowers, and turned round
quickly. "Do you want an honest answer?"

"Ye-es, I've asked for it."

Mrs. Boulte spoke in a low, even voice for five minutes,
very distinctly, that there might be no misunderstanding her
meaning. When Samson broke the pillars of Gaza, he did a
little thing, and one not to be compared to the deliberate
pulling down of a woman's homestead about her own ears.
There was no wise female friend to advise Mrs. Boulte, the
singularly cautious wife, to hold her hand. She struck at
Boulte's heart, because her own was sick with suspicion of
Kurrell, and worn out with the long strain of watching alone
through the Rains. There was no plan or purpose in her
speaking. The sentences made themselves; and Boulte listened, leaning against the door-post with his hands in his
pockets. When all was over, and Mrs. Boulte began to
breathe through her nose before breaking out into tears, he

laughed and stared straight in front of him at the Dosehri hills.

"Is that all?" he said. "Thanks, I only wanted to know, you know."

"What are you going to do?" said the woman, between her sobs.

"Do! Nothing. What should I do? Kill Kurrell or send you Home, or apply for leave to get a divorce? It's two days' dâk into Narkarra." He laughed again and went on: "I'll tell you what *you* can do. You can ask Kurrell to dinner to-morrow – no, on Thursday, that will allow you time to pack – and you can bolt with him. I give you my word I won't follow."

He took up his helmet and went out of the room, and Mrs. Boulte sat till the moonlight streaked the floor, thinking and thinking and thinking. She had done her best upon the spur of the moment to pull the house down; but it would not fall. Moreover, she could not understand her husband, and she was afraid. Then the folly of her useless truthfulness struck her, and she was ashamed to write to Kurrell, saying: "I have gone mad and told everything. My husband says that I am free to elope with you. Get a dâk for Thursday, and we will fly after dinner." There was a cold-bloodedness about that procedure which did not appeal to her. So she sat still in her own house and thought.

At dinner-time Boulte came back from his walk, white and worn and haggard, and the woman was touched at his distress. As the evening wore on, she muttered some expression of sorrow, something approaching to contrition. Boulte came out of a brown study and said, "Oh, *that*! I wasn't thinking about that. By the way, what does Kurrell say to the elopement?"

"I haven't seen him," said Mrs. Boulte. "Good God! is that all?"

But Boulte was not listening, and her sentence ended in a gulp.

The next day brought no comfort to Mrs. Boulte, for

Kurrell did not appear, and the new life that she, in the five minutes' madness of the previous evening, had hoped to build out of the ruins of the old, seemed to be no nearer.

Boulte ate his breakfast, advised her to see her Arab pony fed in the verandah, and went out. The morning wore through, and at midday the tension became unendurable. Mrs. Boulte could not cry. She had finished her crying in the night, and now she did not want to be left alone. Perhaps the Vansuythen Woman would talk to her; and, since talking opens the heart, perhaps there might be some comfort to be found in her company. She was the only other woman in the Station.

In Kashima there are no regular calling-hours. Every one can drop in upon every one else at pleasure. Mrs. Boulte put on a big *terai* hat, and walked across to the Vansuythens' house to borrow last week's "Queen." The two compounds touched, and instead of going up the drive, she crossed through the gap in the cactus-hedge, entering the house from the back. As she passed through the dining-room, she heard, behind the *purdah* that cloaked the drawing-room door, her husband's voice, saying –

"But on my Honour! On my Soul and Honour, I tell you she doesn't care for me. She told me so last night. I would have told you then if Vansuythen hadn't been with you. If it is for *her* sake that you'll have nothing to say to me, you can make your mind easy. It's Kurrell —"

"What?" said Mrs. Vansuythen, with an hysterical little laugh. "Kurrell! Oh, it can't be! You two must have made some horrible mistake. Perhaps you – you lost your temper, or misunderstood, or something. Things *can't* be as wrong as you say."

Mrs. Vansuythen had shifted her defence to avoid the man's pleading, and was desperately trying to keep him to a side-issue.

"There must be some mistake," she insisted, "and it can be all put right again."

Boulte laughed grimly.

"It can't be Captain Kurrell! He told me that he had never taken the least – the least interest in your wife, Mr. Boulte. Oh, *do* listen! He said he had not. He swore he had not," said Mrs. Vansuythen.

The *purdah* rustled, and the speech was cut short by the entry of a little, thin woman, with big rings round her eyes. Mrs. Vansuythen stood up with a gasp.

"What was that you said?" asked Mrs. Boulte. "Never mind that man. What did Ted say to you? What did he say to you? What did he say to you?"

Mrs. Vansuythen sat down helplessly on the sofa, overborne by the trouble of her questioner.

"He said – I can't remember exactly what he said – but I understood him to say – that is – But, really, Mrs. Boulte, isn't it rather a strange question?"

"*Will* you tell me what he said?" repeated Mrs. Boulte. Even a tiger will fly before a bear robbed of her whelps, and Mrs. Vansuythen was only an ordinarily good woman. She began in a sort of desperation: "Well, he said that he never cared for you at all, and, of course, there was not the least reason why he should have, and – and – that was all."

"You said he *swore* he had not cared for me. Was that true?"

"Yes," said Mrs. Vansuythen very softly.

Mrs. Boulte wavered for an instant where she stood, and then fell forward fainting.

"What did I tell you?" said Boulte, as though the conversation had been unbroken. "You can see for yourself. She cares for *him*." The light began to break into his dull mind, and he went on – "And he – what was *he* saying to you?"

But Mrs. Vansuythen, with no heart for explanations or impassioned protestations, was kneeling over Mrs. Boulte.

"Oh, you brute!" she cried. "Are *all* men like this? Help me to get her into my room – and her face is cut against the table. Oh, *will* you be quiet, and help me to carry her? I hate you, and I hate Captain Kurrell. Lift her up carefully and now – go! Go away!"

Boulte carried his wife into Mrs. Vansuythen's bedroom, and departed before the storm of that lady's wrath and disgust, impenitent and burning with jealousy. Kurrell had been making love to Mrs. Vansuythen – would do Vansuythen as great a wrong as he had done Boulte, who caught himself considering whether Mrs. Vansuythen would faint if she discovered that the man she loved had forsworn her.

In the middle of these meditations, Kurrell came cantering along the road and pulled up with a cheery, "Good-mornin'. 'Been mashing Mrs. Vansuythen as usual, eh? Bad thing for a sober, married man, that. What will Mrs. Boulte say?"

Boulte raised his head and said slowly, "Oh, you liar!" Kurrell's face changed. "What's that?" he asked quickly.

"Nothing much," said Boulte. "Has my wife told you that you two are free to go off whenever you please? She has been good enough to explain the situation to me. You've been a true friend to me, Kurrell – old man – haven't you?"

Kurrell groaned, and tried to frame some sort of idiotic sentence about being willing to give "satisfaction." But his interest in the woman was dead, had died out in the Rains, and, mentally, he was abusing her for her amazing indiscretion. It would have been so easy to have broken off the thing gently and by degrees, and now he was saddled with – Boulte's voice recalled him.

"I don't think I should get any satisfaction from killing you, and I'm pretty sure you'd get none from killing me."

Then in a querulous tone, ludicrously disproportioned to his wrongs, Boulte added –

" 'Seems rather a pity that you haven't the decency to keep to the woman, now you've got her. You've been a true friend to *her* too, haven't you?"

Kurrell stared long and gravely. The situation was getting beyond him.

"What do you mean?" he said.

Boulte answered, more to himself than to the questioner:

"My wife came over to Mrs. Vansuythen's just now; and it seems you'd been telling Mrs. Vansuythen that you'd never cared for Emma. I suppose you lied, as usual. What had Mrs. Vansuythen to do with you, or you with her? Try to speak the truth for once in a way."

Kurrell took the double insult without wincing, and replied by another question: "Go on. What happened?"

"Emma fainted," said Boulte simply. "But, look here, what had you been saying to Mrs. Vansuythen?"

Kurrell laughed. Mrs. Boulte had, with unbridled tongue, made havoc of his plans; and he could at least retaliate by hurting the man in whose eyes he was humiliated and shown dishonourable.

"Said to her? What *does* a man tell a lie like that for? I suppose I said pretty much what you've said, unless I'm a good deal mistaken."

"I spoke the truth," said Boulte, again more to himself than to Kurrell. "Emma told me she hated me. She has no right in me."

"No! I suppose not. You're only her husband, y'know. And what did Mrs. Vansuythen say after you had laid your disengaged heart at her feet?"

Kurrell felt almost virtuous as he put the question.

"I don't think that matters," Boulte replied; "and it doesn't concern you."

"But it does! I tell you it does —" began Kurrell shamelessly.

The sentence was cut by a roar of laughter from Boulte's lips. Kurrell was silent for an instant, and then he, too, laughed — laughed long and loudly, rocking in his saddle. It was an unpleasant sound — the mirthless mirth of these men on the long, white line of the Narkarra Road. There were no strangers in Kashima, or they might have thought that captivity within the Dosehri hills had driven half the European population mad. The laughter ended abruptly, and Kurrell was the first to speak.

"Well, what are you going to do?"

Boulte looked up the road, and at the hills. "Nothing," said he quietly; "what's the use? It's too ghastly for anything. We must let the old life go on. I can only call you a hound and a liar, and I can't go on calling you names for ever. Besides which, I don't feel that I'm much better. We can't get out of this place. What *is* there to do?"

Kurrell looked round the rat-pit of Kashima and made no reply. The injured husband took up the wondrous tale.

"Ride on, and speak to Emma if you want to. God knows *I* don't care what you do."

He walked forward, and left Kurrell gazing blankly after him. Kurrell did not ride on either to see Mrs. Boulte or Mrs. Vansuythen. He sat in his saddle and thought, while his pony grazed by the roadside.

The whir of approaching wheels roused him. Mrs. Vansuythen was driving home Mrs. Boulte, white and wan, with a cut on her forehead.

"Stop, please," said Mrs. Boulte, "I want to speak to Ted."

Mrs. Vansuythen obeyed, but as Mrs. Boulte leaned forward, putting her hand upon the splashboard of the dog-cart, Kurrell spoke.

"I've seen your husband, Mrs. Boulte."

There was no necessity for any further explanation. The man's eyes were fixed, not upon Mrs. Boulte, but her companion. Mrs. Boulte saw the look.

"Speak to him!" she pleaded, turning to the woman at her side. "Oh, speak to him! Tell him what you told me just now. Tell him you hate him. Tell him you hate him!"

She bent forward and wept bitterly, while the *sais*, impassive, went forward to hold the horse. Mrs. Vansuythen turned scarlet and dropped the reins. She wished to be no party to such unholy explanations.

"I've nothing to do with it," she began coldly; but Mrs. Boulte's sobs overcame her, and she addressed herself to the man. "I don't know what I am to say, Captain Kurrell. I don't know what I can call you. I think you've – you've behaved abominably, and she has cut her forehead terribly against the table."

"It doesn't hurt. It isn't anything," said Mrs. Boulte feebly. "*That* doesn't matter. Tell him what you told me. Say you don't care for him. Oh, Ted, *won't* you believe her?"

"Mrs. Boulte has made me understand that you were – that you were fond of her once upon a time," went on Mrs. Vansuythen.

"Well!" said Kurrell brutally. "It seems to me that Mrs. Boulte had better be fond of her own husband first."

"Stop!" said Mrs. Vansuythen. "Hear me first. I don't care – I don't want to know anything about you and Mrs. Boulte; but I want *you* to know that I hate you, that I think you are a cur, and that I'll never, *never* speak to you again. Oh, I don't care to say what I think of you, you — man!"

"I want to speak to Ted," moaned Mrs. Boulte, but the dog-cart rattled on, and Kurrell was left on the road, shamed, and boiling with wrath against Mrs. Boulte.

He waited till Mrs. Vansuythen was driving back to her own house, and, she being freed from the embarrassment of Mrs. Boulte's presence, learned for the second time her opinion of himself and his actions.

In the evenings it was the wont of all Kashima to meet at the platform on the Narkarra Road, to drink tea and discuss the trivialities of the day. Major Vansuythen and his wife found themselves alone at the gathering-place for almost the first time in their remembrance; and the cheery Major, in the teeth of his wife's remarkably reasonable suggestion that the rest of the Station might be sick, insisted upon driving round to the two bungalows and unearthing the population.

"Sitting in the twilight!" said he, with great indignation, to the Boultes. "That'll never do! Hang it all, we're one family here! You *must* come out, and so must Kurrell. I'll make him bring his banjo."

So great is the power of honest simplicity and a good digestion over guilty consciences that all Kashima did turn out, even down to the banjo; and the Major embraced the company in one expansive grin. As he grinned, Mrs. Vansuythen raised her eyes for an instant and looked at all Kashima. Her meaning was clear. Major Vansuythen would never know anything. He was to be the outsider in that happy family whose cage was the Dosehri hills.

"You're singing villainously out of tune, Kurrell," said the Major truthfully. "Pass me that banjo."

And he sang in excruciating-wise till the stars came out and all Kashima went to dinner.

* * *

That was the beginning of the New Life of Kashima – the life that Mrs. Boulte made when her tongue was loosened in the twilight.

Mrs. Vansuythen has never told the Major; and since he insists upon keeping up a burdensome geniality, she has been compelled to break her vow of not speaking to Kurrell. This speech, which must of necessity preserve the semblance of politeness and interest, serves admirably to keep alight the flame of jealousy and dull hatred in Boulte's bosom, as it awakens the same passions in his wife's heart. Mrs. Boulte hates Mrs. Vansuythen because she has taken Ted from her, and, in some curious fashion, hates her because Mrs. Vansuythen – and here the wife's eyes see far more clearly than the husband's – detests Ted. And Ted – that gallant captain and honourable man – knows now that it is possible to hate a woman once loved, to the verge of wishing to silence her for ever with blows. Above all, is he shocked that Mrs. Boulte cannot see the error of her ways.

Boulte and he go out tiger-shooting together in all friendship. Boulte has put their relationship on a most satisfactory footing.

"You're a blackguard," he says to Kurrell, "and I've lost any self-respect I may ever have had; but when you're with me, I can feel certain that you are not with Mrs. Vansuythen, or making Emma miserable."

Kurrell endures anything that Boulte may say to him. Sometimes they are away for three days together, and then the Major insists upon his wife going over to sit with Mrs. Boulte, although Mrs. Vansuythen has repeatedly declared that she prefers her husband's company to any in the world. From the way in which she clings to him, she would certainly seem to be speaking the truth.

But of course, as the Major says, "in a little Station we must all be friendly."

BAA BAA, BLACK SHEEP

BAA BAA, BLACK SHEEP

* * *

Baa Baa, Black Sheep,
Have you any wool?
Yes, Sir, yes, Sir, three bags full.
One for the Master, one for the Dame —
None for the Little Boy that cries down the lane.

Nursery Rhyme

THE FIRST BAG

When I was in my father's house, I was in a better place.

THEY were putting Punch to bed – the *ayah* and the *hamal* and Meeta, the big *Surti* boy with the red and gold turban. Judy, already tucked inside her mosquito-curtains, was nearly asleep. Punch had been allowed to stay up for dinner. Many privileges had been accorded to Punch within the last ten days, and a greater kindness from the people of his world had encompassed his ways and works, which were mostly obstreperous. He sat on the edge of his bed and swung his bare legs defiantly.

"Punch-*baba* going to bye-lo?" said the *ayah* suggestively.

"No," said Punch. "Punch-*baba* wants the story about the Ranee that was turned into a tiger. Meeta must tell it, and the *hamal* shall hide behind the door and make tiger-noises at the proper time."

"But Judy-*baba* will wake up," said the *ayah*.

"Judy-*baba* is waked," piped a small voice from the mosquito-curtains. "There was a Ranee that lived at Delhi. Go on, Meeta," and she fell fast asleep again while Meeta began the story.

407

Never had Punch secured the telling of that tale with so little opposition. He reflected for a long time. The *hamal* made the tiger-noises in twenty different keys.

" 'Top!" said Punch authoritatively. "Why doesn't Papa come in and say he is going to give me *put-put*?"

"Punch-*baba* is going away," said the *ayah*. "In another week there will be no Punch-*baba* to pull my hair any more." She sighed softly, for the boy of the household was very dear to her heart.

"Up the Ghauts in a train?" said Punch, standing on his bed. "All the way to Nassick where the Ranee-Tiger lives?"

"Not to Nassick this year, little Sahib," said Meeta, lifting him on his shoulder. "Down to the sea where the cocoanuts are thrown, and across the sea in a big ship. Will you take Meeta with you to *Belait*?"

"You shall all come," said Punch, from the height of Meeta's strong arms. "Meeta and the *ayah* and the *hamal* and Bhini-in-the-Garden, and the salaam-Captain-Sahib-snake-man."

There was no mockery in Meeta's voice when he replied – "Great is the Sahib's favour," and laid the little man down in the bed, while the *ayah*, sitting in the moonlight at the doorway, lulled him to sleep with an interminable canticle such as they sing in the Roman Catholic Church at Parel. Punch curled himself into a ball and slept.

Next morning Judy shouted that there was a rat in the nursery, and thus he forgot to tell her the wonderful news. It did not much matter, for Judy was only three and she would not have understood. But Punch was five; and he knew that going to England would be much nicer than a trip to Nassick.

* * *

Papa and Mamma sold the brougham and the piano, and stripped the house, and curtailed the allowance of crockery

for the daily meals, and took long council together over a
bundle of letters bearing the Rocklington postmark.

"The worst of it is that one can't be certain of anything,"
said Papa, pulling his moustache. "The letters in themselves
are excellent, and the terms are moderate enough."

"The worst of it is that the children will grow up away
from me," thought Mamma: but she did not say it aloud.

"We are only one case among hundreds," said Papa bitterly. "You shall go Home again in five years, dear."

"Punch will be ten then – and Judy eight. Oh, how long
and long and long the time will be! And we have to leave
them among strangers."

"Punch is a cheery little chap. He's sure to make friends
wherever he goes."

"And who could help loving my Ju?"

They were standing over the cots in the nursery late at
night, and I think that Mamma was crying softly. After Papa
had gone away, she knelt down by the side of Judy's cot. The
ayah saw her and put up a prayer that the Memsahib might
never find the love of her children taken away from her and
given to a stranger.

Mamma's own prayer was a slightly illogical one. Sum-
marised it ran: "Let strangers love my children and be as
good to them as I should be, but let *me* preserve their love
and their confidence for ever and ever. Amen." Punch
scratched himself in his sleep, and Judy moaned a little.

Next day they all went down to the sea, and there was a
scene at the Apollo Bunder when Punch discovered that
Meeta could not come too, and Judy learned that the *ayah*
must be left behind. But Punch found a thousand fascinating
things in the rope, block, and steam-pipe line on the big
P. and O. steamer long before Meeta and the *ayah* had dried
their tears.

"Come back, Punch-*baba*," said the *ayah*.

"Come back," said Meeta, "and be a *Burra Sahib*" (a big
man).

"Yes," said Punch, lifted up in his father's arms to wave

good-bye. "Yes, I will come back, and I will be a *Burra Sahib Bahadur*!" (a very big man indeed).

At the end of the first day Punch demanded to be set down in England, which he was certain must be close at hand. Next day there was a merry breeze, and Punch was very sick. "When I come back to Bombay," said Punch on his recovery, "I will come by the road – in a broom-*gharri*. This is a very naughty ship."

The Swedish boatswain consoled him, and he modified his opinions as the voyage went on. There was so much to see and to handle and ask questions about that Punch nearly forgot the *ayah* and Meeta and the *hamal*, and with difficulty remembered a few words of the Hindustani, once his second-speech.

But Judy was much worse. The day before the steamer reached Southampton, Mamma asked her if she would not like to see the *ayah* again. Judy's blue eyes turned to the stretch of sea that had swallowed all her tiny past, and said: "*Ayah!* What *ayah?*"

Mamma cried over her, and Punch marvelled. It was then that he heard for the first time Mamma's passionate appeal to him never to let Judy forget Mamma. Seeing that Judy was young, ridiculously young, and that Mamma, every evening for four weeks past, had come into the cabin to sing her and Punch to sleep with a mysterious rune that he called "Sonny, my soul," Punch could not understand what Mamma meant. But he strove to do his duty; for, the moment Mamma left the cabin, he said to Judy, "Ju, you be-member Mamma?"

" 'Torse I do," said Judy.

"Then *always* bemember Mamma, 'r else I won't give you the paper ducks that the red-haired Captain Sahib cut out for me."

So Judy promised always to "bemember Mamma."

Many and many a time was Mamma's command laid upon Punch, and Papa would say the same thing with an insistence that awed the child.

"You must make haste and learn to write, Punch," said Papa, "and then you'll be able to write letters to us in Bombay."

"I'll come into your room," said Punch, and Papa choked.

Papa and Mamma were always choking in those days. If Punch took Judy to task for not "bemembering," they choked. If Punch sprawled on the sofa in the Southampton lodging-house and sketched his future in purple and gold, they choked; and so they did if Judy put her mouth up for a kiss.

Through many days all four were vagabonds on the face of the earth – Punch with no one to give orders to, Judy too young for anything, and Papa and Mamma grave, distracted, and choking.

"Where," demanded Punch, wearied of a loathsome contrivance on four wheels with a mound of luggage atop – "*where* is our broom-*gharri*? This thing talks so much that *I* can't talk. Where is our *own* broom-*gharri*? When I was at Bandstand before we comed away, I asked Inverarity Sahib why he was sitting in it, and he said it was his own. And I said, 'I will *give* it you,' – I like Inverarity Sahib, – and I said, 'Can you put your legs through the pully-wag loops by the windows?' And Inverarity Sahib said No, and laughed. *I* can put my legs through the pully-wag loops. I can put my legs through *these* pully-wag loops. Look! Oh, Mamma's crying again! I didn't know I wasn't not to do *so*."

Punch drew his legs out of the loops of the four-wheeler; the door opened, and he slid to the earth, in a cascade of parcels, at the door of an austere little villa whose gates bore the legend "Downe Lodge." Punch gathered himself together and eyed the house with disfavour. It stood on a sandy road, and a cold wind tickled his knickerbockered legs.

"Let us go away," said Punch. "This is not a pretty place."

But Mamma and Papa and Judy had left the cab, and all the luggage was being taken into the house. At the doorstep stood a woman in black, and she smiled largely, with dry, chapped lips. Behind her was a man, big, bony, grey, and lame as to one leg – behind him a boy of twelve, black-haired and oily in appearance. Punch surveyed the trio, and advanced without fear, as he had been accustomed to do in Bombay when callers came and he happened to be playing in the verandah.

"How do you do?" said he. "I am Punch." But they were all looking at the luggage – all except the grey man, who shook hands with Punch, and said he was "a smart little fellow." There was much running about and banging of boxes, and Punch curled himself up on the sofa in the dining-room and considered things.

"I don't like these people," said Punch. "But never mind. We'll go away soon. We have always went away soon from everywhere. I wish we was gone back to Bombay *soon*."

The wish bore no fruit. For six days Mamma wept at intervals, and showed the woman in black all Punch's clothes – a liberty which Punch resented. "But p'raps she's a new white *ayah*," he thought. "I'm to call her Antirosa, but she doesn't call *me* Sahib. She says just Punch," he confided to Judy. "What is Antirosa?"

Judy didn't know. Neither she nor Punch had heard anything of an animal called an aunt. Their world had been Papa and Mamma, who knew everything, permitted everything, and loved everybody – even Punch when he used to go into the garden at Bombay and fill his nails with mould after the weekly nail-cutting, because, as he explained between two strokes of the slipper to his sorely tried Father, his fingers "felt so new at the ends."

In an undefined way Punch judged it advisable to keep both parents between himself and the woman in black and the boy in black hair. He did not approve of them. He liked the grey man, who had expressed a wish to be called "Uncle-harri." They nodded at each other when they met, and the grey man showed him a little ship with rigging that took up and down.

"She is a model of the *Brisk* – the little *Brisk* that was sore exposed that day at Navarino." The grey man hummed the last words and fell into a reverie. "I'll tell you about Navarino, Punch, when we go for walks together; and you mustn't touch the ship, because she's the *Brisk*."

Long before that walk, the first of many, was taken, they roused Punch and Judy in the chill dawn of a February morning to say Good-bye; and, of all people in the wide earth, to Papa and Mamma – both crying this time. Punch was very sleepy and Judy was cross.

"Don't forget us," pleaded Mamma. "Oh, my little son, don't forget us, and see that Judy remembers too."

"I've told Judy to bemember," said Punch, wriggling, for his father's beard tickled his neck. "I've told Judy – ten – forty – 'leven thousand times. But Ju's so young – quite a baby – isn't she?"

"Yes," said Papa, "quite a baby, and you must be good to Judy, and make haste to learn to write and – and – and —"

Punch was back in his bed again. Judy was fast asleep, and there was the rattle of a cab below. Papa and Mamma had gone away. Not to Nassick; that was across the sea. To some place much nearer, of course, and equally of course they would return. They came back after dinner-parties, and Papa had come back after he had been to a place called "The Snows," and Mamma with him, to Punch and Judy at Mrs. Inverarity's house in Marine Lines. Assuredly they would come back again. So Punch fell asleep till the true morning, when the black-haired boy met him with the information that Papa and Mamma had gone to Bombay, and that he and Judy were to stay at Downe Lodge "for ever." Antirosa, tearfully appealed to for a contradiction, said that Harry had spoken the truth, and that it behooved Punch to fold up his clothes neatly on going to bed. Punch went out and wept bitterly with Judy, into whose fair head he had driven some ideas of the meaning of separation.

When a matured man discovers that he has been deserted by Providence, deprived of his God, and cast, without help, comfort, or sympathy, upon a world which is new and strange to him, his despair, which may find expression in evil-living, the writing of his experiences, or the more satisfactory diversion of suicide, is generally supposed to be impressive. A child, under exactly similar circumstances as far as its knowledge goes, cannot very well curse God and die. It howls till its nose is red, its eyes are sore, and its head aches. Punch and Judy, through no fault of their own, had lost all their world. They sat in the hall and cried; the black-haired boy looking on from afar.

The model of the ship availed nothing, though the grey man assured Punch that he might pull the rigging up and down as much as he pleased; and Judy was promised free entry into the kitchen. They wanted Papa and Mamma gone to Bombay beyond the seas, and their grief while it lasted was without remedy.

When the tears ceased the house was very still. Antirosa had decided that it was better to let the children "have their cry out," and the boy had gone to school. Punch raised his head from the floor and sniffed mournfully. Judy was nearly asleep. Three short years had not taught her how to bear sorrow with full knowledge. There was a distant, dull boom in the air – a repeated heavy thud. Punch knew that sound in Bombay in the Monsoon. It was the sea – the sea that must be traversed before any one could get to Bombay.

"Quick, Ju!" he cried, "we're close to the sea. I can hear it! Listen! That's where they've went. P'raps we can catch them if we was in time. They didn't mean to go without us. They've only forgot."

"Iss," said Judy. "They've only forgotted. Less go to the sea."

The hall-door was open, and so was the garden-gate.

"It's very, very big, this place," he said, looking cautiously down the road, "and we will get lost; but I will find a man and order him to take me back to my house – like I did in Bombay."

He took Judy by the hand, and the two ran hatless in the

direction of the sound of the sea. Downe Villa was almost the last of a range of newly-built houses running out, through a field of brick-mounds, to a heath where gypsies occasionally camped and where the Garrison Artillery of Rocklington practised. There were few people to be seen, and the children might have been taken for those of the soldiery who ranged far. Half an hour the wearied little legs tramped across heath, potato-patch, and sand-dune.

"I'se so tired," said Judy, "and Mamma will be angry."

"Mamma's *never* angry. I suppose she is waiting at the sea now while Papa gets tickets. We'll find them and go along with. Ju, you mustn't sit down. Only a little more and we'll come to the sea. Ju, if you sit down I'll *thmack* you!" said Punch.

They climbed another dune, and came upon the great grey sea at low tide. Hundreds of crabs were scuttling about the beach, but there was no trace of Papa and Mamma, not even of a ship upon the waters – nothing but sand and mud for miles and miles.

And "Uncleharri" found them by chance – very muddy and very forlorn – Punch dissolved in tears, but trying to divert Judy with an "ickle trab," and Judy wailing to the pitiless horizon for "Mamma, Mamma!" – and again "Mamma!"

THE SECOND BAG

> Ah, well-a-day, for we are souls bereaved!
> Of all the creatures under Heaven's wide scope
> We are most hopeless, who had once most hope,
> And most beliefless, who had most believed.
>
> *The City of Dreadful Night*

ALL this time not a word about Black Sheep. He came later, and Harry the black-haired boy was mainly responsible for his coming.

Judy – who could help loving little Judy? – passed, by

special permit, into the kitchen, and thence straight to Aunty Rosa's heart. Harry was Aunty Rosa's one child, and Punch was the extra boy about the house. There was no special place for him or his little affairs, and he was forbidden to sprawl on sofas and explain his ideas about the manufacture of this world and his hopes for his future. Sprawling was lazy and wore out sofas, and little boys were not expected to talk. They were talked to, and the talking to was intended for the benefit of their morals. As the unquestioned despot of the house at Bombay, Punch could not quite understand how he came to be of no account in this his new life.

Harry might reach across the table and take what he wanted; Judy might point and get what she wanted. Punch was forbidden to do either. The grey man was his great hope and stand-by for many months after Mamma and Papa left, and he had forgotten to tell Judy to "bemember Mamma."

This lapse was excusable, because in the interval he had been introduced by Aunty Rosa to two very impressive things – an abstraction called God, the intimate friend and ally of Aunty Rosa, generally believed to live behind the kitchen range because it was hot there – and a dirty brown book filled with unintelligible dots and marks. Punch was always anxious to oblige everybody. He therefore welded the story of the Creation on to what he could recollect of his Indian fairy tales, and scandalised Aunty Rosa by repeating the result to Judy. It was a sin, a grievous sin, and Punch was talked to for a quarter of an hour. He could not understand where the iniquity came in, but was careful not to repeat the offence, because Aunty Rosa told him that God had heard every word he had said and was very angry. If this were true, why didn't God come and say so, thought Punch, and dismissed the matter from his mind. Afterwards he learned to know the Lord as the only thing in the world more awful than Aunty Rosa – as a Creature that stood in the background and counted the strokes of the cane.

But the reading was, just then, a much more serious matter than any creed. Aunty Rosa sat him upon a table and told him that A B meant ab.

"Why?" said Punch. "A is a and B is bee. *Why* does A B mean ab?"

"Because I tell you it does," said Aunty Rosa, "and you've got to say it."

Punch said it accordingly, and for a month, hugely against his will, stumbled through the brown book, not in the least comprehending what it meant. But Uncle Harry, who walked much and generally alone, was wont to come into the nursery and suggest to Aunty Rosa that Punch should walk with him. He seldom spoke, but he showed Punch all Rocklington, from the mud-banks and the sand of the back-bay to the great harbours where ships lay at anchor, and the dockyards where the hammers were never still, and the marine-store shops, and the shiny brass counters in the Offices where Uncle Harry went once every three months with a slip of blue paper and received sovereigns in exchange; for he held a wound-pension. Punch heard, too, from his lips the story of the battle of Navarino, where the sailors of the Fleet, for three days afterwards, were deaf as posts and could only sign to each other. "That was because of the noise of the guns," said Uncle Harry, "and I have got the wadding of a bullet somewhere inside me now."

Punch regarded him with curiosity. He had not the least idea what wadding was, and his notion of a bullet was a dockyard cannon-ball bigger than his own head. How could Uncle Harry keep a cannon-ball inside him? He was ashamed to ask, for fear Uncle Harry might be angry.

Punch had never known what anger – real anger – meant until one terrible day when Harry had taken his paint-box to paint a boat with, and Punch had protested. Then Uncle Harry had appeared on the scene and, muttering something about "strangers' children," had with a stick smitten the black-haired boy across the shoulders till he wept and yelled, and Aunty Rosa came in and abused Uncle Harry for cruelty to his own flesh and blood, and Punch shuddered to the tips of his shoes. "It wasn't my fault," he explained to the boy, but both Harry and Aunty Rosa said that it was, and that Punch had told tales, and for a week there were no more walks with Uncle Harry.

But that week brought a great joy to Punch.   .

He had repeated till he was thrice weary the statement that "the Cat lay on the Mat and the Rat came in."

"Now I can truly read," said Punch, "and now I will never read anything in the world."

He put the brown book in the cupboard where his school-books lived, and accidentally tumbled out a venerable volume, without covers, labelled "Sharpe's Magazine." There was the most portentous picture of a griffin on the first page, with verses below. The griffin carried off one sheep a day from a German village, till a man came with a "falchion" and split the griffin open. Goodness only knew what a falchion was, but there was the Griffin, and his history was an improvement upon the eternal Cat.

"This," said Punch, "means things, and now I will know all about everything in all the world." He read till the light failed, not understanding a tithe of the meaning, but tantalised by glimpses of new worlds hereafter to be revealed.

"What is a 'falchion'? What is a 'e-wee lamb'? What is a 'base *us*surper'? What is a 'verdant me-ad'?" he demanded with flushed cheeks, at bedtime, of the astonished Aunty Rosa.

"Say your prayers and go to sleep," she replied, and that was all the help Punch then or afterwards found at her hands in the new and delightful exercise of reading.

"Aunty Rosa only knows about God and things like that," argued Punch. "Uncle Harry will tell me."

The next walk proved that Uncle Harry could not help either; but he allowed Punch to talk, and even sat down on a bench to hear about the Griffin. Other walks brought other stories as Punch ranged further afield, for the house held large store of old books that no one ever opened – from "Frank Fairlegh" in serial numbers, and the earlier poems of

Tennyson, contributed anonymously to "Sharpe's Magazine," to '62 Exhibition Catalogues, gay with colours and delightfully incomprehensible, and odd leaves of "Gulliver's Travels."

As soon as Punch could string a few pot-hooks together, he wrote to Bombay, demanding by return of post "all the books in all the world." Papa could not comply with this modest indent, but sent "Grimm's Fairy Tales" and a Hans Andersen. That was enough. If he were only left alone, Punch could pass, at any hour he chose, into a land of his own, beyond reach of Aunty Rosa and her God, Harry and his teasements, and Judy's claims to be played with.

"Don't disturve me, I'm reading. Go and play in the kitchen," grunted Punch. "Aunty Rosa lets *you* go there." Judy was cutting her second teeth and was fretful. She appealed to Aunty Rosa, who descended on Punch.

"I was reading," he explained, "reading a book. I *want* to read."

"You're only doing that to show off," said Aunty Rosa. "But we'll see. Play with Judy now, and don't open a book for a week."

Judy did not pass a very enjoyable playtime with Punch, who was consumed with indignation. There was a pettiness at the bottom of the prohibition which puzzled him.

"It's what I like to do," he said, "and she's found out that and stopped me. Don't cry, Ju – it wasn't your fault – *please* don't cry, or she'll say I made you."

Ju loyally mopped up her tears, and the two played in their nursery, a room in the basement and half underground, to which they were regularly sent after the midday dinner while Aunty Rosa slept. She drank wine – that is to say, something from a bottle in the cellaret – for her stomach's sake, but if she did not fall asleep she would sometimes come into the nursery to see that the children were really playing. Now bricks, wooden hoops, ninepins, and chinaware cannot amuse for ever, especially when all Fairyland is to be won by the mere opening of a book, and, as often as not, Punch would be discovered reading to Judy or telling her interminable tales. That was an offence in the eyes of the law, and Judy would be whisked off by Aunty Rosa, while Punch was left to play alone, "and be sure that I hear you doing it."

It was not a cheering employ, for he had to make a playful noise. At last, with infinite craft, he devised an arrangement whereby the table could be supported as to three legs on toy bricks, leaving the fourth clear to bring down on the floor. He could work the table with one hand and hold a book with the other. This he did till an evil day when Aunty Rosa pounced upon him unawares and told him that he was "acting a lie."

"If you're old enough to do that," she said – her temper was always worst after dinner – "you're old enough to be beaten."

"But – I'm – I'm not a animal!" said Punch, aghast. He remembered Uncle Harry and the stick, and turned white. Aunty Rosa had hidden a light cane behind her, and Punch was beaten then and there over the shoulders. It was a revelation to him. The room-door was shut, and he was left to weep himself into repentance and work out his own gospel of life.

Aunty Rosa, he argued, had the power to beat him with many stripes. It was unjust and cruel, and Mamma and Papa would never have allowed it. Unless perhaps, as Aunty Rosa seemed to imply, they had sent secret orders. In which case he was abandoned indeed. It would be discreet in the future to propitiate Aunty Rosa, but then, again, even in matters in which he was innocent, he had been accused of wishing to "show off." He had "shown off" before visitors when he had attacked a strange gentleman – Harry's uncle, not his own – with requests for information about the Griffin and the falchion, and the precise nature of the Tilbury in which Frank Fairlegh rode – all points of paramount interest which he was bursting to understand. Clearly it would not do to pretend to care for Aunty Rosa.

At this point Harry entered and stood afar off, eyeing

Punch, a dishevelled heap in the corner of the room, with disgust.

"You're a liar – a young liar," said Harry, with great unction, "and you're to have tea down here because you're not fit to speak to us. And you're not to speak to Judy again till Mother gives you leave. You'll corrupt her. You're only fit to associate with the servant. Mother says so."

Having reduced Punch to a second agony of tears, Harry departed upstairs with the news that Punch was still rebellious.

Uncle Harry sat uneasily in the dining-room. "Damn it all, Rosa," said he at last, "can't you leave the child alone? He's a good enough little chap when I meet him."

"He puts on his best manners with you, Henry," said Aunty Rosa, "but I'm afraid, I'm very much afraid, that he is the Black Sheep of the family."

Harry heard and stored up the name for future use. Judy cried till she was bidden to stop, her brother not being worth tears; and the evening concluded with the return of Punch to the upper regions and a private sitting at which all the blinding horrors of Hell were revealed to Punch with such store of imagery as Aunty Rosa's narrow mind possessed.

Most grievous of all was Judy's round-eyed reproach, and Punch went to bed in the depths of the Valley of Humiliation. He shared his room with Harry, and knew the torture in store. For an hour and a half he had to answer that young gentleman's questions as to his motives for telling a lie, and a grievous lie, the precise quantity of punishment inflicted by Aunty Rosa, and had also to profess his deep gratitude for such religious instruction as Harry thought fit to impart.

From that day began the downfall of Punch, now Black Sheep.

"Untrustworthy in one thing, untrustworthy in all," said Aunty Rosa, and Harry felt that Black Sheep was delivered into his hands. He would wake him up in the night to ask him why he was such a liar.

"I don't know," Punch would reply.

"Then don't you think you ought to get up and pray to God for a new heart?"

"Y-yess."

"Get out and pray, then!" And Punch would get out of bed with raging hate in his heart against all the world, seen and unseen. He was always tumbling into trouble. Harry had a knack of cross-examining him as to his day's doings, which seldom failed to lead him, sleepy and savage, into half a dozen contradictions – all duly reported to Aunty Rosa next morning.

"But it *wasn't* a lie," Punch would begin, charging into a laboured explanation that landed him more hopelessly in the mire. "I said that I didn't say my prayers *twice* over in the day, and *that* was on Tuesday. *Once* I did. I *know* I did, but Harry said I didn't," and so forth, till the tension brought tears, and he was dismissed from the table in disgrace.

"You usen't to be as bad as this," said Judy, awe-stricken at the catalogue of Black Sheep's crimes. "Why are you so bad now?"

"I don't know," Black Sheep would reply. "I'm not, if I only wasn't bothered upside down. I knew what I *did*, and I want to say so; but Harry always makes it out different somehow, and Aunty Rosa doesn't believe a word I say. Oh, Ju! don't *you* say I'm bad too."

"Aunty Rosa says you are," said Judy. "She told the Vicar so when he came yesterday."

"Why does she tell all the people outside the house about me? It isn't fair," said Black Sheep. "When I was in Bombay, and was bad – *doing* bad, not made-up bad like this – Mamma told Papa, and Papa told me he knew, and that was all. *Outside* people didn't know too – even Meeta didn't know."

"I don't remember," said Judy wistfully. "I was all little then. Mamma was just as fond of you as she was of me, wasn't she?"

"'Course she was. So was Papa. So was everybody."

"Aunty Rosa likes me more than she does you. She says

that you are a Trial and a Black Sheep, and I'm not to speak to you more than I can help."

"Always? Not outside of the times when you mustn't speak to me at all?"

Judy nodded her head mournfully. Black Sheep turned away in despair, but Judy's arms were round his neck.

"Never mind, Punch," she whispered. "I *will* speak to you just the same as ever and ever. You're my own own brother, though you are – though Aunty Rosa says you're Bad, and Harry says you're a little coward. He says that if I pulled your hair hard, you'd cry."

"Pull, then," said Punch.

Judy pulled gingerly.

"Pull harder – as hard as you can! There! I don't mind how much you pull it *now*. If you'll speak to me same as ever I'll let you pull it as much as you like – pull it out if you like. But I know if Harry came and stood by and made you do it, I'd cry."

So the two children sealed the compact with a kiss, and Black Sheep's heart was cheered within him, and by extreme caution and careful avoidance of Harry he acquired virtue, and was allowed to read undisturbed for a week. Uncle Harry took him for walks, and consoled him with rough tenderness, never calling him Black Sheep. "It's good for you, I suppose, Punch," he used to say. "Let us sit down. I'm getting tired." His steps led him now not to the beach, but to the Cemetery of Rocklington, amid the potato-fields. For hours the grey man would sit on a tombstone, while Black Sheep read epitaphs, and then with a sigh would stump home again.

"I shall lie there soon," said he to Black Sheep, one winter evening, when his face showed white as a worn silver coin under the light of the lych-gate. "You needn't tell Aunty Rosa."

A month later, he turned sharp round, ere half a morning walk was completed, and stumped back to the house. "Put me to bed, Rosa," he muttered. "I've walked my last. The wadding has found me out."

They put him to bed, and for a fortnight the shadow of his sickness lay upon the house, and Black Sheep went to and fro unobserved. Papa had sent him some new books, and he was told to keep quiet. He retired into his own world, and was perfectly happy. Even at night his felicity was unbroken. He could lie in bed and string himself tales of travel and adventure while Harry was downstairs.

"Uncle Harry's going to die," said Judy, who now lived almost entirely with Aunty Rosa.

"I'm very sorry," said Black Sheep soberly. "He told me that a long time ago."

Aunty Rosa heard the conversation. "Will nothing check your wicked tongue?" she said angrily. There were blue circles round her eyes.

Black Sheep retreated to the nursery and read "Cometh up as a Flower" with deep and uncomprehending interest. He had been forbidden to open it on account of its "sinfulness," but the bonds of the Universe were crumbling, and Aunty Rosa was in great grief.

"I'm glad," said Black Sheep. "She's unhappy now. It wasn't a lie, though. *I* knew. He told me not to tell."

That night Black Sheep woke with a start. Harry was not in the room, and there was a sound of sobbing on the next floor. Then the voice of Uncle Harry, singing the song of the Battle of Navarino, came through the darkness: –

> "Our vanship was the Asia –
> The Albion and Genoa!"

"He's getting well," thought Black Sheep, who knew the song through all its seventeen verses. But the blood froze at his little heart as he thought. The voice leapt an octave, and rang shrill as a boatswain's pipe: –

> "And next came on the lovely Rose,
> The Philomel, her fire-ship, closed,
> And the little Brisk was sore exposed
> That day at Navarino."

"That day at Navarino, Uncle Harry!" shouted Black Sheep, half wild with excitement and fear of he knew not what.

A door opened, and Aunty Rosa screamed up the staircase: "Hush! For God's sake hush, you little devil. Uncle Harry is *dead*!"

THE THIRD BAG

Journeys end in lovers' meeting,
Every wise man's son doth know.

"I WONDER what will happen to me now," thought Black Sheep, when semi-pagan rites peculiar to the burial of the Dead in middle-class houses had been accomplished, and Aunty Rosa, awful in black crape, had returned to this life. "I don't think I've done anything bad that she knows of. I suppose I will soon. She will be very cross after Uncle Harry's dying, and Harry will be cross too. I'll keep in the nursery."

Unfortunately for Punch's plans, it was decided that he should be sent to a day-school which Harry attended. This meant a morning walk with Harry, and perhaps an evening one; but the prospect of freedom in the interval was refreshing. "Harry'll tell everything I do, but I won't do anything," said Black Sheep. Fortified with this virtuous resolution, he went to school only to find that Harry's version of his character had preceded him, and that life was a burden in consequence. He took stock of his associates. Some of them were unclean, some of them talked in dialect, many dropped their h's, and there were two Jews and a negro, or some one quite as dark, in the assembly. "That's a *hubshi*," said Black Sheep to himself. "Even Meeta used to laugh at a *hubshi*. I don't think this is a proper place." He was indignant for at least an hour, till he reflected that any expostulation on his part would be by Aunty Rosa construed into "showing off," and that Harry would tell the boys.

"How do you like school?" said Aunty Rosa at the end of the day.

"I think it is a very nice place," said Punch quietly.

"I suppose you warned the boys of Black Sheep's character?" said Aunty Rosa to Harry.

"Oh, yes," said the censor of Black Sheep's morals. "They know all about him."

"If I was with my father," said Black Sheep, stung to the quick, "I shouldn't *speak* to those boys. He wouldn't let me. They live in shops. I saw them go into shops – where their fathers live and sell things."

"You're too good for that school, are you?" said Aunty Rosa, with a bitter smile. "You ought to be grateful, Black Sheep, that those boys speak to you at all. It isn't every school that takes little liars."

Harry did not fail to make much capital out of Black Sheep's ill-considered remark; with the result that several boys, including the *hubshi*, demonstrated to Black Sheep the eternal equality of the human race by smacking his head, and his consolation from Aunty Rosa was that it "served him right for being vain." He learned, however, to keep his opinions to himself, and by propitiating Harry in carrying books and the like to get a little peace. His existence was not too joyful. From nine till twelve he was at school, and from two to four, except on Saturdays. In the evenings he was sent down into the nursery to prepare his lessons for the next day, and every night came the dreaded cross-questionings at Harry's hand. Of Judy he saw but little. She was deeply religious – at six years of age Religion is easy to come by – and sorely divided between her natural love for Black Sheep and her love for Aunty Rosa, who could do no wrong.

The lean woman returned that love with interest, and Judy, when she dared, took advantage of this for the remission of Black Sheep's penalties. Failures in lessons at school were punished at home by a week without reading other than school-books, and Harry brought the news of such a failure with glee. Further, Black Sheep was then bound to

repeat his lessons at bedtime to Harry, who generally succeeded in making him break down, and consoled him by
gloomiest forebodings for the morrow. Harry was at once
spy, practical joker, inquisitor, and Aunty Rosa's deputy ex-
ecutioner. He filled his many posts to admiration. From his
actions, now that Uncle Harry was dead, there was no appeal.
Black Sheep had not been permitted to keep any self-respect
at school: at home he was of course utterly discredited, and
grateful for any pity that the servant-girls – they changed
frequently at Downe Lodge because they, too, were liars –
might show. "You're just fit to row in the same boat with
Black Sheep," was a sentiment that each new Jane or Eliza
might expect to hear, before a month was over, from Aunty
Rosa's lips; and Black Sheep was used to ask new girls
whether they had yet been compared to him. Harry was
"Master Harry" in their mouths; Judy was officially "Miss
Judy"; but Black Sheep was never anything more than Black
Sheep *tout court*.

As time went on and the memory of Papa and Mamma
became wholly overlaid by the unpleasant task of writing
them letters, under Aunty Rosa's eye, each Sunday, Black
Sheep forgot what manner of life he had led in the beginning
of things. Even Judy's appeals to "try and remember about
Bombay" failed to quicken him.

"I can't remember," he said. "I know I used to give orders
and Mamma kissed me."

"Aunty Rosa will kiss you if you are good," pleaded Judy.

"Ugh! I don't want to be kissed by Aunty Rosa. She'd say
I was doing it to get something more to eat."

The weeks lengthened into months, and the holidays
came; but just before the holidays Black Sheep fell into deadly sin.

Among the many boys whom Harry had incited to "punch
Black Sheep's head because he daren't hit back" was one,
more aggravating than the rest, who, in an unlucky moment,
fell upon Black Sheep when Harry was not near. The blows
stung, and Black Sheep struck back at random with all the

power at his command. The boy dropped and whimpered.
Black Sheep was astounded at his own act, but, feeling the
unresisting body under him, shook it with both his hands in
blind fury and then began to throttle his enemy, meaning
honestly to slay him. There was a scuffle, and Black Sheep
was torn off the body by Harry and some colleagues, and
cuffed home tingling but exultant. Aunty Rosa was out:
pending her arrival, Harry set himself to lecture Black Sheep
on the sin of murder – which he described as the offence of
Cain.

"Why didn't you fight him fair? What did you hit him
when he was down for, you little cur?"

Black Sheep looked up at Harry's throat and then at a
knife on the dinner-table.

"I don't understand," he said wearily. "You always set
him on me and told me I was a coward when I blubbed. Will
you leave me alone until Aunty Rosa comes in? She'll beat
me if you tell her I ought to be beaten; so it's all right."

"It's all wrong," said Harry magisterially. "You nearly
killed him, and I shouldn't wonder if he dies."

"Will he die?" said Black Sheep.

"I dare say," said Harry, "and then you'll be hanged, and
go to Hell."

"All right," said Black Sheep, picking up the table-knife.
"Then I'll kill *you* now. You say things and do things, and –
and *I* don't know how things happen, and you never leave
me alone – and I don't care *what* happens!"

He ran at the boy with the knife, and Harry fled upstairs
to his room, promising Black Sheep the finest thrashing in
the world when Aunty Rosa returned. Black Sheep sat at the
bottom of the stairs, the table-knife in his hand, and wept for
that he had not killed Harry. The servant-girl came up from
the kitchen, took the knife away, and consoled him. But
Black Sheep was beyond consolation. He would be badly
beaten by Aunty Rosa; then there would be another beating
at Harry's hands; then Judy would not be allowed to speak
to him; then the tale would be told at school, and then —

There was no one to help and no one to care, and the best way out of the business was by death. A knife would hurt, but Aunty Rosa had told him, a year ago, that if he sucked paint he would die. He went into the nursery, unearthed the now disused Noah's Ark, and sucked the paint off as many animals as remained. It tasted abominable, but he had licked Noah's Dove clean by the time Aunty Rosa and Judy returned. He went upstairs and greeted them with: "Please, Aunty Rosa, I believe I've nearly killed a boy at school, and I've tried to kill Harry, and when you've done all about God and Hell, will you beat me and get it over?"

The tale of the assault as told by Harry could only be explained on the ground of possession by the Devil. Wherefore Black Sheep was not only most excellently beaten, once by Aunty Rosa and once, when thoroughly cowed down, by Harry, but he was further prayed for at family prayers, together with Jane, who had stolen a cold rissole from the pantry and snuffled audibly as her sin was brought before the Throne of Grace. Black Sheep was sore and stiff, but triumphant. He would die that very night and be rid of them all. No, he would ask for no forgiveness from Harry, and at bedtime would stand no questioning at Harry's hands, even though addressed as "Young Cain."

"I've been beaten," said he, "and I've done other things. I don't care what I do. If you speak to me to-night, Harry, I'll get out and try to kill you. Now you can kill me if you like."

Harry took his bed into the spare room, and Black Sheep lay down to die.

It may be that the makers of Noah's Arks know that their animals are likely to find their way into young mouths, and paint them accordingly. Certain it is that the common, weary next morning broke through the windows and found Black Sheep quite well and a good deal ashamed of himself, but richer by the knowledge that he could, in extremity, secure himself against Harry for the future.

When he descended to breakfast on the first day of the

holidays, he was greeted with the news that Harry, Aunty Rosa, and Judy were going away to Brighton, while Black Sheep was to stay in the house with the servant. His latest outbreak suited Aunty Rosa's plans admirably. It gave her good excuse for leaving the extra boy behind. Papa in Bombay, who really seemed to know a young sinner's wants to the hour, sent, that week, a package of new books. And with these, and the society of Jane on board-wages, Black Sheep was left alone for a month.

The books lasted for ten days. They were eaten too quickly in long gulps of twelve hours at a time. Then came days of doing absolutely nothing, of dreaming dreams and marching imaginary armies up and down stairs, of counting the number of banisters, and of measuring the length and breadth of every room in handspans – fifty down the side, thirty across, and fifty back again. Jane made many friends, and, after receiving Black Sheep's assurance that he would not tell of her absences, went out daily for long hours. Black Sheep would follow the rays of the sinking sun from the kitchen to the dining-room and thence upward to his own bedroom until all was grey dark, and he ran down to the kitchen fire and read by its light. He was happy in that he was left alone and could read as much as he pleased. But, later, he grew afraid of the shadows of window-curtains and the flapping of doors and the creaking of shutters. He went out into the garden, and the rustling of the laurel-bushes frightened him.

He was glad when they all returned – Aunty Rosa, Harry, and Judy – full of news, and Judy laden with gifts. Who could help loving loyal little Judy? In return for all her merry babblement, Black Sheep confided to her that the distance from the hall-door to the top of the first landing was exactly one hundred and eighty-four handspans. He had found it out himself.

Then the old life recommenced; but with a difference, and a new sin. To his other iniquities Black Sheep had now added a phenomenal clumsiness – was as unfit to trust in action as he was in word. He himself could not account for spilling everything he touched, upsetting glasses as he put his hand out, and bumping his head against doors that were manifestly shut. There was a grey haze upon all his world, and it narrowed month by month, until at last it left Black Sheep almost alone with the flapping curtains that were so like ghosts, and the nameless terrors of broad daylight that were only coats on pegs after all.

Holidays came and holidays went, and Black Sheep was taken to see many people whose faces were all exactly alike; was beaten when occasion demanded, and tortured by Harry on all possible occasions; but defended by Judy through good and evil report, though she thereby drew upon herself the wrath of Aunty Rosa.

The weeks were interminable, and Papa and Mamma were clean forgotten. Harry had left school and was a clerk in a Banking-Office. Freed from his presence, Black Sheep resolved that he should no longer be deprived of his allowance of pleasure-reading. Consequently when he failed at school he reported that all was well, and conceived a large contempt for Aunty Rosa as he saw how easy it was to deceive her. "She says I'm a little liar when I don't tell lies, and now I do, she doesn't know," thought Black Sheep. Aunty Rosa had credited him in the past with petty cunning and stratagem that had never entered into his head. By the light of the sordid knowledge that she had revealed to him he paid her back full tale. In a household where the most innocent of his motives, his natural yearning for a little affection, had been interpreted into a desire for more bread and jam or to ingratiate himself with strangers and so put Harry into the background, his work was easy. Aunty Rosa could penetrate certain kinds of hypocrisy, but not all. He set his child's wits against hers, and was no more beaten. It grew monthly more and more of a trouble to read the school-books, and even the pages of the open-print story-books danced and were dim. So Black Sheep brooded in the shadows that fell about him and cut him off from the world, inventing horrible punishments for "dear Harry," or plotting another line of the tangled web of deception that he wrapped round Aunty Rosa.

Then the crash came and the cobwebs were broken. It was impossible to foresee everything. Aunty Rosa made personal enquiries as to Black Sheep's progress, and received information that startled her. Step by step, with a delight as keen as when she convicted an underfed housemaid of the theft of cold meats, she followed the trail of Black Sheep's delinquencies. For weeks and weeks, in order to escape banishment from the book-shelves, he had made a fool of Aunty Rosa, of Harry, of God, of all the world! Horrible, most horrible, and evidence of an utterly depraved mind.

Black Sheep counted the cost. "It will only be one big beating, and then she'll put a card with 'Liar' on my back, same as she did before. Harry will whack me and pray for me, and she will pray for me at prayers and tell me I'm a Child of the Devil and give me hymns to learn. But I've done all my reading, and she never knew. She'll say she knew all along. She's an old liar too," said he.

For three days Black Sheep was shut in his own bedroom – to prepare his heart. "That means two beatings. One at school and one here. *That* one will hurt most." And it fell even as he thought. He was thrashed at school before the Jews and the *hubshi*, for the heinous crime of bringing home false reports of progress. He was thrashed at home by Aunty Rosa on the same count, and then the placard was produced. Aunty Rosa stitched it between his shoulders and bade him go for a walk with it upon him.

"If you make me do that," said Black Sheep very quietly, "I shall burn this house down, and perhaps I'll kill you. I don't know whether I *can* kill you – you're so bony – but I'll try."

No punishment followed this blasphemy, though Black Sheep held himself ready to work his way to Aunty Rosa's withered throat, and grip there till he was beaten off. Perhaps Aunty Rosa was afraid, for Black Sheep, having reached the Nadir of Sin, bore himself with a new recklessness.

In the midst of all the trouble there came a visitor from

over the seas to Downe Lodge, who knew Papa and Mamma, and was commissioned to see Punch and Judy. Black Sheep was sent to the drawing-room and charged into a solid tea-table laden with china.

"Gently, gently, little man," said the visitor, turning Black Sheep's face to the light slowly. "What's that big bird on the palings?"

"What bird?" asked Black Sheep.

The visitor looked deep down into Black Sheep's eyes for half a minute, and then said suddenly: "Good God, the little chap's nearly blind!"

It was a most business-like visitor. He gave orders, on his own responsibility, that Black Sheep was not to go to school or open a book until Mamma came home. "She'll be here in three weeks, as you know of course," said he, "and I'm In-verarity Sahib. I ushered you into this wicked world, young man, and a nice use you seem to have made of your time. You must do nothing whatever. Can you do that?"

"Yes," said Punch in a dazed way. He had known that Mamma was coming. There was a chance, then, of another beating. Thank Heaven, Papa wasn't coming too. Aunty Rosa had said of late that he ought to be beaten by a man.

For the next three weeks Black Sheep was strictly allowed to do nothing. He spent his time in the old nursery looking at the broken toys, for all of which account must be rendered to Mamma. Aunty Rosa hit him over the hands if even a wooden boat were broken. But that sin was of small import-ance compared to the other revelations, so darkly hinted at by Aunty Rosa.

"When your Mother comes, and hears what I have to tell her, she may appreciate you properly," she said grimly, and mounted guard over Judy lest that small maiden should at-tempt to comfort her brother, to the peril of her soul.

And Mamma came — in a four-wheeler — fluttered with tender excitement. Such a Mamma! She was young, frivol-ously young, and beautiful, with delicately flushed cheeks, eyes that shone like stars, and a voice that needed no appeal of outstretched arms to draw little ones to her heart. Judy ran straight to her, but Black Sheep hesitated.

Could this wonder be "showing off"? She would not put out her arms when she knew of his crimes. Meantime was it possible that by fondling she wanted to get anything out of Black Sheep? Only all his love and all his confidence; but that Black Sheep did not know. Aunty Rosa withdrew and left Mamma, kneeling between her children, half laughing, half crying, in the very hall where Punch and Judy had wept five years before.

"Well, Chicks, do you remember me?"

"No," said Judy frankly, "but I said, 'God bless Papa and Mamma,' ev'vy night."

"A little," said Black Sheep. "Remember I wrote to you every week, anyhow. That isn't to show off, but 'cause of what comes afterwards."

"What comes after? What should come after, my darling boy?" And she drew him to her again. He came awkwardly, with many angles. "Not used to petting," said the quick Mother-soul. "The girl is."

"She's too little to hurt any one," thought Black Sheep, "and if I said I'd kill her, she'd be afraid. I wonder what Aunty Rosa will tell."

There was a constrained late dinner, at the end of which Mamma picked up Judy and put her to bed with endearments manifold. Faithless little Judy had shown her defection from Aunty Rosa already. And that lady resented it bitterly. Black Sheep rose to leave the room.

"Come and say good-night," said Aunty Rosa, offering a withered cheek.

"Huh!" said Black Sheep. "I never kiss you, and I'm not going to show off. Tell that woman what I've done, and see what she says."

Black Sheep climbed into bed feeling that he had lost Heaven after a glimpse through the gates. In half an hour "that woman" was bending over him. Black Sheep flung up his right arm. It wasn't fair to come and hit him in the dark. Even Aunty Rosa never tried that. But no blow followed.

"Are you showing off? I won't tell you anything more than Aunty Rosa has, and *she* doesn't know everything," said Black Sheep as clearly as he could for the arms round his neck.

"Oh, my son – my little, little son! It was my fault – *my* fault, darling — and yet how could we help it? Forgive me, Punch." The voice died out in a broken whisper, and two hot tears fell on Black Sheep's forehead.

"Has she been making you cry too!" he asked. "You should see Jane cry. But you're nice, and Jane is a Born Liar – Aunty Rosa says so."

"Hush, Punch, hush! My boy, don't talk like that. Try to love me a little bit – a little bit. You don't know how I want it. Punch-*baba*, come back to me! I am your Mother – your own Mother – and never mind the rest. I know – yes, I know, dear. It doesn't matter now. Punch, won't you care for me a little?"

It is astonishing how much petting a big boy of ten can endure when he is quite sure that there is no one to laugh at him. Black Sheep had never been made much of before, and here was this beautiful woman treating him – Black Sheep, the Child of the Devil and the inheritor of undying flame – as though he were a small God.

"I care for you a great deal, Mother dear," he whispered at last, "and I'm glad you've come back; but are you sure Aunty Rosa told you everything?"

"Everything. What *does* it matter? But" – the voice broke with a sob that was also laughter – "Punch, my poor, dear, half-blind darling, don't you think it was a little foolish of you?"

"*No*. It saved a lickin'."

Mamma shuddered and slipped away in the darkness to write a long letter to Papa. Here is an extract: –

. . . Judy is a dear, plump little prig who adores the woman, and wears with as much gravity as her religious opinions – only eight, Jack!

– a venerable horse-hair atrocity which she calls her Bustle! I have just burnt it, and the child is asleep in my bed as I write. She will come to me at once. Punch I cannot quite understand. He is well nourished, but seems to have been worried into a system of small deceptions which the woman magnifies into deadly sins. Don't you recollect our own upbringing, dear, when the Fear of the Lord was so often the beginning of falsehood? I shall win Punch to me before long. I am taking the children away into the country to get them to know me, and, on the whole, I am content, or shall be when you come home, dear boy, and then, thank God, we shall be all under one roof again at last!

Three months later, Punch, no longer Black Sheep, has discovered that he is the veritable owner of a real, live, lovely Mamma, who is also a sister, comforter, and friend, and that he must protect her till the Father comes home. Deception does not suit the part of a protector, and, when one can do anything without question, where is the use of deception?

"Mother would be awfully cross if you walked through that ditch," says Judy, continuing a conversation.

"Mother's never angry," says Punch. "She'd just say, 'You're a little *pagal*'; and that's not nice, but I'll show."

Punch walks through the ditch and mires himself to the knees. "Mother, dear," he shouts, "I'm just as dirty as I can pos-*sib*-ly be!"

"Then change your clothes as quickly as you pos-*sib*-ly can!" Mother's clear voice rings out from the house. "And don't be a little *pagal*!"

"There! 'Told you so," says Punch. "It's all different now, and we are just as much Mother's as if she had never gone."

Not altogether, O Punch, for when young lips have drunk deep of the bitter waters of Hate, Suspicion, and Despair, all the Love in the world will not wholly take away that knowledge; though it may turn darkened eyes for a while to the light, and teach Faith where no Faith was.

THE BRIDGE-BUILDERS

THE BRIDGE-BUILDERS

T HE least that Findlayson, of the Public Works Department, expected was a C.I.E.; he dreamed of a C.S.I.: indeed, his friends told him that he deserved more. For three years he had endured heat and cold, disappointment, discomfort, danger, and disease, with responsibility almost too heavy for one pair of shoulders; and day by day, through that time, the great Kashi Bridge over the Ganges had grown under his charge. Now, in less than three months, if all went well, his Excellency the Viceroy would open the bridge in state, an archbishop would bless it, and the first trainload of soldiers would come over it, and there would be speeches.

Findlayson, C. E., sat in his trolley on a construction line that ran along one of the main revetments – the huge stone-faced banks that flared away north and south for three miles on either side of the river – and permitted himself to think of the end. With its approaches, his work was one mile and three-quarters in length; a lattice-girder bridge, trussed with the Findlayson truss, standing on seven-and-twenty brick piers. Each one of those piers was twenty-four feet in diameter, capped with red Agra stone and sunk eighty feet below the shifting sand of the Ganges' bed. Above them was a railway-line fifteen feet broad; above that, again, a cart-road of eighteen feet, flanked with footpaths. At either end rose towers, of red brick, loopholed for musketry and pierced for big guns, and the ramp of the road was being pushed forward to their haunches. The raw earth-ends were crawling and alive with hundreds upon hundreds of tiny asses climbing out of the yawning borrow-pit below with sackfuls of stuff; and the hot afternoon air was filled with the noise of hooves, the rattle of the drivers' sticks, and the swish and roll-down of the dirt. The river was very low, and on the dazzling white sand between the three centre piers stood squat cribs of railway-sleepers, filled within and daubed without with mud, to support the last of the girders as those were riveted up. In the little deep water left by the drought, an overhead crane travelled to and fro along its spile-pier, jerking sections of iron into place, snorting and backing and grunting as an elephant grunts in the timber-yard. Riveters by the hundred swarmed about the lattice side-work and the iron roof of the railway-line, hung from invisible staging under the bellies of the girders, clustered round the throats of the piers, and rode on the overhang of the footpath-stanchions; their fire-pots and the spurts of flame that answered each hammer-stroke showing no more than pale yellow in the sun's glare. East and west and north and south the construction-trains rattled and shrieked up and down the embankments, the piled trucks of brown and white stone banging behind them till the side-boards were unpinned, and with a roar and a grumble a few thousand tons' more material were flung out to hold the river in place.

Findlayson, C. E., turned on his trolley and looked over the face of the country that he had changed for seven miles around. Looked back on the humming village of five thousand workmen; up stream and down, along the vista of spurs and sand; across the river to the far piers, lessening in the haze; overhead to the guard-towers – and only he knew how strong those were – and with a sigh of contentment saw that his work was good. There stood his bridge before him in the sunlight, lacking only a few weeks' work on the girders of the three middle piers – his bridge, raw and ugly as original sin, but *pukka* – permanent – to endure when all memory of the builder, yea, even of the splendid Findlayson truss, had perished. Practically, the thing was done.

Hitchcock, his assistant, cantered along the line on a little switch-tailed Kabuli pony who through long practice could have trotted securely over a trestle, and nodded to his chief.

"All but," said he, with a smile.

"I've been thinking about it," the senior answered. " 'Not half a bad job for two men, is it?"

"One – and a half. 'Gad, what a Cooper's Hill cub I was when I came on the works!" Hitchcock felt very old in the crowded experiences of the past three years, that had taught him power and responsibility.

"You *were* rather a colt," said Findlayson. "I wonder how you'll like going back to office-work when this job's over."

"I shall hate it!" said the young man, and as he went on his eye followed Findlayson's, and he muttered, "Isn't it damned good?"

"I think we'll go up the service together," Findlayson said to himself. "You're too good a youngster to waste on another man. Cub thou wast; assistant thou art. Personal assistant, and at Simla, thou shalt be, if any credit comes to me out of the business!"

Indeed, the burden of the work had fallen altogether on Findlayson and his assistant, the young man whom he had chosen because of his rawness to break to his own needs. There were labour contractors by the half-hundred – fitters and riveters, European, borrowed from the railway work-shops, with, perhaps, twenty white and half-caste subordinates to direct, under direction, the bevies of workmen – but none knew better than these two, who trusted each other, how the underlings were not to be trusted. They had been tried many times in sudden crises – by slipping of booms, by breaking of tackle, failure of cranes, and the wrath of the river – but no stress had brought to light any man among men whom Findlayson and Hitchcock would have honoured by working as remorselessly as they worked themselves. Find-layson thought it over from the beginning: the months of office-work destroyed at a blow when the Government of India, at the last moment, added two feet to the width of the bridge, under the impression that bridges were cut out of paper, and so brought to ruin at least half an acre of calcu-lations – and Hitchcock, new to disappointment, buried his head in his arms and wept; the heart-breaking delays over the filling of the contracts in England; the futile correspondences hinting at great wealth of commissions if one, only one, rather doubtful consignment were passed; the war that followed the refusal; the careful, polite obstruction at the other end that followed the war, till young Hitchcock, putting one month's leave to another month, and borrowing ten days from Findlayson, spent his poor little savings of a year in a wild dash to London, and there, as his own tongue asserted and the later consignments proved, put the fear of God into a man so great that he feared only Parliament and said so till Hitchcock wrought with him across his own dinner-table, and – he feared the Kashi Bridge and all who spoke in its name. Then there was the cholera that came in the night to the village by the bridge works; and after the cholera smote the small-pox. The fever they had always with them. Hitchcock had been appointed a magistrate of the third class with whipping powers, for the better government of the community, and Findlayson watched him wield his powers temperately, learning what to overlook and what to look after. It was a long, long reverie, and it covered storm, sudden freshets, death in every manner and shape, violent and awful rage against red tape half frenzying a mind that knows it should be busy on other things; drought, sanitation, finance; birth, wedding, burial, and riot in the village of twenty warring castes; argument, expostulation, persuasion, and the blank despair that a man goes to bed upon, thankful that his rifle is all in pieces in the gun-case. Behind everything rose the black frame of the Kashi Bridge – plate by plate, girder by girder, span by span – and each pier of it recalled Hitchcock, the all-round man, who had stood by his chief without failing from the very first to this last.

So the bridge was two men's work – unless one counted Peroo, as Peroo certainly counted himself. He was a Lascar, a Kharva from Bulsar, familiar with every port between Rockhampton and London, who had risen to the rank of serang on the British India boats, but wearying of routine musters and clean clothes, had thrown up the service and gone inland, where men of his calibre were sure of employment. For his knowledge of tackle and the handling of heavy weights, Peroo was worth almost any price he might have chosen to put upon his services; but custom decreed the wage of the overhead-men, and Peroo was not within many silver pieces of his proper value. Neither running water nor extreme heights made him afraid; and, as an ex-serang, he knew how to hold authority. No piece of iron was so big or so badly placed that Peroo could not devise a tackle to lift it – a loose-ended, sagging arrangement, rigged with a scandalous amount of talking, but perfectly equal to the work in hand. It was Peroo who had saved the girder of Number Seven pier from destruction when the new wire-rope jammed in the eye of the crane, and the huge plate tilted in its slings, threatening to slide out sideways. Then the native workmen lost their heads with great shoutings, and Hitchcock's right arm was broken by a falling T-plate, and he buttoned it up in his coat and swooned, and came to and directed for four hours till Peroo, from the top of the crane, reported "All's well," and the plate swung home. There was no one like Peroo, serang, to lash, and guy, and hold, to control the donkey-engines, to hoist a fallen locomotive craftily out of the borrow-pit into which it had tumbled; to strip, and dive, if need be, to see how the concrete blocks round the piers stood the scouring of Mother Gunga, or to adventure upstream on a monsoon night and report on the state of the embankment-facings. He would interrupt the field-councils of Findlayson and Hitchcock without fear, till his wonderful English, or his still more wonderful *lingua-franca*, half Portuguese and half Malay, ran out and he was forced to take string and show the knots that he would recommend. He controlled his own gang of tackle-men – mysterious relatives from Kutch Mandvi gathered month by month and tried to the uttermost. No consideration of family or kin allowed Peroo to keep weak hands or a giddy head on the pay-roll. "My honour is the honour of this bridge," he would say to the about-to-be-dismissed. "What do I care for your honour? Go and work on a steamer. That is all you are fit for."

The little cluster of huts where he and his gang lived

centred round the tattered dwelling of a sea-priest – one who had never set foot on black water, but had been chosen as ghostly counsellor by two generations of sea-rovers all unaffected by port missions or those creeds which are thrust upon sailors by agencies along Thames bank. The priest of the Lascars had nothing to do with their caste, or indeed with anything at all. He ate the offerings of his church, and slept and smoked, and slept again, "for," said Peroo, who had haled him a thousand miles inland, "he is a very holy man. He never cares what you eat so long as you do not eat beef, and that is good, because on land we worship Shiva, we Kharvas; but at sea on the Kumpani's boats we attend strictly to the orders of the Burra Malum [the first mate], and on this bridge we observe what Finlinson Sahib says."

Finlinson Sahib had that day given orders to clear the scaffolding from the guard-tower on the right bank, and Peroo with his mates was casting loose and lowering down the bamboo poles and planks as swiftly as ever they had whipped the cargo out of a coaster.

From his trolley he could hear the whistle of the serang's silver pipe and the creek and clatter of the pulleys. Peroo was standing on the topmost coping of the tower, clad in the blue dungaree of his abandoned service, and as Findlayson motioned to him to be careful, for his was no life to throw away, he gripped the last pole, and, shading his eyes ship-fashion, answered with the long-drawn wail of the fo'c'sle lookout: "*Ham dekhta hai*" ("I am looking out"). Findlayson laughed and then sighed. It was years since he had seen a steamer, and he was sick for home. As his trolley passed under the tower, Peroo descended by a rope, ape-fashion, and cried: "It looks well now, Sahib. Our bridge is all but done. What think you Mother Gunga will say when the rail runs over?"

"She has said little so far. It was never Mother Gunga that delayed us."

"There is always time for her; and none the less there has been delay. Has the Sahib forgotten last autumn's flood, when the stone-boats were sunk without warning – or only a half-day's warning?"

"Yes, but nothing save a big flood could hurt us now. The spurs are holding well on the west bank."

"Mother Gunga eats great allowances. There is always room for more stone on the revetments. I tell this to the Chota Sahib" – he meant Hitchcock – "and he laughs."

"No matter, Peroo. Another year thou wilt be able to build a bridge in thine own fashion."

The Lascar grinned. "Then it will not be in this way – with stonework sunk under water, as the *Quetta* was sunk. I like sus-sus-pen-sheen bridges that fly from bank to bank, with one big step, like a gang-plank. Then no water can hurt. When does the Lord Sahib come to open the bridge?"

"In three months, when the weather is cooler."

"Ho! ho! He is like the Burra Malum. He sleeps below while the work is being done. Then he comes upon the quarter-deck and touches with his finger, and says: 'This is not clean! Dam jibboonwallah!' "

"But the Lord Sahib does not call me a dam jibboon-wallah, Peroo."

"No, Sahib; but he does not come on deck till the work is all finished. Even the Burra Malum of the *Nerbudda* said once at Tuticorin —"

"Bah! Go! I am busy."

"I, also!" said Peroo, with an unshaken countenance. "May I take the light dinghy now and row along the spurs?"

"To hold them with thy hands? They are, I think, sufficiently heavy."

"Nay, Sahib. It is thus. At sea, on the Black Water, we have room to be blown up and down without care. Here we have no room at all. Look you, we have put the river into a dock, and run her between stone sills."

Findlayson smiled at the "we."

"We have bitted and bridled her. She is not like the sea, that can beat against a soft beach. She is Mother Gunga – in irons." His voice fell a little.

"Peroo, thou hast been up and down the world more even than I. Speak true talk, now. How much dost thou in thy heart believe of Mother Gunga?"

"All that our priest says. London is London, Sahib. Sydney is Sydney, and Port Darwin is Port Darwin. Also Mother Gunga is Mother Gunga, and when I come back to her banks I know this and worship. In London I did poojah to the big temple by the river for the sake of the God within. . . . Yes, I will not take the cushions in the dinghy."

Findlayson mounted his horse and trotted to the shed of a bungalow that he shared with his assistant. The place had become home to him in the last three years. He had grilled in the heat, sweated in the rains, and shivered with fever under the rude thatch roof; the lime-wash beside the door was covered with rough drawings and formulæ, and the sentry-path trodden in the matting of the verandah showed where he had walked alone. There is no eight-hour limit to an engineer's work, and the evening meal with Hitchcock was eaten booted and spurred: over their cigars they listened to the hum of the village as the gangs came up from the river-bed and the lights began to twinkle.

"Peroo has gone up the spurs in your dinghy. He's taken a couple of nephews with him, and he's lolling in the stern like a commodore," said Hitchcock.

"That's all right. He's got something on his mind. You'd think that ten years in the British India boats would have knocked most of his religion out of him."

"So it has," said Hitchcock, chuckling. "I overheard him the other day in the middle of a most atheistical talk with that fat old *guru* of theirs. Peroo denied the efficacy of prayer; and wanted the *guru* to go to sea and watch a gale out with him, and see if he could stop a monsoon."

"All the same, if you carried off his *guru* he'd leave us like a shot. He was yarning away to me about praying to the dome of St. Paul's when he was in London."

"He told me that the first time he went into the engine-room of a steamer, when he was a boy, he prayed to the low-pressure cylinder."

"Not half a bad thing to pray to, either. He's propitiating his own Gods now, and he wants to know what Mother Gunga will think of a bridge being run across her. Who's there?" A shadow darkened the doorway, and a telegram was put into Hitchcock's hand.

"She ought to be pretty well used to it by this time. Only a *tar*. It ought to be Ralli's answer about the new rivets. . . . Great Heavens!" Hitchcock jumped to his feet.

"What is it?" said the senior, and took the form. "*That's* what Mother Gunga thinks, is it," he said, reading. "Keep cool, young'un. We've got all our work cut out for us. Let's see. Muir wired half an hour ago: '*Floods on the Ramgunga. Look out.*' Well, that gives us – one, two – nine and a half for the flood to reach Melipur Ghaut and seven's sixteen and a half to Lataoli – say fifteen hours before it comes down to us."

"Curse that hill-fed sewer of a Ramgunga! Findlayson, this is two months before anything could have been expected, and the left bank is littered up with stuff still. Two full months before the time!"

"That's why it comes. I've only known Indian rivers for five-and-twenty years, and I don't pretend to understand. Here comes another *tar*." Findlayson opened the telegram. "Cockran, this time, from the Ganges Canal: '*Heavy rains here. Bad.*' He might have saved the last word. Well, we don't want to know any more. We've got to work the gangs all night and clean up the river-bed. You'll take the east bank and work out to meet me in the middle. Get everything that floats below the bridge: we shall have quite enough river-craft coming down adrift anyhow, without letting the stone-boats ram the piers. What have you got on the east bank that needs looking after?"

"Pontoon – one big pontoon with the overhead crane on it. T'other overhead crane on the mended pontoon, with the cart-road rivets from Twenty to Twenty-three piers – two construction lines, and a turning-spur. The pilework must take its chance," said Hitchcock.

"All right. Roll up everything you can lay hands on. We'll give the gang fifteen minutes more to eat their grub."

Close to the verandah stood a big night-gong, never used except for flood, or fire in the village. Hitchcock had called for a fresh horse, and was off to his side of the bridge when Findlayson took the cloth-bound stick and smote with the rubbing stroke that brings out the full thunder of the metal.

Long before the last rumble ceased every night-gong in the village had taken up the warning. To these were added the hoarse screaming of conches in the little temples; the throbbing of drums and tom-toms; and, from the European quarters, where the riveters lived, McCartney's bugle, a weapon of offence on Sundays and festivals, brayed desperately, calling to "Stables." Engine after engine toiling home along the spurs at the end of her day's work whistled in answer till the whistles were answered from the far bank. Then the big gong thundered thrice for a sign that it was flood and not fire; conch, drum, and whistle echoed the call, and the village quivered to the sound of bare feet running upon soft earth. The order in all cases was to stand by the day's work and wait instructions. The gangs poured by in the dusk; men stopping to knot a loin-cloth or fasten a sandal; gang-foremen shouting to their subordinates as they ran or paused by the tool-issue sheds for bars and mattocks; locomotives creeping down their tracks wheel-deep in the crowd; till the brown torrent disappeared into the dusk of the river-bed, raced over the pilework, swarmed along the lattices, clustered by the cranes, and stood still – each man in his place.

Then the troubled beating of the gong carried the order to take up everything and bear it beyond high-water mark, and the flare-lamps broke out by the hundred between the webs of dull iron as the riveters began a night's work, racing against the flood that was to come. The girders of the three centre piers – those that stood on the cribs – were all but in position. They needed just as many rivets as could be driven into them, for the flood would assuredly wash out their supports, and the ironwork would settle down on the caps of stone if they were not blocked at the ends. A hundred crowbars strained at the sleepers of the temporary line that fed the unfinished piers. It was heaved up in lengths, loaded into trucks, and backed up the bank beyond flood-level by the groaning locomotives. The tool-sheds on the sands melted away before the attack of shouting armies, and with them went the stacked ranks of Government stores, iron-bound boxes of rivets, pliers, cutters, duplicate parts of the riveting-machines, spare pumps and chains. The big crane would be the last to be shifted, for she was hoisting all the heavy stuff up to the main structure of the bridge. The concrete blocks on the fleet of stone-boats were dropped overside, where there was any depth of water, to guard the piers, and the empty boats themselves were poled under the bridge downstream. It was here that Peroo's pipe shrilled loudest, for the first stroke of the big gong had brought the dinghy back at racing speed, and Peroo and his people were stripped to the waist, working for the honour and credit which are better than life.

"I knew she would speak," he cried. "*I* knew, but the telegraph gives us good warning. O sons of unthinkable begetting – children of unspeakable shame – are we here for the look of the thing?" It was two feet of wire-rope frayed at the ends, and it did wonders as Peroo leaped from gunnel to gunnel, shouting the language of the sea.

Findlayson was more troubled for the stone-boats than anything else. McCartney, with his gangs, was blocking up the ends of the three doubtful spans, but boats adrift, if the flood chanced to be a high one, might endanger the girders; and there was a very fleet in the shrunken channel.

"Get them behind the swell of the guard-tower," he shouted down to Peroo. "It will be dead-water there. Get them below the bridge."

"*Accha!* [Very good.] *I* know; we are mooring them with

wire-rope," was the answer. "Heh! Listen to the Chota Sahib. He is working hard."

From across the river came an almost continuous whistling of locomotives, backed by the rumble of stone. Hitchcock at the last minute was spending a few hundred more trucks of Tarakee stone in reinforcing his spurs and embankments.

"The bridge challenges Mother Gunga," said Peroo, with a laugh. "But when *she* talks I know whose voice will be the loudest."

For hours the naked men worked, screaming and shouting under the lights. It was a hot, moonless night; the end of it was darkened by clouds and a sudden squall that made Findlayson very grave.

"She moves!" said Peroo, just before the dawn. "Mother Gunga is awake! Hear!" He dipped his hand over the side of a boat and the current mumbled on it. A little wave hit the side of a pier with a crisp slap.

"Six hours before her time," said Findlayson, mopping his forehead savagely. "Now we can't depend on anything. We'd better clear all hands out of the river-bed."

Again the big gong beat, and a second time there was the rushing of naked feet on earth and ringing iron; the clatter of tools ceased. In the silence, men heard the dry yawn of water crawling over thirsty sand.

Foreman after foreman shouted to Findlayson, who had posted himself by the guard-tower, that his section of the river-bed had been cleaned out, and when the last voice dropped Findlayson hurried over the bridge till the iron plating of the permanent way gave place to the temporary plank-walk over the three centre piers, and there he met Hitchcock.

" 'All clear your side?" said Findlayson. The whisper rang in the box of latticework.

"Yes, and the east channel's filling now. We're utterly out of our reckoning. When is this thing down on us?"

"There's no saying. She's filling as fast as she can. Look!"

Findlayson pointed to the planks below his feet, where the sand, burned and defiled by months of work, was beginning to whisper and fizz.

"What orders?" said Hitchcock.

"Call the roll – count stores – sit on your hunkers – and pray for the bridge. That's all I can think of. Good night. Don't risk your life trying to fish out anything that may go down-stream."

"Oh, I'll be as prudent as you are! 'Night. Heavens, how she's filling! Here's the rain in earnest!"

Findlayson picked his way back to his bank, sweeping the last of McCartney's riveters before him. The gangs had spread themselves along the embankments, regardless of the cold rain of the dawn, and there they waited for the flood. Only Peroo kept his men together behind the swell of the guard-tower, where the stone-boats lay tied fore and aft with hawsers, wire-rope, and chains.

A shrill wail ran along the line, growing to a yell, half fear and half wonder: the face of the river whitened from bank to bank between the stone facings, and the far-away spurs went out in spouts of foam. Mother Gunga had come bank-high in haste, and a wall of chocolate-coloured water was her messenger. There was a shriek above the roar of the water, the complaint of the spans coming down on their blocks as the cribs were whirled out from under their bellies. The stone-boats groaned and ground each other in the eddy that swung round the abutment, and their clumsy masts rose higher and higher against the dim sky-line.

"Before she was shut between these walls we knew what she would do. Now she is thus cramped God only knows what she will do!" said Peroo, watching the furious turmoil round the guard-tower. "Ohé! Fight, then! Fight hard, for it is thus that a woman wears herself out."

But Mother Gunga would not fight as Peroo desired. After the first down-stream plunge there came no more walls of water, but the river lifted herself bodily, as a snake when she drinks in midsummer, plucking and fingering along the revetments, and banking up behind the piers till even Find-layson began to recalculate the strength of his work.

When day came the village gasped. "Only last night," men said, turning to each other, "it was as a town in the river-bed! Look now!"

And they looked and wondered afresh at the deep water, the racing water that licked the throat of the piers. The far-ther bank was veiled by rain, into which the bridge ran out and vanished; the spurs up-stream were marked by no more than eddies and spoutings, and down-stream the pent river, once freed of her guide-lines, had spread like a sea to the horizon. Then hurried by, rolling in the water, dead men and oxen together, with here and there a patch of thatched roof that melted when it touched a pier.

"Big flood," said Peroo, and Findlayson nodded. It was as big a flood as he had any wish to watch. His bridge would stand what was upon her now, but not very much more, and if by any of a thousand chances there happened to be a weakness in the embankments, Mother Gunga would carry his honour to the sea with the other raffle. Worst of all, there was nothing to do except to sit still; and Findlayson sat still under his macintosh till his helmet became pulp on his head, and his boots were over-ankle in mire. He took no count of time, for the river was marking the hours, inch by inch and foot by foot, along the embankment, and he listened, numb and hungry, to the straining of the stone-boats, the hollow thunder under the piers, and the hundred noises that make the full note of a flood. Once a dripping servant brought him food, but he could not eat; and once he thought that he heard a faint toot from a locomotive across the river, and then he smiled. The bridge's failure would hurt his assistant not a little, but Hitchcock was a young man with his big work yet to do. For himself the crash meant everything – everything that made a hard life worth the living. They would say, the men of his own profession . . . he remembered the half-pitying things that he himself had said when Lockhart's new waterworks burst and broke down in brick-heaps and sludge, and Lockhart's spirit broke in him and he died. He remembered what he himself had said when the Sumao Bridge went out in the big cyclone by the sea; and most he remembered poor Hartopp's face three weeks later, when the shame had marked it. His bridge was twice the size of Hartopp's, and it carried the Findlayson truss as well as the new pier-shoe – the Findlayson bolted shoe. There were no excuses in his service. Government might listen, perhaps, but his own kind would judge him by his bridge, as that stood or fell. He went over it in his head, plate by plate, span by span, brick by brick, pier by pier, remembering, comparing, estimating, and recalculating, lest there should be any mistake; and through the long hours and through the flights of formulæ that danced and wheeled before him a cold fear would come to pinch his heart. His side of the sum was beyond question; but what man knew Mother Gunga's arithmetic? Even as he was making all sure by the multiplication-table, the river might be scooping a pot-hole to the very bottom of any one of those eighty-foot piers that carried his reputation. Again a servant came to him with food, but his mouth was dry, and he could only drink and return to the decimals in his brain. And the river was still rising. Peroo, in a mat shelter-coat, crouched at his feet, watching now his face and now the face of the river, but saying nothing.

At last the Lascar rose and floundered through the mud towards the village, but he was careful to leave an ally to watch the boats.

Presently he returned, most irreverently driving before him the priest of his creed – a fat old man, with a grey beard that whipped the wind with the wet cloth that blew over his shoulder. Never was seen so lamentable a *guru*.

"What good are offerings and little kerosene lamps and dry grain," shouted Peroo, "if squatting in the mud is all that thou canst do? Thou hast dealt long with the Gods when they were contented and well-wishing. Now they are angry. Speak to them!"

"What is a man against the wrath of Gods?" whined the

priest, cowering as the wind took him. "Let me go to the temple, and I will pray there."

"Son of a pig, pray *here*! Is there no return for salt fish and curry powder and dried onions? Call aloud! Tell Mother Gunga we have had enough. Bid her be still for the night. I cannot pray, but I have been serving in the Kumpani's boats, and when men did not obey my orders I —" A flourish of the wire-rope colt rounded the sentence, and the priest, breaking free from his disciple, fled to the village.

"Fat pig!" said Peroo. "After all that we have done for him! When the flood is down I will see to it that we get a new *guru*. Finlinson Sahib, it darkens for night now, and since yesterday nothing has been eaten. Be wise, Sahib. No man can endure watching and great thinking on an empty belly. Lie down, Sahib. The river will do what the river will do."

"The bridge is mine; I cannot leave it."

"Wilt thou hold it up with thy hands, then?" said Peroo, laughing. "I was troubled for my boats and sheers *before* the flood came. Now we are in the hands of the Gods. The Sahib will not eat and lie down? Take these, then. They are meat and good toddy together, and they kill all weariness, besides the fever that follows the rain. I have eaten nothing else to-day at all."

He took a small tin tobacco-box from his sodden waist-belt and thrust it into Findlayson's hand, saying: "Nay, do not be afraid. It is no more than opium – clean Malwa opium!"

Findlayson shook two or three of the dark-brown pellets into his hand, and hardly knowing what he did, swallowed them. The stuff was at least a good guard against fever – the fever that was creeping upon him out of the wet mud – and he had seen what Peroo could do in the stewing mists of Autumn on the strength of a dose from the tin box.

Peroo nodded with bright eyes. "In a little – in a little the Sahib will find that he thinks well again. I too will –" He dived into his treasure-box, resettled the rain-coat over his head, and squatted down to watch the boats. It was too dark now to see beyond the first pier, and the night seemed to have given the river new strength. Findlayson stood with his chin on his chest, thinking. There was one point about one of the piers – the seventh – that he had not fully settled in his mind. The figures would not shape themselves to the eye except one by one and at enormous intervals of time. There was a sound rich and mellow in his ears like the deepest note of a double-bass – an entrancing sound upon which he pondered for several hours, as it seemed. Then Peroo was at his elbow, shouting that a wire hawser had snapped and the stone-boats were loose. Findlayson saw the fleet open and swing out fanwise to a long-drawn shriek of wire straining across gunnels.

"A tree hit them. They will all go," cried Peroo. "The main hawser has parted. What does the Sahib do?"

An immensely complex plan had suddenly flashed into Findlayson's mind. He saw the ropes running from boat to boat in straight lines and angles – each rope a line of white fire. But there was one rope which was the master rope. He could see that rope. If he could pull it once, it was absolutely and mathematically certain that the disordered fleet would reassemble itself in the backwater behind the guard-tower. But why, he wondered, was Peroo clinging so desperately to his waist as he hastened down the bank? It was necessary to put the Lascar aside, gently and slowly, because it was necessary to save the boats, and, further, to demonstrate the extreme ease of the problem that looked so difficult. And then – but it was of no conceivable importance – a wire-rope raced through his hand, burning it, the high bank disappeared, and with it all the slowly dispersing factors of the problem. He was sitting in the rainy darkness – sitting in a boat that spun like a top, and Peroo was standing over him.

"I had forgotten," said the Lascar, slowly, "that to those fasting and unused, the opium is worse than any wine. Those who die in Gunga go to the Gods. Still, I have no desire to present myself before such great ones. Can the Sahib swim?"

"What need? He can fly – fly as swiftly as the wind," was the thick answer.

"He is mad!" muttered Peroo, under his breath. "And he threw me aside like a bundle of dung-cakes. Well, he will not know his death. The boat cannot live an hour here even if she strike nothing. It is not good to look at death with a clear eye."

He refreshed himself again from the tin box, squatted down in the bows of the reeling, pegged, and stitched craft, staring through the mist at the nothing that was there. A warm drowsiness crept over Findlayson, the Chief Engineer, whose duty was with his bridge. The heavy raindrops struck him with a thousand tingling little thrills, and the weight of all time since time was made hung heavy on his eyelids. He thought and perceived that he was perfectly secure, for the water was so solid that a man could surely step out upon it, and, standing still with his legs apart to keep his balance – this was the most important point – would be borne with great and easy speed to the shore. But yet a better plan came to him. It needed only an exertion of will for the soul to hurl the body ashore as wind drives paper, to waft it kite-fashion to the bank. Thereafter – the boat spun dizzily – suppose the high wind got under the freed body? Would it tower up like a kite and pitch headlong on the far-away sands, or would it duck about, beyond control, through all eternity? Findlayson gripped the gunnel to anchor himself, for it seemed that he was on the edge of taking the flight before he had settled all his plans. Opium has more effect on the white man than the black. Peroo was only comfortably indifferent to accidents. "She cannot live," he grunted. "Her seams open already. If she were even a dinghy with oars we could have ridden it out; but a box with holes is no good. Finlinson Sahib, she fills."

"*Accha!* I am going away. Come thou also."

In his mind, Findlayson had already escaped from the boat, and was circling high in air to find a rest for the sole of his foot. His body – he was really sorry for its gross helplessness – lay in the stern, the water rushing about its knees.

"How very ridiculous!" he said to himself, from his eyrie – "that – is Findlayson – chief of the Kashi Bridge. The poor beast is going to be drowned, too. Drowned when it's close to shore. I'm – I'm on shore already. Why doesn't it come along?"

To his intense disgust, he found his soul back in his body again, and that body spluttering and choking in deep water. The pain of the reunion was atrocious, but it was necessary, also, to fight for the body. He was conscious of grasping wildly at wet sand, and striding prodigiously, as one strides in a dream, to keep foothold in the swirling water, till at last he hauled himself clear of the hold of the river, and dropped, panting, on wet earth.

"Not this night," said Peroo, in his ear. "The Gods have protected us." The Lascar moved his feet cautiously, and they rustled among dried stumps. "This is some island of last year's indigo-crop," he went on. "We shall find no men here; but have great care, Sahib; all the snakes of a hundred miles have been flooded out. Here comes the lightning, on the heels of the wind. Now we shall be able to look; but walk carefully."

Findlayson was far and far beyond any fear of snakes, or indeed any merely human emotion. He saw, after he had rubbed the water from his eyes, with an immense clearness, and trod, so it seemed to himself, with world-encompassing strides. Somewhere in the night of time he had built a bridge – a bridge that spanned illimitable levels of shining seas; but the Deluge had swept it away, leaving this one island under heaven for Findlayson and his companion, sole survivors of the breed of Man.

An incessant lightning, forked and blue, showed all that there was to be seen on the little patch in the flood – a clump of thorn, a clump of swaying creaking bamboos, and a grey gnarled peepul overshadowing a Hindu shrine, from whose dome floated a tattered red flag. The holy man whose summer resting-place it was had long since abandoned it, and the weather had broken the red-daubed image of his god. The two men stumbled, heavy-limbed and heavy-eyed, over the ashes of a brick-set cooking-place, and dropped down under the shelter of the branches, while the rain and river roared together.

The stumps of the indigo crackled, and there was a smell of cattle, as a huge and dripping Brahminee bull shouldered his way under the tree. The flashes revealed the trident mark of Shiva on his flank, the insolence of head and hump, the luminous stag-like eyes, the brow crowned with a wreath of sodden marigold blooms, and the silky dewlap that almost swept the ground. There was a noise behind him of other beasts coming up from the flood-line through the thicket, a sound of heavy feet and deep breathing.

"Here be more beside ourselves," said Findlayson, his head against the tree-pole, looking through half-shut eyes, wholly at ease.

"Truly," said Peroo, thickly, "and no small ones."

"What are they, then? I do not see clearly."

"The Gods. Who else? Look!"

"Ah, true! The Gods surely – the Gods." Findlayson smiled as his head fell forward on his chest. Peroo was eminently right. After the Flood, who should be alive in the land except the Gods that made it – the Gods to whom his village prayed nightly – the Gods who were in all men's mouths and about all men's ways. He could not raise his head or stir a finger for the trance that held him, and Peroo was smiling vacantly at the lightning.

The Bull paused by the shrine, his head lowered to the damp earth. A green Parrot in the branches preened his wet wings and screamed against the thunder as the circle under the tree filled with the shifting shadows of beasts. There was a black Buck at the Bull's heels – such a Buck as Findlayson in his far-away life upon earth might have seen in dreams – a Buck with a royal head, ebon back, silver belly, and gleaming straight horns. Beside him, her head bowed to the ground, the green eyes burning under the heavy brows, with restless tail switching the dead grass, paced a Tigress, full-bellied and deep-jowled.

The Bull crouched beside the shrine, and there leaped from the darkness a monstrous grey Ape, who seated himself man-wise in the place of the fallen image, and the rain spilled like jewels from the hair of his neck and shoulders.

Other shadows came and went behind the circle, among them a drunken Man flourishing staff and drinking-bottle. Then a hoarse bellow broke out from near the ground. "The flood lessens even now," it cried. "Hour by hour the water falls, and their bridge still stands!"

"My bridge," said Findlayson to himself. "That must be very old work now. What have the Gods to do with my bridge?"

His eyes rolled in the darkness following the roar. A Mugger – the blunt-nosed, ford-haunting Mugger of the Ganges – draggled herself before the beasts, lashing furiously to right and left with her tail.

"They have made it too strong for me. In all this night I have only torn away a handful of planks. The walls stand. The towers stand. They have chained my flood, and the river is not free any more. Heavenly Ones, take this yoke away! Give me clear water between bank and bank! It is I, Mother Gunga, that speak. The Justice of the Gods! Deal me the Justice of the Gods!"

"What said I?" whispered Peroo. "This is in truth a Pun-chayet of the Gods. Now we know that all the world is dead, save you and I, Sahib."

The Parrot screamed and fluttered again, and the Tigress, her ears flat to her head, snarled wickedly.

Somewhere in the shadow, a great trunk and gleaming tusks swayed to and fro, and a low gurgle broke the silence that followed on the snarl.

"We be here," said a deep voice, "the Great Ones. One only and very many. Shiv, my father, is here, with Indra. Kali has spoken already. Hanuman listens also."

"Kashi is without her Kotwal to-night," shouted the Man with the drinking-bottle, flinging his staff to the ground, while the island rang to the baying of hounds. "Give her the Justice of the Gods."

"Ye were still when they polluted my waters," the great Crocodile bellowed. "Ye made no sign when my river was trapped between the walls. I had no help save my own strength, and that failed – the strength of Mother Gunga failed – before their guard-towers. What could I do? I have done everything. Finish now, Heavenly Ones!"

"I brought the death; I rode the spotted sickness from hut to hut of their workmen, and yet they would not cease." A nose-slitten, hide-worn Ass, lame, scissor-legged, and galled, limped forward. "I cast the death at them out of my nostrils, but they would not cease."

Peroo would have moved, but the opium lay heavy upon him.

"Bah!" he said, spitting. "Here is Sitala herself; Mata – the small-pox. Has the Sahib a handkerchief to put over his face?"

"Little help! They fed me the corpses for a month, and I flung them out on my sand-bars, but their work went forward. Demons they are, and sons of demons! And ye left Mother Gunga alone for their fire-carriage to make a mock of. The Justice of the Gods on the bridge-builders!"

The Bull turned the cud in his mouth and answered slowly: "If the Justice of the Gods caught all who made a mock of holy things there would be many dark altars in the land, mother."

"But this goes beyond a mock," said the Tigress, darting forward a griping paw. "Thou knowest, Shiv, and ye, too, Heavenly Ones; ye know that they have defiled Gunga. Surely they must come to the Destroyer. Let Indra judge."

The Buck made no movement as he answered: "How long has this evil been?"

"Three years, as men count years," said the Mugger, close pressed to the earth.

"Does Mother Gunga die, then, in a year, that she is so anxious to see vengeance now? The deep sea was where she runs but yesterday, and to-morrow the sea shall cover her again as the Gods count that which men call time. Can any say that this their bridge endures till to-morrow?" said the Buck.

There was a long hush, and in the clearing of the storm the full moon stood up above the dripping trees.

"Judge ye, then," said the River, sullenly. "I have spoken my shame. The flood falls still. I can do no more."

"For my own part" – it was the voice of the great Ape seated within the shrine – "it pleases me well to watch these men, remembering that I also built no small bridge in the world's youth."

"They say, too," snarled the Tiger, "that these men came of the wreck of thy armies, Hanuman, and therefore thou hast aided —"

"They toil as my armies toiled in Lanka, and they believe that their toil endures. Indra is too high, but Shiv, thou knowest how the land is threaded with their fire-carriages."

"Yea, I know," said the Bull. "Their Gods instructed them in the matter."

A laugh ran round the circle.

"Their Gods! What should their Gods know? They were born yesterday, and those that made them are scarcely yet cold," said the Mugger. "To-morrow their Gods will die."

"Ho!" said Peroo. "Mother Gunga talks good talk. I told that to the padre-sahib who preached on the *Mombassa*, and he asked the Burra Malum to put me in irons for a great rudeness."

"Surely they make these things to please their Gods," said the Bull again.

"Not altogether," the Elephant rolled forth. "It is for the profit of my mahajuns – my fat money-lenders that worship me at each new year, when they draw my image at the head of the account-books. I, looking over their shoulders by lamp-light, see that the names in the books are those of men in far places – for all the towns are drawn together by the fire-carriage, and the money comes and goes swiftly, and the account-books grow as fat as – myself. And I, who am Ganesh of Good Luck, I bless my peoples."

"They have changed the face of the land – which is my land. They have killed and made new towns on my banks," said the Mugger.

"It is but the shifting of a little dirt. Let the dirt dig in the dirt if it pleases the dirt," answered the Elephant.

"But afterwards?" said the Tiger. "Afterwards they will see that Mother Gunga can avenge no insult, and they fall away from her first, and later from us all, one by one. In the end, Ganesh, we are left with naked altars."

The drunken Man staggered to his feet, and hiccupped vehemently.

"Kali lies. My sister lies. Also this my stick is the Kotwal of Kashi, and he keeps tally of my pilgrims. When the time comes to worship Bhairon – and it is always time – the fire-carriages move one by one, and each bears a thousand pilgrims. They do not come afoot any more, but rolling upon wheels, and my honour is increased."

"Gunga, I have seen thy bed at Pryag black with the pilgrims," said the Ape, leaning forward, "and but for the fire-carriage they would have come slowly and in fewer numbers. Remember."

"They come to me always," Bhairon went on thickly. "By day and night they pray to me, all the Common People in the fields and the roads. Who is like Bhairon to-day? What talk is this of changing faiths? Is my staff Kotwal of Kashi for nothing? He keeps the tally, and he says that never were so many altars as to-day, and the fire-carriage serves them well. Bhairon am I – Bhairon of the Common People, and the chiefest of the Heavenly Ones to-day. Also my staff says —"

"Peace, thou!" lowed the Bull. "The worship of the schools is mine, and they talk very wisely, asking whether I be one or many, as is the delight of my people, and ye know what I am. Kali, my wife, thou knowest also."

"Yea, I know," said the Tigress, with lowered head.

"Greater am I than Gunga also. For ye know who moved the minds of men that they should count Gunga holy among the rivers. Who die in that water – ye know how men say – come to us without punishment, and Gunga knows that the fire-carriage has borne to her scores upon scores of such anxious ones; and Kali knows that she has held her chiefest festivals among the pilgrimages that are fed by the fire-carriage. Who smote at Pooree, under the Image there, her thousands in a day and a night, and bound the sickness to the wheels of the fire-carriages, so that it ran from one end of the land to the other? Who but Kali? Before the fire-carriage came it was a heavy toil. The fire-carriages have served thee well, Mother of Death. But I speak for mine own altars, who am not Bhairon of the Common Folk, but Shiv. Men go to and fro, making words and telling talk of strange Gods, and I listen. Faith follows faith among my people in the schools, and I have no anger; for when all words are said, and the new talk is ended, to Shiv men return at the last."

"True. It is true," murmured Hanuman. "To Shiv and to the others, mother, they return. I creep from temple to temple in the North, where they worship one God and His Prophet; and presently my image is alone within their shrines."

"Small thanks," said the Buck, turning his head slowly. "I am that One and His Prophet also."

"Even so, father," said Hanuman. "And to the South I go who am the oldest of the Gods as men know the Gods, and presently I touch the shrines of the New Faith and the Woman whom we know is hewn twelve-armed, and still they call her Mary."

"Small thanks, brother," said the Tigress. "I am that Woman."

"Even so, sister; and I go West among the fire-carriages, and stand before the bridge-builders in many shapes, and because of me they change their faiths and are very wise. Ho! ho! I am the builder of bridges, indeed – bridges between this and that, and each bridge leads surely to Us in the end. Be content, Gunga. Neither these men nor those that follow them mock thee at all."

"Am I alone, then, Heavenly Ones? Shall I smooth out my flood lest unhappily I bear away their walls? Will Indra dry my springs in the hills and make me crawl humbly between their wharfs? Shall I bury me in the sand ere I offend?"

"And all for the sake of a little iron bar with the fire-carriage atop. Truly, Mother Gunga is always young!" said Ganesh the Elephant. "A child had not spoken more foolishly. Let the dirt dig in the dirt ere it return to the dirt. I know only that my people grow rich and praise me. Shiv has said that the men of the schools do not forget; Bhairon is content for his crowd of the Common People; and Hanuman laughs."

"Surely I laugh," said the Ape. "My altars are few beside those of Ganesh or Bhairon, but the fire-carriages bring me new worshippers from beyond the Black Water – the men who believe that their God is toil. I run before them beckoning, and they follow Hanuman."

"Give them the toil that they desire, then," said the River. "Make a bar across my flood and throw the water back upon the bridge. Once thou wast strong in Lanka, Hanuman. Stoop and lift my bed."

"Who gives life can take life." The Ape scratched in the mud with a long forefinger. "And yet, who would profit by the killing? Very many would die."

There came up from the water a snatch of a love-song such as the boys sing when they watch their cattle in the noon heats of late Spring. The Parrot screamed joyously, sidling along his branch with lowered head as the song grew louder, and in a patch of clear moonlight stood revealed the young herd, the darling of the Gopis, the idol of dreaming maids and of mothers ere their children are born – Krishna the Well-beloved. He stooped to knot up his long wet hair, and the Parrot fluttered to his shoulder.

"Fleeting and singing, and singing and fleeting," hiccupped Bhairon. "Those make thee late for the council, brother."

"And then?" said Krishna, with a laugh, throwing back his head. "Ye can do little without me or Karma here." He fondled the Parrot's plumage and laughed again. "What is this sitting and talking together? I heard Mother Gunga roaring in the dark, and so came quickly from a hut where I lay warm. And what have ye done to Karma, that he is so wet and silent? And what does Mother Gunga here? Are the heavens full that ye must come paddling in the mud beastwise? Karma, what do they do?"

"Gunga has prayed for a vengeance on the bridgebuilders, and Kali is with her. Now she bids Hanuman whelm the bridge, that her honour may be made great," cried the Parrot. "I waited here, knowing that thou wouldst come, O my master!"

"And the Heavenly Ones said nothing? Did Gunga and the Mother of Sorrows out-talk them? Did none speak for my people?"

"Nay," said Ganesh, moving uneasily from foot to foot; "I said it was but dirt at play, and why should we stamp it flat?"

"I was content to let them toil – well content," said Hanuman.

"What had I to do with Gunga's anger?" said the Bull.

"I am Bhairon of the Common Folk, and this my staff is Kotwal of all Kashi. I spoke for the Common People."

"Thou?" The young God's eyes sparkled.

"Am I not the first of the Gods in their mouths to-day?" returned Bhairon, unabashed. "For the sake of the Common People I said – very many wise things which I have now forgotten, but this my staff —"

Krishna turned impatiently, saw the Mugger at his feet, and kneeling, slipped an arm round the cold neck. "Mother," he said gently, "get thee to thy flood again. The matter is not for thee. What harm shall thy honour take of this live dirt? Thou hast given them their fields new year after year, and by thy flood they are made strong. They come all to thee at the last. What need to slay them now? Have pity, mother, for a little – and it is only for a little."

"If it be only for a little —" the slow beast began.

"Are they Gods, then?" Krishna returned with a laugh, his eyes looking into the dull eyes of the River. "Be certain that it is only for a little. The Heavenly Ones have heard thee, and presently justice will be done. Go now, mother, to the flood again. Men and cattle are thick on the waters – the banks fall – the villages melt because of thee."

"But the bridge – the bridge stands." The Mugger turned grunting into the undergrowth as Krishna rose.

"It is ended," said the Tigress, viciously. "There is no more justice from the Heavenly Ones. Ye have made shame and sport of Gunga, who asked no more than a few score lives."

"Of *my* people – who lie under the leaf-roofs of the village yonder – of the young girls, and the young men who sing to them in the dark – of the child that will be born next morn – of that which was begotten to-night," said Krishna. "And when all is done, what profit? To-morrow sees them at work. Ay, if ye swept the bridge out from end to end they would begin anew. Hear me! Bhairon is drunk always. Hanuman mocks his people with new riddles."

"Nay, but they are very old ones," the Ape said, laughing.

"Shiv hears the talk of the schools and the dreams of the holy men; Ganesh thinks only of his fat traders; but I – I live with these my people, asking for no gifts, and so receiving them hourly."

"And very tender art thou of thy people," said the Tigress.

"They are my own. The old women dream of me turning in their sleep; the maids look and listen for me when they go to fill their lotahs by the river. I walk by the young men waiting without the gates at dusk, and I call over my shoulder to the white-beards. Ye know, Heavenly Ones, that I alone of us all walk upon the earth continually, and have no pleasure in our heavens so long as a green blade springs here, or there are two voices at twilight in the standing crops. Wise are ye, but ye live far off, forgetting whence ye came. So do I not forget. And the fire-carriage feeds your shrines, ye say? And the fire-carriages bring a thousand pilgrims where but ten came in the old years? True. That is true, to-day."

"But to-morrow they are dead, brother," said Ganesh.

"Peace!" said the Bull, as Hanuman leaned forward again. "And to-morrow, beloved – what of to-morrow?"

"This only. A new word creeping from mouth to mouth among the Common Folk – a word that neither man nor God can lay hold of – an evil word – a little lazy word among the Common Folk, saying (and none know who set that word afoot) that they weary of ye, Heavenly Ones."

The Gods laughed together softly. "And then, beloved?" they said.

"And to cover that weariness they, my people, will bring to thee, Shiv, and to thee, Ganesh, at first greater offerings and a louder noise of worship. But the word has gone abroad, and, after, they will pay fewer dues to your fat Brahmins. Next they will forget your altars, but so slowly that no man can say how his forgetfulness began."

"I knew – I knew! I spoke this also, but they would not hear," said the Tigress. "We should have slain – we should have slain!"

"It is too late now. Ye should have slain at the beginning when the men from across the water had taught our folk nothing. Now my people see their work, and go away thinking. They do not think of the Heavenly Ones altogether. They think of the fire-carriage and the other things that the bridge-builders have done, and when your priests thrust forward hands asking alms, they give a little unwillingly. That is the beginning, among one or two, or five or ten – for I, moving among my people, know what is in their hearts."

"And the end, Jester of the Gods? What shall the end be?" said Ganesh.

"The end shall be as it was in the beginning, O slothful son of Shiv! The flame shall die upon the altars and the

prayer upon the tongue till ye become little Gods again –
Gods of the jungle – names that the hunters of rats and
noosers of dogs whisper in the thicket and among the caves
– rag-Gods, pot Godlings of the tree, and the village-mark,
as ye were at the beginning. That is the end, Ganesh, for
thee, and for Bhairon – Bhairon of the Common People."

"It is very far away," grunted Bhairon. "Also, it is a lie."

"Many women have kissed Krishna. They told him this
to cheer their own hearts when the grey hairs came, and he
has told us the tale," said the Bull, below his breath.

"Their Gods came, and we changed them. I took the
Woman and made her twelve-armed. So shall we twist all
their Gods," said Hanuman.

"Their Gods! This is no question of their Gods – one or
three – man or woman. The matter is with the people. *They*
move, and not the Gods of the bridge-builders," said Krishna.

"So be it. I have made a man worship the fire-carriage as
it stood still breathing smoke, and he knew not that he worshipped me," said Hanuman the Ape. "They will only
change a little the names of their Gods. I shall lead the
builders of the bridges as of old; Shiv shall be worshipped in
the schools by such as doubt and despise their fellows;
Ganesh shall have his mahajuns, and Bhairon the donkey-
drivers, the pilgrims, and the sellers of toys. Beloved, they
will do no more than change the names, and that we have
seen a thousand times."

"Surely they will do no more than change the names,"
echoed Ganesh; but there was an uneasy movement among
the Gods.

"They will change more than the names. Me alone they
cannot kill, so long as a maiden and a man meet together or
the Spring follows the Winter rains. Heavenly Ones, not for
nothing have I walked upon the earth. My people know not
now what they know; but I, who live with them, I read their
hearts. Great Kings, the beginning of the end is born already.
The fire-carriages shout the names of new Gods that are *not*
the old under new names. Drink now and eat greatly! Bathe

your faces in the smoke of the altars before they grow cold! Take dues and listen to the cymbals and the drums, Heavenly Ones, while yet there are flowers and songs. As men count time the end is far off; but as we who know reckon it is to-day. I have spoken."

The young God ceased, and his brethren looked at each other long in silence.

"This I have not heard before," Peroo whispered in his companion's ear. "And yet sometimes, when I oiled the brasses in the engine-room of the *Goorkha*, I have wondered if our priests were so wise – so wise. The day is coming, Sahib. They will be gone by the morning."

A yellow light broadened in the sky, and the tone of the river changed as the darkness withdrew.

Suddenly the Elephant trumpeted aloud as though man had goaded him.

"Let Indra judge. Father of all, speak thou! What of the things we have heard? Has Krishna lied indeed? Or —"

"Ye know," said the Buck, rising to his feet. "Ye know the Riddle of the Gods. When Brahm ceases to dream, the Heavens and the Hells and Earth disappear. Be content. Brahm dreams still. The dreams come and go, and the nature of the dreams changes, but still Brahm dreams. Krishna has walked too long upon earth, and yet I love him the more for the tale he has told. The Gods change, beloved – all save One!"

"Ay, all save one that makes love in the hearts of men," said Krishna, knotting his girdle. "It is but a little time to wait, and ye shall know if I lie."

"Truly it is but a little time, as thou sayest, and we shall know. Get thee to thy huts again, beloved, and make sport for the young things, for still Brahm dreams. Go, my children! Brahm dreams – and till he wakes the Gods die not."

* * *

"Whither went they?" said the Lascar, awestruck, shivering a little with the cold.

"God knows!" said Findlayson. The river and the island lay in full daylight now, and there was never mark of hoof or pug on the wet earth under the peepul. Only a parrot screamed in the branches, bringing down showers of water-drops as he fluttered his wings.

"Up! We are cramped with cold! Has the opium died out? Canst thou move, Sahib?"

Findlayson staggered to his feet and shook himself. His head swam and ached, but the work of the opium was over, and, as he sluiced his forehead in a pool, the Chief Engineer of the Kashi Bridge was wondering how he had managed to fall upon the island, what chances the day offered of return, and, above all, how his work stood.

"Peroo, I have forgotten much. I was under the guard-tower watching the river; and then . . . Did the flood sweep us away?"

"No. The boats broke loose, Sahib, and" (if the Sahib had forgotten about the opium, decidedly Peroo would not remind him) "in striving to retie them, so it seemed to me – but it was dark – a rope caught the Sahib and threw him upon a boat. Considering that we two, with Hitchcock Sahib, built, as it were, that bridge, I came also upon the boat, which came riding on horseback, as it were, on the nose of this island, and so, splitting, cast us ashore. I made a great cry when the boat left the wharf, and without doubt Hitchcock Sahib will come for us. As for the bridge, so many have died in the building that it cannot fall."

A fierce sun, that drew out all the smell of the sodden land, had followed the storm, and in that clear light there was no room for a man to think of the dreams of the dark. Findlayson stared up-stream, across the blaze of moving water, till his eyes ached. There was no sign of any bank to the Ganges, much less of a bridge-line.

"We came down far," he said. "It was wonderful that we were not drowned a hundred times."

"That was the least of the wonder, for no man dies before his time. I have seen Sydney, I have seen London, and twenty great ports, but" – Peroo looked at the damp, discoloured shrine under the peepul – "never man has seen that we saw here."

"What?"

"Has the Sahib forgotten; or do we black men only see the Gods?"

"There was a fever upon me." Findlayson was still looking uneasily across the water. "It seemed that the island was full of beasts and men talking, but I do not remember. A boat could live in this water now, I think."

"Oho! Then it *is* true. 'When Brahm ceases to dream, the Gods die.' Now I know, indeed, what he meant. Once, too, the *guru* said as much to me; but then I did not understand. Now I am wise."

"What?" said Findlayson, over his shoulder.

Peroo went on as if he were talking to himself. "Six – seven – ten monsoons since, I was watch on the fo'c'sle of the *Rewah* – the Kumpani's big boat – and there was a big *tufan;* green and black water beating, and I held fast to the life-lines, choking under the waters. Then I thought of the Gods – of Those whom we saw to-night" – he stared curiously at Findlayson's back, but the white man was looking across the flood. "Yes, I say of Those whom we saw this night past, and I called upon Them to protect me. And while I prayed, still keeping my lookout, a big wave came and threw me forward upon the ring of the great black bow-anchor, and the *Rewah* rose high and high, leaning towards the left-hand side, and the water drew away from beneath her nose, and I lay upon my belly, holding the ring, and looking down into those great deeps. Then I thought, even in the face of death: If I lose hold I die, and for me neither the *Rewah* nor my place by the galley where the rice is cooked, nor Bombay, nor Calcutta, nor even London, will be any more for me. 'How shall I be sure,' I said, 'that the Gods to whom I pray will abide at all?' This I thought, and the *Rewah* dropped her nose as a hammer falls, and all the sea came in and slid me backwards along the fo'c'sle and over the break of the fo'c'sle, and I very badly bruised my shin against the donkey-engine: but I did not die, and I have seen the Gods. They are good for live men, but for the dead . . . They have spoken Themselves. Therefore, when I come to the village I will beat the *guru* for talking riddles which are no riddles. When Brahm ceases to dream the Gods go."

"Look up-stream. The light blinds. Is there smoke yonder?"

Peroo shaded his eyes with his hands. "He is a wise man and quick. Hitchcock Sahib would not trust a rowboat. He has borrowed the Rao Sahib's steam-launch, and comes to look for us. I have always said that there should have been a steam-launch on the bridge works for us."

The territory of the Rao of Baraon lay within ten miles of the bridge; and Findlayson and Hitchcock had spent a fair portion of their scanty leisure in playing billiards and shooting blackbuck with the young man. He had been bear-led by an English tutor of sporting tastes for some five or six years, and was now royally wasting the revenues accumulated during his minority by the Indian Government. His steam-launch, with its silver-plated rails, striped silk awning, and mahogany decks, was a new toy which Findlayson had found horribly in the way when the Rao came to look at the bridge works.

"It's great luck," murmured Findlayson, but he was none the less afraid, wondering what news might be of the bridge.

The gaudy blue-and-white funnel came down-stream swiftly. They could see Hitchcock in the bows, with a pair of opera-glasses, and his face was unusually white. Then Peroo hailed, and the launch made for the tail of the island. The Rao Sahib, in tweed shooting-suit and a seven-hued turban, waved his royal hand, and Hitchcock shouted. But he need have asked no questions, for Findlayson's first demand was for his bridge.

"All serene! 'Gad, I never expected to see you again, Findlayson. You're seven koss down-stream. Yes; there's not a stone shifted anywhere; but how are you? I borrowed the Rao

Sahib's launch, and he was good enough to come along. Jump in."

"Ah, Finlinson, you are very well, eh? That was most unprecedented calamity last night, eh? My royal palace, too, it leaks like the devil, and the crops will also be short all about my country. Now you shall back her out, Hitchcock. I – I do not understand steam-engines. You are wet? You are cold, Finlinson? I have some things to eat here, and you will take a good drink."

"I'm immensely grateful, Rao Sahib. I believe you've saved my life. How did Hitchcock —"

"Oho! His hair was upon end. He rode to me in the middle of the night and woke me up in the arms of Morpheus. I was most truly concerned, Finlinson, so I came too. My head-priest he is very angry just now. We will go quick, Mister Hitchcock. I am due to attend at twelve forty-five in the state temple, where we sanctify some new idol. If not so I would have asked you to spend the day with me. They are dam-bore, these religious ceremonies, Finlinson, eh?"

Peroo, well known to the crew, had possessed himself of the inlaid wheel, and was taking the launch craftily upstream. But while he steered he was, in his mind, handling two feet of partially untwisted wire-rope; and the back upon which he beat was the back of his *guru*.

THE MALTESE CAT

THE MALTESE CAT

THEY had good reason to be proud, and better reason to be afraid, all twelve of them; for though they had fought their way, game by game, up the teams entered for the polo tournament, they were meeting the Archangels that afternoon in the final match; and the Archangels men were playing with half a dozen ponies apiece. As the game was divided into six quarters of eight minutes each, that meant a fresh pony after every halt. The Skidars' team, even supposing there were no accidents, could only supply one pony for every other change; and two to one is heavy odds. Again, as Shiraz, the grey Syrian, pointed out, they were meeting the pink and pick of the polo-ponies of Upper India, ponies that had cost from a thousand rupees each, while they themselves were a cheap lot gathered, often from country-carts, by their masters, who belonged to a poor but honest native infantry regiment.

"Money means pace and weight," said Shiraz, rubbing his black-silk nose dolefully along his neat-fitting boot, "and by the maxims of the game as I know it —"

"Ah, but we aren't playing the maxims," said The Maltese Cat. "We're playing the game; and we've the great advantage of knowing the game. Just think a stride, Shiraz! We've pulled up from bottom to second place in two weeks against all those fellows on the ground here. That's because we play with our heads as well as our feet."

"It makes me feel undersized and unhappy all the same," said Kittiwynk, a mouse-coloured mare with a red browband and the cleanest pair of legs that ever an aged pony owned. "They've twice our style, these others."

Kittiwynk looked at the gathering and sighed. The hard, dusty polo-ground was lined with thousands of soldiers, black and white, not counting hundreds and hundreds of carriages and drags and dog-carts, and ladies with brilliant-coloured parasols, and officers in uniform and out of it, and crowds of natives behind them; and orderlies on camels, who had halted to watch the game, instead of carrying letters up and down the station; and native horse-dealers running about on thin-eared Biluchi mares, looking for a chance to sell a few first-class polo-ponies. Then there were the ponies of thirty teams that had entered for the Upper India Free-for-All Cup – nearly every pony of worth and dignity, from Mhow to Peshawur, from Allahabad to Multan; prize ponies, Arabs, Syrian, Barb, country-bred, Deccanee, Waziri, and Kabul ponies of every colour and shape and temper that you could imagine. Some of them were in mat-roofed stables, close to the polo-ground, but most were under saddle, while their masters, who had been defeated in the earlier games, trotted in and out and told the world exactly how the game should be played.

It was a glorious sight, and the come and go of the little, quick hooves, and the incessant salutations of ponies that had met before on other polo-grounds or race-courses, were enough to drive a four-footed thing wild.

But the Skidars' team were careful not to know their neighbours, though half the ponies on the ground were anxious to scrape acquaintance with the little fellows that had come from the North, and, so far, had swept the board.

"Let's see," said a soft gold-coloured Arab, who had been playing very badly the day before, to The Maltese Cat; "didn't we meet in Abdul Rahman's stable in Bombay, four seasons ago? I won the Paikpattan Cup next season, you may remember?"

"Not me," said The Maltese Cat, politely. "I was at Malta then, pulling a vegetable-cart. I don't race. I play the game."

"Oh!" said the Arab, cocking his tail and swaggering off.

"Keep yourselves to yourselves," said The Maltese Cat to his companions. "We don't want to rub noses with all those goose-rumped half-breeds of Upper India. When we've won this Cup they'll give their shoes to know *us*."

"We sha'n't win the Cup," said Shiraz. "How do you feel?"

"Stale as last night's feed when a muskrat has run over it," said Polaris, a rather heavy-shouldered grey; and the rest of the team agreed with him.

"The sooner you forget that the better," said The Maltese Cat, cheerfully. "They've finished tiffin in the big tent. We shall be wanted now. If your saddles are not comfy, kick. If your bits aren't easy, rear, and let the *saises* know whether your boots are tight."

Each pony had his *sais*, his groom, who lived and ate and slept with the animal, and had betted a good deal more than he could afford on the result of the game. There was no chance of anything going wrong, but to make sure, each *sais* was shampooing the legs of his pony to the last minute. Behind the *saises* sat as many of the Skidars' regiment as had leave to attend the match – about half the native officers, and a hundred or two dark, black-bearded men, with the regimental pipers nervously fingering the big, beribboned bagpipes. The Skidars were what they call a Pioneer regiment, and the bagpipes made the national music of half their men. The native officers held bundles of polo-sticks, long cane-handled mallets, and as the grand stand filled after lunch they arranged themselves by ones and twos at different points round the ground, so that if a stick were broken the player would not have far to ride for a new one. An impatient British Cavalry Band struck up "If you want to know the time, ask a p'leeceman!" and the two umpires in light dust-coats danced out on two little excited ponies. The four players of the Archangels' team followed, and the sight of their beautiful mounts made Shiraz groan again.

"Wait till we know," said The Maltese Cat. "Two of 'em are playing in blinkers, and that means they can't see to get out of the way of their own side, or they *may* shy at the umpires' ponies. They've *all* got white web-reins that are sure to stretch or slip!"

"And," said Kittiwynk, dancing to take the stiffness out

of her, "they carry their whips in their hands instead of on their wrists. Hah!"

"True enough. No man can manage his stick and his reins and his whip that way," said The Maltese Cat. "I've fallen over every square yard of the Malta ground, and I ought to know."

He quivered his little, flea-bitten withers just to show how satisfied he felt; but his heart was not so light. Ever since he had drifted into India on a troop-ship, taken, with an old rifle, as part payment for a racing debt, The Maltese Cat had played and preached polo to the Skidar's team on the Skidars' stony polo-ground. Now a polo-pony is like a poet. If he is born with a love for the game, he can be made. The Maltese Cat knew that bamboos grew solely in order that polo-balls might be turned from their roots, that grain was given to ponies to keep them in hard condition, and that ponies were shod to prevent them slipping on a turn. But, besides all these things, he knew every trick and device of the finest game in the world, and for two seasons had been teaching the others all he knew or guessed.

"Remember," he said for the hundredth time, as the riders came up, "you *must* play together, and you *must* play with your heads. Whatever happens, follow the ball. Who goes out first?"

Kittiwynk, Shiraz, Polaris, and a short high little bay fellow with tremendous hocks and no withers worth speaking of (he was called Corks) were being girthed up, and the soldiers in the background stared with all their eyes.

"I want you men to keep quiet," said Lutyens, the captain of the team, "and especially not to blow your pipes."

"Not if we win, Captain Sahib?" asked the piper.

"If we win you can do what you please," said Lutyens, with a smile, as he slipped the loop of his stick over his wrist, and wheeled to canter to his place. The Archangels' ponies were a little bit above themselves on account of the many-coloured crowd so close to the ground. Their riders were excellent players, but they were a team of crack players instead of a crack team; and that made all the difference in the world. They honestly meant to play together, but it is very hard for four men, each the best of the team he is picked from, to remember that in polo no brilliancy in hitting or riding makes up for playing alone. Their captain shouted his orders to them by name, and it is a curious thing that if you call his name aloud in public after an Englishman you make him hot and fretty. Lutyens said nothing to his men, because it had all been said before. He pulled up Shiraz, for he was playing "back," to guard the goal. Powell on Polaris was half-back, and Macnamara and Hughes on Corks and Kittiwynk were forwards. The tough, bamboo ball was set in the middle of the ground, one hundred and fifty yards from the ends, and Hughes crossed sticks, heads up, with the Captain of the Archangels, who saw fit to play forward; that is a place from which you cannot easily control your team. The little click as the cane-shafts met was heard all over the ground, and then Hughes made some sort of quick wrist-stroke that just dribbled the ball a few yards. Kittiwynk knew that stroke of old, and followed as a cat follows a mouse. While the Captain of the Archangels was wrenching his pony round, Hughes struck with all his strength, and next instant Kittiwynk was away, Corks following close behind her, their little feet pattering like raindrops on glass.

"Pull out to the left," said Kittiwynk between her teeth; "it's coming your way, Corks!"

The back and half-back of the Archangels were tearing down on her just as she was within reach of the ball. Hughes leaned forward with a loose rein, and cut it away to the left almost under Kittiwynk's foot, and it hopped and skipped off to Corks, who saw that if he was not quick it would run beyond the boundaries. That long bouncing drive gave the Archangels time to wheel and send three men across the ground to head off Corks. Kittiwynk stayed where she was; for she knew the game. Corks was on the ball half a fraction of a second before the others came up, and Macnamara, with a backhanded stroke, sent it back across the ground to

Hughes, who saw the way clear to the Archangels' goal, and smacked the ball in before any one quite knew what had happened.

"That's luck," said Corks, as they changed ends. "A goal in three minutes for three hits, and no riding to speak of."

" 'Don't know," said Polaris. "We've made 'em angry too soon. 'Shouldn't wonder if they tried to rush us off our feet next time."

"Keep the ball hanging, then," said Shiraz. "That wears out every pony that is not used to it."

Next time there was no easy galloping across the ground. All the Archangels closed up as one man, but there they stayed, for Corks, Kittiwynk, and Polaris were somewhere on the top of the ball, marking time among the rattling sticks, while Shiraz circled about outside, waiting for a chance.

"We can do this all day," said Polaris, ramming his quarters into the side of another pony. "Where do you think you're shoving to?"

"I'll – I'll be driven in an *ekka* if I know," was the gasping reply, "and I'd give a week's feed to get my blinkers off. I can't see anything."

"The dust is rather bad. Whew! That was one for my off-hock. Where's the ball, Corks?"

"Under my tail. At least, the man's looking for it there! This is beautiful. They can't use their sticks, and it's driving 'em wild. Give old Blinkers a push and then he'll go over."

"Here, don't touch me! I can't see. I'll – I'll back out, I think," said the pony in blinkers, who knew that if you can't see all round your head, you cannot prop yourself against the shock.

Corks was watching the ball where it lay in the dust, close to his near fore-leg, with Macnamara's shortened stick tap-tapping it from time to time. Kittiwynk was edging her way out of the scrimmage, whisking her stump of a tail with nervous excitement.

"Ho! They've got it," she snorted. "Let me out!" and she galloped like a rifle-bullet just behind a tall lanky pony of the

Archangels, whose rider was swinging up his stick for a stroke.

"Not to-day, thank you," said Hughes, as the blow slid off his raised stick, and Kittiwynk laid her shoulder to the tall pony's quarters, and shoved him aside just as Lutyens on Shiraz sent the ball where it had come from, and the tall pony went skating and slipping away to the left. Kittiwynk, seeing that Polaris had joined Corks in the chase for the ball up the ground, dropped into Polaris' place, and then "time" was called.

The Skidars' ponies wasted no time in kicking or fuming. They knew that each minute's rest meant so much gain, and trotted off to the rails, and their *saises* began to scrape and blanket and rub them at once.

"Whew!" said Corks, stiffening up to get all the tickle of the big vulcanite scraper. "If we were playing pony for pony, we would bend those Archangels double in half an hour. But they'll bring up fresh ones and fresh ones and fresh ones after that – you see."

"Who cares?" said Polaris. "We've drawn first blood. Is my hock swelling?"

" 'Looks puffy," said Corks. "You must have had rather a wipe. Don't let it stiffen. You'll be wanted again in half an hour."

"What's the game like?" said The Maltese Cat.

" 'Ground's like your shoe, except where they put too much water on it," said Kittiwynk. "Then it's slippery. Don't play in the centre. There's a bog there. I don't know how their next four are going to behave, but we kept the ball hanging, and made 'em lather for nothing. Who goes out? Two Arabs and a couple of country-breds! That's bad. What a comfort it is to wash your mouth out!"

Kitty was talking with a neck of a lather-covered soda-water bottle between her teeth, and trying to look over her withers at the same time. This gave her a very coquettish air.

"What's bad?" said Grey Dawn, giving to the girth and admiring his well-set shoulders.

"You Arabs can't gallop fast enough to keep yourselves warm – that's what Kitty means," said Polaris, limping to show that his hock needed attention. "Are you playing back, Grey Dawn?"

" 'Looks like it," said Grey Dawn, as Lutyens swung himself up. Powell mounted The Rabbit, a plain bay country-bred much like Corks, but with mulish ears. Macnamara took Faiz-Ullah, a handy, short-backed little red Arab with a long tail, and Hughes mounted Benami, an old and sullen brown beast, who stood over in front more than a polo-pony should.

"Benami looks like business," said Shiraz. "How's your temper, Ben?" The old campaigner hobbled off without answering, and The Maltese Cat looked at the new Arch-angel ponies prancing about on the ground. They were four beautiful blacks, and they saddled big enough and strong enough to eat the Skidars' team and gallop away with the meal inside them.

"Blinkers again," said The Maltese Cat. "Good enough!"

"They're chargers – cavalry chargers!" said Kittiwynk, indignantly. "*They'll* never see thirteen three again."

"They've all been fairly measured, and they've all got their certificates," said The Maltese Cat, "or they wouldn't be here. We must take things as they come along, and keep your eyes on the ball."

The game began, but this time the Skidars were penned to their own end of the ground, and the watching ponies did not approve of that.

"Faiz-Ullah is shirking – as usual," said Polaris, with a scornful grunt.

"Faiz-Ullah is eating whip," said Corks. They could hear the leather-thonged polo-quirt lacing the little fellow's well-rounded barrel. Then The Rabbit's shrill neigh came across the ground.

"I can't do all the work," he cried desperately.

"Play the game – don't talk," The Maltese Cat whickered; and all the ponies wriggled with excitement, and the soldiers and the grooms gripped the railings and shouted. A black pony with blinkers had singled out old Benami, and was interfering with him in every possible way. They could see Benami shaking his head up and down, and flapping his underlip.

"There'll be a fall in a minute," said Polaris. "Benami is getting stuffy."

The game flickered up and down between goal-post and goal-post, and the black ponies were getting more confident as they felt they had the legs of the others. The ball was hit out of a little scrimmage, and Benami and The Rabbit followed it, Faiz-Ullah only too glad to be quiet for an instant.

The blinkered black pony came up like a hawk, with two of his own side behind him, and Benami's eye glittered as he raced. The question was which pony should make way for the other, for each rider was perfectly willing to risk a fall in a good cause. The black, who had been driven nearly crazy by his blinkers, trusted to his weight and his temper; but Benami knew how to apply his weight and how to keep his temper. They met, and there was a cloud of dust. The black was lying on his side, all the breath knocked out of his body. The Rabbit was a hundred yards up the ground with the ball, and Benami was sitting down. He had slid nearly ten yards on his tail, but he had had his revenge, and sat cracking his nostrils till the black pony rose.

"That's what you get for interfering. Do you want any more?" said Benami, and he plunged into the game. Nothing was done that quarter, because Faiz-Ullah would not gallop, though Macnamara beat him whenever he could spare a second. The fall of the black pony had impressed his companions tremendously, and so the Archangels could not profit by Faiz-Ullah's bad behaviour.

But as The Maltese Cat said when "time" was called, and the four came back blowing and dripping, Faiz-Ullah ought to have been kicked all round Umballa. If he did not behave better next time The Maltese Cat promised to pull out his Arab tail by the roots and – eat it.

There was no time to talk, for the third four were ordered out.

The third quarter of a game is generally the hottest, for each side thinks that the others must be pumped; and most of the winning play in a game is made about that time.

Lutyens took over The Maltese Cat with a pat and a hug, for Lutyens valued him more than anything else in the world; Powell had Shikast, a little grey rat with no pedigree and no manners outside polo; Macnamara mounted Bamboo, the largest of the team; and Hughes Who's Who, alias The Animal. He was supposed to have Australian blood in his veins, but he looked like a clothes-horse, and you could whack his legs with an iron crowbar without hurting him.

They went out to meet the very flower of the Archangels' team; and when Who's Who saw their elegantly booted legs and their beautiful satin skins, he grinned a grin through his light, well-worn bridle.

"My word!" said Who's Who. "We must give 'em a little football. These gentlemen need a rubbing down."

"No biting," said The Maltese Cat, warningly; for once or twice in his career Who's Who had been known to forget himself in that way.

"Who said anything about biting? I'm not playing tiddly-winks. I'm playing the game."

The Archangels came down like a wolf on the fold, for they were tired of football, and they wanted polo. They got it more and more. Just after the game began, Lutyens hit a ball that was coming towards him rapidly, and it rolled in the air, as a ball sometimes will, with the whirl of a frightened partridge. Shikast heard, but could not see it for the minute, though he looked everywhere and up into the air as The Maltese Cat had taught him. When he saw it ahead and overhead he went forward with Powell as fast as he could put foot to ground. It was then that Powell, a quiet and level-headed man, as a rule, became inspired, and played a stroke that sometimes comes off successfully after long practice. He took his stick in both hands, and, standing up in his stirrups, swiped at the ball in the air, Munipore fashion. There was one second of paralysed astonishment, and then all four sides of the ground went up in a yell of applause and delight as the ball flew true (you could see the amazed Archangels ducking in their saddles to dodge the line of flight, and looking at it with open mouths), and the regimental pipes of the Skidars squealed from the railings as long as the pipers had breath.

Shikast heard the stroke; but he heard the head of the stick fly off at the same time. Nine hundred and ninety-nine ponies out of a thousand would have gone tearing on after the ball with a useless player pulling at their heads; but Powell knew him, and he knew Powell; and the instant he felt Powell's right leg shift a trifle on the saddle-flap, he headed to the boundary, where a native officer was frantically waving a new stick. Before the shouts had ended, Powell was armed again.

Once before in his life The Maltese Cat had heard that very same stroke played off his own back, and had profited by the confusion it wrought. This time he acted on experience, and leaving Bamboo to guard the goal in case of accidents, came through the others like a flash, head and tail low – Lutyens standing up to ease him – swept on and on before the other side knew what was the matter, and nearly pitched on his head between the Archangels' goal-post as Lutyens kicked the ball in after a straight scurry of a hundred and fifty yards. If there was one thing more than another upon which The Maltese Cat prided himself, it was on this quick, streaking kind of run half across the ground. He did not believe in taking balls round the field unless you were clearly over-matched. After this they gave the Archangels five-minuted football; and an expensive fast pony hates football because it rumples his temper.

Who's Who showed himself even better than Polaris in this game. He did not permit any wriggling away, but bored joyfully into the scrimmage as if he had his nose in a feed-box and was looking for something nice. Little Shikast jumped on the ball the minute it got clear, and every time an Archangel pony followed it, he found Shikast standing over it, asking what was the matter.

"If we can live through this quarter," said The Maltese Cat, "I sha'n't care. Don't take it out of yourselves. Let them do the lathering."

So the ponies, as their riders explained afterwards, "shut-up." The Archangels kept them tied fast in front of their goal, but it cost the Archangels' ponies all that was left of their tempers; and ponies began to kick, and men began to repeat compliments, and they chopped at the legs of Who's Who, and he set his teeth and stayed where he was, and the dust stood up like a tree over the scrimmage until that hot quarter ended.

They found the ponies very excited and confident when they went to their *saises;* and The Maltese Cat had to warn them that the worst of the game was coming.

"Now *we* are all going in for the second time," said he, "and *they* are trotting out fresh ponies. You think you can gallop, but you'll find you can't; and then you'll be sorry."

"But two goals to nothing is a halter-long lead," said Kit-tiwynk, prancing.

"How long does it take to get a goal?" The Maltese Cat answered. "For pity's sake, don't run away with a notion that the game is half-won just because we happen to be in luck *now*! They'll ride you into the grand stand, if they can; you must not give 'em a chance. Follow the ball."

"Football, as usual?" said Polaris. "My hock's half as big as a nose-bag."

"Don't let them have a look at the ball, if you can help it. Now leave me alone. I must get all the rest I can before the last quarter."

He hung down his head and let all his muscles go slack, Shikast, Bamboo, and Who's Who copying his example.

"Better not watch the game," he said. "We aren't playing, and we shall only take it out of ourselves if we grow anxious. Look at the ground and pretend it's fly-time."

They did their best, but it was hard advice to follow. The hooves were drumming and the sticks were rattling all up and down the ground, and yells of applause from the English troops told that the Archangels were pressing the Skidars hard. The native soldiers behind the ponies groaned and grunted, and said things in undertones, and presently they heard a long-drawn shout and a clatter of hurrahs!

"One to the Archangels," said Shikast, without raising his head. "Time's nearly up. Oh, my sire – and *dam*!"

"Faiz-Ullah," said The Maltese Cat, "if you don't play to the last nail in your shoes this time, I'll kick you on the ground before all the other ponies."

"I'll do my best when my time comes," said the little Arab, sturdily.

The *saises* looked at each other gravely as they rubbed their ponies' legs. This was the time when long purses began to tell, and everybody knew it. Kittiwynk and the others came back, the sweat dripping over their hooves and their tails telling sad stories.

"They're better than we are," said Shiraz. "I knew how it would be."

"Shut your big head," said The Maltese Cat; "we've one goal to the good yet."

"Yes; but it's two Arabs and two country-breds to play now," said Corks. "Faiz-Ullah, remember!" He spoke in a biting voice.

As Lutyens mounted Grey Dawn he looked at his men, and they did not look pretty. They were covered with dust and sweat in streaks. Their yellow boots were almost black, their wrists were red and lumpy, and their eyes seemed two inches deep in their heads; but the expression in the eyes was satisfactory.

"Did you take anything at tiffin?" said Lutyens; and the team shook their heads. They were too dry to talk.

"All right. The Archangels did. They are worse pumped than we are."

"They've got the better ponies," said Powell. "I sha'n't be sorry when this business is over."

That fifth quarter was a painful one in every way. Faiz-Ullah played like a little red demon, and The Rabbit seemed to be everywhere at once, and Benami rode straight at anything and everything that came in his way; while the umpires on their ponies wheeled like gulls outside the shifting game. But the Archangels had the better mounts, – they had kept their racers till late in the game, – and never allowed the Skidars to play football. They hit the ball up and down the width of the ground till Benami and the rest were outpaced. Then they went forward, and time and again Lutyens and Grey Dawn were just, and only just, able to send the ball away with a long, spitting backhander. Grey Dawn forgot that he was an Arab, and turned from grey to blue as he galloped. Indeed, he forgot too well, for he did not keep his eyes on the ground as an Arab should, but stuck out his nose and scuttled for the dear honour of the game. They had watered the ground once or twice between the quarters, and a careless waterman had emptied the last of his skinful all in one place near the Skidars' goal. It was close to the end of the play, and for the tenth time Grey Dawn was bolting after the ball, when his near hind foot slipped on the greasy mud, and he rolled over and over, pitching Lutyens just clear of the goal-post; and the triumphant Archangels made their goal. Then "time" was called – two goals all; but Lutyens had to be helped up, and Grey Dawn rose with his near hind leg strained somewhere.

"What's the damage?" said Powell, his arm around Lutyens.

"Collar-bone, *of* course," said Lutyens, between his teeth. It was the third time he had broken it in two years, and it hurt him.

Powell and the others whistled.

" 'Games' up," said Hughes.

"Hold on. We've five good minutes yet, and it isn't my right hand. We'll stick it out."

"I say," said the Captain of the Archangels, trotting up, "are you hurt, Lutyens? We'll wait if you care to put in a substitute. I wish – I mean – the fact is, you fellows deserve this game if any team does. 'Wish we could give you a man, or some of our ponies – or something."

"You're awfully good, but we'll play it to a finish, I think."

The Captain of the Archangels stared for a little. "That's not half bad," he said, and went back to his own side, while Lutyens borrowed a scarf from one of his native officers and made a sling of it. Then an Archangel galloped up with a big bath-sponge, and advised Lutyens to put it under his armpit to ease his shoulder, and between them they tied up his left arm scientifically; and one of the native officers leaped forward with four long glasses that fizzed and bubbled.

The team looked at Lutyens piteously, and he nodded. It was the last quarter, and nothing would matter after that. They drank out the dark golden drink, and wiped their moustaches, and things looked more hopeful.

The Maltese Cat had put his nose into the front of Lutyens' shirt and was trying to say how sorry he was.

"He knows," said Lutyens, proudly. "The beggar knows. I've played him without a bridle before now – for fun."

"It's no fun now," said Powell. "But we haven't a decent substitute."

"No," said Lutyens. "It's the last quarter, and we've got to make our goal and win. I'll trust The Cat."

"If you fall this time, you'll suffer a little," said Macnamara.

"I'll trust The Cat," said Lutyens.

"You hear that?" said The Maltese Cat, proudly, to the others. "It's worth while playing polo for ten years to have that said of you. Now then, my sons, come along. We'll kick up a little bit, just to show the Archangels this team haven't suffered."

And, sure enough, as they went on to the ground, The Maltese Cat, after satisfying himself that Lutyens was home in the saddle, kicked out three or four times, and Lutyens laughed. The reins were caught up anyhow in the tips of his strapped left hand, and he never pretended to rely on them. He knew The Cat would answer to the least pressure of the leg, and by way of showing off – for his shoulder hurt him very much – he bent the little fellow in a close figure-of-eight in and out between the goal-posts. There was a roar from the native officers and men, who dearly loved a piece of *dugabashi* (horse-trick work), as they called it, and the pipes very quietly and scornfully droned out the first bars of a common bazar tune called "Freshly Fresh and Newly New," just as a warning to the other regiments that the Skidars were fit. All the natives laughed.

"And now," said The Maltese Cat, as they took their place, "remember that this is the last quarter, and follow the ball!"

"Don't need to be told," said Who's Who.

"Let me go on. All those people on all four sides will begin to crowd in – just as they did at Malta. You'll hear people calling out, and moving forward and being pushed back; and that is going to make the Archangel ponies very unhappy. But if a ball is struck to the boundary, you go after it, and let the people get out of your way. I went over the pole of a four-in-hand once, and picked a game out of the dust by it. Back me up when I run, and follow the ball."

There was a sort of an all-round sound of sympathy and wonder as the last quarter opened, and then there began exactly what The Maltese Cat had foreseen. People crowded in close to the boundaries, and the Archangels' ponies kept looking sideways at the narrowing space. If you know how a man feels to be cramped at tennis – not because he wants to run out of the court, but because he likes to know that he can at a pinch – you will guess how ponies must feel when they are playing in a box of human beings.

"I'll bend some of those men if I can get away," said Who's Who, as he rocketed behind the ball; and Bamboo nodded without speaking. They were playing the last ounce

in them, and The Maltese Cat had left the goal undefended
to join them. Lutyens gave him every order that he could to
bring him back, but this was the first time in his career that
the little wise grey had ever played polo on his own responsibility, and he was going to make the most of it.

"What are you doing here?" said Hughes, as The Cat
crossed in front of him and rode off an Archangel.

"The Cat's in charge – mind the goal!" shouted Lutyens,
and bowing forward hit the ball full, and followed on, forcing
the Archangels towards their own goal.

"No football," said The Maltese Cat. "Keep the ball by
the boundaries and cramp 'em. Play open order, and drive
'em to the boundaries."

Across and across the ground in big diagonals flew the
ball, and whenever it came to a flying rush and a stroke close
to the boundaries the Archangel ponies moved stiffly. They
did not care to go headlong at a wall of men and carriages,
though if the ground had been open they could have turned
on a sixpence.

"Wriggle her up the sides," said The Cat. "Keep her close
to the crowd. They hate the carriages. Shikast, keep her up
this side."

Shikast and Powell lay left and right behind the uneasy
scuffle of an open scrimmage, and every time the ball was hit
away Shikast galloped on it at such an angle that Powell was
forced to hit it towards the boundary; and when the crowd
had been driven away from that side, Lutyens would send
the ball over to the other, and Shikast would slide desperately
after it till his friends came down to help. It was billiards,
and no football, this time – billiards in a corner pocket; and
the cues were not well chalked.

"If they get us out in the middle of the ground they'll
walk away from us. Dribble her along the sides," cried The
Maltese Cat.

So they dribbled all along the boundary, where a pony
could not come on their right-hand side; and the Archangels
were furious, and the umpires had to neglect the game to

shout at the people to get back, and several blundering mounted policemen tried to restore order, all close to the scrimmage, and the nerves of the Archangels' ponies stretched and broke like cobwebs.

Five or six times an Archangel hit the ball up into the middle of the ground, and each time the watchful Shikast gave Powell his chance to send it back, and after each return, when the dust had settled, men could see that the Skidars had gained a few yards.

Every now and again there were shouts of "Side! Off side!" from the spectators; but the teams were too busy to care, and the umpires had all they could do to keep their maddened ponies clear of the scuffle.

At last Lutyens missed a short easy stroke, and the Skidars had to fly back helter-skelter to protect their own goal, Shikast leading. Powell stopped the ball with a backhander when it was not fifty yards from the goal-posts, and Shikast spun round with a wrench that nearly hoisted Powell out of his saddle.

"Now's our last chance," said The Cat, wheeling like a cockchafer on a pin. "We've got to ride it out. Come along."

Lutyens felt the little chap take a deep breath, and, as it were, crouch under his rider. The ball was hopping towards the right-hand boundary, an Archangel riding for it with both spurs and a whip; but neither spur nor whip would make his pony stretch himself as he neared the crowd. The Maltese Cat glided under his very nose, picking up his hind legs sharp, for there was not a foot to spare between his quarters and the other pony's bit. It was as neat an exhibition as fancy figure-skating. Lutyens hit with all the strength he had left, but the stick slipped a little in his hand, and the ball flew off to the left instead of keeping close to the boundary. Who's Who was far across the ground, thinking hard as he galloped. He repeated stride for stride The Cat's manœuvres with another Archangel pony, nipping the ball away from under his bridle, and clearing his opponent by half a fraction of an inch, for Who's Who was clumsy behind. Then he drove away towards the right as The Maltese Cat came up from the left; and Bamboo held a middle course exactly between them. The three were making a sort of Government-broad-arrow-shaped attack; and there was only the Archangels' back to guard the goal; but immediately behind them were three Archangels racing all they knew, and mixed up with them was Powell sending Shikast along on what he felt was their last hope. It takes a very good man to stand up to the rush of seven crazy ponies in the last quarters of a Cup game, when men are riding with their necks for sale, and the ponies are delirious. The Archangels' back missed his stroke and pulled aside just in time to let the rush go by. Bamboo and Who's Who shortened stride to give The Cat room, and Lutyens got the goal with a clean, smooth, smacking stroke that was heard all over the field. But there was no stopping the ponies. They poured through the goal-posts in one mixed mob, winners and losers together, for the pace had been terrific. The Maltese Cat knew by experience what would happen, and, to save Lutyens, turned to the right with one last effort, that strained a back-sinew beyond hope of repair. As he did so he heard the right-hand goal-post crack as a pony cannoned into it – crack, splinter, and fall like a mast. It had been sawed three parts through in case of accidents, but it upset the pony nevertheless, and he blundered into another, who blundered into the left-hand post, and then there was confusion and dust and wood. Bamboo was lying on the ground, seeing stars; an Archangel pony rolled beside him, breathless and angry; Shikast had sat down dog-fashion to avoid falling over the others, and was sliding along on his little bobtail in a cloud of dust; and Powell was sitting on the ground, hammering with his stick and trying to cheer. All the others were shouting at the top of what was left of their voices, and the men who had been split were shouting too. As soon as the people saw no one was hurt, ten thousand native and English shouted and clapped and yelled, and before any one could stop them the pipers of the Skidars broke on to the ground, with all the native officers and men behind them, and marched up and down, playing a wild Northern tune called "Zakhme Bagán," and through the insolent blaring of the pipes and the high-pitched native yells you could hear the Archangels' band hammering, "For they are all jolly good fellows," and then reproachfully to the losing team, "Ooh, Kafoozalum! Kafoozalum! Kafoozalum!"

Besides all these things and many more, there was a Commander-in-chief, and an Inspector-General of Cavalry, and the principal veterinary officer of all India standing on the top of a regimental coach, yelling like school-boys; and brigadiers and colonels and commissioners, and hundreds of pretty ladies joined the chorus. But The Maltese Cat stood with his head down, wondering how many legs were left to him; and Lutyens watched the men and ponies pick themselves out of the wreck of the two goal-posts, and he patted The Maltese Cat very tenderly.

"I say," said the Captain of the Archangels, spitting a pebble out of his mouth, "will you take three thousand for that pony – as he stands?"

"No, thank you. I've an idea he's saved my life," said Lutyens, getting off and lying down at full length. Both teams were on the ground too, waving their boots in the air, and coughing and drawing deep breaths, as the *saises* ran up to take away the ponies, and an officious water-carrier sprinkled the players with dirty water till they sat up.

"My aunt!" said Powell, rubbing his back, and looking at the stumps of the goal-posts, "that was a game!"

They played it over again, every stroke of it, that night at the big dinner, when the Free-for-All Cup was filled and passed down the table, and emptied and filled again, and everybody made most eloquent speeches. About two in the morning, when there might have been some singing, a wise little, plain little, grey little head looked in through the open door.

"Hurrah! Bring him in," said the Archangels; and his *sais*, who was very happy indeed, patted The Maltese Cat on the flank, and he limped in to the blaze of light and the glittering uniforms, looking for Lutyens. He was used to messes, and men's bedrooms, and places where ponies are not usually encouraged, and in his youth had jumped on and off a mess-table for a bet. So he behaved himself very politely, and ate bread dipped in salt, and was petted all round the table, moving gingerly; and they drank his health, because he had done more to win the Cup than any man or horse on the ground.

That was glory and honour enough for the rest of his days, and The Maltese Cat did not complain much when the veterinary surgeon said that he would be no good for polo any more. When Lutyens married, his wife did not allow him to play, so he was forced to be an umpire; and his pony on these occasions was a flea-bitten grey with a neat polo-tail, lame all round, but desperately quick on his feet, and, as everybody knew, Past Pluperfect Prestissimo Player of the Game.

"IN AMBUSH"

"IN AMBUSH"

I N summer all right-minded boys built huts in the furze-hill behind the College – little lairs whittled out of the heart of the prickly bushes, full of stumps, odd root-ends, and spikes, but, since they were strictly forbidden, palaces of delight. And for the fifth summer in succession, Stalky, McTurk, and Beetle (this was before they reached the dignity of a study) had built like beavers a place of retreat and meditation, where they smoked.

Now, there was nothing in their characters as known to Mr. Prout, their house-master, at all commanding respect; nor did Foxy, the subtle red-haired school Sergeant, trust them. His business was to wear tennis-shoes, carry binoculars, and swoop hawk-like upon evil boys. Had he taken the field alone, that hut would have been raided, for Foxy knew the manners of his quarry; but Providence moved Mr. Prout, whose school-name, derived from the size of his feet, was Hoofer, to investigate on his own account; and it was the cautious Stalky who found the track of his pugs on the very floor of their lair one peaceful afternoon when Stalky would fain have forgotten Prout and his works in a volume of Surtees and a new brierwood pipe. Crusoe, at sight of the footprint, did not act more swiftly than Stalky. He removed the pipes, swept up all loose match-ends, and departed to warn Beetle and McTurk.

But it was characteristic of the boy that he did not approach his allies till he had met and conferred with little Hartopp, President of the Natural History Society, an institution which Stalky held in contempt. Hartopp was more than surprised when the boy meekly, as he knew how, begged to propose himself, Beetle, and McTurk as candidates; confessed to a long-smothered interest in first-flowerings, early butterflies, and new arrivals, and volunteered, if Mr. Hartopp saw fit, to enter on the new life at once. Being a master, Hartopp was suspicious; but he was also an enthusiast, and his gentle little soul had been galled by chance-heard remarks from the three, and specially Beetle. So he was gracious to that repentant sinner, and entered the three names in his book.

Then, and not till then, did Stalky seek Beetle and McTurk in their house form-room. They were stowing away books for a quiet afternoon in the furze, which they called the "wuzzy."

"All up," said Stalky, serenely. "I spotted Heffy's fairy feet round our hut after dinner. 'Blessing they're so big."

"Con-found! Did you hide our pipes?" said Beetle.

"Oh, no. Left 'em in the middle of the hut, of course. What a blind ass you are, Beetle! D'you think nobody thinks but yourself? Well, we can't use the hut any more. Hoofer will be watchin' it."

" 'Bother! Likewise blow!' " said McTurk, thoughtfully, unpacking the volumes with which his chest was cased. The boys carried their libraries between their belt and their collar. "Nice job! This means we're under suspicion for the rest of the term."

"Why? All that Heffy has found is *a* hut. He and Foxy will watch it. It's nothing to do with us; only we mustn't be seen that way for a bit."

"Yes, and where else are we to go?" said Beetle. "You chose that place, too – an' – an' I wanted to read this afternoon."

Stalky sat on a desk drumming his heels on the form.

"You're a despondin' brute, Beetle. Sometimes I think I shall have to drop you altogether. Did you ever know your Uncle Stalky forget you yet? *His rebus infectis* – after I'd seen Heffy's man-tracks marchin' round our hut, I found little Hartopp – *districto ense* – wavin' a butterfly-net. I conciliated Hartopp. 'Told him that you'd read papers to the Bughunters if he'd let you join, Beetle. 'Told him you liked

butterflies, Turkey. Anyhow, I soothed the Hartoffles, and
we're Bug-hunters now."

"What's the good of that?" said Beetle.

"Oh, Turkey, kick him!"

In the interests of science bounds were largely relaxed for
the members of the Natural History Society. They could
wander, if they kept clear of all houses, practically where
they chose; Mr. Hartopp holding himself responsible for
their good conduct.

Beetle began to see this as McTurk began the kicking.

"I'm an ass, Stalky!" he said, guarding the afflicted part.
"*Pax*, Turkey. I'm an ass."

"Don't stop, Turkey. Isn't your Uncle Stalky a great man?"

"Great man," said Beetle.

"All the same bug-huntin's a filthy business," said
McTurk. "How the deuce does one begin?"

"This way," said Stalky, turning to some fags' lockers
behind him. "Fags are dabs at Natural History. Here's young
Braybrooke's botany-case." He flung out a tangle of decayed
roots and adjusted the slide. " 'Gives one no end of a professional air, I think. Here's Clay Minor's geological hammer.
Beetle can carry that. Turkey, you'd better covet a butterfly-
net from somewhere."

"I'm blowed if I do," said McTurk, simply, with immense
feeling. "Beetle, give me the hammer."

"All right. *I'm* not proud. Chuck us down that net on top
of the lockers, Stalky."

"That's all right. It's a collapsible jamboree, too. Beastly
luxurious dogs these fags are. Built like a fishin'-rod. 'Pon
my sainted Sam, but we look the complete Bug-hunters!
Now, listen to your Uncle Stalky! We're goin' along the cliffs
after butterflies. Very few chaps come there. We're goin' to
leg it, too. You'd better leave your book behind."

"Not much!" said Beetle, firmly. "I'm not goin' to be done
out of my fun for a lot of filthy butterflies."

"Then you'll sweat horrid. You'd better carry my Jor-
rocks. 'Twon't make you any hotter."

They all sweated; for Stalky led them at a smart trot west away along the cliffs under the furze-hills, crossing combe after gorsy combe. They took no heed to flying rabbits or fluttering fritillaries, and all that Turkey said of geology was utterly unquotable.

"Are we going to Clovelly?" he puffed at last, and they flung themselves down on the short, springy turf between the drone of the sea below and the light summer wind among the inland trees. They were looking into a combe half full of old, high furze in gay bloom that ran up to a fringe of brambles and a dense wood of mixed timber and hollies. It was as though one-half the combe were filled with golden fire to the cliff's edge. The side nearest to them was open grass, and fairly bristled with notice-boards.

"Fee-rocious old cove, this," said Stalky, reading the near-est. " 'Prosecuted with the utmost rigour of the law. G. M. Dabney, Col., J. P.,' an' all the rest of it. 'Don't seem to me that any chap in his senses would trespass here, does it?"

"You've got to prove damage 'fore you can prosecute for anything! 'Can't prosecute for trespass," said McTurk, whose father held many acres in Ireland. "That's all rot!"

"Glad of that, 'cause this looks like what we wanted. Not straight across, Beetle, you blind lunatic! Any one could spot us half a mile off. This way; and furl up your beastly butter-fly-net."

Beetle disconnected the ring, thrust the net into a pocket, shut up the handle to a two-foot stave, and slid the cane-ring round his waist. Stalky led inland to the wood, which was, perhaps, a quarter of a mile from the sea, and reached the fringe of the brambles.

"Now we can get straight down through the furze, and never show up at all," said the tactician. "Beetle, go ahead and explore. Snf! Snf! Beastly stink of fox somewhere!"

On all fours, save when he clung to his spectacles, Beetle wormed into the gorse, and presently announced between grunts of pain that he had found a very fair fox-track. This was well for Beetle, since Stalky pinched him a tergo. Down that tunnel they crawled. It was evidently a highway for the inhabitants of the combe; and, to their inexpressible joy, ended, at the very edge of the cliff, in a few square feet of dry turf walled and roofed with impenetrable gorse.

"By gum! There isn't a single thing to do except lie down," said Stalky, returning a knife to his pocket. "Look here!"

He parted the tough stems before him, and it was as a window opened on a far view of Lundy, and the deep sea sluggishly nosing the pebbles a couple of hundred feet below. They could hear young jackdaws squawking on the ledges, the hiss and jabber of a nest of hawks somewhere out of sight; and, with great deliberation, Stalky spat on to the back of a young rabbit sunning himself far down where only a cliff-rabbit could have found foothold. Great grey and black gulls screamed against the jackdaws; the heavy-scented acres of bloom round them were alive with low-nesting birds, singing or silent as the shadow of the wheeling hawks passed and returned; and on the naked turf across the combe rabbits thumped and frolicked.

"Whew! What a place! Talk of Natural History; this is it," said Stalky, filling himself a pipe. "Isn't it scrumptious? Good old sea!" He spat again approvingly, and was silent.

McTurk and Beetle had taken out their books and were lying on their stomachs, chin in hand. The sea snored and gurgled; the birds, scattered for the moment by these new animals, returned to their businesses, and the boys read on in the rich, warm, sleepy silence.

"Hullo, here's a keeper," said Stalky, shutting "Handley Cross" cautiously, and peering through the jungle. A man with a gun appeared on the sky-line to the east. "Confound him, he's going to sit down."

"He'd swear we were poachin', too," said Beetle. "What's the good of pheasants' eggs? They're always addled, too."

"Might as well get up to the wood, *I* think," said Stalky. "We don't want G. M. Dabney, Col., J. P., to be bothered about us so soon. Up the wuzzy and keep quiet! He may have followed us, you know."

Beetle was already far up the tunnel. They heard him gasp indescribably: there was the crash of a heavy body leaping through the furze.

"Aie! yeou little red rascal. I see yeou!" The keeper threw the gun to his shoulder, and fired both barrels in their direction. The pellets dusted the dry stems round them as a big fox plunged between Stalky's legs and ran over the cliff-edge.

They said nothing till they reached the wood, torn, dishevelled, hot, but unseen.

"Narrow squeak," said Stalky. "I'll swear some of the pellets went through my hair."

"Did you see him?" said Beetle. "I almost put my hand on him. Wasn't he a whopper! Didn't he stink! Hullo, Turkey, what's the matter? Are you hit?"

McTurk's lean face had turned pearly white; his mouth, generally half open, was tight shut, and his eyes blazed. They had never seen him like this save once in a sad time of civil war.

"Do you know that that was just as bad as murder?" he said, in a grating voice, as he brushed prickles from his head.

"Well, he didn't hit us," said Stalky. "I think it was rather a lark. Here, where are you going?"

"I'm going up to the house, if there is one," said McTurk, pushing through the hollies. "I am going to tell this Colonel Dabney."

"Are you crazy? He'll swear it served us jolly well right. He'll report us. It'll be a public lickin'. Oh, Turkey, don't be an ass! Think of us!"

"You fool!" said McTurk, turning savagely. "D'you suppose I'm thinkin' of *us*? It's the keeper."

"He's cracked," said Beetle, miserably, as they followed. Indeed, this was a new Turkey – a haughty, angular, nose-lifted Turkey – whom they accompanied through a shrubbery on to a lawn, where a white-whiskered old gentleman

with a cleek was alternately putting and blaspheming vigor-
ously.

"Are you Colonel Dabney?" McTurk began in this new
creaking voice of his.

"I — I am, and —" his eyes travelled up and down the boy
— "who — what the devil d'you want? Ye've been disturbing
my pheasants. Don't attempt to deny it. Ye needn't laugh at
it." (McTurk's not too lovely features had twisted themselves
into a horrible sneer at the word pheasant.) "You've been
birds'-nesting. You needn't hide your hat. I can see that you
belong to the College. Don't attempt to deny it. Ye do! Your
name and number at once, sir. Ye want to speak to me — Eh?
You saw my notice-boards? Must have. Don't attempt to
deny it. Ye did! Damnable! Oh, damnable!"

He choked with emotion. McTurk's heel tapped the
lawn and he stuttered a little — two sure signs that he was
losing his temper. But why should he, the offender, be
angry?

"Lo-look here, sir. Do — do you shoot foxes? Because, if
you don't, your keeper does. We've seen him! I do-don't care
what you call us — but it's an awful thing. It's the ruin of
good feelin' among neighbours. A ma-man ought to say once
and for all how he stands about preservin'. It's worse than
murder, because there's no legal remedy." McTurk was
quoting confusedly from his father, while the old gentleman
made noises in his throat.

"Do you know who I am?" he gurgled at last; Stalky and
Beetle quaking.

"No, sorr, nor do I care if ye belonged to the Castle itself.
Answer me now, as one gentleman to another. Do ye shoot
foxes or do ye not?"

And four years before Stalky and Beetle had carefully
kicked McTurk out of his Irish dialect! Assuredly he had
gone mad or taken a sunstroke, and as assuredly he would be
slain — once by the old gentleman and once by the Head. A
public licking for the three was the least they could expect.
Yet — if their eyes and ears were to be trusted — the old

gentleman had collapsed. It might be a lull before the storm, but —

"I do not." He was still gurgling.

"Then you must sack your keeper. He's not fit to live in the same county with a God-fearin' fox. An' a vixen, too – at this time o' year!"

"Did ye come up on purpose to tell me this?"

"Of course I did, ye silly man," with a stamp of the foot. "Would you not have done as much for me if you'd seen that thing happen on my land, now?"

Forgotten – forgotten was the College and the decency due to elders! McTurk was treading again the barren purple mountains of the rainy West coast, where in his holidays he was viceroy of four thousand naked acres, only son of a three-hundred-year-old house, lord of a crazy fishing-boat, and the idol of his father's shiftless tenantry. It was the landed man speaking to his equal – deep calling to deep – and the old gentleman acknowledged the cry.

"I apologise," said he. "I apologise unreservedly – to you, and to the Old Country. Now, will you be good enough to tell me your story?"

"We were in your combe," McTurk began, and he told his tale alternately as a schoolboy and, when the iniquity of the thing overcame him, as an indignant squire; concluding: "So you see he must be in the habit of it. I – we – one never wants to accuse a neighbour's man; but I took the liberty in this case —"

"I see. Quite so. For a reason ye had. Infamous – oh, infamous!" The two had fallen into step beside each other on the lawn, and Colonel Dabney was talking as one man to another. "This comes of promoting a fisherman – a fisherman – from his lobster-pots. It's enough to ruin the reputation of an archangel. Don't attempt to deny it. It is! Your father has brought you up well. He has. I'd much like the pleasure of his acquaintance. Very much, indeed. And these young gentlemen? English they are. Don't attempt to deny it. They came up with you, too? Extraordinary! Extraordinary, now!

In the present state of education I shouldn't have thought any three boys would be well enough grounded. . . . But out of the mouths of – No – no! Not that by any odds. Don't attempt to deny it. Ye're not! Sherry always catches me under the liver, but – beer, now? Eh? What d'you say to beer, and something to eat? It's long since I was a boy – abominable nuisances; but exceptions prove the rule. And a vixen, too!"

They were fed on the terrace by a grey-haired housekeeper. Stalky and Beetle merely ate, but McTurk with bright eyes continued a free and lofty discourse; and ever the old gentleman treated him as a brother.

"My dear man, of *course* ye can come again. Did I not say exceptions prove the rule? The lower combe? Man, dear, anywhere ye please, so long as you do not disturb my pheasants. The two are not incompatible. Don't attempt to deny it. They're not! I'll never allow another gun, though. Come and go as ye please. I'll not see you, and ye needn't see me. Ye've been well brought up. Another glass of beer, now? I tell you a fisherman he was and a fisherman he shall be to-night again. He shall! Wish I could drown him. I'll convoy you to the Lodge. My people are not precisely – ah – broke to boy, but they'll know *you* again."

He dismissed them with many compliments by the high Lodge-gate in the split-oak park palings, and they stood still; even Stalky, who had played second, not to say a dumb, fiddle, regarding McTurk as one from another world. The two glasses of strong home-brewed had brought a melancholy upon the boy, for, slowly strolling with his hands in his pockets, he crooned: – "Oh, Paddy dear, and did ye hear the news that's goin' round?"

Under other circumstances Stalky and Beetle would have fallen upon him, for that song was barred utterly – anathema – the sin of witchcraft. But seeing what he had wrought, they danced round him in silence, waiting till it pleased him to touch earth.

The tea-bell rang when they were still half a mile from

College. McTurk shivered and came out of dreams. The glory of his holiday estate had left him. He was a Colleger of the College, speaking English once more.

"Turkey, it was immense!" said Stalky, generously. "I didn't know you had it in you. You've got us a hut for the rest of the term, where we simply *can't* be collared. Fids! Fids! Oh, Fids! I gloat! Hear me gloat!"

They spun wildly on their heels, jodelling after the accepted manner of a "gloat," which is not unremotely allied to the primitive man's song of triumph, and dropped down the hill by the path from the gasometer just in time to meet their house-master, who had spent the afternoon watching their abandoned hut in the "wuzzy."

Unluckily, all Mr. Prout's imagination leaned to the darker side of life, and he looked on those young-eyed cherubims most sourly. Boys that he understood attended house-matches and could be accounted for at any moment. But he had heard McTurk openly deride cricket – even house-matches; Beetle's views on the honour of the house he knew were incendiary; and he could never tell when the soft and smiling Stalky was laughing at him. Consequently – since human nature is what it is – those boys had been doing wrong somewhere. He hoped it was nothing very serious, but . . .

"*Ti-ra-la-la-i-tu!* I gloat! Hear me!" Stalky, still on his heels, whirled like a dancing dervish to the dining-hall.

"*Ti-ra-la-la-i-tu!* I gloat! Hear me!" Beetle spun behind him with outstretched arms.

"*Ti-ra-la-la-i-tu!* I gloat! Hear me!" McTurk's voice cracked.

Now was there or was there not a distinct flavour of beer as they shot past Mr. Prout?

He was unlucky in that his conscience as a house-master impelled him to consult his associates. Had he taken his pipe and his troubles to little Hartopp's rooms he would, perhaps, have been saved confusion, for Hartopp believed in boys, and knew something about them. His fate led him to King, a fellow house-master, no friend of his, but a zealous hater of Stalky & Co.

"Ah-haa!" said King, rubbing his hands when the tale was told. "Curious! Now *my* house never dreamed of doing these things."

"But you see I've no proof, exactly."

"Proof? With the egregious Beetle! As if one wanted it! I suppose it is not impossible for the Sergeant to supply it? Foxy is considered at least a match for any evasive boy in my house. Of course they were smoking and drinking somewhere. That type of boy always does. They think it manly."

"But they've no following in the school, and they are distinctly – er – brutal to their juniors," said Prout, who had from a distance seen Beetle return, with interest, his butterfly-net to a tearful fag.

"Ah! They consider themselves superior to ordinary delights. Self-sufficient little animals! There's something in McTurk's Hibernian sneer that would make *me* a little annoyed. And they are so careful to avoid all overt acts, too. It's sheer calculated insolence. I am strongly opposed, as you know, to interfering with another man's house; but they need a lesson, Prout. They need a sharp lesson, if only to bring down their overweening self-conceit. Were I you, I should devote myself for a week to their little performances. Boys of that order – and I may flatter myself, but I think I know boys – don't join the Bug-hunters for love. Tell the Sergeant to keep his eye open; and, of course, in my peregrinations I may casually keep mine open, too."

"*Ti-ra-la-la-i-tu!* I gloat! Hear me!" far down the corridor.

"Disgusting!" said King. "Where do they pick up these obscene noises? One sharp lesson is what they want."

The boys did not concern themselves with lessons for the next few days. They had all Colonel Dabney's estate to play with, and they explored it with the stealth of Red Indians and the accuracy of burglars. They could enter either by the Lodge-gates on the upper road – they were careful to

ingratiate themselves with the Lodge-keeper and his wife –
drop down into the combe, and return along the cliffs; or
they could begin at the combe, and climb up into the road.

They were careful not to cross the Colonel's path – he had
served his turn, and they would not outwear their welcome
– nor did they show up on the sky-line when they could
move in cover. The shelter of the gorse by the cliff-edge was
their chosen retreat. Beetle christened it the Pleasant Isle of
Aves, for the peace and the shelter of it; and here, the pipes
and tobacco once cachéd in a convenient ledge an arm's
length down the cliff, their position was legally unassailable.

For, observe, Colonel Dabney had not invited them to
enter his house. Therefore, they did not need to ask specific
leave to go visiting; and school rules were strict on that point.
He had merely thrown open his grounds to them; and, since
they were lawful Bug-hunters, their extended bounds ran up
to his notice-boards in the combe and his Lodge-gates on the
hill.

They were amazed at their own virtue.

"And even if it wasn't," said Stalky, flat on his back,
staring into the blue. "Even suppose we were miles out of
bounds, no one could get at us through this wuzzy, unless he
knew the tunnel. Isn't this better than lyin' up just behind
the Coll – in a blue funk every time we had a smoke? Isn't
your Uncle Stalky —"

"No," said Beetle – he was stretched at the edge of the
cliff spitting thoughtfully. "We've got to thank Turkey for
this. Turkey is the Great Man. Turkey, dear, you're distressing Heffles."

"Gloomy old ass!" said McTurk, deep in a book.

"They've got us under suspicion," said Stalky. "Hoophats
is so suspicious somehow; and Foxy always makes every stalk
he does a sort of – sort of —"

"Scalp," said Beetle. "Foxy's a giddy Chingangook."

"Poor Foxy," said Stalky. "He's goin' to catch us one of
these days. 'Said to me in the Gym last night, 'I've got my
eye on you, Mister Corkran. I'm only warning you for your

good.' Then I said: 'Well, you jolly well take it off again, or you'll get into trouble. I'm only warnin' you for your good.' Foxy was wrath."

"Yes, but it's only fair sport for Foxy," said Beetle. "It's Hefflelinga that has the evil mind. 'Shouldn't wonder if he thought we got tight."

"I never got squiffy but once – that was in the holidays," said Stalky, reflectively; "an' it made me horrid sick. 'Pon my sacred Sam, though, it's enough to drive a man to drink, havin' an animal like Hoof for house-master."

"If we attended the matches an' yelled, 'Well hit, sir,' an' stood on one leg an' grinned every time Heffy said, 'So ho, my sons. Is it thus?' an' said, 'Yes, sir,' an' 'No, sir,' an' 'O, sir,' an' 'Please, sir,' like a lot o' filthy fa-ags, Heffy 'ud think no end of us," said McTurk, with a sneer.

"Too late to begin that."

"It's all right. The Hefflelinga means well. *But* he is an ass. *And* we show him that we think he's an ass. An' *so* Heffy don't love us. 'Told me last night after prayers that he was *in loco parentis*," Beetle grunted.

"The deuce he did!" cried Stalky. "That means he's ma-turin' something unusual dam' mean. Last time he told me that he gave me three hundred lines for dancin' the cachucha in Number Ten dormitory. *Loco parentis*, by gum! But what's the odds as long as you're 'appy? *We're* all right."

They were, and their very rightness puzzled Prout, King, and the Sergeant. Boys with bad consciences show it. They slink out past the Fives Court in haste, and smile nervously when questioned. They return, disordered, in bare time to save a call-over. They nod and wink and giggle one to the other, scattering at the approach of a master. But Stalky and his allies had long outlived these manifestations of youth. They strolled forth unconcernedly, and returned in excellent shape after a light refreshment of strawberries and cream at the Lodge.

The Lodge-keeper had been promoted to keeper, *vice* the murderous fisherman, and his wife made much of the boys.

The man, too, gave them a squirrel, which they presented to the Natural History Society; thereby checkmating little Hartopp, who wished to know what they were doing for Science. Foxy faithfully worked some deep Devon lanes behind a lonely cross-roads inn; and it was curious that Prout and King, members of Common-room seldom friendly, walked together in the same direction – that is to say, northeast. Now, the Pleasant Isle of Aves lay due southwest.

"They're deep – day-vilish deep," said Stalky. "Why are they drawin' those covers?"

"Me," said Beetle, sweetly. "I asked Foxy if he had ever tasted the beer there. That was enough for Foxy, and it cheered him up a little. He and Heffy were sniffin' round our old hut so long I thought they'd like a change."

"Well, it can't last for ever," said Stalky. "Heffy's bankin' up like a thunder-cloud, an' King goes rubbin' his beastly hands, an' grinnin' like a hyena. It's shockin' demoralisin' for King. He'll burst some day."

That day came a little sooner than they expected – came when the Sergeant, whose duty it was to collect defaulters, did not attend an afternoon call-over.

"Tired of pubs, eh? He's gone up to the top of the hill with his binoculars to spot us," said Stalky. "Wonder he didn't think of that before. Did you see old Heffy cock his eye at us when we answered our names? Heffy's in it, too. *Ti-ra-la-la-i-tu!* I gloat! Hear me! Come on!"

"Aves?" said Beetle.

"Of course, but I'm not smokin' *aujourd'hui. Parce que je* jolly well *pense* that we'll be *suivi*. We'll go along the cliffs, slow, an' give Foxy lots of time to parallel us above."

They strolled towards the swimming-baths, and presently overtook King.

"Oh, don't let *me* interrupt you," he said. "Engaged in scientific pursuits, of course? I trust you will enjoy yourselves, my young friends."

"You see!" said Stalky, when they were out of ear-shot. "He *can't* keep a secret. He's followin' to cut off our line of retreat. He'll wait at the baths till Heffy comes along. They've tried every blessed place except along the cliffs, and now they think they've bottled us. No need to hurry."

They walked leisurely over the combes till they reached the line of notice-boards.

"Listen a shake. Foxy's up wind comin' down-hill like beans. When you hear him move in the bushes, go straight across to Aves. They want to catch us *flagrante delicto*."

They dived into the gorse at right angles to the tunnel, openly crossing the grass, and lay still in Aves.

"What did I tell you?" Stalky carefully put away the pipes and tobacco. The Sergeant, out of breath, was leaning against the fence, raking the furze with his binoculars, but he might as well have tried to see through a sand-bag. Anon, Prout and King appeared behind him. They conferred.

"Aha! Foxy don't like the notice-boards, and he don't like the prickles either. Now we'll cut up the tunnel and go to the Lodge. Hullo! They've sent Foxy into cover."

The Sergeant was waist-deep in crackling, swaying furze, his ears filled with the noise of his own progress. The boys reached the shelter of the wood, and looked down through a belt of hollies.

"Hellish noise!" said Stalky, critically. " 'Don't think Colonel Dabney will like it. I move we go into the Lodge and get something to eat. We might as well see the fun out."

Suddenly the keeper passed them at a trot.

"Who'm they to combe-bottom for Lard's sake? Master'll be crazy," he said.

"Poachers simly," Stalky replied in the broad Devon that was the boy's *langue de guerre*.

"I'll poach 'em to raights!" He dropped into the funnel-like combe, which presently began to fill with noises, notably King's voice crying: "Go on, Sergeant! Leave him alone, you, sir. He is executing *my* orders."

"Who'm yeou to give arders here, gingy whiskers? Yeou come up to the master. Come out o' that wuzzy! [This is to the Sergeant.] Yiss, I reckon us knows the boys yeou'm after.

They've tu long ears an' vuzzy bellies, an' you nippies they
in yeour pockets when they'm dead. Come on up to master!
He'll boy yeou all yeou'm a mind to. Yeou other folk bide
your side fence."

"Explain to the proprietor. You can explain, Sergeant,"
shouted King. Evidently the Sergeant had surrendered to the
major force.

Beetle lay at full length on the turf behind the Lodge,
literally biting the earth in spasms of joy.

Stalky kicked him upright. There was nothing of levity
about Stalky or McTurk save a stray muscle twitching on the
cheek.

They tapped at the Lodge-door, where they were always
welcome.

"Come yeou right in an' set down, my little dearrs,"
said the woman. "They'll niver touch my man. He'll poach
'em to rights. Iss fai! Fresh berries an' cream. Us Dartymoor
folk niver forget their friends. But them Bidevor poachers,
they've no hem to their garments. Sugar? My man he've
digged a badger for yeou, my dearrs. 'Tis in the linhay in
a box."

"Us'll take un with us when we'm finished here. I reckon
yeou'm busy. We'll bide here an' – 'tis washin' day with
yeou, simly," said Stalky. "We'm no company to make all
vitty for. Never yeou mind us. Yiss. There's plenty cream."

The woman withdrew, wiping her pink hands on her
apron, and left them in the parlour. There was a scuffle of
feet on the gravel outside the heavily leaded diamond panes,
and then the voice of Colonel Dabney, something clearer
than a bugle.

"Ye can read? You've eyes in your head? Don't attempt
to deny it. Ye have!"

Beetle snatched a crochet-work antimacassar from the
shiny horsehair sofa, stuffed it into his mouth, and rolled out
of sight.

"You saw my notice-boards. Your duty? Curse your im-
pudence, sir. Your duty was to keep off my grounds. Talk of

duty to *me*! Why – why – why, ye misbegotten poacher, ye'll be teachin' me my A B C next! Roarin' like a bull in the bushes down there! Boys? Boys? Boys? Keep your boys at home, then! *I'm* not responsible for your boys! But I don't believe it – I don't believe a word of it. Ye've a furtive look in your eye – a furtive, sneakin', poachin' look in your eye, that 'ud ruin the reputation of an archangel! Don't attempt to deny it! Ye have! A sergeant? More shame to you, then, an' the worst bargain Her Majesty ever made! A sergeant, to run about the country poachin' – on your pension! Damnable! Oh, damnable! But I'll be considerate. I'll be merciful. By gad, I'll be the very essence o' humanity! Did ye, or did ye not, see my notice-boards? Don't attempt to deny it! Ye did. Silence, Sergeant!"

Twenty-one years in the army had left their mark on Foxy. He obeyed.

"Now. March!"

The high Lodge-gate shut with a clang. "My duty! A sergeant to tell me my duty!" puffed Colonel Dabney. "Good Lard! more sergeants!"

"It's King! It's King!" gulped Stalky, his head on the horsehair pillow. McTurk was eating the rag-carpet before the speckless hearth, and the sofa heaved to the emotions of Beetle. Through the thick glass the figures without showed blue, distorted, and menacing.

"I – I protest against this outrage." King had evidently been running uphill. "The man was entirely within his duty. Let – let me give you my card."

"He's in flannels!" Stalky buried his head again.

"Unfortunately – *most* unfortunately – I have not one with me, but my name is King, sir, a house-master of the College, and you will find me prepared – fully prepared – to answer for this man's action. We've seen three —"

"*Did* ye see my notice-boards?"

"I admit we did; but under the circumstances —"

"I stand *in loco parentis*." Prout's deep voice was added to the discussion. They could hear him pant.

"F'what?" Colonel Dabney was growing more and more Irish.

"I'm responsible for the boys under my charge."

"Ye are, are ye? Then all I can say is that ye set them a very bad example – a dam' bad example, if I may say so. I do not own your boys. I've not seen your boys, an' I tell you that if there was a boy grinnin' in every bush on the place, *still* ye've no shadow of a right here, comin' up from the combe that way, an' frightenin' everything in it. Don't attempt to deny it. Ye did. Ye should have come to the Lodge an' seen me like Christians, instead of chasin' your dam' boys through the length and breadth of my covers. *In loco parentis* ye are? Well, I've not forgotten my Latin either, an' I'll say to you: '*Quis custodiet ipsos custodes*.' If the masters trespass, how can we blame the boys?"

"But if I could speak to you privately," said Prout.

"I'll have nothing private with you! Ye can be as private as ye please on the other side o' that gate an' – I wish ye a very good afternoon."

A second time the gate clanged. They waited till Colonel Dabney had returned to the house, and fell into one another's arms, crowing for breath.

"Oh, my Soul! Oh, my King! Oh, my Heffy! Oh, my Foxy! Zeal, all zeal, Mr. Simple." Stalky wiped his eyes. "Oh! Oh! Oh! – 'I *did* boil the exciseman!' We must get out of this or we'll be late for tea."

"Ge-ge-get the badger and make little Hartopp happy. Ma-ma-make 'em all happy," sobbed McTurk, groping for the door and kicking the prostrate Beetle before him.

They found the beast in an evil-smelling box, left two half-crowns for payment, and staggered home. Only the badger grunted most marvellous like Colonel Dabney, and they dropped him twice or thrice with shrieks of helpless laughter. They were but imperfectly recovered when Foxy met them by the Fives Court with word that they were to go up to their dormitory and wait till sent for.

"Well, take this box to Mr. Hartopp's rooms, then. We've

done something for the Natural History Society, at any rate," said Beetle.

" 'Fraid that won't save you, young gen'elmen," Foxy answered, in an awful voice. He was sorely ruffled in his mind.

"All sereno, Foxibus." Stalky had reached the extreme stage of hiccups. "We – we'll never desert you, Foxy. Hounds choppin' foxes in cover is more a proof of vice, ain't it? . . . No, you're right. I'm – I'm not quite well."

"They've gone a bit too far this time," Foxy thought to himself. "Very far gone, I'd say, excep' there was no smell of liquor. An' yet it isn't like 'em – somehow. King and Prout they 'ad their dressin'-down same as me. That's one comfort."

"Now, we must pull up," said Stalky, rising from the bed on which he had thrown himself. "We're injured innocence – as usual. We don't know what we've been sent up here for, do we?"

"No explanation. Deprived of tea. Public disgrace before the house," said McTurk, whose eyes were running over. "It's dam' serious."

"Well, hold on, till King loses his temper," said Beetle. "He's a libellous old rip, an' he'll be in a ravin' paddywhack. Prout's too beastly cautious. Keep your eye on King, and, if he gives us a chance, appeal to the Head. That always makes 'em sick."

They were summoned to their house-master's study, King and Foxy supporting Prout, and Foxy had three canes under his arm. King leered triumphantly, for there were tears, undried tears of mirth, on the boys' cheeks. Then the examination began.

Yes, they had walked along the cliffs. Yes, they had entered Colonel Dabney's grounds. Yes, they had seen the notice-boards (at this point Beetle sputtered hysterically). For what purpose had they entered Colonel Dabney's grounds? "Well, sir, there was a badger."

Here King, who loathed the Natural History Society

because he did not like Hartopp, could no longer be restrained. He begged them not to add mendacity to open insolence. But the badger was in Mr. Hartopp's rooms, sir. The Sergeant had kindly taken it up for them. That disposed of the badger, and the temporary check brought King's temper to boiling-point. They could hear his foot on the floor while Prout prepared his lumbering inquiries. They had settled into their stride now. Their eyes ceased to sparkle; their faces were blank; their hands hung beside them without a twitch. They were learning, at the expense of a fellow-countryman, the lesson of their race, which is to put away all emotion and entrap the alien at the proper time.

So far good. King was importing himself more freely into the trial, being vengeful where Prout was grieved. They knew the penalties of trespassing? With a fine show of irresolution, Stalky admitted that he had gathered some information vaguely bearing on this head, but he thought—The sentence was dragged out to the uttermost: Stalky did not wish to play his trump with such an opponent. Mr. King desired no buts, nor was he interested in Stalky's evasions. They, on the other hand, might be interested in his poor views. Boys who crept – who sneaked – who lurked – out of bounds, even the generous bounds of the Natural History Society, which they had falsely joined as a cloak for their misdeeds – their vices – their villainies – their immoralities —

"He'll break cover in a minute," said Stalky to himself. "Then we'll run into him before he gets away."

Such boys, scabrous boys, moral lepers – the current of his words was carrying King off his feet – evil-speakers, liars, slow-bellies – yea, incipient drunkards . . .

He was merely working up to a peroration, and the boys knew it; but McTurk cut through the frothing sentence, the others echoing:

"I appeal to the Head, sir."

"I appeal to the Head, sir."

"I appeal to the Head, sir."

It was their unquestioned right. Drunkenness meant expulsion after a public flogging. They had been accused of it. The case was the Head's, and the Head's alone.

"Thou hast appealed unto Cæsar: unto Cæsar shalt thou go." They had heard that sentence once or twice before in their careers. "None the less," said King, uneasily, "you would be better advised to abide by our decision, my young friends."

"Are we allowed to associate with the rest of the school till we see the Head, sir?" said McTurk to his house-master, disregarding King. This at once lifted the situation to its loftiest plane. Moreover, it meant no word, for moral leprosy was strictly quarantined, and the Head never executed judgment till twenty-four cold hours later.

"Well – er – if you persist in your defiant attitude," said King, with a loving look at the canes under Foxy's arm. "There is no alternative."

Ten minutes later the news was over the whole school. Stalky & Co. had fallen at last – fallen by drink. They had been drinking. They had returned blind-drunk from a hut. They were even now lying hopelessly intoxicated on the dormitory floor. A few bold spirits crept up to look, and received boots about the head from the criminals.

"We've got him – got him on the Caudine Toasting-Fork!" said Stalky, after those hints were taken. "King'll have to prove his charges up to the giddy hilt."

"Too much ticklee, him bust," Beetle quoted from a book of his reading. "Didn't I say he'd go pop if we lat un bide?"

"No prep., either, O ye incipient drunkards," said McTurk, "and it's trig night, too. Hullo! Here's our dear friend Foxy. More tortures, Foxibus?"

"I've brought you something to eat, young gentlemen," said the Sergeant from behind a crowded tray. Their wars had ever been waged without malice, and a suspicion floated in Foxy's mind that boys who allowed themselves to be tracked so easily might, perhaps, hold something in reserve.

Foxy had served through the Mutiny, when early and accurate information was worth much.

"I – I noticed you 'adn't 'ad anything to eat, an' I spoke to Gumbly, an' he said you wasn't exactly cut off from supplies. So I brought up this. It's your potted 'am tin, ain't it, Mr. Corkran?"

"Why, Foxibus, you're a brick," said Stalky. "I didn't think you had this much – what's the word, Beetle?"

"Bowels," Beetle replied promptly. "Thank you, Sergeant. That's young Carter's potted ham, though."

"There was a C on it. I thought it was Mr. Corkran's. This is a very serious business, young gentlemen. That's what it is. I didn't know, perhaps, but there might be something on your side which you hadn't said to Mr. King or Mr. Prout, maybe."

"There is. Heaps, Foxibus." This from Stalky through a full mouth.

"Then you see, if that was the case, it seemed to me I might represent it, quiet so to say, to the 'Ead when he asks me about it. I've got to take 'im the charges to-night, an' – it looks bad on the face of it."

" 'Trocious bad, Foxy. Twenty-seven cuts in the Gym before all the school, and public expulsion. 'Wine is a mocker, strong drink is ragin',' " quoth Beetles.

"It's nothin' to make fun of, young gentlemen. I 'ave to go to the 'Ead with the charges. An' – an' you mayn't be aware, per'aps, that I was followin' you this afternoon; havin' my suspicions."

"Did ye see the notice-boards?" croaked McTurk, in the very brogue of Colonel Dabney.

"Ye've eyes in your head. Don't attempt to deny it. Ye did!" said Beetle.

"A sergeant! To run about poachin' on your pension! Damnable! Oh, damnable!" said Stalky, without pity.

"Good Lord!" said the Sergeant, sitting heavily upon a bed. "Where – where the devil *was* you? I might ha' known it was a do – somewhere."

"Oh, you clever maniac!" Stalky resumed. "We mayn't be aware you were followin' us this afternoon, mayn't we? 'Thought you were stalkin' us, eh? Why, we led you bung into it, of course. Colonel Dabney – don't you think he's a nice man, Foxy? – Colonel Dabney's our pet particular friend. We've been goin' there for weeks and weeks. He invited us. You and your duty! Curse your duty, sir! Your duty was to keep off his covers."

"You'll never be able to hold up your head again, Foxy. The fags'll hoot at you," said Beetle. "Think of your giddy prestige!"

The Sergeant was thinking – hard.

"Look 'ere, young gentlemen," he said earnestly. "You aren't surely ever goin' to tell, are you? Wasn't Mr. Prout and Mr. King in – in it too?"

"Foxibusculus, they *was*. They was – singular horrid. Caught it worse than you. We heard every word of it. You got off easy, considerin'. If I'd been Dabney I swear I'd ha' quodded you. I think I'll suggest it to him to-morrow."

"An' it's all goin' up to the 'Ead. Oh, Good Lord!"

"Every giddy word of it, my Chingangook," said Beetle, dancing. "Why shouldn't it? *We've* done nothing wrong. *We* ain't poachers. *We* didn't cut about blastin' the characters of poor, innocent boys – sayin' they were drunk."

"That I didn't," said Foxy. "I – I only said that you be'aved uncommon odd when you come back with that badger. Mr. King may have taken the wrong hint from that."

" 'Course he did; an' he'll jolly well shove all the blame on you when he finds out he's wrong. We know King, if you don't. I'm ashamed of you. You ain't fit to be a sergeant," said McTurk.

"Not with three thorough-goin' young devils like you, I ain't. I've been had. I've been ambuscaded. Horse, foot, an' guns, I've been had, an' – an' there'll be no holdin' the junior forms after this. M'r'over, the 'Ead will send me with a note to Colonel Dabney to ask if what you say about bein' invited was true."

"Then you'd better go in by the Lodge-gates this time, instead of chasin' your dam' boys – oh, that was the Epistle to King – so it was. We-el, Foxy?" Stalky put his chin on his hands and regarded the victim with deep delight.

"*Ti-ra-la-la-i-tu!* I gloat! Hear me!" said McTurk. "Foxy brought us tea when we were moral lepers. Foxy has a heart. Foxy has been in the Army, too."

"I wish I'd ha' had you in my company, young gentlemen," said the Sergeant from the depths of his heart; "I'd ha' given you something."

"Silence at drum-head court-martial," McTurk went on. "I'm advocate for the prisoner; and, besides, this is much too good to tell all the other brutes in the Coll. They'd *never* understand. They play cricket, and say: 'Yes, sir,' and 'O, sir,' and 'No, sir.' "

"Never mind that. Go ahead," said Stalky.

"Well, Foxy's a good little chap when he does not esteem himself so as to be clever."

" 'Take not out your 'ounds on a werry windy day,' " Stalky struck in. "*I* don't care if you let him off."

"Nor me," said Beetle. "Heffy is my only joy – Heffy and King."

"I 'ad to do it," said the Sergeant, plaintively.

"Right, O! Led away by bad companions in the execution of his duty or – or words to that effect. You're dismissed with a reprimand, Foxy. *We* won't tell about *you*. I swear we won't," McTurk concluded. "Bad for the discipline of the school. Horrid bad."

"Well," said the Sergeant, gathering up the tea-things, "knowin' what I know o' the young dev – gentlemen of the College, I'm very glad to 'ear it. But what am I to tell the 'Ead?"

"Anything you jolly well please, Foxy. *We* aren't the criminals."

To say that the Head was annoyed when the Sergeant appeared after dinner with the day's crime-sheet would be putting it mildly.

"Corkran, McTurk & Co., I see. Bounds as usual. Hullo! What the deuce is this? Suspicion of drinking. Whose charge?"

"Mr. King's, sir. I caught 'em out of bounds, sir; at least that was 'ow it looked. But there's a lot be'ind, sir." The Sergeant was evidently troubled.

"Go on," said the Head. "Let us have your version."

He and the Sergeant had dealt with one another for some seven years; and the Head knew that Mr. King's statements depended very largely on Mr. King's temper.

"I thought they were out of bounds along the cliffs. But it come out they wasn't, sir. I saw them go into Colonel Dabney's woods, and – Mr. King and Mr. Prout come along – and – the fact was, sir, we was mistook for poachers by Colonel Dabney's people – Mr. King and Mr. Prout and me. There was some words, sir, on both sides. The young gentlemen slipped 'ome somehow, and they seemed 'ighly humorous, sir. Mr. King was mistook by Colonel Dabney himself – Colonel Dabney bein' strict. Then they preferred to come straight to you, sir, on account of what – what Mr. King may 'ave said about their 'abits afterwards in Mr. Prout's study. I only said they was 'ighly humorous, laughin' an' gigglin', an' a bit above 'emselves. They've since told me, sir, in a humorous way, that they was invited by Colonel Dabney to go into 'is woods."

"I see. They didn't tell their house-master that, of course."

"They took up Mr. King on appeal just as soon as he spoke about their – 'abits. Put in the appeal at once, sir, an' asked to be sent to the dormitory waitin' for you. I've since gathered, sir, in their humorous way, sir, that some'ow or other they've 'eard about every word Colonel Dabney said to Mr. King and Mr. Prout when he mistook 'em for poachers. I – I might ha' known when they led me on so that they 'eld the inner line of communications. It's – it's a plain do, sir, if you ask *me*; an' they're gloatin' over it in the dormitory."

The Head saw – saw even to the uttermost farthing – and his mouth twitched a little under his moustache.

"Send them to me at once, Sergeant. This case needn't wait over."

"Good evening," said he when the three appeared under escort. "I want your undivided attention for a few minutes. You've known me for five years, and I've known you for – twenty-five. I think we understand one another perfectly. I am now going to pay you a tremendous compliment (the brown one, please, Sergeant. Thanks. You needn't wait). I'm going to execute you without rhyme, Beetle, or reason. I know you went to Colonel Dabney's covers because you were invited. I'm not even going to send the Sergeant with a note to ask if your statement is true; because I am convinced that on this occasion you have adhered strictly to the truth. I know, too, that you were not drinking. (You can take off that virtuous expression, McTurk, or I shall begin to fear you don't understand me.) There is not a flaw in any of your characters. And that is why I am going to perpetrate a howling injustice. Your reputations have been injured, haven't they? You have been disgraced before the house, haven't you? You have a peculiarly keen regard for the honour of your house, haven't you? Well, *now* I am going to lick you."

Six apiece was their portion upon that word.

"And this I think" – the Head replaced the cane, and flung the written charge into the waste-paper basket – "covers the situation. When you find a variation from the normal – this will be useful to you in later life – always meet him in an abnormal way. And that reminds me. There are a pile of paper-backs on that shelf. You can borrow them if you put them back. I don't think they'll take any harm from being read in the open. They smell of tobacco rather. You will go to prep. this evening as usual. Good night," said that amazing man.

"Good night, and thank you, sir."

"I swear I'll pray for the Head to-night," said Beetle.

"Those last two cuts were just flicks on my collar. There's a 'Monte Cristo' in that lower shelf. I saw it. Bags I, next time we go to Aves!"

"Dearr man!" said McTurk. "No gating. No impots. No beastly questions. All settled. Hullo! what's King goin' in to him for – King and Prout?"

Whatever the nature of that interview, it did not improve either King's or Prout's ruffled plumes, for, when they came out of the Head's house, six eyes noted that the one was red and blue with emotion as to his nose, and that the other was sweating profusely. That sight compensated them amply for the Imperial Jaw with which they were favoured by the two. It seems – and who so astonished as they? – that they had held back material facts; that they were guilty both of *suppressio veri* and *suggestio falsi* (well-known gods against whom they often offended); further, that they were malignant in their dispositions, untrustworthy in their characters, pernicious and revolutionary in their influences, abandoned to the devils of wilfulness, pride, and a most intolerable conceit. Ninthly, and lastly, they were to have a care and to be very careful.

They were careful, as only boys can be when there is a hurt to be inflicted. They waited through one suffocating week till Prout and King were their royal selves again; waited till there was a house-match – their own house, too – in which Prout was taking part; waited, further, till he had buckled on his pads in the pavilion and stood ready to go forth. King was scoring at the window, and the three sat on a bench without.

Said Stalky to Beetle: "I say, Beetle, *quis custodiet ipsos custodes?*"

"Don't ask me," said Beetle. "I'll have nothin' private with you. Ye can be as private as ye please the other end of the bench; and I wish ye a very good afternoon."

McTurk yawned.

"Well, ye should ha' come up to the Lodge like Christians instead o' chasin' your – a-hem – boys through the length an'

breadth of my covers. *I* think these house-matches are all rot.
Let's go over to Colonel Dabney's an' see if he's collared any
more poachers."

That afternoon there was joy in Aves.

A SAHIBS' WAR

A SAHIBS' WAR

PASS? Pass? Pass? I have one pass already, allowing me to go by the *rêl* from Kroonstadt to Eshtellenbosch, where the horses are, where I am to be paid off, and whence I return to India. I am a – trooper of the Gurgaon Rissala (cavalry regiment), the One Hundred and Forty-first Punjab Cavalry. Do not herd me with these black Kaffirs. I am a Sikh – a trooper of the State. The Lieutenant-Sahib does not understand my talk? Is there *any* Sahib on this train who will interpret for a trooper of the Gurgaon Rissala going about his business in this devil's devising of a country, where there is no flour, no oil, no spice, and red pepper, and no respect paid to a Sikh? Is there no help? . . . God be thanked, here is such a Sahib! Protector of the Poor! Heaven-born! Tell the young Lieutenant-Sahib that my name is Umr Singh; I am – I was servant to Kurban Sahib, now dead; and I have a pass to go to Eshtellenbosch, where the horses are. Do not let him herd me with these black Kaffirs! . . . Yes, I will sit by this truck till the Heaven-born has explained the matter to the young Lieutenant-Sahib who does not understand our tongue.

* * *

What orders? The young Lieutenant-Sahib will not detain me? Good! I go down to Eshtellenbosch by the next *terain*? Good! I go with the Heaven-born? Good! Then for this day I am the Heaven-born's servant. Will the Heaven-born bring the honour of his presence to a seat? Here is an empty truck; I will spread my blanket over one corner thus – for the sun is hot, though not so hot as our Punjab in May. I will prop it up thus, and I will arrange this hay thus, so the Presence can sit at ease till God sends us a *terain* for Eshtellenbosch. . . .

The Presence knows the Punjab? Lahore? Amritzar?

531

Attaree, belike? My village is north over the fields three miles from Attaree, near the big white house which was copied from a certain place of the Great Queen's by – by – I have forgotten the name. Can the Presence recall it? Sirdar Dyal Singh Attareewalla! Yes, that is the very man; but how does the Presence know? Born and bred in Hind, was he? O-o-oh! This is quite a different matter. The Sahib's nurse was a Surtee woman from the Bombay side? That was a pity. She should have been an up-country wench; for those make stout nurses. There is no land like the Punjab. There are no people like the Sikhs. Umr Singh is my name, yes. An old man? Yes. A trooper only after all these years? Ye-es. Look at my uniform, if the Sahib doubts. Nay – nay; the Sahib looks too closely. All marks of rank were picked off it long ago, but – but it is true – mine is not a common cloth such as troopers use for their coats, and – the Sahib has sharp eyes – that black mark is such a mark as a silver chain leaves when long worn on the breast. The Sahib says that troopers do not wear silver chains? No-o. Troopers do not wear the Arder of Beritish India? No. The Sahib should have been in the Police of the Punjab. I am not a trooper, but I have been a Sahib's servant for nearly a year – bearer, butler, sweeper, any and all three. The Sahib says that Sikhs do not take menial service? True; but it was for Kurban Sahib – my Kurban Sahib – dead these three months!

* * *

Young – of a reddish face – with blue eyes, and he lilted a little on his feet when he was pleased, and cracked his finger-joints. So did his father before him, who was Deputy-Commissioner of Jullundur in my father's time when I rode with the Gurgaon Rissala. *My* father? Jwala Singh. A Sikh of Sikhs – he fought against the English at Sobraon and carried the mark to his death. So we were knit as it were by a blood-tie, I and my Kurban Sahib. Yes, I was a trooper first – nay, I had risen to a Lance-Duffadar, I remember – and my father gave me a dun stallion of his own breeding on that day; and *he* was a little baba, sitting upon a wall by the parade-ground with his ayah – all in white, Sahib – laughing at the end of our drill. And his father and mine talked together, and mine beckoned to me, and I dismounted, and the baba put his hand into mine – eighteen – twenty-five – twenty-seven years gone now – Kurban Sahib – my Kurban Sahib! Oh, we were great friends after that! He cut his teeth on my sword-hilt, as the saying is. He called me Big Umr Singh – Buwwa Umwa Singh, for he could not speak plain. He stood only this high, Sahib, from the bottom of this truck, but he knew all our troopers by name – every one. . . . And he went to England, and he became a young man, and back he came, lilting a little in his walk, and cracking his finger-joints – back to his own regiment and to me. He had not forgotten either our speech or our customs. He was a Sikh at heart, Sahib. He was rich, open-handed, just, a friend of poor troopers, keen-eyed, jestful, and careless. *I* could tell tales about him in his first years. There was very little he hid from *me*. I was his Umr Singh, and when we were alone he called me Father, and I called him Son. Yes, that was how we spoke. We spoke freely together on everything – about war, and women, and money, and advancement, and such all.

We spoke about this war, too, long before it came. There were many box-wallas, pedlars, with Pathans a few, in this country, notably at the city of Yunasbagh (Johannesburg), and they sent news in every week how the Sahibs lay without weapons under the heel of the Boer-log; and how big guns were hauled up and down the streets to keep Sahibs in order; and how a Sahib called Eger Sahib (Edgar?) was killed for a jest by the Boer-log. The Sahib knows how we of Hind hear all that passes over the earth? There was not a gun cocked in Yunasbagh that the echo did not come into Hind in a month. The Sahibs are very clever, but they forget their own cleverness has created the *dak* (the post), and that for an anna or two all things become known. We of Hind listened and heard and wondered; and when it was a sure thing, as reported by the pedlars and the vegetable-sellers, that the Sahibs of Yunasbagh lay in bondage to the Boer-log, certain among us asked questions and waited for signs. Others of us mistook the meaning of those signs. *Wherefore, Sahib, came the long war in the Tirah!* This Kurban Sahib knew, and we talked together. He said, "There is no haste. Presently we shall fight, and we shall fight for all Hind in that country round Yunasbagh." Here he spoke truth. Does the Sahib not agree? Quite so. It is for Hind that the Sahibs are fighting this war. Ye cannot in one place rule and in another bear service. Either ye must everywhere rule or everywhere obey. God does not make the nations ringstraked. True – true – true!

So did matters ripen – a step at a time. It was nothing to me, except I think – and the Sahib sees this, too? – that it is foolish to make an army and break their hearts in idleness. Why have they not sent for the men of the Tochi – the men of the Tirah – the men of Buner? Folly, a thousand times. *We* could have done it all so gently – so gently.

Then, upon a day, Kurban Sahib sent for me and said, "Ho, Dada, I am sick, and the doctor gives me a certificate for many months." And he winked, and I said, "I will get leave and nurse thee, Child. Shall I bring my uniform?" He said, "Yes, and a sword for a sick man to lean on. We go to Bombay, and thence by sea to the country of the Hubshis" (niggers). Mark his cleverness! He was first of all our men among the native regiments to get leave for sickness and to come here. Now they will not let our officers go away, sick or well, except they sign a bond not to take part in this war-game upon the road. But *he* was clever. There was no whisper of war when he took his sick-leave. I came also? Assuredly. I went to my Colonel, and sitting in the chair (I am – I was – of that rank for which a chair is placed when we speak with the Colonel) I said, "My child goes sick. Give me leave, for I am old and sick also."

And the Colonel, making the word double between English and our tongue, said, "Yes, thou art truly *Sikh*"; and he called me an old devil – jestingly, as one soldier may jest with another; and he said my Kurban Sahib was a liar as to his health (that was true, too), and at long last he stood up and shook my hand, and bade me go and bring my Sahib safe again. My Sahib back again – aie me!

So I went to Bombay with Kurban Sahib, but there, at sight of the Black Water, Wajib Ali, his bearer, checked, and said that his mother was dead. Then I said to Kurban Sahib, "What is one Mussulman pig more or less? Give me the keys of the trunks, and I will lay out the white shirts for dinner." Then I beat Wajib Ali at the back of Watson's Hotel, and that night I prepared Kurban Sahib's razors. I say, Sahib, that I, a Sikh of the Khalsa, an unshorn man, prepared the razors. But I did not put on my uniform while I did it. On the other hand, Kurban Sahib took for me, upon the steamer, a room in all respects like to his own, and would have given me a servant. We spoke of many things on the way to this country; and Kurban Sahib told me what he perceived would be the conduct of the war. He said, "They have taken men afoot to fight men ahorse, and they will foolishly show mercy to these Boer-log because it is believed that they are white." He said, "There is but one fault in this war, and that is that the Government have not employed *us*, but have made it altogether a Sahibs' war. Very many men will thus be killed, and no vengeance will be taken." True talk – true talk! It fell as Kurban Sahib foretold.

And we came to this country, even to Cape Town over yonder, and Kurban Sahib said, "Bear the baggage to the big dak-bungalow, and I will look for employment fit for a sick man." I put on the uniform of my rank and went to the big dak-bungalow, called Maun Nihâl Seyn, and I caused the heavy baggage to be bestowed in that dark lower place – is it known to the Sahib? – which was already full of the swords and baggage of officers. It is fuller now – dead men's kit all! I was careful to secure a receipt for all three pieces. I have it in my belt. They must go back to the Punjab.

Anon came Kurban Sahib, lilting a little in his step, which sign I knew, and he said, "We are born in a fortunate hour.

We go to Eshtellenbosch to oversee the despatch of horses."
Remember, Kurban Sahib was squadron-leader of the Gurgaon Rissala, and *I* was Umr Singh. So I said, speaking as
we do – we did – when none was near, "Thou art a groom
and I am a grass-cutter, but is this any promotion, Child?"
At this he laughed, saying, "It is the way to better things.
Have patience, Father." (Aye, he called me father when none
were by.) "This war ends not to-morrow nor the next day. I
have seen the new Sahibs," he said, "and they are fathers of
owls – all – all – all!"

So we went to Eshtellenbosch, where the horses are; Kurban Sahib doing the service of servants in that business. And
the whole business was managed without forethought by new
Sahibs from God knows where, who had never seen a tent
pitched or a peg driven. They were full of zeal, but empty
of all knowledge. Then came, little by little from Hind, those
Pathans – they are just like those vultures up there, Sahib –
they always follow slaughter. And there came to Eshtellenbosch some Sikhs – Muzbees, though – and some Madras
monkey-men. They came with horses. Puttiala sent horses.
Jhind and Nabha sent horses. All the nations of the Khalsa
sent horses. All the ends of the earth sent horses. God knows
what the army did with them, unless they ate them raw.
They used horses as a courtesan uses oil: with both hands.
These horses needed many men. Kurban Sahib appointed
me to the command (what a command for me!) of certain
woolly ones – *Hubshis* – whose touch and shadow are pollution. They were enormous eaters; sleeping on their bellies;
laughing without cause; wholly like animals. Some were
called Fingoes, and some, I think, Red Kaffirs, but they
were all Kaffirs – filth unspeakable. I taught them to water
and feed, and sweep and rub down. Yes, I oversaw the work
of sweepers – a *jemadar* of *mehtars* (head-man of a refuse-
gang) was I, and Kurban Sahib little better, for five months.
Evil months! The war went as Kurban Sahib had said. Our
new men were slain and no vengeance was taken. It was a
war of fools armed with the weapons of magicians. Guns that

slew at half a day's march, and men who, being new, walked
blind into high grass and were driven off like cattle by the
Boer-log! As to the city of Eshtellenbosch, I am not a Sahib
– only a Sikh. I would have quartered one troop only of the
Gurgaon Rissala in that city – one little troop – and I would
have schooled that city till its men learned to kiss the shadow
of a Government horse upon the ground. There are many
mullahs (priests) in Eshtellenbosch. They preached the Jehad
against us. This is true – all the camp knew it. And most of
the houses were thatched! A war of fools indeed!

At the end of five months my Kurban Sahib, who had
grown lean, said, "The reward has come. We go up towards
the front with horses to-morrow, and, once away, I shall be
too sick to return. Make ready the baggage." Thus we got
away, with some Kaffirs in charge of new horses for a certain
new regiment that had come in a ship. The second day by
terain, when we were watering at a desolate place without any
sort of a bazar to it, slipped out from the horse-boxes one
Sikandar Khan, that had been a *jemadar* of *saises* (head-
groom) at Eshtellenbosch, and was by service a trooper in a
Border regiment. Kurban Sahib gave him big abuse for his
desertion; but the Pathan put up his hands as excusing himself, and Kurban Sahib relented and added him to our service. So there were three of us – Kurban Sahib, I, and
Sikandar Khan – Sahib, Sikh, and *Sag* (dog). But the man
said truly, "We be far from our homes and both servants of
the Raj. Make truce till we see the Indus again." I have eaten
from the same dish as Sikandar Khan – beef, too, for aught
I know! He said, on the night he stole some swine's flesh in
a tin from a mess-tent, that in his Book, the Koran, it is
written that whoso engages in a holy war is freed from ceremonial obligations. Wah! He had no more religion than the
sword-point picks up of sugar and water at baptism. He stole
himself a horse at a place where there lay a new and very raw
regiment. I also procured myself a grey gelding there. They
let their horses stray too much, those new regiments.

Some shameless regiments would indeed have made away

with *our* horses on the road! They exhibited indents and requisitions for horses, and once or twice would have uncoupled the trucks; but Kurban Sahib was wise, and I am not altogether a fool. There is not much honesty at the front. Notably, there was one congregation of hard-bitten horse-thieves; tall, light Sahibs, who spoke through their noses for the most part, and upon all occasions they said, "Oah Hell!" which, in our tongue, signifies *Jehannum ko jao*. They bore each man a vine-leaf upon their uniforms, and they rode like Rajputs. Nay, they rode like Sikhs. They rode like the Ustrelyahs! The Ustrelyahs, whom we met later, also spoke through their noses not little, and they were tall, dark men, with grey, clear eyes, heavily eyelashed like camel's eyes – very proper men – a new brand of Sahib to me. They said on all occasions, "No fee-ah," which in our tongue means *Durro mut* ("Do not be afraid"), so we called them the *Durro Muts*. Dark, tall men, most excellent horsemen, hot and angry, waging war *as* war, and drinking tea as a sandhill drinks water. Thieves? A little, Sahib. Sikandar Khan swore to me; and he comes of a horse-stealing clan for ten generations; he swore a Pathan was a babe beside a *Durro Mut* in regard to horse-lifting. The *Durro Muts* cannot walk on their feet at all. They are like hens on the high road. Therefore they must have horses. Very proper men, with a just lust for the war. Aah – "No fee-ah," say the *Durro Muts*. *They* saw the worth of Kurban Sahib. *They* did not ask him to sweep stables. They would by no means let him go. He did substitute for one of their troop-leaders who had a fever, one long day in a country full of little hills – like the mouth of the Khaibar; and when they returned in the evening, the *Durro Muts* said, "Wallah! This is a man. Steal him!" So they stole my Kurban Sahib as they would have stolen anything else that they needed, and they sent a sick officer back to Eshtellenbosch in his place. Thus Kurban Sahib came to his own again, and I was his bearer, and Sikandar Khan was his cook. The law was strict that this was a Sahibs' war, but there was no order that a bearer and a cook should not ride with their Sahib – and we had naught to wear but our uniforms. We rode up and down this accursed country, where there is no bazar, no pulse, no flour, no oil, no spice, no red pepper, no firewood; nothing but raw corn and a little cattle. There were no great battles as I saw it, but a plenty of gun-firing. When we were many, the Boer-log came out with coffee to greet us, and to show us *purwanas* (permits) from foolish English Generals who had gone that way before, certifying they were peaceful and well-disposed. When we were few, they hid behind stones and shot us. Now the order was that they were Sahibs, and this was a Sahibs' war. Good! But, as I understand it, when a Sahib goes to war, he puts on the cloth of war, and only those who wear that cloth may take part in the war. Good! That also I understand. But these people were as they were in Burma, or as the Afridis are. They shot at their pleasure, and when pressed hid the gun and exhibited *purwanas*, or lay in a house and said they were farmers. Even such farmers as cut up the Madras troops at Hlinedatalone in Burma! Even such farmers as slew Cavagnari Sahib and the Guides at Kabul! We schooled *those* men, to be sure – fifteen, aye, twenty of a morning pushed off the verandah in front of the Bala Hissar. I looked that the Jung-i-lat Sahib (the Commander-in-Chief) would have remembered the old days; but – no. All the people shot at us everywhere, and he issued proclamations saying that he did not fight the people, but a certain army, which army, in truth, was all the Boer-log, who, between them, did not wear enough of uniform to make a loin-cloth. A fool's war from first to last; for it is manifest that he who fights should be hung if he fights with a gun in one hand and a *purwana* in the other, as did all these people. Yet we, when they had had their bellyful for the time, received them with honour, and gave them permits, and refreshed them and fed their wives and their babes, and severely punished our soldiers who took their fowls. So the work was to be done not once with a few dead, but thrice and four times over. I talked much with Kurban Sahib on this, and he said, "It is a Sahibs' war. That

is the order"; and one night, when Sikandar Khan would
have lain out beyond the pickets with his knife and shown
them how it is worked on the Border, he hit Sikandar Khan
between the eyes and came near to breaking in his head.
Then Sikandar Khan, a bandage over his eyes, so that he
looked like a sick camel, talked to him half one march, and
he was more bewildered than I, and vowed he would return
to Eshtellenbosch. But privately to me Kurban Sahib said we
should have loosed the Sikhs and the Gurkhas on these
people till they came in with their foreheads in the dust. For
the war was not of that sort which they comprehended.

They shot us? Assuredly they shot us from houses
adorned with a white flag; but when they came to know our
custom, their widows sent word by Kaffir runners, and presently there was not quite so much firing. *No fee-ah!* All the
Boer-log with whom we dealt had *purwanas* signed by mad
Generals attesting that they were well-disposed to the State.
They had also rifles not a few, and cartridges, which they hid
in the roof. The women wept very greatly when we burned
such houses, but they did not approach too near after the
flames had taken good hold of the thatch, for fear of the
bursting cartridges. The women of the Boer-log are very
clever. They are more clever than the men. The Boer-log
are clever? Never, never, no! It is the Sahibs who are fools.
For their own honour's sake the Sahibs must say that the
Boer-log are clever; but it is the Sahibs' wonderful folly that
has made the Boer-log. The Sahibs should have sent *us* into
the game.

But the *Durro Muts* did well. They dealt faithfully with
all that country thereabouts – not in any way as we of Hind
should have dealt, but they were not altogether fools. One
night when we lay on the top of a ridge in the cold, I saw far
away a light in a house that appeared for the sixth part of an
hour and was obscured. Anon it appeared again thrice for the
twelfth part of an hour. I showed this to Kurban Sahib, for
it was a house that had been spared – the people having many
permits and swearing fidelity at our stirrup-leathers. I said to

Kurban Sahib, "Send half a troop, Child, and finish that house. They signal to their brethren." And he laughed where he lay and said, "If I listened to my bearer Umr Singh, there would not be left ten houses in all this land." I said, "What need to leave one? This is as it was in Burma. They are farmers to-day and fighters to-morrow. Let us deal justly with them." He laughed and curled himself up in his blanket, and I watched the far light in the house till day. I have been on the Border in eight wars, not counting Burma. The first Afghan War; the second Afghan War; two Mahsud Waziri wars (that is four); two Black Mountain wars, if I remember right; the Malakand and Tirah. I do not count Burma, or some small things. *I* know when house signals to house!

I pushed Sikandar Khan with my foot, and he saw it too. He said, "One of the Boer-log who brought pumpkins for the mess, which I fried last night, lives in yonder house." I said, "How dost thou know?" He said, "Because he rode out of the camp another way, but I marked how his horse fought with him at the turn of the road; and before the light fell I stole out of the camp for evening prayer with Kurban Sahib's glasses, and from a little hill I saw the pied horse of that pumpkin-seller hurrying to that house." I said naught, but took Kurban Sahib's glasses from his greasy hands and cleaned them with a silk handkerchief and returned them to their case. Sikandar Khan told me that he had been the first man in the Zenab valley to use glasses – whereby he finished two blood-feuds cleanly in the course of three months' leave. But he was otherwise a liar.

That day Kurban Sahib, with some ten troopers, was sent on to spy the land for our camp. The *Durro Muts* moved slowly at that time. They were weighted with grain and forage and carts, and they greatly wished to leave these all in some town and go on light to other business which pressed. So Kurban Sahib sought a short cut for them, a little off the line of march. We were twelve miles before the main body, and we came to a house under a high bushed hill, with a nullah, which they call a donga, behind it, and an old sangar of piled stones, which they call a kraal, before it. Two thorn bushes grew on either side of the door, like babul bushes, covered with a golden-coloured bloom, and the roof was all of thatch. Before the house was a valley of stones that rose to another bush-covered hill. There was an old man in the verandah – an old man with a white beard and a wart upon the left side of his neck; and a fat woman with the eyes of a swine and the jowl of a swine; and a tall young man deprived of understanding. His head was hairless, no larger than an orange, and the pits of his nostrils were eaten away by a disease. He laughed and slavered and he sported sportively before Kurban Sahib. The man brought coffee and the woman showed us *purwanas* from three General Sahibs, certifying that they were people of peace and goodwill. Here are the *purwanas*, Sahib. Does the Sahib know the Generals who signed them?

They swore the land was empty of Boer-log. They held up their hands and swore it. That was about the time of the evening meal. I stood near the verandah with Sikandar Khan, who was nosing like a jackal on a lost scent. At last he took my arm and said, "See yonder! There is the sun on the window of the house that signalled last night. This house can see that house from here," and he looked at the hill behind him all hairy with bushes, and sucked in his breath. Then the idiot with the shrivelled head danced by me and threw back that head, and regarded the roof and laughed like a hyena, and the fat woman talked loudly, as it were, to cover some noise. After this I passed to the back of the house on pretence to get water for tea, and I saw fresh horse-dung on the ground, and that the ground was cut with the new marks of hoofs; and there had dropped in the dirt one cartridge. Then Kurban Sahib called to me in our tongue, saying, "Is this a good place to make tea?" and I replied, knowing what he meant, "There are over many cooks in the cook-house. Mount and go, Child." Then I returned, and he said, smiling to the woman, "Prepare food, and when we have loosened our girths we will come in and eat"; but to his men he said in a whisper, "Ride away!" No. He did not cover the old man or the fat woman with his rifle. That was not his custom. Some fool of the *Durro Muts*, being hungry, raised his voice to dispute the order to flee, and before we were in our saddles many shots came from the roof – from rifles thrust through the thatch. Upon this we rode across the valley of stones, and men fired at us from the nullah behind the house, and from the hill behind the nullah, as well as from the roof of the house – so many shots that it sounded like a drumming in the hills. Then Sikandar Khan, riding low, said, "This play is not for us alone, but for the rest of the *Durro Muts*," and I said, "Be quiet. Keep place!" for his place was behind me, and I rode behind Kurban Sahib. But these new bullets will pass through five men arow! We were not hit – not one of us – and we reached the hill of rocks and scattered among the stones, and Kurban Sahib turned in his saddle and said, "Look at the old man!" He stood in the verandah firing swiftly with a gun, the woman beside him and the idiot also – both with guns. Kurban Sahib laughed, and I caught him by the wrist, but – his fate was written at that hour. The bullet passed under my arm-pit and struck him in the liver, and I pulled him backward between two great rocks atilt – Kurban Sahib, my Kurban Sahib! From the nullah behind the house and from the hills came our Boer-log in number more than a hundred, and Sikandar Khan said, "*Now* we see the meaning of last night's signal. Give me the rifle." He took Kurban Sahib's rifle – in this war of fools only the doctors carry swords – and lay belly-flat to the work, but Kurban Sahib turned where he lay and said, "Be still. It is a Sahibs' war," and Kurban Sahib put up his hand – thus; and then his eyes rolled on me, and I gave him water that he might pass the more quickly. And at the drinking his Spirit received permission. . . .

Thus went our fight, Sahib. We *Durro Muts* were on a ridge working from the north to the south, where lay our main body, and the Boer-log lay in a valley working from east to west. There were more than a hundred, and our men were

ten, but they held the Boer-log in the valley while they swiftly passed along the ridge to the south. I saw three Boers drop
in the open. Then they all hid again and fired heavily at the
rocks that hid our men; but our men were clever and did not
show, but moved away and away, always south; and the noise
of the battle withdrew itself southward, where we could hear
the sound of big guns. So it fell stark dark, and Sikandar
Khan found a deep old jackal's earth amid rocks, into which
we slid the body of Kurban Sahib upright. Sikandar Khan
took his glasses, and I took his handkerchief and some letters
and a certain thing which I knew hung round his neck, and
Sikandar Khan is witness that I wrapped them all in the
handkerchief. Then we took an oath together, and lay still
and mourned for Kurban Sahib. Sikandar Khan wept till
daybreak – even he, a Pathan, a Mohammedan! All that night
we heard firing to the southward, and when the dawn broke
the valley was full of Boer-log in carts and on horses. They
gathered by the house, as we could see through Kurban
Sahib's glasses, and the old man, who, I take it, was a priest,
blessed them, and preached the holy war, waving his arm;
and the fat woman brought coffee, and the idiot capered
among them and kissed their horses. Presently they went
away in haste; they went over the hills and were not; and a
black slave came out and washed the door-sills with bright
water. Sikandar Khan saw through the glasses that the stain
was blood, and he laughed, saying, "Wounded men lie there.
We shall yet get vengeance."

About noon we saw a thin, high smoke to the southward,
such a smoke as a burning house will make in sunshine,
and Sikandar Khan, who knows how to take a bearing across
a hill, said, "At last we have burned the house of the
pumpkin-seller whence they signalled." And I said: "What
need now that they have slain my child? Let me mourn." It
was a high smoke, and the old man, as I saw, came out into
the verandah to behold it, and shook his clenched hands at
it. So we lay till the twilight, foodless and without water, for
we had vowed a vow neither to eat nor to drink till we had

accomplished the matter. I had a little opium left, of which I gave Sikandar Khan the half, because he loved Kurban Sahib. When it was full dark we sharpened our sabres upon a certain softish rock which, mixed with water, sharpens steel well, and we took off our boots and we went down to the house and looked through the windows very softly. The old man sat reading in a book, and the woman sat by the hearth; and the idiot lay on the floor with his head against her knee, and he counted his fingers and laughed, and she laughed again. So I knew they were mother and son, and I laughed, too, for I had suspected this when I claimed her life and her body from Sikandar Khan, in our discussion of the spoil. Then we entered with bare swords. . . . Indeed, these Boer-log do not understand the steel, for the old man ran towards a rifle in the corner; but Sikandar Khan prevented him with a blow of the flat across the hands, and he sat down and held up his hands, and I put my fingers on my lips to signify they should be silent. But the woman cried, and one stirred in an inner room, and a door opened, and a man, bound about the head with rags, stood stupidly fumbling with a gun. His whole head fell inside the door, and none followed him. It was a very pretty stroke – for a Pathan. Then they were silent, staring at the head upon the floor, and I said to Sikandar Khan, "Fetch ropes! Not even for Kurban Sahib's sake will I defile my sword." So he went to seek and returned with three long leather ones, and said, "Four wounded lie within, and doubtless each has a permit from a General," and he stretched the ropes and laughed. Then I bound the old man's hands behind his back, and unwillingly – for he laughed in my face, and would have fingered my beard – the idiot's. At this the woman with the swine's eyes and the jowl of a swine ran forward, and Sikandar Khan said, "Shall I strike or bind? She was thy property on the division." And I said, "Refrain! I have made a chain to hold her. Open the door." I pushed out the two across the verandah into the darker shade of the thorn-trees, and she followed upon her knees and lay along the ground, and pawed at my boots and howled. Then

Sikandar Khan bore out the lamp, saying that he was a butler and would light the table, and I looked for a branch that would bear fruit. But the woman hindered me not a little with her screechings and plungings, and spoke fast in her tongue, and I replied in my tongue, "I am childless to-night because of thy perfidy, and *my* child was praised among men and loved among women. He would have begotten men – not animals. Thou hast more years to live than I, but my grief is the greater."

I stooped to make sure the noose upon the idiot's neck, and flung the end over the branch, and Sikandar Khan held up the lamp that she might well see. Then appeared suddenly, a little beyond the light of the lamp, the spirit of Kurban Sahib. One hand he held to his side, even where the bullet had struck him, and the other he put forward thus, and said, "No. It is a Sahibs' war." And I said, "Wait a while, Child, and thou shalt sleep." But he came nearer, riding, as it were, upon my eyes, and said, "No. It is a Sahibs' war." And Sikandar Khan said, "Is it too heavy?" and set down the lamp and came to me; and as he turned to tally on the rope, the spirit of Kurban Sahib stood up within arm's reach of us, and his face was very angry, and a third time he said, "No. It is a Sahibs' war." And a little wind blew out the lamp, and I heard Sikandar Khan's teeth chatter in his head.

So we stayed side by side, the ropes in our hand, a very long while, for we could not shape any words. Then I heard Sikandar Khan open his water-bottle and drink; and when his mouth was slaked he passed to me and said, "We are absolved from our vow." So I drank, and together we waited for the dawn in that place where we stood – the ropes in our hand. A little after third cockcrow we heard the feet of horses and gun-wheels very far off, and so soon as the light came a shell burst on the threshold of the house, and the roof of the verandah that was thatched fell in and blazed before the windows. And I said, "What of the wounded Boer-log within?" And Sikandar Khan said, "We have heard the order. It is a Sahibs' war. Stand still." Then came a second shell – good line, but short – and scattered dust upon us where we stood; and then came ten of the little quick shells from the gun that speaks like a stammerer – yes, pompom the Sahibs call it – and the face of the house folded down like the nose and the chin of an old man mumbling, and the forefront of the house lay down. Then Sikandar Khan said, "If it be the fate of the wounded to die in the fire, *I* shall not prevent it." And he passed to the back of the house and presently came back, and four wounded Boer-log came after him, of whom two could not walk upright. And I said, "What hast thou done?" And he said, "I have neither spoken to them nor laid hand on them. They follow in hope of mercy." And I said, "It is a Sahibs' war. Let them wait the Sahibs' mercy." So they lay still, the four men and the idiot, and the fat woman under the thorn-tree, and the house burned furiously. Then began the known sound of cartouches in the roof – one or two at first; then a trill, and last of all one loud noise and the thatch blew here and there, and the captives would have crawled aside on account of the heat that was withering the thorn-trees, and on account of wood and bricks flying at random. But I said, "Abide! Abide! Ye be Sahibs, and this is a Sahibs' war, O Sahibs. There is no order that ye should depart from this war." They did not understand my words. Yet they abode and they lived.

Presently rode down five troopers of Kurban Sahib's command, and one I knew spoke my tongue, having sailed to Calcutta often with horses. So I told him all my tale, using bazar-talk, such as his kidney of Sahib would understand; and at the end I said, "An order has reached us here from the dead that this is a Sahibs' war. I take the soul of my Kurban Sahib to witness that I give over to the justice of the Sahibs these Sahibs who have made me childless." Then I gave him the ropes and fell down senseless, my heart being very full, but my belly was empty, except for the little opium.

They put me into a cart with one of their wounded, and after a while I understood that they had fought against the Boer-log for two days and two nights. It was all one big trap,

Sahib, of which we, with Kurban Sahib, saw no more than the outer edge. They were very angry, the *Durro Muts* – very angry indeed. I have never seen Sahibs so angry. They buried my Kurban Sahib with the rites of his faith upon the top of the ridge overlooking the house, and I said the proper prayers of the faith, and Sikandar Khan prayed in his fashion and stole five signalling-candles, which have each three wicks, and lighted the grave as if it had been the grave of a saint on a Friday. He wept very bitterly all that night, and I wept with him, and he took hold of my feet and besought me to give him a remembrance from Kurban Sahib. So I divided equally with him one of Kurban Sahib's handkerchiefs – not the silk ones, for those were given him by a certain woman; and I also gave him a button from a coat, and a little steel ring of no value that Kurban Sahib used for his keys, and he kissed them and put them into his bosom. The rest I have here in that little bundle, and I must get the baggage from the hotel in Cape Town – some four shirts we sent to be washed, for which we could not wait when we went up-country – and I must give them all to my Colonel-Sahib at Sialkote in the Punjab. For my child is dead – my baba is dead! . . .

I would have come away before; there was no need to stay, the child being dead; but we were far from the rail, and the *Durro Muts* were as brothers to me, and I had come to look upon Sikandar Khan as in some sort a friend, and he got me a horse and I rode up and down with them; but the life had departed. God knows what they called me – orderly, *chaprassi* (messenger), cook, sweeper, I did not know nor care. But once I had pleasure. We came back in a month after wide circles to that very valley. I knew it every stone, and I went up to the grave, and a clever Sahib of the *Durro Muts* (we left a troop there for a week to school those people with *purwanas*) had cut an inscription upon a great rock; and they interpreted it to me, and it was a jest such as Kurban Sahib himself would have loved. Oh! I have the inscription well

copied here. Read it aloud, Sahib, and I will explain the jests.
There are two very good ones. Begin, Sahib:

In Memory of
WALTER DECIES CORBYN
Late Captain 141st Punjab Cavalry

The Gurgaon Rissala, that is. Go on, Sahib.

Treacherously shot near this place by
The connivance of the late
HENDRIK DIRK UYS
A Minister of God
Who thrice took the oath of neutrality
And Piet his son,
This little work

Aha! This is the first jest. The Sahib should see this little
work!

Was accomplished in partial
And inadequate recognition of their loss
By some men who loved him

* * *

Si monumentum requiris circumspice

That is the second jest. It signifies that those who would
desire to behold a proper memorial to Kurban Sahib must
look out at the house. And, Sahib, the house is not there, nor
the well, nor the big tank which they call dams, nor the little
fruit-trees, nor the cattle. There is nothing at all, Sahib,
except the two trees withered by the fire. The rest is like the
desert here – or my hand – or my heart. Empty, Sahib – all
empty!

"WIRELESS"

"WIRELESS"

* * *

KASPAR'S SONG IN "VARDA"

(From the Swedish of Stagnelius)

Eyes aloft, over dangerous places,
    The children follow where Psyche flies,
And, in the sweat of their upturned faces,
    Slash with a net at the empty skies.

So it goes they fall amid brambles,
    And sting their toes on the nettle-tops,
Till after a thousand scratches and scrambles
    They wipe their brows, and the hunting stops.

Then to quiet them comes their father
    And stills the riot of pain and grief,
Saying, "Little ones, go and gather
    Out of my garden a cabbage leaf.

"You will find on it whorls and clots of
    Dull grey eggs that, properly fed,
Turn, by way of the worm, to lots of
    Radiant Psyches raised from the dead."

*

"Heaven is beautiful, Earth is ugly,"
    The three-dimensioned preacher saith,
So we must not look where the snail and the slug lie
    For Psyche's birth. . . . And that is our death!

* * *

"IT's a funny thing, this Marconi business, isn't it?" said
Mr. Shaynor, coughing heavily. "Nothing seems to

make any difference, by what they tell me – storms, hills, or anything; but if that's true we shall know before morning."

"Of course it's true," I answered, stepping behind the counter. "Where's old Mr. Cashell?"

"He's had to go to bed on account of his influenza. He said you'd very likely drop in."

"Where's his nephew?"

"Inside, getting the things ready. He told me that the last time they experimented they put the pole on the roof of one of the big hotels here, and the batteries electrified all the water-supply, and" – he giggled – "the ladies got shocks when they took their baths."

"I never heard of that."

"The hotel wouldn't exactly advertise it, would it? Just now, by what Mr. Cashell tells me, they're tryin' to signal from here to Poole, and they're using stronger batteries than ever. But, you see, he being the guvnor's nephew and all that (and it will be in the papers too), it doesn't matter how they electrify things in this house. Are you going to watch?"

"Very much. I've never seen this game. Aren't you going to bed?"

"We don't close till ten on Saturdays. There's a good deal of influenza in town, too, and there'll be a dozen prescriptions coming in before morning. I generally sleep in the chair here. It's warmer than jumping out of bed every time. Bitter cold, isn't it?"

"Freezing hard. I'm sorry your cough's worse."

"Thank you. I don't mind cold so much. It's this wind that fair cuts me to pieces." He coughed again hard and hackingly, as an old lady came in for ammoniated quinine. "We've just run out of it in bottles, madam," said Mr. Shaynor, returning to the professional tone, "but if you will wait two minutes, I'll make it up for you, madam."

I had used the shop for some time, and my acquaintance with the proprietor had ripened into friendship. It was Mr. Cashell who revealed to me the purpose and power of Apothecaries' Hall what time a fellow-chemist had made an error in a prescription of mine, had lied to cover his sloth, and when error and lie were brought home to him had written vain letters.

"A disgrace to our profession," said the thin, mild-eyed man, hotly, after studying the evidence. "You couldn't do a better service to the profession than report him to Apothecaries' Hall."

I did so, not knowing what djinns I should evoke; and the result was such an apology as one might make who had spent a night on the rack. I conceived great respect for Apothecaries' Hall, and esteem for Mr. Cashell, a zealous craftsman who magnified his calling. Until Mr. Shaynor came down from the North his assistants had by no means agreed with Mr. Cashell. "They forget," said he, "that, first and foremost, the compounder is a medicine-man. On him depends the physician's reputation. He holds it literally in the hollow of his hand, Sir."

Mr. Shaynor's manners had not, perhaps, the polish of the grocery and Italian warehouse next door, but he knew and loved his dispensary work in every detail. For relaxation he seemed to go no farther afield than the romance of drugs – their discovery, preparation, packing, and export – but it led him to the ends of the earth, and on this subject, and the Pharmaceutical Formulary, and Nicholas Culpeper, most confident of physicians, we met.

Little by little I grew to know something of his beginnings and his hopes – of his mother, who had been a school-teacher in one of the northern counties, and of his red-headed father, a small job-master at Kirby Moors, who died when he was a child; of the examinations he had passed and of their exceeding and increasing difficulty; of his dreams of a shop in London; of his hate for the price-cutting Co-operative stores; and, most interesting, of his mental attitude towards customers.

"There's a way you get into," he told me, "of serving them carefully, and I hope, politely, without stopping your own thinking. I've been reading Christie's *New Commercial*

Plants all this Autumn, and that needs keeping your mind on it, I can tell you. So long as it isn't a prescription, of course, I can carry as much as half a page of Christie in my head, and at the same time I could sell out all that window twice over, and not a penny wrong at the end. As to prescriptions, I think I could make up the general run of 'em in my sleep, almost."

For reasons of my own, I was deeply interested in Marconi experiments at their outset in England; and it was of a piece with Mr. Cashell's unvarying thoughtfulness that, when his nephew the electrician appropriated the house for a long-range installation, he should, as I have said, invite me to see the result.

The old lady went away with her medicine, and Mr. Shaynor and I stamped on the tiled floor behind the counter to keep ourselves warm. The shop, by the light of the many electrics, looked like a Paris-diamond mine, for Mr. Cashell believed in all the ritual of his craft. Three superb glass jars – red, green, and blue – of the sort that led Rosamund to parting with her shoes – blazed in the broad plate-glass windows, and there was a confused smell of orris, Kodak films, vulcanite, tooth-powder, sachets, and almond-cream in the air. Mr. Shaynor fed the dispensary stove, and we sucked cayenne-pepper jujubes and menthol lozenges. The brutal east wind had cleared the streets, and the few passers-by were muffled to their puckered eyes. In the Italian warehouse next door some gay-feathered birds and game, hung upon hooks, sagged to the wind across the left edge of our window-frame.

"They ought to take these poultry in – all knocked about like that," said Mr. Shaynor. "Doesn't it make you feel fair perishing? See that old hare! The wind's nearly blowing the fur off him."

I saw the belly-fur of the dead beast blown apart in ridges and streaks as the wind caught it, showing bluish skin underneath. "Bitter cold," said Mr. Shaynor, shuddering. "Fancy going out on a night like this! Oh, here's young Mr. Cashell."

The door of the inner office behind the dispensary opened, and an energetic, spade-bearded man stepped forth, rubbing his hands.

"I want a bit of tin-foil, Shaynor," he said. "Good evening. My uncle told me you might be coming." This to me, as I began the first of a hundred questions.

"I've everything in order," he replied. "We're only waiting until Poole calls us up. Excuse me a minute. You can come in whenever you like – but I'd better be with the instruments. Give me that tin-foil. Thanks."

While we were talking, a girl – evidently no customer – had come into the shop, and the face and bearing of Mr. Shaynor changed. She leaned confidently across the counter.

"But I can't," I heard him whisper uneasily – the flush on his cheek was dull red, and his eyes shone like a drugged moth's. "I can't. I tell you I'm alone in the place."

"No, you aren't. Who's *that*? Let him look after it for half an hour. A brisk walk will do you good. Ah, come now, John."

"But he isn't —"

"I don't care. I want you to; we'll only go round by St. Agnes. If you don't —"

He crossed to where I stood in the shadow of the dispensary counter, and began some sort of broken apology about a lady-friend.

"Yes," she interrupted. "You take the shop for half an hour – to oblige *me*, won't you?"

She had a singularly rich and promising voice that well matched her outline.

"All right," I said. "I'll do it – but you'd better wrap yourself up, Mr. Shaynor."

"Oh, a brisk walk ought to help me. We're only going round by the church." I heard him cough grievously as they went out together.

I refilled the stove, and, after reckless expenditure of Mr. Cashell's coal, drove some warmth into the shop. I explored many of the glass-knobbed drawers that lined the walls, tasted some disconcerting drugs, and, by the aid of a few cardamoms, ground ginger, chloric-ether, and dilute alcohol, manufactured a new and wildish drink, of which I bore a glassful to young Mr. Cashell, busy in the back office. He laughed shortly when I told him that Mr. Shaynor had stepped out – but a frail coil of wire held all his attention, and he had no word for me bewildered among the batteries and rods. The noise of the sea on the beach began to make itself heard as the traffic in the street ceased. Then briefly, but very lucidly, he gave me the names and uses of the mechanism that crowded the tables and the floor.

"When do you expect to get the message from Poole?" I demanded, sipping my liquor out of a graduated glass.

"About midnight, if everything is in order. We've got our installation-pole fixed to the roof of the house. I shouldn't advise you to turn on a tap or anything to-night. We've connected up with the plumbing, and all the water will be electrified." He repeated to me the history of the agitated ladies at the hotel at the time of the first installation.

"But what *is* it?" I asked. "Electricity is out of my beat altogether."

"Ah, if you knew *that* you'd know something nobody knows. It's just It – what we call Electricity, but the magic – the manifestations – the Hertzian waves – are all revealed by *this*. The coherer, we call it."

He picked up a glass tube not much thicker than a thermometer, in which, almost touching, were two tiny silver plugs, and between them an infinitesimal pinch of metallic dust. "That's all," he said, proudly, as though himself responsible for the wonder. "That is the thing that will reveal to us the Powers – whatever the Powers may be – at work – through space – a long distance away."

Just then Mr. Shaynor returned alone and stood coughing his heart out on the mat.

"Serves you right for being such a fool," said young Mr. Cashell, as annoyed as myself at the interruption. "Never mind – we've all the night before us to see wonders."

Shaynor clutched the counter, his handkerchief to his lips. When he brought it away I saw two bright red stains.

"I – I've got a bit of a rasped throat from smoking cigarettes," he panted. "I think I'll try a cubeb."

"Better take some of this. I've been compounding while you've been away." I handed him the brew.

" 'Twon't make me drunk, will it? I'm almost a teetotaller. My word! That's grateful and comforting."

He set down the empty glass to cough afresh.

"Brr! But it was cold out there! I shouldn't care to be lying in my grave a night like this. Don't *you* ever have a sore throat from smoking?" He pocketed the handkerchief after a furtive peep.

"Oh, yes, sometimes," I replied, wondering, while I spoke, into what agonies of terror I should fall if ever I saw those bright red danger-signals under my nose. Young Mr. Cashell among the batteries coughed slightly to show that he was quite ready to continue his scientific explanations, but I was thinking still of the girl with the rich voice and the significantly cut mouth, at whose command I had taken charge of the shop. It flashed across me that she distantly resembled the seductive shape on a gold-framed toilet-water advertisement whose charms were unholily heightened by the glare from the red bottle in the window. Turning to make sure, I saw Mr. Shaynor's eyes bent in the same direction, and by instinct recognised that the flamboyant thing was to him a shrine. "What do you take for your – cough?" I asked.

"Well, I'm the wrong side of the counter to believe much in patent medicines. But there are asthma cigarettes and there are pastilles. To tell you the truth, if you don't object to the smell, which is very like incense, I believe, though I'm not a Roman Catholic, Blaudett's Cathedral Pastilles relieve me as much as anything."

"Let's try." I had never raided a chemist's shop before, so I was thorough. We unearthed the pastilles – brown, gummy cones of benzoin – and set them alight under the toilet-water advertisement, where they fumed in thin blue spirals.

"Of course," said Mr. Shaynor, to my question, "what one uses in the shop for one's self comes out of one's pocket. Why, stock-taking in our business is nearly the same as with jewellers – and I can't say more than that. But one gets them" – he pointed to the pastille-box – "at trade prices." Evidently the censing of the gay, seven-tinted wench with the teeth was an established ritual which cost something.

"And when do we shut up shop?"

"We stay like this all night. The guv – old Mr. Cashell – doesn't believe in locks and shutters as compared with electric light. Besides it brings trade. I'll just sit here in the chair by the stove and write a letter, if you don't mind. Electricity isn't my prescription."

The energetic young Mr. Cashell snorted within, and Shaynor settled himself up in his chair over which he had thrown a staring red, black, and yellow Austrian jute blanket, rather like a table-cover. I cast about, amid patent-medicine pamphlets, for something to read, but finding little, returned to the manufacture of the new drink. The Italian warehouse took down its game and went to bed. Across the street blank shutters flung back the gaslight in cold smears; the dried pavement seemed to rough up in goose-flesh under the scouring of the savage wind, and we could hear, long ere he passed, the policeman flapping his arms to keep himself warm. Within, the flavours of cardamoms and chloric-ether disputed those of the pastilles and a score of drugs and perfume and soap scents. Our electric lights, set low down in the windows before the tun-bellied Rosamund jars, flung inward three monstrous daubs of red, blue, and green, that broke into kaleidoscopic lights on the faceted knobs of the drug-drawers, the cut-glass scent flagons, and the bulbs of the sparklet bottles. They flushed the white-tiled floor in gorgeous patches; splashed along the nickel-silver counter-rails, and turned the polished mahogany counter-panels to the likeness of intricate grained marbles – slabs of porphyry and malachite. Mr. Shaynor unlocked a drawer, and ere he began to write, took out a meagre bundle of letters. From my place by the stove, I could see the scalloped edges of the paper with a flaring monogram in the corner and could even smell the reek of chypre. At each page he turned towards the toilet-water lady of the advertisement and devoured her with over-luminous eyes. He had drawn the Austrian blanket over his shoulders, and among those warring lights he looked more than ever the incarnation of a drugged moth – a tiger-moth as I thought.

He put his letter into an envelope, stamped it with stiff mechanical movements, and dropped it in the drawer. Then I became aware of the silence of a great city asleep – the silence that underlaid the even voice of the breakers along the sea-front – a thick, tingling quiet of warm life stilled down for its appointed time, and unconsciously I moved about the glittering shop as one moves in a sick-room. Young Mr. Cashell was adjusting some wire that crackled from time to time with the tense, knuckle-stretching sound of the electric spark. Upstairs, where a door shut and opened swiftly, I could hear his uncle coughing abed.

"Here," I said, when the drink was properly warmed, "take some of this, Mr. Shaynor."

He jerked in his chair with a start and a wrench, and held out his hand for the glass. The mixture, of a rich port-wine colour, frothed at the top.

"It looks," he said, suddenly, "it looks – those bubbles – like a string of pearls winking at you – rather like the pearls round that young lady's neck." He turned again to the advertisement where the female in the dove-coloured corset had seen fit to put on all her pearls before she cleaned her teeth.

"Not bad, is it?" I said.

"Eh?"

He rolled his eyes heavily full on me, and, as I stared, I beheld all meaning and consciousness die out of the swiftly dilating pupils. His figure lost its stark rigidity, softened into the chair, and, chin on chest, hands dropped before him, he rested open-eyed, absolutely still.

"I'm afraid I've rather cooked Shaynor's goose," I said, bearing the fresh drink to young Mr. Cashell. "Perhaps it was the chloric-ether."

"Oh, he's all right." The spade-bearded man glanced at him pityingly. "Consumptives go off in those sort of dozes very often. It's exhaustion . . . I don't wonder. I daresay the liquor will do him good. It's grand stuff." He finished his share appreciatively. "Well, as I was saying – before he interrupted – about this little coherer. The pinch of dust, you see, is nickel-filings. The Hertzian waves, you see, come out of space from the station that despatches 'em, and all these little particles are attracted together – cohere, we call it – for just so long as the current passes through them. Now, it's important to remember that the current is an induced current. There are a good many kinds of induction —"

"Yes, but what *is* induction?"

"That's rather hard to explain untechnically. But the long and the short of it is that when a current of electricity passes through a wire there's a lot of magnetism present round that wire; and if you put another wire parallel to, and within what we call its magnetic field – why then, the second wire will also become charged with electricity."

"On its own account?"

"On its own account."

"Then let's see if I've got it correctly. Miles off, at Poole, or wherever it is —"

"It will be anywhere in ten years."

"You've got a charged wire —"

"Charged with Hertzian waves which vibrate, say, two hundred and thirty million times a second." Mr. Cashell snaked his forefinger rapidly through the air.

"All right – a charged wire at Poole, giving out these waves into space. Then this wire of yours sticking out into space – on the roof of the house – in some mysterious way gets charged with those waves from Poole —"

"Or anywhere – it only happens to be Poole to-night."

"And those waves set the coherer at work, just like an ordinary telegraph-office ticker?"

"No! That's where so many people make the mistake. The Hertzian waves wouldn't be strong enough to work a great heavy Morse instrument like ours. They can only just make that dust cohere, and while it coheres (a little while for a dot and a longer while for a dash) the current from this battery – the home battery" – he laid his hand on the thing – "can get through to the Morse printing-machine to record the dot or dash. Let me make it clearer. Do you know anything about steam?"

"Very little. But go on."

"Well, the coherer is like a steam-valve. Any child can open a valve and start a steamer's engines, because a turn of the hand lets in the main steam, doesn't it? Now, this home battery here ready to print is the main steam. The coherer is the valve, always ready to be turned on. The Hertzian wave is the child's hand that turns it."

"I see. That's marvellous."

"Marvellous, isn't it? And, remember, we're only at the beginning. There's nothing we sha'n't be able to do in ten years. I want to live – my God, how I want to live, and see it develop!" He looked through the door at Shaynor breathing lightly in his chair. "Poor beast! And he wants to keep company with Fanny Brand."

"Fanny *who*?" I said, for the name struck an obscurely familiar chord in my brain – something connected with a stained handkerchief, and the word "arterial."

"Fanny Brand – the girl you kept shop for." He laughed. "That's all I know about her, and for the life of me I can't see what Shaynor sees in her, or she in him."

"*Can't* you see what he sees in her?" I insisted.

"Oh, yes, if *that's* what you mean. She's a great, big, fat lump of a girl, and so on. I suppose that's why he's so crazy after her. She isn't his sort. Well, it doesn't matter. My uncle says he's bound to die before the year's out. Your drink's given him a good sleep, at any rate." Young Mr. Cashell could not catch Mr. Shaynor's face, which was half turned to the advertisement.

I stoked the stove anew, for the room was growing cold, and lighted another pastille. Mr. Shaynor in his chair, never moving, looked through and over me with eyes as wide and lustreless as those of a dead hare.

"Poole's late," said young Mr. Cashell, when I stepped back. "I'll just send them a call."

He pressed a key in the semi-darkness, and with a rending crackle there leaped between two brass knobs a spark, streams of sparks, and sparks again.

"Grand, isn't it? *That's* the Power – our unknown Power – kicking and fighting to be let loose," said young Mr. Cashell. "There she goes – kick – kick – kick into space. I never get over the strangeness of it when I work a sending-machine – waves going into space, you know. T. R. is our call. Poole ought to answer with L. L. L."

We waited two, three, five minutes. In that silence, of which the boom of the tide was an orderly part, I caught the clear "*kiss – kiss – kiss*" of the halliards on the roof, as they were blown against the installation-pole.

"Poole is not ready. I'll stay here and call you when he is."

I returned to the shop, and set down my glass on a marble slab with a careless clink. As I did so, Shaynor rose to his feet, his eyes fixed once more on the advertisement, where the young woman bathed in the light from the red jar simpered pinkly over her pearls. His lips moved without cessation. I stepped nearer to listen. "And threw – and threw – and threw," he repeated, his face all sharp with some inexplicable agony.

I moved forward astonished. But it was then he found words – delivered roundly and clearly. These:

> And threw warm gules on Madeleine's young breast.

The trouble passed off his countenance, and he returned lightly to his place, rubbing his hands.

It had never occurred to me, though we had many times

discussed reading and prize-competitions as a diversion, that
Mr. Shaynor ever read Keats, or could quote him at all ap-
positely. There was, after all, a certain stained-glass effect of
light on the high bosom of the highly-polished picture which
might, by stretch of fancy, suggest, as a vile chromo recalls
some incomparable canvas, the line he had spoken. Night,
my drink, and solitude were evidently turning Mr. Shaynor
into a poet. He sat down again and wrote swiftly on his
villainous note-paper, his lips quivering.

I shut the door into the inner office and moved up behind
him. He made no sign that he saw or heard. I looked over
his shoulder, and read, amid half-formed words, sentences,
and wild scratches:

> — Very cold it was. Very cold
> The hare – the hare – the hare –
> The birds —

He raised his head sharply, and frowned toward the blank
shutters of the poulterer's shop where they jutted out against
our window. Then one clear line came:

> The hare, in spite of fur, was very cold.

The head, moving machine-like, turned right to the advertisement where the Blaudett's Cathedral pastille reeked
abominably. He grunted, and went on:

> Incense in a censer –
> Before her darling picture framed in gold –
> Maiden's picture – angel's portrait –

"Hsh!" said Mr. Cashell guardedly from the inner office,
as though in the presence of spirits. "There's something
coming through from somewhere; but it isn't Poole." I heard
the crackle of sparks as he depressed the keys of the transmitter. In my own brain, too, something crackled, or it might
have been the hair on my head. Then I heard my own voice,
in a harsh whisper: "Mr. Cashell, there is something coming
through here, too. Leave me alone till I tell you."

"But I thought you'd come to see this wonderful thing – Sir," indignantly at the end.

"Leave me alone till I tell you. Be quiet."

I watched – I waited. Under the blue-veined hand – the dry hand of the consumptive – came away clear, without erasure:

> And my weak spirit fails
> To think how the dead must freeze –

he shivered as he wrote –

> Beneath the churchyard mould.

Then he stopped, laid the pen down, and leaned back.

For an instant, that was half an eternity, the shop spun before me in a rainbow-tinted whirl, in and through which my own soul most dispassionately considered my own soul as that fought with an over-mastering fear. Then I smelt the strong smell of cigarettes from Mr. Shaynor's clothing, and heard, as though it had been the rending of trumpets, the rattle of his breathing. I was still in my place of observation, much as one would watch a rifle-shot at the butts, half-bent, hands on my knees, and head within a few inches of the black, red, and yellow blanket of his shoulder. I was whispering encouragement, evidently to my other self, sounding sentences, such as men pronounce in dreams.

"If he has read Keats, it proves nothing. If he hasn't – like causes *must* beget like effects. There is no escape from this law. *You* ought to be grateful that you know 'St. Agnes Eve' without the book; because, given the circumstances, such as Fanny Brand, who is the key of the enigma, and approximately represents the latitude and longitude of Fanny Brawne; allowing also for the bright red colour of the arterial blood upon the handkerchief, which was just what you were puzzling over in the shop just now; and counting the effect of the professional environment, here almost perfectly duplicated – the result is logical and inevitable. As inevitable as induction."

Still, the other half of my soul refused to be comforted. It was cowering in some minute and inadequate corner – at an immense distance.

Hereafter, I found myself one person again, my hands still gripping my knees, and my eyes glued on the page before Mr. Shaynor. As dreamers accept and explain the upheaval of landscapes and the resurrection of the dead, with excerpts from the evening hymn or the multiplication-table, so I had accepted the facts, whatever they might be, that I should witness, and had devised a theory, sane and plausible to my mind, that explained them all. Nay, I was even in advance of my facts, walking hurriedly before them, assured that they would fit my theory. And all that I now recall of that epoch-making theory are the lofty words: "If he has read Keats it's the chloric-ether. If he hasn't, it's the identical bacillus, or Hertzian wave of tuberculosis, *plus* Fanny Brand and the professional status which, in conjunction with the mainstream of subconscious thought common to all mankind, has thrown up temporarily an induced Keats."

Mr. Shaynor returned to his work, erasing and rewriting as before with swiftness. Two or three blank pages he tossed aside. Then he wrote, muttering:

> The little smoke of a candle that goes out.

"No," he muttered. "Little smoke – little smoke – little smoke. What else?" He thrust his chin forward towards the advertisement, whereunder the last of the Blaudett's Cathedral pastilles fumed in its holder. "Ah!" Then with relief:

> The little smoke that dies in moonlight cold.

Evidently he was snared by the rhymes of his first verse, for he wrote and rewrote "gold – cold – mould" many times. Again he sought inspiration from the advertisement, and set down, without erasure, the line I had overheard:

> And threw warm gules on Madeleine's young breast.

As I remembered the original it is "fair" – a trite word –

instead of "young," and I found myself nodding approval,
though I admitted that the attempt to reproduce "its little
smoke in pallid moonlight died" was a failure.

Followed without a break ten or fifteen lines of bald prose
– the naked soul's confession of its physical yearning for its
beloved – unclean as we count uncleanliness; unwholesome,
but human exceedingly; the raw material, so it seemed to me
in that hour and in that place, whence Keats wove the
twenty-sixth, -seventh, and -eighth stanzas of his poem.
Shame I had none in overseeing this revelation; and my fear
had gone with the smoke of the pastille.

"That's it," I murmured. "That's how it's blocked out.
Go on! Ink it in, man. Ink it in!"

Mr. Shaynor returned to broken verse wherein "loveli-
ness" was made to rhyme with a desire to look upon "her
empty dress." He picked up a fold of the gay, soft blanket,
spread it over one hand, caressed it with infinite tenderness,
thought, muttered, traced some snatches which I could not
decipher, shut his eyes drowsily, shook his head, and
dropped the stuff. Here I found myself at fault, for I could
not then see (as I do now) in what manner a red, black, and
yellow Austrian blanket coloured his dreams.

In a few minutes he laid aside his pen, and, chin on hand,
considered the shop with thoughtful and intelligent eyes. He
threw down the blanket, rose, passed along a line of drug-
drawers, and read the names on the labels aloud. Returning,
he took from his desk Christie's *New Commercial Plants* and
the old Culpeper that I had given him, opened and laid them
side by side with a clerky air, all trace of passion gone from
his face, read first in one and then in the other, and paused
with pen behind his ear.

"What wonder of Heaven's coming now?" I thought.

"Manna – manna – manna," he said at last, under wrinkled brows. "That's what I wanted. Good! Now then! Now
then! Good! Good! Oh, by God, that's good!" His voice rose
and he spoke rightly and fully without a falter:

Candied apple, quince and plum and gourd,
And jellies smoother than the creamy curd,
And lucent syrups tinct with cinnamon,

Manna and dates in Argosy transferred
From Fez; and spiced dainties, every one
From silken Samarcand to cedared Lebanon.

He repeated it once more, using "blander" for "smoother" in the second line; then wrote it down without erasure, but this time (my set eyes missed no stroke of any word) he substituted "soother" for his atrocious second thought, so that it came away under his hand as it is written in the book – as it is written in the book.

A wind went shouting down the street, and on the heels of the wind followed a spurt and rattle of rain.

After a smiling pause – and good right had he to smile – he began anew, always tossing the last sheet over his shoulder:

The sharp rain falling on the window-pane,
Rattling sleet – the wind-blown sleet.

Then prose: "It is very cold of mornings when the wind brings rain and sleet with it. I heard the sleet on the window-pane outside, and thought of you, my darling. I am always thinking of you. I wish we could both run away like two lovers into the storm and get that little cottage by the sea which we are always thinking about, my own dear darling. We could sit and watch the sea beneath our windows. It would be a fairyland all of our own – a fairy sea – a fairy sea. . . ."

He stopped, raised his head, and listened. The steady drone of the Channel along the sea-front that had borne us company so long leaped up a note to the sudden fuller surge that signals the change from ebb to flood. It beat in like the change of step throughout an army – this renewed pulse of the sea – and filled our ears till they, accepting it, marked it no longer.

> A fairyland for you and me
> Across the foam – beyond . . .
> A magic foam, a perilous sea.

He grunted again with effort and bit his underlip. My throat dried, but I dared not gulp to moisten it lest I should break the spell that was drawing him nearer and nearer to the high-water mark but two of the sons of Adam have reached. Remember that in all the millions permitted there are no more than five – five little lines – of which one can say: "These are the pure Magic. These are the clear Vision. The rest is only poetry." And Mr. Shaynor was playing hot and cold with two of them!

I vowed no unconscious thought of mine should influence the blindfold soul, and pinned myself desperately to the other three, repeating and rerepeating:

> A savage spot as holy and enchanted
> As e'er beneath a waning moon was haunted
> By woman wailing for her demon lover.

But though I believed my brain thus occupied, my every sense hung upon the writing under the dry, bony hand, all brown-fingered with chemicals and cigarette-smoke.

> Our windows fronting on the dangerous foam,

(he wrote, after long, irresolute snatches), and then –

> Our open casements facing desolate seas
> Forlorn – forlorn –

Here again his face grew peaked and anxious with that sense of loss I had first seen when the Power snatched him. But this time the agony was tenfold keener. As I watched, it mounted like mercury in the tube. It lighted his face from within till I thought the visibly scourged soul must leap forth naked between his jaws, unable to endure. A drop of sweat trickled from my forehead down my nose and splashed on the back of my hand.

> Our windows facing on the desolate seas
> And pearly foam of magic fairyland –

"Not yet – not yet," he muttered, "wait a minute. *Please*
wait a minute. I shall get it then –

> Our magic windows fronting on the sea,
> The dangerous foam of desolate seas . . .
>   For aye.

Ouh, my God!"

From head to heel he shook – shook from the marrow of
his bones outwards – then leaped to his feet with raised arms,
and slid the chair screeching across the tiled floor where it
struck the drawers behind and fell with a jar. Mechanically,
I stooped to recover it.

As I rose, Mr. Shaynor was stretching and yawning at
leisure.

"I've had a bit of a doze," he said. "How did I come to
knock the chair over? You look rather —"

"The chair startled me," I answered. "It was so sudden in
this quiet."

Young Mr. Cashell behind his shut door was offendedly
silent.

"I suppose I must have been dreaming," said Mr.
Shaynor.

"I suppose you must," I said. "Talking of dreams – I – I
noticed you writing – before —"

He flushed consciously.

"I meant to ask you if you've ever read anything written
by a man called Keats."

"Oh! I haven't much time to read poetry, and I can't say
that I remember the name exactly. Is he a popular writer?"

"Middling. I thought you might know him because he's
the only poet who was ever a druggist. And he's rather
what's called the lover's poet."

"Indeed. I must dip into him. What did he write about?"

"A lot of things. Here's a sample that may interest you."

Then and there, carefully, I repeated the verse he had twice spoken and once written not ten minutes ago.

"Ah. Anybody could see he was a druggist from that line about the tinctures and syrups. It's a fine tribute to our profession."

"I don't know," said young Mr. Cashell, with icy politeness, opening the door one half-inch, "if you still happen to be interested in our trifling experiments. But, should such be the case —"

I drew him aside, whispering, "Shaynor seemed going off into some sort of fit when I spoke to you just now. I thought, even at the risk of being rude, it wouldn't do to take you off your instruments just as the call was coming through. Don't you see?"

"Granted – granted as soon as asked," he said unbending. "I *did* think it a shade odd at the time. So that was why he knocked the chair down?"

"I hope I haven't missed anything," I said.

"I'm afraid I can't say that, but you're just in time for the end of a rather curious performance. You can come in, too, Mr. Shaynor. Listen, while I read it off."

The Morse instrument was ticking furiously. Mr. Cashell interpreted: " '*K.K.V. Can make nothing of your signals.*' " A pause. " '*M.M.V. M.M.V. Signals unintelligible. Purpose anchor Sandown Bay. Examine instruments to-morrow.*' Do you know what that means? It's a couple of men-o'-war working Marconi signals off the Isle of Wight. They are trying to talk to each other. Neither can read the other's messages, but all their messages are being taken in by our receiver here. They've been going on for ever so long. I wish you could have heard it."

"How wonderful!" I said. "Do you mean we're overhearing Portsmouth ships trying to talk to each other – that we're eavesdropping across half South England?"

"Just that. Their transmitters are all right, but their receivers are out of order, so they only get a dot here and a dash there. Nothing clear."

"Why is that?"

"God knows – and Science will know to-morrow. Perhaps the induction is faulty; perhaps the receivers aren't tuned to receive just the number of vibrations per second that the transmitter sends. Only a word here and there. Just enough to tantalise."

Again the Morse sprang to life.

"That's one of 'em complaining now. Listen: '*Disheartening – most disheartening.*' It's quite pathetic. Have you ever seen a spiritualistic seance? It reminds me of that sometimes – odds and ends of messages coming out of nowhere – a word here and there – no good at all."

"But mediums are all impostors," said Mr. Shaynor, in the doorway, lighting an asthma-cigarette. "They only do it for the money they can make. I've seen 'em."

"Here's Poole, at last – clear as a bell. L.L.L. *Now* we sha'n't be long." Mr. Cashell rattled the keys merrily. "Anything you'd like to tell 'em?"

"No, I don't think so," I said. "I'll go home and get to bed. I'm feeling a little tired."

MRS. BATHURST

MRS. BATHURST

✳ ✳ ✳

FROM LYDEN'S "IRENIUS"

ACT III. Sc. II.

GOW: – Had it been your Prince instead of a groom caught in this noose there's not an astrologer of the city—

PRINCE: – Sacked! Sacked! We were a city yesterday.

GOW: – So be it, but I was not governor. Not an astrologer, but would ha' sworn he'd foreseen it at the last versary of Venus, when Vulcan caught her with Mars in the house of stinking Capricorn. But since 'tis Jack of the Straw that hangs, the forgetful stars had it not on their tablets.

PRINCE: – Another life! Were there any left to die? How did the poor fool come by it?

GOW: – *Simpliciter* thus. She that damned him to death knew not that she did it, or would have died ere she had done it. For she loved him. He that hangs him does so in obedience to the Duke, and asks no more than "Where is the rope?" The Duke, very exactly he hath told us, works God's will, in which holy employ he's not to be questioned. We have then left upon this finger, only Jack whose soul now plucks the left sleeve of Destiny in Hell to overtake why she clapped him up like a fly on a sunny wall. Whuff! Sack!

PRINCE: – Your cloak, Ferdinand. I'll sleep now.

FERDINAND: – Sleep, then . . . He too, loved his life?

GOW: – He was born of woman . . . but at the end threw her from him, like your Prince, for a little sleep . . . "Have I any look of a King?" said he, clanking his chain – "to be so baited on all sides by Fortune, that I must e'en die now to live with myself one day longer." I left him railing at Fortune and woman's love.

FERDINAND: – Ah, woman's love!

577

(*Aside*)   Who knows not Fortune, glutted on easy thrones,
             Stealing from feasts as rare to coneycatch,
             Privily in the hedgerows for a clown
             With that same cruel-lustful hand and eye,
             Those nails and wedges, that one hammer and lead,
             And the very gerb of long-stored lightnings loosed
             Yesterday 'gainst some King.

* * *

THE day that I chose to visit H.M.S. *Peridot* in Simon's
    Bay was the day that the Admiral had chosen to send
her up the coast. She was just steaming out to sea as my train
came in, and since the rest of the Fleet were either coaling
or busy at the rifle-ranges a thousand feet up the hill, I found
myself stranded, lunchless, on the sea-front with no hope of
return to Cape Town before five P.M. At this crisis I had the
luck to come across my friend Inspector Hooper, Cape Government Railways, in command of an engine and a brake-van
chalked for repair.

"If you get something to eat," he said, "I'll run you down
to Glengariff siding till the goods comes along. It's cooler
there than here, you see."

I got food and drink from the Greeks who sell all things at a
price, and the engine trotted us a couple of miles up the line
to a bay of drifted sand and a plank- platform half buried in
sand not a hundred yards from the edge of the surf.
Moulded dunes, whiter than any snow, rolled far inland up
a brown and purple valley of splintered rocks and dry scrub.
A crowd of Malays hauled at a net beside two blue-and-green
boats on the beach; a picnic party danced and shouted bare-
foot where a tiny river trickled across the flat, and a circle of
dry hills, whose feet were set in sands of silver, locked us in
against a seven-coloured sea. At either horn of the bay the
railway line cut just above high-water mark, ran round a
shoulder of piled rocks, and disappeared.

"You see there's always a breeze here," said Hooper,

opening the door as the engine left us in the siding on the sand, and the strong south-easter buffeting under Elsie's Peak dusted sand into our tickey beer. Presently he sat down to a file full of spiked documents. He had returned from a long trip up-country, where he had been reporting on damaged rolling-stock, as far away as Rhodesia. The weight of the bland wind on my eyelids; the song of it under the car roof, and high up among the rocks; the drift of fine grains chasing each other musically ashore; the tramp of the surf; the voices of the picnickers; the rustle of Hooper's file, and the presence of the assured sun, joined with the beer to cast me into magical slumber. The hills of False Bay were just dissolving into those of fairyland when I heard footsteps on the sand outside, and the clink of our couplings.

"Stop that!" snapped Hooper, without raising his head from his work. "It's those dirty little Malay boys, you see: they're always playing with the trucks. . . ."

"Don't be hard on 'em. The railway's a general refuge in Africa," I replied.

" 'Tis – up-country at any rate. That reminds me," he felt in his waistcoat-pocket, "I've got a curiosity for you from Wankies – beyond Buluwayo. It's more of a souvenir perhaps than —"

"The old hotel's inhabited," cried a voice. "White men from the language. Marines to the front! Come on, Pritch. Here's your Belmont. Wha – i – i!"

The last word dragged like a rope as Mr. Pyecroft ran round to the open door, and stood looking up into my face. Behind him an enormous Sergeant of Marines trailed a stalk of dried seaweed, and dusted the sand nervously from his fingers.

"What are you doing here?" I asked. "I thought the *Hierophant* was down the coast?"

"We came in last Tuesday – from Tristan D'Acunha – for overhaul, and we shall be in dockyard 'ands for two months, with boiler-seatings."

"Come and sit down." Hooper put away the file.

"This is Mr. Hooper of the Railway," I exclaimed, as Pyecroft turned to haul up the black-moustached sergeant.

"This is Sergeant Pritchard, of the *Agaric*, an old ship-mate," said he. "We were strollin' on the beach." The monster blushed and nodded. He filled up one side of the van when he sat down.

"And this is my friend, Mr. Pyecroft," I added to Hooper, already busy with the extra beer which my prophetic soul had bought from the Greeks.

"*Moi aussi*," quoth Pyecroft, and drew out beneath his coat a labelled quart bottle.

"Why, it's Bass," cried Hooper.

"It was Pritchard," said Pyecroft. "They can't resist him."

"That's not so," said Pritchard mildly.

"Not *verbatim* per'aps, but the look in the eye came to the same thing."

"Where was it?" I demanded.

"Just on beyond here – at Kalk Bay. She was slappin' a rug in a back verandah. Pritch 'adn't more than brought his batteries to bear, before she stepped indoors an' sent it flyin' over the wall."

Pyecroft patted the warm bottle.

"It was all a mistake," said Pritchard. "I shouldn't wonder if she mistook me for Maclean. We're about of a size."

I had heard householders of Muizenburg, St. James's, and Kalk Bay complain of the difficulty of keeping beer or good servants at the seaside, and I began to see the reason. None the less, it was excellent Bass, and I too drank to the health of that large-minded maid.

"It's the uniform that fetches 'em, an' they fetch it," said Pyecroft. "My simple navy blue is respectable, but not fasci-natin'. Now Pritch in 'is Number One rig is always 'purr Mary, on the terrace' – *ex officio* as you might say."

"She took me for Maclean, I tell you," Pritchard insisted. "Why – why – to listen to him you wouldn't think that only yesterday —"

"Pritch," said Pyecroft, "be warned in time. If we begin

tellin' what we know about each other we'll be turned out of the pub. Not to mention aggravated desertion on several occasions —"

"Never anything more than absence without leaf – I defy you to prove it," said the Sergeant hotly. "An' if it comes to that how about Vancouver in '87?"

"How about it? Who pulled bow in the gig going ashore? Who told Boy Niven . . .?"

"Surely you were court-martialled for that?" I said. The story of Boy Niven who lured seven or eight able-bodied seamen and marines into the woods of British Columbia used to be a legend of the Fleet.

"Yes, we were court-martialled to rights," said Pritchard, "but we should have been tried for murder if Boy Niven 'adn't been unusually tough. He told us he had an uncle 'oo'd give us land to farm. 'E said he was born at the back o' Vancouver Island, and *all* the time the beggar was a balmy Barnado Orphan!"

"*But* we believed him," said Pyecroft. "I did – you did – Paterson did – an' 'oo was the Marine that married the cocoanut-woman afterwards – him with the mouth?"

"Oh, Jones, Spit-Kid Jones. I 'aven't thought of 'im in years," said Pritchard. "Yes, Spit-Kid believed it, an' George Anstey and Moon. We were very young an' very curious."

"*But* lovin' an' trustful to a degree," said Pyecroft.

" 'Remember when 'e told us to walk in single file for fear o' bears? 'Remember, Pye, when 'e 'opped about in that bog full o' ferns an' sniffed an' said 'e could smell the smoke of 'is uncle's farm? An' *all* the time it was a dirty little outlyin' uninhabited island. We walked round it in a day, an' come back to our boat lyin' on the beach. A whole day Boy Niven kept us walkin' in circles lookin' for 'is uncle's farm! He said his uncle was compelled by the law of the land to give us a farm!"

"Don't get hot, Pritch. We believed," said Pyecroft.

"He'd been readin' books. He only did it to get a run ashore an' have himself talked of. A day an' a night – eight

of us – followin' Boy Niven round an uninhabited island in
the Vancouver archipelago! Then the picket came for us an'
a nice pack o' idiots we looked!"

"What did you get for it?" Hooper asked.

"Heavy thunder with continuous lightning for two hours.
Thereafter sleet-squalls, a confused sea, and cold, unfriendly
weather till conclusion o' cruise," said Pyecroft. "It was only
what we expected, but what we felt, an' I assure you, Mr.
Hooper, even a sailor-man has a heart to break, was bein' told
that we able seamen an' promisin' marines had misled Boy
Niven. Yes, we poor back-to-the-landers was supposed to
'ave misled him! He rounded on us, o' course, an' got off
easy."

"Excep' for what we gave him in the steerin'-flat when we
came out o' cells. 'Eard anything of 'im lately, Pye?"

"Signal Boatswain in the Channel Fleet, I believe – Mr.
L. L. Niven is."

"An' Anstey died o' fever in Benin," Pritchard mused.
"What come to Moon? Spit-Kid we know about."

"Moon – Moon! Now where did I last . . .? Oh yes, when
I was in the *Palladium*! I met Quigley at Buncrana Station. He told me Moon 'ad run when the *Astrild* sloop
was cruising among the South Seas three years back. He
always showed signs o' bein' a Mormonastic beggar. Yes, he
slipped off quietly an' they 'adn't time to chase him round
the islands even if the navigatin' officer had been equal to the
job."

"Wasn't he?" said Hooper.

"Not so. Accordin' to Quigley the *Astrild* spent half her
commission rompin' up the beach like a she-turtle, an' the
other half hatching turtles' eggs on the top o' numerous
reefs. When she was docked at Sydney her copper looked like
Aunt Maria's washing on the line – an' her 'midship frames
was sprung. The commander swore the dockyard 'ad done it
haulin' the poor thing on to the slips. They *do* do strange
things at sea, Mr. Hooper."

"Ah! I'm not a tax-payer," said Hooper, and opened a

fresh bottle. The Sergeant seemed to be one who had a difficulty in dropping subjects.

"How it all comes back, don't it?" he said. "Why, Moon must 'ave 'ad sixteen years' service before he ran."

"It takes 'em at all ages. Look at – you know," said Pyecroft.

"Who?" I asked.

"A service man within eighteen months of his pension, is the party you're thinkin' of," said Pritchard. "A warrant 'oose name begins with a V, isn't it?"

"But, in a way o' puttin' it, we can't say that he actually did desert," Pyecroft suggested.

"Oh no," said Pritchard. "It was only permanent absence up-country without leaf. That was all."

"Up-country?" said Hooper. "Did they circulate his description?"

"What for?" said Pritchard, most impolitely.

"Because deserters are like columns in the war. They don't move away from the line, you see. I've known a chap caught at Salisbury that way tryin' to get to Nyassa. They tell me, but o' course I don't know, that they don't ask questions on the Nyassa Lake Flotilla up there. I've heard of a P. and O. quartermaster in full command of an armed launch there."

"Do you think Click 'ud ha' gone up that way?" Pritchard asked.

"There's no saying. He was sent up to Bloemfontein to take over some Navy ammunition left in the fort. We know he took it over and saw it into the trucks. Then there was no more Click – then or thereafter. Four months ago it transpired, and thus the *casus belli* stands at present," said Pyecroft.

"What were his marks?" said Hooper again.

"Does the Railway get a reward for returnin' 'em, then?" said Pritchard.

"If I did d'you suppose I'd talk about it?" Hooper retorted angrily.

"You seemed so very interested," said Pritchard with equal crispness.

"Why was he called Click?" I asked, to tide over an uneasy little break in the conversation. The two men were staring at each other very fixedly.

"Because of an ammunition hoist carryin' away," said Pyecroft. "And it carried away four of 'is teeth – on the lower port side, wasn't it, Pritch? The substitutes which he bought weren't screwed home in a manner o' sayin'. When he talked fast they used to lift a little on the bed plate. 'Ence, 'Click.' They called 'im a superior man, which is what we'd call a long, black-'aired, genteely speakin', 'alf-bred beggar on the lower deck."

"Four false teeth on the lower left jaw," said Hooper, his hand in his waistcoat-pocket. "What tattoo marks?"

"Look here," began Pritchard, half rising. "I'm sure we're very grateful to you as a gentleman for your 'orspitality, but per'aps we may 'ave made an error in —"

I looked at Pyecroft for aid. Hooper was crimsoning rapidly.

"If the fat marine now occupying the foc'sle will kindly bring his *status quo* to an anchor yet once more, we may be able to talk like gentlemen – not to say friends," said Pyecroft. "He regards you, Mr. Hooper, as a emissary of the Law."

"I only wish to observe that when a gentleman exhibits such a peculiar, or I should rather say such a *bloomin'* curiosity in identification marks as our friend here —"

"Mr. Pritchard," I interposed, "I'll take all the responsibility for Mr. Hooper."

"An' *you*'ll apologise all round," said Pyecroft. "You're a rude little man, Pritch."

"But how was I —" he began, wavering.

"I don't know an' I don't care. Apologise!"

The giant looked round bewildered and took our little hands into his vast grip, one by one.

"I was wrong," he said meekly as a sheep. "My suspicions was unfounded. Mr. Hooper, I apologise."

"You did quite right to look out for your own end o' the line," said Hooper. "I'd ha' done the same with a gentleman I didn't know, you see. If you don't mind I'd like to hear a little more o' your Mr. Vickery. It's safe with me, you see."

"Why did Vickery run," I began, but Pyecroft's smile made me turn my question to "Who was she?"

"She kep' a little hotel at Hauraki – near Auckland," said Pyecroft.

"By Gawd!" roared Pritchard, slapping his hand on his leg. "Not Mrs. Bathurst!"

Pyecroft nodded slowly, and the Sergeant called all the powers of darkness to witness his bewilderment.

"So far as I could get at it Mrs. B. was the lady in question."

"But Click was married," cried Pritchard.

"An' 'ad a fifteen-year-old daughter. 'E's shown me her photograph. Settin' that aside, so to say, 'ave you ever found these little things make much difference? Because I haven't."

"Good Lord Alive an' Watchin'! . . . Mrs. Bathurst. . . ." Then with another roar: "You can say what you please, Pye, but you don't make me believe it was any of 'er fault. She wasn't *that*!"

"If I was going to say what I please, I'd begin by callin' you a silly ox an' work up to the higher pressures at leisure. I'm trying to say solely what transpired. M'rover, for once you're right. It wasn't her fault."

"You couldn't 'ave made me believe it if it 'ad been," was the answer.

Such faith in a Sergeant of Marines interested me greatly. "Never mind about that," I cried. "Tell me what she was like."

"She was a widow," said Pyecroft. "Left so very young and never re-spliced. She kep' a little hotel for warrants and non-coms close to Auckland, an' she always wore black silk, and 'er neck —"

"You ask what she was like," Pritchard broke in. "Let me give you an instance. I was at Auckland first in '97, at the

end o' the *Marroquin*'s commission, an' as I'd been promoted I went up with the others. She used to look after us
all, an' she never lost by it – not a penny! 'Pay me now,'
she'd say, 'or settle later. I know you won't let me suffer.
Send the money from home if you like.' Why, gentlemen all,
I tell you I've seen that lady take her own gold watch an'
chain off her neck in the bar an' pass it to a bosun 'oo'd come
ashore without 'is ticker an' 'ad to catch the last boat. 'I don't
know your name,' she said, 'but when you've done with it,
you'll find plenty that know me on the front. Send it back
by one o' them.' And it was worth thirty pounds if it was
worth 'arf a crown. The little gold watch, Pye, with the blue
monogram at the back. But, as I was sayin', in those days she
kep' a beer that agreed with me – Slits it was called. One way
an' another I must 'ave punished a good few bottles of it
while we was in the bay – comin' ashore every night or
so. Chaffin' across the bar like, once when we were alone,
'Mrs. B.,' I said, 'when next I call I want you to remember
that this is my particular – just as you're my particular?'
(She'd let you go *that* far!) 'Just as you're my particular,' I
said. 'Oh, thank you, Sergeant Pritchard,' she says, an' put
'er hand up to the curl be'ind 'er ear. Remember that way
she had, Pye?"

"I think so," said the sailor.

"Yes, 'Thank you, Sergeant Pritchard,' she says. 'The
least I can do is to mark it for you in case you change your
mind. There's no great demand for it in the Fleet,' she says,
'but to make sure I'll put it at the back o' the shelf,' an' she
snipped off a piece of her hair ribbon with that old dolphin
cigar cutter on the bar – remember it, Pye? – an' she tied a
bow round what was left – just four bottles. That was '97 –
no, '96. In '98 I was in the *Resiliant* – China station – full
commission. In Nineteen One, mark you, I was in the *Car-
thusian*, back in Auckland Bay again. Of course I went up to
Mrs. B.'s with the rest of us to see how things were goin'.
They were the same as ever. (Remember the big tree on the
pavement by the side-bar, Pye?) I never said anythin' in

special (there was too many of us talkin' to her), but she saw me at once."

"That wasn't difficult?" I ventured.

"Ah, but wait. I was comin' up to the bar, when, 'Ada,' she says to her niece, 'get me Sergeant Pritchard's particular,' and, gentlemen all, I tell you, before I could shake 'ands with the lady, there were those four bottles o' Slits, with 'er 'air ribbon in a bow round each o' their necks, set down in front o' me, an' as she drew the cork she looked at me under her eyebrows in that blindish way she had o' lookin', an', 'Sergeant Pritchard,' she says, 'I do 'ope you 'aven't changed your mind about your particulars.' That's the kind of woman she was – after five years!"

"I don't *see* her yet somehow," said Hooper, but with sympathy.

"She – she never scrupled to feed a lame duck or set 'er foot on a scorpion at any time of 'er life," Pritchard added valiantly.

"That don't help me either. My mother's like that for one."

The giant heaved inside his uniform and rolled his eyes at the car-roof. Said Pyecroft suddenly:

"How many women have you been intimate with all over the world, Pritch?"

Pritchard blushed plum colour to the short hairs of his seventeen-inch neck.

"'Undreds," said Pyecroft. "So've I. How many of 'em can you remember in your own mind, settin' aside the first – an' per'aps the last – *and one more?*"

"Few, wonderful few, now I tax myself," said Sergeant Pritchard, relievedly.

"An' how many times might you 'ave been at Auckland?"

"One – two," he began. "Why, I can't make it more than three times in ten years. But I can remember every time that I ever saw Mrs. B."

"So can I – an' I've only been to Auckland twice – how she stood an' what she was sayin' an' what she looked like.

That's the secret. 'Tisn't beauty, so to speak, nor good talk necessarily. It's just it. Some women'll stay in a man's memory if they once walk down a street, but most of 'em you can live with a month on end, an' next commission you'd be put to it to certify whether they talked in their sleep or not, as one might say."

"Ah," said Hooper. "That's more the idea. I've known just two women of that nature."

"An' it was no fault o' theirs?" asked Pritchard.

"None whatever. I know that!"

"An' if a man gets struck with that kind of woman, Mr. Hooper?" Pritchard went on.

"He goes crazy — or just saves himself," was the slow answer.

"You've hit it," said the Sergeant. "You've seen an' known somethin' in the course o' your life, Mr. Hooper. I'm lookin' at you!" He set down his bottle.

"And how often had Vickery seen her?" I asked.

"That's the dark an' bloody mystery," Pyecroft answered. "I'd never come across him till I come out in the *Hierophant* just now, an' there wasn't any one in the ship who knew much about him. You see, he was what you call a superior man. 'E spoke to me once or twice about Auckland and Mrs. B. on the voyage out. I called that to mind subsequently. There must 'ave been a good deal between 'em, to my way o' thinkin'. Mind you, I'm only giving you my *résumé* of it all, because all I know is second-hand so to speak, or rather I should say more than second-'and."

"How?" said Hooper peremptorily. "You must have seen it or heard it."

"Ye-es," said Pyecroft. "I used to think seein' and hearin' was the only regulation aids to ascertainin' facts, but as we get older we get more accommodatin'. The cylinders work easier, I suppose. . . . Were you in Cape Town last December when Phyllis's Circus came?"

"No — up-country," said Hooper, a little nettled at the change of venue.

"I ask because they had a new turn of a scientific nature called 'Home and Friends for a Tickey.'"

"Oh, you mean the cinematograph – the pictures of prize-fights and steamers. I've seen 'em up-country."

"Biograph or cinematograph was what I was alludin' to. London Bridge with the omnibuses – a troopship goin' to the war – marines on parade at Portsmouth an' the Plymouth Express arrivin' at Paddin'ton."

"Seen 'em all. Seen 'em all," said Hooper impatiently.

"We *Hierophants* came in just before Christmas week an' leaf was easy."

"I think a man gets fed up with Cape Town quicker than anywhere else on the station. Why, even Durban's more like Nature. We was there for Christmas," Pritchard put in.

"Not bein' a devotee of Indian *peeris*, as our Doctor said to the Pusser, I can't exactly say. Phyllis's was good enough after musketry practice at Mozambique. I couldn't get off the first two or three nights on account of what you might call an imbroglio with our Torpedo Lieutenant in the submerged flat, where some pride of the West country had sugared up a gyroscope; but I remember Vickery went ashore with our Carpenter Rigdon – old Crocus we called him. As a general rule Crocus never left 'is ship unless an' until he was 'oisted out with a winch, but *when* 'e went 'e would return noddin' like a lily gemmed with dew. We smothered him down below that night, but the things 'e said about Vickery as a fittin' playmate for a Warrant Officer of 'is cubic capacity, before we got him quiet, was what I should call pointed."

"I've been with Crocus – in the *Redoubtable*," said the Sergeant. "He's a character if there is one."

"Next night I went into Cape Town with Dawson and Pratt; but just at the door of the Circus I came across Vickery. 'Oh!' he says, 'you're the man I'm looking for. Come and sit next me. This way to the shillin' places!' I went astern at once, protestin' because tickey seats better suited my so-called finances. 'Come on,' says Vickery. 'I'm payin'.' Naturally I abandoned Pratt and Dawson in anticipation o' drinks to match the seats. 'No,' he says, when this was 'inted – 'not now. Not now. As many as you please afterwards, but I want you sober for the occasion.' I caught 'is face under a lamp just then, an' the appearance of it quite cured me of my thirsts. Don't mistake. It didn't frighten me. It made me anxious. I can't tell you what it was like, but that was the effect which it 'ad on me. If you want to know, it reminded me of those things in bottles in those herbalistic shops at Plymouth – preserved in spirits of wine. White an' crumply things – previous to birth as you might say."

"You 'ave a beastial mind, Pye," said the Sergeant, re-lighting his pipe.

"Perhaps. We were in the front row, an' 'Home an' Friends' came on early. Vickery touched me on the knee when the number went up. 'If you see anything that strikes you,' he says, 'drop me a hint'; then he went on clicking. We saw London Bridge an' so forth an' so on, an' it was most interestin'. I'd never seen it before. You 'eard a little dynamo like buzzin', but the pictures were the real thing – alive an' movin'."

"I've seen 'em," said Hooper. "Of course they are taken from the very thing itself – you see."

"Then the Western Mail came in to Paddin'ton on the big magic lantern sheet. First we saw the platform empty an' the porters standin' by. Then the engine come in, head on, an' the women in the front row jumped: she headed so straight. Then the doors opened and the passengers came out and the porters got the luggage – just like life. Only – only when any one came down too far towards us that was watchin', they walked right out o' the picture, so to speak. I was 'ighly interested, I can tell you. So were all of us. I watched an old man with a rug 'oo'd dropped a book an' was tryin' to pick it up, when quite slowly, from be'ind two porters – carryin' a little reticule an' lookin' from side to side – comes out Mrs. Bathurst. There was no mistakin' the walk in a hundred thousand. She come forward – right forward – she looked out straight at us with that blindish look which Pritch alluded to.

She walked on and on till she melted out of the picture – like – like a shadow jumpin' over a candle, an' as she went I 'eard Dawson in the tickey seats be'ind sing out: 'Christ! There's Mrs. B!' "

Hooper swallowed his spittle and leaned forward intently.

"Vickery touched me on the knee again. He was clickin' his four false teeth with his jaw down like an enteric at the last kick. 'Are you sure?' says he. 'Sure,' I says; 'didn't you 'ear Dawson give tongue? Why, it's the woman herself.' 'I was sure before,' he says, 'but I brought you to make sure. Will you come again with me to-morrow?'

" 'Willingly,' I says; 'it's like meetin' old friends.'

" 'Yes,' he says, openin' his watch, 'very like. It will be four-and-twenty hours less four minutes before I see her again. Come and have a drink,' he says. 'It may amuse you, but it's no sort of earthly use to me.' He went out shaking his head an' stumblin' over people's feet as if he was drunk already. I anticipated a swift drink an' a speedy return, because I wanted to see the performin' elephants. Instead o' which Vickery began to navigate the town at the rate o' knots, lookin' in at a bar every three minutes approximate Greenwich time. I'm not a drinkin' man, though there are those present" – he cocked his unforgettable eye at me – "who may have seen me more or less imbued with the fragrant spirit. None the less when I drink I like to do it at anchor an' not at an average speed of eighteen knots on the measured mile. There's a tank as you might say at the back o' that big hotel up the hill – what do they call it?"

"The Molteno Reservoir," I suggested, and Hooper nodded.

"That was his limit o' drift. We walked there an' we come down through the Gardens – there was a South-Easter blowin' – an' we finished up by the Docks. Then we bore up the road to Salt River, and wherever there was a pub Vickery put in sweatin'. He didn't look at what he drunk – he didn't look at the change. He walked an' he drunk an' he perspired in rivers. I understood why old Crocus 'ad come back in the condition 'e did, because Vickery an' I 'ad two an' a half hours o' this gipsy manœuvre an' when we got back to the station there wasn't a dry atom on or in me."

"Did he say anything?" Pritchard asked.

"The sum total of 'is conversation from 7.45 P.M. till 11.15 P.M. was 'Let's have another.' Thus the mornin' an' the evenin' were the first day, as Scripture says. . . . To abbreviate a lengthy narrative, I went into Cape Town for five consecutive nights with Master Vickery, and in that time I must 'ave logged about fifty knots over the ground an' taken in two gallon o' all the worst spirits south the Equator. The evolution never varied. Two shilling seats for us two; five minutes o' the pictures, an' perhaps forty-five seconds o' Mrs. B. walking down towards us with that blindish look in her eyes an' the reticule in her hand. Then our walk – and drink till train time."

"What did you think?" said Hooper, his hand fingering his waistcoat-pocket.

"Several things," said Pyecroft. "To tell you the truth, I aren't quite done thinkin' about it yet. Mad? The man was a dumb lunatic – must 'ave been for months – years p'r'aps. I know somethin' o' maniacs, as every man in the Service must. I've been shipmates with a mad skipper – an' a lunatic Number One, but never both together I thank 'Eaven. I could give you the names o' three captains now 'oo ought to be in an asylum, but you don't find me interferin' with the mentally afflicted till they begin to lay about 'em with rammers an' winch-handles. Only once I crept up a little into the wind towards Master Vickery. 'I wonder what she's doin' in England,' I says. 'Don't it seem to you she's lookin' for somebody?' That was in the Gardens again, with the South-Easter blowin' as we were makin' our desperate round. 'She's lookin' for me,' he says, stoppin' dead under a lamp an' clickin'. When he wasn't drinkin', in which case all 'is teeth clicked on the glass, 'e was clickin' 'is four false teeth like a Marconi ticker. 'Yes! lookin' for me,' he said, an' he went on very softly an' as you might say affectionately. '*But*,' he went on, 'in future, Mr. Pyecroft, I should take it kindly of you if you'd confine your remarks to the drinks set before you. Otherwise,' he says, 'with the best will in the world towards you, I may find myself guilty of murder! Do you understand?' he says. 'Perfectly,' I says, 'but would it at all soothe you to know that in such a case the chances o' your being killed are precisely equivalent to the chances o' me being outed?' 'Why, no,' he says, 'I'm almost afraid that 'ud be a temptation.' Then I said – we was right under the lamp by that arch at the end o' the Gardens where the trams come round – 'Assumin' murder was done – or attempted murder – I put it to you that you would still be left so badly crippled, as one might say, that your subsequent capture by the police – to 'oom you would 'ave to explain – would be largely inevitable.' 'That's better,' 'e says, passin' 'is hands over his forehead. 'That's much better, because,' he says, 'do you know, as I am now, Pye, I'm not so sure if I could explain anything much.' Those were the only particular words I had with 'im in our walks as I remember."

"What walks!" said Hooper. "Oh, my soul, what walks!"

"They were chronic," said Pyecroft gravely, "but I didn't anticipate any danger till the Circus left. Then I anticipated that, bein' deprived of 'is stimulant, he might react on me, so to say, with a hatchet. Consequently, after the final performance an' the ensuin' wet walk, I kep' myself aloof from my superior officer on board in the execution of 'is duty as you might put it. Consequently, I was interested when the sentry informs me while I was passin' on my lawful occasions that Click had asked to see the captain. As a general rule warrant officers don't dissipate much of the owner's time, but Click put in an hour and more be'ind that door. My duties kep' me within eyeshot of it. Vickery came out first, an' 'e actually nodded at me an' smiled. This knocked me out o' the boat, because, havin' seen 'is face for five consecutive nights, I didn't anticipate any change there more than a condenser in hell, so to speak. The owner emerged later. His face didn't read off at all, so I fell back on his cox, 'oo'd been eight years with him and knew him better than boat signals. Lamson – that was the cox's name – crossed 'is bows once or twice at low speeds an' dropped down to me visibly concerned. 'He's shipped 'is court-martial face,' says Lamson. 'Some one's goin' to be 'ung. I've never seen that look but once before when they chucked the gun-sights overboard in the *Fantastic*.' Throwin' gun-sights overboard, Mr. Hooper, is the equivalent for mutiny in these degenerate days. It's done to attract the notice of the authorities an' the *Western Mornin' News* – generally by a stoker. Naturally, word went round the lower deck an' we had a private over'aul of our little consciences. But, barrin' a shirt which a second-class stoker said 'ad walked into 'is bag from the marines flat by itself, nothin' vital transpired. The owner went about flyin' the signal for 'attend public execution,' so to say, but there was no corpse at the yard-arm. 'E lunched on the beach an' 'e returned with 'is regulation harbour-routine face about 3 P.M. Thus Lamson lost prestige for raising false alarms. The only person 'oo might 'ave connected the epicycloidal gears correctly was one Pyecroft, when he was told that Mr. Vickery would go up-country that same evening to take over certain naval ammunition left after the war in Bloemfontein Fort. No details was ordered to accompany Master Vickery. He was told off first person singular – as a unit – by himself."

The marine whistled penetratingly.

"That's what I thought," said Pyecroft. "I went ashore with him in the cutter an' 'e asked me to walk through the station. He was clickin' audibly, but otherwise seemed happy-ish.

" 'You might like to know,' he says, stoppin' just opposite the Admiral's front gate, 'that Phyllis's Circus will be performin' at Worcester to-morrow night. So I shall see 'er yet once again. You've been very patient with me,' he says.

" 'Look here, Vickery,' I said, 'this thing's come to be just as much as I can stand. Consume your own smoke. I don't want to know any more.'

" 'You!' he said. 'What have you got to complain of? –

you've only 'ad to watch. I'm *it*,' he says, 'but that's neither here nor there,' he says. 'I've one thing to say before shakin' 'ands. Remember,' 'e says – we were just by the Admiral's garden-gate then – 'remember, that I am *not* a murderer, because my lawful wife died in childbed six weeks after I came out. That much at least I am clear of,' 'e says.

" 'Then what have you done that signifies?' I said. 'What's the rest of it?'

" 'The rest,' 'e says, 'is silence,' an' he shook 'ands and went clickin' into Simons Town station."

"Did he stop to see Mrs. Bathurst at Worcester?" I asked.

"It's not known. He reported at Bloemfontein, saw the ammunition into the trucks, and then 'e disappeared. Went out – deserted, if you care to put it so – within eighteen months of his pension, an' if what 'e said about 'is wife was true he was a free man as 'e then stood. How do you read it off?"

"Poor devil!" said Hooper. "To see her that way every night! I wonder what it was."

"I've made my 'ead ache in that direction many a long night."

"But I'll swear Mrs. B. 'ad no 'and in it," said the Sergeant, unshaken.

"No. Whatever the wrong or deceit was, he did it, I'm sure o' that. I 'ad to look at 'is face for five consecutive nights. I'm not so fond o' navigatin' about Cape Town with a South-Easter blowin' these days. I can hear those teeth click, so to say."

"Ah, those teeth," said Hooper, and his hand went to his waistcoat-pocket once more. "Permanent things false teeth are. You read about 'em in all the murder trials."

"What d'you suppose the captain knew – or did?" I asked.

"I've never turned my searchlight that way," Pyecroft answered unblushingly.

We all reflected together, and drummed on empty beer bottles as the picnic-party, sunburned, wet, and sandy, passed our door singing "The Honeysuckle and the Bee."

"Pretty girl under that kapje," said Pyecroft.

"They never circulated his description?" said Pritchard.

"I was askin' you before these gentlemen came," said Hooper to me, "whether you knew Wankies – on the way to the Zambesi – beyond Buluwayo?"

"Would he pass there – tryin' to get to that Lake what's 'is name?" said Pritchard.

Hooper shook his head and went on: "There's a curious bit o' line there, you see. It runs through solid teak forest – a sort o' mahogany really – seventy-two miles without a curve. I've had a train derailed there twenty-three times in forty miles. I was up there a month ago relievin' a sick inspector, you see. He told me to look out for a couple of tramps in the teak."

"Two?" Pyecroft said. "I don't envy that other man if —"

"We get heaps of tramps up there since the war. The inspector told me I'd find 'em at M'Bindwe siding waiting to go North. He'd give 'em some grub and quinine, you see. I went up on a construction train. I looked out for 'em. I saw them miles ahead along the straight, waiting in the teak. One of 'em was standin' up by the dead-end of the siding an' the other was squattin' down lookin' up at 'im, you see."

"What did you do for 'em?" said Pritchard.

"There wasn't much I could do, except bury 'em. There'd been a bit of a thunderstorm in the teak, you see, and they were both stone dead and as black as charcoal. That's what they really were, you see – charcoal. They fell to bits when we tried to shift 'em. The man who was standin' up had the false teeth. I saw 'em shinin' against the black. Fell to bits he did too, like his mate squatting down an' watchin' him, both of 'em all wet in the rain. Both burned to charcoal, you see. And – that's what made me ask about marks just now – the false-toother was tattooed on the arms and chest – a crown and foul anchor with M. V. above."

"I've seen that," said Pyecroft quickly. "It was so."

"But if he was all charcoal-like?" said Pritchard, shuddering.

"You know how writing shows up white on a burned letter? Well, it was like that, you see. We buried 'em in the teak and I kept ... But he was a friend of you two gentlemen, you see."

Mr. Hooper brought his hand away from his waistcoat-pocket – empty.

Pritchard covered his face with his hands for a moment, like a child shutting out an ugliness.

"And to think of her at Hauraki!" he murmured – "with 'er 'air ribbon on my beer. 'Ada,' she said to her niece ... Oh, my Gawd!" ...

> "On a summer afternoon, when the honeysuckle blooms,
>   And all Nature seems at rest,
> Underneath the bower, 'mid the perfume of the flower,
>   Sat a maiden with the one she loves the best —"

sang the picnic-party waiting for their train at Glengariff.

"Well, I don't know how you feel about it," said Pyecroft, "but 'avin' seen 'is face for five consecutive nights on end, I'm inclined to finish what's left of the beer an' thank Gawd he's dead!"

"SWEPT AND GARNISHED"

"SWEPT AND GARNISHED"

W HEN the first waves of feverish cold stole over Frau
Ebermann she very wisely telephoned for the doctor
and went to bed. He diagnosed the attack as mild influenza,
prescribed the appropriate remedies, and left her to the care
of her one servant in her comfortable Berlin flat. Frau Ebermann, beneath the thick coverlet, curled up with what patience she could until the aspirin should begin to act, and
Anna should come back from the chemist with the forma-
mint, the ammoniated quinine, the eucalyptus, and the little
tin steam-inhaler. Meantime, every bone in her body ached;
her head throbbed; her hot, dry hands would not stay the
same size for a minute together; and her body, tucked into
the smallest possible compass, shrank from the chill of the
well-warmed sheets.

Of a sudden she noticed that an imitation-lace cover
which should have lain mathematically square with the imi-
tation-marble top of the radiator behind the green plush sofa
had slipped away so that one corner hung over the bronze-
painted steam pipes. She recalled that she must have rested
her poor head against the radiator-top while she was taking
off her boots. She tried to get up and set the thing straight,
but the radiator at once receded toward the horizon, which,
unlike true horizons, slanted diagonally, exactly parallel with
the dropped lace edge of the cover. Frau Ebermann groaned
through sticky lips and lay still.

"Certainly, I have a temperature," she said. "Certainly, I
have a grave temperature. I should have been warned by that
chill after dinner."

She resolved to shut her hot-lidded eyes, but opened them
in a little while to torture herself with the knowledge of that
ungeometrical thing against the far wall. Then she saw a
child – an untidy, thin-faced little girl of about ten, who must

have strayed in from the adjoining flat. This proved – Frau Ebermann groaned again at the way the world falls to bits when one is sick – proved that Anna had forgotten to shut the outer door of the flat when she went to the chemist. Frau Ebermann had had children of her own, but they were all grown up now, and she had never been a child-lover in any sense. Yet the intruder might be made to serve her scheme of things.

"Make – put," she muttered thickly, "that white thing straight on the top of that yellow thing."

The child paid no attention, but moved about the room, investigating everything that came in her way – the yellow cut-glass handles of the chest of drawers, the stamped bronze hook to hold back the heavy puce curtains, and the mauve enamel, New Art finger-plates on the door. Frau Ebermann watched indignantly.

"Aie! That is bad and rude. Go away!" she cried, though it hurt her to raise her voice. "Go away by the road you came!" The child passed behind the bed-foot, where she could not see her. "Shut the door as you go. I will speak to Anna, but – first, put that white thing straight."

She closed her eyes in misery of body and soul. The outer door clicked, and Anna entered, very penitent that she had stayed so long at the chemist's. But it had been difficult to find the proper type of inhaler, and —

"Where did the child go?" moaned Frau Ebermann – "the child that was here?"

"There was no child," said startled Anna. "How should any child come in when I shut the door behind me after I go out? All the keys of the flats are different."

"No, no! You forgot this time. But my back is aching, and up my legs also. Besides, who knows what it may have fingered and upset? Look and see."

"Nothing is fingered, nothing is upset," Anna replied, as she took the inhaler from its paper box.

"Yes, there is. Now I remember all about it. Put – put that white thing, with the open edge – the lace, I mean –

quite straight on that —" she pointed. Anna, accustomed to her ways, understood and went to it.

"Now, is it quite straight?" Frau Ebermann demanded.

"Perfectly," said Anna. "In fact, in the very centre of the radiator." Anna measured the equal margins with her knuckle, as she had been told to do when she first took service.

"And my tortoise-shell hair-brushes?" Frau Ebermann could not command her dressing-table from where she lay.

"Perfectly straight, side by side in the big tray, and the comb laid across them. Your watch also in the coralline watch-holder. Everything" – she moved round the room to make sure – "everything is as you have it when you are well." Frau Ebermann sighed with relief. It seemed to her that the room and her head had suddenly grown cooler.

"Good!" said she. "Now warm my nightgown in the kitchen, so it will be ready when I have perspired. And the towels also. Make the inhaler steam, and put in the eucalyptus; that is good for the larynx. Then sit you in the kitchen, and come when I ring. But, first, my hot-water bottle."

It was brought and scientifically tucked in.

"What news?" said Frau Ebermann drowsily. She had not been out that day.

"Another victory," said Anna. "Many more prisoners and guns."

Frau Ebermann purred, one might almost say grunted, contentedly.

"That is good, too," she said; and Anna, after lighting the inhaler lamp, went out.

Frau Ebermann reflected that in an hour or so the aspirin would begin to work, and all would be well. To-morrow – no, the day after – she would take up life with something to talk over with her friends at coffee. It was rare – every one knew it – that she should be overcome by any ailment. Yet in all her distresses she had not allowed the minutest deviation from daily routine and ritual. She would tell her friends – she ran over their names one by one – exactly what measures she had taken against the lace cover on the radiator-top and in regard to her two tortoise-shell hair-brushes and the comb at right angles. How she had set everything in order – everything in order. She roved further afield as she wriggled her toes luxuriously on the hot-water bottle. If it pleased our dear God to take her to Himself, and she was not so young as she had been – there was that plate of the four lower ones in the blue tooth-glass, for instance – He should find all her belongings fit to meet His eye. "Swept and garnished" were the words that shaped themselves in her intent brain. "Swept and garnished for —"

No, it was certainly not for the dear Lord that she had swept; she would have her room swept out to-morrow or the day after, and garnished. Her hands began to swell again into huge pillows of nothingness. Then they shrank, and so did her head, to minute dots. It occurred to her that she was waiting for some event, some tremendously important event, to come to pass. She lay with shut eyes for a long time till her head and hands should return to their proper size.

She opened her eyes with a jerk.

"How stupid of me," she said aloud, "to set the room in order for a parcel of dirty little children!"

They were there – five of them, two little boys and three girls – headed by the anxious-eyed ten-year-old whom she had seen before. They must have entered by the outer door, which Anna had neglected to shut behind her when she returned with the inhaler. She counted them backward and forward as one counts scales – one, two, three, four, five.

They took no notice of her, but hung about, first on one foot then on the other, like strayed chickens, the smaller ones holding by the larger. They had the air of utterly wearied passengers in a railway waiting-room, and their clothes were disgracefully dirty.

"Go away!" cried Frau Ebermann at last, after she had struggled, it seemed to her, for years to shape the words.

"You called?" said Anna at the living-room door.

"No," said her mistress. "Did you shut the flat door when you came in?"

"Assuredly," said Anna. "Besides, it is made to catch of itself."

"Then go away," said she, very little above a whisper. If Anna pretended not to see the children, she would speak to Anna later on.

"And now," she said, turning toward them as soon as the door closed. The smallest of the crowd smiled at her, and shook his head before he buried it in his sister's skirts.

"Why – don't – you – go – away?" she whispered earnestly.

Again they took no notice, but, guided by the elder girl, set themselves to climb, boots and all, on to the green plush sofa in front of the radiator. The little boys had to be pushed, as they could not compass the stretch unaided. They settled themselves in a row, with small gasps of relief, and pawed the plush approvingly.

"I ask you – I ask you why do you not go away – why do you not go away?" Frau Ebermann found herself repeating the question twenty times. It seemed to her that everything in the world hung on the answer. "You know you should not come into houses and rooms unless you are invited. Not houses and bedrooms, you know."

"No," a solemn little six-year-old repeated, "not houses nor bedrooms, nor dining-rooms, nor churches, nor all those places. Shouldn't come in. It's rude."

"Yes, he said so," the younger girl put in proudly. "He said it. He told them only pigs would do that." The line nodded and dimpled one to another with little explosive giggles, such as children use when they tell deeds of great daring against their elders.

"If you know it is wrong, that makes it much worse," said Frau Ebermann.

"Oh yes; much worse," they assented cheerfully, till the smallest boy changed his smile to a baby wail of weariness.

"When will they come for us?" he asked, and the girl at the head of the row hauled him bodily into her square little capable lap.

"He's tired," she explained. "He is only four. He only had his first breeches this Spring." They came almost under his armpits, and were held up by broad linen braces, which, his sorrow diverted for the moment, he patted proudly.

"Yes, beautiful, dear," said both girls.

"Go away!" said Frau Ebermann. "Go home to your father and mother!"

Their faces grew grave at once.

"H'sh! We *can't*," whispered the eldest. "There isn't anything left."

"All gone," a boy echoed, and he puffed through pursed lips. "Like *that*, uncle told me. Both cows too."

"And my own three ducks," the boy on the girl's lap said sleepily.

"So, you see, we came here." The elder girl leaned forward a little, caressing the child she rocked.

"I – I don't understand," said Frau Ebermann. "Are you lost, then? You must tell our police."

"Oh no; we are only waiting."

"But what are you waiting *for*?"

"We are waiting for our people to come for us. They told us to come here and wait for them. So we are waiting till they come," the eldest girl replied.

"Yes. We are waiting till our people come for us," said all the others in chorus.

"But," said Frau Ebermann very patiently – "but now tell me, for I tell you that I am not in the least angry, where do you come from? Where do you come from?"

The five gave the names of two villages of which she had read in the papers.

"That is silly," said Frau Ebermann. "The people fired on us, and they were punished. Those places are wiped out, stamped flat."

"Yes, yes, wiped out, stamped flat. That is why and – I

have lost the ribbon off my pigtail," said the younger girl. She looked behind her over the sofa-back.

"It is not here," said the elder. "It was lost before. Don't you remember?"

"Now, if you are lost, you must go and tell our police. They will take care of you and give you food," said Frau Ebermann. "Anna will show you the way there."

"No," – this was the six-year-old with the smile, – "we must wait here till our people come for us. Mustn't we, sister?"

"Of course. We wait here till our people come for us. All the world knows that," said the eldest girl.

"Yes." The boy in her lap had waked again. "Little children, too – as little as Henri, and *he* doesn't wear trousers yet. As little as all that."

"I don't understand," said Frau Ebermann, shivering. In spite of the heat of the room and the damp breath of the steam-inhaler, the aspirin was not doing its duty.

The girl raised her blue eyes and looked at the woman for an instant.

"You see," she said, emphasising her statements with her fingers, "*they* told *us* to wait *here* till *our* people came for us. So we came. We wait till our people come for us."

"That is silly again," said Frau Ebermann. "It is no good for you to wait here. Do you know what this place is? You have been to school? It is Berlin, the capital of Germany."

"Yes, yes," they all cried; "Berlin, capital of Germany. We know that. That is why we came."

"So, you see, it is no good," she said triumphantly, "because your people can never come for you here."

"They told us to come here and wait till our people came for us." They delivered this as if it were a lesson in school. Then they sat still, their hands orderly folded on their laps, smiling as sweetly as ever.

"Go away! Go away!" Frau Ebermann shrieked.

"You called?" said Anna, entering.

"No. Go away! Go away!"

"Very good, old cat," said the maid under her breath. "Next time you *may* call," and she returned to her friend in the kitchen.

"I ask you – ask you, *please* to go away," Frau Ebermann pleaded. "Go to my Anna through that door, and she will give you cakes and sweeties. It is not kind of you to come into my room and behave so badly."

"Where else shall we go now?" the elder girl demanded, turning to her little company. They fell into discussion. One preferred the broad street with trees, another the railway station; but when she suggested an Emperor's palace, they agreed with her.

"We will go then," she said, and added half apologetically to Frau Ebermann, "You see, they are so little they like to meet all the others."

"What others?" said Frau Ebermann.

"The others – hundreds and hundreds and thousands and thousands of the others."

"That is a lie. There cannot be a hundred even, much less a thousand," cried Frau Ebermann.

"So?" said the girl politely.

"Yes. *I* tell you; and I have very good information. I know how it happened. You should have been more careful. You should not have run out to see the horses and guns passing. That is how it is done when our troops pass through. My son has written me so."

They had clambered down from the sofa, and gathered round the bed with eager, interested eyes.

"Horses and guns going by – how fine!" some one whispered.

"Yes, yes; believe me, *that* is how the accidents to the children happen. You must know yourself that it is true. One runs out to look —"

"But I never saw any at all," a boy cried sorrowfully. "Only one noise I heard. That was when Aunt Emmeline's house fell down."

"But listen to me. *I* am telling you! One runs out to look, because one is little and cannot see well. So one peeps between the man's legs, and then – you know how close those big horses and guns turn the corners – then one's foot slips and one gets run over. That's how it happens. Several times it had happened, but not many times; certainly not a hundred, perhaps not twenty. So, you see, you *must* be all. Tell me now that you are all that there are, and Anna shall give you the cakes."

"Thousands," a boy repeated monotonously. "Then we all come here to wait till our people come for us."

"But now we will go away from here. The poor lady is tired," said the elder girl, plucking his sleeve.

"Oh, you hurt, you hurt!" he cried, and burst into tears.

"What is that for?" said Frau Ebermann. "To cry in a room where a poor lady is sick is very inconsiderate."

"Oh, but look, lady!" said the elder girl.

Frau Ebermann looked and saw.

"*Au revoir*, lady." They made their little smiling bows and curtseys undisturbed by her loud cries. "*Au revoir*, lady. We will wait till our people come for us."

When Anna at last ran in, she found her mistress on her knees, busily cleaning the floor with the lace cover from the radiator, because, she explained, it was all spotted with the blood of five children – she was perfectly certain there could not be more than five in the whole world – who had gone away for the moment, but were now waiting round the corner, and Anna was to find them and give them cakes to stop the bleeding, while her mistress swept and garnished that Our dear Lord when He came might find everything as it should be.

MARY POSTGATE

MARY POSTGATE

O F Miss Mary Postgate, Lady McCausland wrote that
she was "thoroughly conscientious, tidy, companionable, and ladylike. I am very sorry to part with her, and shall
always be interested in her welfare."

Miss Fowler engaged her on this recommendation, and to
her surprise, for she had had experience of companions,
found that it was true. Miss Fowler was nearer sixty than
fifty at the time, but though she needed care she did not
exhaust her attendant's vitality. On the contrary, she gave
out, stimulatingly and with reminiscences. Her father had
been a minor Court official in the days when the Great Exhibition of 1851 had just set its seal on Civilisation made
perfect. Some of Miss Fowler's tales, none the less, were not
always for the young. Mary was not young, and though her
speech was as colourless as her eyes or her hair, she was
never shocked. She listened unflinchingly to every one; said
at the end, "How interesting!" or "How shocking!" as the
case might be, and never again referred to it, for she prided
herself on a trained mind, which "did not dwell on these
things." She was, too, a treasure at domestic accounts, for
which the village tradesmen, with their weekly books, loved
her not. Otherwise she had no enemies; provoked no jealousy
even among the plainest; neither gossip nor slander had ever
been traced to her; she supplied the odd place at the Rector's
or the Doctor's table at half an hour's notice; she was a sort
of public aunt to very many small children of the village
street, whose parents, while accepting everything, would
have been swift to resent what they called "patronage"; she
served on the Village Nursing Committee as Miss Fowler's
nominee when Miss Fowler was crippled by rheumatoid
arthritis, and came out of six months' fortnightly meetings
equally respected by all the cliques.

And when Fate threw Miss Fowler's nephew, an unlovely orphan of eleven, on Miss Fowler's hands, Mary Postgate stood to her share of the business of education as practised in private and public schools. She checked printed clothes-lists, and unitemised bills of extras; wrote to Head and House masters, matrons, nurses and doctors, and grieved or rejoiced over half-term reports. Young Wyndham Fowler repaid her in his holidays by calling her "Gatepost," "Postey," or "Packthread," by thumping her between her narrow shoulders, or by chasing her bleating, round the garden, her large mouth open, her large nose high in air, at a stiff-necked shamble very like a camel's. Later on he filled the house with clamour, argument, and harangues as to his personal needs, likes and dislikes, and the limitations of "you women," reducing Mary to tears of physical fatigue, or, when he chose to be humorous, of helpless laughter. At crises, which multiplied as he grew older, she was his ambassadress and his interpretress to Miss Fowler, who had no large sympathy with the young; a vote in his interest at the councils on his future; his sewing-woman, strictly accountable for mislaid boots and garments; always his butt and his slave.

And when he decided to become a solicitor, and had entered an office in London; when his greeting had changed from "Hullo, Postey, you old beast," to "Mornin', Packthread," there came a war which, unlike all wars that Mary could remember, did not stay decently outside England and in the newspapers, but intruded on the lives of people whom she knew. As she said to Miss Fowler, it was "most vexatious." It took the Rector's son who was going into business with his elder brother; it took the Colonel's nephew on the eve of fruit-farming in Canada; it took Mrs. Grant's son who, his mother said, was devoted to the ministry; and, very early indeed, it took Wynn Fowler, who announced on a postcard that he had joined the Flying Corps and wanted a cardigan waistcoat.

"He must go, and he must have the waistcoat," said Miss Fowler. So Mary got the proper-sized needles and wool, while Miss Fowler told the men of her establishment — two gardeners and an odd man, aged sixty — that those who could join the Army had better do so. The gardeners left. Cheape, the odd man, stayed on, and was promoted to the gardener's cottage. The cook, scorning to be limited in luxuries, also left, after a spirited scene with Miss Fowler, and took the housemaid with her. Miss Fowler gazetted Nellie, Cheape's seventeen-year-old daughter, to the vacant post; Mrs. Cheape to the rank of cook, with occasional cleaning bouts; and the reduced establishment moved forward smoothly.

Wynn demanded an increase in his allowance. Miss Fowler, who always looked facts in the face, said, "He must have it. The chances are he won't live long to draw it, and if three hundred makes him happy —"

Wynn was grateful, and came over, in his tight-buttoned uniform, to say so. His training centre was not thirty miles away, and his talk was so technical that it had to be explained by charts of the various types of machines. He gave Mary such a chart.

"And you'd better study it, Postey," he said. "You'll be seeing a lot of 'em soon." So Mary studied the chart, but when Wynn next arrived to swell and exalt himself before his womenfolk, she failed badly in cross-examination, and he rated her as in the old days.

"You *look* more or less like a human being," he said in his new Service voice. "You *must* have had a brain at some time in your past. What have you done with it? Where d'you keep it? A sheep would know more than you do, Postey. You're lamentable. You are less use than an empty tin can, you dowey old cassowary."

"I suppose that's how your superior officer talks to *you*?" said Miss Fowler from her chair.

"But Postey doesn't mind," Wynn replied. "Do you, Packthread?"

"Why? Was Wynn saying anything? I shall get this right next time you come," she muttered, and knitted her pale brows again over the diagrams of Taubes, Farmans, and Zeppelins.

In a few weeks the mere land and sea battles which she read to Miss Fowler after breakfast passed her like idle breath. Her heart and her interest were high in the air with Wynn, who had finished "rolling" (whatever that might be) and had gone on from a "taxi" to a machine more or less his own. One morning it circled over their very chimneys, alighted on Vegg's Heath, almost outside the garden gate, and Wynn came in, blue with cold, shouting for food. He and she drew Miss Fowler's bath-chair, as they had often done, along the Heath foot-path to look at the biplane. Mary observed that "it smelt very badly."

"Postey, I believe you think with your nose," said Wynn. "I know you don't with your mind. Now what type's that?"

"I'll go and get the chart," said Mary.

"You're hopeless! You haven't the mental capacity of a white mouse," he cried, and explained the dials and the sockets for bomb-dropping till it was time to mount and ride the wet clouds once more.

"Ah!" said Mary, as the stinking thing flared upward. "Wait till our Flying Corps gets to work! Wynn says it's much safer than in the trenches."

"I wonder," said Miss Fowler. "Tell Cheape to come and tow me home again."

"It's all downhill. I can do it," said Mary, "if you put the brake on." She laid her lean self against the pushing-bar and home they trundled.

"Now, be careful you aren't heated and catch a chill," said overdressed Miss Fowler.

"Nothing makes me perspire," said Mary. As she bumped the chair under the porch she straightened her long back. The exertion had given her a colour, and the wind had loosened a wisp of hair across her forehead. Miss Fowler glanced at her.

"What do you ever think of, Mary?" she demanded suddenly.

"Oh, Wynn says he wants another three pairs of stockings – as thick as we can make them."

"Yes. But I mean the things that women think about. Here you are, more than forty —"

"Forty-four," said truthful Mary.

"Well?"

"Well?" Mary offered Miss Fowler her shoulder as usual.

"And you've been with me ten years now."

"Let's see," said Mary. "Wynn was eleven when he came. He's twenty now, and I came two years before that. It must be eleven."

"Eleven! And you've never told me anything that matters in all that while. Looking back, it seems to me that *I've* done all the talking."

"I'm afraid I'm not much of a conversationalist. As Wynn says, I haven't the mind. Let me take your hat."

Miss Fowler, moving stiffly from the hip, stamped her rubber-tipped stick on the tiled hall floor. "Mary, aren't you *anything* except a companion? Would you *ever* have been anything except a companion?"

Mary hung up the garden hat on its proper peg. "No," she said after consideration. "I don't imagine I ever should. But I've no imagination, I'm afraid."

She fetched Miss Fowler her eleven-o'clock glass of Contrexéville.

That was the wet December when it rained six inches to the month, and the women went abroad as little as might be. Wynn's flying chariot visited them several times, and for two mornings (he had warned her by postcard) Mary heard the thresh of his propellers at dawn. The second time she ran to the window, and stared at the whitening sky. A little blur passed overhead. She lifted her lean arms towards it.

That evening at six o'clock there came an announcement in an official envelope that Second Lieutenant W. Fowler had been killed during a trial flight. Death was instantaneous. She read it and carried it to Miss Fowler.

"I never expected anything else," said Miss Fowler; "but I'm sorry it happened before he had done anything."

The room was whirling round Mary Postgate, but she found herself quite steady in the midst of it.

"Yes," she said. "It's a great pity he didn't die in action after he had killed somebody."

"He was killed instantly. That's one comfort," Miss Fowler went on.

"But Wynn says the shock of a fall kills a man at once – whatever happens to the tanks," quoted Mary.

The room was coming to rest now. She heard Miss Fowler say impatiently, "But why can't we cry, Mary?" and herself replying, "There's nothing to cry for. He has done his duty as much as Mrs. Grant's son did."

"And when he died, *she* came and cried all the morning," said Miss Fowler. "This only makes me feel tired – terribly tired. Will you help me to bed, please, Mary? – And I think I'd like the hot-water bottle."

So Mary helped her and sat beside, talking of Wynn in his riotous youth.

"I believe," said Miss Fowler suddenly, "that old people and young people slip from under a stroke like this. The middle-aged feel it most."

"I expect that's true," said Mary, rising. "I'm going to put away the things in his room now. Shall we wear mourning?"

"Certainly not," said Miss Fowler. "Except, of course, at the funeral. I can't go. You will. I want you to arrange about his being buried here. What a blessing it didn't happen at Salisbury!"

Every one, from the Authorities of the Flying Corps to the Rector, was most kind and sympathetic. Mary found herself for the moment in a world where bodies were in the habit of being despatched by all sorts of conveyances to all sorts of places. And at the funeral two young men in buttoned-up uniforms stood beside the grave and spoke to her afterwards.

"You're Miss Postgate, aren't you?" said one. "Fowler

told me about you. He was a good chap – a first-class fellow – a great loss."

"Great loss!" growled his companion. "We're all awfully sorry."

"How high did he fall from?" Mary whispered.

"Pretty nearly four thousand feet, I should think, didn't he? You were up that day, Monkey?"

"All of that," the other child replied. "My bar made three thousand, and I wasn't as high as him by a lot."

"Then *that's* all right," said Mary. "Thank you very much."

They moved away as Mrs. Grant flung herself weeping on Mary's flat chest, under the lych-gate, and cried, "*I* know how it feels! *I* know how it feels!"

"But both his parents are dead," Mary returned, as she fended her off. "Perhaps they've all met by now," she added vaguely as she escaped towards the coach.

"I've thought of that too," wailed Mrs. Grant; "but then he'll be practically a stranger to them. Quite embarrassing!"

Mary faithfully reported every detail of the ceremony to Miss Fowler, who, when she described Mrs. Grant's outburst, laughed aloud.

"Oh, how Wynn would have enjoyed it! He was always utterly unreliable at funerals. D'you remember —" And they talked of him again, each piecing out the other's gaps. "And now," said Miss Fowler, "we'll pull up the blinds and we'll have a general tidy. That always does us good. Have you seen to Wynn's things?"

"Everything – since he first came," said Mary. "He was never destructive – even with his toys."

They faced that neat room.

"It can't be natural not to cry," Mary said at last. "I'm *so* afraid you'll have a reaction."

"As I told you, we old people slip from under the stroke. It's you I'm afraid for. Have you cried yet?"

"I can't. It only makes me angry with the Germans."

"That's sheer waste of vitality," said Miss Fowler. "We

must live till the war's finished." She opened a full wardrobe. "Now, I've been thinking things over. This is my plan. All his civilian clothes can be given away – Belgian refugees, and so on."

Mary nodded. "Boots, collars, and gloves?"

"Yes. We don't need to keep anything except his cap and belt."

"They came back yesterday with his Flying Corps clothes" – Mary pointed to a roll on the little iron bed.

"Ah, but keep his Service things. Some one may be glad of them later. Do you remember his sizes?"

"Five feet eight and a half; thirty-six inches round the chest. But he told me he's just put on an inch and a half. I'll mark it on a label and tie it on his sleeping-bag."

"So that disposes of *that*," said Miss Fowler, tapping the palm of one hand with the ringed third finger of the other. "What waste it all is! We'll get his old school trunk to-morrow and pack his civilian clothes."

"And the rest?" said Mary. "His books and pictures and the games and the toys – and – and the rest?"

"My plan is to burn every single thing," said Miss Fowler. "Then we shall know where they are and no one can handle them afterwards. What do you think?"

"I think that would be much the best," said Mary. "But there's such a lot of them."

"We'll burn them in the destructor," said Miss Fowler.

This was an open-air furnace for the consumption of refuse; a little circular four-foot tower of pierced brick over an iron grating. Miss Fowler had noticed the design in a gardening journal years ago, and had had it built at the bottom of the garden. It suited her tidy soul, for it saved unsightly rubbish-heaps, and the ashes lightened the stiff clay soil.

Mary considered for a moment, saw her way clear, and nodded again. They spent the evening putting away well-remembered civilian suits, underclothes that Mary had marked, and the regiments of very gaudy socks and ties. A second trunk was needed, and, after that, a little packing-

case, and it was late next day when Cheape and the local
carrier lifted them to the cart. The Rector luckily knew of a
friend's son, about five feet eight and a half inches high, to
whom a complete Flying Corps outfit would be most accept-
able, and sent his gardener's son down with a barrow to take
delivery of it. The cap was hung up in Miss Fowler's bedroom, the belt in Miss Postgate's; for, as Miss Fowler said,
they had no desire to make tea-party talk of them.

"That disposes of *that*," said Miss Fowler. "I'll leave the
rest to you, Mary. I can't run up and down the garden.
You'd better take the big clothes-basket and get Nellie to
help you."

"I shall take the wheel-barrow and do it myself," said
Mary, and for once in her life closed her mouth.

Miss Fowler, in moments of irritation, had called Mary
deadly methodical. She put on her oldest waterproof and
gardening-hat and her ever-slipping goloshes, for the weather
was on the edge of more rain. She gathered fire-lighters from
the kitchen, a half-scuttle of coals, and a faggot of brush-
wood. These she wheeled in the barrow down the mossed
paths to the dank little laurel shrubbery where the destructor
stood under the drip of three oaks. She climbed the wire
fence into the Rector's glebe just behind, and from his tenant's rick pulled two large armfuls of good hay, which she
spread neatly on the fire-bars. Next, journey by journey, passing Miss Fowler's white face at the morning-room window
each time, she brought down in the towel-covered clothes-
basket, on the wheel-barrow, thumbed and used Hentys,
Marryats, Levers, Stevensons, Baroness Orczys, Garvices,
schoolbooks, and atlases, unrelated piles of the *Motor Cyclist*,
the *Light Car*, and catalogues of Olympia Exhibitions; the
remnants of a fleet of sailing-ships from ninepenny cutters to
a three-guinea yacht; a prep.-school dressing-gown; bats
from three-and-sixpence to twenty-four shillings; cricket and
tennis balls; disintegrated steam and clockwork locomotives
with their twisted rails; a grey and red tin model of a sub-
marine; a dumb gramophone and cracked records; golf-clubs

that had to be broken across the knee, like his walking-sticks, and an assegai; photographs of private and public school cricket and football elevens, and his O.T.C. on the line of march; kodaks, and film-rolls; some pewters, and one real silver cup, for boxing competitions and Junior Hurdles; sheaves of school photographs; Miss Fowler's photograph; her own which he had borne off in fun and (good care she took not to ask!) had never returned; a playbox with a secret drawer; a load of flannels, belts, and jerseys, and a pair of spiked shoes unearthed in the attic; a packet of all the letters that Miss Fowler and she had ever written to him, kept for some absurd reason through all these years; a five-day attempt at a diary; framed pictures of racing motors in full Brooklands career, and load upon load of undistinguishable wreckage of tool-boxes, rabbit-hutches, electric batteries, tin soldiers, fret-saw outfits, and jig-saw puzzles.

Miss Fowler at the window watched her come and go, and said to herself, "Mary's an old woman. I never realised it before."

After lunch she recommended her to rest.

"I'm not in the least tired," said Mary. "I've got it all arranged. I'm going to the village at two o'clock for some paraffin. Nellie hasn't enough, and the walk will do me good."

She made one last quest round the house before she started, and found that she had overlooked nothing. It began to mist as soon as she had skirted Vegg's Heath, where Wynn used to descend — it seemed to her that she could almost hear the beat of his propellers overhead, but there was nothing to see. She hoisted her umbrella and lunged into the blind wet till she had reached the shelter of the empty village. As she came out of Mr. Kidd's shop with a bottle full of paraffin in her string shopping-bag, she met Nurse Eden, the village nurse, and fell into talk with her, as usual, about the village children. They were just parting opposite the "Royal Oak," when a gun, they fancied, was fired immediately behind the house. It was followed by a child's shriek dying into a wail.

"Accident!" said Nurse Eden promptly, and dashed through the empty bar, followed by Mary. They found Mrs. Gerritt, the publican's wife, who could only gasp and point to the yard, where a little cart-lodge was sliding sideways amid a clatter of tiles. Nurse Eden snatched up a sheet drying before the fire, ran out, lifted something from the ground, and flung the sheet round it. The sheet turned scarlet and half her uniform too, as she bore the load into the kitchen. It was little Edna Gerritt, aged nine, whom Mary had known since her perambulator days.

"Am I hurted bad?" Edna asked, and died between Nurse Eden's dripping hands. The sheet fell aside and for an instant, before she could shut her eyes, Mary saw the ripped and shredded body.

"It's a wonder she spoke at all," said Nurse Eden. "What in God's name was it?"

"A bomb," said Mary.

"One o' the Zeppelins?"

"No. An aeroplane. I thought I heard it on the Heath, but I fancied it was one of ours. It must have shut off its engines as it came down. That's why we didn't notice it."

"The filthy pigs!" said Nurse Eden, all white and shaken. "See the pickle I'm in! Go and tell Dr. Hennis, Miss Postgate." Nurse looked at the mother, who had dropped face down on the floor. "She's only in a fit. Turn her over."

Mary heaved Mrs. Gerritt right side up, and hurried off for the doctor. When she told her tale, he asked her to sit down in the surgery till he got her something.

"But I don't need it, I assure you," said she. "I don't think it would be wise to tell Miss Fowler about it, do you? Her heart is so irritable in this weather."

Dr. Hennis looked at her admiringly as he packed up his bag.

"No. Don't tell anybody till we're sure," he said, and hastened to the "Royal Oak," while Mary went on with the paraffin. The village behind her was as quiet as usual, for the news had not yet spread. She frowned a little to herself, her large nostrils expanded uglily, and from time to time she muttered a phrase which Wynn, who never restrained himself before his womenfolk, had applied to the enemy. "Bloody pagans! They *are* bloody pagans. But," she continued, falling back on the teaching that had made her what she was, "one mustn't let one's mind dwell on these things."

Before she reached the house Dr. Hennis, who was also a special constable, overtook her in his car.

"Oh, Miss Postgate," he said, "I wanted to tell you that that accident at the 'Royal Oak' was due to Gerritt's stable tumbling down. It's been dangerous for a long time. It ought to have been condemned."

"I thought I heard an explosion too," said Mary.

"You might have been misled by the beams snapping. I've been looking at 'em. They were dry-rotted through and through. Of course, as they broke, they would make a noise just like a gun."

"Yes?" said Mary politely.

"Poor little Edna was playing underneath it," he went on, still holding her with his eyes, "and that and the tiles cut her to pieces, you see?"

"I saw it," said Mary, shaking her head. "I heard it too."

"Well, we cannot be sure." Dr. Hennis changed his tone completely. "I know both you and Nurse Eden (I've been speaking to her) are perfectly trustworthy, and I can rely on you not to say anything – yet at least. It is no good to stir up people unless —"

"Oh, I never do – anyhow," said Mary, and Dr. Hennis went on to the county town.

After all, she told herself, it might, just possibly, have been the collapse of the old stable that had done all those things to poor little Edna. She was sorry she had even hinted at other things, but Nurse Eden was discretion itself. By the time she reached home the affair seemed increasingly remote by its very monstrosity. As she came in, Miss Fowler told her that a couple of aeroplanes had passed half an hour ago.

"I thought I heard them," she replied. "I'm going down to the garden now. I've got the paraffin."

"Yes, but – what *have* you got on your boots? They're soaking wet. Change them at once."

Not only did Mary obey but she wrapped the boots in a newspaper, and put them into the string bag with the bottle. So, armed with the longest kitchen poker, she left.

"It's raining again," was Miss Fowler's last word, "but – I know you won't be happy till that's disposed of."

"It won't take long. I've got everything down there, and I've put the lid on the destructor to keep the wet out."

The shrubbery was filling with twilight by the time she had completed her arrangements and sprinkled the sacrificial oil. As she lit the match that would burn her heart to ashes, she heard a groan or a grunt behind the dense Portugal laurels.

"Cheape?" she called impatiently, but Cheape, with his ancient lumbago, in his comfortable cottage would be the last man to profane the sanctuary. "Sheep," she concluded, and threw in the fusee. The pyre went up in a roar, and the immediate flame hastened night around her.

"How Wynn would have loved this!" she thought, stepping back from the blaze.

By its light she saw, half hidden behind a laurel not five paces away, a bareheaded man sitting very stiffly at the foot of one of the oaks. A broken branch lay across his lap – one booted leg protruding from beneath it. His head moved ceaselessly from side to side, but his body was as still as the tree's trunk. He was dressed – she moved sideways to look more closely – in a uniform something like Wynn's, with a flap buttoned across the chest. For an instant, she had some idea that it might be one of the young flying men she had met at the funeral. But their heads were dark and glossy. This man's was as pale as a baby's, and so closely cropped that she could see the disgusting pinky skin beneath. His lips moved.

"What do you say?" Mary moved towards him and stooped.

"Laty! Laty! Laty!" he muttered, while his hands picked at the dead wet leaves. There was no doubt as to his nationality. It made her so angry that she strode back to the destructor, though it was still too hot to use the poker there. Wynn's books seemed to be catching well. She looked up at the oak behind the man; several of the light upper and two or three rotten lower branches had broken and scattered their rubbish on the shrubbery path. On the lowest fork a helmet with dependent strings, showed like a bird's-nest in the light of a long-tongued flame. Evidently this person had fallen through the tree. Wynn had told her that it was quite possible for people to fall out of aeroplanes. Wynn told her too, that trees were useful things to break an aviator's fall, but in this case the aviator must have been broken or he would have moved from his queer position. He seemed helpless except for his horrible rolling head. On the other hand, she could see a pistol case at his belt – and Mary loathed pistols. Months ago, after reading certain Belgian reports together, she and Miss Fowler had had dealings with one – a huge revolver with flat-nosed bullets, which latter, Wynn said, were forbidden by the rules of war to be used against civilised enemies. "They're good enough for us," Miss Fowler had replied. "Show Mary how it works." And Wynn, laughing at the mere possibility of any such need, had led the craven winking Mary into the Rector's disused quarry, and had shown her how to fire the terrible machine. It lay now in the top-left-hand drawer of her toilet-table – a memento not included in the burning. Wynn would be pleased to see how she was not afraid.

She slipped up to the house to get it. When she came through the rain, the eyes in the head were alive with expectation. The mouth even tried to smile. But at sight of the revolver its corners went down just like Edna Gerritt's. A tear trickled from one eye, and the head rolled from shoulder to shoulder as though trying to point out something.

"Cassée. Tout cassée," it whimpered.

"What do you say?" said Mary disgustedly, keeping well to one side, though only the head moved.

"Cassée," it repeated. "Che me rends. Le médecin! Toctor!"

"Nein!" said she, bringing all her small German to bear with the big pistol. "Ich haben der todt Kinder gesehn."

The head was still. Mary's hand dropped. She had been careful to keep her finger off the trigger for fear of accidents. After a few moments' waiting, she returned to the destructor, where the flames were falling, and churned up Wynn's charring books with the poker. Again the head groaned for the doctor.

"Stop that!" said Mary, and stamped her foot. "Stop that, you bloody pagan!"

The words came quite smoothly and naturally. They were Wynn's own words, and Wynn was a gentleman who for no consideration on earth would have torn little Edna into those vividly coloured strips and strings. But this thing hunched under the oak-tree had done that thing. It was no question of reading horrors out of newspapers to Miss Fowler. Mary had seen it with her own eyes on the "Royal Oak" kitchen table. She must not allow her mind to dwell upon it. Now Wynn was dead, and everything connected with him was lumping and rustling and tinkling under her busy poker into red black dust and grey leaves of ash. The thing beneath the oak would die too. Mary had seen death more than once. She came of a family that had a knack of dying under, as she told Miss Fowler, "most distressing circumstances." She would stay where she was till she was entirely satisfied that It was dead – dead as dear papa in the late 'eighties; aunt Mary in 'eighty-nine; mamma in 'ninety-one; cousin Dick in 'ninety-five; Lady McCausland's housemaid in 'ninety-nine; Lady McCausland's sister in nineteen hundred and one; Wynn buried five days ago; and Edna Gerritt still waiting for decent earth to hide her. As she thought – her underlip caught up by one faded canine, brows knit and nostrils wide – she wielded the poker with lunges that jarred the grating at the bottom, and careful scrapes round the brick-work above. She looked at her wrist-watch. It was getting on to half-past four, and the rain was coming down in earnest. Tea would be at five. If It did not die before that time, she would be soaked and would have to change. Meantime, and this occupied her, Wynn's things were burning well in spite of the hissing wet, though now and again a book-back with a quite distinguishable title would be heaved up out of the mass. The exercise of stoking had given her a glow which seemed to reach to the marrow of her bones. She hummed – Mary never had a voice – to herself. She had never believed in all those advanced views – though Miss Fowler herself leaned a little that way – of woman's work in the world; but now she saw there was much to be said for them. This, for instance, was *her* work – work which no man, least of all Dr. Hennis, would ever have done. A man, at such a crisis, would be what Wynn called a "sportsman"; would leave everything to fetch help, and would certainly bring It into the house. Now a woman's business was to make a happy home for – for a husband and children. Failing these – it was not a thing one should allow one's mind to dwell upon – but –

"Stop it!" Mary cried once more across the shadows. "Nein, I tell you! Ich haben der todt Kinder gesehn."

But it was a fact. A woman who had missed these things could still be useful – more useful than a man in certain respects. She thumped like a paviour through the settling ashes at the secret thrill of it. The rain was damping the fire, but she could feel – it was too dark to see – that her work was done. There was a dull red glow at the bottom of the destructor, not enough to char the wooden lid if she slipped it half over against the driving wet. This arranged, she leaned on the poker and waited, while an increasing rapture laid hold on her. She ceased to think. She gave herself up to feel. Her long pleasure was broken by a sound that she had waited for in agony several times in her life. She leaned forward and listened, smiling. There could be no mistake. She closed her eyes and drank it in. Once it ceased abruptly.

"Go on," she murmured, half aloud. "That isn't the end."

Then the end came very distinctly in a lull between two rain-gusts. Mary Postgate drew her breath short between her teeth and shivered from head to foot. "*That's* all right," said she contentedly, and went up to the house, where she scandalised the whole routine by taking a luxurious hot bath before tea, and came down looking, as Miss Fowler said when she saw her lying all relaxed on the other sofa, "quite handsome!"

* * *

THE BEGINNINGS

It was not part of their blood,
  It came to them very late
With long arrears to make good,
  When the English began to hate.

They were not easily moved,
  They were icy willing to wait
Till every count should be proved,
  Ere the English began to hate.

Their voices were even and low,
  Their eyes were level and straight.
There was neither sign nor show,
  When the English began to hate.

It was not preached to the crowd,
  It was not taught by the State.
No man spoke it aloud,
  When the English began to hate.

It was not suddenly bred,
  It will not swiftly abate,
Through the chill years ahead,
  When Time shall count from the date
  That the English began to hate.

"DYMCHURCH FLIT"

"DYMCHURCH FLIT"

JUST at dusk, a soft September rain began to fall on the hop-pickers. The mothers wheeled the bouncing perambulators out of the gardens; bins were put away, and tally-books made up. The young couples strolled home, two to each umbrella, and the single men walked behind them laughing. Dan and Una, who had been picking after their lessons, marched off to roast potatoes at the oast-house, where old Hobden, with Blue-eyed Bess, his lurcher-dog, lived all the month through, drying the hops.

They settled themselves, as usual, on the sack-strewn cot in front of the fires, and, when Hobden drew up the shutter, stared, as usual, at the flameless bed of coals spouting its heat up the dark well of the old-fashioned roundel. Slowly he cracked off a few fresh pieces of coal, packed them, with fingers that never flinched, exactly where they would do most good; slowly he reached behind him till Dan tilted the potatoes into his iron scoop of a hand; carefully he arranged them round the fire, and then stood for a moment, black against the glare. As he closed the shutter, the oast-house seemed dark before the day's end, and he lit the candle in the lanthorn. The children liked all these things because they knew them so well.

The Bee Boy, Hobden's son, who is not quite right in his head, though he can do anything with bees, slipped in like a shadow. They only guessed it when Bess's stump-tail wagged against them.

A big voice began singing outside in the drizzle:–

"Old Mother Laidinwool had nigh twelve months been dead,
She heard the hops were doing well, and then popped up her head."

"There can't be two people made to holler like that!" cried old Hobden, wheeling round.

633

> "For, says she, 'The boys I've picked with when I was young and
>   fair,
> They're bound to be at hoppin', and I'm —' ' "

A man showed at the doorway.

"Well, well! They do say hoppin'll draw the very deadest; and now I belieft 'em. You, Tom? Tom Shoesmith!" Hobden lowered his lanthorn.

"You're a hem of a time makin' your mind to it, Ralph!" The stranger strode in – three full inches taller than Hobden, a grey-whiskered, brown-faced giant with clear blue eyes. They shook hands, and the children could hear the hard palms rasp together.

"You ain't lost none o' your grip," said Hobden. "Was it thirty or forty year back you broke my head at Peasmarsh Fair?"

"Only thirty, an' no odds 'tween us regardin' heads neither. You had it back at me with a hop-pole. How did we get home that night? Swimmin'?"

"Same way the pheasant come into Gubbs's pocket – by a little luck an' a deal o' conjurin'." Old Hobden laughed in his deep chest.

"I see you've not forgot your way about the woods. D'ye do any o' *this* still?" The stranger pretended to look along a gun.

Hobden answered with a quick movement of the hand as though he were pegging down a rabbit-wire.

"No. *That's* all that's left me now. Age she must as Age she can. An' what's your news since all these years?"

> "Oh, I've bin to Plymouth, I've bin to Dover –
> I've bin ramblin', boys, the wide world over,"

the man answered cheerily. "I reckon I know as much of Old England as most." He turned towards the children and winked boldly.

"I lay they told you a sight o' lies, then. I've been into England fur as Wiltsheer once. I was cheated proper over a pair of hedging-gloves," said Hobden.

"There's fancy-talkin' everywhere. *You've* cleaved to your own parts pretty middlin' close, Ralph."

"Can't shift an old tree 'thout it dyin'," Hobden chuckled. "An' I be no more anxious to die than you look to be to help me with my hops to-night."

The great man leaned against the brickwork of the roundel, and swung his arms abroad. "Hire me!" was all he said, and they stumped upstairs laughing.

The children heard their shovels rasp on the cloth where the yellow hops lie drying above the fires, and all the oasthouse filled with the sweet, sleepy smell as they were turned.

"Who is it?" Una whispered to the Bee Boy.

"Dunno, no more'n you – if *you* dunno," said he, and smiled.

The voices on the drying-floor talked and chuckled together, and the heavy footsteps went back and forth. Presently a hop-pocket dropped through the press-hole overhead, and stiffened and fattened as they shovelled it full. "Clank!" went the press, and rammed the loose stuff into tight cake.

"Gently!" they heard Hobden cry. "You'll bust her crop if you lay on so. You be as careless as Gleason's bull, Tom. Come an' sit by the fires. She'll do now."

They came down, and as Hobden opened the shutter to see if the potatoes were done Tom Shoesmith said to the children, "Put a plenty salt on 'em. That'll show you the sort o' man *I* be." Again he winked, and again the Bee Boy laughed and Una stared at Dan.

"*I* know what sort o' man you be," old Hobden grunted, groping for the potatoes round the fire.

"Do ye?" Tom went on behind his back. "Some of us can't abide Horseshoes, or Church Bells, or Running Water; an' talkin' o' runnin' water" – he turned to Hobden, who was backing out of the roundel – "d'you mind the great floods at Robertsbridge, when the miller's man was drowned in the street?"

"Middlin' well." Old Hobden let himself down on the

coals by the fire door. "I was courtin' my woman on the Marsh that year. Carter to Mus' Plum I was – gettin' ten shillin's week. Mine was a Marsh woman."

"Won'erful odd-gates place – Romney Marsh," said Tom Shoesmith. "I've heard say the world's divided like into Europe, Ashy, Afriky, Ameriky, Australy, an' Romney Marsh."

"The Marsh folk think so," said Hobden. "I had a hem o' trouble to get my woman to leave it."

"Where did she come out of? I've forgot, Ralph."

"Dymchurch under the Wall," Hobden answered, a potato in his hand.

"Then she'd be a Pett – or a Whitgift, would she?"

"Whitgift." Hobden broke open the potato and ate it with the curious neatness of men who make most of their meals in the blowy open. "She growed to be quite reasonable-like after livin' in the Weald awhile, but our first twenty year or two she was odd-fashioned, no bounds. And she was a won'erful hand with bees." He cut away a little piece of potato and threw it out to the door.

"Ah! I've heard say the Whitgifts could see further through a millstone than most," said Shoesmith. "Did she, now?"

"She was honest-innocent of any nigromancin'," said Hobden. "Only she'd read signs and sinnifications out o' birds flyin', stars fallin', bees hivin', and such. An' she'd lie awake – listenin' for calls, she said."

"That don't prove naught," said Tom. "All Marsh folk has been smugglers since time ever lastin'. 'Twould be in her blood to listen out o' nights."

"Nature-ally," old Hobden replied, smiling. "I mind when there was smugglin' a sight nearer us than the Marsh be. But that wasn't my woman's trouble. 'Twas a passel o' no-sense talk," he dropped his voice, "about Pharisees."

"Yes. I've heard Marsh men beleft in 'em." Tom looked straight at the wide-eyed children beside Bess.

"Pharisees," cried Una. "Fairies? Oh, I see!"

"People o' the Hills," said the Bee Boy, throwing half of his potato towards the door.

"There you be!" said Hobden, pointing at him. "My boy, he has her eyes and her out-gate senses. That's what *she* called 'em!"

"And what did you think of it all?"

"Um – um," Hobden rumbled. "A man that uses fields an' shaws after dark as much as I've done, he don't go out of his road excep' for keepers."

"But settin' that aside?" said Tom, coaxingly. "I saw ye throw the Good Piece out-at-doors just now. Do ye believe or – *do* ye?"

"There was a great black eye to that tater," said Hobden, indignantly.

"My liddle eye didn't see un, then. It looked as if you meant it for – for Any One that might need it. But settin' that aside, d'ye believe or – *do* ye?"

"I ain't sayin' nothin', because I've heard naught, an' I've seen naught. But if you was to say there was more things after dark in the shaws than men, or fur, or feather, or fin, I dunno as I'd go far-about to call you a liar. Now turn again, Tom. What's your say?"

"I'm like you. I say nothin'. But I'll tell you a tale, an' you can fit it *as* how you please."

"Passel o' no-sense stuff," growled Hobden, but he filled his pipe.

"The Marsh men they call it Dymchurch Flit," Tom went on slowly. "Hap you've heard it?"

"My woman she've told it me scores o' times. Dunno as I didn't end by belieftin' it – sometimes."

Hobden crossed over as he spoke, and sucked with his pipe at the yellow lanthorn-flame. Tom rested one great elbow on one great knee, where he sat among the coal.

"Have you ever bin in the Marsh?" he said to Dan.

"Only as far as Rye, once," Dan answered.

"Ah, that's but the edge. Back behind of her there's steeples settin' beside churches, an' wise women settin' beside their doors, an' the sea settin' above the land, an' ducks herdin' wild in the diks" (he meant ditches). "The Marsh is justa-bout riddled with diks an' sluices, an' tide-gates an water-lets. You can hear 'em bubblin' an' grummelin' when the tide works in 'em, an' then you hear the sea rangin' left- and right-handed all up along the Wall. You've seen how flat she is – the Marsh? You'd think nothin' easier than to walk eend-on acrost her? Ah, but the diks an' the water-lets, they twists the roads about as ravelly as witch-yarn on the spindles. So ye get all turned round in broad daylight."

"That's because they've dreened the waters into the diks," said Hobden. "When I courted my woman the rushes was green – Eh me! the rushes was green – an' the Bailiff o' the Marshes, he rode up and down as free as the fog."

"Who was he?" said Dan.

"Why, the Marsh fever an' ague. He've clapped me on the shoulder once or twice till I shook proper. But now the dreenin' off of the waters have done away with the fevers; so they make a joke, like, that the Bailiff o' the Marshes broke his neck in a dik. A won'erful place for bees an' ducks 'tis too."

"An' old!" Tom went on. "Flesh an' Blood have been there since Time Everlastin' Beyond. Well, now, speakin' among themselves, the Marshmen say that from Time Ever-lastin' Beyond the Pharisees favoured the Marsh above the rest of Old England. I lay the Marshmen ought to know. They've been out after dark, father an' son, smugglin' some one thing or t'other, since ever wool grew to sheep's backs. They say there was always a middlin' few Pharisees to be seen on the Marsh. Impident as rabbits, they was. They'd dance on the nakid roads in the nakid daytime; they'd flash their liddle green lights along the diks, comin' an' goin', like honest smugglers. Yes, an' times they'd lock the church doors against parson an' clerk of Sundays!"

"That 'ud be smugglers layin' in the lace or the brandy till they could run it out o' the Marsh. I've told my woman so," said Hobden.

"I'll lay she didn't beleft it, then – not if she was a Whitgift. A won'erful choice place for Pharisees, the Marsh, by all accounts, till Queen Bess's father he come in with his Reformatories."

"Would that be a Act o' Parliament like?" Hobden asked.

"Sure-ly! Can't do nothing in Old England without Act, Warrant, an' Summons. He got his Act allowed him, an', they say, Queen Bess's father he used the parish churches something shameful. Justabout tore the gizzards out of I dunnamany. Some folk in England they held with 'en; but some they saw it different, an' it eended in 'em takin' sides an' burnin' each other no bounds, accordin' which side was top, time bein'. That tarrified the Pharisees: for Goodwill among Flesh an' Blood is meat an' drink to 'em, an' ill-will is poison."

"Same as bees," said the Bee Boy. "Bees won't stay by a house where there's hating."

"True," said Tom. "This Reformations tarrified the Pharisees same as the reaper goin' round a last stand o' wheat tarrifies rabbits. They packed into the Marsh from all parts, and they says, 'Fair or foul, we must flit out o' this, for Merry England's done with, an' we're reckoned among the Images.'"

"Did they *all* see it that way?" said Hobden.

"All but one that was called Robin – if you've heard of him. What are you laughing at?" Tom turned to Dan. "The Pharisees' trouble didn't tech Robin, because he'd cleaved middlin' close to people like. No more he never meant to go out of Old England – not he; so he was sent messagin' for help among Flesh an' Blood. But Flesh an' Blood must always think of their own concerns, an' Robin couldn't get *through* at 'em, ye see. They thought it was tide-echoes off the Marsh."

"What did you – what did the fai – Pharisees want?" Una asked.

"A boat to be sure. Their liddle wings could no more cross Channel than so many tired butterflies. A boat an' a crew they desired to sail 'em over to France, where yet awhile folks hadn't tore down the Images. They couldn't abide cruel Canterbury Bells ringin' to Bulverhithe for more pore men an' women to be burnded, nor the King's proud messenger ridin' through the land givin' orders to tear down the Images. They couldn't abide it no shape. Nor yet they couldn't get their boat an' crew to flit by without Leave an' Goodwill from Flesh and Blood; an' Flesh an' Blood came an' went about its own business the while the Marsh was swarvin' up, an' swarvin' up with Pharisees from all England over, striving all means to get *through* at Flesh an' Blood to tell 'en their sore need. . . . I don't know as you've ever heard say Pharisees are like chickens?"

"My woman used to say that too," said Hobden, folding his brown arms.

"They be. You run too many chickens together, an' the ground sickens like, an' you get a squat, an' your chickens die. Same way, you crowd Pharisees all in one place – *they* don't die, but Flesh an' Blood walkin' among 'em is apt to sick up an' pine off. *They* don't mean it, an' Flesh an' Blood don't know it, but that's the truth – as I've heard. The Pharisees through bein' all stenched up an' frighted, an' tryin' to come *through* with their supplications, they nature-ally changed the thin airs and humours in Flesh an' Blood. It lay on the Marsh like thunder. Men saw their churches ablaze with the wildfire in the windows after dark; they saw their cattle scatterin' and no man scarin'; their sheep flockin' and no man drivin'; their horses latherin' an' no man leadin'; they saw the liddle low green lights more than ever in the dik-sides; they heard the liddle feet patterin' more than ever round the houses; an' night an' day, day an' night, 'twas all as though they were bein' creeped up on, and hinted at by some One or Other that couldn't rightly shape their trouble. Oh, I lay they sweated! Man an' maid, woman an' child, their Nature done 'em no service all the weeks while the Marsh was swarvin' up with Pharisees. But they was Flesh an' Blood, and Marsh men before all. They reckoned the signs sinnified trouble for the Marsh. Or that the sea 'ud rear up against Dymchurch Wall an' they'd be drownded like Old Winchelsea; or that the Plague was comin'. So they looked for the meanin' in the sea or in the clouds – far an' high up. They never thought to look near an' knee-high, where they could see naught.

"Now there was a poor widow at Dymchurch under the Wall, which, lacking man or property, she had the more time for feeling; and she come to feel there was a Trouble outside her doorstep bigger an' heavier than aught she'd ever carried over it. She had two sons – one born blind, and t'other struck dumb through fallin' off the Wall when he was liddle. They was men grown, but not wage-earnin', an' she worked for 'em, keepin' bees and answerin' Questions."

"What sort of questions?" said Dan.

"Like where lost things might be found, an' what to put about a crooked baby's neck, an' how to join parted sweethearts. She felt the Trouble on the Marsh same as eels feel thunder. She was a wise woman."

"My woman was won'erful weather-tender, too," said Hobden. "I've seen her brish sparks like off an anvil out of her hair in thunderstorms. But she never laid out to answer Questions."

"This woman was a Seeker like, an' Seekers they sometimes find. One night, while she lay abed, hot an' aching, there come a Dream an' tapped at her window, and 'Widow Whitgift,' it said, 'Widow Whitgift!'

"First, by the wings an' the whistling, she thought it was pewits, but last she arose an' dressed herself, an' opened her door to the Marsh, an' she felt the Trouble an' the Groaning all about her, strong as fever an' ague, an' she calls: 'What is it? Oh, what is it?'

"Then 'twas all like the frogs in the diks peeping: then 'twas all like the reeds in the diks clip-clapping; an' then the great Tide-wave rummelled along the Wall, an' she couldn't hear proper.

"Three times she called, an' three times the Tide-wave

did her down. But she catched the quiet between, an' she cries out, 'What is the Trouble on the Marsh that's been lying down with my heart an' arising with my body this month gone?' She felt a liddle hand lay hold on her gown-hem, and she stooped to the pull o' that liddle hand."

Tom Shoesmith spread his huge fist before the fire and smiled at it.

" 'Will the sea drown the Marsh?' she says. She was a Marsh-woman first an' foremost.

" 'No,' says the liddle voice. 'Sleep sound for all o' that.'

" 'Is the Plague comin' to the Marsh?' she says. Them was all the ills she knowed.

" 'No. Sleep sound for all o' that,' says Robin.

"She turned about, half mindful to go in, but the liddle voices grieved that shrill an' sorrowful she turns back, an' she cries: 'If it is not a Trouble of Flesh an' Blood, what can I do?'

"The Pharisees cried out upon her from all round to fetch them a boat to sail to France, an' come back no more.

" 'There's a boat on the Wall,' she says, 'but I can't push it down to the sea, nor sail it when 'tis there.'

" 'Lend us your sons,' says all the Pharisees. 'Give 'em Leave an' Good-will to sail it for us, Mother – O Mother!'

" 'One's dumb, an' t'other's blind,' she says. 'But all the dearer me for that; and you'll lose them in the big sea.' The voices justabout pierced through her. An' there was children's voices too. She stood out all she could, but she couldn't rightly stand against *that*. So she says: 'If you can draw my sons for your job, I'll not hinder 'em. You can't ask no more of a Mother.'

"She saw them liddle green lights dance an' cross till she was dizzy; she heard them liddle feet patterin' by the thousand; she heard cruel Canterbury Bells ringing to Bulver-hithe, an' she heard the great Tide-wave ranging along the Wall. That was while the Pharisees was workin' a Dream to wake her two sons asleep: an' while she bit on her fingers she saw them two she'd bore come out an' pass her with never a word. She followed 'em, cryin' pitiful, to the old boat on the Wall, an' that they took an' runned down to the Sea.

"When they'd stepped mast an' sail the blind son speaks up: 'Mother, we're waitin' your Leave an' Good-will to take Them over.'"

Tom Shoesmith threw back his head and half shut his eyes.

"Eh, me!" he said. "She was a fine, valiant woman, the Widow Whitgift. She stood twistin' the ends of her long hair over her fingers, an' she shook like a poplar, makin' up her mind. The Pharisees all about they hush their children from cryin' an' they waited dumb-still. She was all their dependence. 'Thout her Leave an' Good-will they could not pass; for she was the Mother. So she shook like a asp-tree makin' up her mind. 'Last she drives the word past her teeth, an' 'Go!' she says. 'Go with my Leave an' Good-will.'

"Then I saw – then, they say, she had to brace back same as if she was wadin' in tidewater; for the Pharisees justabout flowed past her – down the beach to the boat, I dunnamany of 'em – with their wives an' children an' valooables, all escapin' out of cruel Old England. Silver you could hear clinkin', an' liddle bundles hove down dunt on the bottomboards, an' passels o' liddle swords an' shield's raklin', an' liddle fingers an' toes scratchin' on the boatside to board her when the two sons pushed her off. That boat she sunk lower an' lower, but all the Widow could see in it was her boys movin' hampered-like to get at the tackle. Up sail they did, an' away they went, deep as a Rye barge, away into the off-shore mistes, an' the Widow Whitgift she sat down and eased her grief till mornin' light."

"I never heard she was all alone," said Hobden.

"I remember now. The one called Robin he stayed with her, they tell. She was all too grievous to listen to his promises."

"Ah! She should ha' made her bargain beforehand. I allus told my woman so!" Hobden cried.

"No. She loaned her sons for a pure love-loan, bein' as

she sensed the Trouble on the Marshes, an' was simply good-willing to ease it." Tom laughed softly. "She done that. Yes, she done that! From Hithe to Bulverhithe, fretty man an' petty maid, ailin' woman an' wailin' child, they took the advantage of the change in the thin airs just about *as* soon as the Pharisees flitted. Folks come out fresh an' shining all over the Marsh like snails after wet. An' that while the Widow Whitgift sat grievin' on the Wall. She might have beleft us – she might have trusted her sons would be sent back! She fussed, no bounds, when their boat come in after three days."

"And, of course, the sons were both quite cured?" said Una.

"No-o. That would have been out o' Nature. She got 'em back *as* she sent 'em. The blind man he hadn't seen naught of anything, an' the dumb man nature-ally, he couldn't say aught of what he'd seen. I reckon that was why the Pharisees pitched on 'em for the ferrying job."

"But what did you – what did Robin, promise the Widow?" said Dan.

"What *did* he promise, now?" Tom pretended to think. "Wasn't your woman a Whitgift, Ralph? Didn't she say?"

"She told me a passel o' no-sense stuff when he was born." Hobden pointed at his son. "There was always to be one of 'em that could see further into a millstone than most."

"Me! That's me!" said the Bee Boy so suddenly that they all laughed.

"I've got it now!" cried Tom, slapping his knee. "So long as Whitgift blood lasted, Robin promised there would allers be one o' her stock that – that no Trouble 'ud lie on, no Maid 'ud sigh on, no Night could frighten, no Fright could harm, no Harm could make sin, an' no Woman could make a fool."

"Well, ain't that just me?" said the Bee Boy, where he sat in the silver square of the great September moon that was staring into the oast-house door.

"They was the exact words she told me when we first found he wasn't like others. But it beats me how you known 'em," said Hobden.

"Aha! There's more under my hat besides hair!" Tom laughed and stretched himself. "When I've seen these two young folk home, we'll make a night of old days, Ralph, with passin' old tales – eh? An' where might you live?" he said, gravely, to Dan. "An' do you think your Pa 'ud give me a drink for taking you there, Missy?"

They giggled so at this that they had to run out. Tom picked them both up, set one on each broad shoulder, and tramped across the ferny pasture where the cows puffed milky puffs at them in the moonlight.

"Oh, Puck! Puck! I guessed you right from when you talked about the salt. How could you ever do it?" Una cried, swinging along delighted.

"Do what?" he said, and climbed the stile by the pollard oak.

"Pretend to be Tom Shoesmith," said Dan, and they ducked to avoid the two little ashes that grow by the bridge over the brook. Tom was almost running.

"Yes. That's my name, Mus' Dan," he said, hurrying over the silent shining lawn, where a rabbit sat by the big white-thorn near the croquet ground. "Here you be." He strode into the old kitchen yard, and slid them down as Ellen came to ask questions.

"I'm helping in Mus' Spray's oast-house," he said to her. "No, I'm no foreigner. I knowed this country 'fore your Mother was born; an' – yes it's dry work oasting, Miss. Thank you."

Ellen went to get a jug, and the children went in – magicked once more by Oak, Ash, and Thorn!

* * *

A THREE-PART SONG

I'm just in love with all these three,
The Weald and the Marsh and the Down countrie;
Nor I don't know which I love the most,
The Weald or the Marsh or the white chalk coast!

I've buried my heart in a ferny hill,
Twix' a liddle low Shaw an' a great high Gill.
Oh hop-vine yaller and woodsmoke blue,
I reckon you'll keep her middling true!

I've loosed my mind for to out and run,
On a Marsh that was old when Kings begun;
Oh Romney Level and Brenzett reeds,
I reckon you know what my mind needs!

I've given my soul to the Southdown grass,
And sheep-bells tinkled where you pass
Oh Firle an' Ditchling an' sails at sea,
I reckon you'll keep my soul or me!

WITH THE NIGHT MAIL

WITH THE NIGHT MAIL

A STORY OF 2000 A.D.

*(Together with extracts from the magazine
in which it appeared)*

A T nine o'clock of a gusty winter night I stood on the
lower stages of one of the G. P. O. outward mail towers.
My purpose was a run to Quebec in "Postal Packet 162 or
such other as may be appointed"; and the Postmaster-
General himself countersigned the order. This talisman
opened all doors, even those in the despatching-caisson at the
foot of the tower, where they were delivering the sorted Continental mail. The bags lay packed close as herrings in the
long grey underbodies which our G. P. O. still calls
"coaches." Five such coaches were filled as I watched, and
were shot up the guides to be locked on to their waiting
packets three hundred feet nearer the stars.

From the despatching-caisson I was conducted by a court-
eous and wonderfully learned official – Mr. L. L. Geary,
Second Despatcher of the Western Route – to the Captains'
Room (this wakes an echo of old romance), where the mail
captains come on for their turn of duty. He introduces me to
the captain of "162" – Captain Purnall, and his relief, Captain Hodgson. The one is small and dark; the other large and
red; but each has the brooding sheathed glance characteristic
of eagles and aeronauts. You can see it in the pictures of our
racing professionals, from L. V. Rautsch to little Ada Warr-
leigh – that fathomless abstraction of eyes habitually turned
through naked space.

On the notice-board in the Captains' Room, the pulsing
arrows of some twenty indicators register, degree by geo-
graphical degree, the progress of as many homeward-bound
packets. The word "Cape" rises across the face of a dial; a

gong strikes: the South African mid-weekly mail is in at the Highgate Receiving Towers. That is all. It reminds one comically of the traitorous little bell which in pigeon-fanciers' lofts notifies the return of a homer.

"Time for us to be on the move," says Captain Purnall, and we are shot up by the passenger-lift to the top of the despatch-towers. "Our coach will lock on when it is filled and the clerks are aboard." . . .

"No. 162" waits for us in Slip E of the topmost stage. The great curve of her back shines frostily under the lights, and some minute alteration of trim makes her rock a little in her holding-down slips.

Captain Purnall frowns and dives inside. Hissing softly, "162" comes to rest as level as a rule. From her North At-lantic Winter nose-cap (worn bright as diamond with boring through uncounted leagues of hail, snow, and ice) to the inset of her three built-out propeller-shafts is some two hundred and forty feet. Her extreme diameter, carried well forward, is thirty-seven. Contrast this with the nine hundred by ninety-five of any crack liner, and you will realise the power that must drive a hull through all weathers at more than the emergency speed of the *Cyclonic*!

The eye detects no joint in her skin plating save the sweeping hair-crack of the bow-rudder – Magniac's rudder that assured us the dominion of the unstable air and left its inventor penniless and half-blind. It is calculated to Castelli's "gull-wing" curve. Raise a few feet of that all but invisible plate three-eighths of an inch and she will yaw five miles to port or starboard ere she is under control again. Give her full helm and she returns on her track like a whip-lash. Cant the whole forward – a touch on the wheel will suffice – and she sweeps at your good direction up or down. Open the com-plete circle and she presents to the air a mushroom-head that will bring her up all standing within a half mile.

"Yes," says Captain Hodgson, answering my thought, "Castelli thought he'd discovered the secret of controlling aeroplanes when he'd only found out how to steer dirigible balloons. Magniac invented his rudder to help war-boats ram each other; and war went out of fashion and Magniac he went out of his mind because he said he couldn't serve his country any more. I wonder if any of us ever know what we're really doing."

"If you want to see the coach locked you'd better go aboard. It's due now," says Mr. Geary. I enter through the door amidships. There is nothing here for display. The inner skin of the gas-tanks comes down to within a foot or two of my head and turns over just short of the turn of the bilges. Liners and yachts disguise their tanks with decoration, but the G. P. O. serves them raw under a lick of grey official paint. The inner skin shuts off fifty feet of the bow and as much of the stern, but the bow-bulkhead is recessed for the lift-shunting apparatus as the stern is pierced for the shaft-tunnels. The engine-room lies almost amidships. Forward of it, extending to the turn of the bow tanks, is an aperture – a bottomless hatch at present – into which our coach will be locked. One looks down over the coamings three hundred feet to the despatching-caisson whence voices boom upward. The light below is obscured to a sound of thunder, as our coach rises on its guides. It enlarges rapidly from a postage-stamp to a playing-card; to a punt and last a pontoon. The two clerks, its crew, do not even look up as it comes into place. The Quebec letters fly under their fingers and leap into the docketed racks, while both captains and Mr. Geary satisfy themselves that the coach is locked home. A clerk passes the way-bill over the hatch-coaming. Captain Purnall thumb-marks and passes it to Mr. Geary. Receipt has been given and taken. "Pleasant run," says Mr. Geary, and disappears through the door which a foot-high pneumatic compressor locks after him.

"A-ah!" sighs the compressor released. Our holding-down clips part with a tang. We are clear.

Captain Hodgson opens the great colloid underbody port-hole through which I watch over-lighted London slide east-ward as the gale gets hold of us. The first of the low winter clouds cuts off the well-known view and darkens Middlesex. On the south edge of it I can see a postal packet's light ploughing through the white fleece. For an instant she gleams like a star ere she drops toward the Highgate Receiving Towers. "The Bombay Mail," says Captain Hodgson, and looks at his watch. "She's forty minutes late."

"What's our level?" I ask.

"Four thousand. Aren't you coming up on the bridge?"

The bridge (let us ever praise the G. P. O. as a repository of ancientest tradition!) is represented by a view of Captain Hodgson's legs where he stands on the Control Platform that runs thwartships overhead. The bow colloid is unshuttered and Captain Purnall, one hand on the wheel, is feeling for a fair slant. The dial shows 4300 feet.

"It's steep to-night," he mutters, as tier on tier of cloud drops under. "We generally pick up an easterly draught below three thousand at this time o' the year. I hate slathering through fluff."

"So does Van Cutsem. Look at him huntin' for a slant!" says Captain Hodgson. A fog-light breaks cloud a hundred fathoms below. The Antwerp Night Mail makes her signal and rises between two racing clouds far to port, her flanks blood-red in the glare of Sheerness Double Light. The gale will have us over the North Sea in half-an-hour, but Captain Purnall lets her go composedly – nosing to every point of the compass as she rises.

"Five thousand – six, six thousand eight hundred" – the dip-dial reads ere we find the easterly drift, heralded by a flurry of snow at the thousand fathom level. Captain Purnall rings up the engines and keys down the governor on the switch before him. There is no sense in urging machinery when Aeolus himself gives you good knots for nothing. We are away in earnest now – our nose notched home on our chosen star. At this level the lower clouds are laid out, all neatly combed by the dry fingers of the East. Below that again is the strong westerly blow through which we rose. Overhead, a film of southerly drifting mist draws a theatrical gauze across the firmament. The moonlight turns the lower strata to silver without a stain except where our shadow underruns us. Bristol and Cardiff Double Lights (those statelily inclined beams over Severnmouth) are dead ahead of us; for we keep the Southern Winter Route. Coventry Central, the pivot of the English system, stabs upward once in ten seconds its spear of diamond light to the north; and a point or two off our starboard bow The Leek, the great cloud-breaker of Saint David's Head, swings its unmistakable green beam twenty-five degrees each way. There must be half a mile of fluff over it in this weather, but it does not affect The Leek.

"Our planet's overlighted if anything," says Captain Purnall at the wheel, as Cardiff-Bristol slides under. "I remember the old days of common white verticals that 'ud show two or three hundred feet up in a mist, if you knew where to look for 'em. In really fluffy weather they might as well have been under your hat. One could get lost coming home then, an' have some fun. Now, it's like driving down Piccadilly."

He points to the pillars of light where the cloud-breakers bore through the cloud-floor. We see nothing of England's outlines: only a white pavement pierced in all directions by these manholes of variously coloured fire – Holy Island's white and red – St. Bee's interrupted white, and so on as far as the eye can reach. Blessed be Sargent, Ahrens, and the Dubois brothers, who invented the cloud-breakers of the world whereby we travel in security!

"Are you going to lift for The Shamrock?" asks Captain Hodgson. Cork Light (green, fixed) enlarges as we rush to it. Captain Purnall nods. There is heavy traffic hereabouts – the cloud-bank beneath us is streaked with running fissures of flame where the Atlantic boats are hurrying Londonward just clear of the fluff. Mail-packets are supposed, under the Conference rules, to have the five-thousand-foot lanes to themselves, but the foreigner in a hurry is apt to take liberties with English air. "No. 162" lifts to a long-drawn wail of the breeze in the fore-flange of the rudder and we make Valencia (white, green, white) at a safe 7000 feet, dipping our beam to an incoming Washington packet.

There is no cloud on the Atlantic, and faint streaks of cream round Dingle Bay show where the driven seas hammer the coast. A big S. A. T. A. liner (*Société Anonyme des Transports Aëriens*) is diving and lifting half a mile below us in search of some break in the solid west wind. Lower still lies a disabled Dane: she is telling the liner all about it in International. Our General Communication dial has caught her talk and begins to eavesdrop. Captain Hodgson makes a motion to shut it off but checks himself. "Perhaps you'd like to listen," he says.

"*Argol* of St. Thomas," the Dane whimpers. "Report owners three starboard shaft collar-bearings fused. Can make Flores as we are, but impossible further. Shall we buy spares at Fayal?"

The liner acknowledges and recommends inverting the bearings. The *Argol* answers that she has already done so without effect, and begins to relieve her mind about cheap German enamels for collar-bearings. The Frenchman assents cordially, cries "*Courage, mon ami*," and switches off.

Their lights sink under the curve of the ocean.

"That's one of Lundt & Bleamers' boats," says Captain Hodgson. "Serves 'em right for putting German compos in their thrust-blocks. *She* won't be in Fayal to-night! By the way, wouldn't you like to look round the engine-room?"

I have been waiting eagerly for this invitation and I follow Captain Hodgson from the control-platform, stooping low to avoid the bulge of the tanks. We know that Fleury's gas can lift anything, as the world-famous trials of '89 showed, but its almost indefinite powers of expansion necessitate vast tank room. Even in this thin air the lift-shunts are busy taking out one-third of its normal lift, and still "162" must be checked by an occasional downdraw of the rudder or our flight would become a climb to the stars. Captain Purnall prefers an over-lifted to an underlifted ship; but no two captains trim ship alike. "When *I* take the bridge," says Captain Hodgson, "you'll see me shunt forty per cent. of the lift out of the gas and run her on the upper rudder. With a swoop upward instead of a swoop downward, *as* you say. Either way will do. It's only habit. Watch our dip-dial! Tim fetches her down once every thirty knots as regularly as breathing."

So is it shown on the dip-dial. For five or six minutes the arrow creeps from 6700 to 7300. There is the faint "szgee" of the rudder, and back slides the arrow to 6000 on a falling slant of ten or fifteen knots.

"In heavy weather you jockey her with the screws as well," says Captain Hodgson, and, unslipping the jointed bar which divides the engine-room from the bare deck, he leads me on to the floor.

Here we find Fleury's Paradox of the Bulk-headed Vacuum – which we accept now without thought – literally in full blast. The three engines are H. T. & T. assisted-vacuo Fleury turbines running from 3000 to the Limit – that is to say, up to the point when the blades make the air "bell" – cut out a vacuum for themselves precisely as overdriven marine propellers used to do. "162's" Limit is low on account of the small size of her nine screws, which, though handier than the old colloid Thelussons, "bell" sooner. The midships engine, generally used as a reinforce, is not running; so the port and starboard turbine vacuum-chambers draw direct into the return-mains.

The turbines whistle reflectively. From the low-arched expansion-tanks on either side the valves descend pillarwise to the turbine-chests, and thence the obedient gas whirls through the spirals of blades with a force that would whip the teeth out of a power-saw. Behind, is its own pressure held in leash or spurred on by the lift-shunts; before it, the vacuum where Fleury's Ray dances in violet-green bands and whirled turbillons of flame. The jointed U-tubes of the vacuum-chamber are pressure-tempered colloid (no glass would endure the strain for an instant) and a junior engineer with tinted spectacles watches the Ray intently. It is the very heart of the machine – a mystery to this day. Even Fleury who begat it and, unlike Magniac, died a multi-millionaire, could not explain how the restless little imp shuddering in the U-tube can, in the fractional fraction of a second, strike the furious blast of gas into a chill greyish-green liquid that drains (you can hear it trickle) from the far end of the vacuum through the education-pipes and the mains back to the bilges. Here it returns to its gaseous, one had almost written sagacious, state and climbs to work afresh. Bilge-tank, upper tank, dorsal-tank, expansion-chamber, vacuum, main-return (as a liquid), and bilge-tank once more is the ordained cycle. Fleury's Ray sees to that; and the engineer with the tinted spectacles sees to Fleury's Ray. If a speck of oil, if even the natural grease of the human finger touch the hooded terminals, Fleury's Ray will wink and disappear and must be laboriously built up again. This means half a day's work for all hands and an expense of one hundred and seventy-odd pounds to the G. P. O. for radium-salts and such trifles.

"Now look at our thrust-collars. You won't find much German compo there. Full-jewelled, you see," says Captain Hodgson as the engineer shunts open the top of a cap. Our shaft-bearings are C. M. C. (Commercial Minerals Company) stones, ground with as much care as the lens of a telescope. They cost £37 apiece. So far we have not arrived at their term of life. These bearings came from "No. 97," which took them over from the old *Dominion of Light* which had them out of the wreck of the *Perseus* aeroplane in the years when men still flew wooden kites over oil engines!

They are a shining reproof to all low-grade German "ruby" enamels, so-called "boort" facings, and the dangerous and unsatisfactory alumina compounds which please dividend-hunting owners and turn skippers crazy.

The rudder-gear and the gas lift-shunt, seated side by side under the engine-room dials, are the only machines in visible motion. The former sighs from time to time as the oil plunger rises and falls half an inch. The latter, cased and guarded like the U-tube aft, exhibits another Fleury Ray, but inverted and more green than violet. Its function is to shunt the lift out of the gas, and this it will do without watching. That is all! A tiny pump-rod wheezing and whining to itself beside a sputtering green lamp. A hundred and fifty feet aft down the flat-topped tunnel of the tanks a violet light, restless and irresolute. Between the two, three white-painted turbine-trunks, like eel-baskets laid on their side, accentuate the empty perspectives. You can hear the trickle of the liquefied gas flowing from the vacuum into the bilge-tanks and the soft *gluck-glock* of gas-locks closing as Captain Purnall brings "162" down by the head. The hum of the turbines and the boom of the air on our skin is no more than a cotton-wool wrapping to the universal stillness. And we are running an eighteen-second mile.

I peer from the fore end of the engine-room over the hatch-coamings into the coach. The mail-clerks are sorting the Winnipeg, Calgary, and Medicine Hat bags; but there is a pack of cards ready on the table.

Suddenly a bell thrills; the engineers run to the turbine-valves and stand by; but the spectacled slave of the Ray in the U-tube never lifts his head. He must watch where he is. We are hard-braked and going astern; there is language from the Control Platform.

"Tim's sparking badly about something," says the unruffled Captain Hodgson. "Let's look."

Captain Purnall is not the suave man we left half an hour since, but the embodied authority of the G. P. O. Ahead of us floats an ancient, aluminium-patched, twin-screw tramp of the dingiest, with no more right to the 5000-foot lane than has a horse-cart to a modern road. She carries an obsolete "barbette" conning-tower – a six-foot affair with railed platform forward – and our warning beam plays on the top of it as a policeman's lantern flashes on the area sneak. Like a sneak-thief, too, emerges a shock-headed navigator in his shirt-sleeves. Captain Purnall wrenches open the colloid to talk with him man to man. There are times when Science does not satisfy.

"What under the stars are you doing here, you sky-scraping chimney-sweep?" he shouts as we two drift side by side. "Do you know this is a Mail-lane? You call yourself a sailor, sir? You ain't fit to peddle toy balloons to an Esquimaux. Your name and number! Report and get down, and be —!"

"I've been blown up once," the shock-headed man cries, hoarsely, as a dog barking. "I don't care two flips of a contact for anything *you* can do, Postey."

"Don't you, sir? But I'll make you care. I'll have you towed stern first to Disko and broke up. You can't recover insurance if you're broke for obstruction. Do you understand *that*?"

Then the stranger bellows: "Look at my propellers! There's been a wulli-wa down below that has knocked us into umbrella-frames! We've been blown up about forty thousand feet! We're all one conjuror's watch inside! My mate's arm's broke; my engineer's head's cut open; my Ray went out when the engines smashed; and . . . and . . . for pity's sake give me my height, Captain! We doubt we're dropping."

"Six thousand eight hundred. Can you hold it?" Captain Purnall overlooks all insults, and leans half out of the colloid, staring and snuffing. The stranger leaks pungently.

"We ought to blow into St. John's with luck. We're trying to plug the fore-tank now, but she's simply whistling it away," her captain wails.

"She's sinking like a log," says Captain Purnall in an undertone. "Call up the Banks Mark Boat, George." Our dip-dial shows that we, keeping abreast the tramp, have dropped five hundred feet the last few minutes.

Captain Purnall presses a switch and our signal beam begins to swing through the night, twizzling spokes of light across infinity.

"That'll fetch something," he says, while Captain Hodgson watches the General Communicator. He has called up the North Banks Mark Boat, a few hundred miles west, and is reporting the case.

"I'll stand by you," Captain Purnall roars to the long figure on the conning-tower.

"Is it as bad as that?" comes the answer. "She isn't insured. She's mine."

"Might have guessed as much," mutters Hodgson. "Owner's risk is the worst risk of all!"

"Can't I fetch St. John's – not even with this breeze?" the voice quavers.

"Stand by to abandon ship. Haven't you *any* lift in you, fore or aft?"

"Nothing but the midship tanks, and they're none too tight. You see, my Ray gave out and —" he coughs in the reek of the escaping gas.

"You poor devil!" This does not reach our friend. "What does the Mark Boat say, George?"

"Wants to know if there's any danger to traffic. Says she's in a bit of weather herself, and can't quit station. I've turned in a General Call, so even if they don't see our beam some one's bound to help – or else we must. Shall I clear our slings? Hold on! Here we are! A Planet liner, too! She'll be up in a tick!"

"Tell her to have her slings ready," cries his brother captain. "There won't be much time to spare . . . Tie up your mate," he roars to the tramp.

"My mate's all right. It's my engineer. He's gone crazy."

"Shunt the lift out of him with a spanner. Hurry!"

"But I can make St. John's if you'll stand by."

"You'll make the deep, wet Atlantic in twenty minutes. You're less than fifty-eight hundred now. Get your papers."

A Planet liner, east bound, heaves up in a superb spiral and takes the air of us humming. Her underbody colloid is open and her transporter-slings hang down like tentacles. We shut off our beam as she adjusts herself – steering to a hair – over the tramp's conning-tower. The mate comes up, his arm strapped to his side, and stumbles into the cradle. A man with a ghastly scarlet head follows, shouting that he must go back and build up his Ray. The mate assures him that he will find a nice new Ray all ready in the liner's engine-room. The bandaged head goes up wagging excitedly. A youth and a

woman follow. The liner cheers hollowly above us, and we
see the passengers' faces at the saloon colloid.

"That's a pretty girl. What's the fool waiting for now?"
says Captain Purnall.

The skipper comes up, still appealing to us to stand by
and see him fetch St. John's. He dives below and returns –
at which we little human beings in the void cheer louder than
ever – with the ship's kitten. Up fly the liner's hissing slings;
her underbody crashes home and she hurtles away again. The
dial shows less than 3000 feet.

The Mark Boat signals we must attend to the derelict,
now whistling her death-song, as she falls beneath us in long
sick zigzags.

"Keep our beam on her and send out a General Warning," says Captain Purnall, following her down.

There is no need. Not a liner in air but knows the
meaning of that vertical beam and gives us and our quarry a
wide berth.

"But she'll drown in the water, won't she?" I ask.

"Not always," is his answer. "I've known a derelict up-
end and sift her engines out of herself and flicker round the
Lower Lanes for three weeks on her forward tanks only.
We'll run no risks. Pith her, George, and look sharp. There's
weather ahead."

Captain Hodgson opens the underbody colloid, swings the
heavy pithing-iron out of its rack which in liners is generally
cased as a smoking-room settee, and at two hundred feet
releases the catch. We hear the whir of the crescent-shaped
arms opening as they descend. The derelict's forehead is
punched in, starred across, and rent diagonally. She falls
stern first, our beam upon her; slides like a lost soul down
that pitiless ladder of light, and the Atlantic takes her.

"A filthy business," says Hodgson. "I wonder what it
must have been like in the old days?"

The thought had crossed my mind, too. What if that
wavering carcass had been filled with the men of the old
days, each one of them taught (*that* is the horror of it!) that

after death he would very possibly go for ever to unspeakable torment?

And scarcely a generation ago, we (one knows now that we are only our fathers re-enlarged upon the earth), *we*, I say, ripped and rammed and pithed to admiration.

Here Tim, from the Control Platform, shouts that we are to get into our inflators and to bring him his at once.

We hurry into the heavy rubber suits – the engineers are already dressed – and inflate at the air-pump taps. G. P. O. inflators are thrice as thick as a racing man's "flickers," and chafe abominably under the armpits. George takes the wheel until Tim has blown himself up to the extreme of rotundity. If you kicked him off the c. p. to the deck he would bounce back. But it is "162" that will do the kicking.

"The Mark Boat's mad – stark ravin' crazy," he snorts, returning to command. "She says there's a bad blow-out ahead and wants me to pull over to Greenland. I'll see her pithed first! We wasted half an hour fussing over that dead duck down under, and now I'm expected to go rubbin' my back all round the Pole. What does she think a Postal packet's made of? Gummed silk? Tell her we're coming on straight, George."

George buckles him into the Frame and switches on the Direct Control. Now under Tim's left toe lies the port-engine Accelerator; under his left heel the Reverse, and so with the other foot. The lift-shunt stops stand out on the rim of the steering-wheel where the fingers of his left hand can play on them. At his right hand is the midships engine lever ready to be thrown into gear at a moment's notice. He leans forward in his belt, eyes glued to the colloid, and one ear cocked toward the General Communicator. Henceforth he is the strength and direction of "162," through whatever may befall.

The Banks Mark Boat is reeling out pages of A. B. C. Directions to the traffic at large. We are to secure all "loose objects"; hood up our Fleury Rays; and "on no account to attempt to clear snow from our conning-towers till the weather abates." Under-powered craft, we are told, can ascend to the limit of their lift, mail-packets to look out for them accordingly; the lower lanes westward are pitting very badly, "with frequent blow-outs, vortices, laterals, etc."

Still the clear dark holds up unblemished. The only warning is the electric skin-tension (I feel as though I were a lace-maker's pillow) and an irritability which the gibbering of the General Communicator increases almost to hysteria.

We have made eight thousand feet since we pithed the tramp and our turbines are giving us an honest two hundred and ten knots.

Very far to the west an elongated blur of red, low down, shows us the North Banks Mark Boat. There are specks of fire round her rising and falling – bewildered planets about an unstable sun – helpless shipping hanging on to her light for company's sake. No wonder she could not quit station.

She warns us to look out for the back-wash of the bad vortex in which (her beam shows it) she is even now reeling.

The pits of gloom about us begin to fill with very faintly luminous films – wreathing and uneasy shapes. One forms itself into a globe of pale flame that waits shivering with eagerness till we sweep by. It leaps monstrously across the blackness, alights on the precise tip of our nose, pirouettes there an instant, and swings off. Our roaring bow sinks as though that light were lead – sinks and recovers to lurch and stumble again beneath the next blow-out. Tim's fingers on the lift-shunt strike chords of numbers – 1:4:7: – 2:4:6: – 7:5:3, and so on; for he is running by his tanks only, lifting or lowering her against the uneasy air. All three engines are at work, for the sooner we have skated over this thin ice the better. Higher we dare not go. The whole upper vault is charged with pale krypton vapours, which our skin-friction may excite to unholy manifestations. Between the upper and lower levels – 5000 and 7000, hints the Mark Boat – we may perhaps bolt through if . . . Our bow clothes itself in blue flame and falls like a sword. No human skill can keep pace with the changing tensions. A vortex has us by the beak and we dive down a two-thousand-foot slant at an angle (the dip-dial and my bouncing body record it) of thirty-five. Our turbines scream shrilly; the propellers cannot bite on the thin air; Tim shunts the lift out of five tanks at once and by sheer weight drives her bulletwise through the maelstrom till she cushions with a jar on an up-gust, three thousand feet below.

"*Now* we've done it," says George in my ear. "Our skin-friction, that last slide, has played Old Harry with the tensions! Look out for laterals, Tim; she'll want some holding."

"I've got her," is the answer. "Come *up*, old woman."

She comes up nobly, but the laterals buffet her left and right like the pinions of angry angels. She is jolted off her course four ways at once, and cuffed into place again, only to be swung aside and dropped into a new chaos. We are never without a corposant grinning on our bows or rolling head over heels from nose to midships, and to the crackle of electricity around and within us is added once or twice the rattle of hail – hail that will never fall on any sea. Slow we must or we may break our back, pitch-poling.

"Air's a perfectly elastic fluid," roars George above the tumult. "About as elastic as a head sea off the Fastnet, ain't it?"

He is less than just to the good element. If one intrudes on the Heavens when they are balancing their volt-accounts; if one disturbs the High Gods' market-rates by hurling steel hulls at ninety knots across tremblingly adjusted electric tensions, one must not complain of any rudeness in the reception. Tim met it with an unmoved countenance, one corner of his under lip caught up on a tooth, his eyes fleeting into the blackness twenty miles ahead, and the fierce sparks flying from his knuckles at every turn of the hand. Now and again he shook his head to clear the sweat trickling from his eyebrows, and it was then that George, watching his chance, would slide down the life-rail and swab his face quickly with a big red handkerchief. I never imagined that a human being could so continuously labour and so collectedly think as did Tim through that Hell's half-hour when the flurry was at its worst. We were dragged hither and yon by warm or frozen suctions, belched up on the tops of wulli-was, spun down by vortices and clubbed aside by laterals under a dizzying rush of stars in the company of a drunken moon. I heard the rushing click of the midship-engine-lever sliding in and out, the low growl of the lift-shunts, and, louder than the yelling winds without, the scream of the bow-rudder gouging into any lull that promised hold for an instant. At last we began to claw up on a cant, bow-rudder and port-propeller together; only the nicest balancing of tanks saved us from spinning like the rifle-bullet of the old days.

"We've got to hitch to windward of that Mark Boat somehow," George cried.

"There's no windward," I protested feebly, where I swung shackled to a stanchion. "How can there be?"

He laughed – as we pitched into a thousand foot blow-out – that red man laughed beneath his inflated hood!

"Look!" he said. "We must clear those refugees with a high lift."

The Mark Boat was below and a little to the sou'west of us, fluctuating in the centre of her distraught galaxy. The air was thick with moving lights at every level. I take it most of them were trying to lie head to wind, but, not being hydras, they failed. An under-tanked Moghrabi boat had risen to the limit of her lift, and, finding no improvement, had dropped a couple of thousand. There she met a superb wulli-wa, and was blown up spinning like a dead leaf. Instead of shutting off she went astern and, naturally, rebounded as from a wall almost into the Mark Boat, whose language (our G. C. took it in) was humanly simple.

"If they'd only ride it out quietly it 'ud be better," said George in a calm, while we climbed like a bat above them all. "But some skippers *will* navigate without enough lift. What does that Tad-boat think she is doing, Tim?"

"Playin' kiss in the ring," was Tim's unmoved reply. A Trans-Asiatic Direct liner had found a smooth and butted into it full power. But there was a vortex at the tail of that smooth, so the T. A. D. was flipped out like a pea from off a finger-nail, braking madly as she fled down and all but over-ending.

"Now I hope she's satisfied," said Tim. "I'm glad I'm not a Mark Boat . . . Do I want help?" The General Communicator dial had caught his ear. "George, you may tell that gentleman with my love – love, remember, George – that I do not want help. Who *is* the officious sardine-tin?"

"A Rimouski drogher on the look-out for a tow."

"Very kind of the Rimouski drogher. This postal packet isn't being towed at present."

"Those droghers will go anywhere on a chance of salvage," George explained. "We call 'em kittiwakes."

A long-beaked, bright steel ninety-footer floated at ease for one instant within hail of us, her slings coiled ready for rescues, and a single hand in her open tower. He was smoking. Surrendered to the insurrection of the airs through which we tore our way, he lay in absolute peace. I saw the smoke of his pipe ascend untroubled ere his boat dropped, it seemed, like a stone in a well.

We had just cleared the Mark Boat and her disorderly neighbours when the storm ended as suddenly as it had begun. A shooting-star to northward filled the sky with the green blink of a meteorite dissipating itself in our atmosphere.

Said George: "That may iron out all the tensions." Even as he spoke, the conflicting winds came to rest; the levels filled; the laterals died out in long, easy swells; the air-ways were smoothed before us. In less than three minutes the covey round the Mark Boat had shipped their power-lights and whirred away upon their businesses.

"What's happened?" I gasped. The nerve-storm within and the volt-tingle without had passed: my inflators weighed like lead.

"God, He knows!" said Captain George soberly. "That old shooting-star's skin-friction has discharged the different levels. I've seen it happen before. Phew! What a relief!"

We dropped from ten to six thousand and got rid of our clammy suits. Tim shut off and stepped out of the Frame. The Mark Boat was coming up behind us. He opened the colloid in that heavenly stillness and mopped his face.

"Hello, Williams!" he cried. "A degree or two out o' station, ain't you?"

"May be," was the answer from the Mark Boat. "I've had some company this evening."

"So I noticed. Wasn't that quite a little draught?"

"I warned you. Why didn't you pull out north? The east-bound packets have."

"Me? Not till I'm running a Polar consumptives' sanatorium boat. I was squinting through a colloid before you were out of your cradle, my son."

"I'd be the last man to deny it," the captain of the Mark Boat replies softly. "The way you handled her just now – I'm a pretty fair judge of traffic in a volt-hurry – it was a thousand revolutions beyond anything even *I*'ve ever seen."

Tim's back supples visibly to this oiling. Captain George on the c. p. winks and points to the portrait of a singularly attractive maiden pinned up on Tim's telescope bracket above the steering-wheel.

I see. Wholly and entirely do I see!

There is some talk overhead of "coming round to tea on Friday," a brief report of the derelict's fate, and Tim volunteers as he descends: "For an A. B. C. man young Williams is less of a high-tension fool than some. . . . Were you thinking of taking her on, George? Then I'll just have a look round that port-thrust – seems to me it's a trifle warm – and we'll jog along."

The Mark Boat hums off joyously and hangs herself up in her appointed eyrie. Here she will stay a shutterless observatory; a life-boat station; a salvage tug; a court of ultimate appeal-cum-meteorological bureau for three hundred miles in all directions, till Wednesday next when her relief slides across the stars to take her buffeted place. Her black hull, double conning-tower, and ever-ready slings represent all that remains to the planet of that odd old word authority. She is responsible only to the Aerial Board of Control – the A. B. C. of which Tim speaks so flippantly. But that semi-elected, semi-nominated body of a few score of persons of both sexes, controls this planet. "Transportation is Civilisation," our motto runs. Theoretically, we do what we please so long as we do not interfere with the traffic *and all it implies*. Practically, the A. B. C. confirms or annuls all international arrangements and, to judge from its last report, finds our tolerant, humorous, lazy little planet only too ready to shift the whole burden of public administration on its shoulders.

I discuss this with Tim, sipping maté on the c. p. while George fans her along over the white blur of the Banks in beautiful upward curves of fifty miles each. The dip-dial translates them on the tape in flowing freehand.

Tim gathers up a skein of it and surveys the last few feet, which record "162's" path through the volt-flurry.

"I haven't had a fever-chart like this to show up in five years," he says ruefully.

A postal packet's dip-dial records every yard of every run. The tapes then go to the A. B. C., which collates and makes composite photographs of them for the instruction of captains. Tim studies his irrevocable past, shaking his head.

"Hello! Here's a fifteen-hundred-foot drop at fifty-five degrees! We must have been standing on our heads then, George."

"You don't say so," George answers. "I fancied I noticed it at the time."

George may not have Captain Purnall's catlike swiftness, but he is all an artist to the tips of the broad fingers that play on the shunt-stops. The delicious flight-curves come away on the tape with never a waver. The Mark Boat's vertical spindle of light lies down to eastward, setting in the face of the following stars. Westward, where no planet should rise, the triple verticals of Trinity Bay (we keep still to the Southern route) make a low-lifting haze. We seem the only thing at rest under all the heavens; floating at ease till the earth's revolution shall turn up our landing-towers.

And minute by minute our silent clock gives us a sixteen-second mile.

"Some fine night," says Tim, "we'll be even with that clock's Master."

"He's coming now," says George, over his shoulder. "I'm chasing the night west."

The stars ahead dim no more than if a film of mist had been drawn under unobserved, but the deep air-boom on our skin changes to a joyful shout.

"The dawn-gust," says Tim. "It'll go on to meet the Sun. Look! Look! There's the dark being crammed back over our bows! Come to the after-colloid. I'll show you something."

The engine-room is hot and stuffy; the clerks in the coach are asleep, and the Slave of the Ray is ready to follow them. Tim slides open the aft colloid and reveals the curve of the world – the ocean's deepest purple – edged with fuming and intolerable gold. Then the Sun rises and through the colloid strikes out our lamps. Tim scowls in his face.

"Squirrels in a cage," he mutters. "That's all we are. Squirrels in a cage! He's going twice as fast as us. Just you wait a few years, my shining friend, and we'll take steps that will amaze you. *We*'ll Joshua you!"

Yes, that is our dream: to turn all earth into the Vale of Ajalon at our pleasure. So far, we can drag out the dawn to twice its normal length in these latitudes. But some day – even on the Equator – we shall hold the Sun level in his full stride.

Now we look down on a sea thronged with heavy traffic. A big submersible breaks water suddenly. Another and another follows with a swash and a suck and a savage bubbling of relieved pressures. The deep-sea freighters are rising to lung up after the long night, and the leisurely ocean is all patterned with peacock's eyes of foam.

"We'll lung up, too," says Tim, and when we return to the c. p. George shuts off, the colloids are opened, and the

fresh air sweeps her out. There is no hurry. The old contracts (they will be revised at the end of the year) allow
twelve hours for a run which any packet can put behind her
in ten. So we breakfast in the arms of an easterly slant which
pushes us along at a languid twenty.

To enjoy life, and tobacco, begin both on a sunny morning half a mile or so above the dappled Atlantic cloud-belts
and after a volt-flurry which has cleared and tempered your
nerves. While we discussed the thickening traffic with the
superiority that comes of having a high level reserved to
ourselves, we heard (and I for the first time) the morning
hymn on a Hospital boat.

She was cloaked by a skein of ravelled fluff beneath us and
we caught the chant before she rose into the sunlight. "*Oh,
ye Winds of God,*" sang the unseen voices: "*bless ye the Lord!
Praise Him and magnify Him for ever!*"

We slid off our caps and joined in. When our shadow fell
across her great open platforms they looked up and stretched
out their hands neighbourly while they sang. We could see
the doctors and the nurses and the white-button-like faces of
the cot-patients. She passed slowly beneath us, heading
northward, her hull, wet with the dews of the night, all
ablaze in the sunshine. So took she the shadow of a cloud
and vanished, her song continuing. "*Oh, ye holy and humble
men of heart, bless ye the Lord! Praise Him and magnify Him
for ever.*"

"She's a public lunger or she wouldn't have been singing
the *Benedicite*; and she's a Greenlander or she wouldn't
have snow-blinds over her colloids," said George at last.
"She'll be bound for Frederikshavn or one of the Glacier
sanatoria for a month. If she was an accident ward she'd be
hung up at the eight-thousand-foot level. Yes – consumptives."

"Funny how the new things are the old things. I've read
in books," Tim answered, "that savages used to haul their
sick and wounded up to the tops of hills because microbes
were fewer there. We hoist 'em into sterilised air for a while.

Same idea. How much do the doctors say we've added to the average life of a man?"

"Thirty years," says George with a twinkle in his eye. "Are we going to spend 'em all up here, Tim?"

"Flap ahead, then. Flap ahead. Who's hindering?" the senior captain laughed, as we went in.

We held a good lift to clear the coastwise and Continental shipping; and we had need of it. Though our route is in no sense a populated one, there is a steady trickle of traffic this way along. We met Hudson Bay furriers out of the Great Preserve, hurrying to make their departure from Bonavista with sable and black fox for the insatiable markets. We over-crossed Keewatin liners, small and cramped; but their captains, who see no land between Trepassy and Blanco, know what gold they bring back from West Africa. Trans-Asiatic Directs we met, soberly ringing the world round the Fiftieth Meridian at an honest seventy knots; and white-painted Ackroyd & Hunt fruiters out of the south fled beneath us, their ventilated hulls whistling like Chinese kites. Their market is in the North among the northern sanatoria where you can smell their grape-fruit and bananas across the cold snows. Argentine beef boats we sighted too, of enormous capacity and unlovely outline. They, too, feed the northern health stations in icebound ports where submersibles dare not rise.

Yellow-bellied ore-flats and Ungava petrol-tanks punted down leisurely out of the north, like strings of unfrightened wild duck. It does not pay to "fly" minerals and oil a mile farther than is necessary; but the risks of transhipping to submersibles in the ice-pack off Nain or Hebron are so great that these heavy freighters fly down to Halifax direct, and scent the air as they go. They are the biggest tramps aloft except the Athabasca grain-tubs. But these last, now that the wheat is moved, are busy, over the world's shoulder, timber-lifting in Siberia.

We held to the St. Lawrence (it is astonishing how the old water-ways still pull us children of the air), and followed his broad line of black between its drifting ice-blocks, all down the Park that the wisdom of our fathers – but every one knows the Quebec run.

We dropped to the Heights Receiving Towers twenty minutes ahead of time, and there hung at ease till the Yokohoma Intermediate Packet could pull out and give us our proper slip. It was curious to watch the action of the holding-down clips all along the frosty river front as the boats cleared or came to rest. A big Hamburger was leaving Pont Levis and her crew, unshipping the platform railings, began to sing "Elsinore" – the oldest of our chanteys. You know it of course:

> *Mother Rugen's tea-house on the Baltic –*
> *Forty couple waltzing on the floor!*
> *And you can watch my Ray,*
> *For I must go away*
> *And dance with Ella Sweyn at Elsinore!*

Then, while they sweated home the covering-plates:

> *Nor-Nor-Nor-Nor-*
> *West from Sourabaya to the Baltic –*
> *Ninety knot an hour to the Skaw!*
> *Mother Rugen's tea-house on the Baltic*
> *And a dance with Ella Sweyn at Elsinore!*

The clips parted with a gesture of indignant dismissal, as though Quebec, glittering under her snows, were casting out these light and unworthy lovers. Our signal came from the Heights. Tim turned and floated up, but surely then it was with passionate appeal that the great tower arms flung open – or did I think so because on the upper staging a little hooded figure also opened her arms wide toward her father?

* * *

In ten seconds the coach with its clerks clashed down to the receiving-caisson; the hostlers displaced the engineers at the idle turbines, and Tim, prouder of this than all, introduced me to the maiden of the photograph on the shelf. "And by the way," said he to her, stepping forth in sunshine under

the hat of civil life, "I saw young Williams in the Mark Boat.
I've asked him to tea on Friday."

AERIAL BOARD OF CONTROL

Lights

No changes in English Inland lights for week ending
Dec. 18th.

CAPE VERDE – Week ending Dec. 18. Verde inclined guide-
light changes from 1st proximo to triple flash – green
white green – in place of occulting red as heretofore.
The warning light for Harmattan winds will be continuous vertical glare (white) on all oases of trans-
Saharan N. E. by E. Main Routes.

INVERCARGIL (N. Z.) – From 1st prox.: extreme southerly
light (double red) will exhibit white beam inclined 45
degrees on approach of Southerly Buster. Traffic flies
high off this coast between April and October.

TABLE BAY – Devil's Peak Glare removed to Simonsberg.
Traffic making Table Mountain coastwise keep all lights
from Three Anchor Bay at least two thousand feet under,
and do not round to till East of E. shoulder Devil's Peak.

SANDHEADS LIGHT – Green triple verticle marks new private
landing-stage for Bay and Burma traffic only.

SNAEFFELL JOKUL – White occulting light withdrawn for
winter.

PATAGONIA – No summer light south Cape Pilar. This includes Staten Island and Port Stanley.

C. NAVARIN – Quadruple fog flash (white), one minute intervals (new).

EAST CAPE – Fog flash – single white with single bomb, 30
sec. intervals (new).

MALAYAN ARCHIPELAGO – Lights unreliable owing erup-
tions. Lay from Cape Somerset to Singapore direct,
keeping highest levels.

For the Board:

$$\left.\begin{array}{l} \text{CATTERTHUN} \\ \text{ST. JUST} \\ \text{VAN HEDDER} \end{array}\right\} \textit{Lights.}$$

Casualties

Week ending Dec. 18th.

SABLE ISLAND – Green single barbette-tower freighter, number indistinguishable, up-ended, and fore-tank pierced after collision, passed 300-ft. level 2 P.M. Dec. 15th. Watched to water and pithed by Mark Boat.

N. F. BANKS – Postal Packet 162 reports *Halma* freighter (Fowey – St. John's) abandoned, leaking after weather, 46° 15′ N. 50° 15′ W. Crew rescued by Planet liner *Asteroid*. Watched to water and pithed by Postal Packet, Dec. 14th.

KERGUELEN, MARK BOAT reports last call from *Cymena* freighter (Gayer Tong Huk & Co.) taking water and sinking in snow-storm South McDonald Islands. No wreckage recovered. Messages and wills of crew at all A. B. C. offices.

FEZZAN – T. A. D. freighter *Ulema* taken ground during Harmattan on Akakus Range. Under plates strained. Crew at Ghat where repairing Dec. 13th.

BISCAY, MARK BOAT reports *Carducci* (Valandingham Line) slightly spiked in western gorge Point de Benasque. Passengers transferred *Andorra* (Fulton Line). Barcelona Mark Boat salving cargo Dec. 12th.

ASCENSION, MARK BOAT – Wreck of unknown racing-plane, Parden rudder, wire-stiffened xylonite vans, and Harliss engine-seating, sighted and salved 7° 20′ S. 18° 41′ W. Dec. 15th. Photos at all A. B. C. offices.

Missing

No answer to General Call having been received during the last week from following overdues, they are posted as missing:

Atlantis, W. 17630. . . . Canton – Valparaiso
Audhumla, W. 889. . . . Stockholm – Odessa
Berenice, W. 2206. . . . Riga – Vladivostock
Draco, E. 446. . . . . Coventry – Puntas Arenas
Tontine, E. 3068. . . . C. Wrath – Ungava
Wu-Sung, E. 41776. . . . . Hankow – Lobito Bay

General Call (all Mark Boats) out for:

Jane Eyre, W. 6990 . . . Port Rupert – City of Mexico
Santander, W. 5514 . . . Gobi-Desert – Manila
V. Edmundsun, E. 9690 . . Kandahar – Fiume

Broke for Obstruction, and Quitting Levels

VALKYRIE (racing plane), A. J. Hartley owner, New York (twice warned).

GEISHA (racing plane), S. van Cott owner, Philadelphia (twice warned).

MARVEL OF PERU (racing plane), J. X. Peixoto owner, Rio de Janeiro (twice warned).

For the Board:

LAZAREFF
McKEOUGH   } *Traffic*.
GOLDBLATT

NOTES

High-Level Sleet

The Northern weather so far shows no sign of improvement. From all quarters come complaints of the unusual prevalence of sleet at the higher levels. Racing-planes and digs alike have suffered severely – the former from unequal deposits of half-frozen slush on their vans (and only those who have "held up" a badly balanced plane in a cross-wind know what that means), and the latter from loaded bows and snow-cased bodies. As a consequence, the Northern and Northwestern upper levels have been practically abandoned, and the high fliers have returned to the ignoble security of the Three, Five, and Six hundred foot levels. But there remain a few undaunted sun-hunters who, in spite of frozen stays and ice-jammed connecting-rods, still haunt the blue empyrean.

Bat-Boat Racing

The scandals of the past few years have at last moved the yachting world to concerted action in regard to "bat" boat racing.

We have been treated to the spectacle of what are practically keeled racing-planes driven a clear five foot or more above the water, and only eased down to touch their so-called "native element" as they near the line. Judges and starters have been conveniently blind to this absurdity, but the public demonstration off St. Catherine's Light at the Autumn Regattas has borne ample, if tardy, fruit. In the future the "bat" is to be a boat, and the long-unheeded demand of the true sportsman for "no daylight under mid-keel in smooth water" is in a fair way to be conceded. The new rule severely restricts plane area and lift alike. The gas compartments are permitted both fore and aft, as in the old type, but the water-ballast central tank is rendered obligatory. These things work, if not for perfection, at least for the evolution of a sane and wholesome *waterborne* cruiser. The type of rudder is unaffected by the new rules, so we may expect to see the Long-Davidson make (the patent on which has just expired) come largely into use henceforward, though the strain on the stern-post in turning at speeds over forty miles an hour is admittedly very severe. But bat-boat racing has a great future before it.

Crete and the A. B. C.

The story of the recent Cretan crisis, as told in the *A. B. C. Monthly Report*, is not without humour. Till the 25th October Crete, as all our planet knows, was the sole surviving European repository of "autonomous institutions," "local self-government," and the rest of the archaic lumber devised in the past for the confusion of human affairs. She has lived practically on the tourist traffic attracted by her annual pageants of Parliaments, Boards, Municipal Councils, etc., etc. Last summer the islanders grew wearied, as their premier explained, of "playing at being savages for pennies," and proceeded to pull down all the landing-towers on the island and shut off general communication till such time as the A. B. C. should annex them. For side-splitting comedy we would refer our readers to the correspondence between the Board of Control and the Cretan premier during the "war." However, all's well that ends well. The A. B. C. have taken over the administration of Crete on normal lines; and tourists must go elsewhere to witness the "debates," "resolutions," and "popular movements" of the old days. The only people to suffer will be the Board of Control, which is grievously overworked already. It is easy enough to condemn the Cretans for their laziness; but when one recalls the large, prosperous, and presumably public-spirited communities which during the last few years have deliberately thrown themselves into the hands of the A. B. C., one cannot be too hard upon St. Paul's old friends.

THE HOUSE SURGEON

THE HOUSE SURGEON

O N an evening after Easter Day, I sat at a table in a homeward bound steamer's smoking-room, where half a dozen of us told ghost stories. As our party broke up a man, playing Patience in the next alcove, said to me: "I didn't quite catch the end of that last story about the Curse on the family's first-born."

"It turned out to be drains," I explained. "As soon as new ones were put into the house the Curse was lifted, I believe. I never knew the people myself."

"Ah! I've had *my* drains up twice; I'm on gravel too."

"You don't mean to say you've a ghost in your house? Why didn't you join our party?"

"Any more orders, gentlemen, before the bar closes?" the steward interrupted.

"Sit down again, and have one with me," said the Patience player. "No, it isn't a ghost. Our trouble is more depression than anything else."

"How interesting! Then it's nothing any one can see?"

"It's – it's nothing worse than a little depression. And the odd part is that there hasn't been a death in the house since it was built – in 1863. The lawyer said so. That decided me – my good lady, rather – and he made me pay an extra thousand for it."

"How curious. Unusual, too!" I said.

"Yes; ain't it? It was built for three sisters – Moultrie was the name – three old maids. They all lived together; the eldest owned it. I bought it from her lawyer a few years ago, and if I've spent a pound on the place first and last, I must have spent five thousand. Electric light, new servants' wing, garden – all that sort of thing. A man and his family ought to be happy after so much expense, ain't it?" He looked at me through the bottom of his glass.

"Does it affect your family much?"

"My good lady – she's a Greek, by the way – and myself are middle-aged. We can bear up against depression; but it's hard on my little girl. I say little; but she's twenty. We send her visiting to escape it. She almost lived at hotels and hydros last year, but that isn't pleasant for her. She used to be a canary – a perfect canary – always singing. You ought to hear her. She doesn't sing now. That sort of thing's unwholesome for the young, ain't it?"

"Can't you get rid of the place?" I suggested.

"Not except at a sacrifice, and we are fond of it. Just suits us three. We'd love it if we were allowed."

"What do you mean by not being allowed?"

"I mean because of the depression. It spoils everything."

"What's it like exactly?"

"I couldn't very well explain. It must be seen to be appreciated, as the auctioneers say. Now, I was much impressed by the story you were telling just now."

"It wasn't true," I said.

"My tale is true. If you would do me the pleasure to come down and spend a night at my little place, you'd learn more than you would if I talked till morning. Very likely 'twouldn't touch your good self at all. You might be – immune, ain't it? On the other hand, if this influenza-influence *does* happen to affect you, why, I think it will be an experience."

While he talked he gave me his card, and I read his name was L. Maxwell M'Leod, Esq., of Holmescroft. A City address was tucked away in a corner.

"My business," he added, "used to be furs. If you are interested in furs – I've given thirty years of my life to 'em."

"You're very kind," I murmured.

"Far from it, I assure you. I can meet you next Saturday afternoon anywhere in London you choose to name, and I'll be only too happy to motor you down. It ought to be a delightful run at this time of year – the rhododendrons will be out. I mean it. You don't know how truly I mean it. Very probably – it won't affect you at all. And – I think I may say I have the finest collection of narwhal tusks in the world. All the best skins and horns have to go through London, and L. Maxwell M'Leod, he knows where they come from, and where they go to. That's his business."

For the rest of the voyage up–channel Mr. M'Leod talked to me of the assembling, preparation, and sale of the rarer furs; and told me things about the manufacture of fur-lined coats which quite shocked me. Somehow or other, when we landed on Wednesday, I found myself pledged to spend that weekend with him at Holmescroft.

On Saturday he met me with a well-groomed motor, and ran me out, in an hour and a half, to an exclusive residential district of dustless roads and elegantly designed country villas, each standing in from three to five acres of perfectly appointed land. He told me land was selling at eight hundred pounds the acre, and the new golf links, whose Queen Anne pavilion we passed, had cost nearly twenty-four thousand pounds to create.

Holmescroft was a large, two-storeyed, low, creeper-covered residence. A verandah at the south side gave on to a garden and two tennis courts, separated by a tasteful iron fence from a most park-like meadow of five or six acres, where two Jersey cows grazed. Tea was ready in the shade of a promising copper beech, and I could see groups on the lawn of young men and maidens appropriately clothed, playing lawn tennis in the sunshine.

"A pretty scene, ain't it?" said Mr. M'Leod. "My good lady's sitting under the tree, and that's my little girl in pink on the far court. But I'll take you to your room, and you can see 'em all later."

He led me through a wide parquet-floored hall furnished in pale lemon, with huge Cloisonnée vases, an ebonised and gold grand piano, and banks of pot flowers in Benares brass bowls, up a pale oak staircase to a spacious landing, where there was a green velvet settee trimmed with silver. The blinds were down, and the light lay in parallel lines on the floors.

He showed me my room, saying cheerfully: "You may be a little tired. One often is without knowing it after a run through traffic. Don't come down till you feel quite restored. We shall all be in the garden."

My room was rather warm, and smelt of perfumed soap. I threw up the window at once, but it opened so close to the floor and worked so clumsily that I came within an ace of pitching out, where I should certainly have ruined a rather lop-sided laburnum below. As I set about washing off the journey's dust, I began to feel a little tired. But, I reflected, I had not come down here in this weather and among these new surroundings to be depressed; so I began to whistle.

And it was just then that I was aware of a little grey shadow, as it might have been a snowflake seen against the light, floating at an immense distance in the background of my brain. It annoyed me, and I shook my head to get rid of it. Then my brain telegraphed that it was the forerunner of a swift-striding gloom which there was yet time to escape if I would force my thoughts away from it, as a man leaping for life forces his body forward and away from the fall of a wall. But the gloom overtook me before I could take in the meaning of the message. I moved toward the bed, every nerve already aching with the foreknowledge of the pain that was to be dealt it, and sat down, while my amazed and angry soul dropped, gulf by gulf, into that horror of great darkness which is spoken of in the Bible, and which, as auctioneers say, must be experienced to be appreciated.

Despair upon despair, misery upon misery, fear after fear, each causing their distinct and separate woe, packed in upon me for an unrecorded length of time, until at last they blurred together, and I heard a click in my brain like the click in the ear when one descends in a diving bell, and I knew that the pressures were equalised within and without, and that, for the moment, the worst was at an end. But I knew also that at any moment the darkness might come down anew; and while I dwelt on this speculation precisely as a man torments a raging tooth with his tongue, it ebbed away into the little grey shadow on the brain of its first coming, and once more I heard my brain, which knew what would recur, telegraph to every quarter for help, release or diversion.

The door opened, and M'Leod reappeared. I thanked him politely, saying I was charmed with my room, anxious to meet Mrs. M'Leod, much refreshed with my wash, and so on and so forth. Beyond a little stickiness at the corners of my mouth, it seemed to me that I was managing my words admirably, the while that I myself cowered at the bottom of unclimbable pits. M'Leod laid his hand on my shoulder, and said: "You've got it now already, ain't it?"

"Yes," I answered. "It's making me sick!"

"It will pass off when you come outside. I give you my word it will then pass off. Come!"

I shambled out behind him, and wiped my forehead in the hall.

"You mustn't mind," he said. "I expect the run tired you. My good lady is sitting there under the copper beech."

She was a fat woman in an apricot-coloured gown, with a heavily powdered face, against which her black long-lashed eyes showed like currants in dough. I was introduced to many fine ladies and gentlemen of those parts. Magnificently appointed landaus and covered motors swept in and out of the drive, and the air was gay with the merry outcries of the tennis players.

As twilight drew on they all went away, and I was left alone with Mr. and Mrs. M'Leod, while tall menservants and maidservants took away the tennis and tea things. Miss M'Leod had walked a little down the drive with a light-haired young man, who apparently knew everything about every South American railway stock. He had told me at tea that these were the days of financial specialisation.

"I think it went off beautifully, my dear," said Mr.

M'Leod to his wife; and to me: "You feel all right now, ain't it? Of course you do."

Mrs. M'Leod surged across the gravel. Her husband skipped nimbly before her into the south verandah, turned a switch, and all Holmescroft was flooded with light.

"You can do that from your room also," he said as they went in. "There is something in money, ain't it?"

Miss M'Leod came up behind me in the dusk. "We have not yet been introduced," she said, "but I suppose you are staying the night?"

"Your father was kind enough to ask me," I replied.

She nodded. "Yes, *I* know; and you know too, don't you? I saw your face when you came to shake hands with mamma. You felt the depression very soon. It is simply frightful in that bedroom sometimes. What do you think it is – bewitchment? In Greece, where I was a little girl, it might have been; but not in England, do you think? Or *do* you?"

"I don't know what to think," I replied. "I never felt anything like it. Does it happen often?"

"Yes, sometimes. It comes and goes."

"Pleasant!" I said, as we walked up and down the gravel at the lawn edge. "What has been your experience of it?"

"That is difficult to say, but – sometimes that – that depression is like as it were" – she gesticulated in most un-English fashion – "a light. Yes, like a light turned into a room – only a light of blackness, do you understand? – into a happy room. For sometimes we are so happy, all we three – so very happy. Then this blackness, it is turned on us just like – ah, I know what I mean now – like the headlamp of a motor, and we are eclipsed. And there is another thing —"

The dressing-gong roared, and we entered the over-lighted hall. My dressing was a brisk athletic performance, varied with outbursts of song – careful attention paid to articulation and expression. But nothing happened. As I hurried downstairs, I thanked Heaven that nothing had happened.

Dinner was served breakfast fashion; the dishes were

placed on the sideboard over heaters, and we helped our-selves.

"We always do this when we are alone, so we talk better," said Mr. M'Leod.

"And we are always alone," said the daughter.

"Cheer up, Thea. It will all come right," he insisted.

"No, papa." She shook her dark head. "Nothing is right while *it* comes."

"It is nothing that we ourselves have ever done in our lives – that I will swear to you," said Mrs. M'Leod suddenly. "And we have changed our servants several times. So we know it is not *them*."

"Never mind. Let us enjoy ourselves while we can," said Mr. M'Leod, opening the champagne.

But we did not enjoy ourselves. The talk failed. There were long silences.

"I beg your pardon," I said, for I thought some one at my elbow was about to speak.

"Ah! That is the other thing!" said Miss M'Leod. Her mother groaned.

We were silent again, and, in a few seconds it must have been, a live grief beyond words – not ghostly dread or horror, but aching, helpless grief – overwhelmed us, each, I felt, according to his or her nature, and held steady like the beam of a burning-glass. Behind that pain I was conscious there was a desire on somebody's part to explain something on which some tremendously important issue hung.

Meantime I rolled bread pills and remembered my sins; M'Leod considered his own reflection in a spoon; his wife seemed to be praying, and the girl fidgeted desperately with hands and feet, till the darkness passed on – as though the malignant rays of a burning-glass had been shifted from us.

"There," said Miss M'Leod, half rising. "Now you see what makes a happy home. Oh, sell it – sell it, father mine, and let us go away!"

"But I've spent thousands on it. You shall go to Harrogate next week, Thea dear."

"I'm only just back from hotels. I am *so* tired of packing."

"Cheer up, Thea. It is over. You know it does not often come here twice in the same night. I think we shall dare now to be comfortable."

He lifted a dish-cover, and helped his wife and daughter. His face was lined and fallen like an old man's after debauch, but his hand did not shake, and his voice was clear. As he worked to restore us by speech and action, he reminded me of a grey-muzzled collie herding demoralised sheep.

After dinner we sat round the dining-room fire – the drawing-room might have been under the Shadow for aught we knew – talking with the intimacy of gipsies by the way-side, or of wounded comparing notes after a skirmish. By eleven o'clock the three between them had given me every name and detail they could recall that in any way bore on the house, and what they knew of its history.

We went to bed in a fortifying blaze of electric light. My one fear was that the blasting gust of depression would return – the surest way, of course, to bring it. I lay awake till dawn, breathing quickly and sweating lightly, beneath what De Quincey inadequately describes as "the oppression of inexpiable guilt." Now as soon as the lovely day was broken, I fell into the most terrible of all dreams – that joyous one in which all past evil has not only been wiped out of our lives, but has never been committed; and in the very bliss of our assured innocence, before our loves shriek and change countenance, we wake to the day we have earned.

It was a coolish morning, but we preferred to breakfast in the south verandah. The forenoon we spent in the garden, pretending to play games that come out of boxes, such as croquet and clock golf. But most of the time we drew together and talked. The young man who knew all about South American railways took Miss M'Leod for a walk in the afternoon, and at five M'Leod thoughtfully whirled us all up to dine in town.

"Now, don't say you will tell the Psychological Society,

and that you will come again," said Miss M'Leod, as we parted. "Because I know you will not."

"You should not say that," said her mother.

"You should say, 'Good-bye, Mr. Perseus. Come again.' "

"Not him!" the girl cried. "He has seen the Medusa's head!"

Looking at myself in the restaurant's mirrors, it seemed to me that I had not much benefited by my week-end. Next morning I wrote out all my Holmescroft notes at fullest length, in the hope that by so doing I could put it all behind me. But the experience worked on my mind, as they say certain imperfectly understood rays work on the body.

I am less calculated to make a Sherlock Holmes than any man I know, for I lack both method and patience, yet the idea of following up the trouble to its source fascinated me. I had no theory to go on, except a vague idea that I had come between two poles of a discharge, and had taken a shock meant for some one else. This was followed by a feeling of intense irritation. I waited cautiously on myself, expecting to be overtaken by horror of the supernatural, but my self persisted in being humanly indignant, exactly as though it had been the victim of a practical joke. It was in great pains and upheavals – that I felt in every fibre – but its dominant idea, to put it coarsely, was to get back a bit of its own. By this I knew that I might go forward if I could find the way.

After a few days it occurred to me to go to the office of Mr. J. M. M. Baxter – the solicitor who had sold Holmescroft to M'Leod. I explained I had some notion of buying the place. Would he act for me in the matter?

Mr. Baxter, a large, greyish, throaty-voiced man, showed no enthusiasm. "I sold it to Mr. M'Leod," he said. "It 'ud scarcely do for me to start on the running-down tack now. But I can recommend —"

"I know he's asking an awful price," I interrupted, "and atop of it he wants an extra thousand for what he calls your clean bill of health."

Mr. Baxter sat up in his chair. I had all his attention.

"Your guarantee with the house. Don't you remember it?"

"Yes, yes. That no death had taken place in the house since it was built. I remember perfectly."

He did not gulp as untrained men do when they lie, but his jaws moved stickily, and his eyes, turning towards the deed boxes on the wall, dulled. I counted seconds, one, two, three – one, two, three – up to ten. A man, I knew, can live through ages of mental depression in that time.

"I remember perfectly." His mouth opened a little as though it had tasted old bitterness.

"Of course *that* sort of thing doesn't appeal to me." I went on. "*I* don't expect to buy a house free from death."

"Certainly not. No one does. But it was Mr. M'Leod's fancy – his wife's rather, I believe; and since we could meet it – it was my duty to my clients – at whatever cost to my own feelings – to make him pay."

"That's really why I came to you. I understood from him you knew the place well."

"Oh, yes. Always did. It originally belonged to some connections of mine."

"The Misses Moultrie, I suppose. How interesting! They must have loved the place before the country round about was built up."

"They were very fond of it indeed."

"I don't wonder. So restful and sunny. I don't see how they could have brought themselves to part with it."

Now it is one of the most constant peculiarities of the English that in polite conversation – and I had striven to be polite – no one ever does or sells anything for mere money's sake.

"Miss Agnes – the youngest – fell ill" (he spaced his words a little), "and, as they were very much attached to each other, that broke up the home."

"Naturally. I fancied it must have been something of that kind. One doesn't associate the Staffordshire Moultries" (my Demon of Irresponsibility at that instant created 'em) "with – with being hard up."

"I don't know whether we're related to them," he answered importantly. "We may be, for our branch of the family comes from the Midlands."

I give this talk at length, because I am so proud of my first attempt at detective work. When I left him, twenty minutes later, with instructions to move against the owner of Holmescroft, with a view to purchase, I was more bewildered than any Doctor Watson at the opening of a story.

Why should a middle-aged solicitor turn plovers' egg colour and drop his jaw when reminded of so innocent and festal a matter as that no death had ever occurred in a house that he had sold? If I knew my English vocabulary at all, the tone in which he said the youngest sister "fell ill" meant that she had gone out of her mind. That might explain his change of countenance, and it was just possible that her demented influence still hung about Holmescroft; but the rest was beyond me.

I was relieved when I reached M'Leod's City office, and could tell him what I had done – not what I thought.

M'Leod was quite willing to enter into the game of the pretended purchase, but did not see how it would help if I knew Baxter.

"He's the only living soul I can get at who was connected with Holmescroft," I said.

"Ah! Living soul is good," said M'Leod. "At any rate our little girl will be pleased that you are still interested in us. Won't you come down some day this week?"

"How is it there now?" I asked.

He screwed up his face. "Simply frightful!" he said. "Thea is at Droitwich."

"I should like it immensely, but I must cultivate Baxter for the present. You'll be sure and keep him busy your end, won't you?"

He looked at me with quiet contempt. "Do not be afraid. I shall be a good Jew. I shall be my own solicitor."

Before a fortnight was over, Baxter admitted ruefully that M'Leod was better than most firms in the business. We buyers were coy, argumentative, shocked at the price of Holmescroft, inquisitive, and cold by turns, but Mr. M'Leod the seller easily met and surpassed us; and Mr. Baxter entered every letter, telegram, and consultation at the proper rates in a cinematograph-film of a bill. At the end of a month he said it looked as though M'Leod, thanks to him, were really going to listen to reason. I was many pounds out of pocket, but I had learned something of Mr. Baxter on the human side. I deserved it. Never in my life have I worked to conciliate, amuse, and flatter a human being as I worked over my solicitor.

It appeared that he golfed. Therefore, I was an enthusiastic beginner, anxious to learn. Twice I invaded his office with a bag (M'Leod lent it) full of the spelicans needed in this detestable game, and a vocabulary to match. The third time the ice broke, and Mr. Baxter took me to his links, quite ten miles off, where in a maze of tramway lines, railroads, and nursery-maids, we skelped our divoted way round nine holes like barges plunging through head seas. He played vilely and had never expected to meet any one worse; but as he realised my form, I think he began to like me, for he took me in hand by the two hours together. After a fortnight he could give me no more than a stroke a hole, and when, with this allowance, I once managed to beat him by one, he was honestly glad, and assured me that I should be a golfer if I stuck to it. I was sticking to it for my own ends, but now and again my conscience pricked me; for the man was a nice man. Between games he supplied me with odd pieces of evidence, such as that he had known the Moultries all his life, being their cousin, and that Miss Mary, the eldest, was an unforgiving woman who would never let bygones be. I naturally wondered what she might have against him; and somehow connected him unfavourably with mad Agnes.

"People ought to forgive and forget," he volunteered one day between rounds. "Specially where, in the nature of things, they can't be sure of their deductions. Don't you think so?"

"It all depends on the nature of the evidence on which one forms one's judgement," I answered.

"Nonsense!" he cried. "I'm lawyer enough to know that there's nothing in the world so misleading as circumstantial evidence. Never was."

"Why? Have you ever seen men hanged on it?"

"Hanged? People have been supposed to be eternally lost on it." His face turned grey again. "I don't know how it is with you, but my consolation is that God must know. He *must*! Things that seem on the face of 'em like murder, or say suicide, may appear different to God. Heh?"

"That's what the murderer and the suicide can always hope – I suppose."

"I have expressed myself clumsily as usual. The facts as God knows 'em – may *be* different – even after the most clinching evidence. I've always said that – both as a lawyer and a man, but some people won't – I don't want to judge 'em – we'll say they can't – believe it; whereas *I* say there's always a working chance – a certainty – that the worst hasn't happened." He stopped and cleared his throat. "Now, let's come on! This time next week I shall be taking my holiday."

"What links?" I asked carelessly, while twins in a perambulator got out of our line of fire.

"A potty little nine-hole affair at a hydro in the Midlands. My cousins stay there. Always will. Not but what the fourth and the seventh holes take some doing. You could manage it, though," he said encouragingly. "You're doing much better. It's only your approach shots that are weak."

"You're right. I can't approach for nuts! I shall go to pieces while you're away – with no one to coach me," I said mournfully.

"I haven't taught you anything," he said, delighted with the compliment.

"I owe all I've learned to you, anyhow. When will you come back?"

"Look here," he began. "I don't know your engagements, but I've no one to play with at Burry Mills. Never have. Why couldn't you take a few days off and join me there? I warn you it will be rather dull. It's a throat and gout place – baths, massage, electricity, and so forth. But the fourth and the seventh holes really take some doing."

"I'm for the game," I answered valiantly; Heaven well knowing that I hated every stroke and word of it.

"That's the proper spirit. As their lawyer I must ask you not to say anything to my cousins about Holmescroft. It upsets 'em. Always did. But speaking as man to man, it would be very pleasant for me if you could see your way to —"

I saw it as soon as decency permitted, and thanked him sincerely. According to my now well-developed theory he had certainly misappropriated his aged cousins' monies under power of attorney, and had probably driven poor Agnes Moultrie out of her wits, but I wished that he was not so gentle, and good-tempered, and innocent-eyed.

Before I joined him at Burry Mills Hydro, I spent a night at Holmescroft. Miss M'Leod had returned from her Hydro, and first we made very merry on the open lawn in the sunshine over the manners and customs of the English resorting to such places. She knew dozens of hydros, and warned me how to behave in them, while Mr. and Mrs. M'Leod stood aside and adored her.

"Ah! That's the way she always comes back to us," he said. "Pity it wears off so soon, ain't it? You ought to hear her sing 'With mirth thou pretty bird.'"

We had the house to face through the evening, and there we neither laughed nor sung. The gloom fell on us as we entered, and did not shift till ten o'clock, when we crawled out, as it were, from beneath it.

"It has been bad this summer," said Mrs. M'Leod in a whisper after we realised that we were freed. "Sometimes I think the house will get up and cry out – it is so bad."

"How?"

"Have you forgotten what comes after the depression?"

So then we waited about the small fire, and the dead air in the room presently filled and pressed down upon us with

the sensation (but words are useless here) as though some
dumb and bound power were striving against gag and bond
to deliver its soul of an articulate word. It passed in a few
minutes, and I fell to thinking about Mr. Baxter's conscience
and Agnes Moultrie, gone mad in the well-lit bedroom that
waited me. These reflections secured me a night during
which I rediscovered how, from purely mental causes, a man
can be physically sick; but the sickness was bliss compared to
my dreams when the birds waked. On my departure,
M'Leod gave me a beautiful narwhal's horn, much as a nurse
gives a child sweets for being brave at a dentist's.

"There's no duplicate of it in the world," he said, "else it
would have come to old Max M'Leod," and he tucked it into
the motor. Miss M'Leod on the far side of the car whispered,
"Have you found out anything, Mr. Perseus?"

I shook my head.

"Then I shall be chained to my rock all my life," she went
on. "Only don't tell papa."

I supposed she was thinking of the young gentleman who
specialised in South American rails, for I noticed a ring on
the third finger of her left hand.

I went straight from that house to Burry Mills Hydro,
keen for the first time in my life on playing golf, which is
guaranteed to occupy the mind. Baxter had taken me a room
communicating with his own, and after lunch introduced me
to a tall, horse-headed elderly lady of decided manners,
whom a white-haired maid pushed along in a bath-chair
through the park-like grounds of the Hydro. She was Miss
Mary Moultrie, and she coughed and cleared her throat just
like Baxter. She suffered – she told me it was a Moultrie
caste-mark – from some obscure form of chronic bronchitis,
complicated with spasm of the glottis; and, in a dead, flat
voice, with a sunken eye that looked and saw not, told me
what washes, gargles, pastilles, and inhalations she had
proved most beneficial. From her I was passed on to her
younger sister, Miss Elizabeth, a small and withered thing
with twitching lips, victim, she told me, to very much the

same sort of throat, but secretly devoted to another set of medicines. When she went away with Baxter and the bath-chair, I fell across a major of the Indian army with gout in his glassy eyes, and a stomach which he had taken all round the Continent. He laid everything before me; and him I escaped only to be confided in by a matron with a tendency to follicular tonsilitis and eczema. Baxter waited hand and foot on his cousins till five o'clock, trying, as I saw, to atone for his treatment of the dead sister. Miss Mary ordered him about like a dog.

"I warned you it would be dull," he said when we met in the smoking-room.

"It's tremendously interesting," I said. "But how about a look round the links?"

"Unluckily damp always affects my eldest cousin. I've got to buy her a new bronchitis-kettle. Arthurs broke her old one yesterday."

We slipped out to the chemist's shop in the town, and he bought a large glittering tin thing whose workings he explained.

"I'm used to this sort of work. I come up here pretty often," he said. "I've the family throat too."

"You're a good man," I said. "A very good man."

He turned towards me in the evening light among the beeches, and his face was changed to what it might have been a generation before.

"You see," he said huskily, "there was the youngest – Agnes. Before she fell ill, you know. But she didn't like leaving her sisters. Never would." He hurried on with his odd-shaped load and left me among the ruins of my black theories. The man with that face had done Agnes Moultrie no wrong.

* * *

We never played our game. I was waked between two and three in the morning from my hygienic bed by Baxter in an ulster over orange and white pyjamas, which I should never have suspected from his character.

"My cousin has had some sort of a seizure," he said. "Will you come? I don't want to wake the doctor. Don't want to make a scandal. Quick!"

So I came quickly, and led by the white-haired Arthurs in a jacket and petticoat, entered a double-bedded room reeking with steam and Friar's Balsam. The electrics were all on. Miss Mary – I knew her by her height – was at the open window, wrestling with Miss Elizabeth, who gripped her round the knees. Miss Mary's hand was at her own throat, which was streaked with blood.

"She's done it. She's done it too!" Miss Elizabeth panted. "Hold her! Help me!"

"Oh, I say! Women don't cut their throats," Baxter whispered.

"My God! Has she cut her throat?" the maid cried out, and with no warning rolled over in a faint. Baxter pushed her under the wash-basins, and leaped to hold the gaunt woman who crowed and whistled as she struggled towards the window. He took her by the shoulder, and she struck out wildly.

"All right! She's only cut her hand," he said. "Wet towel – quick!"

While I got that he pushed her backwards. Her strength seemed almost as great as his. I swabbed at her throat when I could, and found no mark; then helped him to control her a little. Miss Elizabeth leaped back to bed, wailing like a child.

"Tie up her hand somehow," said Baxter. "Don't let it drip about the place. She" – he stepped on broken glass in his slippers, "she must have smashed a pane."

Miss Mary lurched towards the open window again, dropped on her knees, her head on the sill, and lay quiet, surrendering the cut hand to me.

"What did she do?" Baxter turned towards Miss Elizabeth in the far bed.

"She was going to throw herself out of the window," was

the answer. "I stopped her, and sent Arthurs for you. Oh, we can never hold up our heads again!"

Miss Mary writhed and fought for breath. Baxter found a shawl which he threw over her shoulders.

"Nonsense!" said he. "That isn't like Mary"; but his face worked when he said it.

"You wouldn't believe about Aggie, John. Perhaps you will now!" said Miss Elizabeth. "I *saw* her do it, and she's cut her throat too!"

"She hasn't," I said. "It's only her hand."

Miss Mary suddenly broke from us with an indescribable grunt, flew, rather than ran, to her sister's bed, and there shook her as one furious schoolgirl would shake another.

"No such thing," she croaked. "How dare you think so, you wicked little fool?"

"Get into bed, Mary," said Baxter. "You'll catch a chill."

She obeyed, but sat up with the grey shawl round her lean shoulders, glaring at her sister. "I'm better now," she panted. "Arthurs let me sit out too long. Where's Arthurs? The kettle."

"Never mind Arthurs," said Baxter. "*You* get the kettle." I hastened to bring it from the side table. "Now, Mary, as God sees you, tell me what you've done."

His lips were dry, and he could not moisten them with his tongue.

Miss Mary applied herself to the mouth of the kettle, and between indraws of steam said: "The spasm came on just now, while I was asleep. I was nearly choking to death. So I went to the window. I've done it often before, without waking any one. Bessie's such an old maid about draughts. I tell you I was choking to death. I couldn't manage the catch, and I nearly fell out. That window opens too low. I cut my hand trying to save myself. Who has tied it up in this filthy hand-kerchief? I wish you had my throat, Bessie. I never was nearer dying!" She scowled on us all impartially, while her sister sobbed.

From the bottom of the bed we heard a quivering voice:

"Is she dead? Have they took her away? Oh, I never could bear the sight o' blood!"

"Arthurs," said Miss Mary, "you are an hireling. Go away!"

It is my belief that Arthurs crawled out on all fours, but I was busy picking up broken glass from the carpet.

Then Baxter, seated by the side of the bed, began to cross-examine in a voice I scarcely recognised. No one could for an instant have doubted the genuine rage of Miss Mary against her sister, her cousin, or her maid; and that a doctor should have been called in – for she did me the honour of calling me doctor – was the last drop. She was choking with her throat; had rushed to the window for air; had near pitched out, and in catching at the window bars had cut her hand. Over and over she made this clear to the intent Baxter. Then she turned on her sister and tongue-lashed her savagely.

"You mustn't blame me," Miss Bessie faltered at last. "You know what we think of night and day."

"I'm coming to that," said Baxter. "Listen to me. What *you* did, Mary, misled four people into thinking you – you meant to do away with yourself."

"Isn't one suicide in the family enough? Oh God, help and pity us! You *couldn't* have believed that!" she cried.

"The evidence was complete. Now, don't you think," Baxter's finger wagged under her nose – "*can't* you think that poor Aggie did the same thing at Holmescroft when she fell out of the window?"

"She had the same throat," said Miss Elizabeth. "Exactly the same symptoms. Don't you remember, Mary?"

"Which was her bedroom?" I asked of Baxter in an under-tone.

"Over the south verandah, looking on to the tennis lawn."

"I nearly fell out of that very window when I was at Holmescroft – opening it to get some air. The sill doesn't come much above your knees," I said.

"You hear that, Mary? Mary, do you hear what this gentleman says? Won't you believe that what nearly happened to you must have happened to poor Aggie that night? For God's sake – for her sake – Mary, *won't* you believe?"

There was a long silence while the steam kettle puffed.

"If I could have proof – if I could have proof," said she, and broke into most horrible tears.

Baxter motioned to me, and I crept away to my room, and lay awake till morning, thinking more specially of the dumb Thing at Holmescroft which wished to explain itself. I hated Miss Mary as perfectly as though I had known her for twenty years, but I felt that, alive or dead, I should not like her to condemn me.

Yet at mid-day, when I saw Miss Mary in her bath-chair, Arthurs behind and Baxter and Miss Elizabeth on either side, in the park-like grounds of the Hydro, I found it difficult to arrange my words.

"Now that you know all about it," said Baxter aside, after the first strangeness of our meeting was over, "it's only fair to tell you that my poor cousin did not die in Holmescroft at all. She was dead when they found her under the window in the morning. Just dead."

"Under that laburnum outside the window?" I asked, for I suddenly remembered the crooked evil thing.

"Exactly. She broke the tree in falling. But no death has ever taken place *in* the house, so far as we were concerned. You can make yourself quite easy on that point. Mr. M'Leod's extra thousand for what you called the 'clean bill of health' was something towards my cousins' estate when we sold. It was my duty as their lawyer to get it for them – at any cost to my own feelings."

I know better than to argue when the English talk about their duty. So I agreed with my solicitor.

"Their sister's death must have been a great blow to your cousins," I went on. The bath-chair was behind me.

"Unspeakable," Baxter whispered. "They brooded on it day and night. No wonder. If their theory of poor Aggie making away with herself was correct, she was eter-nally lost!"

"Do you believe that she made away with herself?"

"No, thank God! Never have! And after what happened to Mary last night, I see perfectly what happened to poor Aggie. She had the family throat too. By the way, Mary thinks you are a doctor. Otherwise she wouldn't like your having been in her room."

"Very good. Is she convinced now about her sister's death?"

"She'd give anything to be able to believe it, but she's a hard woman, and brooding along certain lines makes one groovy. I have sometimes been afraid of her reason – on the religious side, don't you know. Elizabeth doesn't matter. Brain of a hen. Always had."

Here Arthurs summoned me to the bath-chair, and the ravaged face, beneath its knitted Shetland wool hood, of Miss Mary Moultrie.

"I need not remind you, I hope, of the seal of secrecy – absolute secrecy – in your profession," she began. "Thanks to my cousin's and my sister's stupidity, you have found out—" She blew her nose.

"Please don't excite her, sir," said Arthurs at the back.

"But, my dear Miss Moultrie, I only know what I've seen, of course, but it seems to me that what you thought was a tragedy in your sister's case, turns out, on your own evidence, so to speak, to have been an accident – a dreadfully sad one – but absolutely an accident."

"Do you believe that too?" she cried. "Or are you only saying it to comfort me?"

"I believe it from the bottom of my heart. Come down to Holmescroft for an hour – for half an hour – and satisfy yourself."

"Of what? You don't understand. I see the house every day – every night. I am always there in spirit – waking or sleeping. I couldn't face it in reality."

"But you must," I said. "If you go there in the spirit the greater need for you to go there in the flesh. Go to your sister's room once more, and see the window – I nearly fell out of it myself. It's – it's awfully low and dangerous. That would convince you," I pleaded.

"Yet Aggie had slept in that room for years," she interrupted.

"You've slept in your room here for a long time, haven't you? But you nearly fell out of the window when you were choking."

"That is true. That is one thing true," she nodded. "And I might have been killed as – perhaps – Aggie was killed."

"In that case your own sister and cousin and maid would have said you had committed suicide, Miss Moultrie. Come down to Holmescroft, and go over the place just once."

"You are lying," she said quite quietly. "You don't want me to come down to see a window. It is something else. I warn you we are Evangelicals. We don't believe in prayers for the dead. 'As the tree falls —' "

"Yes. I daresay. But you persist in thinking that your sister committed suicide —"

"No! No! I have always prayed that I might have misjudged her."

Arthurs at the bath-chair spoke up: "Oh, Miss Mary! you *would* 'ave it from the first that poor Miss Aggie 'ad made away with herself; an', of course, Miss Bessie took the notion from you. Only Master – Mister John stood out, and – and I'd 'ave taken my Bible oath *you* was making away with yourself last night."

Miss Mary leaned towards me, one finger on my sleeve.

"If going to Holmescroft kills me," she said, "you will have the murder of a fellow-creature on your conscience for all eternity."

"I'll risk it," I answered. Remembering what torment the mere reflection of her torments had cast on Holmescroft, and remembering, above all, the dumb Thing that filled the house with its desire to speak, I felt that there might be worse things.

Baxter was amazed at the proposed visit, but at a nod from

that terrible woman went off to make arrangements. Then I sent a telegram to M'Leod bidding him and his vacate Holmescroft for that afternoon. Miss Mary should be alone with her dead, as I had been alone.

I expected untold trouble in transporting her, but to do her justice, the promise given for the journey, she underwent it without murmur, spasm, or unnecessary word. Miss Bessie, pressed in a corner by the window, wept behind her veil, and from time to time tried to take hold of her sister's hand. Baxter wrapped himself in his newly found happiness as selfishly as a bridegroom, for he sat still and smiled.

"So long as I know that Aggie didn't make away with herself," he explained, "I tell you frankly I don't care what happened. She's as hard as a rock – Mary. Always was. *She* won't die."

We led her out on to the platform like a blind woman, and so got her into the fly. The half-hour crawl to Holmescroft was the most racking experience of the day. M'Leod had obeyed my instructions. There was no one visible in the house or the gardens; and the front door stood open.

Miss Mary rose from beside her sister, stepped forth first, and entered the hall.

"Come, Bessie," she cried.

"I daren't. Oh, I daren't."

"Come!" Her voice had altered. I felt Baxter start. "There's nothing to be afraid of."

"Good heavens!" said Baxter. "She's running up the stairs. We'd better follow."

"Let's wait below. She's going to the room."

We heard the door of the bedroom I knew open and shut, and we waited in the lemon-coloured hall, heavy with the scent of flowers.

"I've never been into it since it was sold," Baxter sighed. "What a lovely, restful place it is! Poor Aggie used to arrange the flowers."

"Restful?" I began, but stopped of a sudden, for I felt all over my bruised soul that Baxter was speaking truth. It was a light, spacious, airy house, full of the sense of well-being and peace – above all things, of peace. I ventured into the dining-room where the thoughtful M'Leods had left a small fire. There was no terror there, present or lurking; and in the drawing-room, which for good reasons we had never cared to enter, the sun and the peace and the scent of the flowers worked together as is fit in an inhabited house. When I re-turned to the hall, Baxter was sweetly asleep on a couch, looking most unlike a middle-aged solicitor who had spent a broken night with an exacting cousin.

There was ample time for me to review it all – to felicitate myself upon my magnificent acumen (barring some errors about Baxter as a thief and possibly a murderer), before the door above opened, and Baxter, evidently a light sleeper, sprang awake.

"I've had a heavenly little nap," he said, rubbing his eyes with the backs of his hands like a child. "Good Lord! That's not *their* step!"

But it was. I had never before been privileged to see the Shadow turned backward on the dial – the years ripped bodily off poor human shoulders – old sunken eyes filled and alight – harsh lips moistened and human.

"John," Miss Mary called, "I know now. Aggie didn't do it!" and "She didn't do it!" echoed Miss Bessie, and giggled.

"I did not think it wrong to say a prayer," Miss Mary continued. "Not for her soul, but for our peace. Then I was convinced."

"Then we got conviction," the younger sister piped.

"We've misjudged poor Aggie, John. But I feel she knows now. Wherever she is, she knows that we know she is guilt-less."

"Yes, she knows. I felt it too," said Miss Elizabeth.

"I never doubted," said John Baxter, whose face was beau-tiful at that hour. "Not from the first. Never have!"

"You never offered me proof, John. Now, thank God, it will not be the same any more. I can think henceforward of Aggie without sorrow." She tripped, absolutely tripped, across the hall. "What ideas these Jews have of arranging furniture!" She spied me behind a big Cloisonnée vase.

"I've seen the window," she said remotely. "You took a great risk in advising me to undertake such a journey. However, as it turns out . . . I forgive you, and I pray you may never know what mental anguish means! Bessie! Look at this peculiar piano! Do you suppose, Doctor, these people would offer one tea? I miss mine."

"I will go and see," I said, and explored M'Leod's new-built servants' wing. It was in the servants' hall that I unearthed the M'Leod family, bursting with anxiety.

"Tea for three, quick," I said. "If you ask me any questions now, I shall have a fit!" So Mrs. M'Leod got it, and I was butler, amid murmured apologies from Baxter, still smiling and self-absorbed, and the cold disapproval of Miss Mary, who thought the pattern of the china vulgar. However, she ate well, and even asked me whether I would not like a cup of tea for myself.

They went away in the twilight – the twilight that I had once feared. They were going to an hotel in London to rest after the fatigues of the day, and as their fly turned down the drive, I capered on the door step, with the all-darkened house behind me.

Then I heard the uncertain feet of the M'Leods and bade them not to turn on the lights, but to feel – to feel what I had done; for the Shadow was gone, with the dumb desire in the air. They drew short, but afterwards deeper, breaths, like bathers entering chill water, separated one from the other, moved about the hall, tiptoed upstairs, raced down, and then Miss M'Leod, and I believe her mother, though she denies this, embraced me. I know M'Leod did.

It was a disgraceful evening. To say we rioted through the house is to put it mildly. We played a sort of Blind Man's Buff along the darkest passages, in the unlighted drawing-room, and little dining-room, calling cheerily to each other after each exploration that here, and here, and here, the trouble had removed itself. We came up to *the* bedroom –

mine for the night again – and sat, the women on the bed, and we men on chairs, drinking in blessed draughts of peace and comfort and cleanliness of soul, while I told them my tale in full, and received fresh praise, thanks, and blessings.

When the servants, returned from their day's outing, gave us a supper of cold fried fish, M'Leod had sense enough to open no wine. We had been practically drunk since nightfall, and grew incoherent on water and milk.

"I like that Baxter," said M'Leod. "He's a sharp man. The death wasn't in the house, but he ran it pretty close, ain't it?"

"And the joke of it is that he supposes I want to buy the place from you," I said. "Are you selling?"

"Not for twice what I paid for it – now," said M'Leod. "I'll keep you in furs all your life, but not our Holmescroft."

"No – never our Holmescroft," said Miss M'Leod. "We'll ask *him* here on Tuesday, mamma." They squeezed each other's hands.

"Now tell me," said Mrs. M'Leod – "that tall one I saw out of the scullery window – did *she* tell you she was always here in the spirit? I hate her. She made all this trouble. It was not her house after she had sold it. What do you think?"

"I suppose," I answered, "she brooded over what she believed was her sister's suicide night and day – she confessed she did – and her thoughts being concentrated on this place, they felt like a – like a burning-glass."

"Burning-glass is good," said M'Leod.

"I said it was like a light of blackness turned on us," cried the girl, twiddling her ring. "That must have been when the tall one thought worst about her sister and the house."

"Ah, the poor Aggie!" said Mrs. M'Leod. "The poor Aggie, trying to tell every one it was not so! No wonder we felt Something wished to say Something. Thea, Max, do you remember that night —"

"We need not remember any more," M'Leod interrupted. "It is not our trouble. They have told each other now."

"Do you think, then," said Miss M'Leod, "that those two,

the living ones, were actually told something – upstairs – in your – in the room?"

"I can't say. At any rate they were made happy, and they ate a big tea afterwards. As your father says, it is not our trouble any longer – thank God!"

"Amen!" said M'Leod. "Now, Thea, let us have some music after all these months. 'With mirth, thou pretty bird,' ain't it? You ought to hear that."

And in the half-lighted hall, Thea sang an old English song that I had never heard before.

> With mirth, thou pretty bird, rejoice
>   Thy Maker's praise enhanced;
> Lift up thy shrill and pleasant voice,
>   Thy God is high advanced!
> Thy food before He did provide,
> And gives it in a fitting side,
>   Wherewith be thou sufficed!
>
> Why shouldst thou now unpleasant be,
>   Thy wrath against God venting,
> That He a little bird made thee,
>   Thy silly head tormenting,
> Because He made thee not a man?
> Oh, Peace! He hath well thought thereon,
>   Therewith be thou sufficed!

* * *

THE RABBI'S SONG

> If thought can reach to Heaven,
>   On Heaven let it dwell,
> For fear that Thought be given
>   Like power to reach to Hell.
> For fear the desolation
>   And darkness of thy mind,
> Perplex an habitation
>   Which thou hast left behind.

Let nothing linger after –
  No whispering ghost remain,
In wall, or beam, or rafter,
  Of any hate or pain:

Cleanse and call home thy spirit,
  Deny her leave to cast,
On aught thy heirs inherit,
  The shadow of her past.

For think, in all thy sadness,
  What road our griefs may take;
Whose brain reflect our madness,
  Or whom our terrors shake.
For think, lest any languish
  By cause of thy distress –
The arrows of our anguish
  Fly farther than we guess.

Our lives, our tears, as water,
  Are spilled upon the ground;
God giveth no man quarter,
  Yet God a means hath found;
Though faith and hope have vanished,
  And even love grows dim;
A means whereby His banished
  Be not expelled from Him!

THE WISH HOUSE

THE WISH HOUSE

* * *

"LATE CAME THE GOD"

Late came the God, having sent his forerunners who were not
　　regarded –
　Late, but in wrath;
Saying: "The wrong shall be paid, the contempt be rewarded
　On all that she hath."
He poisoned the blade and struck home, the full bosom receiving
The wound and the venom in one, past cure or relieving.

He made treaty with Time to stand still that the grief might be
　　fresh –
Daily renewed and nightly pursued through her soul to her flesh –
Mornings of memory, noontides of agony, midnights unslaked
　　for her,
Till the stones of the Streets of her Hells and her Paradise ached
　　for her.

So she lived while her body corrupted upon her.
　And she called on the Night for a sign, and a Sign was
　　allowed,
And she builded an Altar and served by the light of her Vision –
　Alone, without hope of regard or reward, but uncowed,
Resolute, selfless, divine.
　These things she did in Love's honour . . .
What is a God beside Woman? Dust and derision!

* * *

THE new Church Visitor had just left after a twenty
minutes' call. During that time, Mrs. Ashcroft had used
such English as an elderly, experienced, and pensioned cook

should, who had seen life in London. She was the readier, therefore, to slip back into easy, ancient Sussex ("t"s softening to "d"s as one warmed) when the 'bus brought Mrs. Fettley from thirty miles away for a visit, that pleasant March Saturday. The two had been friends since childhood; but, of late, destiny had separated their meetings by long intervals.

Much was to be said, and many ends, loose since last time, to be ravelled up on both sides, before Mrs. Fettley, with her bag of quilt-patches, took the couch beneath the window commanding the garden, and the football-ground in the valley below.

"Most folk got out at Bush Tye for the match there," she explained, "so there weren't no one for me to cushion agin, the last five mile. An' she *do* just-about bounce ye."

"You've took no hurt," said her hostess. "You don't brittle by agein', Liz."

Mrs. Fettley chuckled and made to match a couple of patches to her liking. "No, or I'd ha' broke twenty year back. You can't ever mind when I was so's to be called round, can ye?"

Mrs. Ashcroft shook her head slowly – she never hurried – and went on stitching a sack-cloth lining into a list-bound rush tool-basket. Mrs. Fettley laid out more patches in the Spring light through the geraniums on the window-sill, and they were silent awhile.

"What like's this new Visitor o' yourn?" Mrs. Fettley inquired, with a nod towards the door. Being very short-sighted, she had, on her entrance, almost bumped into the lady.

Mrs. Ashcroft suspended the big packing-needle judicially on high, ere she stabbed home. "Settin' aside she don't bring much news with her yet, I dunno as I've anythin' special agin her."

"Ourn, at Keyneslade," said Mrs. Fettley, "she's full o' words an' pity, but she don't stay for answers. Ye can get on with your thoughts while she clacks."

"This 'un don't clack. She's aimin' to be one o' those High Church nuns, like."

"Ourn's married, but, by what they say, she've made no

great gains of it . . . " Mrs. Fettley threw up her sharp chin. "Lord! How they dam' cherubim do shake the very bones o' the place!"

The tile-sided cottage trembled at the passage of two specially chartered forty-seat charabancs on their way to the Bush Tye match; a regular Saturday "shopping" 'bus, for the county's capital, fumed behind them; while, from one of the crowded inns, a fourth car backed out to join the procession, and held up the stream of through pleasure-traffic.

"You're as free-tongued as ever, Liz," Mrs. Ashcroft observed.

"Only when I'm with you. Otherwhiles, I'm Granny – three times over. I lay that basket's for one o' your gran'chiller – ain't it?"

" 'Tis for Arthur – my Jane's eldest."

"But he ain't workin' nowheres, is he?"

"No. 'Tis a picnic-basket."

"You're let off light. My Willie, he's allus at me for money for them aireated wash-poles folk puts up in their gardens to draw the music from Lunnon, like. An' I give it 'im – pore fool me!"

"An' he forgets to give you the promise-kiss after, don't he?" Mrs. Ashcroft's heavy smile seemed to strike inwards.

"He do. 'No odds 'twixt boys now an' forty year back. 'Take all an' give naught – an' we to put up with it! Pore fool we! Three shillin' at a time Willie'll ask me for!"

"They don't make nothin' o' money these days," Mrs. Ashcroft said.

"An' on'y last week," the other went on, "me daughter, she ordered a quarter pound suet at the butchers's; an' she sent it back to 'im to be chopped. She said she couldn't bother with choppin' it."

"I lay he charged her, then."

"I lay he did. She told me there was a whisk-drive that afternoon at the Institute, an' she couldn't bother to do the choppin'."

"Tck!"

Mrs. Ashcroft put the last firm touches to the basket-lining. She had scarcely finished when her sixteen-year-old grandson, a maiden of the moment in attendance, hurried up the garden-path shouting to know if the thing were ready, snatched it, and made off without acknowledgment. Mrs. Fettley peered at him closely.

"They're goin' picnickin' somewheres," Mrs. Ashcroft explained.

"Ah," said the other, with narrowed eyes. "I lay *he* won't show much mercy to any he comes across, either. Now 'oo the dooce do he remind me of, all of a sudden?"

"They must look arter theirselves — 'same as we did." Mrs. Ashcroft began to set out the tea.

"No denyin' *you* could, Gracie," said Mrs. Fettley.

"What's in your head now?"

"Dunno . . . But it come over me, sudden-like — about dat woman from Rye — I've slipped the name — Barnsley, wadn't it?"

"Batten — Polly Batten, you're thinkin' of."

"That's it — Polly Batten. That day she had it in for you with a hay-fork — 'time we was all hayin' at Smalldene — for stealin' her man."

"But you heered me tell her she had my leave to keep him?" Mrs. Ashcroft's voice and smile were smoother than ever.

"I did — an' we was all looking that she'd prod the fork spang through your breastes when you said it."

"No-oo. She'd never go beyond bounds — Polly. She shruck too much for reel doin's."

"Allus seems to *me*," Mrs. Fettley said after a pause, "that a man 'twixt two fightin' women is the foolishest thing on earth. 'Like a dog bein' called two ways."

"Mebbe. But what set ye off on those times, Liz?"

"That boy's fashion o' carryin' his head an' arms. I haven't rightly looked at him since he's growed. Your Jane never showed it, but — *him*! Why, 'tis Jim Batten and his tricks come to life again! . . . Eh?"

"Mebbe. There's some that would ha' made it out so – bein' barren-like, themselves."

"Oho! Ah well! Dearie, dearie me, now! . . . An' Jim Batten's been dead this —"

"Seven and twenty year," Mrs. Ashcroft answered briefly. "Won't ye draw up, Liz?"

Mrs. Fettley drew up to buttered toast, currant bread, stewed tea, bitter as leather, some home-preserved pears, and a cold boiled pig's tail to help down the muffins. She paid all the proper compliments.

"Yes. I dunno as I've ever owed me belly much," said Mrs. Ashcroft thoughtfully. "We only go through this world once."

"But don't it lay heavy on ye, sometimes?" her guest suggested.

"Nurse says I'm a sight liker to die o' me indigestion than me leg." For Mrs. Ashcroft had a long-standing ulcer on her shin, which needed regular care from the Village Nurse, who boasted (or others did, for her) that she had dressed it one hundred and three times already during her term of office.

"An' you that *was* so able, too! It's all come on ye before your full time, like. *I've* watched ye goin'." Mrs. Fettley spoke with real affection.

"Somethin's bound to find ye sometime. I've me 'eart left me still," Mrs. Ashcroft returned.

"You was always big-hearted enough for three. That's somethin' to look back on at the day's eend."

"I reckon you've *your* back-lookin's, too," was Mrs. Ashcroft's answer.

"You know it. But I don't think much regardin' such matters excep' when I'm along with you, Gra'. 'Takes two sticks to make a fire."

Mrs. Fettley stared, with jaw half-dropped, at the grocer's bright calendar on the wall. The cottage shook again to the roar of the motor-traffic, and the crowded football-ground below the garden roared almost as loudly; for the village was well set to its Saturday leisure.

* * *

Mrs. Fettley had spoken very precisely for some time without interruption, before she wiped her eyes. "And," she concluded, "they read 'is death-notice to me, out o' the paper last month. O' course it wadn't any o' *my* becomin' concerns – let be I 'adn't set eyes on him for so long. O' course *I* couldn't say nor show nothin'. Nor I've no rightful call to go to Eastbourne to see 'is grave, either. I've been schemin' to slip over there by the 'bus some day; but they'd ask questions at 'ome past endurance. So I 'aven't even *that* to stay me."

"But you've 'ad your satisfactions?"

"Godd! Yess! Those four years 'e was workin' on the rail near us. An' the other drivers they gave him a brave funeral, too."

"Then you've naught to cast-up about. 'Nother cup o' tea?"

* * *

The light and air had changed a little with the sun's descent, and the two elderly ladies closed the kitchen-door against chill. A couple of jays squealed and skirmished through the undraped apple-trees in the garden. This time, the word was with Mrs. Ashcroft, her elbows on the tea-table, and her sick leg propped on a stool . . .

"Well I never! But what did your 'usband say to that?" Mrs. Fettley asked, when the deep-toned recital halted.

"'E said I might go where I pleased for all of 'im. But seein' 'e was bedrid, I said I'd 'tend 'im out. 'E knowed I wouldn't take no advantage of 'im in that state. 'E lasted eight or nine week. Then he was took with a seizure-like; an' laid stone-still for days. Then 'e propped 'imself up abed an' says: 'You pray no man'll ever deal with you like you've dealed with some.' 'An' you?' I says, for *you* know, Liz, what a rover 'e was. 'It cuts both ways,' says 'e, 'but *I'm* death-wise, an' I can see what's comin' to you.' He died a–Sunday

an' was buried a-Thursday . . . An' yet I'd set a heap by him
– one time or – did I ever?"

"You never told me that before," Mrs. Fettley ventured.

"I'm payin' ye for what ye told me just now. Him bein'
dead, I wrote up, sayin' I was free for good, to that Mrs.
Marshall in Lunnon – which gave me my first place as
kitchen-maid – Lord, how long ago! She was well pleased,
for they two was both gettin' on, an' I knowed their ways.
You remember, Liz, I used to go to 'em in service between
whiles, for years – when we wanted money, or – or my
'usband was away – on occasion."

" 'E *did* get that six months at Chichester, didn't 'e?" Mrs.
Fettley whispered. "We never rightly won to the bottom
of it."

" 'E'd ha' got more, but the man didn't die."

" 'None o' your doin's, was it, Gra'?"

"No! 'Twas the woman's husband this time. An' so, my
man bein' dead, I went back to them Marshalls, as cook, to
get me legs under a gentleman's table again, and be called
with a handle to me name. That was the year you shifted to
Portsmouth."

"Cosham," Mrs. Fettley corrected. "There was a middlin'
lot o' new buildin' bein' done there. My man went first, an'
got the room, an' I follered."

"Well, then, I was a year-abouts in Lunnon, all at a
breath, like, four meals a day an' livin' easy. Then, 'long
towards Autumn, they two went travellin', like, to France;
keepin' me on, for they couldn't do without me. I put the
house to rights for the caretaker, an' then I slipped down 'ere
to me sister Bessie – me wages in me pockets, an' all 'ands
glad to be 'old of me."

"That would be when I was at Cosham," said Mrs.
Fettley.

"*You* know, Liz, there wasn't no cheap-dog pride to folk,
those days, no more than there was cinemas nor whisk-
drives. Man or woman 'ud lay hold o' any job that promised
a shillin' to the backside of it, didn't they? I was all peaked

up after Lunnon, an' I thought the fresh airs 'ud serve me. So I took on at Smalldene, obligin' with a hand at the early potato-liftin', stubbin' hens, an' such-like. They'd ha' mocked me sore in my kitchen in Lunnon, to see me in men's boots, an' me petticoats all shorted."

"Did it bring ye any good?" Mrs. Fettley asked.

" 'Twadn't for that I went. You know, 's'well's me, that na'un happens to ye till it '*as* 'appened. Your mind don't warn ye before'and of the road ye've took, till you're at the far eend of it. We've only a backwent view of our proceedin's."

" 'Oo was it?"

" 'Arry Mockler." Mrs. Ashcroft's face puckered to the pain of her sick leg.

Mrs. Fettley gasped. " 'Arry? Bert Mockler's son! An' *I* never guessed!"

Mrs. Ashcroft nodded. "An' I told myself – *an'* I beleft it – that I wanted field-work."

"What did ye get out of it?"

"The usuals. Everythin' at first – worse than naught after. I had signs an' warnings a-plenty, but I took no heed of 'em. For we was burnin' rubbish one day, just when we'd come to know how 'twas with – with both of us. 'Twas early in the year for burnin', an' I said so. 'No!' says he. 'The sooner dat old stuff's off an' done with,' 'e says, 'the better.' 'Is face was harder'n rocks when he spoke. Then it come over me that I'd found me master, which I 'adn't ever before. I'd allus owned 'em, like."

"Yes! Yes! They're yourn or you're theirn," the other sighed. "I like the right way best."

"I didn't. But 'Arry did . . . 'Long then, it come time for me to go back to Lunnon. I couldn't. I clean couldn't! So, I took an' tipped a dollop o' scaldin' water out o' the copper one Monday mornin' over me left 'and and arm. Dat stayed me where I was for another fortnight."

"Was it worth it?" said Mrs. Fettley, looking at the silvery scar on the wrinkled fore-arm.

Mrs. Ashcroft nodded. "An' after that, we two made it up 'twixt us so's 'e could come to Lunnon for a job in a liv'ry-stable not far from me. 'E got it. *I* 'tended to that. There wadn't no talk nowhere. His own mother never suspicioned how 'twas. He just slipped up to Lunnon, an' there we abode that Winter, not 'alf a mile 'tother from each."

"Ye paid 'is fare an' all, though"; Mrs. Fettley spoke convincedly.

Again Mrs. Ashcroft nodded. "Dere wadn't much I didn't do for him. 'E was me master, an' – O God, help us! – we'd laugh over it walkin' together after dark in them paved streets, an' me corns fair wrenchin' in me boots! I'd never been like that before. Ner he! Ner he!"

Mrs. Fettley clucked sympathetically.

"An' when did ye come to the eend?" she asked.

"When 'e paid it all back again, every penny. Then I knowed, but I wouldn't *suffer* meself to know. 'You've been mortal kind to me,' he says. 'Kind!' I said. ' 'Twixt *us*?' But 'e kep' all on tellin' me 'ow kind I'd been an' 'e'd never forget it all his days. I held it from off o' me for three evenin's, because I would *not* believe. Then 'e talked about not bein' satisfied with 'is job in the stables, an' the men there puttin' tricks on 'im, an' all they lies which a man tells when 'e's leavin' ye. I heard 'im out, neither 'elpin' nor 'inderin'. At the last, I took off a liddle brooch which he'd give me an' I says: 'Dat'll do. *I* ain't askin' na'un'.' An' I turned me round an' walked off to me own sufferin's. 'E didn't make 'em worse. 'E didn't come nor write after that. 'E slipped off 'ere back 'ome to 'is mother again."

"An' 'ow often did ye look for 'en to come back?" Mrs. Fettley demanded mercilessly.

"More'n once – more'n once! Goin' over the streets we'd used, I thought de very pave-stones 'ud shruck out under me feet."

"Yes," said Mrs. Fettley. "I dunno but dat don't 'urt as much as aught else. An' dat was all ye got?"

"No. 'Twadn't. That's the curious part, if you'll believe it, Liz."

"I do. I lay you're further off lyin' now than in all your life, Gra'."

"I am . . . An' I suffered, like I'd not wish my most arrantest enemies to. God's Own Name! I went through the hoop that Spring! One part of it was headaches which I'd never known all me days before. Think o' *me* with an 'eddick! But I come to be grateful for 'em. They kep' me from thinkin' . . ."

" 'Tis like a tooth," Mrs. Fettley commented. "It must rage an' rugg till it tortures itself quiet on ye; an' then – then there's na'un left."

"*I* got enough lef' to last me all *my* days on earth. It come about through our charwoman's liddle girl – Sophy Ellis was 'er name – all eyes an' elbers an' hunger. I used to give 'er vittles. Otherwhiles, I took no special notice of 'er, an' a sight less, o' course, when me trouble about 'Arry was on me. But – you know how liddle maids first feel it sometimes – she come to be crazy-fond o' me, pawin' an' cuddlin' all whiles; an' I 'adn't the 'eart to beat 'er off . . . One afternoon, early in Spring 'twas, 'er mother 'ad sent 'er round to scutchel up what vittles she could off of us. I was settin' by the fire, me apern over me head, half-mad with the 'eddick, when she slips in. I reckon I was middlin' short with 'er. 'Lor!' she says. 'Is *that* all? I'll take it off you in two-twos!' I told her not to lay a finger on me, for I thought she'd want to stroke my forehead; an' – I ain't that make. '*I* won't tech ye,' she says, an' slips out again. She 'adn't been gone ten minutes 'fore me old 'eddick took off quick as bein' kicked. So I went about my work. Prasin'ly, Sophy comes back, an' creeps into my chair quiet as a mouse. 'Er eyes was deep in 'er 'ead an' 'er face all drawed. I asked 'er what 'ad 'appened. 'Nothin',' she says. 'On'y *I*'ve got it now.' 'Got what?' I says. 'Your 'eddick,' she says, all hoarse an' sticky-lipped. 'I've took it on me.' 'Nonsense,' I says, 'it went of itself when you was out. Lay still an' I'll make ye a cup o' tea.' ' 'Twon't do no good,' she says, 'till your time's up. 'Ow long do *your* 'eddicks last?' 'Don't talk silly,' I says, 'or I'll send for the Doctor.' It looked to me like she might be hatchin' de measles. 'Oh, Mrs. Ashcroft,' she says, stretchin' out 'er liddle thin arms. 'I *do* love ye.' There wasn't any holdin' again that. I took 'er into me lap an' made much of 'er. 'Is it truly gone?' she says. 'Yes,' I says, 'an' if 'twas you took it away, I'm truly grateful.' ' '*Twas* me,' she says, layin' 'er cheek to mine. 'No one but me knows how.' An' then she said she'd changed me 'eddick for me at a Wish 'Ouse."

"Whatt?" Mrs. Fettley spoke sharply.

"A Wish House. No! *I* 'adn't 'eard o' such things, either. I couldn't get it straight at first, but, puttin' all together, I made out that a Wish 'Ouse 'ad to be a house which 'ad stood unlet an' empty long enough for Some One, like, to come an' in'abit there. She said, a liddle girl that she'd played with in the livery-stables where 'Arry worked 'ad told 'er so. She said the girl 'ad belonged in a caravan that laid up, o' winters, in Lunnon. Gipsy, I judge."

"Ooh! There's no sayin' what Gippos know, but *I*'ve never 'eard of a Wish 'Ouse, an' I know – some things," said Mrs. Fettley.

"Sophy said there was a Wish 'Ouse in Wadloes Road – just a few streets off, on the way to our green-grocer's. All you 'ad to do, she said, was to ring the bell an' wish your wish through the slit o' the letter-box. I asked 'er if the fairies give it 'er? 'Don't ye know,' she says, 'there's no fairies in a Wish 'Ouse? There's on'y a Token.' "

"Goo' Lord A'mighty! Where did she come by *that* word?" cried Mrs. Fettley; for a Token is a wraith of the dead or, worse still, of the living.

"The caravan-girl 'ad told 'er, she said. Well, Liz, it troubled me to 'ear 'er, an' lyin' in me arms she must ha' felt it. 'That's very kind o' you,' I says, holdin' 'er tight, 'to wish me 'eddick away. But why didn't ye ask somethin' nice for yourself?' 'You can't do that,' she says. 'All you'll get at a Wish 'Ouse is leave to take someone else's trouble. I've took Ma's 'ea-daches, when she's been kind to me; but this is the first time I've been able to do aught for you. Oh, Mrs. Ashcroft, I *do* just-about love you.' An' she goes on all like that. Liz, I tell you my 'air e'en a'most stood on end to 'ear 'er. I asked 'er what like a Token was. 'I dunno,' she says, 'but after you've ringed the bell, you'll 'ear it run up from the basement, to the front door. Then say your wish,' she says, 'an' go away.' 'The Token don't open de door to ye, then?' I says. 'Oh no,' she says. 'You on'y 'ear gigglin', like, be'ind the front door. Then you say you'll take the trouble off of 'ooever 'tis you've chose for your love; an' ye'll get it,' she says. I didn't ask no more – she was too 'ot an' fevered. I made much of 'er till it come time to light de gas, an' a liddle after that, 'er 'eddick – mine, I suppose – took off, an' she got down an' played with the cat."

"Well I never!" said Mrs. Fettley. "Did – did ye foller it up, anyways?"

"She askt me to, but I wouldn't 'ave no such dealin's with a child."

"What *did* ye do, then?"

" 'Sat in me own room 'stid o' the kitchen when me 'ed-dicks come on. But it lay at de back o' me mind."

" 'Twould. Did she tell ye more, ever?"

"No. Besides what the Gippo girl 'ad told 'er, she knew naught, 'cept that the charm worked. An', next after that – in May 'twas – I suffered the summer out in Lunnon. 'Twas hot an' windy for weeks, an' the streets stinkin' o' dried 'orse-dung blowin' from side to side an' lyin' level with the kerb. We don't get that nowadays. I 'ad my 'ol'day just before hoppin', an' come down 'ere to stay with Bessie again. She noticed I'd lost flesh, an' was all poochy under the eyes."

"Did ye see 'Arry?"

Mrs. Ashcroft nodded. "The fourth – no, the fifth day. Wednesday 'twas. I knowed 'e was workin' at Smalldene again. I asked 'is mother in the street, bold as brass. She 'adn't room to say much, for Bessie – you know 'er tongue – was talkin' full-clack. But that Wednesday, I was walkin' with one o' Bessie's chillern hangin' on me skirts, at de back o' Chanter's Tot. Prasin'ly, I felt 'e was be'ind me on the footpath, an' I knowed by 'is tread 'e'd changed 'is nature. I slowed, an' I heard 'im slow. Then I fussed a piece with the child, to force him past me, like. So 'e 'ad to come past. 'E just says 'Good-evenin'', and goes on, tryin' to pull 'isself together."

"Drunk, was he?" Mrs. Fettley asked.

"Never! S'runk an' wizen; 'is clothes 'angin' on 'im like bags, an' the back of 'is neck whiter'n chalk. 'Twas all I could do not to oppen my arms an' cry after him. But I swallered me spittle till I was back 'ome again an' the chillern abed. Then I says to Bessie, after supper, 'What in de world's come to 'Arry Mockler?' Bessie told me 'e'd been a-Hospital for two months, 'long o' cuttin' 'is foot wid a spade, muckin' out the old pond at Smalldene. There was poison in de dirt, an' it rooshed up 'is leg, like, an' come out all over him. 'E 'adn't been back to 'is job – carterin' at Smalldene – more'n a fortnight. She told me the Doctor said he'd go off, likely, with the November frostes; an' 'is mother 'ad told 'er that 'e didn't rightly eat nor sleep, an' sweated 'imself into pools, no odds 'ow chill 'e lay. An' spit terrible o' mornin's. 'Dearie me,' I says. 'But, mebbe, hoppin' 'll set 'im right again,' an' I licked me thread-point an' I fetched me needle's eye up to it an' I threads me needle under de lamp, steady as rocks. An' dat night (me bed was in de wash-house) I cried an' I cried. An' you know, Liz – for you've been with me in my throes – it takes summat to make me cry."

"Yes; but chile-bearin' is on'y just pain," said Mrs. Fettley.

"I come round by cock-crow, an' dabbed cold tea on me eyes to take away the signs. Long towards nex' evenin' – I was settin' out to lay some flowers on me 'usband's grave, for the look o' the thing – I met 'Arry over against where the War Memorial is now. 'E was comin' back from 'is 'orses, so 'e couldn't not see me. I looked 'im all over, an' ' 'Arry,' I says twix' me teeth, 'come back an' rest-up in Lunnon.' 'I won't take it,' he says, 'for I can give ye naught.' 'I don't ask it,' I says. 'By God's Own Name, I don't ask na'un! On'y come up an' see a Lunnon doctor.' 'E lifts 'is two 'eavy eyes at me: ' 'Tis past that, Gra',' 'e says. 'I've but a few months left.' ' 'Arry!' I says. '*My* man!' I says. I couldn't say no more. 'Twas all up in me throat. 'Thank ye kindly, Gra',' 'e says (but 'e never says 'my woman'), an' 'e went on up-street an' 'is mother – Oh, damn 'er! – she was watchin' for 'im, an' she shut de door be'ind 'im."

Mrs. Fettley stretched an arm across the table, and made to finger Mrs. Ashcroft's sleeve at the wrist, but the other moved it out of reach.

"So I went on to the churchyard with my flowers, an' I remembered my 'usband's warnin' that night he spoke. 'E *was* death-wise, an' it '*ad* 'appened as 'e said. But as I was settin' down de jam-pot on the grave-mound, it come over me there was one thing I *could* do for 'Arry. Doctor or no Doctor, I thought I'd make a trial of it. So I did. Nex' mornin', a bill came down from our Lunnon green-grocer. Mrs. Marshall, she'd lef' me petty cash for suchlike – o' course – but I tole Bess 'twas for me to come an' open the 'ouse. So I went up, afternoon train."

"An' – but I know you 'adn't – 'adn't you no fear?"

"What for? There was nothin' front o' me but my own shame an' God's croolty. I couldn't ever get 'Arry – 'ow *could* I? I knowed it must go on burnin' till it burned me out."

"Aie!" said Mrs. Fettley, reaching for the wrist again, and this time Mrs. Ashcroft permitted it.

"Yit 'twas a comfort to know I could try *this* for 'im. So I went an' I paid the green-grocer's bill, an' put 'is receipt in me hand-bag, an' then I stepped round to Mrs. Ellis – our char – an' got the 'ouse-keys an' opened the 'ouse. First, I made me bed to come back to (God's Own Name! Me bed to lie upon!). Nex' I made me a cup o' tea an' sat down in the kitchen thinkin', till 'long towards dusk. Terrible close, 'twas. Then I dressed me an' went out with the receipt in me 'and-bag, feignin' to study it for an address, like. Fourteen, Wadloes Road, was the place – a liddle basement-kitchen 'ouse, in a row of twenty-thirty such, an' tiddy strips o'

walled garden in front – the paint off the front doors, an'
na'un done to na'un since ever so long. There wasn't 'ardly no
one in the streets 'cept the cats. 'Twas 'ot, too! I turned into the
gate bold as brass; up de steps I went an' I ringed the front-
door bell. She pealed loud, like it do in an empty house.
When she'd all ceased, I 'eard a cheer, like, pushed back on
de floor o' the kitchen. Then I 'eard feet on de kitchen-stairs,
like it might ha' been a heavy woman in slippers. They come
up to de stair-head, acrost the hall – I 'eard the bare boards
creak under 'em – an' at de front door dey stopped. I stooped
me to the letter-box slit, an' I says: 'Let me take everythin'
bad that's in store for my man, 'Arry Mockler, for love's
sake.' Then, whatever it was t'other side de door let its
breath out, like, as if it 'ad been holdin' it for to 'ear better."

"Nothin' was *said* to ye?" Mrs. Fettley demanded.

"Na'un. She just breathed out – a sort of *A-ah*, like. Then
the steps went back an' downstairs to the kitchen – all draggy
– an' I heard the cheer drawed up again."

"An' you abode on de doorstep, throughout all, Gra'?"

Mrs. Ashcroft nodded.

"Then I went away, an' a man passin' says to me: 'Didn't
you know that house was empty?' 'No,' I says. 'I must ha'
been give the wrong number.' An' I went back to our 'ouse,
an' I went to bed; for I was fair flogged out. 'Twas too 'ot to
sleep more'n snatches, so I walked me about, lyin' down
betweens, till crack o' dawn. Then I went to the kitchen to
make me a cup o' tea, an' I hitted meself just above the ankle
on an old roastin'-jack o' mine that Mrs. Ellis had moved out
from the corner, her last cleanin'. An' so – nex' after that –
I waited till the Marshalls come back o' their holiday."

"Alone there? I'd ha' thought you'd 'ad enough of empty
houses," said Mrs. Fettley, horrified.

"Oh, Mrs. Ellis an' Sophy was runnin' in an' out soon's I
was back, an' 'twixt us we cleaned de house again top-to-
bottom. There's allus a hand's turn more to do in every
house. An' that's 'ow 'twas with me that Autumn an' Winter,
in Lunnon."

"Then na'un hap – overtook ye for your doin's?"

Mrs. Ashcroft smiled. "No. Not then. 'Long in November I sent Bessie ten shillin's."

"You was allus free-'anded," Mrs. Fettley interrupted.

"An' I got what I paid for, with the rest o' the news. She said the hoppin' 'ad set 'im up wonderful. 'E'd 'ad six weeks of it, and now 'e was back again carterin' at Smalldene. No odds to me '*ow* it 'ad 'appened – 'slong's it '*ad*. But I dunno as my ten shillin's eased me much. 'Arry bein' *dead*, like, 'e'd ha' been mine, till Judgement. 'Arry bein' alive, 'e'd like as not pick up with some woman middlin' quick. I raged over that. Come Spring, I 'ad somethin' else to rage for. I'd growed a nasty little weepin' boil, like, on me shin, just above the boot-top, that wouldn't heal no shape. It made me sick to look at it, for I'm clean-fleshed by nature. Chop me all over with a spade, an' I'd heal like turf. Then Mrs. Marshall she set 'er own doctor at me. 'E said I ought to ha' come to him at first go-off, 'stead o' drawin' all manner o' dyed stockin's over it for months. 'E said I'd stood up too much to me work, for it was settin' very close atop of a big swelled vein, like, behither the small o' me ankle. 'Slow come, slow go,' 'e says. 'Lay your leg up on high an' rest it,' he says, 'an 'twill ease off. Don't let it close up too soon. You've got a very fine leg, Mrs. Ashcroft,' 'e says. An' he put wet dressin's on it."

" 'E done right." Mrs. Fettley spoke firmly. "Wet dressin's to wet wounds. They draw de humours, same's a lamp-wick draws de oil."

"That's true. An' Mrs. Marshall was allus at me to make me set down more, an' dat nigh healed it up. An' then after a while they packed me off down to Bessie's to finish the cure; for I ain't the sort to sit down when I ought to stand up. You was back in the village then, Liz."

"I was. I was, but – never did I guess!"

"I didn't desire ye to." Mrs. Ashcroft smiled. "I saw 'Arry once or twice in de street, wonnerful fleshed up an' restored back. Then, one day I didn't see 'im, an' 'is mother told me one of 'is 'orses 'ad lashed out an' caught 'im on the 'ip. So 'e was abed an' middlin' painful. An' Bessie, she says to his mother, 'twas a pity 'Arry 'adn't a woman of 'is own to take the nursin' off 'er. And the old lady *was* mad! She told us that 'Arry 'ad never looked after any woman in 'is born days, an' as long as she was atop the mowlds, she'd contrive for 'im till 'er two 'ands dropped off. So I knowed she'd do watch-dog for me, 'thout askin' for bones."

Mrs. Fettley rocked with small laughter.

"That day," Mrs. Ashcroft went on, "I'd stood on me feet nigh all the time, watchin' the doctor go in an' out; for they thought it might be 'is ribs, too. That made my boil break again, issuin' an' weepin'. But it turned out 'twadn't ribs at all, an' 'Arry 'ad a good night. When I heard that, nex' mornin', I says to meself, 'I won't lay two an' two together *yit*. I'll keep me leg down a week, an' see what comes of it.' It didn't hurt me that day, to speak of – 'seemed more to draw the strength out o' me like – an' 'Arry 'ad another good night. That made me persevere; but I didn't dare lay two an' two together till the week-end, an' then, 'Arry come forth e'en a'most 'imself again – na'un hurt outside ner in of him. I nigh fell on me knees in de wash-house when Bessie was up-street. 'I've got ye now, my man,' I says. 'You'll take your good from me 'thout knowin' it till my life's end. O God send me long to live for 'Arry's sake!' I says. An' I dunno that didn't still me ragin's."

"For good?" Mrs. Fettley asked.

"They come back, plenty times, but, let be how 'twould, I knowed I was doin' for 'im. I *knowed* it. I took an' worked me pains on an' off, like regulatin' my own range, till I learned to 'ave 'em at my commandments. An' that was funny, too. There was times, Liz, when my trouble 'ud all s'rink an' dry up, like. First, I used to try an' fetch it on again; bein' fearful to leave 'Arry alone too long for anythin' to lay 'old of. Prasin'ly I come to see that was a sign he'd do all right awhile, an' so I saved myself."

" 'Ow long for?" Mrs. Fettley asked, with deepest interest.

"I've gone de better part of a year onct or twice with na'un more to show than the liddle weepin' core of it, like. *All* s'rinked up an' dried off. Then he'd inflame up – for a warnin' – an' I'd suffer it. When I couldn't no more – an' I *'ad* to keep on goin' with my Lunnon work – I'd lay me leg high on a cheer till it eased. Not too quick. I knowed by the feel of it, those times, dat 'Arry was in need. Then I'd send another five shillin's to Bess, or somethin' for the chillern, to find out if, mebbe, 'e'd took any hurt through my neglects. 'Twas *so*! Year in, year out, I worked it dat way, Liz, an' 'e got 'is good from me 'thout knowin' – for years and years."

"But what did *you* get out of it, Gra'?" Mrs. Fettley almost wailed. "Did ye see 'im reg'lar?"

"Times – when I was 'ere on me 'ol'days. An' more, now that I'm 'ere for good. But 'e's never looked at me, ner any other woman 'cept 'is mother. 'Ow I used to watch an' listen! So did she."

"Years an' years!" Mrs. Fettley repeated. "An' where's 'e workin' at now?"

"Oh, 'e's give up carterin' quite a while. He's workin' for one o' them big tractorisin' firms – ploughin' sometimes, an' sometimes off with lorries – fur as Wales, I've 'eard. He comes 'ome to 'is mother 'tween whiles; but I don't set eyes on him now, fer weeks on end. No odds! 'Is job keeps 'im from continuin' in one stay anywheres."

"But – just for de sake o' sayin' somethin' – s'pose 'Arry *did* get married?" said Mrs. Fettley.

Mrs. Ashcroft drew her breath sharply between her still even and natural teeth. "*Dat* ain't been required of me," she answered. "I reckon my pains 'ull be counted agin that. Don't *you*, Liz?"

"It ought to be, dearie. It ought to be."

"It *do* 'urt sometimes. You shall see it when Nurse comes. She thinks I don't know it's turned."

Mrs. Fettley understood. Human nature seldom walks up to the word "cancer."

"Be ye certain sure, Gra'?" she asked.

"I was sure of it when old Mr. Marshall 'ad me up to 'is study an' spoke a long piece about my faithful service. I've obliged 'em on an' off for a goodish time, but not enough for a pension. But they give me a weekly 'lowance for life. I knew what *that* sinnified – as long as three years ago."

"Dat don't *prove* it, Gra'."

"To give fifteen bob a week to a woman 'oo'd live twenty year in the course o' nature? It *do*!"

"You're mistook! You're mistook!" Mrs. Fettley insisted.

"Liz, there's *no* mistakin' when the edges are all heaped up, like – same as a collar. You'll see it. An' I laid out Dora Wickwood, too. *She* 'ad it under the arm-pit, like."

Mrs. Fettley considered awhile, and bowed her head in finality.

" 'Ow long d'you reckon 'twill allow ye, countin' from now, dearie?"

"Slow come, slow go. But if I don't set eyes on ye 'fore next hoppin', this'll be goodbye, Liz."

"Dunno as I'll be able to manage by then – not 'thout I have a liddle dog to lead me. For de chillern, dey won't be troubled, an' – O Gra'! – I'm blindin' up – I'm blindin' up!"

"Oh, *dat* was why you didn't more'n finger with your quilt patches all this while! I was wonderin' . . . But the pain *do* count, don't ye think, Liz? The pain *do* count to keep 'Arry – where I want 'im. Say it can't be wasted, like."

"I'm sure of it – sure of it, dearie. You'll 'ave your reward."

"I don't want no more'n this – *if* de pain is taken into de reckonin'."

" 'Twill be – 'twill be, Gra'."

There was a knock on the door.

"That's Nurse. She's before 'er time," said Mrs. Ashcroft. "Open to 'er."

The young lady entered briskly, all the bottles in her bag clicking. "Evenin', Mrs. Ashcroft," she began. "I've come raound a little earlier than usual because of the Institute dance to-na-ite. You won't ma-ind, will you?"

"Oh, no. Me dancin' days are over." Mrs. Ashcroft was

the self-contained domestic at once. "My old friend, Mrs. Fettley 'ere, has been settin' talkin' with me a while."

"I hope she 'asn't been fatiguing you?" said the Nurse a little frostily.

"Quite the contrary. It 'as been a pleasure. Only – only – just at the end I felt a bit – a bit flogged out like."

"Yes, yes." The Nurse was on her knees already, with the washes to hand. "When old ladies get together they talk a deal too much, I've noticed."

"Mebbe we do," said Mrs. Fettley, rising. "So, now, I'll make myself scarce."

"Look at it first, though," said Mrs. Ashcroft feebly. "I'd like ye to look at it."

Mrs. Fettley looked, and shivered. Then she leaned over, and kissed Mrs. Ashcroft once on the waxy yellow forehead, and again on the faded grey eyes.

"It *do* count, don't it – de pain?" The lips that still kept trace of their original moulding hardly more than breathed the words.

Mrs. Fettley kissed them and moved towards the door.

* * *

RAHERE

Rahere, King Henry's Jester, feared by all the Norman Lords
For his eye that pierced their bosoms, for his tongue that shamed their swords;
Fed and flattered by the Churchmen – well they knew how deep he stood
In dark Henry's crooked counsels – fell upon an evil mood.

Suddenly, his days before him and behind him seemed to stand
Stripped and barren, fixed and fruitless, as those leagues of naked sand
When St Michael's ebb slinks outward to the bleak horizon-bound,
And the trampling wide-mouthed waters are withdrawn from sight and sound.

Then a Horror of Great Darkness sunk his spirit and, anon,
(Who had seen him wince and whiten as he turned to walk alone)
Followed Gilbert the Physician, and muttered in his ear,
"Thou hast it, O my brother?" "Yea, I have it," said Rahere.
"So it comes," said Gilbert smoothly, "man's most immanent
     distress.
'Tis a humour of the Spirit which abhorreth all excess;
And, whatever breed the surfeit – Wealth, or Wit, or Power, or
     Fame
(And thou hast each) the Spirit laboureth to expel the same.

"Hence the dulled eye's deep self-loathing – hence the loaded
     leaden brow;
Hence the burden of Wanhope that aches thy soul and body now.
Ay, the merriest fool must face it, and the wisest Doctor learn;
For it comes – it comes," said Gilbert, "as it passes – to return."

But Rahere was in his torment, and he wandered, dumb and far,
Till he came to reeking Smithfield where the crowded gallows are.
(Followed Gilbert the Physician) and beneath the wry-necked
     dead,
Sat a leper and his woman, very merry, breaking bread.

He was cloaked from chin to ankle – faceless, fingerless, obscene –
Mere corruption swaddled man-wise, but the woman whole and
     clean;
And she waited on him crooning, and Rahere beheld the twain,
Each delighting in the other, and he checked and groaned again.

"So it comes, – it comes," said Gilbert, "as it came when Life
     began.
'Tis a motion of the Spirit that revealeth God to man
In the shape of Love exceeding, which regards not taint or fall,
Since in perfect Love, saith Scripture, can be no excess at all.

"Hence the eye that sees no blemish – hence the hour that holds
     no shame.
Hence the Soul assured the Essence and the Substance are the
     same.
Nay, the meanest need not miss it, though the mightier pass it by;
For it comes – it comes," said Gilbert, "and, thou seest, it does
     not die!"

THE JANEITES

THE JANEITES

* * *

THE SURVIVAL

Securely, after days
   Unnumbered, I behold
Kings mourn that promised praise
   Their cheating bards foretold.

Of earth-constricting wars,
   Of Princes passed in chains,
Of deeds out-shining stars,
   No word or voice remains.

Yet furthest times receive
   And to fresh praise restore,
Mere flutes that breathe at eve,
   Mere seaweed on the shore.

A smoke of sacrifice;
   A chosen myrtle-wreath;
An harlot's altered eyes;
   A rage 'gainst love or death;

Glazed snow beneath the moon;
   The surge of storm-bowed trees –
The Caesars perished soon,
   And Rome Herself: But these

Endure while Empires fall
   And Gods for Gods make room . . .
Which greater God than all
   Imposed the amazing doom?

Horace, Ode 22, Bk V

* * *

Jane lies in Winchester – blessed be her shade!
Praise the Lord for making her, and her for all she made!

And while the stones of Winchester, or Milsom Street, remain,
Glory, love, and honour unto England's Jane!

In the Lodge of Instruction attached to "Faith and Works No. 5837 E.C.," which has already been described, Saturday afternoon was appointed for the weekly clean-up, when all visiting Brethren were welcome to help under the direction of the Lodge Officer of the day: their reward was light refreshment and the meeting of companions.

This particular afternoon – in the autumn of '20 – Brother Burges, P.M., was on duty and, finding a strong shift present, took advantage of it to strip and dust all hangings and curtains, to go over every inch of the Pavement – which was stone, not floorcloth – by hand; and to polish the Columns, Jewels, Working outfit and organ. I was given to clean some Officer's Jewels – beautiful bits of old Georgian silver-work humanised by generations of elbow-grease – and retired to the organ loft; for the floor was like the quarter-deck of a battleship on the eve of a ball. Half-a-dozen brethren had already made the Pavement as glassy as the aisle of Greenwich Chapel; the brazen chapiters winked like pure gold at the flashing Marks on the Chairs; and a morose one-legged brother was attending to the Emblems of Mortality with, I think, rouge.

"They ought," he volunteered to Brother Burges as we passed, "to be betwixt the colour of ripe apricots an' a half-smoked meerschaum. That's how we kept 'em in my Mother-Lodge – a treat to look at."

"I've never seen spit-and-polish to touch this," I said.

"Wait till you see the organ," Brother Burges replied. "You could shave in it when they've done. Brother Anthony's in charge up there – the taxi-owner you met here last month. I don't think you've come across Brother Humberstall, have you?"

"I don't remember –" I began.

"You wouldn't have forgotten him if you had. He's a hair-dresser now, somewhere at the back of Ebury Street. 'Was Garrison Artillery. 'Blown up twice."

"Does he show it?" I asked at the foot of the organ-loft stairs.

"No-o. Not much more than Lazarus did, I expect." Brother Burges fled off to set someone else to a job.

Brother Anthony, small, dark, and hump-backed, was hissing groom-fashion while he treated the rich acacia-wood panels of the Lodge organ with some sacred, secret composition of his own. Under his guidance Humberstall, an enormous, flat-faced man, carrying the shoulders, ribs, and loins of the old Mark '14 Royal Garrison Artillery, and the eyes of a bewildered retriever, rubbed the stuff in. I sat down to my task on the organ-bench, whose purple velvet cushion was being vacuum-cleaned on the floor below.

"Now," said Anthony, after five minutes' vigorous work on the part of Humberstall. "*Now* we're gettin' somethin' worth lookin' at! Take it easy, an' go on with what you was tellin' me about that Macklin man."

"I – I 'adn't anything against 'im," said Humberstall, "excep' he'd been a toff by birth; but that never showed till he was bosko absoluto. Mere bein' drunk on'y made a common 'ound of 'im. But when bosko, it all came out. Otherwise, he showed me my duties as mess-waiter very well on the 'ole."

"Yes, yes. But what in 'ell made you go *back* to your Circus? The Board gave you down-an'-out fair enough, you said, after the dump went up at Eatables?"

"Board or no Board, *I* 'adn't the nerve to stay at 'ome – not with mother chuckin' 'erself round all three rooms like a rabbit every time the Gothas tried to get Victoria; an' sister writin' me aunts four pages about it next day. Not for *me*, thank you! till the war was over. So I slid out with a draft – they wasn't particular in '17, so long as the tally was correct – and I joined up again with our Circus somewhere at the back of Lar Pug Noy, I think it was." Humberstall paused for some seconds and his brow wrinkled. "Then I – I went sick, or somethin' or other, they told me; but I know *when* I reported for duty, our Battery Sergeant Major says that I wasn't expected back, an' – an', one thing leadin' to another – to cut a long story short – I went up before our Major – Major – I shall forget my own name next – Major —"

"Never mind," Anthony interrupted. "Go on! It'll come back in talk!"

" 'Alf a mo'. 'Twas on the tip o' my tongue then."

Humberstall dropped the polishing-cloth and knitted his brows again in most profound thought. Anthony turned to me and suddenly launched into a sprightly tale of his taxi's collision with a Marble Arch refuge on a greasy day after a three-yard skid.

" 'Much damage?" I asked.

"Oh no! Ev'ry bolt an' screw an' nut on the chassis strained; *but* nothing carried away, you understand me, an' not a scratch on the body. You'd never 'ave guessed a thing wrong till you took 'er in hand. It *was* a wop too: 'ead-on – like this!" And he slapped his tactful little forehead to show what a knock it had been.

"Did your Major dish you up much?" he went on over his shoulder to Humberstall who came out of his abstraction with a slow heave.

"We-ell! He told me I wasn't expected back either; an' he said 'e couldn't 'ang up the 'ole Circus till I'd rejoined; an' he said that my ten-inch Skoda which I'd been Number Three of, before the dump went up at Eatables, had 'er full crowd. But, 'e said, as soon as a casualty occurred he'd remember me. 'Meantime,' says he, 'I particularly want you for actin' mess-waiter.'

" 'Beggin' your pardon, sir,' I says perfectly respectful; 'but I didn't exactly come back for *that*, sir.'

" 'Beggin' *your* pardon, 'Umberstall,' says 'e, 'but I 'appen to command the Circus! Now, you're a sharp-witted man,' he says; 'an' what we've suffered from fool-waiters in Mess 'as been somethin' cruel. You'll take on, from now – under instruction to Macklin 'ere.' So this man, Macklin, that I was tellin' you about, showed me my duties . . . 'Ammick! I've got it! 'Ammick was our Major, an' Mosse was Captain!" Humberstall celebrated his recapture of the name by labouring at the organ-panel on his knee.

"Look out! You'll smash it," Anthony protested.

"Sorry! Mother's often told me I didn't know my strength. Now, here's a curious thing. This Major of ours – it's all comin' back to me – was a high-up divorce-court lawyer; an' Mosse, our Captain, was Number One o' Mosse's Private Detective Agency. You've heard of it? 'Wives watched while you wait, an' so on. Well, these two 'ad been registerin' together, so to speak, in the Civil line for years on end, but hadn't ever met till the War. Consequently, at Mess their talk was mostly about famous cases they'd been mixed up in. 'Ammick told the Law-courts' end o' the business, an' all what had been left out of the pleadin's; an' Mosse 'ad the actual facts concernin' the errin' parties – in hotels an' so on. I've heard better talk in our Mess than ever before or since. It comes o' the Gunners bein' a scientific corps."

"That be damned!" said Anthony. "If anythin' 'appens to 'em they've got it all down in a book. There's no book when your lorry dies on you in the 'Oly Land. *That's* brains."

"Well, *then*," Humberstall continued, "come on this secret society business that I started tellin' you about. When those two – 'Ammick an' Mosse – 'ad finished about their matrimonial relations – and, mind you, they weren't radishes – they seldom or ever repeated – they'd begin, as often as not, on this Secret Society woman I was tellin' you of – this Jane. She was the only woman I ever 'eard 'em say a good word for. 'Cordin' to them Jane was a none-such. *I* didn't know then she was a Society. 'Fact is, I only 'ung out 'arf an ear in their direction at first, on account of bein' under instruction for mess-duty to this Macklin man. What drew *my* attention to her was a new Lieutenant joinin' up. We called 'im 'Gander' on account of his profeel, which was the identical

bird. 'E'd been a nactuary – workin' out 'ow long civilians
'ad to live. Neither 'Ammick nor Mosse wasted words on 'im
at Mess. They went on talking as usual, an' in due time, *as*
usual, they got back to Jane. Gander cocks one of his big
chilblainy ears an' cracks his cold finger-joints. 'By God!
Jane?' says 'e. 'Yes, Jane,' says 'Ammick pretty short an'
senior. 'Praise 'Eaven!' says Gander. 'It was "Bubbly" where
I've come from down the line.' (Some damn review or other,
I expect.) Well, neither 'Ammick nor Mosse was easy-
mouthed, or for that matter mealy-mouthed; but no sooner
'ad Gander passed that remark than they both shook 'ands
with the young squirt across the table an' called for the port
back again. It *was* a password, all right! Then they went at it
about Jane – all three, regardless of rank. That made me
listen. Presently, I 'eard 'Ammick say —"

" ' 'Arf a mo'," Anthony cut in. "But what was *you* doin'
in Mess?"

"Me an' Macklin was refixin' the sand-bag screens to the
dug-out passage in case o' gas. We never knew when we'd
cop it in the 'Eavies, don't you see. But we knew we 'ad been
looked for for some time, an' it might come any minute. But,
as I was sayin', 'Ammick says what a pity 'twas Jane 'ad died
barren. 'I deny that,' says Mosse. 'I maintain she was fruitful
in the 'ighest sense o' the word.' An' Mosse knew about such
things, too. 'I'm inclined to agree with 'Ammick,' says young
Gander. 'Any'ow, she's left no direct an' lawful prog'ny.' I
remember every word they said, on account o' what 'appened
subsequently. I 'adn't noticed Macklin much, or I'd ha' seen
he was bosko absoluto. Then '*e* cut in, leanin' over a packin'-
case with a face on 'im like a dead mackerel in the dark.
'Pa-hardon me, gents,' Macklin says, 'but this *is* a matter on
which I *do* 'appen to be moderately well-informed. She *did*
leave lawful issue in the shape o' one son; an' 'is name was
'Enery James.'

" 'By what sire! Prove it,' says Gander, before 'is senior
officers could get in a word.

" 'I will,' says Macklin, surgin' on 'is two thumbs. *An*',

mark you, none of 'em spoke! I forget whom he said was the
sire of this 'Enery James-man; but 'e delivered 'em a lecture
on this Jane-woman for more than a quarter of an hour. I
know the exact time, because my old Skoda was on duty at
ten-minute intervals reachin' after some Jerry formin'-up
area; and her blast always put out the dug-out candles. I relit
'em once, an' again at the end. In conclusion, this Macklin
fell flat forward on 'is face, which was how 'e generally
wound up 'is notion of a perfect day. Bosko absoluto!

" 'Take 'im away,' says 'Ammick to me. ' 'E's sufferin'
from shell-shock.'

"To cut a long story short, *that* was what first put the
notion into my 'ead. Wouldn't it you? Even 'ad Macklin been
a 'igh-up Mason —"

"Wasn't 'e, then?" said Anthony, a little puzzled.

" 'E'd never gone beyond the Blue Degrees, 'e told me.
Any'ow, 'e'd lectured 'is superior officers up an' down; 'e'd
as good as called 'em fools most o' the time, in 'is toff's voice.
I 'eard 'im an' I saw 'im. An' all he got was – me told off to
put 'im to bed! And all on account o' Jane! Would *you* have
let a thing like that get past you? Nor me, either! Next mornin', when his stummick was settled, I was at him full-cry to
find out 'ow it was worked. Toff or no toff, 'e knew his end
of a bargain. First, 'e wasn't takin' any. He said I wasn't fit
to be initiated into the Society of the Janeites. That only
meant five bob more – fifteen up to date.

" 'Make it one Bradbury,' 'e says. 'It's dirt-cheap. You
saw me 'old the Circus in the 'ollow of me 'and?'

"No denyin' it. I *'ad*. So, for one pound, he communicated me the Pass-word of the First Degree which was *Tilniz
an' trap-doors.*

" 'I know what a trap-door is,' I says to 'im, 'but what in
'ell's *Tilniz?*'

" 'You obey orders,' 'e says, 'an' next time I ask you what
you're thinkin' about you'll answer, "*Tilniz an' trap-doors,*"
in a smart and soldierly manner. I'll spring that question at
me own time. All you've got to do is to be distinck.'

"We settled all this while we was skinnin' spuds for dinner at the back o' the rear-truck under our camouflage-screens. Gawd, 'ow that glue-paint did stink! Otherwise, 'twasn't so bad, with the sun comin' through our pantomime-leaves, an' the wind marcelling the grasses in the cutting. Well, one thing leading to another, nothin' further 'appened in this direction till the afternoon. We 'ad a high standard o' livin' in Mess – an' in the Group, for that matter. I was takin' away Mosse's lunch – dinner 'e would never call it – an' Mosse was fillin' 'is cigarette-case previous to the afternoon's duty. Macklin, in the passage, comin' in as if 'e didn't know Mosse was there, slings 'is question at me, an' I give the countersign in a low but quite distinck voice, makin' as if I 'adn't seen Mosse. Mosse looked at me through and through, with his cigarette-case in his 'and. Then 'e jerks out 'arf a dozen – best Turkish – on the table an' exits. I pinched 'em an' divvied with Macklin.

" 'You see 'ow it works,' says Macklin. 'Could you 'ave invested a Bradbury to better advantage?'

" 'So far, no,' I says. 'Otherwise, though, if they start provin' an' tryin' me, I'm a dead bird. There must be a lot more to this Janeite game.'

" ' 'Eaps an' 'eaps,' he says. 'But to show you the sort of 'eart I 'ave, I'll communicate you all the 'Igher Degrees among the Janeites, includin' the Charges, for another Bradbury; but you'll 'ave to work, Dobbin.' "

" 'Pretty free with your Bradburys, wasn't you?" Anthony grunted disapprovingly.

"What odds? *Ac*-tually, Gander told us, we couldn't expect to av'rage more than six weeks' longer apiece, an', any'ow, *I* never regretted it. But make no mistake – the preparation was somethin' cruel. In the first place, I come under Macklin for direct instruction *re* Jane."

"Oh! Jane *was* real, then?" Anthony glanced for an instant at me as he put the question. "I couldn't quite make that out."

"Real!" Humberstall's voice rose almost to a treble. "Jane?

Why, she was a little old maid 'oo'd written 'alf a dozen books about a hundred years ago. 'Twasn't as if there was anythin' *to* 'em, either. *I* know. I had to read 'em. They weren't adventurous, nor smutty, nor what you'd call even interestin' – all about girls o' seventeen (they begun young then, I tell you), not certain 'oom they'd like to marry; an' their dances an' card-parties an' picnics, and their young blokes goin' off to London on 'orseback for 'air-cuts an' shaves. It took a full day in those days, if you went to a proper barber. They wore wigs, too, when they was chemists or clergymen. All that interested me on account o' me profession, an' cuttin' the men's 'air every fortnight. Macklin used to chip me about bein' an 'air-dresser. 'E *could* pass remarks, too!"

Humberstall recited with relish a fragment of what must have been a superb commination-service, ending with, "You lazy-minded, lousy-headed, long-trousered, perfumed perookier."

"An' you took it?" Anthony's quick eyes ran over the man.

"Yes. I was after my money's worth; an' Macklin, havin' put 'is 'and to the plough, wasn't one to withdraw it. Otherwise, if I'd pushed 'im, I'd ha' slew 'im. Our Battery Sergeant Major nearly did. For Macklin had a wonderful way o' passing remarks on a man's civil life; an' he put it about that our B.S.M. had run a dope an' dolly-shop with a Chinese woman, the wrong end o' Southwark Bridge. Nothin' you could lay 'old of, o' course; but —" Humberstall let us draw our own conclusions.

"That reminds me," said Anthony, smacking his lips. "I 'ad a bit of a fracas with a fare in the Fulham Road last month. He called me a paras-tit-ic Forder. I informed 'im I was owner-driver, an' 'e could see for 'imself the cab was quite clean. That didn't suit 'im. 'E said it was crawlin'."

"What happened?" I asked.

"One o' them blue-bellied Bolshies of post-war Police (neglectin' point-duty, as usual) asked us to flirt a little quieter. My joker chucked some Arabic at 'im. That was when we signed the Armistice. 'E'd been a Yeoman – a perishin' Gloucestershire Yeoman – that I'd helped gather in the orange crop with at Jaffa, in the 'Oly Land!"

"And after that?" I continued.

"It 'ud be 'ard to say. I know 'e lived at Hendon or Cricklewood. I drove 'im there. We must 'ave talked Zionism or somethin', because at seven next mornin' him an' me was tryin' to get petrol out of a milkshop at St. Albans. They 'adn't any. In lots o' ways this war has been a public noosance, as one might say, but there's no denyin' it 'elps you slip through life easier. The dairyman's son 'ad done time on Jordan with camels. So he stood us rum an' milk."

"Just like 'avin' the Password, eh?" was Humberstall's comment.

"That's right! Ours was *Imshee kelb*. Not so 'ard to remember as your Jane stuff."

"Jane wasn't so very 'ard – not the way Macklin used to put 'er," Humberstall resumed. "I 'ad only six books to remember. I learned the names by 'eart as Macklin placed 'em. There was one, called *Persuasion*, first; an' the rest in a bunch, except another about some Abbey or other – last by three lengths. But, as I was sayin', what beat me was there was nothin' *to* 'em nor *in* 'em. Nothin' at all, believe me."

"You seem good an' full of 'em, any'ow," said Anthony.

"I mean that 'er characters was no *use*! They was only just like people you run across any day. One of 'em was a curate – the Reverend Collins – always on the make an' lookin' to marry money. Well, when I was a Boy Scout, 'im or 'is twin brother was our troop-leader. An' there was an upstandin' 'ard-mouthed Duchess or a Baronet's wife that didn't give a curse for anyone 'oo wouldn't do what she told 'em to; the Lady – Lady Catherine (I'll get it in a minute) De Bugg. Before Ma bought the 'air-dressin' business in London I used to know of an 'olesale grocer's wife near Leicester (I'm Leicestershire myself) that might 'ave been 'er duplicate. And – oh yes – there was a Miss Bates; just an old maid runnin' about like a hen with 'er 'ead cut off, an' her tongue loose at both ends. I've got an aunt like 'er. Good as gold – but, *you* know."

"Lord, yes!" said Anthony, with feeling. "An' did you find out what *Tilniz* meant? I'm always huntin' after the meanin' of things meself."

"Yes, 'e was a swine of a Major-General, retired, and on the make. They're all on the make, in a quiet way, in Jane. 'E was so much of a gentleman by 'is own estimation that 'e was always be'avin' like a hound. *You* know the sort. 'Turned a girl out of 'is own 'ouse because she 'adn't any money – *after*, mark you, encouragin' 'er to set 'er cap at his son, because 'e thought she had."

"But that 'appens all the time," said Anthony. "Why, me own mother —"

"That's right. So would mine. But this Tilney was a man, an' some'ow Jane put it down all so naked it made you ashamed. I told Macklin that, an' he said I was shapin' to be a good Janeite. 'Twasn't *his* fault if I wasn't. 'Nother thing, too; 'avin' been at the Bath Mineral Waters 'Ospital in 'Sixteen, with trench-feet, was a great advantage to me, because I knew the names o' the streets where Jane 'ad lived. There was one of 'em – Laura, I think, or some other girl's name – which Macklin said was 'oly ground. 'If you'd been initiated *then*,' he says, 'you'd ha' felt your flat feet tingle every time you walked over those sacred pavin'-stones.'

" 'My feet tingled right enough,' I said, 'but not on account of Jane. Nothin' remarkable about that,' I says.

" ' 'Eaven lend me patience!' he says, combin' 'is 'air with 'is little hands. 'Every dam' thing about Jane is remarkable to a pukka Janeite! It was there,' he says, 'that Miss What's-her-Name' (he had the name; I've forgotten it) 'made up 'er engagement again, after nine years, with Captain T'other Bloke.' An' he dished me out a page an' a half of one of the books to learn by 'eart – *Persuasion*, I think it was."

" 'You quick at gettin' things off by 'eart?" Anthony demanded.

"Not as a rule. I was then, though, or else Macklin knew 'ow to deliver the Charges properly. 'E said 'e'd been some sort o' schoolmaster once, and he'd make my mind resume work or break 'imself. That was just before the Battery Sergeant Major 'ad it in for him on account o' what he'd been sayin' about the Chinese wife an' the dolly-shop."

"What did Macklin really say?" Anthony and I asked together. Humberstall gave us a fragment. It was hardly the stuff to let loose on a pious post-war world without revision.

"And what had your B.S.M. been in civil life?" I asked at the end.

" 'Ead-embalmer to an 'olesale undertaker in the Midlands," said Humberstall; "but, o' course, *when* he thought 'e saw his chance he naturally took it. He came along one mornin' lickin' 'is lips. 'You don't get past me this time,' 'e says to Macklin. 'You're for it, Professor.'

" ' 'Ow so, me gallant Major,' says Macklin; 'an' what for?'

" 'For writin' obese words on the breech o' the ten-inch,' says the B.S.M. She was our old Skoda that I've been tellin' you about. We called 'er 'Bloody Eliza.' She 'ad a badly wore obturator an' blew through a fair treat. I knew by Macklin's face the B.S.M. 'ad dropped it somewhere, but all he vow'saifed was, 'Very good, Major. We will consider it in Common Room.' The B.S.M. couldn't ever stand Macklin's toff's way o' puttin' things; so he goes off rumblin' like 'ell's bells in an 'urricane, as the Marines say. Macklin put it to me at once, what had I been doin'? Some'ow he could read me like a book.

"Well, all *I*'d done – an' I told 'im *he* was responsible for it – was to chalk the guns. Ammick never minded what the men wrote up on 'em. 'E said it gave 'em an interest in their job. You'd see all sorts of remarks chalked on the side-plates or the gear-casin's."

"What sort of remarks?" said Anthony keenly.

"Oh! 'Ow Bloody Eliza, or Spittin' Jim – that was our old Mark Five Nine-point-two – felt that morning, an' such things. But it 'ad come over me – more to please Macklin than anythin' else – that it was time we Janeites 'ad a look in. So, as I was tellin' you, I'd taken an' rechristened all three of 'em, on my own, early that mornin'. Spittin' Jim I 'ad chalked 'The Reverend Collins' – that Curate I was tellin' you about; an' our cut-down Navy Twelve, 'General Tilney', because it was worse wore in the groovin' than anything I'd ever seen. The Skoda (an' that was where I dropped it) I 'ad chalked up 'The Lady Catherine De Bugg'. I made a clean breast of it all to Macklin. He reached up an' patted me on the shoulder. 'You done nobly,' he says. 'You're bringin' forth abundant fruit, like a good Janeite. But I'm afraid your spellin' has misled our worthy B.S.M. *That's* what it is,' 'e says, slappin' 'is little leg. ' 'Ow might you 'ave spelt De Burgh for example?'

"I told 'im. 'Twasn't right; an' 'e nips off to the Skoda to make it so. When 'e comes back, 'e says that the Gander 'ad been before 'im an' corrected the error. But we two come up before the Major, just the same, that afternoon after lunch; 'Ammick in the chair, so to speak, Mosse in another, an' the B.S.M. chargin' Macklin with writin' obese words on His Majesty's property, on active service. When it transpired that me an' not Macklin was the offendin' party, the B.S.M. turned 'is hand in and sulked like a baby. 'E as good as told 'Ammick 'e couldn't hope to preserve discipline unless examples was made – meanin', o' course, Macklin."

"Yes, I've heard all that," said Anthony, with a contemptuous grunt. "The worst of it is, a lot of it's true."

" 'Ammick took 'im up sharp about Military Law, which he said was even more fair than the civilian article."

"My Gawd!" This came from Anthony's scornful midmost bosom.

" 'Accordin' to the unwritten law of the 'Eavies,' says 'Ammick, 'there's no objection to the men chalkin' the guns, if decency is preserved. On the other 'and,' says he, 'we 'aven't yet settled the precise status of individuals entitled so to do. I 'old that the privilege is confined to combatants only.'

" 'With the permission of the Court,' says Mosse, who was another born lawyer, 'I'd like to be allowed to join issue on that point. Prisoner's position is very delicate an' doubtful, an' he has no legal representative.'

" 'Very good,' says 'Ammick. 'Macklin bein' acquitted —'

" 'With submission, me lud,' says Mosse. 'I hope to prove 'e was accessory before the fact.'

" '*As* you please,' says 'Ammick. 'But in that case, 'oo the 'ell's goin' to get the port I'm tryin' to stand the Court?'

" 'I submit,' says Mosse, 'prisoner, bein' under direct observation o' the Court, could be temporarily enlarged for that duty.'

"So Macklin went an' got it, an' the B.S.M. had 'is glass with the rest. Then they argued whether mess servants an' non-combatants was entitled to chalk the guns ('Ammick *versus* Mosse). After a bit, 'Ammick as C.O. give 'imself best, an' me an' Macklin was severely admonished for trespassin' on combatants' rights, an' the B.S.M. was warned that if we repeated the offence 'e could deal with us summ'rily. He 'ad some glasses o' port an' went out quite 'appy. Then my turn come, while Macklin was gettin' them their tea; an' one thing leadin' to another, 'Ammick put me through all the Janeite Degrees, you might say. 'Never 'ad such a doin' in my life.'

"Yes, but what did you tell 'em?" said Anthony. "I can't ever *think* my lies quick enough when I'm for it."

"No need to lie. I told 'em that the backside view o' the Skoda, when she was run up, put Lady De Bugg into my 'ead. They gave me right there, but they said I was wrong about General Tilney. 'Cordin' to them, our Navy twelve-inch ought to 'ave been christened Miss Bates. I said the same idea 'ad crossed my mind, till I'd seen the General's groovin'. Then I felt it had to be the General or nothin'. But they give me full marks for the Reverend Collins – our Nine-point-two."

"An' you fed 'em *that* sort o' talk?" Anthony's fox-coloured eyebrows climbed almost into his hair.

"While I was assistin' Macklin to get tea – yes. Seein' it was an examination, I wanted to do 'im credit as a Janeite."

"An' – an' what did they say?"

"They said it was 'ighly creditable to us both. I don't drink, so they give me about a hundred fags."

"Gawd! What a Circus you must 'ave been," was Anthony's gasping comment.

"It *was* a 'appy little Group. I wouldn't 'a changed with any other."

Humberstall sighed heavily as he helped Anthony slide back the organ-panel. We all admired it in silence, while Anthony repocketed his secret polishing mixture, which lived in a tin tobacco-box. I had neglected my work for listening to Humberstall. Anthony reached out quietly and took over a Secretary's Jewel and a rag. Humberstall studied his reflection in the glossy wood.

"Almost," he said critically, holding his head to one side.

"Not with an Army. You could with a Safety, though," said Anthony. And, indeed, as Brother Burges had foretold, one might have shaved in it with comfort.

"Did you ever run across any of 'em afterwards, any time?" Anthony asked presently.

"Not so many of 'em left to run after, now. With the 'Eavies it's mostly neck or nothin'. We copped it. In the neck. In due time."

"Well, *you* come out of it all right." Anthony spoke both stoutly and soothingly; but Humberstall would not be comforted.

"That's right; but I almost wish I 'adn't," he sighed. "I was 'appier there than ever before or since. Jerry's March push in 'Eighteen did us in; an' yet, 'ow could we 'ave expected it? 'Ow *could* we 'ave expected it? We'd been sent back for rest an' runnin'-repairs, back pretty near our base; an' our old loco' that used to shift us about o' nights, she'd gone down the line for repairs. But for 'Ammick we wouldn't even 'ave 'ad our camouflage-screens up. He told our Brigadier that, whatever 'e might be in the Gunnery line, as a leadin' Divorce lawyer he never threw away a point in argument. So 'e 'ad us all screened in over in a cuttin' on a little spur-line near a wood; an' e' saw to the screens 'imself. The leaves weren't more than comin' out then, an' the sun used to make our glue-paint stink. Just like actin' in a theatre, it was! But 'appy. *But* 'appy! I expect if we'd been caterpillars, like the new big six-inch hows, they'd ha' remembered us. But we was the old La Bassee '15 Mark o' Heavies that ran on rails – not much more good than scrap-iron that late in the war. An', believe me, gents – or Brethren, as I should say – we copped it cruel. Look 'ere! It was in the afternoon, an' I was watchin' Gander instructin' a class in new sights at Lady Catherine. All of a sudden I 'eard our screens rip overhead, an' a runner on a motor-bike come sailin', sailin' through the air – like that bloke that used to bicycle off Brighton Pier – and landed one awful wop almost atop o' the class. ' 'Old 'ard,' says Gander. 'That's no way to report. What's the fuss?' 'Your screens 'ave broke my back, for one thing,' says the bloke on the ground; 'an' for another, the 'ole front's gone.' 'Nonsense,' says Gander. 'E 'adn't more than passed the remark when the man was vi'lently sick an' conked out. 'E 'ad plenty papers on 'im from Brigadiers and C.O.s reporting 'emselves cut off an' askin' for orders. 'E was right both ways – his back an' our front. The 'ole Somme front washed out as clean as kiss-me-'and!" His huge hand smashed down open on his knee.

"We 'eard about it at the time in the 'Oly Land. Was it reelly as quick as all that?" said Anthony.

"Quicker! Look 'ere! The motor-bike dropped in on us about four pip-emma. After that, we tried to get orders o' some kind or other, but nothin' came through excep' that all available transport was in use and not likely to be released. *That* didn't 'elp us any. About nine o'clock comes along a young Brass 'At in brown gloves. We was quite a surprise to 'im. 'E said they were evacuating the area and we'd better shift. 'Where to?' says 'Ammick, rather short.

" 'Oh, somewhere Amiens way,' he says. 'Not that I'd guarantee Amiens for any length o' time; but Amiens might do to begin with.' I'm giving you the very words. Then 'e goes off swingin' 'is brown gloves, and 'Ammick sends for Gander and orders 'im to march the men through Amiens to Dieppe; book thence to New'aven, take up positions be'ind Seaford, an' carry on the war. Gander said 'e'd see 'im damned first. 'Ammick says 'e'd see 'im court-martialled after. Gander says what 'e meant to say was that the men 'ud see all an' sundry damned before they went into Amiens with their gunsights wrapped up in their putties. 'Ammick says 'e 'adn't said a word about putties, an' carryin' off the gunsights was purely optional. 'Well, anyhow,' says Gander, 'putties or drawers, they ain't goin' to shift a step unless you lead the procession.'

" 'Mutinous 'ounds,' says 'Ammick. 'But we live in a democratic age. D'you suppose they'd object to kindly diggin' 'emselves in a bit?' 'Not at all,' says Gander. 'The B.S.M.'s kept 'em at it like terriers for the last three hours.' 'That bein' so,' says 'Ammick, 'Macklin'll now fetch us small glasses o' port.' Then Mosse comes in – he could smell port a mile off – an' he submits we'd only add to the congestion in Amiens if we took our crowd there, whereas, if we lay doggo where we was, Jerry might miss us, though he didn't seem to be missin' much that evenin'.

"The 'ole country was pretty noisy, an' our dumps we'd lit ourselves flarin' Heavens high as far as you could see. Lyin' doggo was our best chance. I believe we might ha' pulled it off, if we'd been left alone, but along towards midnight – there was some small stuff swishin' about, but nothin' particular – a nice little bald-headed old gentleman in uniform pushes into the dug-out wipin' his glasses an' sayin' e' was thinkin' o' formin' a defensive flank on our left with 'is battalion which 'ad just come up. 'Ammick says 'e wouldn't form much if 'e was 'im. 'Oh, don't say that,' says the old gentleman, very shocked. 'One must support the Guns, mustn't one?' 'Ammick says we was refittin' an' about as effective, just then, as a public lav'tory. 'Go into Amiens,' he says, 'an' defend 'em there.' 'Oh no,' says the old gentleman, 'me an' my laddies *must* make a defensive flank for you,' an' he flips out of the dug-out like a performin' bullfinch, chirruppin' for his 'laddies.' Gawd in 'Eaven knows what sort o' push they was – little boys mostly – but they 'ung on to 'is coat-tails like a Sunday-school treat, an' we 'eard 'em muckin' about in the open for a bit. Then a pretty tight barrage was slapped down for ten minutes, an' 'Ammick thought the laddies had copped it already. 'It'll be our turn next,' says Mosse. 'There's been a covey o' Gothas messin' about for the last 'alf-hour – lookin' for the Railway Shops, I expect. They're just as likely to take us.' 'Arisin' out o' that,' says 'Ammick, 'one of 'em sounds pretty low down now. We're for it, me learned colleagues!' 'Jesus!' says Gander, 'I believe you're right, sir.' And that was the last word *I* 'eard on the matter."

"Did they cop you then?" said Anthony.

"They did. I expect Mosse was right, an' they took us for the Railway Shops. When I come to, I was lyin' outside the cuttin', which was pretty well filled up. The Reverend Collins was all right; but Lady Catherine and the General was past prayin' for. I lay there, takin' it in, till I felt cold an' I looked at meself. Otherwise, I 'adn't much on excep' me boots. So I got up an' walked about to keep warm. Then I saw somethin' like a mushroom in the moonlight. It was the nice old gentleman's bald 'ead. I patted it. 'Im and 'is laddies 'ad copped it right enough. Some battalion run out in a 'urry from England, I suppose. They 'adn't even begun to dig in – pore little perishers! I dressed myself off 'em there, an' topped off with a British warm. Then I went back to the cuttin' an' someone says to me: 'Dig, you ox, dig! Gander's under.' So I 'elped shift things till I threw up blood an' bile mixed. Then I dropped, an' they brought Gander out – dead – an' laid 'im next me. 'Ammick 'ad gone too – fair tore in 'alf, the B.S.M. said; but the funny thing was he talked quite a lot before 'e died, an' nothin' to 'im below 'is stummick, they told me. Mosse we never found. 'E'd been standing by Lady Catherine. She'd up-ended an' gone back on 'em, with 'alf the cuttin' atop of 'er, by the look of things."

"And what come to Macklin?" said Anthony.

"Dunno . . . 'E was with 'Ammick. I expect I must ha' been blown clear of all by the first bomb; for I was the on'y Janeite left. We lost about half our crowd, either under, or after we'd got 'em out. The B.S.M. went off 'is rocker when mornin' came, an' he ran about from one to another sayin': 'That was a good push! That was a great crowd! Did ye ever know any push to touch 'em?' An' then 'e'd cry. So what was left of us made off for ourselves, an' I came across a lorry, pretty full, but they took me in."

"Ah!" said Anthony with pride. " 'They all take a taxi when it's rainin'.' 'Ever 'eard that song?"

"They went a long way back. Then I walked a bit, an' there was a hospital-train fillin' up, an' one of the Sisters – a grey-headed one – ran at me wavin' 'er red 'ands an' sayin' there wasn't room for a louse in it. I was past carin'. But she went on talkin' and talkin' about the war, an' her pa in Ladbroke Grove, an' 'ow strange for 'er at 'er time of life to be doin' this work with a lot o' men, an' next war, 'ow the nurses 'ud 'ave to wear khaki breeches on account o' the mud, like the Land Girls; an' that reminded 'er, she'd boil me an egg if she could lay 'ands on one, for she'd run a chicken-farm once. You never 'eard anythin' like it – outside o' Jane. It set me off laughin' again. Then a woman with a nose an' teeth on 'er, marched up. 'What's all this?' she says. 'What do you want?' 'Nothing,' I says, 'only make Miss Bates, there, stop talkin' or I'll die.' 'Miss Bates?' she says. 'What in 'Eaven's name makes you call 'er that?' 'Because she is,' I says. 'D'you know what you're sayin'?' she says, an' slings her bony arm round me to get me off the ground. ' 'Course I do,' I says, 'an' if you knew Jane you'd know too.' 'That's enough,' says she. 'You're comin' on this train if I have to kill a Brigadier for you,' an' she an' an ord'ly fair hove me into the train, on to a stretcher close to the cookers.

That beef-tea went down well! Then she shook 'ands with me an' said I'd hit off Sister Molyneux in one, an' then she pinched me an extra blanket. It was 'er own 'ospital pretty much. I expect she was the Lady Catherine de Burgh of the area. Well, an' so, to cut a long story short, nothing further transpired."

" 'Adn't you 'ad enough by then?" asked Anthony.

"I expect so. Otherwise, if the old Circus 'ad been carryin' on, I might 'ave 'ad another turn with 'em before Armistice. Our B.S.M. was right. There never was a 'appier push. 'Ammick an' Mosse an' Gander an' the B.S.M. an' that pore little Macklin-man makin' an' passin' an' raisin' me an' gettin' me on to the 'ospital train after 'e was dead, all for a couple of Bradburys. I lie awake nights still, reviewing matters. There never was a push to touch ours – never!"

Anthony handed me back the Secretary's Jewel resplendent.

"Ah," said he. "No denyin' that Jane business was more useful to you than the Roman Eagles or the Star an' Garter. 'Pity there wasn't any of you Janeites in the 'Oly Land. I never come across 'em."

"Well, as pore Macklin said, it's a very select Society, an' you've got to be a Janeite in your 'eart, or you won't have any success. An' yet he made me a Janeite! I read all her six books now for pleasure 'tween times in the shop; an' it brings it all back – down to the smell of the glue-paint on the screens. You take it from me, Brethren, there's no one to touch Jane when you're in a tight place. Gawd bless 'er, whoever she was."

Worshipful Brother Burges, from the floor of the Lodge, called us all from Labour to Refreshment. Humberstall hove himself up – so very a cart-horse of a man one almost expected to hear the harness creak on his back – and descended the steps.

He said he could not stay for tea because he had promised his mother to come home for it, and she would most probably be waiting for him now at the Lodge door.

"One or other of 'em always comes for 'im. He's apt to miss 'is gears sometime," Anthony explained to me, as we followed.

"Goes on a bust, d'you mean?"

" 'Im! He's no more touched liquor than 'e 'as women since 'e was born. No, 'e's liable to a sort o' quiet fits, like. They came on after the dump blew up at Eatables. But for them, 'e'd ha' been Battery Sergeant Major."

"Oh!" I said. "I couldn't make out why he took on as mess-waiter when he got back to his guns. That explains things a bit."

" 'Is sister told me the dump goin' up knocked all 'is Gunnery instruction clean out of 'im. The only thing 'e stuck to was to get back to 'is old crowd. Gawd knows 'ow 'e worked it, but 'e did. He fair deserted out of England to 'em, she says; an' when they saw the state 'e was in, they 'adn't the 'eart to send 'im back or into 'ospital. They kep' 'im for a mascot, as you might say. That's *all* dead-true. 'Is sister told me so. But I can't guarantee that Janeite business, excep' 'e never told a lie since 'e was six. 'Is sister told me so. What do *you* think?"

"He isn't likely to have made it up out of his own head," I replied.

"But people don't get so crazy-fond o' books as all that, do they? 'E's made 'is sister try to read 'em. She'd do anythin' to please him. But, as I keep tellin' 'er, so'd 'is mother. D'you 'appen to know anything about Jane?"

"I believe Jane was a bit of a match-maker in a quiet way when she was alive, and I know all her books are full of match-making," I said. "*You'd* better look out."

"Oh, *that's* as good as settled," Anthony replied, blushing.

* * *

JANE'S MARRIAGE

Jane went to Paradise:
  That was only fair.
Good Sir Walter met her first,
  And led her up the stair.

Henry and Tobias,
  And Miguel of Spain,
Stood with Shakespeare at the top
  To welcome Jane –

Then the Three Archangels,
  Offered out of hand,
Anything in Heaven's gift
  That she might command.
Azrael's eyes upon her,
  Raphael's wings above,
Michael's sword against her heart,
  Jane said: "Love."

Instantly the under-
  standing Seraphim
Laid their fingers on their lips
  And went to look for him.
Stole across the Zodiac,
  Harnessed Charles's Wain,
And whispered round the Nebulae
  "Who loved Jane?"

In a private limbo
  Where none had thought to look,
Sat a Hampshire gentleman
  Reading of a book.
It was called *Persuasion*,
  And it told the plain
Story of the love between
  Him and Jane.

He heard the question
  Circle Heaven through –
Closed the book and answered:
  "I did – and do!"
Quietly but speedily
  (As Captain Wentworth moved)
Entered into Paradise
  The man Jane loved!

THE BULL THAT THOUGHT

THE BULL THAT THOUGHT

WESTWARD from a town by the Mouths of the Rhône, runs a road so mathematically straight, so barometrically level, that it ranks among the world's measured miles and motorists use it for records.

I had attacked the distance several times, but always with a Mistral blowing, or the unchancy cattle of those parts on the move. But once, running from the East, into a high-piled, almost Egyptian, sunset, there came a night which it would have been sin to have wasted. It was warm with the breath of summer in advance; moonlit till the shadow of every rounded pebble and pointed cypress wind-break lay solid on that vast flat-floored waste; and my Mr. Leggatt, who had slipped out to make sure, reported that the road-surface was unblemished.

"*Now*," he suggested, "we might see what she'll do under strict road-conditions. She's been pullin' like the Blue de Luxe all day. Unless I'm all off, it's her night out."

We arranged the trial for after dinner – thirty kilometres as near as might be; and twenty-two of them without even a level crossing.

There sat beside me at table d'hôte an elderly, bearded Frenchman wearing the rosette of by no means the lowest grade of the Legion of Honour, who had arrived in a talkative Citroën. I gathered that he had spent much of his life in the French Colonial Service in Annam and Tonquin. When the war came, his years barring him from the front line, he had supervised Chinese wood-cutters who, with axe and dynamite, deforested the centre of France for trench-props. He said my chauffeur had told him that I contemplated an experiment. He was interested in cars – had admired mine – would, in short, be greatly indebted to me if I permitted him to assist as an observer. One could not well refuse; and, knowing my Mr. Leggatt, it occurred to me there might also be a bet in the background.

While he went to get his coat, I asked the proprietor his name. "Voiron – Monsieur André Voiron," was the reply. "And his business?" "Mon Dieu! He is Voiron! He is all those things, there!" The proprietor waved his hands at brilliant advertisements on the dining-room walls, which declared that Voiron Frères dealt in wines, agricultural implements, chemical manures, provisions and produce throughout that part of the globe.

He said little for the first five minutes of our trip, and nothing at all for the next ten – it being, as Leggatt had guessed, Esmeralda's night out. But, when her indicator climbed to a certain figure and held there for three blinding kilometres, he expressed himself satisfied, and proposed to me that we should celebrate the event at the hotel. "I keep yonder," said he, "a wine on which I should value your opinion."

On our return, he disappeared for a few minutes, and I heard him rumbling in a cellar. The proprietor presently invited me to the dining-room, where, beneath one frugal light, a table had been set with local dishes of renown. There was, too, a bottle beyond most known sizes, marked black on red, with a date. Monsieur Voiron opened it, and we drank to the health of my car. The velvety, perfumed liquor, between fawn and topaz, neither too sweet nor too dry, creamed in its generous glass. But I knew no wine composed of the whispers of angels' wings, the breath of Eden and the foam and pulse of Youth renewed. So I asked what it might be.

"It is champagne," he said gravely.

"Then what have I been drinking all my life?"

"If you were lucky, before the War, and paid thirty shillings a bottle, it is possible you may have drunk one of our better-class *tisanes.*"

"And where does one get this?"

"Here, I am happy to say. Elsewhere, perhaps, it is not so

easy. We growers exchange these real wines among ourselves."

I bowed my head in admiration, surrender, and joy. There stood the most ample bottle, and it was not yet eleven o'clock. Doors locked and shutters banged throughout the establishment. Some last servant yawned on his way to bed. Monsieur Voiron opened a window and the moonlight flooded in from a small pebbled court outside. One could almost hear the town of Chambres breathing in its first sleep. Presently, there was a thick noise in the air, the passing of feet and hooves, lowings, and a stifled bark or two. Dust rose over the courtyard wall, followed by the strong smell of cattle.

"They are moving some beasts," said Monsieur Voiron, cocking an ear. "Mine, I think. Yes, I hear Christophe. Our beasts do not like automobiles – so we move at night. You do not know our country – the Crau, here, or the Camargue? I was – I am now, again – of it. All France is good; but this is the best." He spoke, as only a Frenchman can, of his own loved part of his own lovely land.

"For myself, if I were not so involved in all these affairs" – he pointed to the advertisements – "I would live on our farm with my cattle, and worship them like a Hindu. You know our cattle of the Camargue, Monsieur? No? It is not an acquaintance to rush upon lightly. There are no beasts like them. They have a mentality superior to that of others. They graze and they ruminate, by choice, facing our Mistral, which is more than some automobiles will do. Also they have in them the potentiality of thought – and when cattle think – I have seen what arrives."

"Are they so clever as all that?" I asked idly.

"Monsieur, when your sportif chauffeur camouflaged your limousine so that she resembled one of your Army lorries, I would not believe her capacities. I bet him – ah – two to one – she would not touch ninety kilometres. It was proved that she could. I can give you no proof, but will you believe me if I tell you what a beast who thinks can achieve?"

"After the War," said I spaciously, "everything is credible."

"That is true! Everything inconceivable has happened; but still we learn nothing and we believe nothing. When I was a child in my father's house – before I became a Colonial Administrator – my interest and my affection were among our cattle. We of the old rock live here – have you seen? – in big farms like castles. Indeed, some of them may have been Saracenic. The barns group round them – great white-walled barns, and yards solid as our houses. One gate shuts all. It is a world apart; an administration of all that concerns beasts. It was there I learned something about cattle. You see, they are our playthings in the Camargue and the Crau. The boy measures his strength against the calf that butts him in play among the manure-heaps. He moves in and out among the cows, who are – not so amiable. He rides with the herdsmen in the open to shift the herds. Sooner or later, he meets as bulls the little calves that knocked him over. So it was with me – till it became necessary that I should go to our Colonies." He laughed. "Very necessary. That is a good time in youth, Monsieur, when one does these things which shock our parents. Why is it always Papa who is so shocked and has never heard of such things – and Mamma who supplies the excuses? . . . And when my brother – my elder who stayed and created the business – begged me to return and help him, I resigned my Colonial career gladly enough. I returned to our own lands, and my well-loved, wicked white and yellow cattle of the Camargue and the Crau. My Faith, I could talk of them all night, for this stuff unlocks the heart, without making repentance in the morning . . . Yes! It was after the War that this happened. There was a calf, among Heaven knows how many of ours – a bull-calf – an infant indistinguishable from his companions. He was sick, and he had been taken up with his mother into the big farm-yard at home with us. Naturally the children of our herdsmen practised on him from the first. It is in their blood. The Spaniards make a cult of bull-fighting. Our little devils down here bait bulls as automatically as the English child kicks or throws balls. This calf would chase them with his eyes open, like a cow when she hunts a man. They would take refuge behind our tractors and wine-carts in the centre of the yard: he would chase them in and out as a dog hunts rats. More than that, he would study their psychology, his eyes in their eyes. Yes, he watched their faces to divine which way they would run. He himself, also, would pretend sometimes to charge directly at a boy. Then he would wheel right or left – one could never tell – and knock over some child pressed against a wall who thought himself safe. After this, he would stand over him, knowing that his companions must come to his aid; and when they were all together, waving their jackets across his eyes and pulling his tail, he would scatter them – how he would scatter them! He could kick, too, sideways like a cow. He knew his ranges as well as our gunners, and he was as quick on his feet as our Carpentier. I observed him often. Christophe – the man who passed just now – our chief herdsman, who had taught me to ride with our beasts when I was ten – Christophe told me that he was descended from a yellow cow of those days that had chased us once into the marshes. 'He kicks just like her,' said Christophe. 'He can side-kick as he jumps. Have you seen, too, that he is not deceived by the jacket when a boy waves it? He uses it to find the boy. They think they are feeling him. He is feeling them always. He thinks, that one.' I had come to the same conclusion. Yes – the creature was a thinker along the lines necessary to his sport; and he was a humorist also, like so many natural murderers. One knows the type among beasts as well as among men. It possesses a curious truculent mirth – almost indecent but infallibly significant —"

Monsieur Voiron replenished our glasses with the great wine that went better at each descent.

"They kept him for some time in the yards to practise upon. Naturally he became a little brutal; so Christophe turned him out to learn manners among his equals in the grazing lands, where the Camargue joins the Crau. How old was he then? About eight or nine months, I think. We met again a few months later – he and I. I was riding one of our little half-wild horses, along a road of the Crau, when I found myself almost unseated. It was he! He had hidden himself behind a wind-break till we passed, and had then charged my horse from behind. Yes, he had deceived even my little horse! But I recognised him. I gave him the whip across the nose, and I said: 'Apis, for this thou goest to Arles! It was unworthy of thee, between us two.' But that creature had no shame. He went away laughing, like an Apache. If he had dismounted me, I do not think it is I who would have laughed – yearling as he was."

"Why did you want to send him to Arles?" I asked.

"For the bull-ring. When your charming tourists leave us, we institute our little amusements there. Not a real bull-fight, you understand, but young bulls with padded horns, and our boys from hereabouts and in the city go to play with them. Naturally, before we send them we try them in our yards at home. So we brought up Apis from his pastures. He knew at once that he was among the friends of his youth – he almost shook hands with them – and he submitted like an angel to padding his horns. He investigated the carts and tractors in the yards, to choose his lines of defence and attack. And then – he attacked with an *élan*, and he defended with a tenacity and forethought that delighted us. In truth, we were so pleased that I fear we trespassed upon his patience. We desired him to repeat himself, which no true artist will tolerate. But he gave us fair warning. He went out to the centre of the yard, where there was some dry earth; he kneeled down and – you have seen a calf whose horns fret him thrusting and rooting into a bank? He did just that, very deliberately, till he had rubbed the pads off his horns. Then he rose, dancing on those wonderful feet that twinkled, and he said: 'Now, my friends, the buttons are off the foils. Who begins?' We understood. We finished at once. He was turned out again on the pastures till it should be time to amuse them at our little metropolis. But, some time before he went to

Arles – yes, I think I have it correctly – Christophe, who had been out on the Crau, informed me that Apis had assassinated a young bull who had given signs of developing into a rival. That happens, of course, and our herdsmen should prevent it. But Apis had killed in his own style – at dusk, from the ambush of a wind-break – by an oblique charge from behind which knocked the other over. He had then disembowelled him. All very possible, *but* – the murder accomplished – Apis went to the bank of a wind-break, knelt, and carefully, as he had in our yard, cleaned his horns in the earth. Christophe, who had never seen such a thing, at once borrowed (do you know, it is most efficacious when taken that way?) some Holy Water from our little chapel in those pastures, sprinkled Apis (whom it did not affect), and rode in to tell me. It was obvious that a thinker of that bull's type would also be meticulous in his toilette; so, when he was sent to Arles, I warned our consignees to exercise caution with him. Happily, the change of scene, the music, the general attention, and the meeting again with old friends – all our bad boys attended – agreeably distracted him. He became for the time a pure *farceur* again; but his wheelings, his rushes, his rat-huntings were more superb than ever. There was in them now, you understand, a breadth of technique that comes of reasoned art, and, above all, the passion that arrives after experience. Oh, he had learned, out there on the Crau! At the end of his little turn, he was, according to local rules, to be handled in all respects except for the sword, which was a stick, as a professional bull who must die. He was manoeuvred into, or he posed himself in, the proper attitude; made his rush; received the point on his shoulder and then – turned about and cantered toward the door by which he had entered the arena. He said to the world: 'My friends, the representation is ended. I thank you for your applause. I go to repose myself.' But our Arlesians, who are – not so clever as some, demanded an encore, and Apis was headed back again. We others from his country, we knew what would happen. He went to the centre of the ring, kneeled, and, slowly, with full parade, plunged his horns alternately in the dirt till the pads came off. Christophe shouts: 'Leave him alone, you straight-nosed imbeciles! Leave him before you must.' But they required emotion; for Rome has always debauched her loved Provincia with bread and circuses. It was given. Have you, Monsieur, ever seen a servant, with pan and broom, sweeping round the base-board of a room? In a half-minute Apis has them all swept out and over the barrier. Then he demands once more that the door shall be opened to him. It is opened and he retires as though – which, truly, is the case – loaded with laurels."

Monsieur Voiron refilled the glasses, and allowed himself a cigarette, which he puffed for some time.

"And afterwards?" I said.

"I am arranging it in my mind. It is difficult to do it justice. Afterwards – yes, afterwards – Apis returned to his pastures and his mistresses and I to my business. I am no longer a scandalous old 'sportif' in shirt-sleeves howling encouragement to the yellow son of a cow. I revert to Voiron Frères – wines, chemical manures, *et cetera*. And next year, through some chicane which I have not the leisure to unravel, and also, thanks to our patriarchal system of paying our older men out of the increase of the herds, old Christophe possesses himself of Apis. Oh, yes, he proves it through descent from a certain cow that my father had given his father before the Republic. Beware, Monsieur, of the memory of the illiterate man! An ancestor of Christophe had been a soldier under our Soult against your Beresford, near Bayonne. He fell into the hands of Spanish guerrillas. Christophe and his wife used to tell me the details on certain Saints' Days when I was a child. Now, as compared with our recent war, Soult's campaign and retreat across the Bidassoa —"

"But did you allow Christophe just to annex the bull?" I demanded.

"You do not know Christophe. He had sold him to the Spaniards before he informed me. The Spaniards pay in coin

– douros of very pure silver. Our peasants mistrust our paper. You know the saying: 'A thousand francs paper; eight hundred metal, and the cow is yours.' Yes, Christophe sold Apis, who was then two and a half years old, and to Christophe's knowledge thrice at least an assassin."

"How was that?" I said.

"Oh, his own kind only; and always, Christophe told me, by the same oblique rush from behind, the same sideways overthrow, and the same swift disembowelment, followed by this levitical cleaning of the horns. In human life he would have kept a manicurist – this Minotaur. And so, Apis disappears from our country. That does not trouble me. I know in due time I shall be advised. Why? Because, in this land, Monsieur, not a hoof moves between Berre and the Saintes Maries without the knowledge of specialists such as Christophe. The beasts are the substance and the drama of their lives to them. So when Christophe tells me, a little before Easter Sunday, that Apis makes his début in the bull-ring of a small Catalan town on the road to Barcelona, it is only to pack my car and trundle there across the frontier with him. The place lacked importance and manufactures, but it had produced a matador of some reputation, who was condescending to show his art in his native town. They were even running one special train to the place. Now our French railway system is only execrable, but the Spanish —"

"You went down by road, didn't you?" said I.

"Naturally. It was not too good. Villamarti was the matador's name. He proposed to kill two bulls for the honour of his birthplace. Apis, Christophe told me, would be his second. It was an interesting trip, and that little city by the sea was ravishing. Their bull-ring dates from the middle of the seventeenth century. It is full of feeling. The ceremonial too – when the horsemen enter and ask the Mayor in his box to throw down the keys of the bull-ring – that was exquisitely conceived. You know, if the keys are caught in the horseman's hat, it is considered a good omen. They were perfectly caught. Our seats were in the front row beside the gates where the bulls enter, so we saw everything.

Villamarti's first bull was not too badly killed. The second matador, whose name escapes me, killed his without distinction – a foil to Villamarti. And the third, Chisto, a laborious, middle-aged professional who had never risen beyond a certain dull competence, was equally of the background. Oh, they are as jealous as the girls of the Comédie Française, these matadors! Villamarti's troupe stood ready for his second bull. The gates opened, and we saw Apis, beautifully balanced on his feet, peer coquettishly round the corner, as though he were at home. A picador – a mounted man with the long lance-goad – stood near the barrier on his right. He had not even troubled to turn his horse, for the capeadors – the men with the cloaks – were advancing to play Apis – to feel his psychology and intentions, according to the rules that are made for bulls who do not think . . . I did not realise the murder before it was accomplished! The wheel, the rush, the oblique charge from behind, the fall of horse and man were simultaneous. Apis leaped the horse, with whom he had no quarrel, and alighted, all four feet together (it was enough), between the man's shoulders, changed his beautiful feet on the carcass, and was away, pretending to fall nearly on his nose. Do you follow me? In that instant, by that stumble, he produced the impression that his adorable assassination was a mere bestial blunder. Then, Monsieur, I began to comprehend that it was an artist we had to deal with. He did not stand over the body to draw the rest of the troupe. He chose to reserve that trick. He let the attendants bear out the dead, and went on to amuse himself among the capeadors. Now to Apis, trained among our children in the yards, the cloak was simply a guide to the boy behind it. He pursued, you understand, the person, not the propaganda – the proprietor, not the journal. If a third of our electors of France were as wise, my friend! . . . But it was done leisurely, with humour and a touch of truculence. He romped after one man's cloak as a clumsy dog might do, but I observed that he kept the man on his terrible left side. Christophe whispered to me: 'Wait for his mother's kick. When he has made the fellow confident it will arrive.' It arrived in the middle of a gambol. My God! He lashed out in the air as he frisked. The man dropped like a sack, lifted one hand a little towards his head, and – that was all. So you see, a body was again at his disposition; a second time the cloaks ran up to draw him off, but, a second time, Apis refused his grand scene. A second time he acted that his murder was accident and – he convinced his audience! It was as though he had knocked over a bridge-gate in the marshes by mistake. Unbelievable? I saw it."

The memory sent Monsieur Voiron again to the champagne, and I accompanied him.

"But Apis was not the sole artist present. They say Villamarti comes of a family of actors. I saw him regard Apis with a new eye. He, too, began to understand. He took his cloak and moved out to play him before they should bring on another picador. He had his reputation. Perhaps Apis knew it. Perhaps Villamarti reminded him of some boy with whom he had practised at home. At any rate Apis permitted it – up to a certain point; but he did not allow Villamarti the stage. He cramped him throughout. He dived and plunged clumsily and slowly, but always with menace and always closing in. We could see that the man was conforming to the bull – not the bull to the man; for Apis was playing him towards the centre of the ring, and, in a little while – I watched his face – Villamarti knew it. But I could not fathom the creature's motive. 'Wait,' said old Christophe. 'He wants that picador on the white horse yonder. When he reaches his proper distance he will get him. Villamarti is his cover. He used me once that way.' And so it was, my friend! With the clang of one of our own Seventy-fives, Apis dismissed Villamarti with his chest – breasted him over – and had arrived at his objective near the barrier. The same oblique charge; the head carried low for the sweep of the horns; the immense sideways fall of the horse, broken-legged and half-paralysed; the senseless man on the ground, and – behold Apis between them, backed against the barrier – his right covered by the horse; his left by the body of the man at his feet. The simplicity of it! Lacking the carts and tractors of his early parade-grounds he, being a genius, had extemporised with the materials at hand, and dug himself in. The troupe closed up again, their left wing broken by the kicking horse, their right immobilised by the man's body which Apis bestrode with significance. Villamarti almost threw himself between the horns, but – it was more an appeal than an attack. Apis refused him. He held his base. A picador was sent at him – necessarily from the front, which alone was open. Apis charged – he who, till then, you realise, had not used the horn! The horse went over backwards, the man half beneath him. Apis halted, hooked him under the heart, and threw him to the barrier. We heard his head crack, but he was dead before he hit the wood. There was no demonstration from the audience. They, also, had begun to realise this Foch among bulls! The arena occupied itself again with the dead. Two of the troupe irresolutely tried to play him – God knows in what hope! – but he moved out to the centre of the ring. 'Look!' said Christophe. 'Now he goes to clean himself. That always frightened me.' He knelt down; he began to clean his horns. The earth was hard. He worried at it in an ecstasy of absorption. As he laid his head along and rattled his ears, it was as though he were interrogating the Devils themselves upon their secrets, and always saying impatiently: 'Yes, I know that – and *that* – and *that*! Tell me more – *more*!' In the silence that covered us, a woman cried: 'He digs a grave! Oh, Saints, he digs a grave!' Some others echoed this – not loudly – as a wave echoes in a grotto of the sea.

"And when his horns were cleaned, he rose up and studied poor Villamarti's troupe, eyes in eyes, one by one, with the gravity of an equal in intellect and the remote and merciless resolution of a master in his art. This was more terrifying than his toilette."

"And they – Villamarti's men?" I asked.

"Like the audience, were dominated. They had ceased to

posture, or stamp, or address insults to him. They conformed to him. The two other matadors stared. Only Chisto, the oldest, broke silence with some call or other, and Apis turned his head towards him. Otherwise he was isolated, immobile – sombre – meditating on those at his mercy. Ah!

"For some reason the trumpet sounded for the *bandilleras* – those gay hooked darts that are planted in the shoulders of bulls who do not think, after their neck-muscles are tired by lifting horses. When such bulls feel the pain, they check for an instant, and, in that instant, the men step gracefully aside. Villamarti's bandillero answered the trumpet mechanically – like one condemned. He stood out, poised the darts and stammered the usual patter of invitation . . . And after? I do not assert that Apis shrugged his shoulders, but he reduced the episode to its lowest elements, as could only a bull of Gaul. With his truculence was mingled always – owing to the shortness of his tail – a certain Rabelaisian abandon, especially when viewed from the rear. Christophe had often commented upon it. Now, Apis brought that quality into play. He circulated round that boy, forcing him to break up his beautiful poses. He studied him from various angles, like an incompetent photographer. He presented to him every portion of his anatomy except his shoulders. At intervals he feigned to run in upon him. My God, he was cruel! But his motive was obvious. He was playing for a laugh from the spectators which should synchronise with the fracture of the human morale. It was achieved. The boy turned and ran towards the barrier. Apis was on him before the laugh ceased; passed him; headed him – what do I say? – herded him off to the left, his horns beside and a little in front of his chest: he did not intend him to escape into refuge. Some of the troupe would have closed in, but Villamarti cried: 'If he wants him he will take him. Stand!' They stood. Whether the boy slipped or Apis nosed him over I could not see. But he dropped, sobbing. Apis halted like a car with four brakes, struck a pose, smelt him very completely and turned away. It was dismissal more ignominious than degradation at the head of one's battalion. The representation was finished. Remained only for Apis to clear his stage of the subordinate characters.

"Ah! His gesture then! He gave a dramatic start – this Cyrano of the Camargue – as though he was aware of them for the first time. He moved. All their beautiful breeches twinkled for an instant along the top of the barrier. He held the stage alone! But Christophe and I, we trembled! For, observe, he had now involved himself in a stupendous drama of which he only could supply the third act. And, except for an audience on the razor-edge of emotion, he had exhausted his material. Molière himself – we have forgotten, my friend, to drink to the health of that great soul – might have been at a loss. And Tragedy is but a step behind Failure. We could see the four or five Civil Guards, who are sent always to keep order, fingering the breeches of their rifles. They were but waiting a word from the Mayor to fire on him, as they do sometimes at a bull who leaps the barrier among the spectators. They would, of course, have killed or wounded several people – but that would not have saved Apis."

Monsieur Voiron drowned the thought at once, and wiped his beard.

"At that moment Fate – the Genius of France, if you will – sent to assist in the incomparable finale, none other than Chisto, the eldest, and I should have said (but never again will I judge!) the least inspired of all; mediocrity itself but, at heart – and it is the heart that conquers always, my friend – at heart an artist. He descended stiffly into the arena, alone and assured. Apis regarded him, his eyes in his eyes. The man took stance, with his cloak, and called to the bull as to an equal: 'Now, Señor, we will show these honourable caballeros something together.' He advanced thus against this thinker who at a plunge – a kick – a thrust – could, we all knew, have extinguished him. My dear friend, I wish I could convey to you something of the unaffected bonhomie, the humour, the delicacy, the consideration bordering on respect even, with which Apis, the supreme artist, responded to this invitation. It was the Master, wearied after a strenuous hour in the atelier, unbuttoned and at ease with some not inexpert but limited disciple. The telepathy was instantaneous between them. And for good reason! Christophe said to me: 'All's well. That Chisto began among the bulls. I was sure of it when I heard him call just now. He has been a herdsman. He'll pull it off.' There was a little feeling and adjustment, at first, for mutual distances and allowances.

"Oh, yes! And here occurred a gross impertinence of Villamarti. He had, after an interval, followed Chisto – to retrieve his reputation. My Faith! I can conceive the elder Dumas slamming his door on an intruder precisely as Apis did. He raced Villamarti into the nearest refuge at once. He stamped his feet outside it, and he snorted: 'Go! I am engaged with an artist.' Villamarti went – his reputation left behind for ever.

"Apis returned to Chisto saying: 'Forgive the interruption. I am not always master of my time, but you were about to observe, my dear confrère . . .?' Then the play began. Out of compliment to Chisto, Apis chose as his objective (every bull varies in this respect) the inner edge of the cloak – that nearest to the man's body. This allows but a few millimetres clearance in charging. But Apis trusted himself as Chisto trusted him, and, this time, he conformed to the man, with inimitable judgement and temper. He allowed himself to be played into the shadow or the sun, as the delighted audience demanded. He raged enormously; he feigned defeat; he despaired in statuesque abandon, and thence flashed into fresh paroxysms of wrath – but always with the detachment of the true artist who knows he is but the vessel of an emotion whence others, not he, must drink. And never once did he forget that honest Chisto's cloak was to him the gauge by which to spare even a hair on the skin. He inspired Chisto too. My God! His youth returned to that meritorious beef-sticker – the desire, the grace, and the beauty of his early dreams. One could almost see that girl of the past for whom he was rising, rising to these present heights of skill and daring. It was his hour too – a miraculous hour of dawn returned to gild the sunset. All he knew was at Apis' disposition. Apis acknowledged it with all that he had learned at home, at Arles and in his lonely murders on our grazing-grounds. He flowed round Chisto like a river of death – round his knees, leaping at his shoulders, kicking just clear of one side or the other of his head; behind his back hissing as he shaved by; and once or twice – inimitable! – he reared wholly up before him while Chisto slipped back from beneath the avalanche of that instructed body. Those two, my dear friend, held five thousand people dumb with no sound but of their breathings – regular as pumps. It was unbearable. Beast and man realised together that we needed a change of note – a *détente*. They relaxed to pure buffoonery. Chisto fell back and talked to him outrageously. Apis pretended he had never heard such language. The audience howled with delight. Chisto slapped him; he took liberties with his short tail, to the end of which he clung while Apis pirouetted; he played about him in all postures; he had become the herdsman again – gross, careless, brutal, but comprehending. Yet Apis was always the more consummate clown. All that time (Christophe and I saw it) Apis drew off towards the gates of the *toril* where so many bulls enter but – have you ever heard of one that returned? *We* knew that Apis knew that as he had saved Chisto, so Chisto would save him. Life is sweet to us all; to the artist who lives many lives in one, sweetest. Chisto did not fail him. At the last, when none could laugh any longer, the man threw his cape across the bull's back, his arm round his neck. He flung up a hand at the gate, as Villamarti, young and commanding but *not* a herdsman, might have raised it, and he cried: 'Gentlemen, open to me and my honourable little donkey.' They opened – I have misjudged Spaniards in my time! – those gates opened to the man and the bull together, and closed behind them. And then? From the Mayor to the Guarda Civile they went mad for five minutes, till the trumpets blew and the fifth bull rushed out – an unthinking black Andalusian. I suppose someone killed him. My friend, my very dear friend, to whom I have opened my heart, I confess that I did not watch. Christophe and I, we were weeping together like children of the same Mother. Shall we drink to Her?"

* * *

ALNASCHAR AND THE OXEN

There's a pasture in a valley where the hanging woods divide,
    And a Herd lies down and ruminates in peace;
Where the pheasant rules the nooning, and the owl the twilight tide,
    And the war-cries of our world die out and cease.
Here I cast aside the burden that each weary week-day brings
    And, delivered from the shadows I pursue,
On peaceful, postless Sabbaths I consider Weighty Things –
    Such as Sussex Cattle feeding in the dew!

At the gate beside the river where the trouty shallows brawl,
    I know the pride that Lobengula felt,
When he bade the bars be lowered of the Royal Cattle Kraal,
    And fifteen mile of oxen took the veldt.
From the walls of Bulawayo in unbroken file they came
    To where the Mount of Council cuts the blue . . .
I have only six and twenty, but the principle's the same
    With my Sussex Cattle feeding in the dew!

To a luscious sound of tearing, where the clovered herbage rips,
    Level-backed and level-bellied watch 'em move –
See those shoulders, guess that heart-girth, praise those loins, admire those hips,
    And the tail set low for flesh to make above!
Count the broad unblemished muzzles, test the kindly mellow skin
    And, where yon heifer lifts her head at call,
Mark the bosom's just abundance 'neath the gay and clean-cut chin,
    And those eyes of Juno, overlooking all!

Here is colour, form and substance! I will put it to the proof
   And, next season, in my lodges shall be born
Some very Bull of Mithras, flawless from his agate hoof
   To his even-branching, ivory, dusk-tipped horn.
He shall mate with block-square virgins – kings shall seek his
     like in vain,
   While I multiply his stock a thousandfold,
Till an hungry world extol me, builder of a lofty strain
   That turns one standard ton at two years old!

There's a valley, under oakwood, where a man may dream his
   dream,
   In the milky breath of cattle laid at ease,
Till the moon o'ertops the alders, and her image chills the stream,
   And the river-mist runs silver round their knees!
Now the footpaths fade and vanish; now the ferny clumps deceive;
   Now the hedgerow-folk possess their fields anew;
Now the Herd is lost in darkness, and I bless them as I leave,
   My Sussex Cattle feeding in the dew!

A MADONNA OF THE TRENCHES

A MADONNA OF THE TRENCHES

***

GIPSY VANS

Unless you come of the gipsy stock
   That steals by night and day,
Lock your heart with a double lock
   And throw the key away.
Bury it under the blackest stone
   Beneath your father's hearth,
And keep your eyes on your lawful own
   And your feet to the proper path.
    Then you can stand at your door and mock
      When the gipsy-vans come through . . .
    For it isn't right that the Gorgio stock
      Should live as the Romany do.

Unless you come of the gipsy blood
   That takes and never spares,
Bide content with your given good
   And follow your own affairs.
Plough and harrow and roll your land,
   And sow what ought to be sowed;
But never let loose your heart from your hand,
   Nor flitter it down the road!
    Then you can thrive on your boughten food
      As the gipsy-vans come through . . .
    For it isn't nature the Gorgio blood
      Should love as the Romany do.

Unless you carry the gipsy eyes
   That see but seldom weep,
Keep your head from the naked skies
   Or the stars'll trouble your sleep.
Watch your moon through your window-pane
   And take what weather she brews;

777

But don't run out in the midnight rain
  Nor home in the morning dews.

Then you can huddle and shut your eyes
  As the gipsy-vans come through . . .
For it isn't fitting the Gorgio ryes
  Should walk as the Romany do.

Unless you come of the gipsy race
  That counts all time the same,
Be you careful of Time and Place
  And Judgment and Good Name:
Lose your life for to live your life
  The way that you ought to do;
And when you are finished, your God and your wife
  And the Gipsies 'll laugh at you!
    Then you can rot in your burying-place
      As the gipsy-vans come through . . .
    For it isn't reason the Gorgio race
      Should die as the Romany do.

* * *

Whatever a man of the sons of men
  Shall say to his heart of the lords above,
They have shown man, verily, once and again,
  Marvellous mercy and infinite love.

O sweet one love, O my life's delight,
  Dear, though the days have divided us,
Lost beyond hope, taken far out of sight,
  Not twice in the world shall the Gods do thus.
              Swinburne, "Les Noyades."

Seeing how many unstable ex-soldiers came to the Lodge of
Instruction (attached to Faith and Works E.C. 5837) in the
years after the war, the wonder is there was not more trouble
from Brethren whom sudden meetings with old comrades
jerked back into their still raw past. But our round, torpedo-

bearded local Doctor – Brother Keede, Senior Warden – always stood ready to deal with hysteria before it got out of hand; and when I examined Brethren unknown or imperfectly vouched for on the Masonic side, I passed on to him anything that seemed doubtful. He had had his experience as medical officer of a South London Battalion, during the last two years of the war; and, naturally, often found friends and acquaintances among the visitors.

Brother C. Strangwick, a young, tallish, new-made Brother, hailed from some South London Lodge. His papers and his answers were above suspicion, but his red-rimmed eyes had a puzzled glare that might mean nerves. So I introduced him particularly to Keede, who discovered in him a Headquarters Orderly of his old Battalion, congratulated him on his return to fitness – he had been discharged for some infirmity or other – and plunged at once into Somme memories.

"I hope I did right, Keede," I said when we were robing before Lodge.

"Oh, quite. He reminded me that I had him under my hands at Sampoux in 'Eighteen, when he went to bits. He was a Runner."

"Was it shock?" I asked.

"Of sorts – but not what he wanted me to think it was. No, he wasn't shamming. He had Jumps to the limit – but he played up to mislead me about the reason of 'em . . . Well, if we could stop patients from lying, medicine would be too easy, I suppose."

I noticed that, after Lodge-working, Keede gave him a seat a couple of rows in front of us, that he might enjoy a lecture on the Orientation of King Solomon's Temple, which an earnest Brother thought would be a nice interlude between labour and the high tea that we called our "Banquet." Even helped by tobacco it was a dreary performance. About half-way through, Strangwick, who had been fidgeting and twitching for some minutes, rose, drove back his chair grinding across the tesselated floor, and yelped: "Oh, My Aunt! I can't stand this any longer." Under cover of a general laugh of assent he brushed past us and stumbled towards the door.

"I thought so!" Keede whispered to me. "Come along!" We overtook him in the passage, crowing hysterically and wringing his hands. Keede led him into the Tyler's Room, a small office where we stored odds and ends of regalia and furniture, and locked the door.

"I'm – I'm all right," the boy began, piteously.

" 'Course you are." Keede opened a small cupboard which I had seen called upon before, mixed sal volatile and water in a graduated glass, and, as Strangwick drank, pushed him gently on to an old sofa. "There," he went on. "It's nothing to write home about. I've seen you ten times worse. I expect our talk has brought things back."

He hooked up a chair behind him with one foot, held the patient's hands in his own, and sat down. The chair creaked.

"Don't!" Strangwick squealed. "I can't stand it! There's nothing on earth creaks like they do! And – and when it thaws we – we've got to slap 'em back with a spa-ade! 'Remember those Frenchmen's little boots under the duck-boards? . . . What'll I do? What'll I do about it?"

Someone knocked at the door, to know if all were well.

"Oh, quite, thanks!" said Keede over his shoulder. "But I shall need this room awhile. Draw the curtains, please."

We heard the rings of the hangings that drape the passage from Lodge to Banquet Room click along their poles, and what sound there had been, of feet and voices, was shut off.

Strangwick, retching impotently, complained of the frozen dead who creak in the frost.

"He's playing up still," Keede whispered. "*That's* not his real trouble – any more than 'twas last time."

"But surely," I replied, "men get those things on the brain pretty badly. 'Remember in October —"

"This chap hasn't, though. I wonder what's really helling him. What are you thinking of?" said Keede peremptorily.

"French End an' Butcher's Row," Strangwick muttered.

"Yes, there were a few there. But, suppose we face Bogey

instead of giving him best every time." Keede turned towards me with a hint in his eye that I was to play up to his leads.

"What was the trouble with French End?" I opened at a venture.

"It was a bit by Sampoux, that we had taken over from the French. They're tough, but you wouldn't call 'em tidy as a nation. They had faced both sides of it with dead to keep the mud back. All those trenches were like gruel in a thaw. Our people had to do the same sort of thing – elsewhere; but Butcher's Row in French End was the – er – showpiece. Luckily, we pinched a salient from Jerry just then, an' straightened things out – so we didn't need to use the Row after November. You remember, Strangwick?"

"My God, yes! When the duckboard-slats were missin' you'd tread on 'em, an' they'd creak."

"They're bound to. Like leather," said Keede. "It gets on one's nerves a bit, but —"

"Nerves? It's real! It's real!" Strangwick gulped.

"But at your time of life, it'll all fall behind you in a year or so. I'll give you another sip of – paregoric, an' we'll face it quietly. Shall we?"

Keede opened his cupboard again and administered a carefully dropped dark dose of something that was not sal volatile. "This'll settle you in a few minutes," he explained. "Lie still, an' don't talk unless you feel like it."

He faced me, fingering his beard.

"Ye-es. Butcher's Row wasn't pretty," he volunteered. "Seeing Strangwick here, has brought it all back to me again. 'Funny thing! We had a Platoon Sergeant of Number Two – what the deuce was his name? – an elderly bird who must have lied like a patriot to get out to the front at his age; but he was a first-class Non-Com., and the last person, you'd think, to make mistakes. Well, he was due for a fortnight's home leave in January, 'Eighteen. You were at B.H.Q. then, Strangwick, weren't you?"

"Yes. I was Orderly. It was January twenty-first"; Strangwick spoke with a thickish tongue, and his eyes burned. Whatever drug it was, had taken hold.

"About then," Keede said. "Well, this Sergeant, instead of coming down from the trenches the regular way an' joinin' Battalion Details after dark, an' takin' that funny little train for Arras, thinks he'll warm himself first. So he gets into a dug-out, in Butcher's Row, that used to be an old French dressing-station, and fugs up between a couple of braziers of pure charcoal! As luck 'ud have it, that was the only dug-out with an inside door opening inwards – some French anti-gas fitting, I expect – and, by what we could make out, the door must have swung to while he was warming. Anyhow, he didn't turn up at the train. There was a search at once. We couldn't afford to waste Platoon Sergeants. We found him in the morning. He'd got his gas all right. A machine-gunner reported him, didn't he, Strangwick?"

"No, sir. Corporal Grant – o' the Trench Mortars."

"So it was. Yes, Grant – the man with that little wen on his neck. 'Nothing wrong with your memory, at any rate. What was the Sergeant's name?"

"Godsoe – John Godsoe," Strangwick answered.

"Yes, that was it. I had to see him next mornin' – frozen stiff between the two braziers – and not a scrap of private papers on him. *That* was the only thing that made me think it mightn't have been – quite an accident."

Strangwick's relaxing face set, and he threw back at once to the Orderly Room manner.

"I give my evidence – at the time – to you, sir. He passed – overtook me, I should say – comin' down from supports, after I'd warned him for leaf. I thought he was goin' through Parrot Trench as usual; but 'e must 'ave turned off into French End where the old bombed barricade was."

"Yes. I remember now. You were the last man to see him alive. That was on the twenty-first of January, you say? Now, *when* was it that Dearlove and Billings brought you to me – clean out of your head?" . . . Keede dropped his hand, in the style of magazine detectives, on Strangwick's shoulder. The boy looked at him with cloudy wonder, and muttered: "I was took to you on the evenin' of the twenty-fourth of January. But you don't think I did him in, do you?"

I could not help smiling at Keede's discomfiture; but he recovered himself. "Then what the dickens *was* on your mind that evening – before I gave you the hypodermic?"

"The – the things in Butcher's Row. They kept on comin' over me. You've seen me like this before, sir."

"But I knew that it was a lie. You'd no more got stiffs on the brain then than you have now. You've got something, but you're hiding it."

" 'Ow do *you* know, Doctor?" Strangwick whimpered.

"D'you remember what you said to me, when Dearlove and Billings were holding you down that evening?"

"About the things in Butcher's Row?"

"Oh, no! You spun me a lot of stuff about corpses creaking; but you let yourself go in the middle of it – when you pushed that telegram at me. What did you mean, f'rinstance, by asking what advantage it was for you to fight beasts of officers if the dead didn't rise?"

"Did I say 'Beasts of Officers'?"

"You did. It's out of the Burial Service."

"I suppose, then, I must have heard it. As a matter of fact, I 'ave." Strangwick shuddered extravagantly.

"Probably. And there's another thing – that hymn you were shouting till I put you under. It was something about Mercy and Love. 'Remember it?"

"I'll try," said the boy obediently, and began to paraphrase, as nearly as possible thus: " 'Whatever a man may say in his heart unto the Lord, yea verily I say unto you – Gawd hath shown man, again and again, marvellous mercy an' – an' somethin' or other love.' " He screwed up his eyes and shook.

"Now where did you get *that* from?" Keede insisted.

"From Godsoe – on the twenty-first Jan. . . . 'Ow could *I* tell what 'e meant to do?" he burst out in a high, unnatural key – "Any more than I knew *she* was dead."

"Who was dead?" said Keede.

"Me Auntie Armine."

"The one the telegram came to you about, at Sampoux, that you wanted me to explain – the one that you were talking of in the passage out here just now when you began: 'O Auntie,' and changed it to 'O Gawd,' when I collared you?"

"That's her! I haven't a chance with you, Doctor. *I* didn't know there was anything wrong with those braziers. How could I? We're always usin' 'em. Honest to God, I thought at first go–off he might wish to warm himself before the leaf-train. I – I didn't know Uncle John meant to start – 'ouse-keepin'." He laughed horribly, and then the dry tears came.

Keede waited for them to pass in sobs and hiccoughs before he continued: "Why? Was Godsoe your Uncle?"

"No," said Strangwick, his head between his hands. "Only we'd known him ever since we were born. Dad 'ad known him before that. He lived almost next street to us. Him an' Dad an' Ma an' – an' the rest had always been friends. So we called him Uncle – like children do."

"What sort of man was he?"

"One o' *the* best, sir. 'Pensioned Sergeant with a little money left him – quite independent – and very superior. They had a sittin'-room full o' Indian curios that him and his wife used to let sister an' me see when we'd been good."

"Wasn't he rather old to join up?"

"That made no odds to him. He joined up as Sergeant Instructor at the first go–off, an' when the Battalion was ready he got 'imself sent along. He wangled me into 'is Platoon when I went out – early in 'Seventeen. Because Ma wanted it, I suppose."

"I'd no notion you knew him that well," was Keede's comment.

"Oh, it made no odds to him. He 'ad no pets in the Platoon, but 'e'd write 'ome to Ma about me an' all the doin's. You see" – Strangwick stirred uneasily on the sofa –

"we'd known him all our lives – lived in the next street an' all . . . An' him well over fifty. Oh dear me! *Oh* dear me! What a bloody mix-up things are, when one's as young as me!" he wailed of a sudden.

But Keede held him to the point. "He wrote to your mother about you?"

"Yes. Ma's eyes had gone bad followin' on air-raids. 'Blood-vessels broke behind 'em from sittin' in cellars an' bein' sick. She had to 'ave 'er letters read to her by Auntie. Now I think of it, that was the only thing that you might have called anything at all —"

"Was that the Aunt that died, and that you got the wire about?" Keede drove on.

"Yes – Auntie Armine – Ma's younger sister, an' she nearer fifty than forty. What a mix-up! An' if I'd been asked any time about it, I'd 'ave sworn there wasn't a single sol'tary item concernin' her that everybody didn't know an' hadn't known all along. No more conceal to her doin's than – than so much shop-front. She'd looked after sister an' me, when needful – hoopin' cough an' measles – just the same as Ma. We was in an' out of her house like rabbits. You see, Uncle Armine is a cabinet-maker, an' second-'and furniture, an' we liked playin' with the things. She 'ad no children, and when the war came, she said she was glad of it. But she never talked much of her feelin's. She kept herself to herself, you understand." He stared most earnestly at us to help out our understandings.

"What was she like?" Keede inquired.

"A biggish woman, an' had been 'andsome, I believe, but, bein' used to her, we two didn't notice much – except, per'aps, for one thing. Ma called her 'er proper name, which was Bella; but Sis an' me always called 'er Auntie Armine. See?"

"What for?"

"We thought it sounded more like her – like somethin' movin' slow, in armour."

"Oh! And she read your letters to your mother, did she?"

"Every time the post came in she'd slip across the road from opposite an' read 'em. An' – an' I'll go bail for it that that was all there was to it for as far back as *I* remember. Was I to swing tomorrow, I'd go bail for *that*! 'Tisn't fair of 'em to 'ave unloaded it all on me, because – because – if the dead *do* rise, why, what in 'ell becomes of me an' all I've believed all me life? I want to know *that*! I – I —"

But Keede would not be put off. "Did the Sergeant give you away at all in his letters?" he demanded, very quietly.

"There was nothin' to give away – we was too busy – but his letters about me were a great comfort to Ma. I'm no good at writin'. I saved it all up for my leafs. I got me fourteen days every six months an' one over . . . I was luckier than most, that way."

"And when you came home, used you to bring 'em news about the Sergeant?" said Keede.

"I expect I must have; but I didn't think much of it at the time. I was took up with me own affairs – naturally. Uncle John always wrote to me once each leaf, tellin' me what was doin' an' what I was li'ble to expect on return, an' Ma 'ud 'ave that read to her. Then o' course I had to slip over to his wife an' pass her the news. An' then there was the young lady that I'd thought of marryin' if I came through. We'd got as far as pricin' things in the windows together."

"And you didn't marry her – after all?"

Another tremor shook the boy. "*No!*" he cried. " 'Fore it ended, I knew what reel things reelly mean! I – I never dreamed such things could be! . . . An' she nearer fifty than forty an' me own Aunt! . . . But there wasn't a sign nor a hint from first to last, so 'ow *could* I tell? Don't you *see* it? All she said to me after me Christmas leaf in '18, when I come to say goodbye – all Auntie Armine said to me was: 'You'll be seein' Mister Godsoe soon?' 'Too soon for my likings,' I says. 'Well then, tell 'im from me,' she says, 'that I expect to be through with my little trouble by the twenty-first of next month, an' I'm dyin' to see him as soon as possible after that date.' "

"What sort of trouble was it?" Keede turned professional at once.

"She'd 'ad a bit of a gatherin' in 'er breast, I believe. But she never talked of 'er body much to any one."

"*I* see," said Keede. "And she said to you?"

Strangwick repeated: " 'Tell Uncle John I hope to be finished of my drawback by the twenty-first, an' I'm dying to see 'im as soon as 'e can after that date.' An' then she says, laughin': 'But you've a head like a sieve. I'll write it down, an' you can give it him when you see 'im.' So she wrote it on a bit o' paper an' I kissed 'er goodbye – I was always her favourite, you see – an' I went back to Sampoux. The thing hardly stayed in my mind at all, d'you see. But the next time I was up in the front line – I was a Runner, d'ye see – our platoon was in North Bay Trench an' I was up with a message to the Trench Mortar there that Corporal Grant was in charge of. Followin' on receipt of it, he borrowed a couple of men off the platoon, to slue 'er round or somethin'. I give Uncle John Auntie Armine's paper, an' I give Grant a fag, an' we warmed up a bit over a brazier. Then Grant says to me: 'I don't like it'; an' he jerks 'is thumb at Uncle John in the bay studyin' Auntie's message. Well, *you* know, sir, you had to speak to Grant about 'is way of prophesyin' things – after Rankine shot himself with the Very light."

"I did," said Keede, and he explained to me: "Grant had the Second Sight – confound him! It upset the men. I was glad when he got pipped. What happened after that, Strangwick?"

"Grant whispers to me: 'Look, you damned Englishman. 'E's for it.' Uncle John was leanin' up against the bay, an' hummin' that hymn I was tryin' to tell you just now. He looked different all of a sudden – as if 'e'd got shaved. *I* don't know anything of these things, but I cautioned Grant as to his style of speakin', if an officer 'ad 'eard him, an' I went on. Passin' Uncle John in the bay, 'e nods an' smiles, which he didn't often, an' he says, pocketin' the paper: 'This suits *me*. I'm for leaf on the twenty-first, too.' "

"He said that to you, did he?" said Keede.

"*Pre*cisely the same as passin' the time o' day. O' course I returned the agreeable about hopin' he'd get it, an' in due course I returned to 'Eadquarters. The thing 'ardly stayed in my mind a minute. That was the eleventh January – three days after I'd come back from leaf. You remember, sir, there wasn't anythin' doin' either side round Sampoux the first part o' the month. Jerry was gettin' ready for his March Push, an' as long as he kept quiet, we didn't want to poke 'im up."

"I remember that," said Keede. "But what about the Sergeant?"

"I must have met him, on an' off, I expect, goin' up an' down, through the ensuin' days, but it didn't stay in me mind. Why needed it? And on the twenty-first Jan., his name was on the leaf-paper when I went up to warn the leaf-men. I noticed *that*, o' course. Now that very afternoon Jerry 'ad been tryin' a new trench-mortar, an' before our 'Eavies could out it, he'd got a stinker into a bay an' mopped up 'alf a dozen. They were bringin' 'em down when I went up to the supports, an' that blocked Little Parrot, same as it always did. *You* remember, sir?"

"Rather! And there was that big machine-gun behind the Half-House waiting for you if you got out," said Keede.

"I remembered that too. But it was just on dark an' the fog was comin' off the Canal, so I hopped out of Little Parrot an' cut across the open to where those four dead Warwicks are heaped up. But the fog turned me around, an' the next thing I knew I was knee-over in that old 'alf-trench that runs west o' Little Parrot into French End. I dropped into it – almost atop o' the machine-gun platform by the side o' the old sugar boiler an' the two Zoo-ave skel'tons. That gave me my bearin's, an' so I went through French End, all up those missin' duckboards, into Butcher's Row where the *poy-looz* was laid in six deep each side, an' stuffed under the duckboards. It had froze tight, an' the drippin's had stopped, an' the creakin's had begun."

"Did that really worry you at the time?" Keede asked.

"No," said the boy with professional scorn. "If a Runner starts noticin' such things he'd better chuck. In the middle of the Row, just before the old dressin'-station you referred to, sir, it come over me that somethin' ahead on the duck-boards was just like Auntie Armine, waitin' beside the door; an' I thought to meself 'ow truly comic it would be if she could be dumped where I was then. In 'alf a second I saw it was only the dark an' some rags o' gas-screen, 'angin' on a bit of board, 'ad played me the trick. So I went on up to the supports an' warned the leaf-men there, includin' Uncle John. Then I went up Rake Alley to warn 'em in the front line. I didn't hurry because I didn't want to get there till Jerry 'ad quieted down a bit. Well, then a Company Relief dropped in – an' the officer got the wind up over some lights on the flank, an' tied 'em into knots, an' I 'ad to hunt up me leaf-men all over the blinkin' shop. What with one thing an' another, it must 'ave been 'alf-past eight before I got back to the supports. There I run across Uncle John, scrapin' mud off himself, havin' shaved – quite the dandy. He asked about the Arras train, an' I said, if Jerry was quiet, it might be ten o'clock. 'Good!' says 'e. 'I'll come with you.' So we started back down the old trench that used to run across Halnaker, back of the support dug-outs. *You* know, sir."

Keede nodded.

"Then Uncle John says something to me about seein' Ma an' the rest of 'em in a few days, an' had I any messages for 'em? Gawd knows what made me do it, but I told 'im to tell Auntie Armine I never expected to see anything like *her* up in our part of the world. And while I told him I laughed. That's the last time I *'ave* laughed. 'Oh – you've seen 'er, 'ave you?' says he, quite natural-like. Then I told 'im about the sand-bags an' rags in the dark, playin' the trick. 'Very likely,' says he, brushin' the mud off his puttees. By this time, we'd got to the corner where the old barricade into French End was – before they bombed it down, sir. He turns right an' climbs across it. 'No, thanks,' says I. 'I've been there once this evenin'.' But he wasn't attendin' to me. He felt behind the rubbish an' bones just inside the barricade, an' when he straightened up, he had a full brazier in each hand.

" 'Come on, Clem,' he says, an' he very rarely give me me own name. 'You aren't afraid, are you?' he says. 'It's just as short, an' if Jerry starts up again he won't waste stuff here. He knows it's abandoned.' 'Who's afraid now?' I says. 'Me for one,' says he. 'I don't want *my* leaf spoiled at the last minute.' Then 'e wheels round an' speaks that bit you said come out o' the Burial Service."

For some reason Keede repeated it in full, slowly: "If, after the manner of men, I have fought with beasts at Ephesus, what advantageth it me if the dead rise not?"

"That's it," said Strangwick. "So we went down French End together – everything froze up an' quiet, except for their creakin's. I remember thinkin' —" His eyes began to flicker.

"Don't think. Tell what happened," Keede ordered.

"Oh! Beg y' pardon! He went on with his braziers, hummin' his hymn, down Butcher's Row. Just before we got to the old dressin'-station he stops and sets 'em down an' says: 'Where did you say she was, Clem? Me eyes ain't as good as they used to be.'

" 'In 'er bed at 'ome,' I says. 'Come on down. It's perishin' cold, an' *I'm* not due for leaf.'

" 'Well, I am,' 'e says. '*I* am . . .' An' then – 'give you me word I didn't recognise the voice – he stretches out 'is neck a bit, in a way 'e 'ad, an' says: 'Why, Bella!' 'e says. 'Oh, Bella!' 'e says. 'Thank Gawd!' 'e says. Just like that! An' then I saw – I tell you I *saw* – Auntie Armine herself standin' by the old dressin'-station door where first I'd thought I'd seen her. He was lookin' at 'er an' she was lookin' at him. I saw it, an' me soul turned over inside me because – because it knocked out everything I'd believed in. I 'ad nothin' to lay 'old of, d'ye see? An' 'e was lookin' at 'er as though he could 'ave et 'er, an' she was lookin' at 'im the same way, out of 'er eyes. Then he says: 'Why, Bella,' 'e says, 'this must be only the second time we've been alone together in all these years.' An' I saw 'er half hold out her arms to 'im in that perishin' cold. An' she nearer fifty than forty an' me own Aunt! You can shop me for a lunatic to-morrow, but I saw it – I *saw* 'er answerin' to his spoken word! . . . Then 'e made a snatch to unsling 'is rifle. Then 'e cuts 'is hand away saying: 'No! Don't tempt me, Bella. We've all Eternity ahead of us. An hour or two won't make any odds.' Then he picks up the braziers an' goes on to the dug-out door. He'd finished with me. He pours petrol on 'em, an' lights it with a match, an' carries 'em inside, flarin'. All that time Auntie Armine stood with 'er arms out – an' a look in 'er face! *I* didn't know such things was or could be! Then he comes out an' says: 'Come in, my dear'; an' she stoops an' goes into the dug-out with that look on her face – that look on her face! An' then 'e shuts the door from inside an' starts wedgin' it up. So 'elp me Gawd, I saw an' 'eard all these things with my own eyes an' ears!"

He repeated his oath several times. After a long pause Keede asked him if he recalled what happened next.

"It was a bit of a mix-up, for me, from then on. I must have carried on – they told me I did, but – but I was – I felt a – a long way inside of meself, like – if you've ever had that feelin'. I wasn't rightly on the spot at all. They woke me up sometime next morning, because 'e 'adn't showed up at the train; an' someone had seen him with me. I wasn't 'alf cross-examined by all an' sundry till dinner-time.

"Then, I think, I volunteered for Dearlove, who 'ad a sore toe, for a front-line message. I had to keep movin', you see, because I hadn't anything to hold *on* to. Whilst up there, Grant informed me how he'd found Uncle John with the door wedged an' sand-bags stuffed in the cracks. I hadn't waited for that. The knockin' when 'e wedged up was enough for me. 'Like Dad's coffin."

"No one told *me* the door had been wedged." Keede spoke severely.

"No need to black a dead man's name, sir."

"What made Grant go to Butcher's Row?"

"Because he'd noticed Uncle John had been pinchin' charcoal for a week past an' layin' it up behind the old barricade there. So when the 'unt began, he went that way straight as a string, an' when he saw the door shut, he knew. He told me he picked the sand-bags out of the cracks an' shoved 'is hand through and shifted the wedges before anyone come along. It looked all right. You said yourself, sir, the door must 'ave blown to."

"Grant knew what Godsoe meant, then?" Keede snapped.

"Grant knew Godsoe was for it; an' nothin' earthly could 'elp or 'inder. He told me so."

"And then what did you do?"

"I expect I must 'ave kept on carryin' on, till Headquarters give me that wire from Ma – about Auntie Armine dyin'."

"When had your Aunt died?"

"On the mornin' of the twenty-first. The mornin' of the twenty-first! That tore it, d'ye see? As long as I could think, I had kep' tellin' myself it was like those things you lectured about at Arras when we was billeted in the cellars – the Angels of Mons, and so on. But that wire tore it."

"Oh! Hallucinations! I remember. And that wire tore it?" said Keede.

"Yes! You see" – he half lifted himself off the sofa – "there wasn't a single gor-dam thing left abidin' for me to take hold of, here or hereafter. If the dead *do* rise – and I saw 'em – why – why *anything* can 'appen. Don't you understand?"

He was on his feet now, gesticulating stiffly.

"For I saw 'er," he repeated. "I saw 'im an' 'er – she dead since mornin' time, an' he killin' 'imself before my livin' eyes so's to carry on with 'er for all Eternity – an' she 'oldin' out 'er arms for it! I want to know where I'm *at*! Look 'ere, you two – why stand *we* in jeopardy every hour?"

"God knows," said Keede to himself.

"Hadn't we better ring for someone?" I suggested. "He'll go off the handle in a second."

"No, he won't. It's the last kick-up before it takes hold. I know how the stuff works. Hul-lo!"

Strangwick, his hands behind his back and his eyes set, gave tongue in the strained, cracked voice of a boy reciting. "Not twice in the world shall the Gods do thus," he cried again and again.

"And I'm damned if it's goin' to be even once for me!" he went on with sudden insane fury. "*I* don't care whether we '*ave* been pricin' things in the windows . . . *Let* 'er sue if she likes! She don't know what reel things mean. *I* do – I've 'ad occasion to notice 'em . . . *No*, I tell you! I'll 'ave 'em when I want 'em, an' be done with 'em; but not till I see that look on a face . . . that look . . . I'm not takin' any. The reel thing's life an' death. It *begins* at death, d'ye see. *She* can't understand . . . Oh, go on an' push off to Hell, you an' your lawyers. I'm fed up with it – fed up!"

He stopped as abruptly as he had started, and the drawn face broke back to its natural irresolute lines. Keede, holding both his hands, led him back to the sofa, where he dropped like a wet towel, took out some flamboyant robe from a press, and drew it neatly over him.

"Ye-es. *That's* the real thing at last," said Keede. "Now he's got it oV his mind he'll sleep. By the way, who introduced him?"

"Shall I go and find out?" I suggested.

"Yes; and you might ask him to come here. There's no need for us to stand to all night."

So I went to the Banquet which was in full swing, and was seized by an elderly, precise Brother from a South London Lodge who followed me, concerned and apologetic. Keede soon put him at his ease.

"The boy's had trouble," our visitor explained. "I'm most mortified he should have performed his bad turn here. I thought he'd put it be'ind him."

"I expect talking about old days with me brought it all back," said Keede. "It does sometimes."

"Maybe! Maybe! But over and above that, Clem's had post-war trouble, too."

"Can't he get a job? He oughtn't to let that weigh on him, at his time of life," said Keede cheerily.

" 'Tisn't that – he's provided for – but" – he coughed confidentially behind his dry hand – "as a matter of fact, Worshipful Sir, he's – he's implicated for the present in a little breach of promise action."

"Ah! That's a different thing," said Keede.

"Yes. That's his reel trouble. No reason given, you understand. The young lady in every way suitable, an' she'd make him a good little wife too, if I'm any judge. But he says she ain't his ideel or something. 'No getting at what's in young people's minds these days, is there?"

"I'm afraid there isn't," said Keede. "But he's all right now. He'll sleep. You sit by him, and when he wakes, take him home quietly . . . Oh, we're used to men getting a little upset here. You've nothing to thank us for, Brother – Brother –"

"Armine," said the old gentleman. "He's my nephew by marriage."

"That's all that's wanted!" said Keede.

Brother Armine looked a little puzzled. Keede hastened to explain. "As I was saying, all he wants now is to be kept quiet till he wakes."

* * *

GOW'S WATCH

Act V Scene 3

After the Battle.
The PRINCESS *by the Standard on the Ravelin.*
Enter GOW, *with the Crown of the Kingdom.*

GOW: Here's earnest of the Queen's submission.
This by her last herald – and in haste.

PRINCESS: 'Twas ours already. Where is the woman?

GOW: 'Fled with her horse. They broke at dawn.

Noon has not struck, and you're Queen questionless.

PRINCESS: By you – through you. How shall I honour *you*?

GOW: Me? But for what?

PRINCESS: For all – all – all –

Since the realm sunk beneath us! Hear him! "For what?"

Your body 'twixt my bosom and her knife,

Your lips on the cup she proffered for my death;

Your one cloak over me, that night in the snows,

We held the Pass at Bargi. Every hour

New strengths, to this most unbelievable last.

"Honour him?" I will honour – will honour you – . . .

'Tis at your choice.

GOW: Child, mine was long ago.

(*Enter* FERDINAND, *as from horse.*)

But here's one worthy honour. Welcome, Fox!

FERDINAND: And to you, Watchdog. This day clenches all.

We've made it and seen it.

GOW: Is the city held?

FERDINAND: Loyally. Oh, they're drunk with loyalty yonder.

A virtuous mood. Your bombards helped 'em to it . . .

But here's my word for you. The Lady Frances —

PRINCESS: I left her sick in the city. No harm, I pray.

FERDINAND: Nothing that she called harm. In truth, so little

That (*to* GOW) I am bidden to tell you, she'll be here

Almost as soon as I.

GOW: She says it?

FERDINAND: Writes.

This. (*Gives him letter.*) Yester eve.

'Twas given me by the priest –

He with her in her hour.

GOW: So? (*Reads*) So it is.

She will be here. (*To* FERDINAND) And all is safe in the city?

FERDINAND: As thy long sword and my lean wits can make

it.

You've naught to stay for. Is it the road again?

GOW: Ay. This time, not alone . . . She will be here.

PRINCESS: I am here. You have not looked at me awhile.

GOW: The rest is with you, Ferdinand . . . Then free.

PRINCESS: And at my service more than ever. I claim —
(Our wars have taught me) – being your Queen, now,
claim
You wholly mine.

GOW: Then free . . . She will be here! A little while —

PRINCESS (to FERDINAND): He looks beyond, not at me.

FERDINAND: Weariness.
We are not so young as once was. 'Two days' fight –
A worthy servitor – to be allowed
Some freedom.

PRINCESS: I have offered him all he would.

FERDINAND: He takes what he has taken.
(The Spirit of the LADY FRANCES appears to GOW.)

GOW: Frances!

PRINCESS: Distraught!

FERDINAND: An old head-blow, may be. He has dealt in
them.

GOW (to the Spirit): What can the Grave against us, O my
Heart,
Comfort and light and reason in all things
Visible and invisible – my one God?
Thou that wast I these barren unyoked years
Of triflings now at end! Frances!

PRINCESS: She's old.

FERDINAND: True. By most reckonings old.
They must keep other count.

PRINCESS: He kisses his hand to the air!

FERDINAND: His ring, rather, he kisses. Yes – for sure – the
ring.

GOW: Dear and most dear. And now, those very arms. (Dies.)

PRINCESS: Oh, look! He faints. Haste, you! Unhelm him!
Help!

FERDINAND: Needless. No help
Avails against that poison. He is sped.

PRINCESS: By his own hand? *This* hour? When I had
  offered —
FERDINAND: He had made other choice – an old, old choice,
  Ne'er swerved from, and now patently sealed in death.
PRINCESS: He called on – the Lady Frances was it? Where-
  fore?
FERDINAND: Because she was his life. Forgive, my friend –
  (*covers* GOW's *face*).
  God's uttermost beyond me in all faith,
  Service and passion – if I unveil at last
The secret. (*To the* PRINCESS) Thought – dreamed you, it was
  for *you*
  He poured himself – for you resoldered the Crown?
  Struck here, held there, amended, broke, built up
  His multiplied imaginings for *you*?
PRINCESS: I thought – I thought he —
FERDINAND: Looked beyond. *Her* wish
  Was the sole Law he knew. *She* did not choose
  Your House should perish. Therefore he bade it stand.
  Enough for him when she had breathed a word:
  'Twas his to make it iron, stone, or fire,
  Driving our flesh and blood before his ways
  As the wind straws. Her one face unregarded
  Waiting you with your mantle or your glove —
  That is the God whom he is gone to worship.
(*Trumpets without. Enter the Prince's Heralds.*)
  And here's the work of Kingship begun again.
  These from the Prince of Bargi – to whose sword
  You owe such help as may, he thinks, be paid . . .
  He's equal in blood, in fortune more than peer,
  Young, most well favoured, with a heart to love –
  And two States in the balance. Do you meet him?
PRINCESS: God and my Misery! I have seen Love at last.
  What shall content me after?

THE EYE OF ALLAH

THE EYE OF ALLAH

* * *

UNTIMELY

Nothing in life has been made by man for man's using
But it was shown long since to man in ages
Lost as the name of the maker of it,

Who received oppression and scorn for his wages —
Hate, avoidance, and scorn in his daily dealings —
Until he perished, wholly confounded.

More to be pitied than he are the wise
Souls which foresaw the evil of loosing
Knowledge or Art before time, and aborted
Noble devices and deep-wrought healings,
Lest offence should arise.

Heaven delivers on earth the Hour that cannot be thwarted,
Neither advanced, at the price of a world or a soul, and its Prophet
Comes through the blood of the vanguards who dreamed — too soon
  — it had sounded.

* * *

T HE Cantor of St. Illod's being far too enthusiastic a
  musician to concern himself with its Library, the Sub-
Cantor, who idolised every detail of the work, was tidying
up, after two hours' writing and dictation in the Scriptorium.
The copying-monks handed him in their sheets — it was a
plain Four Gospels ordered by an Abbot at Evesham — and
filed out to vespers. John Otho, better known as John of
Burgos, took no heed. He was burnishing a tiny boss of gold

801

in his miniature of the Annunciation for his Gospel of St. Luke, which it was hoped that Cardinal Falcodi, the Papal Legate, might later be pleased to accept.

"Break off, John," said the Sub-Cantor in an undertone.

"Eh? Gone, have they? I never heard. Hold a minute, Clement."

The Sub-Cantor waited patiently. He had known John more than a dozen years, coming and going at St. Illod's, to which monastery John, when abroad, always said he belonged. The claim was gladly allowed for, more even than other Fitz Otho's, he seemed to carry all the Arts under his hand, and most of their practical receipts under his hood.

The Sub-Cantor looked over his shoulder at the pinned-down sheet where the first words of the Magnificat were built up in gold washed with red-lac for a background to the Virgin's hardly yet fired halo. She was shown, hands joined in wonder, at a lattice of infinitely intricate arabesque, round the edges of which sprays of orange-bloom seemed to load the blue hot air that carried back over the minute parched landscape in the middle distance.

"You've made her all Jewess," said the Sub-Cantor, studying the olive-flushed cheek and the eyes charged with foreknowledge.

"What else was Our Lady?" John slipped out the pins. "Listen, Clement. If I do not come back, this goes into my Great Luke, whoever finishes it." He slid the drawing between its guard-papers.

"Then you're for Burgos again – as I heard?"

"In two days. The new Cathedral yonder – but they're slower than the Wrath of God, those masons – is good for the soul."

"*Thy* soul?" The Sub-Cantor seemed doubtful.

"Even mine, by your permission. And down south – on the edge of the Conquered Countries – Granada way – there's some Moorish diaper-work that's wholesome. It allays vain thought and draws it toward the picture – as you felt, just now, in my Annunciation."

"She – it was very beautiful. No wonder you go. But you'll not forget your absolution, John?"

"Surely." This was a precaution John no more omitted on the eve of his travels than he did the recutting of the tonsure which he had provided himself with in his youth, somewhere near Ghent. The mark gave him privilege of clergy at a pinch, and a certain consideration on the road always.

"You'll not forget, either, what we need in the Scriptorium. There's no more true ultramarine in this world now. They mix it with that German blue. And as for vermilion —"

"I'll do my best always."

"And Brother Thomas" (this was the Infirmarian in charge of the monastery hospital) "he needs —"

"He'll do his own asking. I'll go over his side now, and get me re-tonsured."

John went down the stairs to the lane that divides the hospital and cook-house from the back-cloisters. While he was being barbered, Brother Thomas (St. Illod's meek but deadly persistent Infirmarian) gave him a list of drugs that he was to bring back from Spain by hook, crook, or lawful purchase. Here they were surprised by the lame, dark Abbot Stephen, in his fur-lined night-boots. Not that Stephen de Sautré was any spy; but as a young man he had shared an unlucky Crusade, which had ended, after a battle at Mansura, in two years' captivity among the Saracens at Cairo where men learn to walk softly. A fair huntsman and hawker, a reasonable disciplinarian, but a man of science above all, and a Doctor of Medicine under one Ranulphus, Canon of St. Paul's, his heart was more in the monastery's hospital work than its religious. He checked their list interestedly, adding items of his own. After the Infirmarian had withdrawn, he gave John generous absolution, to cover lapses by the way; for he did not hold with chance-bought Indulgences.

"And what seek you *this* journey?" he demanded, sitting on the bench beside the mortar and scales in the little warm cell for stored drugs.

"Devils, mostly," said John, grinning.

"In Spain? Are not Abana and Pharphar —?"

John, to whom men were but matter for drawings, and well-born to boot (since he was a de Sanford on his mother's side), looked the Abbot full in the face and — "Did *you* find it so?" said he.

"No. They were in Cairo too. But what's your special need of 'em?"

"For my Great Luke. He's the master-hand of all Four when it comes to devils."

"No wonder. He was a physician. You're not."

"Heaven forbid! But I'm weary of our Church-pattern devils. They're only apes and goats and poultry conjoined. 'Good enough for plain red-and-black Hells and Judgement Days – but not for me."

"What makes you so choice in them?"

"Because it stands to reason and Art that there are all musters of devils in Hell's dealings. Those Seven, for example, that were haled out of the Magdalene. They'd be she-devils – no kin at all to the beaked and horned and bearded devils-general."

The Abbot laughed.

"And see again! The devil that came out of the dumb man. What use is snout or bill to *him*? He'd be faceless as a leper. Above all – God send I live to do it! – the devils that entered the Gadarene swine. They'd be – they'd be – I know not yet what they'd be, but they'd be surpassing devils. I'd have 'em diverse as the Saints themselves. But now, they're all one pattern, for wall, window, or picture-work."

"Go on, John. You're deeper in this mystery than I."

"Heaven forbid! But I say there's respect due to devils, damned tho' they be."

"Dangerous doctrine."

"My meaning is that if the shape of anything be worth man's thought to picture to man, it's worth his best thought."

"That's safer. But I'm glad I've given you Absolution."

"There's less risk for a craftsman who deals with the out-side shapes of things – for Mother Church's glory."

"Maybe so, but John" – the Abbot's hand almost touched John's sleeve – "tell me, now, is – is she Moorish or – or Hebrew?"

"She's mine," John returned.

"Is that enough?"

"I have found it so."

"Well – ah well! It's out of my jurisdiction, but – how do they look at it down yonder?"

"Oh, they drive nothing to a head in Spain – neither Church nor King, bless them! There's too many Moors and Jews to kill them all, and if they chased 'em away there'd be no trade nor farming. Trust me, in the Conquered Countries, from Seville to Granada, we live lovingly enough together – Spaniard, Moor, and Jew. Ye see, *we* ask no questions."

"Yes – yes," Stephen sighed. "And always there's the hope, she may be converted."

"Oh yes, there's always hope."

The Abbot went on into the hospital. It was an easy age before Rome tightened the screw as to clerical connections. If the lady were not too forward, or the son too much his father's beneficiary in ecclesiastical preferments and levies, a good deal was overlooked. But, as the Abbot had reason to recall, unions between Christian and Infidel led to sorrow. None the less, when John with mule, mails, and man, clat-tered off down the lane for Southampton and the sea, Stephen envied him.

* * *

He was back, twenty months later, in good hard case, and loaded down with fairings. A lump of richest lazuli, a bar of orange-hearted vermilion, and a small packet of dried beetles which make most glorious scarlet, for the Sub-Cantor. Besides that, a few cubes of milky marble, with yet a pink flush in them, which could be slaked and ground down to incomparable background-stuff. There were quite half the drugs that the Abbot and Thomas had demanded, and there was a long deep-red cornelian necklace for the Abbot's Lady – Anne of Norton. She received it graciously, and asked where John had come by it.

"Near Granada," he said.

"You left all well there?" Anne asked. (Maybe the Abbot had told her something of John's confession.)

"I left all in the hands of God."

"Ah me! How long since?"

"Four months less eleven days."

"Were you – with her?"

"In my arms. Childbed."

"And?"

"The boy too. There is nothing now."

Anne of Norton caught her breath.

"I think you'll be glad of that," she said after a while.

"Give me time, and maybe I'll compass it. But not now."

"You have your handwork and your art and – John – remember there's no jealousy in the grave."

"Ye-es! I have my Art, and Heaven knows I'm jealous of none."

"Thank God for that at least," said Anne of Norton, the always ailing woman who followed the Abbot with her sunk eyes. "And be sure I shall treasure this" – she touched the beads – "as long as I shall live."

"I brought – trusted – it to you for that," he replied, and took leave. When she told the Abbot how she had come by it, he said nothing, but as he and Thomas were storing the drugs that John handed over in the cell which backs on to the hospital kitchen-chimney, he observed, of a cake of dried poppy-juice: "This has power to cut off all pain from a man's body."

"I have seen it," said John.

"But for pain of the soul there is, outside God's Grace, but one drug; and that is a man's craft, learning, or other helpful motion of his own mind."

"That is coming to me, too," was the answer.

John spent the next fair May day out in the woods with the monastery swineherd and all the porkers; and returned loaded with flowers and sprays of spring, to his own carefully kept place in the north bay of the Scriptorium. There, with his travelling sketch-books under his left elbow, he sunk himself past all recollections in his Great Luke.

Brother Martin, Senior Copyist (who spoke about once a fortnight), ventured to ask, later, how the work was going.

"All here!" John tapped his forehead with his pencil. "It has been only waiting these months to – ah God! – be born. Are ye free of your plain-copying, Martin?"

Brother Martin nodded. It was his pride that John of Burgos turned to him, in spite of his seventy years, for really good page-work.

"Then see!" John laid out a new vellum – thin but flawless. "There's no better than this sheet from here to Paris. Yes! Smell it if you choose. Wherefore – give me the compasses and I'll set it out for you – if ye make one letter lighter or darker than its next, I'll stick ye like a pig."

"Never, John!" the old man beamed happily.

"But I will! Now, follow! Here and here, as I prick, and in script of just this height to the hair's-breadth, ye'll scribe the thirty-first and thirty-second verses of Eighth Luke."

"Yes, the Gadarene Swine! '*And they besought him that he would not command them to go out into the abyss. And there was a herd of many swine*' " — Brother Martin naturally knew all the Gospels by heart.

"Just so! Down to '*and he suffered them.*' Take your time to it. My Magdalene has to come off my heart first."

Brother Martin achieved the work so perfectly that John stole some soft sweetmeats from the Abbot's kitchen for his reward. The old man ate them; then repented; then confessed and insisted on penance. At which, the Abbot, knowing there was but one way to reach the real sinner, set him a book called *De Virtutibus Herbarum* to fair-copy. St. Illod's had borrowed it from the gloomy Cistercians, who do not hold with pretty things, and the crabbed text kept Martin busy just when John wanted him for some rather specially spaced letterings.

"See now," said the Sub-Cantor improvingly. "You should not do such things, John. Here's Brother Martin on penance for your sake —"

"No – for my Great Luke. But I've paid the Abbot's cook. I've drawn him till his own scullions cannot keep straight-faced. *He*'ll not tell again."

"Unkindly done! And you're out of favour with the Abbot too. He's made no sign to you since you came back – never asked you to high table."

"I've been busy. Having eyes in his head, Stephen knew it. Clement, there's no Librarian from Durham to Torre fit to clean up after you."

The Sub-Cantor stood on guard; he knew where John's compliments generally ended.

"But outside the Scriptorium —"

"Where I never go." The Sub-Cantor had been excused even digging in the garden, lest it should mar his wonderful book-binding hands.

"In all things outside the Scriptorium you are the master-fool of Christendie. Take it from me, Clement. I've met many."

"I take everything from you," Clement smiled benignly. "You use me worse than a singing-boy."

They could hear one of that suffering breed in the cloister below, squalling as the Cantor pulled his hair.

"God love you! So I do! But have you ever thought how I lie and steal daily on my travels – yes, and for aught you know, murder – to fetch you colours and earths?"

"True," said just and conscience-stricken Clement. "I have often thought that were I in the world – which God forbid! – I might be a strong thief in some matters."

Even Brother Martin, bent above his loathed *De Virtutibus*, laughed.

* * *

But about mid-summer, Thomas the Infirmarian conveyed to John the Abbot's invitation to supper in his house that night, with the request that he would bring with him anything that he had done for his Great Luke.

"What's toward?" said John, who had been wholly shut up in his work.

"Only one of his 'wisdom' dinners. You've sat at a few since you were a man."

"True: and mostly good. How would Stephen have us —?"

"Gown and hood over all. There will be a doctor from Salerno – one Roger, an Italian. Wise and famous with the knife on the body. He's been in the Infirmary some ten days, helping me – even me!"

" 'Never heard the name. But our Stephen's *physicus* before *sacerdos*, always."

"And his Lady has a sickness of some time. Roger came hither in chief because of her."

"Did he? Now I think of it, I have not seen the Lady Anne for a while."

"Ye've seen nothing for a long while. She has been housed near a month – they have to carry her abroad now."

"So bad as that, then?"

"Roger of Salerno will not yet say what he thinks. But —"

"God pity Stephen! . . . Who else at table, beside thee?"

"An Oxford friar. Roger is his name also. A learned and famous philosopher. And he holds his liquor too, valiantly."

"Three doctors – counting Stephen. I've always found that means two atheists."

Thomas looked uneasily down his nose. "That's a wicked proverb," he stammered. "You should not use it."

"Hoh! Never come you the monk over me, Thomas! You've been Infirmarian at St. Illod's eleven years – and a lay-brother still. Why have you never taken orders, all this while?"

"I – I am not worthy."

"Ten times worthier than that new fat swine – Henry Who's-his-name – that takes the Infirmary Masses. He bullocks in with the Viaticum, under your nose, when a sick man's only faint from being bled. So the man dies – of pure fear. Ye know it! I've watched your face at such times. Take Orders, Didymus. You'll have a little more medicine and a little less Mass with your sick then; and they'll live longer."

"I am unworthy – unworthy," Thomas repeated pitifully.

"Not you – but – to your own master you stand or fall. And now that my work releases me for awhile, I'll drink with any philosopher out of any school. And Thomas," he coaxed, "a hot bath for me in the Infirmary before vespers."

* * *

When the Abbot's perfectly cooked and served meal had ended, and the deep-fringed naperies were removed, and the Prior had sent in the keys with word that all was fast in the Monastery, and the keys had been duly returned with the word, "Make it so till Prime," the Abbot and his guests went out to cool themselves in an upper cloister that took them, by way of the leads, to the South Choir side of the Triforium. The summer sun was still strong, for it was barely six o'clock, but the Abbey Church, of course, lay in her wonted darkness. Lights were being lit for choir-practice thirty feet below.

"Our Cantor gives them no rest," the Abbot whispered. "Stand by this pillar and we'll hear what he's driving them at now."

"Remember all!" the Cantor's hard voice came up. "This is the soul of Bernard himself, attacking our evil world. Take it quicker than yesterday, and throw all your words clean-bitten from you. In the loft there! Begin!"

The organ broke out for an instant, alone and raging. Then the voices crashed together into that first fierce line of the "*De Contemptu Mundi*."

"*Hora novissima – tempora pessima*" – a dead pause till the assenting *sunt* broke, like a sob, out of the darkness, and one boy's voice, clearer than silver trumpets, returned the long-drawn *vigilemus*.

"*Ecce minaciter, imminet Arbiter*" (organ and voices were leashed together in terror and warning, breaking away liquidly to the "*ille supremus*"). Then the tone-colours shifted for the prelude to – "*Imminet, imminet, ut mala terminet* —"

"Stop! Again!" cried the Cantor; and gave his reasons a little more roundly than was natural at choir-practice.

"Ah! Pity o' man's vanity! He's guessed we are here. Come away!" said the Abbot. Anne of Norton, in her carried chair, had been listening too, further along the dark Triforium, with Roger of Salerno. John heard her sob. On the way back, he asked Thomas how her health stood. Before Thomas could reply the sharp-featured Italian doctor pushed between them. "Following on our talk together, I judged it best to tell her," said he to Thomas.

"What?" John asked simply enough.

"What she knew already." Roger of Salerno launched into a Greek quotation to the effect that every woman knows all about everything.

"I have no Greek," said John stiffly. Roger of Salerno had been giving them a good deal of it, at dinner.

"Then I'll come to you in Latin. Ovid hath it neatly. '*Utque malum late solet immedicable cancer* —' but doubtless you know the rest, worthy Sir."

"Alas! My school-Latin's but what I've gathered by the way from fools professing to heal sick women. '*Hocus-pocus* —' but doubtless you know the rest, worthy Sir."

Roger of Salerno was quite quiet till they regained the dining-room, where the fire had been comforted and the dates, raisins, ginger, figs, and cinnamon-scented sweetmeats set out, with the choicer wines, on the after-table. The Abbot seated himself, drew off his ring, dropped it, that all might hear the tinkle, into an empty silver cup, stretched his feet towards the hearth, and looked at the great gilt and carved rose in the barrel-roof. The silence that keeps from Compline to Matins had closed on their world. The bull-necked Friar watched a ray of sunlight split itself into colours on the rim of a crystal salt-cellar; Roger of Salerno had re-opened some discussion with Brother Thomas on a type of spotted fever that was baffling them both in England and abroad; John took note of the keen profile, and – it might serve as a note for the Great Luke – his hand moved to his bosom. The Abbot saw, and nodded permission. John whipped out silver-point and sketch-book.

"Nay – modesty is good enough – but deliver your own opinion," the Italian was urging the Infirmarian. Out of courtesy to the foreigner nearly all the talk was in table-Latin; more formal and more copious than monk's patter. Thomas began with his meek stammer.

"I confess myself at a loss for the cause of the fever unless – as Varro saith in his *De Re Rustica* – certain small animals which the eye cannot follow enter the body by nose and mouth, and set up grave diseases. On the other hand, this is not in Scripture."

Roger of Salerno hunched head and shoulders like an angry cat. "Always *that*!" he said, and John snatched down the twist of the thin lips.

"Never at rest, John," the Abbot smiled at the artist. "You should break off every two hours for prayers, as we do. St. Benedict was no fool. Two hours is all that a man can carry the edge of his eye or hand."

"For copyists – yes. Brother Martin is not sure after one hour. But when a man's work takes him, he must go on till it lets him go."

"Yes, that is the Demon of Socrates," the Friar from Oxford rumbled above his cup.

"The doctrine leans toward presumption," said the Abbot. "Remember, 'Shall mortal man be more just than his Maker?'"

"There is no danger of justice"; the Friar spoke bitterly. "But at least Man might be suffered to go forward in his Art or his thought. Yet if Mother Church sees or hears him move anyward, what says she? 'No!' Always 'No.' "

"But if the little animals of Varro be invisible" – this was Roger of Salerno to Thomas – "how are we any nearer to a cure?"

"By experiment" – the Friar wheeled round on them suddenly. "By reason and experiment. The one is useless without the other. But Mother Church ——"

"Ay!" Roger de Salerno dashed at the fresh bait like a pike. "Listen, Sirs. Her bishops – our Princes – strew our roads in Italy with carcasses that they make for their pleasure or wrath. Beautiful corpses! Yet if I – if we doctors – so much as raise the skin of one of them to look at God's fabric beneath, what says Mother Church? 'Sacrilege! Stick to your pigs and dogs, or you burn!' "

"And not Mother Church only!" the Friar chimed in. "*Every* way we are barred – barred by the words of some man, dead a thousand years, which are held final. Who is any son of Adam that his one say-so should close a door towards truth? I would not except even Peter Peregrinus, my own great teacher."

"Nor I Paul of Aegina," Roger of Salerno cried. "Listen, Sirs! Here is a case to the very point. Apuleius affirmeth, if a man eat fasting of the juice of the cut-leaved buttercup – *sceleratus* we call it, which means 'rascally' " – this with a condescending nod towards John – "his soul will leave his body laughing. Now this is the lie more dangerous than truth, since truth of a sort is in it."

"He's away!" whispered the Abbot despairingly.

"For the juice of that herb, I know by experiment, burns, blisters, and wries the mouth. I know also the *rictus*, or pseudo-laughter on the face of such as have perished by the strong poisons of herbs allied to this ranunculus. Certainly that spasm resembles laughter. It seems then, in my judgement, that Apuleius, having seen the body of one thus poisoned, went off at score and wrote that the man died laughing."

"Neither staying to observe, nor to confirm observation by experiment," added the Friar, frowning.

Stephen the Abbot cocked an eyebrow toward John.

"How think *you*?" said he.

"I'm no doctor," John returned, "but I'd say Apuleius in all these years might have been betrayed by his copyists. They take short-cuts to save 'emselves trouble. Put case that Apuleius wrote the soul *seems to* leave the body laughing, after this poison. There's not three copyists in five (*my* judgement) would not leave out the 'seems to'. For who'd question Apuleius? If it seemed so to him, so it must be. Otherwise any child knows cut-leaved buttercup."

"Have you knowledge of herbs?" Roger of Salerno asked curtly.

"Only, that when I was a boy in convent, I've made tetters round my mouth and on my neck with buttercup-juice, to save going to prayer o' cold nights."

"Ah!" said Roger. "I profess no knowledge of tricks." He turned aside, stiffly.

"No matter! Now for your own tricks, John," the tactful Abbot broke in. "You shall show the doctors your Magdalene and your Gadarene Swine and the devils."

"Devils? Devils? *I* have produced devils by means of drugs; and have abolished them by the same means. Whether devils be external to mankind or immanent, I have not yet pronounced." Roger of Salerno was still angry.

"Ye dare not," snapped the Friar from Oxford. "Mother Church makes Her own devils."

"Not wholly! Our John has come back from Spain with brand-new ones." Abbot Stephen took the vellum handed to him, and laid it tenderly on the table. They gathered to look. The Magdalene was drawn in palest, almost transparent, grisaille, against a raging, swaying background of woman-faced devils, each broke to and by her special sin, and each, one could see, frenziedly straining against the Power that compelled her.

"I've never seen the like of this grey shadow work," said the Abbot. "How came you by it?"

"*Non nobis!* It came to me," said John, not knowing he was a generation or so ahead of his time in the use of that medium.

"Why is she so pale?" the Friar demanded.

"Evil has all come out of her – she'd take any colour now."

"Ay, like light through glass. *I* see."

Roger of Salerno was looking in silence – his nose nearer and nearer the page. "It is so," he pronounced finally. "Thus it is in epilepsy – mouth, eyes, and forehead – even to the droop of her wrist there. Every sign of it! She will need restoratives, that woman, and, afterwards, sleep natural. No poppy-juice, or she will vomit on her waking. And thereafter – but I am not in my Schools." He drew himself up. "Sir," said he, "you should be of Our calling. For, by the Snakes of Aesculapius, you *see*!"

The two struck hands as equals.

"And how think you of the Seven Devils?" the Abbot went on.

These melted into convoluted flower- or flame-like bodies, ranging in colour from phosphorescent green to the black purple of outworn iniquity, whose hearts could be traced beating through their substance. But, for sign of hope and the sane workings of life, to be regained, the deep border was of conventionalised spring flowers and birds, all crowned by a kingfisher in haste, atilt through a clump of yellow iris.

Roger of Salerno identified the herbs and spoke largely of their virtues.

"And now, the Gadarene Swine," said Stephen. John laid the picture on the table.

Here were devils dishoused, in dread of being abolished to the Void, huddling and hurtling together to force lodgment by every opening into the brute bodies offered. Some of the swine fought the invasion, foaming and jerking; some were surrendering to it, sleepily, as to a luxurious back-scratching; others, wholly possessed, whirled off in bucking droves for the lake beneath. In one corner the freed man stretched out his limbs all restored to his control, and Our Lord, seated, looked at him as questioning what he would make of his deliverance.

"Devils indeed!" was the Friar's comment. "But wholly a new sort."

Some devils were mere lumps, with lobes and protuberances – a hint of a fiend's face peering through jelly-like walls. And there was a family of impatient, globular devillings who had burst open the belly of their smirking parent, and were revolving desperately toward their prey. Others patterned themselves into rods, chains and ladders, single or conjoined, round the throat and jaws of a shrieking sow, from whose ear emerged the lashing, glassy tail of a devil that had made good his refuge. And there were granulated and conglomerate devils, mixed up with the foam and slaver where the attack was fiercest. Thence the eye carried on to the insanely active backs of the downward-racing swine, the swineherd's aghast face, and his dog's terror.

Said Roger of Salerno, "I pronounce that these were begotten of drugs. They stand outside the rational mind."

"Not these," said Thomas the Infirmarian, who as a servant of the Monastery should have asked his Abbot's leave to speak. "Not *these* – look! – in the bordure."

The border to the picture was a diaper of irregular but balanced compartments or cellules, where sat, swam, or weltered, devils in blank, so to say – things as yet uninspired by Evil – indifferent, but lawlessly outside imagination. Their shapes resembled, again, ladders, chains, scourges, diamonds, aborted buds, or gravid phosphorescent globes – some well-nigh star-like.

Roger of Salerno compared them to the obsessions of a Churchman's mind.

"Malignant?" the Friar from Oxford questioned.

" 'Count everything unknown for horrible,' " Roger quoted with scorn.

"Not I. But they are marvellous – marvellous. I think —"

The Friar drew back. Thomas edged in to see better, and half opened his mouth.

"Speak," said Stephen, who had been watching him. "We are all in a sort doctors here."

"I would say then" – Thomas rushed at it as one putting out his life's belief at the stake – "that these lower shapes in the bordure may not be so much hellish and malignant as models and patterns upon which John has tricked out and embellished his proper devils among the swine above there!"

"And that would signify?" said Roger of Salerno sharply.

"In my poor judgement, that he may have seen such shapes – without help of drugs."

"Now who – *who*," said John of Burgos, after a round and unregarded oath, "has made thee so wise of a sudden, my Doubter?"

"I wise? God forbid! Only John, remember – one winter six years ago – the snow-flakes melting on your sleeve at the cookhouse-door. You showed me them through a little crystal, that made small things larger."

"Yes. The Moors call such a glass the Eye of Allah," John confirmed.

"You showed me them melting – six-sided. You called them, then, your patterns."

"True. Snow-flakes melt six-sided. I have used them for diaper-work often."

"Melting snow-flakes as seen through a glass? By art optical?" the Friar asked.

"Art optical? *I* have never heard!" Roger of Salerno cried.

"John," said the Abbot of St. Illod's commandingly, "was it – is it so?"

"In some sort," John replied, "Thomas has the right of it. Those shapes in the bordure were my workshop-patterns for the devils above. In *my* craft, Salerno, we dare not drug. It kills hand and eye. My shapes are to be seen honestly, in nature."

The Abbot drew a bowl of rose-water towards him. "When I was prisoner with – with the Saracens after Mansura," he began, turning up the fold of his long sleeve, "there were certain magicians – physicians – who could show –" he dipped his third finger delicately in the water – "all the firmament of Hell, as it were, in –" he shook off one drop from his polished nail on to the polished table – "even such a supernaculum as this."

"But it must be foul water – not clean," said John.

"Show us then – all – all," said Stephen. "I would make sure – once more." The Abbot's voice was official.

John drew from his bosom a stamped leather box, some six or eight inches long, wherein, bedded on faded velvet, lay what looked like silver-bound compasses of old box-wood, with a screw at the head which opened or closed the legs to minute fractions. The legs terminated, not in points, but spoon-shapedly, one spatula pierced with a metal-lined hole less than a quarter of an inch across, the other with a half-inch hole. Into this latter John, after carefully wiping with a silk rag, slipped a metal cylinder that carried glass or crystal, it seemed, at each end.

"Ah! Art optic!" said the Friar. "But what is that beneath it?"

It was a small swivelling sheet of polished silver no bigger than a florin, which caught the light and concentrated it on the lesser hole. John adjusted it without the Friar's proffered help.

"And now to find a drop of water," said he, picking up a small brush.

"Come to my upper cloister. The sun is on the leads still," said the Abbot, rising.

They followed him there. Half-way along, a drip from a gutter had made a greenish puddle in a worn stone. Very carefully, John dropped a drop of it into the smaller hole of the compass-leg, and, steadying the apparatus on a coping, worked the screw in the compass-joint, screwed the cylinder, and swung the swivel of the mirror till he was satisfied.

"Good!" He peered through the thing. "My Shapes are all here. Now look, Father! If they do not meet your eye at first, turn this nicked edge here, left- or right-handed."

"I have not forgotten," said the Abbot, taking his place. "Yes! They are here – as they were in my time – my time past. There is no end to them, I was told . . . There *is* no end!"

"The light will go. Oh, let me look! Suffer me to see, also!" the Friar pleaded, almost shouldering Stephen from the eye-piece. The Abbot gave way. His eyes were on time past. But the Friar, instead of looking, turned the apparatus in his capable hands.

"Nay, nay," John interrupted, for the man was already fiddling at the screws. "Let the Doctor see."

Roger of Salerno looked, minute after minute. John saw his blue-veined cheek-bones turn white. He stepped back at last, as though stricken.

"It is a new world – a new world and – Oh, God Unjust! – I am old!"

"And now Thomas," Stephen ordered.

John manipulated the tube for the Infirmarian, whose hands shook, and he too looked long. "It is Life," he said presently in a breaking voice. "No Hell! Life created and rejoicing – the work of the Creator. They live, even as I have dreamed. Then it was no sin for me to dream. No sin – O God – no sin!"

He flung himself on his knees and began hysterically the *Benedicite omnia Opera*.

"And now I will see how it is actuated," said the Friar from Oxford, thrusting forward again.

"Bring it within. The place is all eyes and ears," said Stephen.

They walked quietly back along the leads, three English counties laid out in evening sunshine around them; church upon church, monastery upon monastery, cell after cell, and the bulk of a vast cathedral moored on the edge of the banked shoals of sunset.

When they were at the after-table once more they sat down, all except the Friar who went to the window and huddled bat-like over the thing. "I see! I see!" he was repeating to himself.

"He'll not hurt it," said John. But the Abbot, staring in front of him, like Roger of Salerno, did not hear. The Infirmarian's head was on the table between his shaking arms.

John reached for a cup of wine.

"It was shown to me," the Abbot was speaking to himself, "in Cairo, that man stands ever between two Infinities – of greatness and littleness. Therefore, there is no end – either to life – or —"

"And *I* stand on the edge of the grave," snarled Roger of Salerno. "Who pities *me*?"

"Hush!" said Thomas the Infirmarian. "The little creatures shall be sanctified – sanctified to the service of His sick."

"What need?" John of Burgos wiped his lips. "It shows no more than the shapes of things. It gives good pictures. I had it at Granada. It was brought from the East, they told me."

Roger of Salerno laughed with an old man's malice. "What of Mother Church? Most Holy Mother Church? If it comes to Her ears that we have spied into Her Hell without Her leave, where do we stand?"

"At the stake," said the Abbot of St. Illod's, and, raising his voice a trifle, "You hear that? Roger Bacon, heard you that?"

The Friar turned from the window, clutching the compasses tighter.

"No, no!" he appealed. "Not with Falcodi – not with our English-hearted Foulkes made Pope. He's wise – he's learned. He reads what I have put forth. Foulkes would never suffer it."

"'Holy Pope is one thing, Holy Church another,'" Roger quoted.

"But, I – I can bear witness it is no Art Magic," the Friar went on. "Nothing is it, except Art optical – wisdom after trial and experiment, mark you. I can prove it, and – my name weighs with men who dare think."

"Find them!" croaked Roger of Salerno. "Five or six in all the world. That makes less than fifty pounds by weight of ashes at the stake. I have watched such men – reduced."

"I will not give this up!" The Friar's voice cracked in passion and despair. "It would be to sin against the Light."

"No, no! Let us – let us sanctify the little animals of Varro," said Thomas.

Stephen leaned forward, fished his ring out of the cup, and slipped it on his finger. "My sons," said he, "we have seen what we have seen."

"That it is no magic but simple Art," the Friar persisted.

" 'Avails nothing. In the eyes of Mother Church we have seen more than is permitted to man."

"But it was Life – created and rejoicing," said Thomas.

"To look into Hell as we shall be judged – as we shall be proved – to have looked, is for priests only."

"Or green-sick virgins on the road to sainthood who, for cause any midwife could give you —"

The Abbot's half-lifted hand checked Roger of Salerno's outpouring.

"Nor may even priests see more in Hell than Church knows to be there. John, there is respect due to Church as well as to Devils."

"My trade's the outside of things," said John quietly. "I have my patterns."

"But you may need to look again for more," the Friar said.

"In my craft, a thing done is done with. We go on to new shapes after that."

"And if we trespass beyond bounds, even in thought, we lie open to the judgment of the Church," the Abbot continued.

"But thou knowest – *knowest*!" Roger of Salerno had returned to the attack. "Here's all the world in darkness concerning the causes of things – from the fever across the lane to thy Lady's – thine own Lady's – eating malady. Think!"

"I have thought upon it, Salerno! I have thought indeed."

Thomas the Infirmarian lifted his head again; and this time he did not stammer at all. "As in the water, so in the blood must they rage and war with each other! I have dreamed these ten years – I thought it was a sin – but my dreams and Varro's are true! Think on it again! Here's the Light under our very hand!"

"Quench it! You'd no more stand to roasting than – any other. I'll give you the case as Church – as I myself – would frame it. Our John here returns from the Moors, and shows us a hell of devils contending in the compass of one drop of water. Magic past clearance! You can hear the faggots crackle."

"But thou knowest! Thou hast seen it all before! For man's poor sake! For old friendship's sake – Stephen!" The Friar was trying to stuff the compasses into his bosom as he appealed.

"What Stephen de Sautré knows, you his friends know also. I would have you, now, obey the Abbot of St. Illod's. Give to me!" He held out his ringed hand.

"May I – may John here – not even make a drawing of one – one screw?" said the broken Friar, in spite of himself.

"Nowise!" Stephen took it over. "Your dagger, John. Sheathed will serve."

He unscrewed the metal cylinder, laid it on the table, and with the dagger's hilt smashed some crystal to sparkling dust which he swept into a scooped hand and cast behind the hearth.

"It would seem," said he, "the choice lies between two sins. To deny the world a Light which is under our hand, or to enlighten the world before her time. What you have seen, I saw long since among the physicians at Cairo. And I know what doctrine they drew from it. Hast *thou* dreamed, Thomas? I also – with fuller knowledge. But this birth, my sons, is untimely. It will be but the mother of more death, more torture, more division, and greater darkness in this dark age. Therefore I, who know both my world and the Church, take this Choice on my conscience. Go! It is finished."

He thrust the wooden part of the compasses deep among the beech logs till all was burned.

* * *

THE LAST ODE

(Nov. 27, B.C. 8)
Horace, Ode 31, Bk V

As watchers couched beneath a Bantine oak,
　　Hearing the dawn-wind stir,
Know that the present strength of night is broke
　　Though no dawn threaten her
Till dawn's appointed hour – so Virgil died,
Aware of change at hand, and prophesied

Change upon all the Eternal Gods had made
　　And on the Gods alike –
Fated as dawn but, as the dawn, delayed
　　Till the just hour should strike –

A Star new-risen above the living and dead;
　　And the lost shades that were our loves restored
As lovers, and for ever. So he said;
　　Having received the word . . .

Maecenas waits me on the Esquiline:
　　Thither to-night go I . . .
And shall this dawn restore us, Virgil mine,
　　To dawn? Beneath what sky?

THE GARDENER

THE GARDENER

* * *

> One grave to me was given,
>   One watch till Judgement Day;
> And God looked down from Heaven
>   And rolled the stone away.
>
> *One day in all the years,*
>   *One hour in that one day,*
> *His Angel saw my tears,*
>   *And rolled the stone away!*

EVERY ONE in the village knew that Helen Turrell did her duty by all her world, and by none more honourably than by her only brother's unfortunate child. The village knew, too, that George Turrell had tried his family severely since early youth, and were not surprised to be told that, after many fresh starts given and thrown away, he, an Inspector of Indian Police, had entangled himself with the daughter of a retired non-commissioned officer, and had died of a fall from a horse a few weeks before his child was born. Mercifully, George's father and mother were both dead, and though Helen, thirty-five and independent, might well have washed her hands of the whole disgraceful affair, she most nobly took charge, though she was, at the time, under threat of lung trouble which had driven her to the South of France. She arranged for the passage of the child and a nurse from Bombay, met them at Marseilles, nursed the baby through an attack of infantile dysentery due to the carelessness of the nurse, whom she had had to dismiss, and at last, thin and worn but triumphant, brought the boy late in the Autumn, wholly restored, to her Hampshire home.

All these details were public property, for Helen was as open as the day, and held that scandals are only increased by hushing them up. She admitted that George had always been rather a black sheep, but things might have been much worse if the mother had insisted on her right to keep the boy. Luckily, it seemed that people of that class would do almost anything for money, and, as George had always turned to her in his scrapes, she felt herself justified – her friends agreed with her – in cutting the whole non-commissioned officer connection, and giving the child every advantage. A christening, by the Rector, under the name of Michael, was the first step. So far as she knew herself, she was not, she said, a child-lover, but, for all his faults, she had been very fond of George, and she pointed out that little Michael had his father's mouth to a line; which made something to build upon.

As a matter of fact, it was the Turrell forehead, broad, low, and well-shaped, with the widely spaced eyes beneath it, that Michael had most faithfully reproduced. His mouth was somewhat better cut than the family type. But Helen, who would concede nothing good to his mother's side, vowed he was a Turrell all over, and, there being no one to contradict, the likeness was established.

In a few years Michael took his place, as accepted as Helen had always been – fearless, philosophical, and fairly good-looking. At six, he wished to know why he could not call her "Mummy," as other boys called their mothers. She explained that she was only his auntie, and that aunties were not quite the same as mummies, but that, if it gave him pleasure, he might call her "Mummy" at bedtime, for a pet-name between themselves.

Michael kept his secret most loyally, but Helen, as usual, explained the fact to her friends; which when Michael heard, he raged.

"Why did you tell? *Why* did you tell?" came at the end of the storm.

"Because it's always best to tell the truth," Helen answered, her arm round him as he shook in his cot.

"All right, but when the troof's ugly I don't think it's nice."

"Don't you, dear?"

"No, I don't, and" – she felt the small body stiffen – "now you've told, I won't call you 'Mummy' any more – not even at bedtimes."

"But isn't that rather unkind?" said Helen softly.

"I don't care! I don't care! You've hurted me in my insides and I'll hurt you back. I'll hurt you as long as I live!"

"Don't, oh, don't talk like that, dear! You don't know what —"

"I will! And when I'm dead I'll hurt you worse!"

"Thank goodness, I shall be dead long before you, darling."

"Huh! Emma says, ' 'Never know your luck.' " (Michael had been talking to Helen's elderly, flat-faced maid.) "Lots of little boys die quite soon. So'll I. *Then* you'll see!"

Helen caught her breath and moved towards the door, but the wail of "Mummy! Mummy!" drew her back again, and the two wept together.

* * *

At ten years old, after two terms at a prep. school, something or somebody gave him the idea that his civil status was not quite regular. He attacked Helen on the subject, breaking down her stammered defences with the family directness.

" 'Don't believe a word of it," he said, cheerily, at the end. "People wouldn't have talked like they did if my people had been married. But don't you bother, Auntie. I've found out all about my sort in English Hist'ry and the Shakespeare bits. There was William the Conqueror to begin with, and – oh, heaps more, and they all got on first-rate. 'Twon't make any difference to you, my being *that* – will it?"

"As if anything could —" she began.

"All right. We won't talk about it any more if it makes you cry." He never mentioned the thing again of his own will, but when, two years later, he skilfully managed to have measles in the holidays, as his temperature went up to the appointed one hundred and four he muttered of nothing else, till Helen's voice, piercing at last his delirium, reached him with assurance that nothing on earth or beyond could make any difference between them.

The terms at his public school and the wonderful Christmas, Easter, and Summer holidays followed each other, variegated and glorious as jewels on a string; and as jewels Helen treasured them. In due time Michael developed his own interests, which ran their courses and gave way to others; but his interest in Helen was constant and increasing throughout. She repaid it with all that she had of affection or could command of counsel and money; and since Michael was no fool, the War took him just before what was like to have been a most promising career.

He was to have gone up to Oxford, with a scholarship, in October. At the end of August he was on the edge of joining the first holocaust of public-school boys who threw themselves into the Line; but the captain of his O.T.C., where he had been sergeant for nearly a year, headed him off and steered him directly to a commission in a battalion so new that half of it still wore the old Army red, and the other half was breeding meningitis through living overcrowdedly in damp tents. Helen had been shocked at the idea of direct enlistment.

"But it's in the family," Michael laughed.

"You don't mean to tell me that you believed that old story all this time?" said Helen. (Emma, her maid, had been dead now several years.) "I gave you my word of honour – and I give it again – that – that it's all right. It is indeed."

"Oh, *that* doesn't worry me. It never did," he replied valiantly. "What I meant was, I should have got into the show earlier if I'd enlisted – like my grandfather."

"Don't talk like that! Are you afraid of its ending so soon, then?"

"No such luck. You know what K. says."

"Yes. But my banker told me last Monday it couldn't *possibly* last beyond Christmas – for financial reasons."

" 'Hope he's right, but our Colonel – and he's a Regular – says it's going to be a long job."

Michael's battalion was fortunate in that, by some chance which meant several "leaves," it was used for coast-defence among shallow trenches on the Norfolk coast; thence sent north to watch the mouth of a Scotch estuary, and, lastly, held for weeks on a baseless rumour of distant service. But, the very day that Michael was to have met Helen for four whole hours at a railway-junction up the line, it was hurled out, to help make good the wastage of Loos, and he had only just time to send her a wire of farewell.

In France luck again helped the battalion. It was put down near the Salient, where it led a meritorious and unexacting life, while the Somme was being manufactured; and enjoyed the peace of the Armentières and Laventie sectors when that battle began. Finding that it had sound views on protecting its own flanks and could dig, a prudent Commander stole it out of its own Division, under pretence of helping to lay telegraphs, and used it round Ypres at large.

A month later, and just after Michael had written Helen that there was nothing special doing and therefore no need to worry, a shell-splinter dropping out of a wet dawn killed him at once. The next shell uprooted and laid down over the body what had been the foundation of a barn wall, so neatly that none but an expert would have guessed that anything unpleasant had happened.

* * *

By this time the village was old in experience of war, and, English fashion, had evolved a ritual to meet it. When the postmistress handed her seven-year-old daughter the official telegram to take to Miss Turrell, she observed to the Rector's gardener: "It's Miss Helen's turn now." He replied, thinking of his own son: "Well, he's lasted longer than some." The child herself came to the front-door weeping aloud, because Master Michael had often given her sweets. Helen, presently, found herself pulling down the house-blinds one after one with great care, and saying earnestly to each: "Missing *always* means dead." Then she took her place in the dreary procession that was impelled to go through an inevitable series of unprofitable emotions. The Rector, of course, preached hope and prophesied word, very soon, from a prison camp. Several friends, too, told her perfectly truthful tales, but always about other women, to whom, after months and months of silence, their missing had been miraculously restored. Other people urged her to communicate with infallible Secretaries of organisations who could communicate with benevolent neutrals, who could extract accurate information from the most secretive of Hun prison commandants. Helen did and wrote and signed everything that was suggested or put before her.

Once, on one of Michael's leaves, he had taken her over a munition factory, where she saw the progress of a shell from blank-iron to the all but finished article. It struck her at the time that the wretched thing was never left alone for a single second; and "I'm being manufactured into a bereaved next of kin," she told herself, as she prepared her documents.

In due course, when all the organisations had deeply or sincerely regretted their inability to trace, etc., something gave way within her and all sensation – save of thankfulness for the release – came to an end in blessed passivity. Michael had died and her world had stood still and she had been one with the full shock of that arrest. Now she was standing still and the world was going forward, but it did not concern her – in no way or relation did it touch her. She knew this by the ease with which she could slip Michael's name into talk and incline her head to the proper angle, at the proper murmur of sympathy.

In the blessed realisation of that relief, the Armistice with all its bells broke over her and passed unheeded. At the end of another year she had overcome her physical loathing of the living and returned young, so that she could take them by the hand and almost sincerely wish them well. She had no interest in any aftermath, national or personal, of the war, but, moving at an immense distance, she sat on various relief committees and held strong views – she heard herself delivering them – about the site of the proposed village War Memorial.

Then there came to her, as next of kin, an official intimation, backed by a page of a letter to her in indelible pencil, a silver identity-disc, and a watch, to the effect that the body of Lieutenant Michael Turrell had been found, identified, and re-interred in Hagenzeele Third Military Cemetery – the letter of the row and the grave's number in that row duly given.

So Helen found herself moved on to another process of the manufacture – to a world full of exultant or broken relatives, now strong in the certainty that there was an altar upon earth where they might lay their love. These soon told her, and by means of time-tables made clear, how easy it was and how little it interfered with life's affairs to go and see one's grave.

"*So* different," as the Rector's wife said, "if he'd been killed in Mesopotamia, or even Gallipoli."

The agony of being waked up to some sort of second life drove Helen across the Channel, where, in a new world of abbreviated titles, she learnt that Hagenzeele Third could be comfortably reached by an afternoon train which fitted in with the morning boat, and that there was a comfortable little hotel not three kilometres from Hagenzeele itself, where one could spend quite a comfortable night and see one's grave next morning. All this she had from a Central Authority who lived in a board and tar-paper shed on the skirts of a razed city full of whirling lime-dust and blown papers.

"By the way," said he, "you know your grave, of course?"

"Yes, thank you," said Helen, and showed its row and number typed on Michael's own little typewriter. The officer would have checked it, out of one of his many books; but a large Lancashire woman thrust between them and bade him tell her where she might find her son, who had been corporal in the A.S.C. His proper name, she sobbed, was Anderson, but, coming of respectable folk, he had of course enlisted under the name of Smith; and had been killed at Dickiebush, in early 'Fifteen. She had not his number nor did she know which of his two Christian names he might have used with his alias; but her Cook's tourist ticket expired at the end of Easter week, and if by then she could not find her child she should go mad. Whereupon she fell forward on Helen's breast; but the officer's wife came out quickly from a little bedroom behind the office, and the three of them lifted the woman on to the cot.

"They are often like this," said the officer's wife, loosening the tight bonnet-strings. "Yesterday she said he'd been killed at Hooge. Are you sure you know your grave? It makes such a difference."

"Yes, thank you," said Helen, and hurried out before the woman on the bed should begin to lament again.

* * *

Tea in a crowded mauve and blue striped wooden structure, with a false front, carried her still further into the nightmare. She paid her bill beside a stolid, plain-featured English-woman, who, hearing her inquire about the train to Hagen-zeele, volunteered to come with her.

"I'm going to Hagenzeele myself," she explained. "Not to Hagenzeele Third; mine is Sugar Factory, but they call it La Rosière now. It's just south of Hagenzeele Three. Have you got your room at the hotel there?"

"Oh yes, thank you. I've wired."

"That's better. Sometimes the place is quite full, and at others there's hardly a soul. But they've put bathrooms into the old Lion d'Or – that's the hotel on the west side of Sugar Factory – and it draws off a lot of people, luckily."

"It's all new to me. This is the first time I've been over."

"Indeed! This is my ninth time since the Armistice. Not on my own account. I haven't lost any one, thank God – but, like every one else, I've a lot of friends at home who have.

Coming over as often as I do, I find it helps them to have someone just look at the place and tell them about it afterwards. And one can take photos for them, too. I get quite a list of commissions to execute." She laughed nervously and tapped her slung Kodak. "There are two or three to see at Sugar Factory this time, and plenty of others in the cemeteries all about. My system is to save them up, and arrange them, you know. And when I've got enough commissions for one area to make it worth while, I pop over and execute them. It *does* comfort people."

"I suppose so," Helen answered, shivering as they entered the little train.

"Of course it does. (Isn't it lucky we've got window-seats?) It must do or they wouldn't ask one to do it, would they? I've a list of quite twelve or fifteen commissions here" – she tapped the Kodak again – "I must sort them out to-night. Oh, I forgot to ask you. What's yours?"

"My nephew," said Helen. "But I was very fond of him."

"Ah, yes! I sometimes wonder whether *they* know after death? What do you think?"

"Oh, I don't – I haven't dared to think much about that sort of thing," said Helen, almost lifting her hands to keep her off.

"Perhaps that's better," the woman answered. "The sense of loss must be enough, I expect. Well, I won't worry you any more."

Helen was grateful, but when they reached the hotel Mrs. Scarsworth (they had exchanged names) insisted on dining at the same table with her, and after the meal, in the little, hideous salon full of low-voiced relatives, took Helen through her "commissions" with biographies of the dead, where she happened to know them, and sketches of their next of kin. Helen endured till nearly half-past nine, ere she fled to her room.

Almost at once there was a knock at her door and Mrs. Scarsworth entered; her hands, holding the dreadful list, clasped before her.

"Yes – yes – *I* know," she began. "You're sick of me, but I want to tell you something. You – you aren't married, are you? Then perhaps you won't . . . But it doesn't matter. I've *got* to tell someone. I can't go on any longer like this."

"But please —" Mrs. Scarsworth had backed against the shut door, and her mouth worked dryly.

"In a minute," she said. "You – you know about these graves of mine I was telling you about downstairs, just now? They really *are* commissions. At least several of them are." Her eye wandered round the room. "What extraordinary wall-papers they have in Belgium, don't you think? . . . Yes. I swear they are commissions. But there's *one*, d'you see, and – and he was more to me than anything else in the world. Do you understand?"

Helen nodded.

"More than anyone else. And, of course, he oughtn't to have been. He ought to have been nothing to me. But he *was*. He *is*. That's why I do the commissions, you see. That's all."

"But why do you tell me?" Helen asked desperately.

"Because I'm *so* tired of lying. Tired of lying – always lying – year in and year out. When I don't tell lies I've got to act 'em and I've got to think 'em, always. *You* don't know what that means. He was everything to me that he oughtn't to have been – the one real thing – the only thing that ever happened to me in all my life; and I've had to pretend he wasn't. I've had to watch every word I said, and think out what lie I'd tell next, for years and years!"

"How many years?" Helen asked.

"Six years and four months before, and two and three-quarters after. I've gone to him eight times, since. To-morrow'll make the ninth, and – and I can't – I *can't* go to him again with nobody in the world knowing. I want to be honest with someone before I go. Do you understand? It doesn't matter about *me*. I was never truthful, even as a girl. But it isn't worthy of *him*. So – so I – I had to tell you. I can't keep it up any longer. Oh, I can't!"

She lifted her joined hands almost to the level of her mouth, and brought them down sharply, still joined, to full arms' length below her waist. Helen reached forward, caught them, bowed her head over them, and murmured: "Oh, my dear! My dear!" Mrs. Scarsworth stepped back, her face all mottled.

"My God!" said she. "Is *that* how you take it?"

Helen could not speak, and the woman went out; but it was a long while before Helen was able to sleep.

* * *

Next morning Mrs. Scarsworth left early on her round of commissions, and Helen walked alone to Hagenzeele Third. The place was still in the making, and stood some five or six feet above the metalled road, which it flanked for hundreds of yards. Culverts across a deep ditch served for entrances through the unfinished boundary wall. She climbed a few wooden-faced earthen steps and then met the entire crowded level of the thing in one held breath. She did not know that Hagenzeele Third counted twenty-one thousand dead already. All she saw was a merciless sea of black crosses, bearing little strips of stamped tin at all angles across their faces. She could distinguish no order or arrangement in their mass; nothing but a waist-high wilderness as of weeds stricken dead, rushing at her. She went forward, moved to the left and the right hopelessly, wondering by what guidance she should ever come to her own. A great distance away there was a line of whiteness. It proved to be a block of some two or three hundred graves whose headstones had already been set, whose flowers were planted out, and whose new-sown grass showed green. Here she could see clear-cut letters at the ends of the rows, and, referring to her slip, realised that it was not here she must look.

A man knelt behind a line of headstones – evidently a gardener, for he was firming a young plant in the soft earth. She went towards him, her paper in her hand. He rose at her approach and without prelude or salutation asked: "Who are you looking for?"

"Lieutenant Michael Turrell – my nephew," said Helen slowly and word for word, as she had many thousands of times in her life.

The man lifted his eyes and looked at her with infinite compassion before he turned from the fresh-sown grass toward the naked black crosses.

"Come with me," he said, "and I will show you where your son lies."

* * *

When Helen left the Cemetery she turned for a last look. In the distance she saw the man bending over his young plants; and she went away, supposing him to be the gardener.

* * *

THE BURDEN

One grief on me is laid
　　Each day of every year,
Wherein no soul can aid,
　　Whereof no soul can hear:
Whereto no end is seen
　　Except to grieve again –
Ah, Mary Magdalene,
　　Where is there greater pain?

To dream on dear disgrace
　　Each hour of every day –
To bring no honest face
　　To aught I do or say:
To lie from morn till e'en –
　　To know my lies are vain –
Ah, Mary Magdalene,
　　Where can be greater pain?

To watch my steadfast fear
  Attend my every way
Each day of every year –
  Each hour of every day:
To burn, and chill between –
  To quake and rage again –
Ah, Mary Magdalene,
  Where shall be greater pain?

One grave to me was given –
  To guard till Judgement Day –
But God looked down from Heaven
  And rolled the Stone away!

One day of all my years –
  One hour of that one day –
His Angel saw my tears
  And rolled the Stone away!

DAYSPRING MISHANDLED

DAYSPRING MISHANDLED

* * *

C'est moi, c'est moi, c'est moi!
  Je suis la Mandragore!
La fille des beaux jours qui s'éveille à l'aurore –
  Et qui chante pour toi!

C. Nodier

I N the days beyond compare and before the Judgments, a
genius called Graydon foresaw that the advance of education and the standard of living would submerge all mind-
marks in one mudrush of standardised reading-matter, and
so created the Fictional Supply Syndicate to meet the demand.

Since a few days' work for him brought them more money
than a week's elsewhere, he drew many young men – some
now eminent – into his employ. He bade them keep their
eyes on the Sixpenny Dream Book, the Army and Navy
Stores Catalogue (this for backgrounds and furniture as they
changed), and *The Hearthstone Friend*, a weekly publication
which specialised unrivalledly in the domestic emotions. Yet,
even so, youth would not be denied, and some of the collaborated love-talk in "Passion Hath Peril," and "Ena's Lost
Lovers," and the account of the murder of the Earl in "The
Wickwire Tragedies" – to name but a few masterpieces now
never mentioned for fear of blackmail – was as good as anything to which their authors signed their real names in more
distinguished years.

Among the young ravens driven to roost awhile on Graydon's ark was James Andrew Manallace – a darkish, slow

northerner of the type that does not ignite, but must be detonated. Given written or verbal outlines of a plot, he was useless; but, with a half-dozen pictures round which to write his tale, he could astonish.

And he adored that woman who afterwards became the mother of Vidal Benzaguen,* and who suffered and died because she loved one unworthy. There was, also, among the company a mannered, bellied person called Alured Castorley, who talked and wrote about "Bohemia," but was always afraid of being "compromised" by the weekly suppers at Neminaka's Café in Hestern Square, where the Syndicate work was apportioned, and where every one looked out for himself. He, too, for a time, had loved Vidal's mother, in his own way.

Now, one Saturday at Neminaka's, Graydon, who had given Manallace a sheaf of prints – torn from an extinct children's book called *Philippa's Queen* – on which to improvise, asked for results. Manallace went down into his ulster-pocket, hesitated a moment, and said the stuff had turned into poetry on his hands.

"Bosh!"

"That's what it isn't," the boy retorted. "It's rather good."

"Then it's no use to us." Graydon laughed. "Have you brought back the cuts?"

Manallace handed them over. There was a castle in the series; a knight or so in armour; an old lady in a horned head-dress; a young ditto; a very obvious Hebrew; a clerk, with pen and inkhorn, checking wine-barrels on a wharf; and a Crusader. On the back of one of the prints was a note, "If he doesn't want to go, why can't he be captured and held to ransom?" Graydon asked what it all meant.

"I don't know yet. A comic opera, perhaps," said Manallace.

Graydon, who seldom wasted time, passed the cuts on to someone else, and advanced Manallace a couple of sovereigns

*"The Village that Voted the Earth was Flat." *A Diversity of Creatures.*

to carry on with, as usual; at which Castorley was angry and would have said something unpleasant but was suppressed. Half-way through supper, Castorley told the company that a relative had died and left him an independence; and that he now withdrew from "hackwork" to follow "Literature." Generally, the Syndicate rejoiced in a comrade's good fortune, but Castorley had gifts of waking dislike. So the news was received with a vote of thanks, and he went out before the end, and, it was said, proposed to 'Dal Benzaguen's mother, who refused him. He did not come back. Manallace, who had arrived a little exalted, got so drunk before midnight that a man had to stay and see him home. But liquor never touched him above the belt, and when he had slept awhile, he recited to the gas-chandelier the poetry he had made out of the pictures; said that, on second thoughts, he would convert it into comic opera; deplored the Upas-tree influence of Gilbert and Sullivan; sang somewhat to illustrate his point; and – after words, by the way, with a negress in yellow satin – was steered to his rooms.

In the course of a few years, Graydon's foresight and genius were rewarded. The public began to read and reason upon higher planes, and the Syndicate grew rich. Later still, people demanded of their printed matter what they expected in their clothing and furniture. So, precisely as the three guinea handbag is followed in three weeks by its thirteen and sevenpence ha'penny indistinguishable sister, they enjoyed perfect synthetic substitutes for Plot, Sentiment, and Emotion. Graydon died before the Cinema-caption school came in, but he left his widow twenty-seven thousand pounds.

Manallace made a reputation, and, more important, money for Vidal's mother when her husband ran away and the first symptoms of her paralysis showed. His line was the jocundly-sentimental Wardour Street brand of adventure, told in a style that exactly met, but never exceeded, every expectation.

As he once said when urged to "write a real book": "I've got my label, and I'm not going to chew it off. If you save people thinking, you can do anything with 'em." His output apart, he was genuinely a man of letters. He rented a small cottage in the country and economised on everything, except the care and charges of Vidal's mother.

Castorley flew higher. When his legacy freed him from "hackwork," he became first a critic – in which calling he loyally scalped all his old associates as they came up – and then looked for some speciality. Having found it (Chaucer was the prey), he consolidated his position before he occupied it, by his careful speech, his cultivated bearing, and the whispered words of his friends whom he, too, had saved the trouble of thinking. It followed that, when he published his first serious articles on Chaucer, all the world which is interested in Chaucer said: "This is an authority." But he was no impostor. He learned and knew his poet and his age; and in a month-long dog-fight in an austere literary weekly, met and mangled a recognised Chaucer expert of the day. He also, "for old sake's sake," as he wrote to a friend, went out of his way to review one of Manallace's books with an intimacy of unclean deduction (this was before the days of Freud) which long stood as a record. Some member of the extinct Syndicate took occasion to ask him if he would – for old sake's sake – help Vidal's mother to a new treatment. He answered that he had "known the lady very slightly and the calls on his purse were so heavy that," etc. The writer showed the letter to Manallace, who said he was glad Castorley hadn't interfered. Vidal's mother was then wholly paralysed. Only her eyes could move, and those always looked for the husband who had left her. She died thus in Manallace's arms in April of the first year of the War.

During the War he and Castorley worked as some sort of departmental dishwashers in the Office of Co-ordinated Supervisals. Here Manallace came to know Castorley again. Castorley, having a sweet tooth, cadged lumps of sugar for his tea from a typist, and when she took to giving them to a younger man, arranged that she should be reported for smoking in unauthorised apartments. Manallace possessed himself

of every detail of the affair, as compensation for the review
of his book. Then there came a night when, waiting for a big
air-raid, the two men had talked humanly, and Manallace
spoke of Vidal's mother. Castorley said something in reply,
and from that hour – as was learned several years later –
Manallace's real life-work and interests began.

The War over, Castorley set about to make himself Supreme Pontiff on Chaucer by methods not far removed from
the employment of poison-gas. The English Pope was silent,
through private griefs, and influenza had carried off the
learned Hun who claimed continental allegiance. Thus Castorley crowed unchallenged from Upsala to Seville, while
Manallace went back to his cottage with the photo of Vidal's
mother over the mantelpiece. She seemed to have emptied
out his life, and left him only fleeting interests in trifles. His
private diversions were experiments of uncertain outcome,
which, he said, rested him after a day's gadzooking and
vitalstapping. I found him, for instance, one week-end, in his
toolshed-scullery, boiling a brew of slimy barks which were,
if mixed with oak-galls, vitriol and wine, to become an ink-
powder. We boiled it till the Monday, and it turned into an
adhesive stronger than birdlime, and entangled us both.

At other times, he would carry me off, once in a few
weeks, to sit at Castorley's feet, and hear him talk about
Chaucer. Castorley's voice, bad enough in youth, when it
could be shouted down, had, with culture and tact, grown
almost insupportable. His mannerisms, too, had multiplied
and set. He minced and mouthed, postured and chewed his
words throughout those terrible evenings; and poisoned not
only Chaucer, but every shred of English literature which he
used to embellish him. He was shameless, too, as regarded
self-advertisement and "recognition" – weaving elaborate in-
trigues; forming petty friendships and confederacies, to be
dissolved next week in favour of more promising alliances;
fawning, snubbing, lecturing, organising and lying as unrest-
ingly as a politician, in chase of the Knighthood due not to
him (he always called on his Maker to forbid such a thought)

but as tribute to Chaucer. Yet, sometimes, he could break
from his obsession and prove how a man's work will try to
save the soul of him. He would tell us charmingly of copyists
of the fifteenth century in England and the Low Countries,
who had multiplied the Chaucer MSS., of which there remained – he gave us the exact number – and how each scribe
could by him (and, he implied, by him alone) be distinguished from every other by some peculiarity of letter-
formation, spacing or like trick of pen-work; and how he
could fix the dates of their work within five years. Sometimes
he would give us an hour of really interesting stuff and then
return to his overdue "recognition." The changes sickened
me, but Manallace defended him, as a master in his own line
who had revealed Chaucer to at least one grateful soul.

This, as far as I remembered, was the Autumn when Manallace holidayed in the Shetlands or the Faroes, and came
back with a stone "quern" – a hand corn-grinder. He said it
interested him from the ethnological standpoint. His whim
lasted till next harvest, and was followed by a religious spasm
which, naturally, translated itself into literature. He showed
me a battered and mutilated Vulgate of 1485, patched up the
back with bits of legal parchments, which he had bought for
thirty-five shillings. Some monk's attempt to rubricate chapter-initials had caught, it seemed, his forlorn fancy, and he
dabbled in shells of gold and silver paint for weeks.

That also faded out, and he went to the Continent to get
local colour for a love-story, about Alva and the Dutch, and
the next year I saw practically nothing of him. This released
me from seeing much of Castorley, but, at intervals, I would
go there to dine with him, when his wife – an unappetising,
ash-coloured woman – made no secret that his friends
wearied her almost as much as he did. But at a later meeting,
not long after Manallace had finished his Low Countries'
novel, I found Castorley charged to bursting-point with
triumph and high information hardly withheld. He confided
to me that a time was at hand when great matters would be
made plain, and "recognition" would be inevitable. I as-

sumed, naturally, that there was fresh scandal or heresy afoot in Chaucer circles, and kept my curiosity within bounds.

In time, New York cabled that a fragment of a hitherto unknown Canterbury Tale lay safe in the steel-walled vaults of the seven-million-dollar Sunnapia Collection. It was news on an international scale – the New World exultant – the Old deploring the "burden of British taxation which drove such treasures, etc.", and the lighter-minded journals disporting themselves according to their publics; for "our Dan," as one earnest Sunday editor observed, "lies closer to the national heart than we wot of." Common decency made me call on Castorley, who, to my surprise, had not yet descended into the arena. I found him, made young again by joy, deep in just-passed proofs.

Yes, he said, it was all true. He had, of course, been in it from the first. There had been found one hundred and seven new lines of Chaucer tacked on to an abridged end of *The Persone's Tale*, the whole the work of Abraham Mentzius, better known as Mentzel of Antwerp (1388–1438/9) – I might remember he had talked about him – whose distinguishing peculiarities were a certain Byzantine formation of his *g*'s, the use of a "sickle-slanted" reed-pen, which cut into the vellum at certain letters; and, above all, a tendency to spell English words on Dutch lines, whereof the manuscript carried one convincing proof. For instance (he wrote it out for me), a girl praying against an undesired marriage, says:

> "Ah Jesu-Moder, pitie my oe peyne.
> Daiespringe mishandeelt cometh nat agayne."

Would I, please, note the spelling of "mishandeelt"? Stark Dutch and Mentzel's besetting sin! But in *his* position one took nothing for granted. The page had been part of the stiffening of the side of an old Bible, bought in a parcel by Dredd, the big dealer, because it had some rubricated chapter-initials, and by Dredd shipped, with a consignment of similar odds and ends, to the Sunnapia Collection, where they were making a glass-cased exhibit of the whole history of illumination and did not care how many books they gutted for that purpose. There, someone who noticed a crack in the back of the volume had unearthed it. He went on: "They didn't know what to make of the thing at first. But they knew about *me*! They kept quiet till I'd been consulted. You might have noticed I was out of England for three months.

"I was over there, of course. It was what is called a 'spoil' – a page Mentzel had spoiled with his Dutch spelling – I expect he had had the English dictated to him – then had evidently used the vellum for trying out his reeds; and then, I suppose, had put it away. The 'spoil' had been doubled, pasted together, and slipped in as stiffening to the old book-cover. I had it steamed open, and analysed the wash. It gave the flour-grains in the paste – coarse, because of the old millstone – and there were traces of the grit itself. What? Oh, possibly a handmill of Mentzel's own time. He may have doubled the spoilt page and used it for part of a pad to steady wood-cuts on. It may have knocked about his workshop for years. That, indeed, is practically certain because a beginner from the Low Countries has tried his reed on a few lines of some monkish hymn – not a bad lilt tho' – which must have been common form. Oh yes, the page may have been used in other books before it was used for the Vulgate. That doesn't matter, but *this* does. Listen! I took a wash, for analysis, from a blot in one corner – that would be after Mentzel had given up trying to make a possible page of it, and had grown care-less – and I got the actual *ink* of the period! It's a practically eternal stuff compounded on – I've forgotten his name for the minute – the scribe at Bury St. Edmunds, of course – hawthorn bark and wine. Anyhow, on *his* formula. *That* wouldn't interest you either, but, taken with all the other testimony, it clinches the thing. (You'll see it all in my State-ment to the Press on Monday.) Overwhelming, isn't it?"

"Overwhelming," I said, with sincerity. "Tell me what the tale was about, though. That's more in my line."

"I know it; but *I* have to be equipped on all sides. The verses are relatively easy for one to pronounce on. The freshness, the fun, the humanity, the fragrance of it all, cries – no, shouts – itself as Dan's work. Why 'Daiespringe mishandled' alone stamps it from Dan's mint. Plangent as doom, my dear boy – plangent as doom! It's all in my Statement. Well, substantially, the fragment deals with a girl whose parents wish her to marry an elderly suitor. The mother isn't so keen on it, but the father, an old Knight, is. The girl, of course, is in love with a younger and a poorer man. Common form? Granted. Then the father, who doesn't in the least want to, is ordered off to a Crusade and, by way of passing on the kick, as we used to say during the War, orders the girl to be kept in duresse till his return or her consent to the old suitor. Common form, again? Quite so. That's too much for her mother. She reminds the old Knight of his age and infirmities, and the discomforts of Crusading. Are you sure I'm not boring you?"

"Not at all," I said, though time had begun to whirl backwards through my brain to a red-velvet, pomatum-scented side-room at Neminaka's and Manallace's set face intoning to the gas.

"You'll read it all in my Statement next week. The sum is that the old lady tells him of a certain Knight-adventurer on the French coast, who, for a consideration, waylays Knights who don't relish crusading and holds them to impossible ransoms till the trooping-season is over, or they are returned sick. He keeps a ship in the Channel to pick 'em up and transfers his birds to his castle ashore, where he has a reputation for doing 'em well. As the old lady points out:

'And if perchance thou fall into his honde
By God how canstow ride to Holilonde?'

"You see? Modern in essence as Gilbert and Sullivan, but handled as only Dan could! And she reminds him that 'Honour and olde bones' parted company long ago. He makes one splendid appeal for the spirit of chivalry:

Lat all men change as Fortune may send,
But Knighthood beareth service to the end,

and *then*, of course, he gives in:

> For what his woman willeth to be don
> Her manne must or wauken Hell anon.

"Then she hints that the daughter's young lover, who is in the Bordeaux wine-trade, could open negotiations for a kidnapping without compromising him. And *then* that careless brute Mentzel spoils his page and chucks it! But there's enough to show what's going to happen. You'll see it all in my Statement. Was there ever anything in literary finds to hold a candle to it? . . . And they give grocers Knighthoods for selling cheese!"

I went away before he could get into his stride on that course. I wanted to think, and to see Manallace. But I waited till Castorley's Statement came out. He had left himself no loophole. And when, a little later, his (nominally the Sunnapia people's) "scientific" account of their analyses and tests appeared, criticism ceased, and some journals began to demand "public recognition." Manallace wrote to me on this subject, and I went down to his cottage, where he at once asked me to sign a Memorial on Castorley's behalf. With luck, he said, we might get him a K.B.E. in the next Honours List. Had I read the Statement?

"I have," I replied. "But I want to ask you something first. Do you remember the night you got drunk at Neminaka's, and I stayed behind to look after you?"

"Oh, *that* time," said he, pondering. "Wait a minute! I remember Graydon advancing me two quid. He was a generous paymaster. And I remember – now, who the devil rolled me under the sofa – and what for?"

"We all did," I replied. "You wanted to read us what you'd written to those Chaucer cuts."

"I don't remember that. No! I don't remember anything after the sofa-episode . . . *You* always said that you took me home – didn't you?"

"I did, and you told Kentucky Kate outside the old

Empire that you had been faithful, Cynara, in your fashion."

"Did I?" said he. "My God! Well, I suppose I have." He stared into the fire. "What else?"

"Before we left Neminaka's you recited me what you had made out of the cuts – the whole tale! So – you see?"

"Ye-es." He nodded. "What are you going to do about it?"

"What are *you*?"

"I'm going to help him get his Knighthood – first."

"Why?"

"I'll tell you what he said about 'Dal's mother – the night there was an air-raid on the offices."

He told it.

"That's why," he said. "Am I justified?"

He seemed to me entirely so.

"But after he gets his Knighthood?" I went on.

"That depends. There are several things I can think of. It interests me."

"Good Heavens! I've always imagined you a man without interests."

"So I was. I owe my interests to Castorley. He gave me every one of 'em except the tale itself."

"How did *that* come?"

"Something in those ghastly cuts touched off something in me – a sort of possession, I suppose. I was in love too. No wonder I got drunk that night. I'd *been* Chaucer for a week! Then I thought the notion might make a comic opera. But Gilbert and Sullivan were too strong."

"So I remember you told me at the time."

"I kept it by me, and it made me interested in Chaucer – philologically and so on. I worked on it on those lines for years. There wasn't a flaw in the wording even in '14. I hardly had to touch it after that."

"Did you ever tell it to any one except me?"

"No, only 'Dal's mother – when she could listen to any-thing – to put her to sleep. But when Castorley said – what he did about her, I thought I might use it. 'Twasn't difficult. *He* taught me. D'you remember my birdlime experiments, and the stuff on our hands? I'd been trying to get that ink for more than a year. Castorley told me where I'd find the formula. And your falling over the quern, too?"

"That accounted for the stone-dust under the microscope?"

"Yes. I grew the wheat in the garden here, and ground it myself. Castorley gave me Mentzel complete. He put me on to an MS. in the British Museum which he said was the finest sample of his work. I copied his 'Byzantine *g*'s' for months."

"And what's a 'sickle-slanted' pen?" I asked.

"You nick one edge of your reed till it drags and scratches on the curves of the letters. Castorley told me about Mentzel's spacing and margining. I only had to get the hang of his script."

"How long did that take you?"

"On and off – some years. I was too ambitious at first – I wanted to give the whole poem. That would have been risky. Then Castorley told me about spoiled pages and I took the hint. I spelt 'Dayspring mishandeelt' Mentzel's way – to make sure of him. It's not a bad couplet in itself. Did you see how he admires the 'plangency' of it?"

"Never mind him. Go on!" I said.

He did. Castorley had been his unfailing guide throughout, specifying in minutest detail every trap to be set later for his own feet. The actual vellum was an Antwerp find, and its introduction into the cover of the Vulgate was begun after a long course of amateur bookbinding. At last, he bedded it under pieces of an old deed, and a printed page (1686) of Horace's *Odes*, legitimately used for repairs by different owners in the seventeenth and eighteenth centuries; and at the last moment, to meet Castorley's theory that spoiled pages were used in workshops by beginners, he had written a few Latin words in fifteenth-century script – the Statement gave the exact date – across an open part of the fragment. The thing ran: "*Illa alma Mater ecca, secum afferens me acceptum. Nicolaus Atrib.*" The disposal of the thing was easiest of all. He had merely hung about Dredd's dark bookshop of fifteen rooms, where he was well known, occasionally buying but generally browsing, till, one day, Dredd Senior showed him a case of cheap black-letter stuff, English and Continental – being packed for the Sunnapia people – into which Manallace tucked his contribution, taking care to wrench the back enough to give a lead to an earnest seeker.

"And then?" I demanded.

"After six months or so Castorley sent for me. Sunnapia had found it, and as Dredd had missed it, and there was no money-motive sticking out, they were half convinced it was genuine from the start. But they invited him over. He conferred with their experts, and suggested the scientific tests. *I* put that into his head, before he sailed. That's all. And now, will you sign our Memorial?"

I signed. Before we had finished hawking it round there was a host of influential names to help us, as well as the impetus of all the literary discussion which arose over every detail of the glorious trove. The upshot was a K.B.E.* for Castorley in the next Honours List; and Lady Castorley, her cards duly printed, called on friends that same afternoon.

Manallace invited me to come with him, a day or so later, to convey our pleasure and satisfaction to them both. We were rewarded by the sight of a man relaxed and ungirt – not to say wallowing naked – on the crest of Success. He assured us that "The Title" should not make any difference to our future relations, seeing it was in no sense personal, but, as he had often said, a tribute to Chaucer; "and, after all," he pointed out, with a glance at the mirror over the mantelpiece, "Chaucer was the prototype of the 'verray parfit gentil Knight' of the British Empire so far as that then existed."

*Officially it was on account of his good works in the Department of Co-ordinated Supervisals, but all true lovers of literature knew the real reason, and told the papers so.

On the way back, Manallace told me he was considering either an unheralded revelation in the baser Press which should bring Castorley's reputation about his own ears some breakfast-time, or a private conversation, when he would make clear to Castorley that he must now back the forgery as long as he lived, under the threat of Manallace's betraying it if he flinched.

He favoured the second plan. "If I pull the string of the shower-bath in the papers," he said, "Castorley might go off his verray parfit gentil nut. I want to keep his intellect."

"What about your own position? The forgery doesn't matter so much. But if you tell this you'll kill him," I said.

"I intend that. Oh – my position? I've been dead since – April, Fourteen, it was. But there's no hurry. What was it *she* was saying to you just as we left?"

"She told me how much your sympathy and understanding had meant to him. She said she thought that even Sir Alured did not realise the full extent of his obligations to you."

"She's right, but I don't like her putting it that way."

"It's only common form – as Castorley's always saying."

"Not with *her*. She can hear a man think."

"She never struck me in that light."

"*You* aren't playing against her."

"Guilty conscience, Manallace?"

"H'm! I wonder. Mine or hers? I *wish* she hadn't said that. 'More even than *he* realises it.' I won't call again for a while."

He kept away till we read that Sir Alured, owing to slight indisposition, had been unable to attend a dinner given in his honour.

Inquiries brought word that it was but natural reaction, after strain, which, for the moment, took the form of nervous dyspepsia, and he would be glad to see Manallace at any time. Manallace reported him as rather pulled and drawn, but full of his new life and position, and proud that his efforts should have martyred him so much. He was going to collect, collate, and expand all his pronouncements and inferences into one authoritative volume.

"I must make an effort of my own," said Manallace. "I've collected nearly all his stuff about the Find that has appeared in the papers, and he's promised me everything that's missing. I'm going to help him. It will be a new interest."

"How will you treat it?" I asked.

"I expect I shall quote his deductions on the evidence, and parallel 'em with my experiments – the ink and the paste and the rest of it. It ought to be rather interesting."

"But even then there will only be your word. It's hard to catch up with an established lie," I said. "Especially when you've started it yourself."

He laughed. "I've arranged for *that* – in case anything happens to me. Do you remember the 'Monkish Hymn'?"

"Oh yes! There's quite a literature about it already."

"Well, you write those ten words above each other, and read down the first and second letters of 'em; and see what you get.* My Bank has the formula."

He wrapped himself lovingly and leisurely round his new task, and Castorley was as good as his word in giving him help. The two practically collaborated, for Manallace suggested that all Castorley's strictly scientific evidence should be in one place, with his deductions and dithyrambs as appendices. He assured him that the public would prefer this arrangement, and, after grave consideration, Castorley agreed.

"That's better," said Manallace to me. "Now I shan't have so many hiatuses in my extracts. Dots always give the reader

*Illa
alma
Mater
ecca
secum
afferens
me
acceptum
Nicolaus
Atrib.

the idea you aren't dealing fairly with your man. I shall merely quote him solid, and rip him up, proof for proof, and date for date, in parallel columns. His book's taking more out of him than I like, though. He's been doubled up twice with tummy attacks since I've worked with him. And he's just the sort of flatulent beast who may go down with appendicitis."

We learned before long that the attacks were due to gall-stones, which would necessitate an operation. Castorley bore the blow very well. He had full confidence in his surgeon, an old friend of theirs; great faith in his own constitution; a strong conviction that nothing would happen to him till the book was finished, and, above all, the Will to Live.

He dwelt on these assets with a voice at times a little out of pitch and eyes brighter than usual beside a slightly-sharpening nose.

I had only met Gleeag, the surgeon, once or twice at Castorley's house, but had always heard him spoken of as a most capable man. He told Castorley that his trouble was the price exacted, in some shape or other, from all who had served their country; and that, measured in units of strain, Castorley had practically been at the Front through those three years he had served in the Office of Co-ordinated Supervisals. However, the thing had been taken betimes, and in a few weeks he would worry no more about it.

"But suppose he dies?" I suggested to Manallace.

"He won't. I've been talking to Gleeag. He says he's all right."

"Wouldn't Gleeag's talk be common form?"

"I *wish* you hadn't said that. But, surely, Gleeag wouldn't have the face to play with me – or her."

"Why not? I expect it's been done before."

But Manallace insisted that, in this case, it would be impossible.

The operation was a success and, some weeks later, Castorley began to recast the arrangement and most of the material of his book. "Let me have my way," he said, when Manallace protested. "They are making too much of a baby

of me. I really don't need Gleeag looking in every day now."
But Lady Castorley told us that he required careful watching. His heart had felt the strain, and fret or disappointment
of any kind must be avoided. "Even," she turned to Manallace, "though you know ever so much better how his book
should be arranged than he does himself."

"But really," Manallace began. "I'm very careful not to
fuss —"

She shook her finger at him playfully. "You don't think
you do; but, remember, he tells me everything that you tell
him, just the same as he told me everything that he used to
tell *you*. Oh, I don't mean the things that men talk about. I
mean about his Chaucer."

"I didn't realise that," said Manallace, weakly.

"I thought you didn't. He never spares me anything; but
I don't mind," she replied with a laugh, and went off to
Gleeag, who was paying his daily visit. Gleeag said he had
no objection to Manallace working with Castorley on the
book for a given time – say, twice a week – but supported
Lady Castorley's demand that he should not be over-taxed
in what she called "the sacred hours." The man grew more
and more difficult to work with, and the little check he had
heretofore set on his self-praise went altogether.

"He says there has never been anything in the History of
Letters to compare with it," Manallace groaned. "He wants
now to inscribe – he never dedicates, you know – inscribe it
to me, as his 'most valued assistant.' The devil of it is that
she backs him up in getting it out soon. Why? How much do
you think she knows?"

"Why should she know anything at all?"

"You heard her say he had told her everything that he told
me about Chaucer? (I *wish* she hadn't said that!) If she puts
two and two together, she can't help seeing that every one of
his notions and theories has been played up to. But then –
but then . . . Why is she trying to hurry publication? She
talks about me fretting him. *She's* at him, all the time, to be
quick."

Castorley must have over-worked, for, after a couple of months, he complained of a stitch in his right side, which Gleeag said was a slight sequel, a little incident of the operation. It threw him back awhile, but he returned to his work undefeated.

The book was due in the Autumn. Summer was passing, and his publisher urgent, and – he said to me, when after a longish interval I called – Manallace had chosen this time, of all, to take a holiday. He was not pleased with Manallace, once his indefatigable *aide*, but now dilatory, and full of time-wasting objections. Lady Castorley had noticed it, too.

Meantime, with Lady Castorley's help, he himself was doing the best he could to expedite the book; but Manallace had mislaid (did I think through jealousy?) some essential stuff which had been dictated to him. And Lady Castorley wrote Manallace, who had been delayed by a slight motor accident abroad, that the fret of waiting was prejudicial to her husband's health. Manallace, on his return from the Continent, showed me that letter.

"He has fretted a little, I believe," I said.

Manallace shuddered. "If I stay abroad, I'm helping to kill him. If I help him to hurry up the book, I'm expected to kill him. *She* knows," he said.

"You're mad. You've got this thing on the brain."

"I have not! Look here! You remember that Gleeag gave me from four to six, twice a week, to work with him. She called them the 'sacred hours.' You heard her? Well, they *are*! They are Gleeag's and hers. But she's so infernally plain, and I'm such a fool, it took me weeks to find it out."

"That's their affair," I answered. "It doesn't prove she knows anything about the Chaucer."

"She *does*! He told her everything that he had told me when I was pumping him, all those years. She put two and two together when the thing came out. She saw exactly how I had set my traps. I know it! She's been trying to make me admit it."

"What did you do?"

"Didn't understand what she was driving at, of course. And then she asked Gleeag, before me, if he didn't think the delay over the book was fretting Sir Alured. He didn't think so. He said getting it out might deprive him of an interest. He had that much decency. *She's* the devil!"

"What do you suppose is her game, then?"

"If Castorley knows he's been had, it'll kill him. She's at me all the time, indirectly, to let it out. I've told you she wants to make it a sort of joke between us. Gleeag's willing to wait. He knows Castorley's a dead man. It slips out when they talk. They say 'He was,' not 'He is.' Both of 'em know it. But *she* wants him finished sooner."

"I don't believe it. What are you going to do?"

"What can I? I'm not going to have him killed, though."

Manlike, he invented compromises whereby Castorley might be lured up by-paths of interest, to delay publication. This was not a success. As Autumn advanced Castorley fretted more, and suffered from returns of his distressing colics. At last, Gleeag told him that he thought they might be due to an overlooked gallstone working down. A second comparatively trivial operation would eliminate the bother once and for all. If Castorley cared for another opinion, Gleeag named a surgeon of eminence. "And then," said he, cheerily, "the two of us can talk you over." Castorley did not want to be talked over. He was oppressed by pains in his side, which, at first, had yielded to the liver-tonics Gleeag prescribed; but now they stayed – like a toothache – behind everything. He felt most at ease in his bedroom-study, with his proofs round him. If he had more pain than he could stand, he would consider the second operation. Meantime Manallace – "the meticulous Manallace," he called him – agreed with him in thinking that the Mentzel page-facsimile, done by the Sunnapia Library, was not quite good enough for the great book, and the Sunnapia people were, very decently, having it re-processed. This would hold things back

862   RUDYARD KIPLING

till early spring, which had its advantages, for he could run a fresh eye over all in the interval.

One gathered these news in the course of stray visits as the days shortened. He insisted on Manallace keeping to the "sacred hours," and Manallace insisted on my accompanying him when possible. On these occasions he and Castorley would confer apart for half an hour or so, while I listened to an unendurable clock in the drawing-room. Then I would join them and help wear out the rest of the time, while Castorley rambled. His speech, now, was often clouded and uncertain – the result of the "liver-tonics"; and his face came to look like old vellum.

It was a few days after Christmas – the operation had been postponed till the following Friday – that we called together. She met us with word that Sir Alured had picked up an irritating little winter cough, due to a cold wave, but we were not, therefore, to abridge our visit. We found him in steam perfumed with Friar's Balsam. He waved the old Sunnapia facsimile at us. We agreed that it ought to have been more worthy. He took a dose of his mixture, lay back and asked us to lock the door. There was, he whispered, something wrong somewhere. He could not lay his finger on it, but it was in the air. He felt he was being played with. He did not like it. There was something wrong all round him. Had we noticed it? Manallace and I severally and slowly denied that we had noticed anything of the sort.

With no longer break than a light fit of coughing, he fell into the hideous, helpless panic of the sick – those worse than captives who lie at the judgment and mercy of the hale for every office and hope. He wanted to go away. Would we help him to pack his Gladstone? Or, if that would attract too much attention in certain quarters, help him to dress and go out? There was an urgent matter to be set right, and now that he had The Title and knew his own mind it would all end happily and he would be well again. *Please* would we let him go out, just to speak to – he named her; he named her by her "little" name out of the old Neminaka days? Manallace quite agreed, and recommended a pull at the "liver-tonic" to brace him after so long in the house. He took it, and Manallace suggested that it would be better if, after his walk, he came down to the cottage for a week-end and brought the revise with him. They could then retouch the last chapter. He answered to that drug and to some praise of his work, and presently simpered drowsily. Yes, it *was* good – though he said it who should not. He praised himself awhile till, with a puzzled forehead and shut eyes, he told us that *she* had been saying lately that it was too good – the whole thing, if we understood, was *too* good. He wished us to get the exact shade of her meaning. She had suggested, or rather implied, this doubt. She had said – he would let us draw our own inferences – that the Chaucer find had "antici-pated the wants of humanity." Johnson, of course. No need to tell *him* that. But what the hell was her implication? Oh God! Life had always been one long innuendo! *And* she had said that a man could do anything with any one if he saved him the trouble of thinking. What did she mean by that? *He* had never shirked thought. He had thought sustainedly all his life. It *wasn't* too good, was it? Manallace didn't think it was too good – did he? But this pick-pick-picking at a man's brain and work was too bad, wasn't it? *What* did she mean? Why did she always bring in Manallace, who was only a friend – no scholar, but a lover of the game – Eh? Manallace could confirm this if he were here, instead of loafing on the Continent just when he was most needed.

"I've come back," Manallace interrupted, unsteadily. "I can confirm every word you've said. You've nothing to worry about. It's *your* find – *your* credit – *your* glory and – all the rest of it."

"Swear you'll tell her so then," said Castorley. "She doesn't believe a word I say. She told me she never has since before we were married. Promise!"

Manallace promised, and Castorley added that he had named him his literary executor, and proceeds of the book to go to his wife. "All profits without deduction," he gasped.

"Big sales if it's properly handled. *You* don't need money . . . Graydon'll trust *you* to any extent. It 'ud be a long . . ."

He coughed, and, as he caught breath, his pain broke through all the drugs, and the outcry filled the room. Manallace rose to fetch Gleeag, when a full, high, affected voice, unheard for a generation, accompanied, as it seemed, the clamour of a beast in agony, saying: "I wish to God someone would stop that old swine howling down there! *I* can't . . . I was going to tell you fellows that it would be a dam' long time before Graydon advanced *me* two quid."

We escaped together, and found Gleeag waiting, with Lady Castorley, on the landing. He telephoned me, next morning, that Castorley had died of bronchitis, which his weak state made it impossible for him to throw off. "Perhaps it's just as well," he added, in reply to the condolences I asked him to convey to the widow. "We might have come across something we couldn't have coped with."

Distance from that house made me bold.

"You knew all along, I suppose? What was it, really?"

"Malignant kidney-trouble – generalised at the end. No use worrying him about it. We let him through as easily as possible. Yes! A happy release . . . What? . . . Oh! Cremation. Friday, at eleven."

There, then, Manallace and I met. He told me that she had asked him whether the book need now be published; and he had told her this was more than ever necessary, in her interests as well as Castorley's.

"She is going to be known as his widow – for a while, at any rate. Did I perjure myself much with him?"

"Not explicitly," I answered.

"Well, I have now – with *her* – explicitly," said he, and took out his black gloves . . .

As, on the appointed words, the coffin crawled sideways, through the noiselessly-closing doorflaps, I saw Lady Castorley's eyes turn towards Gleeag.

* * *

GERTRUDE'S PRAYER

(Modernised from the "Chaucer" of Manallace.)

That which is marred at birth Time shall not mend,
    Nor water out of bitter well make clean;
All evil thing returneth at the end,
    Or elseway walketh in our blood unseen.
Whereby the more is sorrow in certaine –
Dayspring mishandled cometh not againe.

To-bruizèd be that slender, sterting spray
    Out of the oake's rind that should betide
A branch of girt and goodliness, straightway
    Her spring is turnèd on herself, and wried
And knotted like some gall or veiney wen –
Dayspring mishandled cometh not agen.

Noontide repayeth never morning-bliss –
    Sith noon to morn is incomparable;
And, so it be our dawning goeth amiss,
    None other after-hour serveth well.
Ah! Jesu-Moder, pitie my oe paine –
Dayspring mishandled cometh not againe!

THE CHURCH THAT WAS AT
ANTIOCH

THE CHURCH THAT WAS AT ANTIOCH

* * *

"But when Peter was come to Antioch, I withstood him to the face, because he was to be blamed."

– St Paul's Epistle to the Galatians 2:11

H IS mother, a devout and well-born Roman widow, decided that he was doing himself no good in an Eastern Legion so near to free-thinking Constantinople, and got him seconded for civil duty in Antioch, where his uncle, Lucius Sergius, was head of the urban Police. Valens obeyed as a son and as a young man keen to see life, and, presently, cast up at his uncle's door.

"That sister-in-law of mine," said the elder, "never remembers me till she wants something. What have you been doing?"

"Nothing, Uncle."

"Meaning everything?"

"That's what Mother thinks. But I haven't."

"We shall see. Your quarters are across the inner court-yard. Your – er – baggage is there already . . . Oh, I shan't interfere with your private arrangements! I'm not the uncle with the rough tongue. Get your bath. We'll talk at supper."

But before that hour "Father Serga," as the Prefect of Police was called, learned from the Treasury that his nephew had marched overland from Constantinople in charge of a treasure-convoy which, after a brush with brigands in the pass outside Tarsus, he had duly delivered.

"Why didn't you tell me about it?" his uncle asked at the meal.

"I had to report to the Treasury first," was the answer.

Serga looked at him. "Gods! You *are* like your father," said he. "Cilicia is scandalously policed."

"So I noticed. They ambushed us not five miles from Tarsus town. Are we given to that sort of thing here?"

"You make yourself at home early. No. *We* are not, but Syria is a Non-regulation Province – under the Emperor – not the Senate. We've the entire unaccountable East to one side; the scum of the Mediterranean on the other; and all hell-cat Judaea southward. Anything can happen in Syria. D'you like the prospect?"

"I shall – under you."

"It's in the blood. The same with men as horses. Now what have you done that distresses your mother so?"

"She's a little behind the times, sir. She follows the old school, of course – the home-worships, and the strict Latin Trinity. I don't think she recognises any Gods outside Jupiter, Juno, and Minerva."

"I don't either – officially."

"Nor I, as an officer, sir. But one wants more than that, and – and – what I learned in Byzant squared with what I saw with the Fifteenth."

"You needn't go on. All Eastern Legions are alike. You mean you follow Mithras – eh?"

The young man bowed his head slightly.

"No harm, boy. It's a soldier's religion, even if it comes from outside."

"So I thought. But Mother heard of it. She didn't approve and – I suppose that's why I'm here."

"Off the trident and into the net! Just like a woman! All Syria is stuffed with Mithraism. *My* objection to fancy religions is that they mostly meet after dark, and that means more work for the Police. We've a College here of stiff-necked Hebrews who call themselves Christians."

"I've heard of them," said Valens. "There isn't a

ceremony or symbol they haven't stolen from the Mithras ritual."

"No news to *me*! Religions are part of my office-work; and they'll be part of yours. Our Synagogue Jews are fighting like Scythians over this new faith."

"Does that matter much?"

"So long as they fight each other, we've only to keep the ring. Divide and rule – especially with Hebrews. Even these Christians are divided now. You see – one part of their worship is to eat together."

"Another theft! The Supper is the essential Symbol with us," Valens interrupted.

"With *us*, it's the essential symbol of trouble for your uncle, my dear. Any one can become a Christian. A Jew may; but he still lives by his Law of Moses (I've had to master that cursed code, too), and it regulates all his doings. Then he sits down at a Christian love-feast beside a Greek or Westerner, who doesn't kill mutton or pig – No! No! Jews don't touch pork – as the Jewish Law lays down. Then the tables are broken up – but not by laughter – No! No! Riot!"

"That's childish," said Valens.

"Wish it were. But my lictors are called in to keep order, and I have to take the depositions of Synagogue Jews, denouncing Christians as traitors to Caesar. If I chose to act on half the stuff their Rabbis swear to, I'd have respectable little Jew shop-keepers up every week for conspiracy. *Never* decide on the evidence, when you're dealing with Hebrews! Oh, you'll get your bellyful of it! You're for Market-duty tomorrow in the Little Circus ward, all among 'em. And now, sleep you well! I've been on this frontier as far back as any one remembers – that's why they call me the Father of Syria – and oh – it's good to see a sample of the old stock again!"

Next morning, and for many weeks after, Valens found himself on Market-inspection duty with a fat Aedile, who flew into rages because the stalls were not flushed down at the proper hour. A couple of his uncle's men were told off to him, and, of course, introduced him to the thieves' and prostitutes' quarters, to the leading gladiators, and so forth.

One day, behind the Little Circus, near Singon Street, he ran into a mob, where a race-course gang were trying to collect, or evade, some bets on recent chariot-races. The Aedile said it was none of his affair and turned back. The lictors closed up behind Valens, but left the situation in his charge. Then a small hard man with eyebrows was punted on to his chest, amid howls from all around that he was the ringleader of a conspiracy. "Yes," said Valens, "that was an old trick in Byzant; but I think we'll take *you*, my friend." Turning the small man loose, he gathered in the loudest of his accusers to appear before his uncle.

"You were quite right," said Serga next day. "That gentleman was put up to the job – by someone else. I ordered him one Roman dozen. Did you get the name of the man they were trying to push off on you?"

"Yes. Gaius Julius Paulus. Why?"

"I guessed as much. He's an old acquaintance of mine, a Cilician from Tarsus. Well-born – a citizen by descent, and well-educated, but his people have disowned him. So he works for his living."

"He spoke like a well-born. He's in splendid training, too. Felt him. All muscle."

"Small wonder. He can outmarch a camel. He is really the Prefect of this new sect. He travels all over our Eastern Provinces starting their Colleges and keeping them up to the mark. That's why the Synagogue Jews are hunting him. If they could run him in on the political charge, it would finish him."

"Is he seditious, then?"

"Not in the least. Even if he were, I wouldn't feed him to the Jews just because they wanted it. One of our Governors tried that game down-coast – for the sake of peace – some years ago. He didn't get it. Do you like your Market-work, my boy?"

"It's interesting. D'you know, Uncle, I think the Synagogue Jews are better at their slaughterhouse arrangements than we."

"They are. That's what makes 'em so tough. A dozen stripes are nothing to Apella, though he'll howl the yard down while he's getting 'em. You've the Christians' College in your quarter. How do they strike you?"

"Quiet enough. They're worrying a bit over what they ought to eat at their love-feasts."

"I know it. Oh, I meant to tell you – we mustn't try 'em too high just now, Valens. My office reports that Paulus, your small friend, is going down-country for a few days to meet another priest of the College, and bring him back to help smooth over their difficulties about their victuals. That means their congregation will be at loose ends till they return. Mass without mind always comes a cropper. So, *now* is when the Synagogue Jews will try to compromise them. I don't want the poor devils stampeded into what can be made to look like political crime. Understand?"

Valens nodded. Between his uncle's discursive evening talks, studded with kitchen-Greek and out-of-date Roman society-verses; his morning tours with the puffing Aedile; and the confidences of his lictors at all hours; he fancied he understood Antioch.

So he kept an eye on the rooms in the colonnade behind the Little Circus, where the new faith gathered. One of the many Jew butchers told him that Paulus had left affairs in the hands of some man called Barnabas, but that he would come back with one, Petrus – evidently a well-known character – who would settle all the food-differences between Greek and Hebrew Christians. The butcher had no spite against Greek Christians as such, if they would only kill their meat like decent Jews.

Serga laughed at this talk, but lent Valens an extra man or two, and said that this lion would be his to tackle, before long.

The boy found himself rushed into the arena one hot dusk, when word had come that this was to be a night of trouble. He posted his lictors in an alley within signal, and entered the common-room of the College, where the love-feasts were held. Every one seemed as friendly as a Christian – to use the slang of the quarter – and Barnabas, a smiling, stately man by the door, specially so.

"I am glad to meet you," he said. "You helped our Paulus in that scuffle the other day. We can't afford to lose *him*. I wish he were back!"

He looked nervously down the hall, as it filled with people, of middle and low degree, setting out their evening meal on the bare tables, and greeting each other with a special gesture.

"I assure you," he went on, his eyes still astray, "*we*'ve no intention of offending any of the brethren. Our differences can be settled if only —"

As though on a signal, clamour rose from half a dozen tables at once, with cries of "Pollution! Defilement! Heathen! The Law! The Law! Let Caesar know!" As Valens backed against the wall, the crowd pelted each other with broken meats and crockery, till at last stones appeared from nowhere.

"It's a put-up affair," said Valens to Barnabas.

"Yes. They come in with stones in their breasts. Be careful! They're throwing your way," Barnabas replied. The crowd was well embroiled now. A section of it bore down to where they stood, yelling for the Justice of Rome. His two lictors slid in behind Valens, and a man leaped at him with a knife.

Valens struck up the hand, and the lictors had the man helpless as the weapon fell on the floor. The clash of it stilled the tumult a little. Valens caught the lull, speaking slowly: "Oh, citizens," he called, "*must* you begin your love-feasts with battle? Our tripe-sellers' burial-club has better manners."

A little laughter relieved the tension.

"The Synagogue has arranged this," Barnabas muttered. "The responsibility will be laid on me."

"Who is the Head of your College?" Valens called to the crowd.

The cries rose against each other.

"Paulus! Saul! *He* knows the world – No! No! Petrus! Our Rock! *He* won't betray us. Petrus, the Living Rock."

"When do they come back?" Valens asked. Several dates were given, sworn to, and denied.

"Wait to fight till they return. I'm not a priest; but if you don't tidy up these rooms, our Aedile" (Valens gave him his gross nick-name in the quarter) "will fine the sandals off your feet. And you mustn't trample good food either. When you've finished, I'll lock up after you. Be quick. *I* know our Prefect if you don't."

They toiled, like children rebuked. As they passed out with baskets of rubbish, Valens smiled. The matter would not be pressed further.

"Here is our key," said Barnabas at the end. "The Synagogue will swear I hired this man to kill you."

"Will they? Let's look at him."

The lictors pushed their prisoner forward.

"Ill-fortune!" said the man. "I owed you for my brother's death in Tarsus Pass."

"Your brother tried to kill me," Valens retorted.

The fellow nodded.

"Then we'll call it even-throws," Valens signed to the lictors, who loosed hold. "Unless you *really* want to see my uncle?"

The man vanished like a trout in the dusk. Valens returned the key to Barnabas, and said:

"If I were you, I shouldn't let your people in again till your leaders come back. You don't know Antioch as I do."

He went home, the grinning lictors behind him, and they told his uncle, who grinned also, but said that he had done the right thing – even to patronising Barnabas.

"Of course, *I* don't know Antioch as you do; but, seriously, my dear, I think you've saved their Church for the Christians this time. I've had three depositions already that your

Cilician friend was a Christian hired by Barnabas. Just as well for Barnabas that you let the brute go."

"You told me you didn't want them stampeded into trouble. Besides, it was fair-throws. I may have killed his brother after all. We had to kill two of 'em."

"Good! You keep a level head in a tight corner. You'll need it. There's no lying about in secluded parks for *us*! I've got to see Paulus and Petrus when they come back, and find out what they've decided about their infernal feasts. Why can't they all get decently drunk and be done with it?"

"They talk of them both down-town as though they were Gods. By the way, Uncle, all the riot was worked up by Synagogue Jews sent from Jerusalem – not by our lot at all."

"You *don't* say so? Now, perhaps, you understand why I put you on market-duty with old Sow-Belly! You'll make a Police-officer yet."

Valens met the sacred, mixed congregation round the fountains and stalls as he went about his quarter. They were rather relieved at being locked out of their rooms for the time; as well as by the news that Paulus and Petrus would report to the Prefect of Police before addressing them on the great food-question.

Valens was not present at the first part of that interview, which was official. The second, in the cool, awning-covered courtyard, with drinks and *hors-d'oeuvre*, all set out beneath the vast lemon and lavender sunset, was much less formal.

"You have met, I think," said Serga to the little lean Paulus as Valens entered.

"Indeed, yes. Under God, we are twice your debtors," was the quick reply.

"Oh, that was part of my duty. I hope you found our roads good on your journey," said Valens.

"Why, yes. I think they were." Paulus spoke as if he had not noticed them.

"We should have done better to come by boat," said his companion, Petrus, a large fleshy man, with eyes that seemed to see nothing, and a half-palsied right hand that lay idle in his lap.

"Valens came overland from Byzant," said his uncle. "He rather fancies his legs."

"He ought to at his age. What was your best day's march on the Via Sebaste?" Paulus asked interestedly, and, before he knew, Valens was reeling off his mileage on mountain-roads every step of which Paulus seemed to have trod.

"That's good," was the comment. "And I expect you march in heavier order than I."

"What would you call your best day's work?" Valens asked in turn.

"I have covered . . ." Paulus checked himself. "And yet not I but the God," he muttered. "It's hard to cure oneself of boasting."

A spasm wrenched Petrus's face.

"Hard indeed," said he. Then he addressed himself to Paulus as though none other were present. "It is true I have eaten with Gentiles and as the Gentiles ate. Yet, at the time, I doubted if it were wise."

"That is behind us now," said Paulus gently. "The decision has been taken for the Church – that little Church which you saved, my son." He turned on Valens with a smile that half-captured the boy's heart. "Now – as a Roman and a Police-officer – what think you of us Christians?"

"That I have to keep order in my own ward."

"Good! Caesar must be served. But – as a servant of Mithras, shall we say – how think you about our food-disputes?"

Valens hesitated. His uncle encouraged him with a nod. "As a servant of Mithras I eat with any initiate, so long as the food is clean," said Valens.

"But," said Petrus, "*that* is the crux."

"Mithras also tells us," Valens went on, "to share a bone covered with dirt, if better cannot be found."

"You observe no difference, then, between peoples at your feasts?" Paulus demanded.

"How dare we? We are all His children. Men make laws. Not Gods," Valens quoted from the old Ritual.

"Say that again, child!"

"Gods do not make laws. They change men's hearts. The rest is the Spirit."

"You heard it, Petrus? You heard that? It is the utter Doctrine itself!" Paulus insisted to his dumb companion.

Valens, a little ashamed of having spoken of his faith, went on:

"They tell me the Jew butchers here want the monopoly of killing for your people. Trade feeling's at the bottom of most of it."

"A little more than that perhaps," said Paulus. "Listen a minute." He threw himself into a curious tale about the God of the Christians, Who, he said, had taken the shape of a Man, and Whom the Jerusalem Jews, years ago, had got the authorities to deal with as a conspirator. He said that he himself, at that time a right Jew, quite agreed with the sentence, and had denounced all who followed the new God. But one day the Light and the Voice of the God broke over him, and he experienced a rending change of heart – precisely as in the Mithras creed. Then he met, and had been initiated by, some men who had walked and talked and, more particularly, had eaten, with the new God before He was killed, and who had seen Him after, like Mithras, He had risen from His grave. Paulus and those others – Petrus was one of them – had next tried to preach Him to the Jews, but that was no success; and, one thing leading to another, Paulus had gone back to his home at Tarsus, where his people disowned him for a renegade. There he had broken down with overwork and despair. Till then, he said, it had never occurred to any of them to show the new religion to any except right Jews; for their God had been born in the shape of a Jew. Paulus himself only came to realise the possibilities of outside work, little by little. He said he had all the foreign preaching in his charge now, and was going to change the whole world by it.

Then he made Petrus finish the tale, who explained, speaking very slowly, that he had, some years ago, received orders from the God to preach to a Roman officer of Irregulars down-country; after which that officer and most of his people wanted to become Christians. So Petrus had initiated them the same night, although none of them were Hebrews. "And," Petrus ended, "I saw there is nothing under heaven that we dare call unclean."

Paulus turned on him like a flash and cried:

"You admit it! Out of your own mouth it is evident." Petrus shook like a leaf and his right hand almost lifted.

"Do *you* too twit me with my accent?" he began, but his face worked and he choked.

"Nay! God forbid! And God once more forgive *me*!" Paulus seemed as distressed as he, while Valens stared at the extraordinary outbreak.

"Talking of clean and unclean," his uncle said tactfully, "there's that ugly song come up again in the City. They were singing it on the city-front yesterday, Valens. Did you notice?"

He looked at his nephew, who took the hint.

"If it was 'Pickled Fish,' sir, they were. Will it make trouble?"

"As surely as these fish" – a jar of them stood on the table – "make one thirsty. How does it go? Oh yes." Serga hummed:

"Oie-eaah!
From the Shark and the Sardine – the clean and the unclean –
   To the Pickled Fish of Galilee, said Petrus, shall be mine."

He twanged it off to the proper gutter-drawl.

"(Ha-ow?)
In the nets or on the line,
Till the Gods Themselves decline.
(Whe-en?)
When the Pickled Fish of Galilee ascend the Esquiline!"

That'll be something of a flood – worse than live fish in trees! Hey?"

"It will happen one day," said Paulus.

He turned from Petrus, whom he had been soothing tenderly, and resumed in his natural, hardish voice:

"Yes. We owe a good deal to that Centurion being converted when he was. It taught us that the whole world could receive the God; and it showed *me* my next work. I came over from Tarsus to teach here for a while. And I shan't forget how good the Prefect of Police was to us then."

"For one thing, Cornelius was an early colleague," Serga smiled largely above his strong cup. " 'Prime companion' – how does it go? – 'we drank the long, long Eastern day out together,' and so on. For another, I know a good workman when I see him. That camel-kit you made for my desert-tours, Paul, is as sound as ever. And for a third – which to a man of my habits is most important – that Greek doctor you recommended me is the only one who understands my tumid liver."

He passed a cup of all but unmixed wine, which Paulus handed to Petrus, whose lips were flaky-white at the corners.

"But your trouble," the Prefect went on, "will come from your own people. Jerusalem never forgives. They'll get you run in on the charge of *laesa majestatis* soon or late."

"Who knows better than I?" said Petrus. "And the decision we *all* have taken about our love-feasts may unite Hebrew and Greek against us. As I told you, Prefect, we are asking Christian Greeks not to make the feasts difficult for Christian Hebrews by eating meat that has not been lawfully killed. (Our way is much more wholesome, anyhow.) Still, we may get round that. But there's *one* vital point. Some of our Greek Christians bring food to the love-feasts that they've bought from your priests, after your sacrifices have been offered. That we can't allow."

Paulus turned to Valens imperiously.

"You mean they buy Altar-scraps," the boy said. "But only the very poor do it; and it's chiefly block-trimmings.

The sale's a perquisite of the Altar-butchers. They wouldn't like its being stopped."

"Permit separate tables for Hebrew and Greek, as I once said," Petrus spoke suddenly.

"That would end in separate churches. There shall be but *one* Church," Paulus spoke over his shoulder, and the words fell like rods. "You think there may be trouble, Valens?"

"My uncle —" Valens began.

"No, no!" the Prefect laughed. "Singon Street Markets are your Syria. Let's hear what our Legate thinks of his Province."

Valens flushed and tried to pull his wits together.

"Primarily," he said, "it's pig, I suppose. Hebrews hate pork."

"Quite right, too. Catch *me* eating pig east the Adriatic! *I* don't want to die of worms. Give me a young Sabine tush-ripe boar! I have spoken!"

Serga mixed himself another raw cup and took some pickled Lake fish to bring out the flavour.

"But, still," Petrus leaned forward like a deaf man, "if we admitted Hebrew and Greek Christians to separate tables we should escape —"

"Nothing, except salvation," said Paulus. "We have broken with the whole Law of Moses. We live in and through and by our God only. Else we are nothing. What is the sense of harking back to the Law at meal-times? Whom do we deceive? Jerusalem? Rome? The God? You yourself have eaten with Gentiles! You yourself have said —"

"One says more than one means when one is carried away," Petrus answered, and his face worked again.

"This time you will say precisely what is meant," Paulus spoke between his teeth. "We will keep the Churches *one* – in and through the Lord. You dare not deny this?"

"I dare nothing – the God knows! But I have denied Him . . . I denied Him . . . And He said – He said I was the Rock on which His Church should stand."

"*I* will see that it stands, and yet not I —" Paulus's voice dropped again. "To-morrow you will speak to the one Church of the one Table the world over."

"That's *your* business," said the Prefect. "But I warn you again, it's your own people who will make you trouble."

Paulus rose to say farewell, but in the act he staggered, put his hand to his forehead and, as Valens steered him to a divan, collapsed in the grip of that deadly Syrian malaria which strikes like a snake. Valens, having suffered, called to his rooms for his heavy travelling-fur. His girl, whom he had bought in Constantinople a few months before, fetched it. Petrus tucked it awkwardly round the shivering little figure; the Prefect ordered lime-juice and hot water, and Paulus thanked them and apologised, while his teeth rattled on the cup.

"Better to-day than to-morrow," said the Prefect. "Drink – sweat – and sleep here the night. Shall I send for my doctor?"

But Paulus said that the fit would pass naturally, and as soon as he could stand he insisted on going away with Petrus, late though it was, to prepare their announcement to the Church.

"Who was that big, clumsy man?" his girl asked Valens as she took up the fur. "He made more noise than the small one, who was really suffering."

"He's a priest of the new College by the Little Circus, dear. He believes, Uncle told me, that he once denied his God, Who, he says, died for him."

She halted in the moonlight, the glossy jackal skins over her arm.

"Does he? *My* God bought me from the dealers like a horse. Too much, too, he paid. Didn't he? 'Fess, thou?"

"No, thee!" emphatically.

"But I wouldn't deny *my* God – living or dead! . . . Oh – but *not* dead! My God's going to live – for me. Live – live thou, my heart's blood, for ever!"

It would have been better had Paulus and Petrus not left the Prefect's house so late; for the rumour in the city, as the

Prefect knew, and as the long conference seemed to confirm, was that Caesar's own Secretary of State in Rome was, through Paulus, arranging for a general defilement of the Hebrew with the Greek Christians, and that after this had been effected, by promiscuous eating of unlawful foods, all Jews would be lumped together as Christians – members, that is, of a mere free-thinking sect instead of the very particular and troublesome "Nation of Jews within the Empire." Eventually, the story went, they would lose their rights as Roman citizens, and could then be sold on any slave-stand.

"Of course," Serga explained to Valens next day, "that has been put about by the Jerusalem Synagogue. Our Antioch Jews aren't clever enough. Do you see their game? Petrus is a defiler of the Hebrew nation. If he is cut down to-night by some properly primed young zealot so much the better."

"He won't be," said Valens. "I'm looking after him."

"Hope so. But, if he isn't knifed," Serga went on, "they'll try to work up city riots on the grounds that, when all the Jews have lost their civil rights, he'll set up as a sort of King of the Christians."

"At Antioch? In the present year of Rome? That's crazy, Uncle."

"*Every* crowd is crazy. What else do we draw pay for? But, listen. Post a Mounted Police patrol at the back of the Little Circus. Use 'em to keep the people moving when the congregation comes out. Post two of your men in the Porch of their College itself. Tell Paulus and Petrus to wait there with them, till the streets are clear. Then fetch 'em both over here. Don't hit till you have to. Hit hard *before* the stones fly. Don't get my little horses knocked about more than you can help, and – look out for 'Pickled Fish'!"

Knowing his own quarter, it seemed to Valens as he went on duty that evening that his uncle's precautions had been excessive. The Christian Church, of course, was full, and a large crowd waited outside for word of the decision about the feasts. Most of them seemed to be Christians of sorts, but there was an element of gesticulating Antiochene loafers, and like all crowds they amused themselves with popular songs while they waited. Things went smoothly, till a group of Christians raised a rather explosive hymn, which ran:

> "Enthroned above Caesar and Judge of the Earth!
> We wait on Thy coming – oh tarry not long!
> As the Kings of the Sunrise
> Drew sword at Thy Birth,
> So we arm in this midnight of insult and wrong!"

"Yes – and if one of their fish-stalls is bumped over by a camel – it's *my* fault!" said Valens. "Now they've started it!"

Sure enough, voices on the outskirts broke into "Pickled Fish," but before Valens could speak, they were suppressed by someone crying:

"Quiet there, or you'll get your pickle before your fish."

It was close on twilight when a cry rose from within the packed Church, and its congregation breasted out into the crowd. They all talked about the new orders for their love-feasts, most of them agreeing that they were sensible and easy. They agreed, too, that Petrus (Paulus did not seem to have taken much part in the debate) had spoken like one inspired, and they were all extremely proud of being Christians. Some of them began to link arms across the alley, and strike into the "Enthroned above Caesar" chorus.

"And this, I *think*," Valens called to the young Commandant of the Mounted Patrol, "is where we'll begin to steer 'em home. Oh! And 'Let night also have her well-earned hymn,' as Uncle 'ud say."

There filed out from behind the Little Circus four blaring trumpets, a standard, and a dozen Mounted Police. Their wise little grey Arabs sidled, passaged, shouldered, and nosed softly into the mob, as though they wanted petting, while the trumpets deafened the narrow street. An open square, near by, eased the pressure before long. Here the Patrol broke into fours, and gridironed it, saluting the images of the Gods at each corner and in the centre. People stopped, as usual, to watch how cleverly the incense was cast down over the withers into the spouting cressets; children reached up to pat horses which they said they knew; family groups re-found each other in the smoky dusk; hawkers offered cooked suppers; and soon the crowd melted into the main traffic avenues. Valens went over to the Church porch, where Petrus and Paulus waited between his lictors.

"That was well done," Paulus began.

"How's the fever?" Valens asked.

"I was spared for to-day. I think, too, that by The Blessing we have carried our point."

"Good hearing! My uncle bids me say you are welcome at his house."

"That is always a command," said Paulus, with a quick down-country gesture. "Now that this day's burden is lifted, it will be a delight."

Petrus joined up like a weary ox. Valens greeted him, but he did not answer.

"Leave him alone," Paulus whispered. "The virtue has gone out of me – him – for the while." His own face looked pale and drawn.

The street was empty, and Valens took a short cut through an alley, where light ladies leaned out of windows and laughed. The three strolled easily together, the lictors behind them, and far off they heard the trumpets of the Night Horse saluting some statue of a Caesar, which marked the end of their round. Paulus was telling Valens how the whole Roman Empire would be changed by what the Christians had agreed to about their love-feasts, when an impudent little Jew boy stole up behind them, playing "Pickled Fish" on some sort of desert bag-pipe.

"Can't you stop that young pest, one of you?" Valens asked laughing. "You shan't be mocked on this great night of yours, Paulus."

The lictors turned back a few paces, and shook a torch at

the brat, but he retreated and drew them on. Then they heard Paulus shout, and when they hurried back, found Valens prostrate and coughing – his blood on the fringe of the kneeling Paulus's robe. Petrus stooped, waving a helpless hand above them.

"Someone ran out from behind that well-head. He stabbed him as he ran, and ran on. Listen!" said Paulus.

But there was not even the echo of a footfall for clue, and the Jew boy had vanished like a bat. Said Valens from the ground:

"Home! Quick! I have it!"

They tore a shutter out of a shop-front, lifted and carried him, while Paulus walked beside. They set him down in the lighted inner courtyard of the Prefect's house, and a lictor hurried for the Prefect's physician.

Paulus watched the boy's face, and, as Valens shivered a little, called to the girl to fetch last night's fur rug. She brought it, laid the head on her breast, and cast herself beside Valens.

"It isn't bad. It doesn't bleed much. So it *can't* be bad – can it?" she repeated. Valens's smile reassured her, till the Prefect came and recognised the deadly upward thrust under the ribs. He turned on the Hebrews.

"To-morrow you will look for where your Church stood," said he.

Valens lifted the hand that the girl was not kissing.

"No – no!" he gasped. "The Cilician did it! For his brother! He said it."

"The Cilician you let go to save these Christians because I —?" Valens signed to his uncle that it was so, while the girl begged him to steal strength from her till the doctor should come.

"Forgive me," said Serga to Paulus. "None the less I wish your God in Hades once for all . . . But what am I to write his mother? Can't either of you two talking creatures tell me what I'm to tell his mother?"

"What has *she* to do with him?" the slave-girl cried. "He

is mine – mine! I testify before all Gods that he bought me! I am his. He is mine."

"We can deal with the Cilician and his friends later," said one of the lictors. "But what now?"

For some reason, the man, though used to butcher-work, looked at Petrus.

"Give him drink and wait," said Petrus. "I have – seen such a wound." Valens drank and a shade of colour came to him. He motioned the Prefect to stoop.

"What is it? Dearest of lives, what troubles?"

"The Cilician and his friends . . . Don't be hard on them . . . They get worked up . . . They don't know what they are doing . . . Promise!"

"This is not I, child. It is the Law."

"No odds. You're Father's brother . . . Men make laws – not Gods . . . Promise! . . . It's finished with me."

Valens's head eased back on its yearning pillow.

Petrus stood like one in a trance. The tremor left his face as he repeated:

" 'Forgive them, for they know not what they do.' Heard you *that*, Paulus? He, a heathen and an idolater, said it!"

"I heard. What hinders now that we should baptise him?" Paulus answered promptly.

Petrus stared at him as though he had come up out of the sea.

"Yes," he said at last. "It is the little maker of tents . . . And what does he *now* – command?"

Paulus repeated the suggestion.

Painfully, that other raised the palsied hand that he had once held up in a hall to deny a charge.

"Quiet!" said he. "Think you that one who has spoken Those Words needs such as *we* are to certify him to any God?"

Paulus cowered before the unknown colleague, vast and commanding, revealed after all these years.

"As you please – as you please," he stammered, overlooking the blasphemy. "Moreover there is the concubine."

The girl did not heed, for the brow beneath her lips was chilling, even as she called on her God who had bought her at a price that he should not die but live.

* * *

THE DISCIPLE

He that hath a Gospel,
　　To loose upon Mankind,
Though he serve it utterly –
　　Body, soul, and mind –
Though he go to Calvary
　　Daily for its gain –
It is His Disciple
　　Shall make his labour vain.

He that hath a Gospel,
　　For all earth to own –
Though he etch it on the steel,
　　Or carve it on the stone –
Not to be misdoubted
　　Through the after-days –
It is His Disciple
　　Shall read it many ways.

It is His Disciple
　　(Ere Those Bones are dust)
Who shall change the Charter,
　　Who shall split the Trust –
Amplify distinctions,
　　Rationalise the Claim,
Preaching that the Master
　　Would have done the same.

It is His Disciple
  Who shall tell us how
Much the Master would have scrapped
  Had he lived till now –
What he would have modified
  Of what he said before –
It is His Disciple
  Shall do this and more . . .

He that hath a Gospel
  Whereby Heaven is won

(Carpenter, or Cameleer,
  Or Maya's dreaming son),
Many swords shall pierce Him,
  Mingling blood with gall;
But His Own Disciple
  Shall wound Him worst of all!

THE MANNER OF MEN

THE MANNER OF MEN

* * *

"If after the manner of men I have fought with beasts."

I Corinthians 15:32

H ER cinnabar-tinted topsail, nicking the hot blue horizon, showed she was a Spanish wheat-boat hours before
she reached Marseilles mole. There, her mainsail brailed
itself, a spritsail broke out forward, and a handy driver aft;
and she threaded her way through the shipping to her berth
at the quay as quietly as a veiled woman slips through a bazar.

The blare of her horns told her name to the port. An
elderly hook-nosed Inspector came aboard to see if her cargo
had suffered in the run from the South, and the senior ship-
cat purred round her captain's legs as the after-hatch was
opened.

"If the rest is like this —" the Inspector sniffed — "you had
better run out again to the mole and dump it."

"That's nothing," the captain replied. "All Spanish wheat
heats a little. They reap it very dry."

"Pity you don't keep it so, then. What would you call *that*
— crop or pasture?"

The Inspector pointed downwards. The grain was in bulk,
and deck-leakage, combined with warm weather, had
sprouted it here and there in sickly green films.

"So much the better," said the captain brazenly. "That
makes it waterproof. Pare off the top two inches, and the rest
is as sweet as a nut."

"*I* told that lie, too, when I was your age. And how does
she happen to be loaded?"

The young Spaniard flushed, but kept his temper.

"She happens to be ballasted, under my eye, on lead-pigs and bagged copper-ores."

"I don't know that they much care for verdigris in their dole-bread at Rome. But – you were saying?"

"I was trying to tell you that the bins happen to be grain-tight, two-inch chestnut, floored and sided with hides."

"Meaning dressed African leathers on your private account?"

"What has that got to do with you? We discharge at Port of Rome, not here."

"So your papers show. And what might you have stowed in the wings of her?"

"Oh, apes! Circumcised apes – just like you!"

"Young monkey! Well, if you are not above taking an old ape's advice, next time you happen to top off with wool and screw in more bales than are good for her, get your ship undergirt before you sail. I know it doesn't look smart coming into Port of Rome, but it'll save your decks from lifting worse than they are."

There was no denying that the planking and waterways round the after-hatch had lifted a little. The captain lost his temper.

"I know your breed!" he stormed. "You promenade the quays all summer at Caesar's expense, jamming your Jew-bow into everybody's business; and when the norther blows, you squat over your brazier and let us skippers hang in the wind for a week!"

"You have it! Just that sort of a man am I now," the other answered. "That'll do, the quarter-hatch!"

As he lifted his hand the falling sleeve showed the broad gold armlet with the triple vertical gouges which is only worn by master mariners who have used all three seas – Middle, Western, and Eastern.

"Gods!" the captain saluted. "I thought you were —"

"A Jew, of course. Haven't you used Eastern ports long enough to know a Red Sidonian when you see one?"

"Mine the fault – yours be the pardon, my father!" said the Spaniard impetuously. "Her topsides *are* a trifle strained. There was a three days' blow coming up. I meant to have had her undergirt off the Islands, but hawsers slow a ship so – and one hates to spoil a good run."

"To whom do you say it?" The Inspector looked the young man over between horny sun and salt-creased eyelids like a brooding pelican. "But if you care to get up your girt-hawsers to-morrow, I can find men to put 'em overside. It's no work for open sea. Now! Main-hatch, there! . . . I thought so. She'll need another girt abaft the foremast." He motioned to one of his staff, who hurried up the quay to where the port Guard-boat basked at her mooring-ring. She was a stoutly-built, single-banker, eleven a side, with a short punching ram; her duty being to stop riots in harbour and piracy along the coast.

"Who commands her?" the captain asked.

"An old shipmate of mine, Sulinor – a River man. We'll get his opinion."

In the Mediterranean (Nile keeping always her name) there is but one river – that shifty-mouthed Danube, where she works through her deltas into the Black Sea. Up went the young man's eyebrows.

"Is he any kin to a Sulinor of Tomi, who used to be in the flesh-traffic – and a Free Trader? My uncle has told me of him. He calls him Mango."

"That man. He was my second in the wheat-trade my last five voyages, after the Euxine grew too hot to hold him. But he's in the Fleet now . . . You know your ship best. Where do you think the after-girts ought to come?"

The captain was explaining, when a huge dish-faced Dacian, in short naval cuirass, rolled up the gangplank, carefully saluting the bust of Caesar on the poop, and asked the captain's name.

"Baeticus, for choice," was the answer.

They all laughed, for the sea, which Rome mans with foreigners, washes out many shore-names.

"My trouble is this —" Baeticus began, and they went into committee, which lasted a full hour. At the end, he led them to the poop, where an awning had been stretched, and wines set out with fruits and sweet shore water.

They drank to the Gods of the Sea, Trade, and Good Fortune, spilling those small cups overside, and then settled at ease.

"Girting's an all-day job, if it's done properly," said the Inspector. "Can you spare a real working-party by dawn to-morrow, Mango?"

"But surely – for you, Red."

"I'm thinking of the wheat," said Quabil curtly. He did not like nick-names so early.

"Full meals *and* drinks," the Spanish captain put in.

"Good! Don't return 'em too full. By the way" – Sulinor lifted a level cup – "where do you get this liquor, Spaniard?"

"From our Islands (the Balearics). Is it to your taste?"

"It is." The big man unclasped his gorget in solemn preparation.

Their talk ran professionally, for though each end of the Mediterranean scoffs at the other, both unite to mock landward, wooden-headed Rome and her stiff-jointed officials.

Sulinor told a tale of taking the Prefect of the Port, on a breezy day, to Forum Julii, to see a lady, and of his lamentable condition when landed.

"Yes," Quabil sneered. "Rome's mistress of the world – as far as the foreshore."

"If Caesar ever came on patrol with me," said Sulinor, "he might understand there was such a thing as the Fleet."

"Then he'd officer it with well-born young Romans," said Quabil. "Be grateful you are left alone. *You* are the last man in the world to want to see Caesar."

"Except one," said Sulinor, and he and Quabil laughed.

"What's the joke?" the Spaniard asked.

Sulinor explained.

"We had a passenger, our last trip together, who wanted to see Caesar. It cost us our ship and freight. That's all."

"Was he a warlock – a wind-raiser?"

"Only a Jew Philosopher. But he *had* to see Caesar. He said he had; and he piled up the *Eirene* on his way."

"Be fair," said Quabil. "I don't like the Jews – they lie too close to my own hold – but it was Caesar lost me my ship." He turned to Baeticus. "There was a proclamation, our end of the world, two seasons back, that Caesar wished the Eastern wheat-boats to run through the winter, and he'd guarantee all loss. Did *you* get it, youngster?"

"No. Our stuff is all in by September. I wager Caesar never paid you! How late did you start?"

"I left Alexandria across the bows of the Equinox – well down in the pickle, with Egyptian wheat – half pigeon's dung – and the usual load of Greek sutlers and their women. The second day out the sou'-wester caught me. I made across it north for the Lycian coast, and slipped into Myra till the wind should let me get back into the regular grain-track again."

Sailor-fashion, Quabil began to illustrate his voyage with date and olive stones from the table.

"The wind went into the north, as I knew it would, and I got under way. You remember, Mango? My anchors were apeak when a Lycian patrol threshed in with Rome's order to us to wait on a Sidon packet with prisoners and officers. Mother of Carthage, I cursed him!"

"Shouldn't swear at Rome's Fleet. Weatherly craft, those Lycian racers! Fast, too. I've been hunted by them! Never thought I'd command one," said Sulinor, half aloud.

"And now I'm coming to the leak in *my* decks, young man." Quabil eyed Baeticus sternly. "Our slant north had strained her, and I should have undergirt her at Myra. Gods know why I didn't! I set up the chain-staples in the cable-tier for the prisoners. I even had the girt-hawsers on deck – which saved time later; but the thing I should have done, that I did *not*."

"Luck of the Gods!" Sulinor laughed. "It was because our little philosopher wanted to see Caesar in his own way at our expense."

"Why did he want to see him?" said Baeticus.

"As far as I ever made out from him and the centurion, he wanted to argue with Caesar – about philosophy."

"He was a prisoner, then?"

"A political suspect – with a Jew's taste for going to law," Quabil interrupted. "No orders for irons. Oh, a little shrimp of a man, but – but he seemed to take it for granted that he led everywhere. He messed with us."

"And he was worth talking to, Red," said Sulinor.

"*You* thought so; but he had the woman's trick of taking the tone and colour of whoever he talked to. Now – as I was saying . . ."

There followed another illustrated lecture on the difficulties that beset them after leaving Myra. There was always too much west in the Autumn winds, and the *Eirene* tacked against it as far as Cnidus. Then there came a northerly slant, on which she ran through the Aegean Islands, for the tail of Crete; rounded that, and began tacking up the south coast.

"Just darning the water again, as we had done from Myra to Cnidus," said Quabil ruefully. "I daren't stand out. There was the bone-yard of all the Gulf of Africa under my lee. But at last we worked into Fairhaven – by that cork yonder. Late as it was, *I* should have taken her on, but I had to call a ship-council as to lying up for the Winter. That Rhodian law may have suited open boats and cock-crow coasters,* but it's childish for ocean-traffic."

"*I* never allow it in any command of mine," Baeticus spoke quietly. "The cowards give the order, and the captain bears the blame."

Quabil looked at him keenly. Sulinor took advantage of the pause.

"We were in harbour, you see. So our Greeks tumbled out and voted to stay where we were. It was my business to show

---

*Quabil meant the coasters who worked their way by listening to the cocks crowing on the beaches they passed. The insult is nearly as old as sail.

them that the place was open to many winds, and that if it came on to blow we should drive ashore."

"Then I," broke in Quabil, with a large and formidable smile, "advised pushing on to Phenike, round the cape, only forty miles across the bay. My mind was that, if I could get her undergirt there, I might later – er – coax them out again on a fair wind, and hit Sicily. But the undergirting came first. She was beginning to talk too much – like me now."

Sulinor chafed a wrist with his hand.

"She was a hard-mouthed old water-bruiser in any sea," he murmured.

"She could lie within six points of any wind," Quabil retorted, and hurried on. "What made Paul vote with those Greeks? He said we'd be sorry if we left harbour."

"Every passenger says that, if a bucketful comes aboard," Baeticus observed.

Sulinor refilled his cup, and looked at them over the brim, under brows as candid as a child's, ere he set it down.

"Not Paul. He did not know fear. He gave me a dose of my own medicine once. It was a morning watch coming down through the Islands. We had been talking about the cut of our topsail – he was right – it held too much lee wind – and then he went to wash before he prayed. I said to him: 'You seem to have both ends and the bight of most things coiled down in your little head, Paul. If it's a fair question, what *is* your trade ashore?' And he said: 'I've been a man-hunter – Gods forgive me; and now that I think The God has forgiven me, I am man-hunting again.' Then he pulled his shirt over his head, and I saw his back. Did *you* ever see his back, Quabil?"

"I expect I did – that last morning, when we all stripped; but I don't remember."

"*I* shan't forget it! There was good, sound lictor's work and criss-cross Jew scourgings like gratings; and a stab or two; and, besides those, old dry bites – when they get good hold and rugg you. That showed he must have dealt with the Beasts. So, whatever he'd done, he'd paid for. I was just wondering what he *had* done, when he said: 'No; not your sort of man-hunting.' 'It's your own affair,' I said: 'but *I* shouldn't care to see Caesar with a back like that. I should hear the Beasts asking for me.' 'I may that, too, some day,' he said, and began sluicing himself, and – then – What's brought the girls out so early? Oh, I remember!"

There was music up the quay, and a wreathed shore-boat put forth full of Arlesian women. A long-snouted three-banker was hauling from a slip till her trumpets warned the benches to take hold. As they gave way, the *hrmph-hrmph* of the oars in the oar-ports reminded Sulinor, he said, of an elephant choosing his man in the Circus.

"She has been here re-masting. They've no good rough-tree at Forum Julii," Quabil explained to Baeticus. "The girls are singing her out."

The shallop ranged alongside her, and the banks held water, while a girl's voice came across the clock-calm harbour-face:

"Ah, would swift ships had never been about the seas to rove!
For then these eyes had never seen nor ever wept their love.
Over the ocean-rim he came – beyond that verge he passed,
And I who never knew his name must mourn him to the last!"

"And you'd think they meant it," said Baeticus, half to himself.

"That's a pretty stick," was Quabil's comment as the man-of-war opened the island athwart the harbour. "But she's overmasted by ten foot. A trireme's only a bird-cage."

"Luck of the Gods I'm not singing in one now," Sulinor muttered. They heard the yelp of a bank being speeded up to the short sea-stroke.

"I wish there was some way to save mainmasts from rack-ing." Baeticus looked up at his own, bangled with copper wire.

"The more reason to undergirt, my son," said Quabil. "*I* was going to undergirt that morning at Fairhaven. You re-member, Sulinor? I'd given orders to overhaul the hawsers the night before. My fault! Never say 'Tomorrow.' The Gods hear you. And then the wind came out of the south, mild as milk. All we had to do was to slip round the headland to Phenike – and be safe."

Baeticus made some small motion, which Quabil noticed, for he stopped.

"My father," the young man spread apologetic palms, "is not that lying wind the in-draught of Mount Ida? It comes up with the sun, but later —"

"You need not tell *me*! We rounded the cape, our decks like a fair (it was only half a day's sail), and then, out of Ida's bosom the full north-easter stamped on us! Run? What else? I needed a lee to clean up in. Clauda was a few miles down wind; but whether the old lady would bear up when she got there, I was not so sure."

"She did." Sulinor rubbed his wrists again. "We were towing our longboat half-full. I steered somewhat that day."

"What sail were you showing?" Baeticus demanded.

"Nothing – and twice too much at that. But she came round when Sulinor asked her, and we kept her jogging in the lee of the island. I said, didn't I, that my girt-hawsers were on deck?"

Baeticus nodded. Quabil plunged into his campaign at long and large, telling every shift and device he had employed. "It was scanting daylight," he wound up, "but I daren't slur the job. Then we streamed our boat alongside, baled her, sweated her up, and secured. You ought to have seen our decks!"

"Panic?" said Baeticus.

"A little. But the whips were out early. The centurion – Julius – lent us his soldiers."

"How did your prisoners behave?" the young man went on.

Sulinor answered him. "Even when a man is being shipped to the Beasts, he does not like drowning in irons. They tried to rive the chain-staples out of her timbers."

"I got the main-yard on deck" – this was Quabil. "That

eased her a little. They stopped yelling after a while, didn't they?"

"They did," Sulinor replied. "Paul went down and told them there was no danger. And they believed him! Those scoundrels believed him! He asked me for the keys of the leg-bars to make them easier. '*I*'ve been through this sort of thing before,' he said, 'but they are new to it down below. Give me the keys.' I told him there was no order for him to have any keys; and I recommended him to line his hold for a week in advance, because we were in the hands of the Gods. 'And when are we ever out of them?' he asked. He looked at me like an old gull lounging just astern of one's taffrail in a full gale. *You* know that eye, Spaniard?"

"Well do I!"

"By that time" – Quabil took the story again – "we had drifted out of the lee of Clauda, and our one hope was to run for it and pray we weren't pooped. None the less, I could have made Sicily with luck. As a gale I have known worse, but the wind never shifted a point, d'ye see? We were flogged along like a tired ox."

"Any sights?" Baeticus asked.

"For ten days not a blink."

"Nearer two weeks," Sulinor corrected. "We cleared the decks of everything except our ground-tackle, and put six hands at the tillers. She seemed to answer her helm – sometimes. Well, it kept *me* warm for one."

"How did your philosopher take it?"

"Like the gull I spoke of. He was there, but outside it all. *You* never got on with him, Quabil?"

"Confessed! I came to be afraid at last. It was not my office to show fear, but I was. *He* was fearless, although I knew that he knew the peril as well as I. When he saw that trying to – er – cheer me made me angry, he dropped it. Like a woman, again. You saw more of him, Mango?"

"Much. When I was at the rudders he would hop up to the steerage, with the lower-deck ladders lifting and lunging a foot at a time, and the timbers groaning like men beneath the Beasts. We used to talk, hanging on till the roll jerked us into the scuppers. Then we'd begin again. What about? Oh! Kings and Cities and Gods and Caesar. He was sure he'd see Caesar. I told him I had noticed that people who worried Those Up Above" – Sulinor jerked his thumb towards the awning – "were mostly sent for in a hurry."

"Hadn't you wit to see he never wanted you for yourself, but to get something out of you?" Quabil snapped.

"Most Jews are like that – and all Sidonians!" Sulinor grinned. "But what *could* he have hoped to get from any one? We were doomed men all. You said it, Red."

"Only when I was at my emptiest. Otherwise I *knew* that with any luck I could have fetched Sicily! But I broke – we broke. Yes, we got ready – you too – for the Wet Prayer."

"How does that run with you?" Baeticus asked, for all men are curious concerning the bride-bed of Death.

"With us of the River," Sulinor volunteered, "we say: 'I sleep; presently I row again.' "

"Ah! At our end of the world we cry: 'Gods, judge me not as a God, but a man whom the Ocean has broken.' " Baeticus looked at Quabil, who answered, raising his cup: "We Sidonians say, 'Mother of Carthage, I return my oar!' But it all comes to the one in the end." He wiped his beard, which gave Sulinor his chance to cut in.

"Yes, we were on the edge of the Prayer when – do you remember, Quabil? – *he* clawed his way up the ladders and said: 'No need to call on what isn't there. My God sends me sure word that I shall see Caesar. *And* he has pledged me all your lives to boot. Listen! No man will be lost.' And Quabil said: 'But what about my ship?' " Sulinor grinned again.

"That's true. I had forgotten the cursed passengers," Quabil confirmed. "But he spoke as though my *Eirene* were a fig-basket. 'Oh, she's bound to go ashore, somewhere,' he said, 'but not a life will be lost. Take this from me, the Servant of the One God.' Mad! Mad as a magician on market-day!"

"No," said Sulinor. "Madmen see smooth harbours and full meals. I have had to – soothe that sort."

"After all," said Quabil, "he was only saying what had been in my head for a long time. I had no way to judge our drift, but we likely might hit something somewhere. Then he went away to spread his cook-house yarn among the crew. It did no harm, or I should have stopped him."

Sulinor coughed, and drawled:

"I don't see any one stopping Paul from what he fancied he ought to do. But it was curious that, on the change of watch, I —"

"No – I!" said Quabil.

"Make it so, then, Red. Between us, at any rate, we felt that the sea had changed. There was a trip and a kick to her dance. *You* know, Spaniard. And then – I *will* say that, for a man half-dead, Quabil here did well."

"I'm a bo'sun-captain, and not ashamed of it. I went to get a cast of the lead. (Black dark and raining marlinspikes!) The first cast warned me, and I told Sulinor to clear all aft for anchoring by the stern. The next – shoaling like a slip-way – sent me back with all hands, and we dropped both bowers and spare and the stream."

"He'd have taken the kedge as well, but I stopped him," said Sulinor.

"I had to stop *her*! They nearly jerked her stern out, but they held. And everywhere I could peer or hear were break-ers, or the noise of tall seas against cliffs. We were trapped! But our people had been starved, soaked, and half-stunned for ten days, and now they were close to a beach. That was enough! They must land on the instant; and was I going to let them drown within reach of safety? *Was* there panic? I spoke to Julius, and his soldiers (give Rome her due!) schooled them till I could hear my orders again. But on the kiss-of-dawn some of the crew said that Sulinor had told them to lay out the kedge in the long-boat."

"I let 'em swing her out," Sulinor confessed. "I wanted 'em for warnings. But Paul told me his God had promised their lives to him along with ours, and any private sacrifice would spoil the luck. So, as soon as she touched water, I cut the rope before a man could get in. She was ashore – stove – in ten minutes."

"Could you make out where you were by then?" Baeticus asked Quabil.

"As soon as I saw the people on the beach – yes. They are my sort – a little removed. Phoenicians by blood. It was Malta – *one* day's run from Syracuse, where I would have been safe! Yes, Malta and my wheat gruel. Good port-of-discharge, eh?"

They smiled, for Melita may mean "mash" as well as "Malta."

"It puddled the sea all round us, while I was trying to get my bearings. But my lids were salt-gummed, and I hic-coughed like a drunkard."

"And drunk you most gloriously were, Red, half an hour later!"

"Praise the Gods – and for once your pet Paul! That little man came to me on the fore-bitts, puffed like a pigeon, and pulled out a breastful of bread, and salt fish, and the wine – the good new wine. 'Eat,' he said, 'and make all your people eat, too. Nothing will come to them except another wetting. They won't notice that, after they're full. Don't worry about *your* work either,' he said. 'You *can't* go wrong today. You are promised to me.' And then he went off to Sulinor."

"He did. He came to me with bread and wine and bacon – good they were! But first he said words over them, and then rubbed his hands with his wet sleeves. I asked him if he were a magician. 'Gods forbid!' he said. 'I am so poor a soul that I flinch from touching dead pig.' As a Jew, he wouldn't like pork, naturally. Was that before or after our people broke into the store-room, Red?"

"Had *I* time to wait on them?" Quabil snorted. "I know they gutted my stores full-hand, and a double blessing of wine atop. But we all took that – deep. Now this is how we lay." Quabil smeared a ragged loop on the table with a wine-wet finger. "Reefs – see, my son – and overfalls to leeward here; something that loomed like a point of land on our right there; and, ahead, the blind gut of a bay with a Cyclops surf hammering it. How we had got in was a miracle. Beaching was our only chance, and meantime she was settling like a tired camel. Every foot I could lighten her meant that she'd take ground closer in at the last. I told Julius. He understood. 'I'll keep order,' he said. 'Get the passengers to shift the wheat as long as you judge it's safe.' "

"Did those Alexandrian achators really work?" said Baeticus.

"I've never seen cargo discharged quicker. It was time. The wind was taking off in gusts, and the rain was putting down the swells. I made out a patch of beach that looked less like death than the rest of the arena, and I decided to drive in on a gust under the spitfire-sprit – and, if she answered her helm before she died on us, to humour her a shade to starboard, where the water looked better. I stayed the fore-mast; set the spritsail fore and aft, as though we were board-ing; told Sulinor to have the rudders down directly he cut the cables; waited till a gust came; squared away the sprit, and drove."

Sulinor carried on promptly:

"I had two hands with axes on each cable, and one on each rudder-lift; and, believe me, when Quabil's pipe went, both blades were down and turned before the cable-ends had fizzed under! She jumped like a stung cow! She drove. She sheared. I think the swell lifted her, and over-ran. She came down, and struck aft. Her stern broke off under my toes, and all the guts of her at that end slid out like a man's paunched by a lion. I jumped forward, and told Quabil there was nothing but small kindlings abaft the quarter hatch, and he shouted: 'Never mind! Look how beautifully I've laid her!' "

"I had. What I took for a point of land to starboard, y'see, turned out to be almost a bridge-islet, with a swell of sea 'twixt it and the main. And that meeting-swill, d'you see, surging in as she drove, gave her four or five foot more to cushion on. I'd hit the exact instant."

"Luck of the Gods, *I* think! Then we began to bustle our people over the bows before she went to pieces. You'll admit Paul was a help there, Red?"

"I dare say he herded the old judies well enough; but he should have lined up with his own gang."

"He did that, too," said Sulinor. "Some fool of an under-officer had discovered that prisoners must be killed if they look like escaping; and he chose that time and place to put it to Julius – sword drawn. Think of hunting a hundred prisoners to death on those decks! It would have been worse than the Beasts!"

"But Julius saw – Julius saw it," Quabil spoke testily. "I heard him tell the man not to be a fool. They couldn't escape further than the beach."

"And how did your philosopher take *that*?" said Baeticus.

"As usual," said Sulinor. "But, you see, we two had dipped our hands in the same dish for weeks; and, on the River, that makes an obligation between man and man."

"In my country also," said Baeticus, rather stiffly.

"So I cleared my dirk – in case I had to argue. Iron always draws iron with me. But *he* said: 'Put it back. They are a little scared.' I said: 'Aren't *you*?' 'What?' he said; 'of being killed, you mean? No. Nothing can touch me till I've seen Caesar.' Then he carried on steadying the ironed men (some were slavering-mad) till it was time to unshackle them by fives, and give 'em their chance. The natives made a chain through the surf, and snatched them out breast-high."

"Not a life lost! Like stepping off a jetty," Quabil proclaimed.

"Not quite. But he had promised no one should drown."

"How *could* they – the way I had laid her – gust and swell and swill together?"

"And was there any salvage?"

"Neither stick nor string, my son. We had time to look, too. We stayed on the island till the first Spring ship sailed for Port of Rome. They hadn't finished Ostia breakwater that year."

"And, of course, Caesar paid you for your ship?"

"I made no claim. I saw it would be hopeless; and Julius, who knew Rome, was against any appeal to the authorities. He said that was the mistake Paul was making. And, I suppose, because I did not trouble them, and knew a little about the sea, they offered me the Port Inspectorship here. There's no money in it – if I were a poor man. Marseilles will never be a port again. Narbo has ruined her for good."

"But Marseilles is far from under-Lebanon," Baeticus suggested.

"The further the better. I lost my boy three years ago in Foul Bay, off Berenice, with the Eastern Fleet. He was rather like you about the eyes, too. You and your circumcised apes!"

"But – honoured one! My master! Admiral! – Father mine – how *could* I have guessed?"

The young man leaned forward to the other's knee in act to kiss it. Quabil made as though to cuff him, but his hand came to rest lightly on the bowed head.

"Nah! Sit, lad! Sit back. It's just the thing the Boy would have said himself. You didn't hear it, Sulinor?"

"I guessed it had something to do with the likeness as soon as I set eyes on him. You don't so often go out of your way to help lame ducks."

"You can see for yourself she needs undergirting, Mango!"

"So did that Tyrian tub last month. And you told her she might bear up for Narbo or bilge for all of you! But he shall have his working-party tomorrow, Red."

Baeticus renewed his thanks. The River man cut him short.

"Luck of the Gods," he said. "Five – four – years ago I might have been waiting for you anywhere in the Long Puddle with fifty River men – and no moon."

Baeticus lifted a moist eye to the slip-hooks on his yardarm, that could hoist and drop weights at a sign.

"You might have had a pig or two of ballast through your benches coming alongside," he said dreamily.

"And where would my overhead-nettings have been?" the other chuckled.

"Blazing – at fifty yards. What are fire-arrows for?"

"To fizzle and stink on my wet sea-weed blindages. Try again."

They were shooting their fingers at each other, like the little boys gambling for olive-stones on the quay beside them.

"Go on – go on, my son! Don't let that pirate board," cried Quabil.

Baeticus twirled his right hand very loosely at the wrist.

"In that case," he countered, "I should have fallen back on my foster-kin – my father's island horsemen."

Sulinor threw up an open palm.

"Take the nuts," he said. "Tell me, is it true that those infernal Balearic slingers of yours can turn a bull by hitting him on the horns?"

"On either horn you choose. My father farms near New Carthage. They come over to us for the summer to work. There are ten in my crew now."

Sulinor hiccoughed and folded his hands magisterially over his stomach.

"Quite proper. Piracy *must* be put down! Rome says so. I do so," said he.

"I see." The younger man smiled. "But tell me, why did you leave the slave – the Euxine trade, O Strategos?"

"That sea is too like a wine-skin. Only one neck. It made mine ache. So I went into the Egyptian run with Quabil here."

"But why take service in the Fleet? Surely the Wheat pays better?"

"I intended to. But I had dysentery at Malta that winter, and Paul looked after me."

"Too much muttering and laying-on of hands for *me*," said Quabil; himself muttering about some Thessalian jugglery with a snake on the island.

"*You* weren't sick, Quabil. When I was getting better, and Paul was washing me off once, he asked if my citizenship were in order. He was a citizen himself. Well, it was and it was not. As second of a wheat-ship I was *ex officio* Roman citizen – for signing bills and so forth. But on the beach, my ship perished, he said I reverted to my original shtay – status – of an extraprovinshal Dacian by a Sich – Sish – Scythian – I think she was – mother. Awkward – what? All the Middle Sea echoes like a public bath if a man is wanted."

Sulinor reached out again and filled. The wine had touched his huge bulk at last.

"But, as I was saying, once *in* the Fleet nowadays one is a Roman with authority – no waiting twenty years for your papers. And Paul said to me: 'Serve Caesar. You are not canvas I can cut to advantage at present. But if you serve Caesar you will be obeying at least some sort of law.' He talked as though I were a barbarian. Weak as I was, I could have snapped his back with my bare hands. I told him so. 'I don't doubt it,' he said. 'But that is neither here nor there. If you take refuge under Caesar at sea, you may have time to think. Then I may meet you again, and we can go on with our talks. But that is as The God wills. What concerns you *now* is that, by taking service, you will be free from the fear that has ridden you all your life.' "

"Was he right?" asked Baeticus after a silence.

"He was. I had never spoken to him of it, but he knew it. *He* knew! Fire – sword – the sea – torture even – one does not think of them too often. But not the Beasts! Aie! *Not* the Beasts! I fought two dog-wolves for the life on a sand-bar when I was a youngster. Look!"

Sulinor showed his neck and chest.

"They set the sheep-dogs on Paul at some place or other once – because of his philosophy! And he was going to see Caesar – going to see Caesar! And he – he had washed me clean after dysentery!"

"Mother of Carthage, you never told me that!" said Quabil.

"Nor should I now, had the wine been weaker."

* * *

AT HIS EXECUTION

I am made all things to all men –
    Hebrew, Roman, and Greek –
    In each one's tongue I speak,
Suiting to each my word,
That some may be drawn to the Lord!

I am made all things to all men –
    In City or Wilderness
    Praising the crafts they profess
That some may be drawn to the Lord –
By any means to my Lord!

Since I was overcome
    By that great Light and Word,
I have forgot or forgone
The self men call their own
(Being made all things to all men)
    So that I might save some
    At such small price, to the Lord,
As being all things to all men.

I was made all things to all men,
But now my course is done –
And now is my reward –
Ah, Christ, when I stand at Thy Throne
With those I have drawn to the Lord,
Restore me my self again!

ABOUT THE INTRODUCER

ROBERT GOTTLIEB is the editor of *The Journal of John Cheever*. He has been the editor-in-chief of Alfred A. Knopf and *The New Yorker*.

TITLES IN EVERYMAN'S LIBRARY